Praise for John

Votan

'The narrative is terse, the colours vivid, the events barbarously splendid … an imagination as rich as it is vivid'   *The Times*

'… excitement, mythology, the splendour and barbarity of the Dark Ages, and vividly imagined adventures'   *Northern Echo*

Not for All the Gold in Ireland

'A thoroughly enjoyable novel, full of exuberance and colourful fantasy'   *Manchester Evening News*

'Crackles with atmosphere and splendidly imaginative writing'
Guardian Journal

Men Went to Cattreath

'A novel of stark imaginative fire'   *The Observer*

'Rich and fascinating and intense'   *Western Mail*

VOTAN
AND OTHER NOVELS

JOHN JAMES

This edition first published in Great Britain in 2014 by
Gollancz
An imprint of the Orion Publishing Group
Orion House, 5 Upper St Martin's Lane,
London WC2H 9EA
An Hachette UK Company

1 3 5 7 9 10 8 6 4 2

A CIP catalogue record for this book
is available from the British Library

ISBN 978 0 575 10550 8

Typeset by Jouve (UK), Milton Keynes

Printed and bound by CPI Group (UK) Ltd, Croydon CR0 4YY

The Orion Publishing Group's policy is to use papers
that are natural, renewable and recyclable products and
made from wood grown in sustainable forests. The logging
and manufacturing processes are expected to conform to
the environmental regulations of the country of origin.

www.orionbooks.co.uk
www.gollancz.co.uk

Contents

Introduction by Neil Gaiman

The hardest part of being a writer, particularly being someone who writes fiction for a living, is that it makes it harder to reread a book you loved. The more you know about the mechanics of fiction, the craft of writing, the way a story is put together, the way words work in sequence to create effects, the harder it is to go back to books that changed you when you were younger. You can see the joins, the rough edges, the clumsy sentences, the paper-thin people. The more you know, the harder it is to appreciate the things that once gave you joy.

But sometimes it's nothing like that at all. Sometimes you return to a book and find that it's better than you remembered, better than you had hoped: all the things that you had loved were still there, but that it's even more packed with things that you appreciate. It's deeper, cleaner, wiser. The book got better because you know more, have experienced more, encountered more. And when you meet one of those books, it's a cause, as they used to say on the back of the book jackets, for celebration.

So. Let's talk about *Votan*.

I'm really late in getting this introduction in, mostly because I've been trying to work out how to introduce *Votan* without giving it all away. One does not want to explain the jokes, nor does one feel the need to assign homework before one gives someone a book to read. But it will not hurt if you are familiar with your Norse myths. They will make *Votan* a deeper book, a game of mirrors and reflections and twice-told tales. It might be a good thing to read the *Mabinogion*, and the Irish *Taín*. They will make you smile wider and shake your head in wonder when you read *Not For All The Gold In Ireland*.

So. First of all, you should feel free to skip this introduction and go and read the book. You are holding a beautiful book here, written by a remarkable writer: it contains three novels. Two novels about a Greek Trader called Photinus, who is at least the equal of, and, dare I say it, a finer rogue and tale-spinner than George McDonald Fraser's Flashman; and a darker retelling, or recreation, of a Welsh epic poem.

I read them as a young man – they were republished as fantasy novels in the early eighties, having been published in the sixties as historical novels. They are not fantasy novels, nor are they strictly historical novels: instead they are novels set in historical periods which people who read fantasy might also appreciate. The Photinus novels (there are only two, with a third novel implied but, alas, never written) are based on mythic and magical stories. (*Men Went to Cattraeth* is bleaker, and based on an old Welsh poem, the *Y Goddodin*.)

Photinus's mind and his point of view, his voice if you will, is not ours. It is this voice that lingers longest for me. His attitudes and his world are those of the past. Occasionally he commits atrocities. He does not have a twenty-first century head. Many characters in historical novels are us, with our point of view, wearing fancy dress. Votan's dress is rarely fancy. The conceit that all protagonists in historical novels should share our values, our prejudices and our desires is a fine one (I've used it myself), and it is much more difficult and much more of an adventure to create characters who are not us, do not believe what we believe, but see things in a way that is alien to us and to our time.

My own novel *American Gods* has a sequence where the hero, Shadow, spends nine nights on the tree, like Odin, a sacrifice to himself: I did not dare to reread *Votan* in the years running up to writing *American Gods*, then once my book was written, it was the first thing I read for pleasure, like a chocolate I had put away as a boy until the perfect time. I was nervous, and should not have been. Instead I discovered a whole world inside a book I already knew. (And yes, I am sure that Shadow's tree-hanging owed a huge debt to Votan's.)

So. Here are the things I will tell you, that might make reading this book more pleasant for you.

Votan is the story of a man called Photinus – a young man, a Greek trader, a magician, heartless and in it for profit – who seeks amber, and finds wealth and companionship and also finds himself Odin Allfather, the Norse god. The sagas and the tales and the poems that tell us about the Aesir, about Odin and Thor (Donar is Donner is Thunder) all reconfigure here, as if seen through a dark mirror: bleak tales they are, and dark.

It is not that James demythologises the stories, strips off all the beauty and the magic. It is more that he gives us reflection. As their best, these books are like holding a conversation with somebody from two thousand years ago. Occasionally, James can be too knowing or too wry (it is worth observing how many of Photinus's observations are common sense and utterly wrong – where amber comes from, for example, or the commercial possibilities of coal) but these moments are swept away into the next glorious story.

And the more you know, the more there is to find. I do not want to give away anything that James hid so well in his text, but here, I shall give you a couple of early ones for free: Loki is of the Aser, but not of them, trading on their behalf from his base in Outgard, not Asgard. In one of the most famous stories, we visit, with Thor, Utgard, where the giants live, and meet the crafty trickster who is also King of the Giants, Utgardloki. (Loki is half giant, half Aesir.) In the Norse sagas, Fenrir (from old norse, meaning fen dweller) is a monstrous wolf, the offspring of Loki, who bites off the hand of Tyr: here, our own Tyr tells the story of his own encounter with Fenris.

The stories of the Norse Gods are dark stories, and they do not end well: there is always Ragnarok waiting, the end of all things, the destruction of Asgard and the Aesir and all they hold dear. While Photinus/Votan become a god, he is doing it as a servant of another god, in this case an aspect of Apollo, who desires chaos, and who is laying, in his own way, the steps that will brng about the end of the world, in fire. We meet the gods in this book, in a way that reminds me of Gene Wolfe's Latro tales.

Remember, when reading these books, Google is your friend. Wikipedia is your friend. If you are curious, look it up. Were there really Celts in Galatea – modern Turkey – that the British would have recognised as cousins, speaking a similar tongue? (Why yes, there were. Wikipedia tells me that three Gaulish tribes travelled south east, the "*Trocmi, Tolistobogii* and *Tectosages*. They were eventually defeated by the *Seleucid* king *Antiochus I*, in a battle where the Seleucid war elephants shocked the Celts.") Were there really *vomitoria*, where Romans went to vomit? (No, there weren't. It's a common misconception. A vomitorium was actually kind of hallway. But this is a rare slip.)

Not For All The Gold In Ireland brings us an older Photinus. I'm not sure that he's wiser, but he's softer, less monstrous. And he's funnier (both books are funny, although the humour of *Votan* is gallows humour). He's off to get back a document, and on the way he's going to wander a long way into a number of stories. He'll become Manawyden, son of Llyr, the hero of several branches of the great Welsh prose work known as the *Mabinogion* (as are many of the people we will meet on the way – Pryderi, for example, and Rhiannon. Taliesin turns up too, centuries before we would expect the legendary Taliesin (but it is a title, we learn, not a name, handed down from bard to bard)).

And there's a strange and glorious achievement here: for the people are human, yes. But they are also mythical, larger than life. Not always in the way that we expect culture heroes and gods to be, but in a new way: they are avatars of gods, avatars of heroes: are these the Odin and the Loki and the Thor of legend, or do they echo them? Do the gods and heroes have a separate existence from Photinus and his crew, and are our protagonist and his friends being pushed through tales that will need to exist?

As the tale goes on, we meet other heroes (is Photinus a hero? He is the hero of his own story) and when we encounter Setanta, the given name of the Irish hero known as Cú Chulainn, we can predict that we will slip, as we do, from the *Mabinogion* into the *Taín*. And *Not For All The Gold In Ireland* concludes itself in a manner that is both a valid conclusion to the book we have been reading and is also a cliffhanger, and perhaps also a set up for another book, one in which, I suspect, Photinus would have found himself Quetzalcoatl of the Azteks and Kukulkan of the Mayans.

That book was never written. John James did not return to Photinus: he wrote other novels, fine and powerful, and different. These are books that have been brought back into print by people who love them, and would not let them be forgotten. If you are willing to walk and ride with Photinus, who was called Votan and Manannan and many other names, and who only wanted to increase his family's wealth, and to bed the willing wives of absent officers, then he will repay you, not with amber, or mammoth ivory, or Irish gold, but with stories, which are the finest gift of all.

Neil Gaiman
New York

VOTAN

Vindabonum

1

Well, if you really want to know how it was I came to be chained to an oak tree, half-way up in the middle of nowhere, with wolves trying to eat me out of it, I'll tell you. Of course, it's not nearly as interesting as what happened afterwards, but you can piece that together yourself if you go down to any of the taverns around the Praetorian barracks and listen to what the soldiers sing. If you can understand German, of course. They sing things like:

> High the Allfather
> Hung in the hornbeam;
> Nine days and no drinking,
> Nine nights and no nurture ...

or:

> Alfege the Earl, Odin-born,
> Great in guile, wise in war ...

I often go down there and listen. It never crosses their minds that it was only me all the time. Half the songs are about me; the other half I made up myself, anyway.

I thought that would make you sit up. It isn't every man you meet who can remember being worshipped as a God – and who still is. And it isn't every day you meet someone who has fathered half a dozen Royal Houses. I haven't spent all my time in the counting house, you know. As a matter of fact, looking back, I seem to have spent most of it in bed. That's where I learnt my German, in bed, with Ursa, in Vindabonum.

I was young, then. We went up to Vindabonum, my father and I, during the reign of his late Sainted Majesty. It was not altogether

3

by our own volition. We were priests of Apollo in the Old City. Not Apollo the Sun only, or Apollo the Music-maker at all, but Apollo the Healer, who is a very specialised God indeed and not to be found in very many shrines. There was a great deal to do there in those days. People came to be healed from quite a distance, sprains and bruises and such like, mostly. My father was very good with these.

'Yes, yes, Photinus,' he would say, 'it's all very well to do these spectacular cures, trepannings and amputations and visitations of boils and sores. But how often do you get a chance to see them? Not often enough to get any practice in, let alone make any money. No, it's these little jobs that are the doctor's bread and oil. They come in every day by the score. They've got to come in, you see. You can follow the plough with boils or even if you're raving mad – you can govern a province like that, you know – but not with a swollen ankle that you can't put to the ground. You've got your choice: come in to the doctor and pay, or lie up for a fortnight, and you can't afford to do that. In you have to go, half a day in the ox cart, see the doctor, pay up your half piece of silver or your pair of chickens, and zut! he jerks it back into place for you. The next day, back you are behind the plough or pitching sheaves into the wagon, and you know that the next winter you won't starve. Time's everything in sowing and harvest; do it when you have to or never do it at all.'

Not that we were too worried about the pairs of chickens. Some of the hill farms had been in the family since the Persians, and a lot of the other charters weren't much later. And there was some confusion, very often, about what was Temple property and what was family. So long as we lived in Vindabonum, the silver came up regularly. From the farm rents, from the olive presses, from the shipping line, from all the agencies we had. Not a bad organisation really. It all came through keeping out of politics.

But it was politics sent us up to Vindabonum. Keeping out of politics is always a bit of a risk. It isn't so much supporting the wrong man as not supporting the right one, and there had been a bit of trouble about not joining up with the right people.

Now doubtless in the days of their late Sainted Majesties

Nero or Galba we might have all been killed where we sat, but by my young days we'd run out of violence. Besides we had a lot of influence in odd places, and it was enough for someone to suggest, quite firmly, that it might be better if we went and lived elsewhere for a time. Not necessarily Vindabonum. They offered us a choice of several places, all quite horrible, like that place south of Leptis Magna, on the edge of the desert, and York. I never did get to York.

Anyway, they were all on frontiers, and we happened to have an agent in Vindabonum, a man called Otho who did a lot of buying of furs and timber and wax across the Danube, and selling cloth and wine and pottery and oil. That's a good trade; you sell the oil and wine *in* the pots, saves carriage. So we went there, up with all our furniture and plate in the wagons from Aquileia, we weren't going to be uncomfortable, and our own servants. We had a dreadful time with them, and in the end we had to send them back and stock up in the local slave market.

That's how we got Ursa. She was a Thuringian who had been carried off by a party of scavenging Marcomen, a big hearty lass, blonde and blue eyed. Don't you believe it when they tell you all Germans have yellow hair. A lot of them have, enough to impress you, but most of them are more mousy. As for red hair, that Tacitus talks about, that's rare too, except among the Picts. Fair skin, though, mostly, and nobody quite as black-haired or black-eyed as we see here in the south.

When we got Ursa, she was none too worried about what had happened. Being hauled off to Vindabonum and sold for rough work in the kitchen was, for her, an entry into the great world. She didn't stay in the kitchen long. I was nineteen at the time, and very much at a loss, and there wasn't anything much she could do about it, even if she had objected. In fact, she seemed really pleased at my picking her up, and somehow the other Germans in the household always treated her as something special. And that's how I learned German.

Once I began to get fluent in German, Vindabonum, too, began to wake up. Hardly any of the locals spoke Greek. A lot of them could be understood in a rather horrid kind of Latin, but mostly it was German or nothing. Once I could get along in

5

German it was different. It was another world, their world. It was a world of small shops and taverns, open markets and bustling people. Savages at bottom, of course, like their cousins across the Danube, noisy and uncontrollable.

I was nineteen, I told you, and there wasn't much of what you might call entertainment. There was a kind of theatre where they had regimental sports twice a year, second-rate gladiators and beasts nobody would risk on a more sophisticated audience. There was a tale locally about a party of actors who had come with some Sophocles, but nobody turned up, and they were last seen walking back to Aquileia, having sold all their costumes to pay their debts, and lucky nobody sold them too.

So the only things to watch were the religious ceremonies, not that there were very many of them either. There were the usual official shrines and the troops had a Mithraeum, but that was private, of course. No use trying to see that unless you're willing to take on more obligations than anyone would in their right minds. I wonder how long it takes to get the bull's blood out of your hair. The Jews were just as private; there were two kinds, the orthodox ones, and the ones who eat anything and worship an ass's head.

There was more fun where the Germans lived, outside the walls, in nasty little slums along the river and the roads. They weren't anything like as bad as the German villages I've seen since, but they shocked me then. They were alive, though, with their little clusters of square thatched houses, and their cooking fires outside and naked children in the dust. If it rained, of course, it was a different matter, and when it snowed it turned quite nasty, especially inside with everyone huddled around the open fires, or braziers if your house doubled as a tavern. But most of the summer and autumn we could sit on the benches outside those taverns, drinking the local brews of barley or rye or plum, and looking at the way these people lived, not lived, camped really, not living in any settled way, squatting under the ramparts.

What did they live on? Well some of them had bits of land out on the edge of the woods, and a lot lived by heavy labour, hauling barges up the Danube or building in the barracks. A lot of them were craftsmen, heavy workers like smiths or potters.

It's always a sign of civilisation when you find men doing the potting. The men who worked the wagons up from Aquileia, with all that lovely red Samian, couldn't afford to buy it and they used the local rather gritty ware.

Most of these people had relations across the river on the Marcfield, as they called it, or even farther north. On feast days we would go to one of the riverside taverns, Rudi's usually, and watch them coming across on the ferry. There were peasants in their best clothes come to see the great city, and a very great city that filthy Vindabonum must have seemed to them. They only saw the native quarter, of course; we never let them within the gates.

There were mothers and fathers up to see their recruit sons in the cavalry barracks, because by that time nobody was very choosy who you recruited for an auxiliary regiment, and they brought in pies and sausages. Sweethearts too, sometimes, but not many of those, because half of the recruits were running from some girl they'd got into trouble, and the other half were eager to see if it felt any different to get a southern girl into the same state.

There were pedlars with leather and carved wood, and cheap silver ornaments beaten out of silver coins, and men with Amber, and there were Holy Men. We usually had a line of legionaries across the quay, picking out at random perhaps one traveller in five or six and making him turn out his bundle for concealed weapons. The people didn't seem to mind this, and we never saw anybody caught with anything, although often enough the odd pie or apple changed hands. It made the job worth while, and was one of the reasons why duty on the river was popular even after ten years of peace. But nobody ever filched a piece of Amber, it wouldn't have been worth it, too much scandal. And nobody ever searched a Holy Man.

You've probably read about the German's religion in authors like Tacitus. But none of these men ever went across the frontier. None of them ever spoke to more than one or two Germans, and those were Latin-speaking civilised ones, and being properly brought up and full of Homer, they tried to make some sense out of what they heard. The fact of the matter is that there's no sense in it at all. No two Germans will agree on who their Gods are. Mostly they have two. One is called Tiwaz, and he is a fine-weather Wind God, and the other is called Wude, and he is a bad-weather Sky God, and you hear him riding overhead with all his dogs howling in any storm. In the north, they also have a kind of Vulcan, a Smith God, who must be very comforting in the winters they have there. And there are a lot of minor Gods for streams and trees and suchlike, but nobody agrees about them at all.

They haven't any real temples; they make offerings at rocks and trees where there has been an epiphany of a God. And they haven't any priests, only these Holy Men. Being a Holy Man might happen to anyone. It starts with an epiphany of the God, a waking one like being struck by lightning, or in a dream. And the God lays a charge on you, and out you are driven to fulfil it. These Holy Men, of course, happen in a lot of lands where the people aren't really settled on the soil or haven't enough to eat. The Jews had them, and some of them wrote down the charges the God put on them. I've seen the Celtic ones, and they are very given to being holier than anyone else, and talk a lot about it. India is full of them. In Germany they are rare.

There are some Holy Men who eat no flesh, and some who live on nothing but fresh blood. There are some who may not touch women, and some who are, conveniently, driven by the God to sow their seed where they can. There are some who wash and some who don't wash. The one I am going to talk about didn't wash.

2

We were sitting outside Rudi's Tavern one day, the last fine day of autumn. There was Aristarchos, prefect of a cavalry cohort, and Meno, from the Legion Headquarters, who was drowned in the Danube the following year. There was a lawyer called Poly-cleites, who didn't tell anyone why he had come up there on the edge of nowhere, though my father knew. We were, in fact, a little Greek club, all speaking Greek, and we were drinking beer and eating hot sausage; sometimes I think I lived on hot sausage in those days.

This Holy Man was worth looking at. He was well over six feet, and he had matted greasy yellow hair down to his waist. He had clothes on, and not all of them bother: a leather breech clout, and a scarlet cloak down to the hips in the German fashion, and that was new and clean.

He walked past the troops as if he didn't see them and they were glad to let him alone; some of these gentry have uncertain tempers. He came to the top of the bank, and he very carefully turned till he was looking straight into the eye of the sun. Then he put up his bare arm, and plucked something large and shining out of the empty air. That's not too difficult if you've been trained to it, as I have. It was too far off to see what. Then, whatever it was, he threw it straight at the sun. We followed its course in the air. Whether it was the wind or some God that held it I do not know, but I swear it changed its course, and it fell, quite gently, on to our table. It didn't even spill anyone's beer. We looked at it. It didn't roll. It was a great piece of Amber, twice the size of your two clenched fists. A king's ransom.

'Generous, isn't he?' said Aristarchos. 'Oh, no, he's coming for it. You can smell him from here.'

You could too. Over he came, and he sat down at the table, pushing in between the two soldiers and opposite me. I felt a bit of a devil, so as he sat down I made a few of the right passes and vanished the Amber, on to my lap under the table.

'Careful,' said Aristarchos. 'You'll be turned into a toad in another minute.'

However, the Holy Man didn't seem surprised. He just sat. There was no harm in being polite.

'Beer, Holy Sir,' I offered.

'Tiwaz has laid it on me. I drink no strong drink.' He had a strong northern accent. One of the tavern servants brought a jug of water, and filled him a beaker.

He'd drawn it half an hour before out of the river. Never drink water unless you've seen it drawn; usually then you don't want to any more. The Holy Man must have had a stomach made of pottery; the water was darker than the beer.

9

He looked at the knives on the table. He leaned across and picked up Polycleites's knife. Polycleites opened his mouth and the other three of us all kicked him under the table. The Holy Man said, in German, 'Iron, iron, iron,' three times, just like that. He spun the knife on the table. When it stopped, the handle pointed to him, the point to me. He did the same thing with Aristarchos's knife, then with Meno's. Each time, the point of the knife looked straight at me. Last, he took my knife. He spun it. This time, the point came to him, the hilt to me. He drank again.

He looked at me. His blue eyes bored into my black. After a while he looked away. He looked at my hair. At that time, it was still possible that I might follow my father in the Temple, and my hair and beard had been uncut since birth. My hair was long as his, black and clean against his dirty yellow.

He asked, 'What is your name, Roman?'

I didn't feel like arguing about Romans and Greeks, they all looked alike to him, anyway. I said,

'I am Photinus.'

'Photan, Votan, Woden, Odin,' he repeated, trying out all the variants which the Germans used. Germans can't learn to speak Greek, their tongues are too short, and they had great difficulty with the initial *Ph* of my name, turning it sometimes into a digamma, sometimes into a double *u* and sometimes a single *u*, sometimes dropping it altogether.

'And what is your name, Holy Sir?'

'I have no name.'

'How do men call you, then?'

'I have no name. Men call me Joy.'

He stood up. He had the Amber in his hand. I had not seen or felt him take it back. It worried me. I stood up with him. I did not want to, I just felt I would. Always, in the north, whatever I did, even when I must have been obeying the command of a God, I felt I was doing what I wished.

He went back to the quay. He stood where he had stood before, this time most carefully placing his back to the sun, so that his shadow fell straight before him. Again he flung the Amber straight up into the air, straight above his head, and the sun caught it and it shone so that we could all mark it and see it

10

curve down into the waters of the Danube. There were a dozen legionaries who spent the next week, all day and every day, diving for it, but they never found it.

There were a lot of people watching, mostly German. Joy turned away from the river. I had been expecting him to go back across the ferry, but no, he walked away, across the German quarter. I followed him. I had to. We came to a place by the Carnuntum road where there was an oak tree in an open space.

When he stopped there were about thirty or forty Germans with us. Two had spades. Without a word they began to dig. They dug a grave, seven feet long and two feet wide. When it was about four feet deep, others came and spread a layer of brushwood and twigs in the bottom. There was a great heap of brushwood too that they left by the graveside.

Joy turned to me and said in quite beautiful Greek, with no trace of an accent:

'I go to my Hesperides. I go to renew my youth.'

Another German came forward with a long rope. Joy tied a noose in it and placed it round his own neck. It struck me that there was something wrong. Joy's vows were to Tiwaz. But hanging was how you sacrificed to Wude, the Wind God; you hanged the victim from a branch, wind about him, wind beneath him, the wind squeezed from his body.

Joy climbed into the tree. He sat astride a branch about ten feet up. He looked about him, and then threw me the end of the rope.

'Hold!' he said.

I passed the end of the rope around my body and braced myself. I felt the jerk as he jumped. The strain lasted a moment. Then a knife flashed and someone cut the rope. I turned to see. A dozen Germans held Joy's rigid body. The face was swollen, the tongue protruded.

I touched him. Born in Apollo's house, I knew where to touch him. In the temple, in the throat, there was the pulse of a day-old chick.

They laid him in the grave. Over him they heaped more brushwood. They covered all with a few inches of earth. We all went away.

Each day I went back at noon to the oak tree. The grave was untouched, the earth drying on the brushwood. On the ninth day the grave was open. In it was a layer of ash and charred twigs. There was no body alive or dead, burnt or unburnt. Where Joy was I did not know.

None of my friends ever mentioned again that struggle in the tavern. None of the Germans under the tree, many of them men I knew, ever mentioned it again. Otho never spoke of it at all. But he knew.

3

There was just one other thing wrong with Vindabonum. Or right, depending on your point of view. There were an awful lot of men, gentlemen, that is, and not many ladies. There were plenty for the legionaries and the Germans, I mean, but not so many that you could really associate with. There were a few local gentry, if you had a low standard for gentrydom, and some of the auxiliary and legionary officers were married, but too many of these had picked up their wives in the fish-market when they were in the ranks. So the really attractive ones were rare, and those honey pots drew a lot of wasps.

The effect of this was not altogether what you might imagine. There wasn't really anything for either men or women to do a great deal of the time. Nothing for the women, except to run small houses with cheap slaves. Very little for officers in third-rate regiments on garrison duty. A few, like Aristarchos, would go out to find something to do, and they didn't stay long, even if they lived. But even that kind of garrison life entails a fair amount of detached duty at isolated posts and all kinds of chances to get out into the country. This didn't mean that the ladies were more accessible. It only meant that the ladies made all the running.

There were a fair variety of doctors in Vindabonum. There were half a dozen Greeks, a couple of Jews, and a whole crowd of Germans, who might be anything from properly trained priests to witches hung with charms. Any of them was perfectly capable of looking after broken arms or sprains or the occasional

12

stab wounds. After every tavern brawl, one of the Greeks, who had been in Egypt and was a specialist, a real specialist recognised by the military, would have a spate of business relieving skull fractures. Most of these were due to Rudi's chucker-out, a man called Donar. He was something of a mystery. He sounded like a northerner, and had been working as a smith, but had thrown this up on a sudden in the autumn to work for Rudi. He was not tall, but burly, very muscular, and he had a fine crop of red hair and beard.

So for routine medicine the town was well provided. But when my father arrived, and they realised that he wasn't going to practise, in spite of all his prestige, the local doctors adopted him as a kind of elder statesman of medicine. The way they showed this was quite simple. When they got anything that was quite incurable like visitations of boils or sores, they would pass it on to him as a superior operator. Once Milo, the trepanning specialist, even sent around a skull fracture he wasn't keen on, just alive, with the brains oozing out. Of course the man died. Luckily the family chose to believe it wasn't my father who killed him, but the bouncing around in the ox wagon from door to door. So they sued Milo, and Polycleites was drunk again that day and lost the case for him. Nobody ever tried to sue Rudi, or Donar.

A lot of other odd cases arrived. There were facial tics and cases of paralysis and just plain madness. Most of them came from citizens, not from Germans. Those were probably afraid that they'd have to pay. Once my father found he was practising again, he began to charge on a swingeing scale.

'Patients don't trust you if they don't pay,' he would tell me. 'If they want to get well, they have to do something about it themselves. The only thing they can do is pay. So I make them pay.'

He would never have me around when he was dealing with these cases, but there was one winter evening when he began to explain his methods.

'There's not much you can do to tics, and so on. I just ask them how it got started. They become so interested in telling me about it that they forget to tic. First of all they have short spells of not twitching. Next they get to the stage when they don't twitch at all in the surgery. Then they get so excited they stop twitching an hour before they get here, in sheer anticipation, and they forget to start twitching again till a couple of hours after they leave.

'There are other things, too. Do you know how these ailments start? Take Julia Scapella, for instance. How much older do you think old Scapellus is than she? Twenty years? There he is, senior centurion of the Legion. Not only that, it makes him chief of staff for six thousand infantry, four cavalry regiments, and heaven knows how many minor posts and storehouses. Think of the pickings.

'Well, now he's static, he begins to think he ought to have a wife to suit his dignity, none of these early marriages with fishwives for him, and off he sends to a broker in Rome, probably the one he got his name through. Up the girl comes, never seen him before, doesn't know a thing, and it comes as a bit of a shock. Then she begins to get boils on her … well, she gets boils. So he begins that round of staff visits, and they get longer and longer, and she begins to appreciate the good things of life she's missing. And now she's looking for treatment. The treatment is obvious. But not to her.'

It was to me, though, and it didn't take long to begin it, not with that bit of inside knowledge, and what I could easily pick up about Scapellus's roster of visits. Not long, either, before Julia was paying a good fee for the complete cure of her boils, and I am pleased to say that my father made no attempt to avoid splitting it two ways. But this was what started all the trouble, in the spring.

4

It was one of the nights Otho came to dinner. He often came to dinner, or we went to him, as he had rented us the house next door to his, close to the west gate. This was a quiet affair, not like the big parties my father often used to give in those days for the other doctors, and people of better standing. There were just the three of us, and we were discussing the general state of trade.

'So what are we in business here for?' Otho asked. He knew

more about the situation than anyone else on the river, which was why we employed him.

'We trade in timber and hides, and wax. Some slaves, ragged savages, some furs, ragged pelts from moth-eaten bears (I will tell you some day how the mother moth finds her way back to her nest in the moving bear). Marcomen bring them down to the ferry, ragged Marcomen. We pay them in pots, wine, silver. Good round silver, beautiful shining silver. We pay them in coins, silver coins. They don't want coin because they want to spend it, it's just that when silver comes in coin they know how pure it is. If those oafs in Rome knew how much trouble they cause each time they debase it. They know all about that, out in Germany. 'We want old denarii,' they tell me. 'Two-horse denarii, one of those or two of the new kind.' They want wine … wine … wine …' I filled his cup.

'They want wine, red wine. They want pottery, red Samian pottery, the lovely red shine of the glaze. And glass, too, glass from Campania, glass they want more than gold. Gold? What do they want with gold? A little piece of gold pays for a lot of hides, and there it is, a little piece. But for the same hides you can have enough silver to make into the mount for a drinking horn or a morse to fasten your cloak with. And if the silver you start off with is coin, two-horse denarii that you melt down, then you know you've got good silver.'

'Silver as a raw material for an industry,' mused my father.

'But there is something that comes down, but not often, and for that I always give silver. It glows … it shines …'

'Amber,' I breathed. 'Perhaps once a month, perhaps less often you see that. High profit, perhaps, but not what you'd call an important article of trade.'

'Not now, not now.' I gave Otho more wine, it was worth staying in for, to hear this kind of thing.

'Sixty, seventy years ago, this was a great place for the Amber trade. Those days, the Romans came up from Aquileia, up the Marc River, to trade for Amber with the Marcomen. There were real Marcomen there, then, my fathers. The Amber came down, Amber by the wagon load, think of it, by the wagon load, red glowing Amber. They paid for the Amber, and then they paid our wagoners to take it down to Aquileia, and then we sold them the oxen out of the wagons, all thin and tired from the journey, as fat stock. Ah, those were the fine days …'

'How did they end?' I asked.

'Herman came. First he beat the Romans up in the north, three legions he cut up and not one word heard of them again. We had our Good King then, my grandfather Maroboduus. Herman defeated him, drove him out. All our fine warriors dead, our women raped, our children sold, all our nobles driven out, scattered, dead, dead. The Good King, he died in Ravenna. They made us all citizens because we hated Herman and so did the Romans, but the Marcomen are ruled now by renegades, people of low birth. And Herman and his Thuringians joined with the Cat King, and they hold all the centre of the great plain, and all the Amber they make goes through their hands and through the Thuringians, and to the Rhine. And it is paying the two sets of duty on it, to the Cat King and to the Thuringians, that makes Amber so expensive. But if we could open the road east of the Cat men, and bring Amber down without paying the dues, if someone could go to the Kings of the Amber Road in the north, why then, think of the profits …'

We thought. It was enticing.

'Could you get anyone to go?' my father asked.

'I've got someone,' said Otho. 'Two men. They know the way to the north and I can trust them. They will take a little silver, but mostly they will go to meet people and find out the way. Occa will go.'

I knew Occa. He was a sergeant-major in Aristarchos's regiment. I had heard he was due for a long leave.

'And the other?'

'Donar.'

A chucker-out? I stopped thinking about the scheme, there was nothing in it, nothing at all.

We gave Otho more wine, and left him crying into his cups that he couldn't find anyone of spirit willing to go, no one of intelligence or learning. He kept looking at me, and I kept ignoring him. There was nothing in the plan at all. Only wind.

5

Two days later it was the first fine day of spring. I had nothing to do, exiles usually haven't. I had watched old Scapellus ride out on a long tour down river, all the posts to Carnuntum. That would keep him out of the way for a few nights, and I had already arranged how to occupy them. Then I had a work-out at the cavalry gymnasium. I had been having a few lessons with the cavalry sword, the long springy one. There's quite a different technique with it. As I came out of the barracks I saw two off-duty legionaries. I wouldn't have noticed them if they hadn't been so obviously taking notice of me.

I went off to Rudi's tavern; I was peckish after the exercise, and as it was so sunny I sat on a bench outside sheltered from the wind, and ordered beer and hot sausages. It was a bit early and while the girl was getting the sausages heated up I ate a couple of salt herrings out of the barrel; they came down from the north too. After a while I looked across the street, and the two legionaries were there, not doing anything but standing against the wall of the house opposite and looking at me. Just looking. They were the same two. Their look made me feel a bit uncomfortable. After a bit, I called the girl and had her move me indoors by the fire. At least it didn't look as if they had chased me away.

It was more cheerful inside. I gossiped with Rudi's number one wife. He made the best of both worlds; he told Romans that polygamy was a German custom, and to the Germans he said that was how the Romans lived at home in the south. Then she chivvied the number three wife, who had just brought me the hot sausages, to go and look after two new customers. I looked over, and they were the same two legionaries asking for beer. They bought half a pint each, the cheapest kind, and one of them made an entry on his tablets as if he was keeping account of his expenses. Then they sat nursing their pots and looking at me.

I looked back. They weren't very formidable in themselves, rather mild in fact. I knew them both by sight. That one looked after living-out permits for legionaries with native wives in the

17

German quarter. The other was with the quartermaster, dealing with arrowheads and other warlike expendable stores. Not the kind of men to beat anybody up, but conscientious, pedantic, reliable, just the kind to use for following. Literate, too, could write a report afterwards.

In this position, how do you get rid of your follower? Easy, I thought, I've never known the soldier yet who'll pass up a free meal. When I finished my sausage, I called over the number three wife.

'Those two gentlemen over there by the door, nearly through their beer. Get them a good big dish of hot sausages, bread, onions. Any radishes? Good, those too. And a quart apiece of best beer, the strong black stuff. Don't mention my name, and keep the change.'

I suppose she thought I was mad, but that didn't matter. She was glad of the tip, since she was saving to buy Rudi another wife so that she'd no longer get all the kicks.

As soon as she got the tray over to their table I got up and slipped out past her. There was enough on that tray to keep them busy for a quarter of an hour at least, even if they gobbled like pigs, and I was barely a furlong from Otho's house, which had a side door into ours. But as I came to the gate, I looked behind me, and there they were on the street corner looking back at me.

When I got into the house, I found Otho was not alone. Donar was there, and another man. If Donar was burly, this one was cubic, the same measurement tall and wide and deep. It was Occa. I don't know what his cavalry regiment rode on; elephants, I should think. He had scars all up his arms; rumour says that he had once tackled a bear single handed, and it was the bear that ran away. Looking at him you could believe it. He was rubbing pig fat into his face. Donar was putting a last edge on a sword with a strop. Otho was weighing out silver pieces into bags, fourteen pounds in a bag.

I stopped and looked at them.

'Off this afternoon?' I asked.

'Tonight,' said Occa.

'Over the wall,' said Donar.

'Over the wall in the dark?' I asked. It was fairly easy, if nobody spotted you; the town wall was one side of Otho's courtyard. 'Why not just walk out of the gates in the morning?'

The three Germans looked at me in a pitying way, as if I had missed the point of something obvious.

'Nonsense,' said Occa. 'No story ever started by stealthily slipping through gates unguarded in day undiminished.'

'Have you no piety?' asked Donar. 'No sense of achievement? A feat at the first gives the Gods greater glory.'

The Germans speak like that when they want to be formal. I could talk their language fairly well by now, and I thought I might try my hand at ceremony one day. At that moment I was content with saying, 'Watch out for your necks on the other side.' And I went up to my room. I had a couple of hours' sleep, and then I began to dress for my visit to Julia. I was still thinking about Donar sneaking out of the town in the dark, probably leaving behind a handful of bad debts and a couple of sweethearts in the family way.

I had some dinner in my room, and then I set out for Julia's. I crossed our courtyard, and the gate keeper opened up for me. I stepped out into the dark street and stood for a moment with the open gate at my back. I looked about. In a sheltered alcove a little way along there were two men standing. They were not in the least concerned with keeping out of the moonlight, but only with keeping out of the wind. They were easy to recognise, even at that distance. As I looked at the two watchers, someone seized my arm from behind and pulled me back into the courtyard.

'Have you no sense?' asked Aristarchos. 'Haven't you seen them?'

'Seen them?' I tried to be reasonable. 'They've been on my trail all day. I paid for their dinner, but they didn't eat it.'

'Two of my lads did. They told me about it. Do you know who they are?'

'Yes. Two clerks from Headquarters Century.'

'Scapellus's century.'

'So? Who's afraid of that weedy pair? I didn't even bring a sword out with me. I don't think either of them has handled a weapon since they did recruit drill.'

'No,' said Aristarchos very slowly, as if he were speaking to a foreigner, or to a child. 'No, not that kind of man. You don't use that kind of man to kill. I don't, anyway, and that's my job, and it's Scapellus's job too, and he's been at it a lot longer than I have. No, that kind of man you use for following and watching, because they do it so well. You use others for killing. I know I would, so Scapellus will.'

'Do you think that illiterate squarehead can get the better of Greeks like us?' Scapellus was half German, they said, and the best part of his education he'd got in the barrackroom. Aristarchos was sounding a bit scornful, so there was no harm in buttering him up a bit, even if he was only a Thracian with a thick accent.

'I don't know what they're watching for, and anyway, Scapellus hasn't any civil jurisdiction … has he …? I've got a week before he comes back, and I never knew a quartermaster who couldn't be bribed.'

'Let us look at this in detail,' said Aristarchos smoothly, very much one Greek to another. 'First of all, they're watching for you to call on Julia. You've been seen before, you know. All Scapellus wants to do is catch you on the premises. Secondly, you haven't got a week. Scapellus didn't go to Carnuntum, he only went as far as the tenth milecastle on the river, and he's coming back by dawn. I did the ration documents for the escort, so that's how I know. And thirdly, it isn't only that pair watching. When Scapellus comes back tomorrow, he's going to find you trussed up and waiting for him.'

'Now, now,' I said, 'that's going a bit far. Julia wouldn't let me down like that. Nor the house slaves either, they're under the thumb.'

'House slaves don't come into it. They're under lock and key. So is Julia, and she's got that Syrian, Publiolus's wife, to chaperone her. You didn't know you'd been seen there too, did you? And then there's Manlius's wife, in our regiment, to chaperone them, and that's how I know. So look, Photinus, don't go up the street tonight, because a couple of those boys will hustle you in through that door whether you like it or not. And if you don't go up the street tonight, walk carefully the next few days. If Scapellus comes home and finds the trap sprung and empty, he might come calling.'

'So what do I do now?'

'Sit tight and stay indoors for a bit. Now it's clouding over, I'm going to run for it. If they let Scapellus think I tipped you off I'm for it.'

He slid through the gate into the dark. I knew that when he had been farther down the river, he had had a reputation as a horse thief. Now he moved like it.

I closed the gate and thought hard. If Julia was crying her heart out with the Syrian, there was no knowing what they were plotting between them. I might not have Scapellus round at once, but I'd probably have Publiolus at the door first thing in the morning. How long was I to stay indoors? A week? A month? Even if I did stay inside, there was nothing to stop Scapellus and his bullies from pushing the door in. And once husbands began to think over Julia's troubles – nothing could hide Scapellus coming back five days early – there was no knowing who might be coming round.

So what was I to do? I could hardly leave Vindabonum; I was, however you looked at it, under arrest. Anywhere else I could just have got out of town, just like I did at Ostia, when the husband came back, and after that unfortunate affair with the pimp in Alexandria, and as for Tyre, I never thought I'd find a Levantine who'd play with my dice. But in each of those places I had a ship to get back to and comrades who were at least as deep in it as I was. But there was no travelling about the Empire for me, with a pack of vengeful husbands all eager to put me under arrest. I was trapped, with the river at my back. Then it struck me. A river is a road, water is a way. I slipped through the internal gate into Otho's courtyard and went into his office. Otho and Donar looked at me curiously. Occa was greasing his boots.

'Don't go for an hour or so,' I told them. 'I'm coming with you.'

21

Germany

1

I went straight back to my own room and called Ursa.

'Quick,' I told her, in German. 'Get me some German clothes. Shirt, trews, short cloak, sandals. Quick.'

Out of the cupboard I heaved a leather bag with a shoulder strap, made for a pack mule once but better this way. In it I put my best sky-blue silk tunic and a spare pair of sandals. I had a few pieces of silver handy, but after what I'd heard I didn't think it worth taking gold. I looked round and found one or two pieces of silver plate, old-fashioned embossed stuff. Then I took a leather water bottle with a strap, one I used to use out hunting.

If I were going north to meet the Amber Kings, I thought, I needed a king's clothes. I had a helmet, no, not a helmet, a cap of boiled leather, all covered and patterned with gold leaf, and this I put in, and a cuirass to match, for show not for war, soft leather and gold wire. These had come from the east somewhere, long ago, and had caught my fancy. I took a sword, the first I learnt to use, a Kopis, pointed, curved, one edge razor-sharp, the other finger-thick, blunt, the bone breaker, a fine hilt, but a plain scabbard. The general effect was of something meant for real use, but I knew well the metal wasn't of the best.

I was writing a letter to my father when Ursa came back with the clothes. She had a complete German suit, red woollen shirt, and red and yellow checked trousers. It was unworn, and a perfect fit; she must have started making it for me weeks before. Trousers are funny things to wear. You can always feel them on your legs. It takes you a long time to get used to riding a horse in them, the cloth spoils the contact with the beast's side.

She didn't bring me a German cloak. They are short. She

22

brought me my own long grey horseman's cloak, down to my heels.

'This is good for blanket, sleep in it,' she told me. I finished the letter to my father. I stood up to go. Ursa threw her arms around my neck.

'Rejoice,' she said; she said it in Greek, it was one of the few words she knew, then in German:

'Rejoice. Joy goes with you. Joy awaits you. Joy sends you on. Rejoice.'

I went down into our courtyard on the soft German sandals. Hobnails are no use out there beyond the Frontier, there are no paved roads. I went through the postern into Otho's courtyard, right under the town wall. The others were there, and a crowd of slaves, all talking at once.

'When do we start?' I asked Occa.

'Now,' he said. 'Somebody's gone to get the ladder.'

This shows what a state the river frontier was like then, you could build houses right up against city walls, inside anyway. One of Otho's slaves brought a ladder and set it against the wall. There was a sentry on top, walking about.

'What about him?' I asked.

'He won't see anything,' said Otho. I wondered how much that had cost. It wasn't only paying the sentry, the firm had probably had to pay the Guard Commander as well, and almost certainly somebody in the Legion Headquarters had a hand in the purse.

'How many has he been paid not to see?' I asked. I didn't want Scapellus over the river after us first thing.

'Any number,' said Otho. 'Up you go.'

I hate ladders on land. It's one thing climbing on a ship, but quite another when you only have the hard ground to fall on. I followed Donar up the ladder clinging on as tight as I could. Occa kept on pushing me. We got on to the top. The sentry turned his back on us. Otho shouted up,

'Have you got the rope?'

Donar threw one end of a rope down, and half a dozen of Otho's slaves tailed on to the end of it. Then one by one we slid down the other side of the wall. We made enough noise to wake

23

Morpheus, especially as each of us was carrying two fourteen-pound bags of silver coin.

We walked down a path to the river side.

'How do we cross it?' I asked. 'The ferry stopped hours ago.'

'You've been at sea,' Occa told me. 'You're going to row.'

If I had, I'd not rowed, I'd sailed like a gentleman. Out to Tyre in furs and honey, Tyre to Alexandria in cedarwood, Alexandria to Ostia in wheat, and a trooping run home. One year at sea, it showed me the world. I didn't want to sink to rowing.

It wasn't as bad as that. There was a small, illegal boat hidden in the reeds just where any legionary would have looked for it – more expense, I thought, and all for sentiment's sake. I was able to let her go down with the current and land up on the other side of a bend, where a man had been showing a lantern at intervals. I suppose it was another of Otho's contacts. He had three horses for us. those small scrubby things, and a great luxury, saddles, which were just coming in in those days. Most people out in the north just rode on blankets thrown over the horses' backs. We mounted and off we went. I was in the middle. The others seemed to know where we were going.

We rode for days. Some people talk as if the lands outside the Empire are quite different. In fact, it's just the same at first. For a couple of days we went along stretches of agger, roads laid by the army in Domitian's campaign ten years before, unused since and now breaking up under weather and time, not wear. All the country was like that. The people were the same as on our side of the river, the clothes were the same, the language, the houses, the food. But it was all a bit shabbier and second-rate. The houses weren't as clean as the German houses around the walls of Vindabonum, and that means they were foul.

After the first few days we didn't pass many houses. When I came back that way I began to realise how skilfully Occa had planned his march to take us out of people's sight and earshot. Usually we rose at dawn and rode off at once. We would stop at noon and rest the horses and eat, and after an hour or two set off again till sunset. We had dried meat and twice-baked bread with us. Once or twice Occa went off with his bow and got a deer, though it was really out of the season, and we called at farms and

24

bartered the meat and hide for carrots and cabbages that had been stored through the winter.

We followed the Marcomen's river, a little east of north through the empty hills. One day, a little before sunset, we came out of the wood, the scrubby patchy stuff you get near a river, into an open space. In the middle there was an oak, a very old oak, dead, blasted and scarred by lightning. Occa stopped and held up his hand.

'The God has been here,' he said.

'That was a long time ago,' I told him.

'Yes, seven years ago, in July,' he replied. I had not realised that his knowledge of the way was so exact or so recent. He went on, 'There is something new. Can a dead tree put forth a new shoot, or the dry rock a living branch? It is new that the oak should send out ash, or the dull rock smite as a smith. From here it looks like a splinter, hanging vertical from the trunk, but it is new. Do as I do.'

As I watched Occa took out his water bottle and poured a few drops out on the ground, as a libation. This was mere politeness, a greeting to the sky-god. As we rode forward behind him we saw that the ground was scattered with horse skulls and bits of faded cloth held down by stones. Beneath the tree was the skeleton of a horse, whole, only a few months dead.

Donar stopped me a dozen yards from the tree. Occa kicked his heels into his horse and rode forward, hard, and as he passed the tree he grasped the spear shaft and pulled it. He let it go just in time to avoid sliding off the horse's back. The spear did not move.

Then Donar rode forward. From where I sat I could see the muscles of his arm and back strain as he pulled, but again the spear did not move. I thought of riding sedately past, uncertain of whether they would appreciate my meddling with their German rites, but Donar shouted to me to come on and have a pull.

I clapped my heels into the horse's ribs and went full tilt at the tree. I grabbed at the shaft, calling on Apollo to let me grasp it, even if I never moved it. My hands felt the smooth shaft, jerked it, slipped a little. I had the spear.

The two Germans shouted, a paean, a warcry, a great ululation. Without looking back we rode away, miles away up the

25

river, none of us speaking till we reached what looked like a good camping place for the night. I sat on my saddle, while the others hobbled the horses and turned them to graze, and I looked at the spear. It was the usual long iron head on a six foot ash shaft. It had not been in the weather very long, perhaps six months at the most, and there was only a very thin coating of rust. I'm not sure it hadn't been greased before it was left. I got some ash and some sand and I began to clean the metal.

Donar and Occa came and sat by me and told me how it must have happened.

'It is our custom, all over Germany,' said Donar, 'that when a man is going out on some desperate journey from which there is no returning, if he goes to join the cavalry, or to do a murder, or to his death ...'

'Or to his marriage.' Occa, in middle age, was a bachelor.

'... he will take a weapon, a knife or an axe, or a spear, and he will thrust it into a tree ...'

'And he will make an offering to the God, don't forget the offering. This one made the horse sacrifice.'

That was the most magnificent and most expensive sacrifice of all, and this had been the most costly: a mare.

'Then every man who passes must try to draw the weapon out of the tree, and only the man for whom the God intends it will be able to take it. That spear was meant for you, Photinus.'

The rust was almost all gone. I showed the ferrule just below the head to Donar.

'What are these marks below the crosspiece?' For it had a crosspiece like a boar spear, and that was not usual.

They both looked at it closely. I know that many people think that the Germans have no writing, but I have the best of reasons for knowing better. Certainly you cannot write German words in Greek or Latin letters, that would be against all reason, but there is a way of writing German in German letters, which are called Runes. This was the first time I had seen Runes, and in my innocence I thought that any German could read them. This time I heard nothing to disturb my delusion, for Occa took one glance and said,

'That means Joy. Joy left that spear. Joy left you his spear. That is why he sought you at the ferry.'

A few days later I asked Donar to take his punches and strike my name into the iron on the other side of the socket. So now Votan lies for ever in the iron with Joy. But only Donar could read it, for in those days in the North every man made his own runes.

2

A few days later we were coming out of the land of no people, the bare mountains, into a land of scattered farms and shepherds. And then, in a few more days, the farms were more frequent, the population thickened, concentrated, condensed almost, out of a cloud of precarious settlers into a vortex, a constellation of permanent farms, hamlets, villages almost, little clusters of houses and barns.

We came to the farm of one of Occa's clansmen, Haro, a man of power and influence in the region. He was, I had been told, Otho's agent among the Marcomen, but he said that Otho was his agent among the Romans. He came himself and unbarred the gates of his stockade – they had been shut specially for the purpose – to let us in. The farmyard was built up feet above the plain on the dung and rubbish of generations. Inside the stockade, the main farmhouse was a great hall, the frame of whole trees, the walls filled in with wattle and daub, the roof thatched with wheat straw. It was twenty paces long, inside, and ten wide. The door was in the middle of the long side, and the hearth at one end, sure sign that Haro had only lately dispensed with the company of his cows at night. They now slept, in winter, in the huts scattered around the yard. At least in some of the huts; we three were put into one, and bidden be ready for a feast that night.

There was a group of women around a fire outside one hut, and I went over and asked for some hot water. They sent the youngest to bring it over, and she set down the pot by the door, and walked away with serious face, steady and erect like a grown-up, she hoped, though it was obvious that one word would have set her giggling, and scurrying back.

We washed the dust away, and I put on my best tunic. Then

27

we sat outside the door and watched the other guests arrive, big proud men, chiefs with their war bands, or at least the pick of their war bands. They all went into the hall. At last, Occa decided dignity would let us appear, and in we went. This was the first time I had been the guest of a German, other than Otho with his Spanish butler and his Syrian cook, and his nearly Roman dining-room with its three tables and couches. This room had three tables, too, one across the width of the hall farthest from the door, and the others at right angles down the sides. Haro met us and offered us that sweet Spanish wine, which those Germans are so keen on as an appetiser. It was very precious there, so no more than one glass was offered, and that a very small one. There was not so much as an eggspoonful of sea water or resin there to blend in it, so I was not sorry that the main drink of the evening was to be beer.

When the wine was drunk with the usual exchange of healths, we guests of honour went to sit on the long benches behind the top table, our backs to the hearth, our faces to a brazier. I moved to the seat to which Haro waved me, and as I sat down, he bellowed, as if introducing the only stranger:

'Photinus the Greek, from the sea and the islands. Far has he travelled, to the lands of the spices. He left behind comfort to sleep in the forest, left behind women, silks, sauces and silver. He overcame Joy to come on this journey, Greek vowed to his God he goes to the Northlands. Spear on shoulder he rides through the mountains, over the plains to the Kings of the Amber.'

I thought this a bit unwise if we were supposed to be going in secret, but Occa assured me that we had only the Cat King to fear, and that all present were Marcomen and Quadi, enemies of the Cat people. So I sat down, and watched what we would have for supper. I must say there was more order and ceremony at this banquet than at any other barbarian feast I ever went to. Each of us was given a pair of silver mounted drinking horns – on the top table, that is; farther down they brought their own. The retainers were crammed together; at least we had room to move our elbows.

First the servants brought salt fish, to give us a thirst, and then filled the horns, one with barley beer, the other with mead. After the fish, gross hunks of roast meat were placed on the table, with loaves of rye bread. My neighbour, with a great effort at courtesy, cut me thick slabs of pig and deer mixed together. He wore a cloak of wolf pelts, with a wolf's head hanging down behind. On a golden chain round his neck were wolf's teeth, dozens of them. He made a sport, he told me, a trade, a livelihood, of wolf hunting, with spear, with bow, with trap, even with poison, winter and summer. His own name he himself had almost forgotten. Everyone now called him Wolf. I could no more applaud his pursuit of wolves than I could approve of Occa's attack on the bear, but in his name I found an omen. He had a healthy respect for his wolves, in spite of the fifty tails sewn on the hem of his cloak.

'Only two good things about wolves. They make good cloaks and they can't climb trees. Bear climbs trees, but not wolf. If you ever want to cheat them, get up a tree. Stay there. Stay there till they go. Hours, days, maybe, but stay there.'

His main topic, that night, was the indignity of having to come, at Haro's insistence, unarmed into the hall. He proudly showed a scar across his scalp, from front to back.

'I got that at a feast, up with the Thuringians, big man he was, good fellow, know him well. Got some of the best wolf hunting this side of the great forest. I'll take you up there one day, great sport. What? The scar? Yes, well, that was after the dinner, we can't remember why, but he hit me with a bench. No swords, but it didn't stop us fighting.'

'If it had been a sword,' my other neighbour observed – his name was Lothar, and, he was delighted to tell me, he had been across the border twice, once on a cattle raid and once into Carnuntum to market – 'if it had been a sword, where would you be now?'

He rolled up his shirt to show a fine scar across his stomach.

'*That* was a sword. It was my wedding feast and my brand new brother-in-law did it. It kept me in bed three weeks – quiet, Wolf, we haven't all got minds like yours. But there, if we'd all been hit on the heads with benches … Here, our guest's plate is empty. Pass the beef – no, try this, a real local delicacy. What? Oh, bulls' testicles, raw.'

'Perhaps he doesn't eat them,' said Wolf in an interested way. 'Oh, yes, he does, though. All right, they always taste like that at first, really. Try some more mead. Go on, drain it! Boy! More mead!'

The mead finished me. The next thing I knew I was struggling out into the courtyard. I don't know how I managed to reach fresh air without disgracing myself. Wolf was at my elbow, not jeering as I feared but bitterly regretting his own lack of capacity.

'Small bladder, that's my trouble, always has been. I can stand up to the liquor itself, strong head I've got, but once over the gallon and a half, out I've got to come. That's right, boy, get it up, get rid of it, you'll feel better then. Only good thing about the south, there's not so much bulk to wine. All right? Let's get back then, there's still some cold roast pork left, and plenty of crackling. There, there, get it up. I thought you were finished for a moment, but … here's some water, clear your taste. What, *over* your head? Are you sure? Well, all right then. No, better not go to lie down, it isn't etiquette. Back we go, I'll make sure they don't press you to any more. Takes a bit of getting used to, I suppose. Here we grow up on it. Just sit still a bit. Lothar! pass me the pork.'

I only wish now that I could recover from a drinking bout the way I could then. A slab of rye bread and a draught of beer, not the rich dark stuff I had been drinking, but the ordinary thin bitter brew, well beer we used to call it, and I was able to watch what was happening again. There was a minstrel now, standing by the fire and singing away, some long involved song about a hero who was killing a dragon, very slowly. For line after monotonous line the sword slid past one scale after another. I must have looked bored, for Haro leant across and said to me:

'Good, isn't he? But what does Greek sound like?'

Now, when people say that to you, as they often do abroad, it's no use saying something like 'No, thank you', because they always want a translation. I had to think of something to suit the company. This was hardly the time or the place for Sappho. Homer, in contrast, was both too near and too far away from them in spirit. I took something which would show them both

30

how near the Greek mood could come to theirs, and at the same time how foreign to them was its precision. I spoke the two lines of the epitaph on the Spartans at Thermopylae:

> Go, tell the Spartans, thou who passest by,
> That here obedient to their laws we lie.

'And what does it mean?' they all shouted together.

'Give me some quiet and I will tell you,' I said. Now was the moment to see if I really could make verse in German. Wolf, with excellent aim after the amount of beer he had taken, threw a mutton bone at the bard, who fell into the brazier, and while some people poured beer over him to put the flames out, and others poured beer into him to revive him, Haro passed me his harp. I tried a few chords. It was not too different from a lyre, provided I only used it to beat out the rhythm. Anyone brought up on hexameters should find German verse easy, I thought, drunk or sober. Whether I was right or wrong is not for me to say, but as far as I remember this is what I sang:

> Men went to battle, there was no returning.
> Go tell in Sparta, low burns our pyre.
> We were three hundred, they ten times ten thousand.
> From sea to mountain set we the shield wall.
> Over the hill flank came the betrayer.
> Broken the shield wall, bloody the sea shore.
> Our Kings commanded us, bear no shield back again.
> Men went to battle, there was no returning.

It didn't leave a dry eye in the place. Men were weeping for their lost comrades, for their own lost youth, for the days when they too might have stood to die in a shield wall, not gone home as soon as they were outnumbered, like sensible married men. To break the ocean of sobbing, Haro shouted:

'Bring a cloak, put down a cloak, let's have a cloak and a couple of them on it.'

Two of the retainers came forward with a cloak, an old thing, stained and torn, but a big one, a horseman's cloak like mine.

31

They spread it on the floor between the brazier and the top table. Out of the confusion at the bottom of the hall, two men were pushed, half reluctant, to stand on the cloak. Each had a shield, one daubed with an eagle, one with a bear. Somebody brought them their swords.

You may not have seen a German sword, not to handle. They are different from ours. Ours have a point; the legionary's is short and stiff, the cavalry trooper's sword is long and springy, but each has a point, and you use them on the move, putting all your own fifteen stone or the speed of your horse behind it, to drive through leather or mail.

Germans, on the contrary, like to fight standing still. They depend on the strength of their arms and the weight of their weapons to do the damage, and so their swords are two-edged, but rounded at the tip, not pointed. The sword is always long, four fingers broad at the hilt, and two fingers at the tip. Down from hilt to tip, on each side, there runs a groove, some say to collect the blood, some say to make the blade stronger, some say because blades were always made that way. The hilts they hang round with charms and rings, and they usually keep them covered with little leather bags to protect the finery.

These two men, Bear-shield and Bird-shield, stood on the cloak. The shields were of limewood, covered with leather, and strengthened with iron. The fight they made was nothing you'll ever see at the games; it was too slow, no audience would ever pay to see it. They stood face to face, on the cloak, a pace apart. When Haro shouted 'Start!' each began to move crabwise to his left, keeping his shield between himself and his opponent. Then Bear-shield struck, a wide slashing blow, and the other turned it on the edge of his shield. They crabbed again, and then Bird-shield had a cut, the weight of that long blade far forward. He leaned forward too far, and almost overbalanced, and I waited for Bear-shield to go for the back of the knee and hamstring him, but no, the idiot stood aside and let his opponent recover. Then they went around again, and Bear-shield had a go, and again the blow was turned. They went on like that, turn and turn about to cut, for what seemed to me like hours, always careful to keep their feet on the cloak.

After a few dozen of these blows, the shields were pretty tattered. Bear-man looked at his shield in disgust, and flung it behind him. It seemed this had to be done when you were due to receive a blow, not when you were about to deal one, and your opponent then had to throw his shield away too. Bird-man wasn't very pleased, obviously, but he struck, and though Bear-man swayed back, the tip of the sword caught him on the ear. The blood ran down his neck, slowly. A number of the audience were down on their hands and knees at the edge of the cloak. Everything was quiet, and the torch flames made everything dance in silence. Then Bear-man had a slash, Bird-man parried with the flat of his blade, but the other with a flick of his wrist changed the direction of his cut in mid-air, and chopped sideways along the Bird-man's arm. The blood spouted down his fingers on to the cloak, and the kneelers shouted and Haro shouted and we all shouted and the two swordsmen embraced and rubbed each other's wounds with the trinkets from their swords. It seemed that drawing first blood didn't mean you'd won; but the man who first dropped blood on the cloak lost.

There were a number of fights after that, and a fair amount of betting. I did well on one fight between a big local man, and a small stranger who was left-handed; I reasoned that the right-hander would be put off, while the left-hander probably fought right-handed men every week. He did too, and won in about three or four cuts.

Then there were a pair of elderly men, rather fat, who were so inept that we just threw mutton bones at them and laughed them off the cloak. They were followed by a grudge fight, in earnest, between the local expert, who elected to fight without a shield and take the firststroke, and a novice who was to keep his shield – there was much bad blood in this one. However, while the expert was circling for his second blow, and that, I am sure, would have been the end of the novice, he put his foot on a mutton bone and down he went. He turned the ankle, and couldn't get up, and there he lay while some argued over the bets, and a gaggle of local doctors talked over whether the poultice would be better mixed with pig's blood or with bull's urine. None of them bothered to look at the patient, so I did. It didn't take a moment to feel what was wrong with that joint, not to anyone with my training. The clever thing was to do something about it. I tipped the wink to Donar, who stood ready to hold the shoulders.

The problem was finding the leg under about seven layers of wrappings, without alarming the patient. How would you do it? Just a bit of skill, and you'd never believe the things I took out of those wrappings. Mutton bones, chicken legs, a drinking horn, all with a flow of more or less obscene patter that got the sufferer and everyone else into fits of laughter. When I had the boot off, even some of the Quadi remarked on the smell, but I merely slipped in '*Venite*' as a signal, and Donar pulled and I twisted and the expert howled and the bone came right.

Then I wrapped the ankle in bandages soaked in cold beer for want of water, and I forbade the expert to walk on it for a week, and for good measure I made up a charm which I have had said over bad sprains of my own since then by Germans who didn't know me, and which went:

> Blood to blood,
> Bone to bone,
> Strength to the sinew,
> Skin strong as stone,
> Oak strong as ash,
> Elm at the end,
> Earth over all.

Everybody within earshot wagged their heads and said what a powerful and efficacious charm that must be, and that you hadn't to worry about who was going to do the magic as long as you had a Greek about, but ask them to do hard work … not likely. Then while Donar was busy helping the patient to a bench, which had to be cleared of novices sitting boasting and rubbing charcoal into their cuts to make them show up better, I slipped out. Me for bed, I thought, if only I can remember which is my hut.

Her warm arm slipped under mine, her warm body pressed to me. Out of the dark she asked:

'Spear-bearer from the South, Greek going north, Joy-knower, Joy-bringer?'

'And if I am?'

There had been no women at the feast. The serving women were not fit to meet the likes of us; nor were the likes of us, strangers, foreigners, of no known clan or lineage, fit to meet Haro's wife or daughters. But this was no serving maid, these hands did not spend the mornings on the quern, grinding out the flour for the day. She smelt sweet, and her voice was gentle not shrill, as she said softly, 'Come, come.'

At that age, that was a call I would never resist. She led me towards a tangle of huts, barns, stables, all mixed together. The tangled clouds raced past the rising moon. The wind caught my hair and hers and mixed them. She pointed up and said:

'You hear the dogs of Wude?'

And indeed the wind sounded faintly, if you wished to think so, like a pack of hunting dogs belling. We came to one hut among many, and she pushed open the unbarred door. The floor was spread with sweet fresh rushes, and the walls hung with embroidered cloths. All round the room were bronze lamps, imported, and probably bought from the family, I thought. They lit her fair skin, her fine face, her long golden hair against my black, as she sank back on the great bed, and spread with furs, furs, a king's ransom in furs, and spread over with silk, an Empress's dowry in fine silk.

I asked her name.

'Gerda,' she told me. The wind howled in the roof.

'Listen,' she cried. 'He rides! The wild hunt rides.'

It was daylight, hardly daylight, the first light. Donar was shaking me, saying:

'Never know where to look for you when you've had a few. Lucky you didn't go for the women, then you would take some finding, bit by bit. Do you know what they do up here?' his voice went maundering on. I looked up at the sky. I lay on a mouldering pile of roof straw in a ruined hut. The door sagged from one leather hinge. Painted plaster peeled damp from the walls. Spring flowers, buds still unopened for the day, sprouted from the turf floor. The wind still howled through the rafters. Where was the huntsman now?

35

We left as soon as it was fairly light. For more days we rode across the uplands, and then through more mountains. Away to the west there rose one great peak that the Germans called the Old Father, the mountain where the world had begun. We left it behind and came down into a country of forests and marshes, and wide rivers.

Then one day about noon we were making along a forest path when there came out of the scrub two horsemen, poor men, in rags, riding on blankets, one red and blue check, the other no particular colour except dirty. They stopped by the side of the path, and watched us as we went by. They were poor. They had no swords, but they carried the long spears of the country, and on their shields the eye of love, or of piety, might make out the shape of a cat. They watched us pass, and we looked them over as we went by, but none of us spoke. Two spears would not fight with three, that was common sense.

That night, and the following night, we set sentries, that is to say we took it in turns to sit by the fire and watch for the Cat King's men, watch the horses grazing hobbled. We had grown soft and lazy, each night we would build us a hut of branches to sleep in, our spears leaning against the door outside at the sentry's back. The second night, Occa was on watch, when he shouted to us to come.

'The horses' he was yelling, 'the horses' – and as we got into the open air we saw that someone had unhobbled them and was driving them away. We all three ran down the slope toward the horses. Then I thought we were fools all to go together, and I turned and sure enough there was someone around the hut. I shouted and ran back, and he went off into the wood like a streak.

All he took was my spear. The other two, being spearmen from boyhood, had grabbed theirs to go after the horses, but I had quite forgotten mine, and gone down drawing my sword.

'Easy come, easy go,' I said. Donar was more worried at the impiety.

'It will bring the thief no luck,' he told us, 'to take something hallowed by the God.'

'More to the point,' said Occa, 'there can only be the two of them now, or they'd have attacked. But they must be expecting more, and they've gone for the others while we can't move.'

For we each of us had, in our bags and in the silver sacks, more than a man will willingly carry for more than a few hundred paces, and there was no going to the north on foot. We argued a bit, and the upshot was that we agreed that Occa should go back on foot to find Marcomen of his own clan, and come in a day or two to rescue us. We two would look after the silver.

Occa rubbed wood ash into the pig fat on his face and arms till he was black as night. He left his cloak and wore only his tunic and trousers. He looked for a while at his sword. It was a fine piece of work, made somewhere in the Lebanon, beaten with the cedar charcoal that makes the iron so hard. The hilt was of beech wood carved into the shape of a coiled serpent, and for a pommel he had a great ball of crystal. The scabbard was of soft leather, embossed with the figures of Leda and the Swan, and all tooled with gold leaf, and sewn with gold wire. It was a lovely thing, and it took him long to decide to leave it on his bag, and go off with his spear and his shield and his long hunting knife. He moved away into the forest, silently.

I sat and talked with Donar.

'Why did you come south?' I asked him. It was no use asking him where he had come south from, or what was his nation, he turned all that aside, though there were some who said he talked like a kingless Vandal.

'I came to learn more about sword making,' he said. 'I wanted to know if there was any magic about the swords of the Legions that carried them through Gaul and on to the edge of Germany.'

'And was there?'

'None at all. Rather poor iron, most of it. We make better. Even the way you fight one by one, push and jab, push and jab, all the time, is more comical than anything else. But in a battle, it's the centurion who fights, and the cohort is his weapon.'

We lay and watched for the dawn.

'Talking of centurions,' I said, 'I wonder what Aristarchos is doing now.'

'Getting out of Julia's bed, I shouldn't wonder. You know, he

37

never expected you to get out of the way so smartly when he told you to.'

'What do you mean?'

'He hired these two men to watch you and then told you some cock-and-bull story about Scapellus coming back. He thought if you didn't turn up, he could get straight into bed with Julia, and if you stayed indoors for a couple of days she'd never look at you again. So he told you Scapellus was coming back … Funny thing, though …'

'What?'

'Old Occa had it from a friend in the Legion headquarters, he wouldn't tell Aristarchos, you know how these legionaries like to spite the cavalry. Scapellus *was* coming back at dawn, after all. I wonder if Aristarchos got up in time. I think it's dawn now. What about breakfast? I think we've got plenty of bacon.'

That day we took it in turns to sit on the kit-bags outside the hut, while turn and turn about we dug a hole in the hut floor, four feet deep, with our knives and our bleeding fingers. There we buried the silver-bags. We stacked our firewood in the hut too. We already had our plan, though we didn't think there would be any need for it for days, if at all. But the other Cat men must have come up sooner than they were expected, because that evening, while Donar was going down to the stream to get some water, they rushed me.

I looked up from where I was sitting, and there they were, a dozen of them, coming at me from the edge of the woods. I knew what to do. I picked a brand from our fire and threw it into the hut, and I shouted:

'Run, Donar, run, hide!' as loudly as I could.

Then one of them came at me with a spear, and I got my sword out, it always would stick and need a tug when I tried it, but that evening it came clean out like a flash. The man with the spear must have met swordsmen before, and when I parried he slipped through my parry, and though he didn't spit me the spear went through my tunic and tore my side. While I was trying not to scream and struggling to get back into the on guard position, someone else must have knocked me on the head. Down I went.

When I knew about things again I just lay still with my eyes shut. After a bit I could open my eyes without moving. That wasn't caution. After you've been knocked out you don't want to do anything but lie still for a long time. And you feel so sick. There was a lot of noise. They were arguing over where the silver had gone. They couldn't look in the hut till the fire died down, and anyway, simple men that they were, they couldn't believe that we'd burn the hut with silver inside. I could see a pair of puttees and very worn shoes near my face. This man was talking.

'We've only got one of them. If we wait around here too long we'll have Occa and half his clan here after us—'

'We've got his sword,' said somebody.

'Aye, good sword that.'

'The King will want that.'

The first man managed to make himself heard again.

'We'll wake this one up and make him tell us where the silver is.'

'Wake him? Make him? How do you do that?'

'How do you think? A bit of fun, that'll be.'

'A bit of fun, and them two listening out there?'

'It'll bring them back.'

'Them, and who else with them? We're not risking that.'

There seemed to be, to say the least, a division of authority in this band.

Someone new put in, the intellectual of the group obviously, with a compromise.

'Take him somewhere else and have your fun there. Don't do it where we can hear it.'

They brought a horse up, and somebody picked me up bodily, grey cloak and all, and slung me across the crupper in front of the rider.

'D'you want his spear?'

'Of course. I stuck him with it, didn't I?'

'They say Donar put his name on it. Stands to reason, don't it, if your name's on it, it'll get you.'

'I'll have his bag, too. The brown one, that's what he was carrying.'

The horse laboured under the load. My wound had begun to clot, but heaving me on to the animal's back had opened it again.

The horse smelt the blood and jibbed, and the jerking about made the wound hurt more, and my head throbbed. As the pain tightened, I went out again.

I opened my eyes on the pale light of dawn. Everything was pain – my head, my side. I saw life through a mist of pain. Carefully through my pain I felt myself beneath my cloak. I still had my knife, the one that had pointed to Joy. I held my knife in my pain. The horse stopped. He got down. I could not remember who or what had given me pain. I only knew that I must increase pain, breed pain, multiply pain, bring pain to its highest power.

He took me by the shoulders to pull me off.

I stabbed him through the cloak, under the ribs and up. The man screamed, the horse screamed. Through pain I knew where pain lived. We fell together. I was on top. I struck and struck as he screamed, to the groin, to the face I slashed at his eyes, he vomited blood, he jetted blood and pain. The knife had gone, I held hair. Through pain I beat his head on the ground, I felt bone break.

He had been a long time dead. He had been long out of pain. The painful river ran with painful noise. The painful sun was high. Somehow I must see what I was left with.

The horse had gone. He was still there. He had a bag, on the ground near him, with sausage. He had a water bottle, full. I washed my face, swilled out my mouth. A little farther was another water bottle; mine, empty.

I felt I could look at him. The flies crawled in his eyes. I took my knife from his armpit. I cleaned it in the ground, I washed the blood with water. I made myself eat some sausage. I brought it up. I ate more. I must.

I turned him over. He stank. His clothes were tattered. My cloak was bloody, but his was foul, drenched in blood and worse. There was a wallet on his belt. I cut it away; a few silver pieces, a lump of Amber. I knew what I was going to do. I wanted rope. I turned him over and over. Round his waist, not rope, a chain, an iron chain, a gang chain, with places for the necks, and a lock. No key. Where to look for the key?

He had a bronze ring. Why should a man wear a bronze ring? Those keys with a finger ring on the end are common enough here, but I found it hard to think of one there. But even in this wilderness, the chain was Roman, the lock was Roman. The key must be Roman.

Those tales you have heard of cutting off a finger from a body to take a ring. They are true. I did it. I had the key. I put it on my own finger.

I could move a little now. I rolled him fifty paces to the edge of the river. It might have been a mile. We were on the outside of a bend, where the stream ran deep and fast and had cut the bank into a low cliff. I pushed him over into the water. He floated away. I never knew his name.

I lowered the water bottles by their straps and filled them. I soaked the shirt away from my wound. It was long and ragged but not deep. If I could lie up somewhere for a few days I might be fit enough to walk back to Haro's farm. Cat men could follow the trail we had left, wolves could smell the blood. I must move on.

I reckoned that I could make perhaps a mile in the hour. It was slower going than that. After a few steps I stepped on my spear lying in the long grass, where it had fallen. I used it as a staff. It was easier then. I moved away from the river, through the scrub, alder and willow. I went up hill. There was nothing to my purpose. I had the set mind of the mad. No sane man would have done what I did.

I came out of the scrub. There was about half a mile of open space before the edge of the forest itself. There were charred stumps, spongy earth. The clearing had been burnt, frequently. No trees, nothing but grass had grown over it. In the centre of the clearing, too old and huge for a grass fire to harm, was an oak tree.

The oak in the burnt land should have warned. The scraps of rag and fur in the branches, the broken jars at the foot, the horse skulls around, should have told what it was. I was mad. Wolves could not climb a tree. Cat men could not see through a curtain of fresh leaves. Who sent me mad?

I got into the crown of the tree, a man's height above the ground. Too high for wolves to jump? Every movement now tore at my knitting side, my brains flowed loose in my skull. I leant

41

against a limb. The chain I passed round my body and the branch, and I locked it. The ring was on my finger. If I could wake three days on the heaving deck pressing down on the steering oar, then I could sleep three days in the still tree.

The light was going. The chain hurt. My head ached, my side burnt. It was bitterly cold. It was dark, darker than night, darker than a cave, darker than death.

4

That night the Most Holy One, the God himself, came to me. There are many appearances of Apollo, and you who have been brought up here in Rome know only Apollo the Youth, the Singer. But you who have never been to the Old City cannot know the God as He stands there in the Sanctuary. The God came from the Islands long ago and chose his own Temple. The God, the Father of Aesculapius, is an old man, long-haired, long-bearded, as indeed I was in those days. He is the Healer and the Destroyer, Apollo Paeon.

He stood before me in the tree, in breech clout and scarlet cloak, as he stands in the Sanctuary. All the night long He stood before me as He so long stood before our Fathers. For He is our Father, we are His sons, and before His son the Father stood the night through.

Near dawn I asked Him:

'Father Paeon, why are you here? Why are we here?'

He answered, 'When you stood with Joy at the river bank, when you took Joy's spear in your hand, did you not vow to go where I should send you? Now shall you pay your vow, and see the Hyperboreans from whence I came.'

'And what shall I do there, my Father?'

'Is not my name Apollo, and does it not mean Destruction? You shall bring destruction to all who are safe and contented. In the shadow of light shall you bring them the darkness of fire.'

Apollo brought the dawn as I hung in my chain. I moistened my lips as the sun came up, and I wished I could risk eating again, but the sausage was salty and my water would last three

42

days at most with great care. Toward noon, Apollo sent a sign. The cloud came over and there was a thunderstorm. My clothes were soaked, I drank the water that poured through my hair. I licked the water from the leaves and I ate. There was a hollow in the tree just in front of me that filled with water and I could just reach it, straining against the chain.

If I let the chain out, if I unlocked it and let it out a link or two, I would still be safe, I could reach the water without rasping the wound. I would – I had no key. There was no key on my finger, or in the wallet. Not on the ground beneath. There it was, a foot beyond my reach, below my reach. It hung on a twig as on a finger. And I could not reach it.

I wriggled and I squirmed. I could not get down to it. I tried to work the chain down, but it wouldn't come, it was stuck on some snag behind the limb. I could not reach round to it. I fought and writhed, and every movement tore at my side, opened the knitting wound, let the blood trickle again down my side. I hung in my chain and looked down. In my agony Apollo had sent a sign. In the grass the hyacinths bloomed as once they bloomed for Amyclos, son of the hyacinth, killed in far Sparta by the disc of Apollo.

As night fell, the God came again, but not as a man. Apollo Lykanthropos came, great grey shadowy forms in the dusk. If you ever come to the Old City and stand in the Sanctuary before the God, you will know what the wolf means to our family.

There were a score of them, and that in the late spring, when they hunt singly. They came and went in the dark. Just before dawn, at the time when Apollo spoke to me, when I was almost asleep in spite of my fear and pain and fatigue, the first one leapt. His teeth tore the toe of my shoe. I pulled up my feet into the crown, but still they leapt, not singly, but two or three at a time snapping and slavering. I could smell them, I could feel their spittle on my legs. For an hour in the twilight, the wolves danced, and to my wrist was still tied the spear which I must not use.

Apollo brought the sun, and there were no wolves. I licked the dew from the leaves. There were no clouds. I struggled with the chain, and brought blood. I could not reach the key. When the sun was high, I risked a pull at the water bottle. It was then

43

that I saw the men. They stood at the edge of the wood, and they danced in my eyes so that I could not count them. I tried to shout, but I had no voice. They were not there any more.

Then it was dark again, and light again. I do not know how often the dark and the light came. Or how often the wolves danced. After a while there was no water in the bottles. Only the dew and sometimes the rain. And the pain. I hung forward on the chain in pain. My head was an expanding flame, my mouth a sea of dust. And there was hunger, the worst hunger of all, for I had food that I dare not touch, the salt sausage.

There were creatures in the tree that crawled on the leaves, the slimy and hairy and creeping things that no man may eat. Yet I think that I tried to eat, and I think I retched. There were squirrels and birds, yet not one that came within reach of my spear. Somewhere in the tree were bees. And there was something in the tree I never saw, though I heard him slither in the branches and once I felt his long body trail across my thighs. Yet he was a comfort, for how should any snake, python or not, harm a man vowed to Apollo?

The wolves danced, and the rain drove through my cloak, and the sun glared down on the empty land. And I saw.

How far can you see from six feet up in an oak tree, on the edge of a forest in the plain? I tell you, I saw from sea to sea and from beginning to end. And the ghosts of the dead may haunt you, and the dread of them bring you to madness; but the ghosts of them who are doomed yet to be born – I tell you what I know, I tell you nothing that I have not seen, and the dread of that is too much for any mortal man. Look at my hair and know how dread it was.

In the east there is nothing. Nothing at all. There are more men than ever you could dream of. But every man looks exactly like his neighbour, and every generation is exactly like every other generation. Nor is there ever any change or ever anything new.

But to the west, the whole land is a pot of porridge and the walls of the Empire are the sides of the pot. Every bubble in the porridge is a nation and nations are born as the bubbles burst. In the end the pot will boil over. For it is not the pot only that boils but the very air.

44

I told you that in those days it was warmer than it is now, and you thought that it was the delusion of an old man trying to keep his bones from freezing.

But I know that Apollo himself comes and goes as he pleases, and that sometimes he withdraws the Chariot of the Sun from the earth, and sometimes comes nearer, and between the warmest and the coldest times may be hundreds of years.

From six feet up in the oak tree, while the snake moved about me and above me and behind me, I saw the cold and the heat come and go, age on age, from the tree to the ocean, and beyond the ocean. For there are lands beyond the ocean. As I hung in my chains, Apollo let me see in my pain that he is even now withdrawing from the earth. As the earth got colder, the porridge boiled over and swamped into the Empire. And as porridge which boils over is burnt and charred and changed into ash, so the barbarians who will boil over into the Empire will be changed and transmuted and charred into new nations, neither Roman nor Barbarian. And every one of these nations that is changed will be led by the sons of Votan, who lead only because they are Votan-born. And the Votan-born will spread over the whole earth, and whatever people they conquer they will turn into something like themselves.

The colder it gets, and the farther Apollo goes from the earth, the more the nations of the Votan-born will turn to the sea, and go out to face the storms of the ocean, and the terrors that lie beyond the ocean. But when Apollo approaches nearer the earth, then they will turn to the east. And in the east they will have little luck. They will conquer no land, nor will they change any nation, but rather will they be changed themselves.

My tree, the oak tree, stood somewhere in the borders between east and west. Beneath it I saw the Votan-born lead their people against the east, and the east ride back over their bodies. And when they had any success and ruled for a time over the east, the east in time always swallowed them up.

Yet the Votan-born ride against the east again and again. Sometimes they ride in the name of an Emperor who was a God, and sometimes in the name of an Emperor who knew no God, and sometimes in the name of a God who could not be an

Emperor, because he was a God of Peace, and sometimes they ride in the names of no one but themselves. But whether they ride cased in furs against the cold or cased in iron against the arrows, whether they fight with swords or with fire, they ride against the east because the east rides against them. And always they die. Some die well, in battle or in bed. Some die ill, of dysentery or plague, or drowned in a ditch or crammed in a barn and burnt. And near the end of time, they will die not well or badly, but miserably, passionlessly, wretchedly, hopelessly, walking in naked columns to choke.

And at the end of time – there will be an end of time. After the Votan-born have made the greatest music, and have painted the greatest pictures and sung the greatest songs that can ever be, then the east will come against them for the last time. And then, knowing clearly what they do, but not knowing whose will they do, the Votan-born will dissolve the whole world in fire, and they will return to the Sun whose sons they are.

Out of that glare of fire I woke to the glare of noon. The men came, and I could not speak to them. They came to the very foot of the tree, and before my dry eyes they poured out cool, clear, bitter beer at the roots. Then they too were gone.

After that my head became very heavy. I saw every thing far away yet very clear as when you look through glass into clear water, at shells and little fishes. I knew I was going to die. I watched the empty land and watched myself die.

At sunset there was a thunderstorm, and the rain ran into the hollow, and I drank. Then I slept till I woke in the darkness. There was someone in the tree. You must know that there cannot be Apollo without Artemis. You cannot love the wolf and hate the bear. I heard her scramble into the branches, and the little twigs break beneath her. I heard her claws scratch on the bark. Then the bear turned to me, hairy chest against my chest, face against my face, breath mixed with my breath, cold teeth smooth against my cheek. She stayed while I might count a hundred. Then she climbed up, and I knew by the sounds that she had found the bees' nest. Honey, wild honey, poured down on to my head and face, and I licked it off. The wolves did not come.

Toward dawn, the God stood before me again, and spoke.

46

'Go north, and begin the End for me. But do not call upon my name till you come again within the cities of the Empire. For long ago I left the Hyperboreans. Where you find peace, you will leave war, and where stability, confusion, and where trust, deceit. But in all you shall do my will.'

Then I felt that the snag at the back of the limb was broken, and the chain ran smoothly up and down the tree. I saw myself alone and wounded and hungry on the great plain, and I thought that it no longer mattered.

5

I was very far gone. The whole world seemed far away. I stood back and looked at myself. I saw how slow I was in thinking and I marvelled at it. I saw that my limbs trembled like an old man's. I watched my own mind work slowly through the argument that if my chain was slack I ought to be able to reach the key. After an hour or more, I saw myself decide to try. Very slowly I worked the chain down the tree. For some reason I was afraid that I might fall.

Little pieces fell out of my time of life, little holes of blackness. My side was a dull glow that fanned into flame every time I moved. There was still some water in the hollow. When I had reached the bottom of the chain's movement, I allowed myself a mouthful.

I touched the key once or twice. I hardly believed it was still there. I put the ring on my finger. I opened the lock. The chain fell away. I let my spear fall after it. I finished the water in the hollow; now I could walk, crawl, to more. I slid to the ground, my feet touched the earth; then my face.

When the blackness was over again, I found my spear and leaned it against the tree. I climbed up it, to my knees, to my feet. The men were there, a dozen of them, big men, with shaven heads and long yellow moustaches, dressed in the German fashion but unbelievably shabby. I waited to be killed.

They stood about ten yards from me. They had no weapons at all. One of them, the oldest, I thought, came forward and said something. I could not understand a word. I said in German:

'Drink … drink …'

One of them, a boy, brought forward a pot. There is nothing like bitter beer for quenching your thirst. I drained it.

The older man then said something in German, very thickly accented. At first I thought he was talking about the Old Father Mountain, and I said 'Yes, Yes' and pointed. He talked on, and I slowly began to follow. He was calling me Old Father – no, he was calling me Allfather. This was wrong. This was what they called the God in Germany. I said: 'No, no, Photinus, I am Photinus,' and the man said,

'Yes, yes, Votan, Votan Allfather. Come, Allfather, come and eat.'

I was too ill to protest any further. I tried to step forward, but I could not move. Some of the men ran back to the edge of the wood, and returned with a litter made of boughs. They helped me on to it, and carried me away. One of the boys carried my spear erect before me. Another picked up my bag, turned it inside out, and under the horrified gaze of his seniors gobbled up the end of sausage left in it. Before the older men, crimson with rage and shame, could begin to scold, I said, 'Eat, eat it all!'

Another man picked up my two water bottles and shook them. There was a swishing sound. One of them still had about a pint of water. Had I, in my delirium, always gone to the same bottle to drink, and always found it empty?

They carried me some miles along the river edge to where they lived in little huts of boughs. They were a wandering people with neither king nor cities nor any possessions, not even any iron, who lived on what they could gather and catch along the river and in the woods. For their clothes and pots, and even for corn, they traded the furs they caught through the winter.

'We take them,' said the headman, who said his name was Tawalz, 'to the Asers, and they give us the good things of life.'

'Who are the Asers?' I asked him, for this was a name I had not heard before. But all Tawalz would say was, 'We take you to Asers, you meet Asers, first you heal.'

In one of the huts, Tawalz and some old women cut and soaked away the shirt from my wound, and – and this shows how poor they were – one of the old women took my shirt away and carefully darned up the tears, and washed it and brought it back to me. First they cared for the scabby weals the chain had made on my chest, and the scratches from the branches and the insect bites. They brought ointment to smear on, but I would not let them use it till I was sure that it was not bear fat.

Over the great festering wound in my side they were more concerned. Tawalz said:

'It is not deep but it will remain open till we can find the healing stone that is upon the sword and lay it upon the wound.'

'It was no sword,' I said. 'It was a spear, and my own spear, that the lad carried into camp.'

So they brought the spear, and just like any civilised doctor Tawalz put ointment on the head and bound it up and vowed the hurt of the wound to the God, and then cleaned the wound itself and bandaged it.

I wanted to sleep, but the old women, all anxious, said through Tawalz that I must eat first. They brought me stewed meat in a bowl, and when I tasted it, it was something that I had not tasted for years, it was horse. I asked them why horse, and Tawalz said:

'Allfather, it is a horse for you.'

They had caught a horse loose in the forest, and while you or I, if we found a stray horse, and there was no danger of being caught, would use it or sell it, they knew no better than to take it to the tree, which was all the temple that they had, and sacrifice it. But to my horror, it became clear that the horse was sacrificed to me, and now they expected me to eat it all. Have you ever tried to eat a whole horse? The old ladies were very insistent that I should. First I could eat it fresh, and then I would have it salt, and with the offal and the intestines they could make sausages, and they were busy cleaning the skin to make a blanket for my bed. I forget what they were going to do with the hooves.

I managed to get over to them the idea that if the sacrifice were to me, then I could do as I liked with it. So I would give a feast to the whole clan. And since it is no use eating flesh alone, I gave some of the silver pieces from the wallet for two of the young men to run twelve hours each way to the nearest German farm, where they had an arrangement, to buy corn, salt and beer. Then they let me sleep.

But before I slept I looked at my hair as it lay on the pillow, and I grew afraid. I asked for a mirror, and of course they had no such thing, but when they understood at last they brought me a bowl of water. When it was still I looked at my reflection in the water. My face was lined and haggard, as I expected. What I did not expect was this, that in those days on the tree, my hair and my beard had changed from black to white. From that day to this, I have been as you see me, a white-haired man, and for years I bore an old man's head on a young man's body. It is not at all a bad thing in many ways. It gives you an authority, a reputation which you would not otherwise possess, and old men and chieftains bow to you and call you Father, or even Allfather. White-haired Photinus I have been ever since, and it was as a white-haired man that I came to the Northern Sea and faced the Asers.

6

I slept for twenty-four hours, as far as I could guess. When I woke, they brought me my clothes, all washed and pressed with smooth stones, and they also brought me all the horse furniture. This was not only the rope harness and iron bit and a few iron fittings, but the blanket too, red and blue check, and my own kit-bag. So I went to their feast in all dignity in my best blue tunic, and I drank from my own silver cup, and I ate off my own silver plate. We ate the horse; forty of us left little of a horse, or of a couple of deer and a few dozen carp with it. There was enough beer for all the adults to drink their fill, and even for the children to taste. The women, as well as the men, sat round the fire to eat.

These people are used to eating but once a day, and that not every day. Their bread was the worst I tasted in the north, being over half acorn and birch pith mixed with the flour. They called themselves the Polyani, from their word for the river meadows in which they lived; and they were proudly distinct from the Rus, who spoke the same language and lived in the same way, but farther east on the wide plains of grass, next to the yellow men, or the Lesny, who lived in the forests between.

I tried to find out who or what they thought I was.

'Joy led us to Allfather, joy told us he was here,' said Tawalz, and I was never sure if I had understood him correctly. 'We come to the tree, and we see Allfather chained there to hunger and to thirst. Yet there is water in his bottles, and there is food in his bag. We see the wolf dance to Allfather, and we see the bear come to feed Allfather and bring him honey. And at the end we see Allfather bend down for his magic and unlock his chain and step from the tree.'

'How many days was I in the tree?' I asked.

'Oh, many days, many days,' said Tawalz. 'Many days – nine days.' But later I realised that nine was an indefinite number to them, more than several and less than many. I was never sure how they regarded me, as the epiphany of a God or as a Holy Man fulfilling a vow. We talked of other things. I told them of cities. They listened, and then said:

'Oh, yes, like Asgard.'

'What is Asgard?' I asked, but they had never been there, they only knew it was where the Asers, most of them, lived, and if it were not a city then it was recognisably like one. I talked about Egypt, and I told them of the elephant. They said, yes, they knew all about elephants, and they drew one in the sand to show that they knew exactly what I meant. They said that far to the north of them was a desert, but a desert of ice, not of sand, and this is reasonable, for the earth is perfect and symmetrical and there must be deserts of cold to balance the deserts of heat. In those deserts too, it seems, there live elephants, but they do not wander about the earth. There they burrow underground, seeking in the heart of the earth the warmth they cannot find on the surface. When they come to the surface the light kills them at once, and so they are often found at the end of the winter, which is one long night, dead half-way out of their burrows in the ground. The Polyani and the Rus call them Mamunt.

The Polyani had no real Gods, only a few spirits of pools and woods and rivers, that were better bribed than worshipped. Where they felt the need, they borrowed the Gods of the richer people around, the Germans, or farther east, the Scyths, or in the south the Greeks. Tawalz said:

'We knew you would come, Allfather, because long ago, in

51

Grandfather's Grandfather's time, a man came talking about a God, who hung on a tree, and was wounded with a spear. He said this God would come to us alive. We do not know it is Allfather.'

I asked who this man was, but they could not tell me, except that he would not eat wild boar. At the end, they had been forced to do what he seemed, to the best of their understanding, to be asking them to do. They ate him and drank his blood. This had been a most repugnant thing for Tawalz's ancestors, and only their excess of courtesy, and their desire to do whatever their guest requested, had brought them to do it. Besides, the tradition was that he tasted vile, and most of him had been decently burnt. They hoped that this minor waste did not offend me. This was the only thing they told me that I found it difficult to believe.

It took another ten days or so after the feast before my side was healed well enough to travel. I was very weak, and I spent the time sitting at the river bank fishing. There are no Votan-born among the Polyani. I watched Tawalz and his brother Olen build the raft on which they would take the winter's catch of furs, bundled up by kind, down river to, they said, Outgard, wherever that might be, to sell, they said, to Loki, whoever he might be.

'Is he an Aser?' I asked, and they hummed and hawed, and were of two minds.

'Is he an Amber King?' I asked, and of that too they were uncertain. They only knew that he was the man who would sell them iron and cloth and salt for their furs. They had very little iron. There was but the one axe in the whole band, and that among people who lived on the forest edge. The raft they built well, of logs jointed and dowelled together, with a little shelter, for us to sleep in.

In the end we went off, Tawalz and Olen and I. There was little poling to do, the river carried us on, and we would stop for the night near the camps of other little bands of Polyani. I could not follow much that they said, but I knew that the tale of the white-haired man who starved on purpose wounded in a tree, attended by wolves and snakes, was travelling well ahead of us. The further we got, the greater the respect with which I was treated, and of course some of this consideration rubbed off on to Tawalz. Later it profited him.

7

One afternoon we came to Outgard. The river was wide and shallow, fordable for a man on foot. We grounded the raft on a sloping beach on the east side of the stream. The two Polyani humped the bales of furs out on to the bank. Tawalz led me up from the water's edge to the beginning of a path paved with logs. At the end of the path well above the flood level was the long black line of a palisade. Olen came behind. I looked back at the bales of furs, abandoned.

'Will they be safe?' I asked.

'Of course,' said Tawalz. 'Look, here come porters. And up there, see? Vandals.'

There were three or four Germans lounging at the gates, different from the crowd of Polyani who passed us as they went to carry the furs in. The men at the gate were big men in all their gear, with spears, shields, and, something I had not seen before in the north, mail shirts. They wore helmets, second-hand legionary pattern, and each had a blue cloak. I found out later that this was a batch of cloth that Loki had bought as a speculation and been unable to sell, so he had paid his Vandals in cloth.

'Loki keeps them here. Nobody steals furs. Loki sits within the gate.'

And he did. By all the rules, looking back, I should have hated Loki. In fact I rather liked him. I kept on liking him, really, right up to the end. He was young then, about thirty, and my build, fair hair and blue eyes, of course. He was the first German I ever met who was a dandy. He was wearing a red shirt and blue trousers, and yellow puttees matching his yellow cloak. He had soft leather knee boots and a soft leather belt, two palms wide, worked with a pattern of silver wire. Round his neck hung a great globe of Amber on a golden chain.

He carried no sword, and I tell you, he was clean. He wasn't as clean, say, as an auxiliary trooper going on duty, but he was about as clean as the Polyani who spend all their time in and out of the water. The Polyani, though, never bothered to brush the mud off. Loki was a great deal cleaner than the Marcomen.

Loki was more like a Greek than any German I ever met. Not, of course, like one of those stupid dolts from Attica or the Peloponnese, but one of your bright lads from Rhodes or Alexandria. He was a merchant, and there he sat at the gate in a kind of booth, with his scales and his measures on the table. He spoke to Tawalz, as soon as we appeared, in the good old beat-'em-down-below-cost manner.

'What do you think you're doing here? Far too late, far too late.'

Tawalz was used to this. He said,

'Furs. Fine furs, you never saw better. Such you never see again.'

'It's been a bad year, all down the river. Poor stuff, take it away.'

'No, all good fur, first rate. It surprised us all. *He* brought it.'

'Who's 'he'?'

I had been standing carefully withdrawn from the scene. With my old grey cloak pulled around me, I leaned on my spear and looked round, inside the palisade. It was a big enclosure, a hundred and fifty paces each way, and all as neat and tidy as a legionary fort. At my right, along one side, was a double row of barns and stables. At the other side were huts, obviously for people. In front of me, at the far side, was a great hall, twice as big as Haro's, with a huddle of kitchens and larders behind. In the open space in front was a kind of market with stalls, and a great throng of men buying and selling.

But Outgard was not a city. In the first place, there were no women, and certainly no confused crowd of children who get under your feet in the smallest German village. Secondly, that palisade was no wall, but a frail fence, built to keep horses in, not thieves out. Like all the houses, the fence had a temporary look. Even the fresh coat of tar merely made it look newer, less rooted. But it was something to look at while I withdrew my gaze from Tawalz who was whispering to Loki about 'Nine days … wolves … bear … honey.' Then Loki called out,

'Hey, you! Greybeard!'

I just didn't hear him, till he used my name and asked, 'Votan! Where do you come from, and where are you going?'

So I paid him for his calculated discourtesy with a long stare, and then:

'If I fight with Mamunt below the earth, or ride the sky beyond the clouds, what is it to you where I go?' And to illustrate, I swung my spear point in a great arc from ground to sky to ground, and everyone watched the shining arc, and nobody saw my hands at all.

Loki didn't try to answer that, he just wanted time to think, now that the rumours he had heard had come true. So he returned,

'No gossiping in business hours. Eat at my right hand to-night. There will be a hut for you, for you alone. Tawalz will show you.'

I turned away, but Loki hadn't finished.

'Hey, that spear. No one goes armed in Outgard. Leave it with the Vandals at the gate!'

There was no harm in leaving him the appearance of authority. I leaned over his table and stood the spear in the corner of his booth, behind his back.

'Take care of it,' I said. 'A God gave it to me. The last man who touched it without leave is dead.'

Off I went toward the market. Nobody who tries to sound as businesslike as that should be allowed an inch of latitude. Five paces from the booth, I turned and called to Loki.

'Keep your eyes on the stock, merchant! Catch!' And I threw him the Amber globe.

8

Now how was I to dine with the Lord of the Amber Road in my rags? I had only two or three silver coins, and my silver cup and plate which I would need. It was like taking a cake from a blind baby. Those poor Germans never knew what hit them.

The first group I came to were playing the old game with three cups and a pea. Now I will not ask you to believe that I invented it; but Autolycus did, and he was staying with the Family at the time. I watched a bit, and gossiped.

'Come far?'

'Thuringia. Back tomorrow, thank heaven.'

I lost a diplomatic denarius.

'What did you bring up?'

'Usual. Linen out, back in furs. Ferdi there, he came up in glass. Risky trade that, but profitable.'

'Any Amber?'

'Not here, you'll have to go to Asgard for it. Loki buys it in from the forest dwellers, and the furs, but he only sells furs. The Amber all goes back to Asgard, and Njord only sells for silver.'

I put the rest of my own silver down. The dealer covered it and I took him. In another four passes I cleaned him out. Then I took the cups and won what the rest of the school had between them. Then I allowed everybody to win something back, and even let the dealer have enough to start again, so I went off letting them all think that the game had been fair.

The next pair were playing the finger game. You know, I shoot out fingers and you shout a number at the same time. If you are right, you win. This sounds like pure chance, but you watch people playing. They think they are shouting at random, but everyone has favourite numbers, and if you watch a man for a little you can always work out his system. Then you can take him as far as you like. I did. I didn't clean them out, just took enough to do the job.

What they lost was mostly silver jewellery, and a very few coins. I went to one of the market stalls. There was a Vandal behind it. All the stalls belonged to Loki. There were Vandals behind them all. I got a grey tunic, grey trousers, good boots, a soft belt. Then something caught my fancy, and I bought a big grey hat with a floppy brim. I asked about a cloak as long as the one I had on, and I was promised delivery next morning. They were fairly popular, the man said, but not in grey, the colour wasn't really worth stocking. No German will wear grey, or that dark blue the Vandals used, if he can possibly help it.

I thought of the two Polyani. I had given Olen my blue tunic because he hadn't got one at all, but his trousers were all right. I got a suit for Tawalz, nothing fancy, but tough, and boots for the pair of them. Then I added a few iron fish hooks and a dozen iron arrow points. You know, they were used to going in after boar with bone-tipped arrows, and they haven't got the penetration to slow the beast up at all.

Then I was down to my last few silver pieces again. But at

least I was respectable. With three silver pieces I could start again. I had a set of loaded dice in my bag. There were two or three likely prospects I'd marked down. There was even one who might go for a gold brick – or would it be a silver one up here? That could wait till an emergency. Did I tell you, once in Alexandria I sold the Pharos to three different people in one day, and another day, the whole Library?

9

So, decent, we went into the hall. And though they firmly settled Olen near the door, the Vandals put Tawalz fairly well up, and me, of course, they led to sit with Loki at the top table.

No, Loki told me, he wasn't a Vandal. He seemed pleased to talk to me, to have somebody new to talk to must have been rare. He said he was an Aser.

'Yes, I came out here some years ago, and I took Outgard over completely when my uncle Bergelmir ... left. It's a bit lonely, but quite comfortable.'

Loki was comfortable. On the top table we had silver-mounted drinking horns, and silver plate. And we had wine to drink, only Italian of course, but still better than beer. I was telling Loki how much better the wine would be with a lacing of sea-water, when a big man, rather drunk, but not so drunk he wasn't nasty, stood in front of us and threw down his cloak on the floor. That, I knew, was a challenge to fight any man in the house. I tried to ignore it, but he didn't ignore me. There were no takers – the man on my right whispered that Grude was a notorious bully – so he leant on the top table and taunted me with cowardice, age, and stupidity. None of which was true. I don't like to say that Loki had arranged this, but there would have been no fight in his hall without his approval, and it was an attractive chance of getting rid of two nuisances at once.

Grude leant over and leaned his elbows on the table and breathed beer all over me with a stream of insults that would have withered the whiskers off a boar. When I sat there like a log, Loki helped by sneering:

'You'll be all right, I'll lend you a mail shirt.'

Of course, I was fool enough to say, 'I have no sword,' and at once there was a Vandal at my elbow with a whole bundle of them which their owners had deposited with him at the door for safe keeping. He offered me the hilts, and I shut my eyes and took one at random.

The God guided my hand. There was a roar of laughter in the hall, and Grude snatched the weapon away from me. It was his own sword. For a moment he looked as if he were going to throw it away, but then he must have felt a bit sheepish and he kept it. Still, it unsettled him for the evening, and I think it was really the death of him.

I turned my head away again, and took another, and again the God guided me. This was no German sword, I thought, this was a Greek Kopis like my own, not too long, pointed, one edge sharp, the other finger-thick, the bone breaker. I had heard that they had been once in fashion all over Germany. Now they only lingered in the far west.

This I could use. The weight of the blade was a little far forward for my liking, but otherwise the balance was perfect. I passed it from hand to hand, tossed it up and caught it, and tried a few wrist flicks. It was then that some people began to realise that this was a real contest, and I heard the odds shorten. I looked around to get a few denarii on before it came down to evens, but somebody got in the way, holding out an oilstone and saying,

'Make her sharp, make my little Jutta sharp.' He was a middle-aged man with a thick north-western accent. 'Treat her well, she is thirsty, my sax.'

It was obvious that he was a little afraid of having the costly blade damaged.

'She'll be all right,' I told him. 'I shed no blood.'

He caught my eye and my meaning. With the look of one craftsman meeting another, he held the sword up and breathed on the blade, below the hilt.

'Look, a snake sword,' and, sure enough, in the torchlight little snakes twisted in the iron.

I held Jutta comfortably and stood on a stain at one corner of the cloak. I kept my back to Loki; I didn't want those eyes on

58

mine. Someone gave me a shield, and I threw it away. This gave Grude first stroke, although he was the challenger, but it forced him to throw away his shield too. He wasn't used to fighting like that, but I was, and what use are rules if you can't use them?

I had to think of tactics. I couldn't try to tire him out, I was still weak from the tree. I didn't want to go moving around over the mutton bones. I knew what to do, but a lot of people were shouting advice, and examples of excellent wit like, 'Show him your stuffing, Votan.' Nobody seemed to be shouting for Grude, and it was just as well, the whole thing didn't last long.

We took guard, Loki shouted, 'Ready!', and Grude tried a downward cut. He was a bit clumsy, and I just pushed his sword away and instead of cutting myself I carried the parry on into a jab-jab-jab at his eyes. I thought I might force him off the cloak, but he'd met this before, and now he tried a cut, roundarm, almost horizontal. So nothing was easier than to counter by bringing the blunt edge of Jutta down on to his wrist, so that we heard the bone crack. The sword went flying and I followed through with all my might on to his kneecap.

He went down like a log, and lay there screaming, which drew some comment, but you will admit that a broken wrist and a smashed kneecap together are rather painful. And then I found out the kind of people I was living with.

A couple of Vandals picked Grude up.

'How is he?' asked Loki.

'His wrist is smashed, and he'll never walk straight again.'

'What use is that to us?' Loki said, and they heaved him up over a bench and somebody cut off his head with his own sword. I believe Loki got hold of his farm after that. They carted out the body and threw sawdust on the floor to stop the dogs licking the blood.

They brought me Grude's belongings, as was right. There was quite a lot of silver coin and a few pieces of gold in a wallet, some scraps of Amber, a gold neck chain, and a gold ring with a big yellow stone in it. Next day, I took Cutha, who owned Jutta, to a goldsmith and he opened the ring and closed it again tightly around the grip, so that shapely sword at last had some adornment. I recited twenty lines of Homer over it, Hector's speech to

Andromache which seemed appropriate, and scratched my name in the soft gold, so that Cutha thought Jutta had a real healing stone at last.

But that night, most of the western Germans crowded around me, laughing and shouting congratulations, and so did some of the Vandals. Some of the others said I had not acted fairly in going straight from a parry into a stroke without waiting, but nobody now dared say it close enough for me to hear.

They brought me Grude's sword and shield. I said I didn't want them, though I did keep the belt, which was better than the one I had bought. When I pushed Grude's sword away, Cutha offered me Jutta in exchange, saying, 'She likes you, she'll go with you,' but he was quite drunk, so I said I would have no sword till Donar made me one. At this, some of the Vandals laughed, as if Donar, some Donar, was dead and done for, but the westerners looked very impressed.

In the end I gave Grude's sword, and the shield, to Tawalz. He was the first of all the Polyani to bear arms like a free man, and the first to make his authority felt over more than one band. Trouble and blood came of that gift and little else.

The chain and the silver I used to buy more gifts for the Polyani, spear heads and axes and iron pots, and bolts of linen and woollen cloth. No pottery or glass, which they would dearly have loved, since there was little chance of their getting all the way back unbroken; but I did send bronze brooches for the old ladies who had nursed me, and a bronze mirror that they might see what one looked like.

The return for the furs Tawalz took in grain and beer. This was little in comparison to the furs, and he decided to leave the rest till later in the year. Loki not only did not allow him interest on this debt, but even charged him a fee for storage. He would have done well in Alexandria.

I gave the belt I'd bought to Tawalz. So I had little gain from the bloody affair, indeed I lost, for no one now would fight with me, and there was no chance of persuading anyone that I was qualified to sell him the Amber mines, or wherever they got the stuff. (I never did find out how you get it, and I think someone must have had a fine time telling Tacitus that tale about picking it up on the sea shore.) So it was as a dangerous man and a well-known one that I left Outgard. And through the Vandals and their wives who lived in the village over the ridge, and through the traders who were there that night, all Germany soon knew of the white-haired man from the tree who had come out of the forest.

10

I had two nights at Outgard. The second evening was quiet, perhaps because I spent most of the day leaning on my spear in front of Loki's booth, and just looking at him as he worked. This unsettled him so much that, in plain language, he offered me a horse to go away to Asgard and annoy somebody else. So I went.

I went in company with the Saxons who had been at the first dinner. They had a packtrain, and a packmaster, a big man with one hand; he had lost his right hand, and carried his shield on his forearm, and his spear in his left. They had been waiting for him to arrive; he came in the day after the fight. As we went the Saxons told me about the Asers. They appeared not sure whether to expect from me omniscience or universal ignorance.

I found out a lot that would have been useful to Otho. The Asers were the lords of the Amber roads. The Polyani lived beyond the river. Beyond them, and to the north-east lived the Scrawlings. North again, across the shallow seas, lived the Goths, who were Germans. It was these peoples who brought in the furs and the Amber. They would only trade with the Asers. The Asers held immense stocks of all they wanted, close to the river and the sea, so that we, if we tried, could never outbid the Asers. All trade had to be through the Asers.

On the other hand, to the traders the Asers supplied packtrains and escorts at low prices, and on the roads between the three great Aser posts, at Outgard, Asgard and Westgard toward the Rhine, they had stopping places for the packtrains.

At one of these we stopped the first night. We rode into a palisade, and there were men to take the horses and stable them, and Vandals to check every bale and put it into the stores. We went into a hall, and we stood in line to receive great platters of stewed meat and vegetables, and bread, and each man his horn of beer. There was as much food as you could eat, as often as you returned for more, but extra beer you had to buy at a counter in the corner. I sat with Cutha and asked, 'Is Loki an Aser?'

'Some say he is, and some say he isn't. He came from Asgard, sure enough, and Njord sent him. And it wasn't long before he drove out Bergelmir, the old man, now he really was an Aser. Where Bergelmir went no one knows, but he strode away vowing vengeance on Njord and Loki and all the Aser house. But Tyr, there, the packtrain leader, now he is an Aser. Look, he's going to tell one of his tales; up on the table, there he goes.'

And up Tyr stood indeed, to give what was always a popular piece, though this was the first time of many that I ever heard it. He had a sausage in his hand, and as he recited he alternately took bites and made obscene gestures.

'It fell, a couple of years ago, at the end of a long wet summer, that Ulla and Hermod and I went to forage down in Thuringia. The pickings weren't very good, not enough to live through the winter, just a few furs and some girls, that we sold off cheap to the Marcomen. All those goods that went straight down, to Carnuntum and Vindabonum, they sold for silver and glass and wine, and all we got was some sausage.'

'What, sausage?' shouted the audience, they weren't subtle and this was the traditional response to Tyr.

'Yes, sausage,' and the one he had was as long as your arm and as thick as your wrist.

'Well, the girls weren't up to much, and we very soon finished the sausage. We hadn't as much as a roof to our heads, when the leaves were beginning to fall. My trousers were full of enormous holes, and Ulla was hardly decent, so Hermod, who was respectable then, said we ought to go on into Dacia. There we'd meet no one who knew us before, and bring no disgrace to our families. At worst we'd beg bread from the peasants and slaves, and we might find a chieftain to feast us.'

'But the people of Dacia are crafty and mean, the crows starve to death in their cornfields. The rags of my bottom were beating my brains out, and the cold struck chill to my liver ...'

62

'To your liver?' and they all cheered.

'To my liver. For a good square meal, I'd have gone past the river to ride for a soldier in Britain. It was then that Hermod found us a horse, a fine black horse with a saddle. The man who rode it was drunk in a ditch, he left us never a penny, and his trousers wouldn't fit any of us, so we went on east by the river. We slept that night in a hole in a ditch, and the horse we hobbled and tethered. We slept in a ditch as beggars do, and that night a Roman robbed us!'

'Robbed you?'

'Aye, robbed us. We woke in the morning, our horse was gone, and our trousers were hung in a treetop. The thief left his runes in the bark of a tree, Aristarchos the son of Demos. Let Romans rob beggars as much as they like, but they ought to stay in their own country. We weren't going to let them do it again, so we went north in a hurry. North we went in hunger and cold, for the snow had come and the winter, till up in the mountains we came to a hall that belonged to a noble named Fenris.'

'Named Fenris?' they all bawled.

'Yes, Fenris. We told him the tale of how we'd been robbed by Romans down by the river. They'd taken our horses, our silver, our gold, they'd taken our horns and our trousers. Only our swords that we slept on at night were left to show we were noble. They'd driven us out in hunger and cold to trudge our way home through the mountains, when all that we wanted was freedom to go, to the east to try Scythian women. But we'll never see Scythian women now, the Polyani have got all the traffic.

'Fenris was warm-hearted and generous, the fool, and he took us into his household. He had seven fine daughters and seven strapping sons, though these last had gone off to … forage.'

'To forage?'

'Yes, to forage.' They passed Tyr up another sausage, he'd finished the first one.

'Now old Fenris lived well, with Amber and bronzes, wine, furs and salt fishes, with silver and salt. He lived on the Asers, though little they knew it. He bribed men and bought men, he raided, he cheated, he swam across rivers and emptied the trap lines, and all that he got he sent down to the Romans, he passed it through Otho to sell at cut prices. No, he had no morals and no sense of beauty, no rings or cartels could appeal to his soul. And so he grew wealthy on crumbs from the table of great Njord Borsson, the Lord of the Asers. Drink all to the Asers, drink to great Njord Borsson.'

Everyone drank, and then of course they went back to the counter for more beer.

'Fenris had one daughter, a lass called Hedwiga, a tall wench and strapping, with skin smooth as marble. Her hair that hung braided in two yellow pigtails hung thick long and fragrant clear down to her bottom. They swayed and they bounced as she walked in the rickyard, her hips swaged, her breasts shimmered, a sight for the starving. I knew she'd come, the way she looked at me, once alone in the barn we'd soon have got … friendly.'

'What, friendly?'

'Yes, friendly. Another loved Ulla, and one wanted Hermod, we'd soon have been talking if not for their father. He had eyes where we had backbones, he had ears where we have toenails, he could hear the sun arising, he could see the grass a-growing, seven daughters on the rampage he could watch and never miss one. How then do you bed a woman when her father watches daily, when her father listens nightly, when she sleeps behind the hangings, and his bed's across the doorway?

'Then Hermod had a brainwave, he always was a genius, we'd get the old man drunk and pass him where he lay. Don't ever drink with Fenris, it really isn't worth it, his legs and feet are hollow, and the beer just drains away. So even drinking three to one, he had us on the floor.

'Then Hermod had a brainwave, he always was a genius, we'd tie the old man up, and let *him* sleep upon the floor. And we said that night to Fenris, when the ale horns were half empty, "Fenris, we know you are a mighty man. You walk the forest with a giant's strength. Oak trees your fingers pluck from out the earth. The winter wind is not more powerful. Has no one ever tried to bind your arms?" "Many have tried," said Fenris, "none succeeded. Tie up my arms with any cord you like and I will break it."

'So we tied him up first with a short length of fish line, thin light and strong – he broke it at once. Then we took twine that

64

we use for the corn sheaves, doubled, re-doubled, an eightfold cord. He strained for a moment, then jerked, and behold it, the eightfold cord was snapped clean away.

'Now Fenris was fuddled and hazy with drinking, so we took some boat line as thick as my thumb. We tied him and wrapped him to look like a parcel, and all was set fair to get into bed. Then Hermod had a brainwave, he always was a genius, said, "Let's put him out, let him sit in the cold for the wolves to eat him," and when he said wolves, old Fenris went mad. He stretched and he strained, he wrenched and he wriggled, his face it went red and his wrists they went white. We three men stopped laughing, the girls they stopped giggling, and then in the silence we heard the knots burst!'

'The knots burst?'

'The knots burst, the rope burst, the hemp strands went flying, the benches went flying, and Fenris went mad. With an axe from the wall he chased us and flailed us, he splintered the tables and split all the stools. He shivered the pillars, he broke up the braziers, he cut up six rats and bisected a dog. The tables were scattered, the floor straw was scattered, and we all were scattered before that big axe. He chopped first at Ulla, overbalanced and missed him, he cut hard at Hermod and cut off – some hair. Then he went after me, all round the tables, and he hacked and he slashed and he *cut off my hand!*'

There was a moment of hush so that you could hear the rats in the roof. In German eyes, Fenris had done something unmentionable in striking a guest. It was Tyr who had behaved honourably in running away, resisting any temptation to strike back or defend himself, the very embodiment of virtuous self-control – or so we were supposed to think.

'Then in the morning we'd all got sober; they cleaned the wound and they sewed up the stump. Poor old Fenris, he *was* broken hearted, and we had to tell him what we'd been about. That started him laughing, he near burst his gut. "What, sleep with my daughters, is that all you wanted? Why didn't you ask me? I'll fix it tonight."

'We did it in style with the horse and the cockerel, with priest and with fire, corn mother and knife. Fenris no more raids the

65

lands of the Asers, we pay him a pension, he stays at home. But I have a wife now, down there with the Quadi, and four healthy sons, one each time I go home.'

In the pandemonium that followed, Tyr came and sat down beside me.

'I always do this some time on the trip,' he told me in a confidential way, while a Vandal came round and poured beer for the pair of us. 'No, no, *you* don't pay here. I take half the profit on the beer sales, and a show like this always improves the trade.'

There were crowds of men around the beer counter, where the Vandals had effectively put up the price by simply not filling the horns so full.

Tyr went on:

'If things are flat tomorrow night, I'll do 'How the Ash became the World Tree', profitable that one, I can manage five toasts in it. The night after, I've got something I've been working on for some time, about Loki and a horse, rather indecent, but quite funny. The next night, Asgard.'

Tyr never asked me anything, who I was or where I came from, he just accepted me as someone who had a right to be there.

The night before the packtrain reached Asgard, I said goodbye to the Saxons. They all urged me to come out to the west and visit them in their islands and marshes.

'You shall have the best seat in the hall, and the saltiest of the salt fish to make you want to drink more of our beer, the finest beer in all Germany,' said Cutha, 'and if I am out on the roads, as well I may be, mention my name to the King, or better, to the Queen.'

'Aye, better to the Queen,' they all said, and laughed; 'better to the Queen.'

11

The next day, as we rode through the pinewoods, I kept changing my place in the packtrain, and cutting across corners, both ways, through the trees, so that no one could say, 'I was the last to see him, and it was there.'

Late in the afternoon I slipped into the wood, and they did not see me go. I found a little hollow where I might sleep, fasting for I came to the judgement time of my life. But the white mare, that Loki gave me, I hobbled and turned out to graze, for she had taken no vow.

But how, unless Apollo watched and counted the days, did I choose, for that Night-Before-Asgard, the night of the Summer Solstice? All across the fields beyond the forest the fires burned, and men and girls leaped the flames till dawn.

An hour after dawn, when I knew the Saxons would be well out on the road again, I rode out of the forest. First I came to the Palisade by the trail, empty now in the morning, except for the Vandals lounging by the gate. And I knew that was not Asgard. And I turned north, at a fork, and in a hundred paces I came out of the scrub to a cluster of houses on the forward face of a ridge. But I knew this was not Asgard.

The path led through the village, past the dirty houses, to the crest of the ridge. Where the path went over the ridge, there was an ash tree on one side, and on the other a Standing Stone, raised by the Men of Old.

I smelt the sea, and that I could see a half mile from the crest. Between the ridge and the sea was a salt marsh. Down from the Standing Stone and across the marsh went a causeway of logs.

In the marsh stood Asgard. The great halls stood above the marsh, on a decking of wood, old and dry, but covered with clay that it might not burn. And this decking was carried on piles that lifted it twice the height of a man above the reeds and the brackish water. No man could come at Asgard, except along the causeway from the land, or along the jetties from the sea. Around the decking went a palisade of tarred wood. The marsh was too deep for a man to wade, and too shallow and full of reeds for a boat. No man came into Asgard unless he were asked.

Asgard

1

I laid my spear against the ash, and tied the mare to the branches. I went to a house where there was a pile of firewood already stacked, and I took it and piled it on the crest of the ridge. I led forward the mare, and I cut her throat with the edge of my spear. Her blood poured out on the ground and her breath mingled with the wind.

I struck fire from the Standing Stone with the blade of the spear, and I kindled the brushwood and the pine billets. And when the smoke of the sacrifice rose to send the mare to draw the everlasting chariot around the earth, I leant on my spear and looked at Asgard.

As I stood with the south-east sun hot on my back and the first dryness in my mouth, I saw a man come out of the gate of Asgard and walk slowly and steadily toward me. He was of middle height and thick built. He wore a mail shirt, and trousers of leather. His helm shone with bronze, and his sword hilt glittered with gold and rings. His shield was painted with an eagle, and his green cloak was worked in gold and silver thread. In his hands he carried a broken crock with a little water, and a crust of rye bread. He came to me and shouted:

'I am Heimdall that keeps the gate of Asgard. I know you, Votan Whitehair. If you come into Asgard my master Njord Borsson may let you eat the crumbs at the bottom of his table.'

But I said, 'I am Votan, the old, the young, the first, the last. Myself a sacrifice to myself, myself dedicated to myself, nine days I hung in the tree. And I tell you, I will not come into Asgard till Njord Borsson himself come out with barley bread and bitter beer to bring me in.'

And he poured out the water on the ground and threw the bread to the dogs, and he went back.

When the sun stood west of south above my head, and my throat was dry in the heat, I saw a man come out of the gate of Asgard and walk slowly and steadily toward me. He was young and golden-haired. His trousers were of blue linen and his shirt of purple silk, and his cloak of fine white wool. There were gold chains about his neck, and gold rings on his fingers. His belt was a chain of Amber links, and the handle of his knife was Amber, and the sheath was carved from one piece of Amber. In one hand he carried a glass of wine and in the other he carried a loaf of white wheaten bread. And he said:

'Votan, Spearbearer, Spearbringer, I am Frederik Njordson, and my father Njord Borsson bids you come into Asgard to dine with him.'

But I replied, 'I am Votan, born and not born, from the south and not from the south. Wounded with my own spear, nine days I hung in the tree. And I tell you, I will not come into Asgard till Njord Borsson come out himself with bitter beer and barley bread to bring me in.'

And he broke the glass of wine on the Standing Stone, and he threw the bread to the sea-gulls, and he went back.

When the level west sun shone in my eyes, and my tongue was a stick in my mouth, I saw a man come out of Asgard and walk slowly and steadily toward me. He was old and frail, a great age, fifty or more, and his hair was white as mine. His trousers were of fine wool, and black, and his tunic of fine linen and black, and his cloak of heavy wool, and black. One gold chain was about his neck, and one gold ring upon his thumb, and a gold circlet in his hair. In his hands was a silver tray, and on the tray was bitter beer in a silver cup, and barley bread on a silver plate. And he said:

'Votan, I am Njord Borsson. Lay your spear on your shoulder, and bear it into Asgard and take your place among the Asers.'

I sprinkled salt upon the bread and I ate, and I drank the beer. I took Njord's right arm, and walked with him across the causeway into Asgard. To one side there were halls, and to the other side there were halls, and in front of us was the great hall of Njord, Valhall.

At the door of Valhall I bowed to Njord and I placed my spear in his hands.

'Well do we know this spear,' he said. 'It is called Gungnir. It was once a sword, a sword of heroes. Many the shields it spoiled in battle, many the heads that rolled before it. Then it grew thin and weak with much honing. Here it was beaten into a spear head, beaten by smiths of immortal cunning.' And he gave me back my spear. And I went into the hall that stood on the right of the door of Valhall, and the Vandals brought me water and lye, and they brought me clothes both grey and gay, and I washed myself and combed out my long white hair, and I dressed in grey.

I walked alone into Valhall, and the sidetables were full of men in rich clothes. Behind the top table sat Njord in a great high-backed chair, and on his left were two chairs, and on his right were two chairs.

Frederik spoke into my ear:

'Go on, Votan; take your rightful place among the Asers.'

Which was my rightful place? Not so difficult. Njord's son must sit at his right hand, so I went to the far left seat, and modestly waited to be moved higher, next to Njord. On my left hand, at right angles to me at the head of the side-table, was One-handed Tyr, and opposite him at the other sidetable was a handsome man in green called, I found, Baldur. We looked down the hall, and Heimdall with a flourish pulled back a curtain, and Freda entered.

Was there ever anyone like Freda? Well, frankly ... no. There may have been others like Edith, and even others like Bithig, difficult though that may be to imagine. And there are ten thousand like Ursa or Gerda in every nation in Germany. But never anyone like Freda.

Freda came up the hall. She was white-clad and gleaming, golden-haired and willowy, shining and splendid in the red and yellow torchlight. Gold rings were on her fingers, gold bracelets on her arms, a great gold brooch was at her shoulder. Behind her were her maidens in yellow or green or crimson. She sat at my right hand between me and Njord.

On the table in front of Njord, Heimdall set a whetstone. A strip of stone a foot long, square, it bellied in the middle to two

70

inches thick, narrowed to the ends. At each end it was carved with four faces under one crown, red painted, gilded. It had never sharpened sword or knife. When the whetstone was on the table, the meal began.

All in the hall ate off silver, but Njord and his children and I ate off gold. All drank from horns, gold-lipped, gold-mounted, but we drank from glass. What we ate or drank that night I cannot remember, but it was probably no different from any barbarian feast that I attended anywhere else.

For that night already I knew I must have Freda. That night she scarcely spoke, and I was drawn only by her beauty, her fragrance, her keen look, her clear grace. Later I found there was a clear mind too behind those great blue eyes, and a complex way of thought you could never guess from a few conventional phrases like, 'Have another boar's head,' or 'Please pass the chickens.' Clear, complex, but, I must admit, limited.

2

Next morning I woke in my new house, and a Vandal brought me bread and beef and beer. I went to Njord and said:

'I am, then, Votan Aser. You, great Njord, have said so. What am I to do in Asgard?'

'Come with me,' he said, 'and see what the Asers do. Whatever we do not do, that do you.'

So all day I watched what the Asers did. All day Njord sat at the gate like Loki, and as the merchants rode in and out, he spoke with them and drank with them.

Baldur rode out. In the village at the top of the ridge, and in a hundred villages, the peasants grew corn and meat for Asgard. Baldur ruled them, and they planted what he told them to plant, and they gathered it when he told them to gather it, and all went well. While the young and handsome Baldur planned, all prospered, and the peasants were well paid in silver and salt for corn and meat; for raw wool came furs and fish, and for raw hides, dyed cloth and made shoes.

One-handed Tyr rode out with a dozen Vandals. These men

were themselves Captains of Vandal escorts, horse-breakers and horse-traders, and packtrain masters. Tyr ruled them, kept the palisades in order, said who should travel and who not, and where and when.

Frederik took a gang of men down to the jetty. Some worked repairing the planking, others unloaded a ship full of salt fish. This was about Frederik's limit. Any brain in that generation had gone to Freda.

Where was Freda? She was working harder than anyone. There were always a hundred mouths in Asgard to feed, and in all the palisades. There was grain to be ground, bread to be baked, beer to be brewed, and all was done under her hands, there was nobody in the kitchens to be trusted.

Trusted? I looked at how things went in the warehouses. Njord sat at the gate, but the trading was done by a crowd of men under Skirmir. I never liked the man. I watched the way it was all done, straight barter of furs against glass, Amber against silver, salt from the Saxon saltpans against wine, salted fish against pots. It was no wonder Skirmir looked so fat and dressed so well. I saw what the Asers did not, what I could do.

I talked to the three I could trust, Tyr and Freda and Njord. I asked Njord if he had bought anything himself lately, or been into the storehouses.

'No, I leave it all to Skirmir. Are you trying to say the Asers are being cheated?'

'Well, not cheating exactly. Let's call it friction. But if you look in the warehouses you see the result. Furs bought by the bale uninspected, common furs at the same price as ermine. Old-fashioned bronze winestrainers nobody will buy from us, black cloth when nobody wears black but you. And grey and dark blue, too. Whoever heard of a German wearing those colours from choice? As long as you go about things this way, by barter, there's always going to be a way for salesmen to bribe our buyers.'

'How do we stop it?' they all asked.

'There are two essential tools of business. One is writing, and the other, we'll begin with that, is ...' I looked at them. 'Have you ever heard of money?'

And of course, they hadn't. Everything went by barter. I couldn't talk about coin, there, of course, but I could talk about weight of silver. It took me the best part of the summer to work out just what we had in the storehouses and calculate prices for everything depending on how big our stocks were. I drew everything out on the sand of the beach.

Soon the merchants began to get used to doing everything in terms of pounds weight of silver. They got used, too, to the idea that ermine was a more profitable proposition than bear, and to the fact that old-fashioned bronze buckets brought only scrap prices, and that thin wine was paid for as vinegar. And at the end of every day, each of our own dealers had to give some explanation of what he had sold, and show what he had bought. Skirmir began to look less prosperous.

After dinner, each evening, I walked with Freda on the jetty. It is not a thing I would recommend to try in any German village. But there, Asgard was not a real German village, Freda's appearance in hall showed that. And I was Votan Aser, Old Man, Young Man, no one knew what, but very definitely a Holy Man and Freda, well, she was Freda, Njord's Daughter, and a law to herself.

We walked and talked on the jetty.

'Why do you do all this, Votan?' she asked. 'What do you want from Asgard?'

'Why, what does anyone else want from Asgard?'

'Anyone else?' she was contemptuous. 'Who else in Asgard would want what you want? Tyr or Baldur, who can think of nothing but corn and horses? Frederik, that blockhead who can't tell copper and glass from gold and diamonds?'

'There are other prizes besides gold and silver, and other Asers besides those.'

'And who has been telling you about them – Tyr?'

'I hear things from Cutha Cuthson.'

'Not much passes Cutha. Votan, Votan, why were you so long in coming?'

73

You cannot ask for a woman's hand when your own is empty. I preached constantly to the Asers the great truth that bullion is the only wealth, that gold and silver are the true aim of all trade. How then could I ask for Freda and not bring gold and silver to Asgard?

I listened to the tales the merchants told, and the songs they sang, especially the men from near the Rhine. I heard again and again the songs of the great battle in the wood, when the three legions went down. What these men told me was one thing. The things they thought I knew were quite another.

I went to Njord.

'Give me a horse,' I said. 'The God has come upon me,' and I knew that he could not deny me. The Aser horse stables were beyond the ridge, in the village. I went there with Freda and Tyr. Njord, once I had come to Asgard, never passed the Standing Stone again but once. At the stable door, with the long line of stalls in front of me, on both sides, I asked Freda to bind my eyes.

I knew I was expected to choose a white mare; this was the usual mount of a Holy Man. The mare under the Tree of the Spear had been white, and it was a white mare Loki had given me. But instead, blindfold, I walked down the aisle between the stalls, and stopped at random. Then I spun on my heel several times, and stretched out both my hands in front of me till I felt a flank. I took off the bandage myself. It was a stallion, and a black, the biggest horse I ever rode on. He was fast too, some people used to say he must have eight legs he went so fast.

I put a bridle on him, and a saddle, and led him over the causeway into the gate of Asgard. Njord looked at him.

'When the spear was made,' he said, 'a mare was brought. When the mare was taken, a colt was left. This is the colt. It is Sleipnir.'

4

I rode west from Asgard. I spent a night at Orm's place, one of our palisades. There I talked with a party of Batavians. They said the same thing as all the other Germans. South and west of Orm's place was the Heath, and across the Heath no packtrain would go.

'Why not?' I asked this party, just looking for confirmation. They all answered, everybody trying to get his own little phrase into the conversation.

'It's haunted.'

'The whole place is a sacrifice.'

'Ghosts walk there.'

'Long, long ago, there was a great King, a great King, greater than all Kings. Out there on the Heath there is a tree. There he sacrificed an army.'

'Aye, with his own hand he devoted them all to the Gods. The men he killed, the horses he killed, all their weapons he broke, and their treasure he scattered before the Gods. And no living men go there.'

'How long ago?' I asked, as I so often asked, but no German has any sense of time.

'Oh, long ago, long, long ago,' they said, as usual.

'Who was the King? What was his name?' and they all went on,

'A great King.'

'Long, long ago.'

'Tall as the sky.'

'Long, long ago.'

'Tall as the sky.'

'Long, long ago.'

'His arm was strong as the sea.'

'At the beginning when the earth was formed.'

'With his own arm he sacrificed them all, thousands on thousands.'

'Long ago.'

'A great King.'

'Long, long ago.'

Once I had thought it all tales. But there were so many who told the same tales, and from so many different places. Next morning, at sunrise, in sight of them all I cast my spear into the face of the sun, into the eye of the day, and I vowed to ride to the centre of the Heath. And they all said,

75

'It's all right for you, look who you are. But no mortal man has ever been there since.'

I asked Orm:

'What *is* at the centre of the Heath?'

'How should I know better than you? Some say there's a tree there, and some say there's a serpent. Some say there's a dragon guarding treasure, and some say there's a hole to the centre of the world. I think there's nothing; no, not just empty land, just nothing, no sky, no land, just nothing.'

It was a bad day to start across the Heath. When I cast my spear into the eye of the sun, I had to guess where the sun might be, for the mist covered everything. You couldn't see far, and you couldn't make much speed. I wrapped my cloak around me and I made south-west as far as I could guess. About noon the sun began to break through, and I could see the kind of place I was in.

It was sandy, gravelly country. The lower places were boggy. The higher ground had some fir trees, but mostly it was heather and coarse grass. There were snakes, too; it was adder country if ever I saw it. They were out sunning themselves on the stones, everywhere. Later, there weren't any trees. There were no people, no birds or big animals. Only snakes. It was dead quiet on the empty heath. There was only Sleipnir to make a sound. Yet I heard things as I heard them on the tree. I didn't see any-thing, only heard them, the sound of a beaten army, men groaning and shouting, wagons creaking as they turned and twisted along roads not yet built. Pressed from all sides, they sought room and space not to fight, not even to die but only to surrender and have rest.

When the sun was north of west and below my shoulder, I came to a boggy pool. Beyond was a plain, and in the centre of the plain, a mile in front of me, at the very centre of the Heath, was a tree. Here the silence was more silent. The beaten army had at last found its rest. The water, yellow in the evening light, looked evil, treacherous, but Sleipnir bent his head and drank. I drank too, and I filled my old water bottle. I ate some of the bread and sausage I had brought, and I wrapped myself in my grey cloak. I turned Sleipnir loose. I did not light a fire, nor in

76

that barren place did I expect wolves or bears. I slept. In that place Apollo sent no dreams.

But in the hour before dawn, the God himself stood before me, in scarlet cloak and breech clout, in long hair and uncut beard, as he stands in the Sanctuary in the Old City.

'Father Paeon,' I asked him, 'do I do thy will?'

He answered:

'Here in my secret place you seek me out. Take what you will to do what I will. What you will take, you will return tenfold when all I will is done.'

He went in the mists of the dawn, the dawn I could not see for mist.

After dawn I drank and ate. Sleipnir came where I knelt at the pool and nuzzled my neck. I mounted and rode toward the tree.

5

A furlong from the tree, Sleipnir stopped dead, and I could not get him to go farther. In such a case you can't make the horse go any farther, even if you get down and pull, so I dismounted and walked forward.

I walked on the things that Sleipnir would not step over. In the long grass things unseen shifted and cracked under my feet. They had been there a long time. The bones were mouldered and etched into the sour soil. The iron helmets rusted into the skulls. Here and there the bronze of armour or cloak fastenings remained, green and greasy, the leather and the cloth long rotted away.

Those bronze strips came from shield rims, oblong convex shields. These had been horses, long rows of them, little but the teeth remaining.

They all lay, men and horses, where they had fallen. Some had gone down quietly, others had writhed or struggled. But the bones were not disarranged, no wolf or bear had feasted, nor vulture nor crow. Only the adders slithered among the bones or sunned themselves on the skulls.

How had they died? No bone was smashed, no skull split, no

neck severed. They had died as the white mare died at the gate of Asgard. Each had faced the tree, and then the quick slash of the knife, the hot blood on the ground and the hot breath in the air. But then not burned, not buried, just left. With all their arms and armour, all their clothes, their boots, even their jewels, just left.

Here a heap of rusty corruption, with fragments of bronze, enamels, jewels, that had been a bundle of swords, every blade broken. That pile of old iron – that had been a mass of spear heads, the shafts broken. This was booty, the plunder from a great battle. They had brought the prizes of war to a sacred tree, and sacrificed it to Wude, to Tiwaz, to all the gods. They killed the horses, they killed the men, they broke and blunted the weapons, they hacked the leather of the shields. Here they had been the pioneers of a legion. The axe edges were turned, the saws heated and their tempers spoilt, the faces of the hammers scored with a cold chisel. In the north they would have thrown it all into a peat bog. Here they had to let it lie on the heath.

How many? The survivors of three legions. The others were up in a peat bog. There had been many nations at that victory, and the plunder was shared. There *were* others, indeed. There was an eagle missing. Two standards, the shafts broken, had been left to lean against a tree.

An army is too big to hang. Some men had been hanged, though, hanged and left to rot in the air. Their bones lay in jumbled heaps on the ground; after all the years you could still see the rope marks on the bough. Not so many years, though. I had known old men who had heard at first hand about old Claudius raving through the palace when he heard, how he cried,

'Varus, Varus, bring me back my legions.'

Well that was Varus now, by the look of the jewels. Just a shapeless pile of rubbish.

Herman was dead now, that great King, whose arm was strong as the sea, who stood tall as the sky. He was no pile of rubbish. They had burned him, and perhaps the dust of his ashes had blown over Varus's bones. Now after three or four generations no one could even remember his name. He had driven the Romans back to the Rhine, he had thrust through the Marcomen to the Danube, the nearest thing to an Emperor the Germans ever had or ever will have. But all forgotten now, dead and forgotten. You have heard those tales of the long memories of people with no writing. False, all false. Who remembers Herman but his enemies?

This was no place to stay, where no wind blew, where no bird or beast moved, only the adders. Varus had a fine gold brooch, with a cameo, the Judgment of Paris. I took that for a gift. Behind the tree in an untidy mound, under the cups and mirrors and trappings of the officers' baggage, were the regimental pay-chests. Into my saddlebags I shovelled the great piles of gold coin, as much as Sleipnir could carry, as much as I could lift. From the regimental plate I took one piece I liked, a boar, silver gilt, a foot long. I went to the standards. The shafts were broken. I couldn't take everything, the crosspieces, the chains and crowns and plaques. I unscrewed the eagles themselves, and put them in my bag. Was there anything else I wanted? I could always come back for it. Only the Holy One of Wude would touch, would receive Wude's sacrifice.

6

It was most of a day and a night again and some of the next day, to Orm's place. That evening I went into the hall and sat at the centre of the high table. I could tell by the language that the room was full of Saxons, and I looked around for a face I knew. I found it and called,

'Cutha! Cutha Cuthson! Come up higher.'

He sat at my left hand, since Orm was on my right, as was only proper, it being his house.

'Well, Allfather,' he said; I was used to being called that by men twice my age and more, it is something that happens when you go white in a night. 'It is good to see you in your proper place at last.'

'All the same, Cutha, you can do something for me, or perhaps Orm can. I want a smith, a good one, a man I can trust.'

'Want one? Buy one?'

79

'Buy one, hire one, steal one, I don't care. And I'll want a carpenter too.'

'What kind of smith?' asked Orm. 'Blacksmith? Sword-smith?'

'No, bronze, and gold. And the gold mostly leaf beating, weeks of beating.'

'I have a nephew,' Orm said. 'He is a maker of anything, in any substance. He would go with you. For wood, look, he made this table, all that carving on the legs. And in bronze, here, Gand … *Gand!!* Too much noise in this hall; Gand! pass me your horn; see? Good enough? His name is Bragi.'

'He'll do you,' said Cutha. 'I knew his mother, Saxon she was. And his father is a Vandal, Orm's brother, and what more do you want?'

The Saxon half would guarantee loyalty, the Vandal half … well, the Vandals are a byword throughout the north for their sensitivity, their love of beautiful things, their craftsmanship. The table and the horn mount were good enough. I saw the man, and he agreed to come with me, and he brought his apprentice, Ingelri, who wasn't so good on the wood but was a promising worker in metal.

It took us days to get back to Asgard. We worked through the forest, marking down stands of timber for charcoal. At the last we went through the woodyards and the piles of weathering timber near Asgard.

'You'll want oak for the frames, and limewood for the back and panels,' Bragi said.

'Here, this oak looks well weathered,' I told him.

'Yes, but not that branch. It's had mistletoe growing on it. You can still see the scar. You couldn't sit on that, it wouldn't be proper.'

'Take it all the same,' I told him. We kept that branch apart, and worked it down into a spear shaft, taking care that the scar showed still. Then we sweated a spear head on to it, a good one, and Bragi made a bronze ferrule, and we gave it to Loki at the next Yule. He was very pleased with it, and called it always his Mistletoe Twig.

7

That night I went into Valhall late, when I knew that Freda was already at her place. I swaggered in and I strutted up the Hall to stand before Njord. To Freda I bowed and I said,

'I bring you a brooch, costly in craftsmanship, in gold and glass cast and carved.'

To Frederik I bowed and I said,

'I bring you a boar from the bushes, gold from the Ghost Land, fetched from the forest and chivvied across the causeway.'

There was a long silence. Then I bowed to Njord, and I began,

'To you, my Father, King of the Amber Road ...' I paused. '... Before the winter is over I will give you a house of gold, and columns that glisten.'

And as I went to sit by Freda I prayed that Bragi was as good a worker as he said; and then I cursed the way that now I could hardly speak ordinary prose, but had to keep on spouting alliterative nonsense, whatever I had to do to the sense.

I looked at Freda, and I caught her eyes. I knew that she might look with interest on any fresh face in the wilderness, that you might take her ear with strange tales or make her wriggle her toes with a kiss, but the way to get at Freda's heart was to satisfy her greed. For jewels she would do anything. That great morse she pinned over her breast. And Frederik proudly placed the golden boar on the table before him, as pleased as if he had won it himself. As Njord his whetstone, so Frederik his boar. What for Votan?

I looked at Freda, and I caught her eyes. I knew I might ask for her when I would, or even take her without asking. But before I asked I had more gifts for the Asers, and they must be ready before the Amber Fleet came in.

8

Next morning, Bragi and I went through the bronze stores, and found sheets of copper, easier to work. We had some Vandals fence off a place on the ridge, and Bragi and Ingelri began to beat out copper tubes.

I went into the village and found the potter. Just as in Vinda-bonum, the merchants brought up Samian pots, but this was too expensive for the peasants, and they used a local gritty ware, rather nasty. The women made it themselves, and I could never persuade any of them to use a wheel. The potter, as she called herself, was the old woman who owned the kiln, and charged others for using it, and made little pottery herself, except for her own use.

I bargained with her for space in the kiln. The first pot I turned out set her quite aback. She stared at it. Then she just squashed it with her foot. Pots, she let me know, were not like that. Pots were like this ... and she made one. I told her no. I wanted magic pots, like this, and this. Now would she please dry them in the sun, and then fire them as usual. Just to show good-will, I'd make a couple of pots of her shape, like this ... and she could have them to sell, or keep if she preferred. Now for more magic pots ... no, they wouldn't hurt the kiln, or the pots in the rest of the batch. I'd make sure of that with a spell, and I recited another twenty lines of Homer. I thought Andromache's lament for Hector most appropriate in the circumstances.

That took till nearly midday. I went into the kitchens of Asgard, and found Freda. I asked her,

'Who does your brewing?'

'I do, who else? Why?'

'I want some mash.'

'Take your pick. Here's the barley mash for the beer, but over here I've got some honey fermenting, and the cranberries are nearly ready.'

I sniffed around and I decided that the honey mash, in great bronze cauldrons, was the best choice. I had it all carried off to our little place behind the ridge, Freda complaining bitterly that she hadn't meant me to take so much.

Two days later the pots were ready, and the piping, and we had got a good supply of charcoal carried in. I found a couple of boys from the village to watch the pots, and we began to make ... well, it's a temple secret, really. The trouble I had making sure that no one person ever saw all the process! It was difficult with the honey mash, up till then I'd only seen it done with grapes, but by hard work we had three jugs filled and sealed when the Amber Fleet came in.

9

There were three Amber Fleets that year. One came from Scania, across the Eastern Sea, and was led by Siggeir, King of that land and of its people, who called themselves Goths. But some of the Goths, a few generations before, had settled on an island, named Borg, and from there had spread across into Germany, on the coasts above Outgard. They called themselves after their island, Burgundians, and their Amber Fleet came in the next day, under their chief, Sigmund Volsungson.

He called himself a king, though there was a certain reluctance in some quarters to acknowledge the title, and there was, to say the least, a coolness between Siggeir and Sigmund. The Goth King resented the independent airs of the Burgundians, and there was some trouble between the two men, over a woman of course, though I never heard the details. Volsung himself had been killed in battle against Siggeir.

But in Valhall, none bore arms, and in Asgard no men might quarrel. There was no fighting or quarrelling on the quays, either. The stockade in the village was full, but not of traders. Vandal spearmen, and Lombard warriors with great axes had been dribbling in from the forest for weeks. It need never take us more than a few days to raise a small army of these hungry men, eager to earn a few pieces of silver, or, better still, grain and salt fish and cloth to help them through the winter. But without them to keep the peace, I would not have given young Sigmund's life more than two minutes' purchase, nor that of his little nation either, if Siggeir and the Goths had ever gone at them in earnest. Still, I thought, some day it might be worth knowing that Siggeir and Sigmund might so easily be brought to fight.

From Siggeir I bought a necklace carved out of ivory, walrus ivory of course, though he swore it was elephant, images of birds all joined together with gold wire. One of Sigmund's men sold me a brooch, a strange piece, not Roman, but from farther east, beyond the Scythians or India or the Silk country. The fool thought it was Gaulish, bronze was bronze to him, he sold it by weight, and stone was stone and worthless. It had a stone, not a gem, but hard stone like marble, all carved into a bird and a flower, as plain as if it were written with a pen on that stone the size of my thumbnail. Hard stone, ten years of a man's life went into carving that, and a drunken Burgundian sold it for two denarii and a horn of strong ale.

There were a few days of frantic trading, carrying up Amber and ivory from the ships, and valuing it in silver. Then we sold them what they wanted, bronze and iron, cloth and pottery, jars of wine and casks of dried fruit. Most precious of all was glass, more precious even than silver plate embossed with Gods and cupids.

On the last night, our own Gods and cupids, our gold and silver plate came out for a last feast. We pushed in more chairs at the top table to seat the Kings on either side of Njord.

Then when the whetstone lay in front of Njord, and the gold boar stood in front of Frederik, but before ale had been poured, I rose and banged my fist on the table. Then Bragi walked up the hall, carrying a tray of small silver cups that we had found at the back of the silver store; they had not sold because the Germans had nothing strong enough to be worth drinking out of them. These cups he set before the Kings and before the Asers, before Baldur and One-handed Tyr as well. Then Ingelri gave Bragi a jug, and he filled the cups.

We all eight drank. And seven of us had never drunk anything like it before, and seven of us didn't believe it. And you, of course, will never have drunk anything like it, unless you have been initiated to one of the secret Gods. It gives a glow inside, rather like drinking a charcoal brazier. You don't get it like that with wine, or from draughts of black bitter beer, even if you make the beer hot in a cauldron as the Germans like doing. When the coughing was over, I told Bragi to set them up again. We soon had two cheerful Kings and five very happy Asers.

Then Njord, who was after all not a King, though he was

richer than ten Kings together, felt that with two Kings at his table he must make some kingly gesture. He flung wide his arms – well, the liquor was more than he had bargained for, and we set him on his legs again – and he made a more restrained gesture and began to speak.

'Votan Whitehair, Votan Aser, for this gift of yours, this – what d'ye call it? Honeydew? – Votan, for this Honeydew ask of the Asers any gift you like.'

This was the time to strike, and to strike with finesse, with ceremony, straight to the heart.

'Njord, great Lord of the Asers, Father of all who guard the Amber Road, as an Aser I ask of the Asers the gift of an Aser. I ask for Freda.'

Njord looked a bit taken aback. I motioned to Bragi to fill up the cups again, and to Ingelri to get another jug ready.

'This is a great thing you ask,' faltered Njord. 'To marry Freda ... and there is Loki ... I thought ...'

Rather than have him stumble on till he sobered, I pushed in,

'Loki is married to Outgard, he would only take her from you. Do I not dwell here in Asgard, to see that you are not cheated? When did Loki bring you silver to double your last year's takings? Do I not heal the strains of your joints and sing you songs without number? Have I not promised a Golden House, and will I not teach you writing? The Honeydew I have poured out here, to loosen your tongues, to grant visions. Freda I ask for my bride, for my own, and in earnest I give her presents.'

And I put the ivory chain around her neck, and I fastened the bronze and stone brooch into her dress, and on her finger I put her ring, that I won from a Friesian at dice, in Orm's place, pale Irish gold with a cameo, Leda and the Swan carved on a sardonyx.

And then I might not have done it. Frederik and Sigmund sat together looking puzzled, fuddled rather, and a fine handsome pair of blockheads they were. But Tyr stood up and flung his one arm around my shoulder, and Baldur called out in that high-pitched voice of his which always irritated me,

'Oh, bother Loki, he's got so tiresome lately.'

Then Siggeir spoke, the great heavy Goth King, blue scars

on his arms and face, and the authority of twenty ancestors behind him.

'You offered, Njord, you offered, you must keep your word. If the girl is willing she must go. And he shall stay here in Valhall for ever, and be an Aser till the end of time, to keep your goods and count your silver heaps.'

And Sigmund, of course he couldn't be outdone by Siggeir, and he too stupid to think, even, of any bargaining, but only thought he ought to say something like a King, he got up and said:

'You have spoken, great Njord, before two Kings you have promised, and your daughter, the Lady of Valhall, you must give Votan.'

Unfortunately, having both overeaten and mixed the Honeydew with great horns of beer, he chose that moment to be sick, all over Frederik. Frederik had made an especial effort to be elegant that night, and had let us know it; he was never so friendly to Sigmund after.

Siggeir ignored this interruption, for he was a King, a real one.

'Now Lady Freda, turn and face this man. Will you take him till the end of time, to be your husband? And if you will, then tell us all the day.'

Freda didn't give a clear answer. She just stood and said,

'I must have time to weave my bridal sheets, and make a bed, and heap it high with furs. There's beer to brew, and sausage, pies and ham … how is it there is never enough ham … I cannot do it under twenty days.'

There was a huge roar throughout the hall at this reluctant bride, and with a final effort at solemnity Siggeir stood again and said,

'Bridal gifts will I bring to you, gold and Amber and ivory, walrus tusks and sealskin cloaks and knives with handles of horn. But you, Votan, you have no shield. I have a shield, of limewood and leather, bossed and bound with bronze, painted and gay with colours and marked with a raven, a bird of bronze and enamel to shine in battle. A shield to protect your bride, to ward off the weather, made by a master, a shield fit for heroes, a shield fit for Votan.'

They were still trying to revive Sigmund, so Agnar Volsungson stood up. Twice the man his brother was, I was quite sorry
the following year when Lyngi Siggeirson and a party of Goths
and Black Danes caught him on the Amber Shores, somewhere
beyond Outgard, and killed him under an ash tree. And there lie
his bones to this day, and the adders crawl through his skull, for
they neither stripped him nor burnt him, but left the body, mail
shirt and helmet and sword and buckler, as an offering ... well,
to me I suppose. And that very night in Valhall I saw Lyngi look
at him, and mark him down for death, even while Agnar said,

'We will bring gold and bronze work, that the men of old
made and buried on Bornholm. We the Volsungas of all the Burgundians are bold to burrow for bronzes.'

What he meant was that only the Royal House were allowed
to rob graves in Bornholm.

Then Njord, obviously feeling that he had been thoroughly
compromised, called for a toast to the happy pair. Siggeir, sweating from the strains of speechmaking, relaxed from a King into
a slightly drunken middle-aged gentleman, and turning to Freda
began,

'Now I remember, long ago, I was young then, going hunting
with your grandfather Bor Burisson, and we raised this boar ...'

On my other side, Tyr and Lyngi were having a technical discussion as to whether a mail shirt was worth wearing for the
protection it gave, being so heavy, or whether it were not better
to follow the Gaulish custom and go into battle stark naked and
helmless, trusting to speed and skill with sword and shield to
keep your skin. The following year, of course, it was naked that
Lyngi went in against Agnar, and gutted him, much, the Danes
told me, to Agnar's surprise.

As a result, relieved of any necessity for conversation, I was
able to look at my reflection in my beer, and say to myself,

'Well, Photinus, what have you done now? You must be mad!'

And to tell you the truth, I was mad the whole time I was
beyond the frontier, and I knew it, and I knew that every single
thing I did and said would have been unthinkable to any sane
man.

This would have been unthinkable to ask for Freda in marriage, to marry a savage. Why did I do it? Well, to start with, Freda was really the first clean woman I had seen since Julia, and certainly the only clean woman in Asgard, the only young woman in Asgard. Then I was stealing a march on Loki, and that put me in everybody's good books, Asers, traders, even some of his own Vandals. Most of all, I had to live, and out there on the edge of the world, there were only two ways for a stranger to live, as a noble, or as a beggar. Marrying Freda, marrying an Aser, made a noble, an Aser, of me for certain.

But why should Freda have married me? She had leapt over the fire on Midsummer Eve, and asked the Gods to send her a man. The obvious man was Loki, but was Loki more than half a man? Ask Baldur.

Then I was a novelty. I was clean, to start with, I wore my pig fat with an air. I was a stranger, mysterious in many ways, with tales of far countries. And in those days, I didn't look too bad, in spite of my white hair. My face had filled out after the time on the tree, and I combed my beard. And though I walked like a young man, I had an old man's head. I had read everything any Greek had written, I knew all that any Greek ever knew, and that made me, in the eyes of the north, a man of great and unfathomable wisdom, a man of experience that no one man could collect in one mortal life.

As I thought that in taking Freda, I was taking power in the north, so Freda thought that she was taking power in me, power of a kind that was never seen in Asgard. But I wasn't powerful. I was mad! Mad! And I knew it.

Ten days later, the third Amber Fleet came in, the Black Danes' fleet from the islands up in the shallow sea. King Sweyn Halffoot came himself. They had called him Sweyn Olafson till a Saxon cut off a slice of his left foot with an axe in a sea fight. Since then he had limped, but that made his hand no less heavy, and his temper was uncertain. It was as well not to mention Cutha Cuthson to him, since the Danes were pushing now toward the Saxon shores, and thought it uncivil of the Saxons to object. There was no Saxon Fleet; the Saxons, on the whole, are incompetent sailors.

Sweyn decided to stay for the wedding, after he had sent the fleet home, and he produced a gift for Freda, a necklace of pearls; not the fresh water mussel pearls, but real oyster pearls from Britain.

Now we had a dozen boys watching the honeydew pots as they bubbled. Ingelri and a dozen of *his* apprentices beat, beat, beat all day at the gold, beating the Roman coins into great sheets, thin as silk.

Bragi was making two great chairs, thrones, one for me and one for Freda. The frames were of oak, and the panels were of limewood, the back panels and the side panels beneath the arms, carved on either side. I had Leda and the Swan on the back panel, carved from Freda's ring, and on the other side of that panel, against my back, Danae and the shower of gold, which symbolised what I was doing for Asgard. On each side piece he carved the tree, leaves and branches and acorns, and the bees and the bear and the snake in it. The end of each arm he carved into a wolf's head, snarling, life size.

On the back panel of Freda's chair, he carved Myself in the Tree, with the wolves dancing around me, and it was much admired and craftsmen came from far away to see it and copy it. The other side of that panel he worked with an Amber ship, and a distaff and a spinning wheel on the arm panels. Above each of Freda's shoulders rose the pillars of the chair, and each of the pillars ended, like the arms, in the life size head of a maiden with streaming hair. The pillars of my chair were bare.

10

How many kings will come to your wedding? Listen, how many kings came to mine.

No Vandal king came. The Vandals were poor, a few thousand starving families, too poor to afford a king. But the whole horde of Vandals came, hoping for a free meal, and we fed them all on the shore, men and women and all the children.

Two Lombard kings came. They themselves were very poor. One owned a sword, and looked down his nose at the other who carried only his big axe. The latter spent his time talking to any

89

other king who would listen about the importance of keeping up the old traditions like this of having one trouser knee always patched in an odd colour. But I noticed that when Baldur gave him a new pair, he wore them, without a patch. Both tried to persuade the wealthier kings to buy mercenaries from them.

A king of the Cherusci came, from beyond the Lombards. He took great pride in being sophisticated. He had once been a sergeant in an auxiliary regiment, and knew the military roads and the inns nearly as far as Milan. He spoke rather bad Latin, slowly, and he kept trying to practise it on me, which made the other kings jealous.

A king of the Friesians came. A rich king this, rich on the herring trade with Britain. He swaggered and clinked with gold chains. He threw chains around my neck and Freda's with a lordly gesture, but with one eye on the Cheruscan, who brought a hundred jars of wine. He swore it was Falernian, but it was only that filthy Gaulish stuff, not much better than ration red. Still, I don't think he knew the difference himself.

The Saxon king didn't come. He sent one of Cutha Cuthson's men with a very tactful message, saying I would understand if he did not sit at the same table as Sweyn. And since he had heard that I always wore grey, he sent me a bridal suit of dove-grey silk, and gold combs set with garnets on which he hoped that Freda would pile her hair.

Sweyn himself stayed. He rarely moved, he spent most of his life sitting on his throne or on his ship and here he always had a chair on the jetty. As a result he had grown now so fat that no horse would bear him. His main interest was in food, and he would sit all day watching the ships and chewing sausage and salt herrings to work up an appetite for supper.

Sigmund did not come. He sent another of his brothers, Gylfi; he died the next year, too, more's the pity. Sigmund, for all he was the eldest, was the runt of that litter. He asked pointedly to be excused since he was needed at home to defend Bornholm in case of an attack by Siggeir.

Siggeir came. He came with only three fast ships, having left all his other ships under Lyngi in case the Burgundians should raid Scania. He brought his Queen, Signy, and this in itself was a wonder, for the Ladies of the north seldom travel, except to their own weddings, and never by sea. But Signy said that it was unthinkable that Freda would be married with no one better than Skirmir's wife to attend her. As if Freda had not governed all the household of Asgard herself for years.

Siggeir also brought a little yellow man who was, he said, a king of the Scrawlings. This peculiar creature spoke no word of any known language, except a few conventional phrases like 'Fill 'em up' or 'Pass the herrings'. Siggeir told me that at home this man ate nothing but a kind of tame deer that gave him milk and meat and horn and leather and served him for both horse and cow. At any rate he wore clothes and shoes of deer skin, and brought us great robes and cloaks of the same material. His name sounded like Jokuhai-inen. A thin man, he ate as much as Sweyn, but it never seemed to do him any good.

Siggeir brought me the shield. A round shield, covered in leather, it had a rim of bronze worked in dragons' heads with garnet eyes. The boss was of iron, and we gilded that ourselves later, with some of the gold leaf we had over after we covered all the pillars of Valhall. Above the boss, in bronze and enamel, flew the raven Siggeir spoke of; below the boss in enamel and bronze crawled a dragon.

Loki did not come.

On the wedding day, we did everything. We leapt over the fire, and broke the jar, we killed the cock and rode the white horse, and ate bread together. We stood under the crown and we shared the cup, and followed every rite anyone present could remember. Where I should have sworn on the sword I swore on Gungnir's point, and seven kings and a queen stood witness.

When all was over we went into the hall. For the first time the kings saw the thrones. For Freda and I sat at the centre of the top table, with Tyr at my side and Signy to support the bride. But now on each pillar of my chair, one above each shoulder, were the eagles I had fetched from the Heath. All looked at them, and the Cheruscan king, who knew well enough, said in his barrack-room grunt:

'What d'ye call those? Tom tits? or black-cocks?'

And it was on the tip of my tongue to say 'carrion crows', but then I remembered the great Goth shield that hung on the wall behind me, and I said,

'No, ravens.'

So ravens they were called ever after, and they might well have been just that, for they were tarnished and black with age, and the filth of a century propped beneath a tree. King Jokuhai-inen got very excited, and babbled away in his peculiar language, and though none of us could understand a word we realised at last that he had names for the birds. The best we could make of what he said was Hoogin and Moonin, and under these gibberish titles the birds were known ever after. And all the better in that they had no meaning or history except in the mind of a Wizard King who could raise the wind when he wished; he showed us, later.

We all sat down together to the wedding feast. No expense had been spared. We had even hired a minstrel so that Blind Hod, who usually sang at our feasts, could join in the banquet without worrying about the effect of beer on his voice. We drank Honeydew from silver cups, with gold-mounted horns of beer or wine for chasers. One Lombard king drank beer, to show how he clung to the old customs. The other drank wine to show he was modern in his ideas.

We ate as I never ate before in Germany. We had oysters from Britain, that came up through Friesia, and Freda found a pearl in one of hers, which was thought to be a sign of luck. We had salmon from the land of Norroway, and eels preserved in a kind of jelly, and stewed seaweed, though I did not care to try this.

There was whalemeat, and that was strange because it was more like beef than fish, but with a rank taste to it. And a strange thing, for the whale, that huge fish that a man may take for an island at sea, has no fat at all in its body. I, who have eaten the meat, tell you that for truth.

There was wheat bread and rye bread and barley bread. By special arrangement, a bowl of wheat porridge, legionary ration style, was served to the Cheruscan sergeant-king. He threw it at the Friesian king, but missed him and it splashed over Sweyn, who licked it off his sleeve and said it was very good and please was there any more?

I had brought quite a lot of food up from Gaul. The fruit

went quite well, figs, and dried plums from Illyria. Nobody else liked the olives, though, and I ate them myself, the whole barrel, as the winter went on. It took me all that time, too, to teach Freda how to fry in decent oil instead of in pig fat.

The Honeydew was a great success. I had flavoured the mash with juniper berries, which improves the taste a great deal. We gave a big cup to the minstrel, who was churning out one of the traditional stories. But under the spell of the Honeydew he, being a Batavian, gave us a highly original version of how the brave Batavians won the great Battle of the Wood, while Herman and the Thuringians only came up after all was over.

Then the Cheruscan king sang us the descent of the Lord Mithras, for he had gone as far as the Dog, but only because you couldn't get promotion any other way.

Jokuhai-inen sang and danced, beating on a little drum, hung with silver bells. None of the others knew what it meant, but I had been watching what he had been refusing, and I knew that he was dancing the Death of the Bear. For his people, once in three years only do they sacrifice the bear in truth, but they may dance the sacrifice on any great occasion when they need good fortune.

Tyr gave us again the song of how he lost his hand. He had now added a great deal of personal and genealogical material on Aristarchos, some of which was to my knowledge untrue, and the rest of which may have been no more than wishful thinking.

Then they called for me to sing, and I think I gave them more than they expected. I sang them of how the Lord Apollo brought to men the gifts of song and music and writing, and when they were all entranced I ended,

> Now I can impart the art of writing
> Not only for Latin or Greek or Egyptian
> But for the God's language, your own tongue, the German,
> Let each King leave a man to stay through the winter
> And learn of Votan the secret of writing
> To return in the spring and teach all the nobles
> The signs of the Gods, the Runes of Valhall.

And so they all agreed, and each of them left behind a noble, except the two Lombard kings, who stayed themselves to save themselves the cost of their keep through the winter, as well as to watch each other. One of them offered to hire out his wife to Jokuhai-inen for the wedding night, and was furious when he found the Scrawling king had already made arrangements with the other. But his rival was even more furious to find that Jokuhai-inen had sublet her to Sweyn and not only enjoyed her himself but made a profit on the transaction.

When all had agreed that a standard runic writing was desirable, and we had drunk all the Honeydew, and the minstrel had been mutton-boned, we went in procession to my house, lit by kings as torchbearers. Signy went in to deck Freda for the bridal bed, while the men made me drink a last horn of ale, and they had a final contest among themselves as to who could drain the biggest horn at one draft. It says a lot for Siggeir's naivety that he thought he could pass me a horn half full of beer and half of Honeydew without my noticing, but I managed to exchange horns with a Lombard king, and he was so naive he drank it, and he was fearfully ill later in the night. So in the end only six kings saw me to my bed.

But as to what happened there, you may learn across the Styx. Whatever Ursa, or Gerda, or any of the others were, remember that Freda was my wife, and my first wife. So don't expect to hear any more about that. In spite of what came after.

Lands Beyond Asgard

1

That first year of my marriage to Freda, the first year of my first marriage, was the best whole year of my life, complete and without flaw. Perhaps I was in the virginity of my powers. Perhaps it was the effect of that first bitter northern winter, cooped up on our pile-based deck above the frozen marsh. It was in that year that I learned how to command kings, how to send kings to their death and kingdoms to destruction. Hear then what I did.

First, in that winter I taught men to write. Asers and kings (even if only Lombard kings) and nobles and traders all sat down before me every morning through the winter, and learnt of me how to write. Of course I could not teach them how to write in Latin, for they cannot learn Latin, their tongues are too short. So I had to make an alphabet that would fit the German sounds. It was only then that I found out how many different kinds of the German language there are, and how many sounds. And, of course, I could not think of using wax tablets. I had to make letters that could be scratched on limewood panels across the grain.

Njord never learnt the trick at all. One of the Lombard kings was nearly as bad. The other learnt very quickly; his name was Hoenir. He had very little to do but work, for his wife, having tasted the sweets of wealth with Sweyn and Jokuhai-inen, had gone off with the Cheruscan king. He passed her on to other military friends, and when I saw her again a few years later, in Rome, she was mistress to a captain in the Praetorian Guard, and doing well on selling permits to beg around the Milvian bridge.

Loki came at Yule. He learnt to read in three weeks. This is their winter festival, when their custom is to burn a tree. This

cult in Asgard, living as we did on a wooden deck above
swamp, in wooden houses, but I had Bragi make a great tray
of bronze and we piled a heap of earth to put it on and we burnt
the tree in that.

We gave Loki his spear, and he was very pleased. He made no
comment on the thrones, or on the marriage, till midway
through the Yule dinner, when he produced a complete set of
silver plate, cups, dishes, wine strainers, bowls, two of everything, all Syrian by the workmanship, and not more than ten
years old by the style. I often wondered where he stole it. Still, it
was a magnificent gift.

When the banquet was well under way, he tried to feed
Hoogin and Moonin with crumbs. Then he got maudlin over
the maidens on Freda's chair, and called them his little Greek
girls. And he used the Greek word too, Kyria, and then he called
them Valhall Kyria, and the name stuck.

2

Among the men who had come in the ships with Sweyn was a
noble named Starkadder. He stayed to learn the Runes, having
nowhere else to go that winter but Sweyn's hall, and ours was as
good. He was a landless man, having lost his farm at dice, as so
often happens. One night, in the hall, I sang the tale of Scylla
and Charybdis, translating Homer as best I could. Starkadder
was most impressed by my description of an octopus, for they do
not live in the seas of the north.

He went away next day, and repainted his shield, which before
had had the usual simple design of an eagle or a boar or some
such thing. He painted on it what he thought an octopus might
be. There was a human face, and from it there came out in all
directions eight human arms, and each of these arms carried a
weapon, one a sword, another a hammer, another an axe, and so
on. The result was most distinctive, and ever after he was known
as Starkadder Eightarms.

He came to me and said,

'Votan Whitehair, that came out of the forest with your spear on your shoulder and now sit in Asgard a Lord of the Amber Road, tell me how I too may win wealth.'

'First,' I told him, 'remember you are not Votan Spearbearer.'

'True,' he answered, 'but I do not wish to be as wealthy as you.'

Therefore I told him how he might become a wealthy man, and I lent him silver, for there is little you can do without capital unless you are the manifestation of some God. What I told him, and how he did it, you shall hear, but it was about this time, in the winter, that I began to learn my power over kings and nations.

3

Donar came in March. He just walked into Valhall one evening just as we sat down to dinner. He came in through the door, and bellowed,

'I am Donar. I bring the sword I promised.'

He walked up the hall and laid the blade on the table in front of me. Then he went around to the seat on the other side of Njord, where Loki usually sat, and settled down in it comfortably. Nobody said a word against him. He never gave any explanation of why he had come.

The sword he brought was, of course, not a whole sword but only a blade, and the tang of the hilt. Donar and Bragi worked together on the hilt, carving it in beechwood to fit my hand, and balancing it to suit my grip exactly. However I would not let them make any rings or healing stones for it. I told them,

'There will be no healing of any blow that I strike with Votan's sword.'

Yet the blade never tasted blood but the one time, while I had it.

Donar also had for me my old sword, my Kopis. He was not very polite about the quality of the blade. I didn't know what to do with it, and in the end I gave it away, to Sigmund, when he came for a few days in the spring, trying to get credit in corn against the winter's Amber sales. He was very grateful, the block-head, incredulous that I should give him my own sword, a sword of Votan's for his own.

I asked Donar how he had got it, indeed how he had got here at all.

'When you shouted,' he told me, 'I went into the woods. I heard one horse go off after a bit, and that must have been you. There was a lot of noise, and a great deal of cursing when they tried to scrape the burning wood out of the hut, and sort through it for the silver. After a bit lying watching them I found out there was someone alongside me. It was Occa. He had gone back a few hours, and met Wolf, who was coming up behind, as, apparently, had already been arranged. I knew there'd be somebody, but they didn't tell me. Wolf had a crowd of men, Vandals as well as Quadi, and his son-in-law too.'

'Who's Wolf's son-in-law?'

'Tyr, of course. Didn't you know, Fenris Wolf cut off his hand? Well, we came up in a circle and rushed them about dawn, but of course we couldn't hold the Vandals back and they killed the lot. We got the silver out and traded it through Tyr, and shipped a fair amount of Amber back to Otho.'

'Do you mean to say that Tyr knew I was coming?'

'Well, we heard some things from the Polyani. The real worry was in case you got to Outgard before Tyr, and you did, but we hear you took care of yourself.'

'And who else knows all this besides Tyr?'

'And what should Tyr know, other than that you are Votan Spearbearer Spearbringer, the marked of Joy?'

No more would he say. And as always around everything I did, everywhere I went in the north, there was the strange feeling that I was expected, that all was prepared, that I was playing a part in a piece I had not written, no, nor yet read.

Donar settled down, as I said, and not only in that seat, but in Asgard. He put up a smithy by the Honeydew sheds, where twenty men watched the pots, and he began to make swords, snake swords. Ingelri left Bragi and went to work under Donar, learning how to make the long ribbons of iron, and interlace them, beating them in the heat of the charcoal. So much charcoal did we need for this that the Lombard axes began to eat visibly into the edge of the great forest. Ingelri became a great swordsmith, and his swords became as famous as Donar's. More famous, because Ingelri, and all his clan, marked the blades with his name, while Donar never learned my Runes.

Donar's own sword was a Sax, a lovely thing. Instead of Runes, he inlaid the blade with patterns in silver and copper wire.

4

One day I went into the hall and Njord said to me,

'Learn now how hard it is to be an Aser. See here these men who come from Sweyn. They say that the Saxons are seizing their saltpans and driving them from their pastures, and Sweyn wishes me to stop trading with the Saxons. And these men come from Edwin the Saxon King, and they say that the Black Danes are seizing their saltpans and driving them from their pastures; and Edwin wishes me to stop trading with the Danes. What then shall I do?'

'Go to your kings,' I told the envoys, 'and tell them that in three weeks from today they will meet me at – are there any sacred places in Denmark?'

'Dozens,' said Hoenir the Lombard, and named one at random.

'Then in three weeks King Hoenir and I will meet King Sweyn and King Edwin there, and we will come to an agreement. And you, Hoenir, will bring fifty of your axemen, and you will stand as witness of any agreement and guard us all while we talk.'

And Njord did not object though I said all this without consulting him in the slightest. He merely said later that he was glad I was going, since he was no longer able to ride, and he did not want Asgard full of kings all through the summer.

I went with Hoenir and fifty of his Lombards, all riding horses borrowed from the Aser stables, much to the dissatisfaction of Tyr who protested that he could not see how to plan the summer's packtrains if he were fifty horses short.

These were hungry men with hungry axes, who left behind hungry wives and hungry children, and who, now the ploughing was over, rode with me to save the food at home, and live on the Asers. We went across the hungry land and we lived on the dry bread and bacon in our saddle bags, and we came to the meeting place.

It was some way from the edge of the woods. There was, of course, a sacred tree, and a little way from it there was a bog. The Lombards cut down young trees and made houses thatched with the green leaves. All the time I was there until the last night I ate no food that a Lombard had not prepared, and drank nothing but water from a spring that trickled down into the bog, and spoke to no one except in Hoenir's hearing.

Three days before the appointed time there came two parties, of Black Danes and of Saxons, and each party brought wagon loads of ready cut timber to build a hall, and the first task I had, and that a hard one, was to persuade them to put all the wood together and build one hall, and not two.

On the appointed day, all the common people went away, except two nobles, one a Black Dane and one a Saxon, who stayed to be witness, and the Lombards took their swords from them, and then spread out in a great circle around to keep the kings safe.

Midway through the morning we saw the kings coming, from opposite directions. Edwin the Saxon King came on horseback, and he was forced to ride in circles to waste time and not arrive before Sweyn, who sat in an ox cart. Edwin was an old man, as old as Njord, and frail.

There was a table and benches. I sat at the head, with Sweyn at my left hand and Edwin at my right. Hoenir sat at the foot, and the Danish noble between him and Edwin, and the Saxon noble opposite him. And I faced to the north-west, so that each king faced his own kingdom.

I avoided any question of priority in speech. I made them throw dice. Sweyn threw a five and a two against two threes, and launched into an oration. It was long and flowery, and he had obviously taken notice of Siggeir's style. He spoke for two hours, and at the end I said,

'Hoenir has written down in Runes what this great king has said. Let us hear it.'

Hoenir cleared his throat and read,

'King Sweyn said the salt beaches were empty when the

100

Danes came. The pastures have paid homage to the Danes from time immemorial.'

King Edwin took the hint. He only spoke for twenty minutes. Hoenir read from his tablets,

'King Edwin said the pastures were empty when the Saxons came. The Saxons have made salt on the beaches from time immemorial.'

I began to question the Kings. How much salt came from the beaches? Whence came the wood to burn to make it? How many cattle grazed the pastures? Who sold the hides, and to whom? How many men? What service? What duty? What protection?

When Hoenir had everything written on his tablets I clapped my hands and a Lombard came with six silver cups and a jug of Honeydew. I poured a drop, a notional gesture, into each cup. We drank, after I had spilled a little on the table in the face of the sun. Then Hoenir and I went apart to another table. I took the jug.

We read the tablets. We talked in whispers. We drank. The others watched us in silence, their tongues hanging out. When I was satisfied, Hoenir wrote down my judgment, three times. Then we went back taking our two full cups. I left the jug.

'Hear my judgment,' I told them. 'Hoenir has written it three times, once for Danes, once for Saxons, once for himself as a witness. Tonight I will read it to all your nobles at the feast.'

'No feast,' said Sweyn. 'He killed two of my brothers.'

'No feast,' said Edwin. 'He killed my only son.'

I sniffed the liquor in my cup. I breathed drink at them.

'There will be no more killing of kings' sons, or of kings' brothers, or of anyone else. Here is a treaty that will keep peace in the north for a thousand years.'

The two kings looked at the jug. They said they would accept my judgment.

'Hear this! The salt beaches belong to Edwin. Sweyn's men may make salt there. Edwin shall send a noble to watch, and one-tenth of all the salt shall be Edwin's, and he may take it, or Sweyn may redeem it for silver.

'The pastures belong to Sweyn. The Saxons shall graze them. Four years in five shall they pay tribute in hides and men to

Edwin, and one year in five to Sweyn, but never shall they march to war for Dane against Saxon, or for Saxon against Black Dane.'

Because this judgment was complex and gave each king the shadow of his ancient title, though the substance was gone, they hailed it as a work of genius. We stood and collected the cups and I poured out the Honeydew, full cups this time, and we all drank to the treaty.

Then the Saxons and Danes came and passed the axe ring and brought sacrifices to seal the treaty. Silver and Amber and furs and bronze they brought, and they threw it all into the bog. They brought two men that had been shipwrecked, the Saxons had a Friesian and the Danes a Goth, and these first they hanged from the tree, and then threw still choking into the bog. And, most magnificent of all, each side brought two white mares, and the four they drove into the bog, and cut their throats as they struggled, and their blood poured out on the ground, and their breath mingled with the wind.

Then, as evening came on, tables were set up for a feast, for both sides had come prepared for a feast, however the kings had objected. I set Hoenir at the head of the high table, with the other kings seated on the sides toward their own kingdoms, and I sat opposite Hoenir, and we ate, and drank beer and Honeydew. And later I moved around among the other nobles, and I learnt many things. Sweyn wanted salt beaches so that he need no longer pay the Saxons for his salt herrings, but sell them himself to the Goths and take Edwin's trade. Edwin wanted the pastures, not for cattle, but so that Cutha Cuthson his man could raise more horses for his packtrains, and not have to buy them from the Black Danes.

When the feast had lasted a long time, an hour before dawn, I went away and passed the axe ring, and I came to the edge of the bog where no man went at night. There the Most Holy One stood before me, as He stands in the sanctuary in the Old City. His cloak was of scarlet, and His hair hung about His shoulders as did my own.

After a while I said,

'Father Paeon, do I do your will?'

He answered,

'All that I wish you to do you have done, and strife do you bring on them that are at peace. This treaty will mean war in the north for a thousand years.'

Both Saxons and Danes pressed us to come back with them. But Hoenir, much on his dignity, said,

'Two kings have the Lombard nation, and only one is at home, yet both must watch the ripening wheat or shall no harvest come.'

The greater kings loaded Hoenir with silver and Amber, and Edwin gave him a great sword, a good sword but two-edged and so quite out of fashion among the Saxons. There the people live among the islands in the marshes, and the sax with its one sharp edge and one blunt is what they need, for cutting reeds as well as for lopping heads, and for breaking lobster shells as well as for breaking bones. So Sweyn gave him a fine shield, good for land fighting but too heavy a thing to strap to your arm at sea. And every Lombard who came on a borrowed Aser horse went back leading it, and riding his own.

But I would take no fee for my judgment.

5

Asgard was boring in summer. Freda was pregnant. There was little to do. I took to riding off into the forest, to the villages. Sometimes I followed the packtrains, sometimes not. Wherever I went, people came to me to have their twisted bones and sprained joints put back into shape. They shared with me their food of acorn bread and salt meat. I began to learn all that went on in the north. People said later that it was my ravens that told me all I knew. It was not; it was those same people themselves, a word here, a phrase there, a change in prices, a move of a clan from one part of the forest to another.

About midsummer, or a little later, two Vandals came to me, and said that Starkadder Eightarms had what I wanted if I would come to get it, at a harbour in the Black Danes' country. So I went with them, and I found Starkadder in a rare good humour. He had done as I had told him, and now he had for me my share of the proceeds.

103

Starkadder had borrowed a ship from a Danish noble, one of the Amber Hunters, a man for whom he had once done a murder but who had not yet paid him. So that this man, out of fear, could not deny Starkadder the use of a ship for one voyage, without any fee. Starkadder with the silver I had lent him was able to gather a band of men, all landless men like himself, Vandals whom even the Asers would not hire, and Lombards who had quarrelled with both their kings, and Saxons and Black Danes, and Scrawlings who had come west to make their fortune, and lost their honour which was all they ever had, and men from Gaul who had come out of the Empire to save their skins, for they never had any honour. They were all men who would kill you for a penny, or sack a town for sixpence.

They took the ship and they caulked her, for she was old and leaky, and they put in some food, but not a lot for they had not much money even then, and they did not want to take anything they might have to bring back. Then they took her to sea, and they worked her north, overloaded, to the coast of the Land of Norroway.

Now whether the Land of Norroway is a part of Germany or an island no man knows, but if the shallow sea balances our central sea, as it must if there is any logic on the earth, then that great desert land, where a man may walk to Scania, must be a Northern Africa. And that is why there are elephants in the north that burrow beneath the earth to escape the cold.

They made the coast of the Land of Norroway, and they were glad to see it, and thought it more than they had hoped to do. They rowed along the coast till they came to King Vikar's hall, where it stood over a large village, on a harbour. There they beached the ship, and half of Starkadder's men came to the shore, but the rest stayed hidden under the bulwarks, and a Scrawling watchman kept everyone away.

King Vikar knew Starkadder as a hard man to have work for you, a man to send to collect your debts. Starkadder had been the King's man once, and eaten his bread, and in his band had learnt the arts of war. When the King saw it was Starkadder, he was pleased, not afraid, and bade him and his men feast in his hall. Starkadder told him that they had been on their way to raid the Scrawlings on the Amber beaches, but that they had been deceived in the mists. King Vikar thought he might have use for Starkadder, and wanted him to go north, and raid another king who had been interfering with Vikar's herring fisheries.

They sat down in the hall, Vikar's men and Starkadder's men together, one and one. Vikar's two daughters carried round the ale, Alfhilda, and Gambara that should have married Harold Edwinson. After the ale had gone round, and Vikar's men had drunk much, and Starkadder's men had drunk little, and I do not know how he managed that, Starkadder brought out four jars of Honeydew that I had given him; his hardest task on the voyage had been to stop his men from drinking it. The Honeydew they poured into the horns of King Vikar and his men.

Then they began to play the games that the Germans like to play after their dinner, and one of Starkadder's men slipped out to give the signal to the ships. It was only twilight, for it was the night before the Midsummer feast.

Starkadder said to King Vikar,

'We have a new game. We call it the game of Votan.'

'What kind of game is that?' asked King Vikar.

'First,' Starkadder told him, 'you must stand with one foot on the table and the other on a bronze bucket.'

'So I will,' said Vikar laughing. 'Bring a bucket,' for if you tell them it is a game these men will submit to any kind of indignity.

'Now you must take a live cockerel in your right hand and a horn brimful of ale in your left.'

King Vikar did so, and in the twilight the men from the ship were coming ashore into the village, with their swords drawn, and ropes coiled round their waists, and their bare axes held before them, axes with two foot blades and cherry wood handles.

'Now,' said Starkadder. 'Let your two principal chiefs make a rope of twisted juniper withies, and put it around your neck,' and this too Vikar had them do, not thinking any harm.

'Now, when I call Go! you must drink the horn of beer at one draught, not spilling a drop nor letting go the cock nor touching the withies with your neck. And I wager you a jar of Honeydew to a piece of silver that you cannot do it.'

'Done,' said Vikar, for he thought that more complex and

absurd the rules, the more likely it was to be a game of skill, worthy of a king, that called for no exertion, but only for dexterity. And now the men from the ships stood all round the hall.

'Go!' said Starkadder Eightarms, and the King began to drink the beer. Then 'Pull!' said Starkadder to the two principal chiefs, and they, overbalancing with laughter, pulled, for they thought it a trick to make the King spill his beer. The King choked and let go the cock as he tried to keep his balance with his face in the horn, and his men laughed and they all watched the cock as it fluttered up to the rafters. Then each of Starkadder's men took the knife with which he cut his meat, that King Vikar had laid before him, and killed his neighbour, King Vikar's man, and Starkadder took a spear from the wall, and said, 'Now I give you to Votan.' And he thrust the King through the body, and then killed the two principal men, so that their blood flowed on the ground and their breath went up into the air.

Then Starkadder and his men went through the village and every man that they found they killed, that there might not be a blood feud against them. But all the women and the boys they drove together, and they collected all the gold and silver and bronze, all the furs and Amber, for Vikar was a rich King, and fit to marry his daughter to the Saxon King's son.

The next day they took King Vikar's ships, and they filled them with prisoners and booty, and they put to sea. The houses, and the corn they could not carry, they burnt. It was midsummer night, and they left only the old women and the babies to leap over the flames.

Then in a day and a night, with a good north wind so that they dared to set the sails, and women and boys in plenty to row, they came down to the harbour where I met them, and which belonged to a trader called Elesa. There they sold all the booty and the people to Elesa, and the ships too, and Starkadder took half and his men half. Yet Starkadder never owned land, for no one would sell it him, nor would any king take his oath or hire him for more than one voyage at a time; for he had once sworn an oath to King Vikar.

I went with Starkadder to see my share of the plunder, four young women, and one of them was Gambara, Vikar's daughter.

I took Gambara to bed that night, but she was so much trouble and so much fuss, that I quite lost my patience with her and told her I would sell her to a brothel in Gaul. After that I went out, and it was an hour before dawn.

The God stood before me as he stands in the Temple in the Old City, in scarlet cloak and his hair about his shoulders. I asked him,

'Father Paeon, have I done what you wished?'

He answered:

'I sent you to bring destruction to the north. Now the seed is sown, and the breeze has begun to blow.'

In the end I got rid of Gambara. I did not dare take her back to Asgard. I told off a couple of Vandals to take her down as a present for Hoenir, whose wife had gone off with the Cheruscan. Now he had a sword, he was pleased enough to have a wife, and a genuine princess at that, even though her royal father ruled over a fish market, died drunk and was flung on a midden. She never showed me the least malice afterwards. Why should she? A maidenhead she was bound to lose anyway was small price to pay for a kingdom, especially since till the Vandals rolled her still bound on Hoenir's floor she thought she was bound for the brothel.

That, I said, was in the midsummer, and in the Spring she gave birth to two sons, Ibor and Agio. When they were of age, Hoenir died, and the other Lombard king came to the funeral. They killed him and his sons, and the heads they threw on the pyre. So the Lombards had two kings of the one blood, and that fresh blood, to hold against the Vandals who pressed them hard from the east. How the Vandals found a king I shall tell you later.

The other three women I took home for Freda, since I thought it wrong she should be less well served than Julia Scapella, and have only Skirmir's wife and a few village girls to do her hair. Freda was delighted, and after she had flogged each of them a few times they became quite devoted to her.

Donar, however, was for some reason most displeased at this story, and let it be widely known, so that Starkadder came no more to Asgard, but kept the seas all the summer in King Vikar's own ship, which was a good one, and in the winter he would go down into the Empire to sell his goods among the Gauls. Alfhilda, Vikar's daughter, he kept with him in his ship.

Donar spent a great deal of our silver in buying back King Vikar's people. Gambara did the same, but what she spent was mostly Lombard blood. Most of the youths and some of the women came back at the last to found a new nation, though a few of the little boys had been gelded.

It was these youths and their sons who years later caught Starkadder on a lee shore on the Amber beaches and killed him and all his men. Alfhilda, who had gone with him willingly on all his voyages, they threw into the ship and burnt, and her children with her, and that satisfied Gambara, who was always jealous. But Starkadder Eightarms they flung dead into the waves for the fishes to eat.

6

After the death of King Vikar, Donar had little to say to me. He seemed bored even with making swords; Ingelri was perfectly capable now of looking after their production. Donar spent a lot of time playing with Freda, and then, when the Amber Fleets came, he went away. All the kings came that year. Only Sigmund did not come, sending one of his brothers, Synfiotli. Even Edwin came, early, with shiploads of salt and salted fish. Sweyn came, wearing King Vikar's chain, for that was his price, but Donar did not know. Siggeir came, but Signy stayed at home, for she was near her time, and for once it had nothing to do with me.

Last of all, Jokuhai-inen came in his own ship. That is to say, he did not come in Siggeir's fleet, but he had hired a Goth ship, and had mixed Scrawling spearmen in among the rowers to guard his cargo of walrus ivory and sealskins. For walrus ivory we had put up the price, and it was worth his while to come himself.

He had brought a gift for Freda, a gift of a Scrawling woman. Not of his own kind, but from somewhere farther east, sallow faced and flat chested, with coarse black hair, but good sport, I tell you that, who know. But Jokuhai-inen brought one and took one, for he persuaded Donar to go back to the north in his ship with him. Donar tried to tell us all why.

'Somewhere up in that land, they say, dwells the Smith God, in a land where fire spouts from the earth and the rivers run hot with steam.' That sounded reasonable enough, for there must be a burning mountain in the north to balance Etna in the logic of the world. But who would want to live in a natural hypocaust?

'So,' Donar went on, 'I will go up there and worship. Then Jokuhai-inen says he will teach me how to catch fish that swim in ice, and trap wild foxes, and milk deer. Up there the nights are half a year long. Think what feasts one can have. How much Honeydew ought I to take for a half-year's feast?'

How Jokuhai-inen told him all that I never knew, for then Donar hardly had two words of the Scrawlings' language, though when he came back he was fluent, and he had learnt it in the best place, in bed. How much sport there must be in bed when each night is half a year long!

We saw Donar go, in Jokuhai-inen's ship. The King sat at the steering oar, much to the dismay of the Goth shipmaster, who protested that Jokuhai-inen had hardly spent two hours in control, and he was sure to run her ashore or foul a jetty or ram another ship. Donar said it would be all right, for he would stand in the bow and beat out the time for the rowers with his hammer on the side of the ship. What *he* knew about it we couldn't guess. He knew only one rate of striking, and he soon had the rowers panting. We cheered and waved and they cheered and waved and the ship heavy laden wallowed out from us into the open sea. And winter came.

7

At the beginning of the winter, when the snow begins to fall, and the cattle are brought in from the forest to the byres to live, if they can, through the winter, the Barbarians keep the Feast of the Dead. This is not a feast of joy, to thank the Dead for their gift of life. It is a feast of fear, when the Dead prowl around the house, and the noise of the feast grows high to drown the noise of the dead feet outside. And games are played, as crazy as the game that killed King Vikar, so that mirth for a moment will whelm the noise of the Dead, the fear of Death.

Yet all that bitter night, the doors of the hall stay open, that the Dead may come in. At the end of Valhall we placed a table, and on that table the plate was of gold and the cups of glass. There was the strongest of the beer, and the whitest of the bread, and the fattest of the meat, and the sweetest of the honey. All this was set out for the Dead to eat. King Vikar, and Grude, and the Cat king's men, and the men they threw in the bog, all dead, dead, dead, and all eating in Valhall.

Then as the minstrel was singing a cheerful doggerel, and the boys were ducking for apples, and everyone was laughing for fear that they might scream in terror, someone did scream in terror and something came into the hall out of the Night of the Dead. The noise stopped as a man's voice stops when the water goes over him. There was a long silence as it stood there, bulky and bloated and white with furs and with snow.

Then while the hall sat in silence, great Valhall sheeted with gold and hung with shields, so silent that the fire ceased to crackle and the straw to rustle, and the very rats in the roof stopped running, the being at the door raised his arm and put back his fur hood. And we should have known that no man but an Aser would have walked abroad on the Night of the Dead, and no Aser but Loki. Yet such was the shock of his entry that it was still in silence that he walked up Valhall, past the silent benches and the silent fires. And the very smell that came to us was not the smell of wet furs but the smell of death.

Four of the Great Asers sat on the top table, Njord and Frederik and Freda and I. At the sidetable nearest the High Table sat the lesser Asers. At my left hand sat One-handed Tyr, and next him Bragi, and his new wife Idun that he had only lately brought in from her village. Opposite Tyr sat Baldur, with his arm around Blind Hod, and between Frederik and Baldur was an empty chair. Not the chair that had been there when I first came to the hall, but one carved and patterned with tongs and hammers and anvils and all the instruments of a smith's art.

Loki then entered the hall, for the first time since Yule. In

110

silence he walked up the hall, past the silent packmen and traders, to the silent Asers, toward the silent High Table and the empty chair. And when he was within three paces of it, when he had only to pass between the tables and take it, someone spoke: Bragi spoke:

'That is Donar's chair.'

Loki stopped short, rigid, his body bowed a little forward, toward the chair that he had almost reached. Then he straightened up very slowly, and he turned to look at Bragi while a man might count five, slowly.

Let me tell you, that in all my years on land and at sea, I have never heard language like Loki used that night. I never did find out what some of the words meant. I may have learnt some German. I certainly learnt a lot about the Asers, and I did not enjoy hearing it. He didn't take long over Bragi. I can't remember the exact words, but the gist of it was,

'And who are you to tell me where to sit, you stupid little Vandal turd? There you sit, chip-chop, chip-chop, all day, and stuff yourself all day with crusts from your betters' table. What do you think you can puff yourself up into? Whoever heard of a carpenter who behaved like a human being? And that bag from the forest with you, heather still growing between her toes, enough dirt there for an oak. Had she ever seen a plate before she came here? And now she dines off silver. There she is, cramming herself. Look at her, with her mouth full, and open too. Wind change, dear?'

Hod was unwise enough to snigger.

'And that blind beggar, harping for ha'pence on the heath he was, never a rag to his back, and even the harp he pawned for a muttonbone and stole it back again in the dark when all men are blind. And who dragged him here like a rat to gnaw at our stores?'

He spat at Baldur and missed.

'You great hermaphroditic bastard, there you sit, shame on you, cuddling him in front of everyone. Once the Spring comes, off you'll go, waggling your fat buttocks around the villages, and as long as it's young and fresh you'll take it.'

In truth, this spite was at the root of all.

111

'Fertility blessings, indeed, any field'll crop if you manure it. Don't like me saying that, do you? And who's going to stop me? Not that fat drunken slob at the gate, snoring like a pig, deserter from the baggage line of some second-rate legion, he couldn't guard a pot of ale.'

Yet Heimdall had come softly into the hall not five paces behind Loki, and now he stood at the door and brought his spear up ready to throw. But Njord moved his finger and the spear came down again. Loki had never noticed, he had rounded on Tyr, and here he really let himself go. He flung at Tyr a stream of precise and circumstantial accusations, a highway robbery here, a rape there, a kidnapping at this place, a merchant who was never seen again after that.

'And your hand, how do you say you lost that? Bitten off by a Wolf? Cut off for theft, more likely. Steal a bone from a dog, a crust from a child, steal anything you like, and not even because you want it, but only because it is there to steal. And as for you, you great stupid block' – this was to Frederik – 'can't count, can't read, can't think, can't fight, can't talk, what use are you to the Asers? What good are you to the world? What good are you to anybody but your father, and only good to him to remind him that once only he played a man's part.'

He spat again, on the Whetstone.

'Njord Borsson, Lord of the dust of the Amber Road! You vain old man, you sit there stroking your beard and looking fine. What do you think you are? You think that because you are the oldest of the Asers you are the greatest of the Asers, that you are the strongest of the Asers. Once indeed you were the strongest of the Asers, when you drove out Bergelmir, when you sent Mymir to drown on the winter sea. Now you are the weakest of the Asers, your strength is gone, you can turn no one out. What are you good for now but to sit at the gate and drink the liquor better men make? For ten years now you have not walked on your own feet. *She* has held you up!

'And look at her, all of you, look at her, where she sits, loaded with rings, hung with gold chains, in linens and silks and furs. How did she get them? Don't you all know? If you want any special favours, any cheap rates, any cut prices, go to Freda, she'll fix the old man. It's no good offering just any silver or bronze or gold; but something to wear, jewels or foreign cloth ... anything, she'll do anything. And if you had something really fine, and there wasn't anything else you really wanted, you could have Freda herself. Hands up any man, Aser or Vandal or serf, who hasn't had Freda? Any man in the Hall? Any man in all Germany? Tyr? Baldur? Heimdall? even Frederik?

'And there Votan sits by her, the fatherless man, come out of the forest from nowhere to be a professional cuckold for the sake of a free dinner every night, come down like a monkey out of the tree to sponge on old monkey Njord. And what's he do for it? He'll give you Honeydew free, and have the shirt off your back, and the skin too, while you sleep it off. He'll not kill himself, but he'll arrange your death for you, so long as he makes a penny profit. And he'll arrange a peace treaty that brings in a hundred years of war, and then he'll sell swords to both sides, and buy in the plunder, cheap. And in between – look at the randy stallion of the Shallow Sea, and watch for your wives. He wants to have as many loves as Freda, but his taste is better; *he* goes for queens. Mark him well. At the end he will bring down Asgard on your heads; but on your heads, not on his.'

And with that he turned and walked down the hall, to leave us all still and silent as if nothing had happened, as if his speech had taken no time at all. Unfortunately his dignity could not resist temptation, and he paused on the way to spit copiously, and, now having had some practice, in Skirmir's eye. That broke the tension and, the tight drumskin of the air once pierced, it was Baldur who stood up and screamed in his high voice,

'And what if Votan has slept with a thousand women? What if every one of us has slept with her? When did you ever sleep with a woman? Or with a grown man, come to that? Little boys are more your line, that can't argue, or worse, the wild beasts of the forest. Are the cattle of Outgard safe? Loki! Who fathered Sleipnir on the Mare?'

Everyone laughed. They laughed and laughed, they beat their hands on the benches, drunk or sober they shouted, they hooted, they rolled about and fell backward. In that gust of laughter, they forgave Loki his blistering scorn. Perhaps I was too sophisticated for that kind of humour, and Loki didn't find it very funny either.

He stood glaring at us all, white-cheeked. Then he did something that checked all laughter, that shook us all into a shocked and frightened silence. Loki sat at the table of the Dead. He drank the wine of the Dead, and he ate the Dead men's bread. He drank of every cup, and he ate of every dish. He poured out the beer of the Dead, and he tore the Dead men's meat with his fingers, as he ate the Meal without Salt, the Meal without Iron, the Meal of Old Time. With every bite, with every sip, he cursed us all, he cursed Asgard, silently, without a word, to death, to misery and poverty and death, death, death.

He went from the hall. Next day there were those who said that he had not come by any mortal means, that he left no footmark in the snow, coming or going. That may well have been true, in that the falling snow covered up any marks he may have made. But from that moment, when Loki went through the door, though we did not see it at once, all our luck left us, and all the threads of our destruction began to draw together.

All that Loki had done, and that was enough, was, not even to tell the truth, but only to shout aloud what each of us knew already in his heart. Who cared where Tyr had lost his hand? Better to say he lost it in a drunken brawl than under the gallows. Better to talk of faith and chastity and honour even if we know of lies and theft and adultery. Once you burrow to see the foundations, the whole wall falls on you.

8

When Donar came back in the spring, the paint was back on our faces, and the lies were true again. Again we were the great Asers, wise and good and rich, and so we must have seemed to the Scrawlings who came in, rowing Donar home themselves. They unloaded ivory, mostly, great bags of it on the jetty. But when Donar came up from the ship two men walked behind him, and another two behind them, and each pair carried between them what no one there but me had ever seen before, and that was an

Elephant Tusk. And what tusks! You have never seen tusks like them, and never will, not out of Africa. Huge they were, and curled, and yellow with age, and each stood two men high.

So Donar came in state, marching to the gate of Asgard. He stopped before us Asers, grouped before Valhall, and the two pairs of bearers brought up one tusk on either side of him, upright, reaching far above our heads. Donar stuck his chest out and said,

'Here are the teeth of the World Serpent. No more will he wander the dark and bring down the hillsides, for I have killed him. With my little hammer I did it, all alone with my little Mollnir,' and he waved the hammer around his head, and I would not have called it a little hammer, though it was not of the largest, but there, I am no craftsman. The Asers all cheered, and the Scrawlings all screamed, and the Vandals shouted their warcries and banged their spear-butts on their shields. That night in Valhall, Donar stood up and told us all about it.

'Here I stand,' he began, 'too drunk to fall.'

'You're not,' shouted a number of the drunker Vandals but indeed he was, for he hadn't stopped drinking since I gave him his first horn, no not a cup, a horn, of Honeydew in the courtyard that morning.

'Here I stand,' he started again, 'as soused as a herring. I am only a poor smith, I can only hammer, I can't make up songs like some I could touch with a short stick, only hammer, hammer, hammer with my little Mollnir.' He was waving the hammer about, and suddenly flung it straight down the Hall. It just missed the minstrel, who flung himself flat in time, but scattered a brazier. And so he got first singed, and then wet, for someone threw over him one of the buckets that we kept standing round in case of fire, full of marsh water to start with, but of course they usually got topped up by anyone who had a skinful of beer and couldn't make it to the open air. But Bragi put out his hand and plucked the hammer out of the air, gently, and sent it back hard and fast to Donar, who went on:

'Here I stand, a poor smith who had some luck in the north. I'm not going to make a song about it, I can't, I can see two whetstones, two boars, four of those horrible birds. We didn't have any birds in the ship, just me and the Scrawlings, and we

115

rowed the old barge north till we came to the edge of the ice. My hands were horny, my bottom was blistered, I'd had enough of rowing I'll tell you that. We left it there, and we got off and walked in the snow, and on our feet we wore great big boats for shoes.

'Far in the north we came to the hall of the Scrawling King. He had not built it of timber and turves and plaster, but of birchen boughs and deer skin over all. There we stopped to feast and to drink all through the winter and all through the night. There were Scrawling matrons to pour us our beer, and Scrawling maidens to help us to bed, and Scrawling magicians who did us great wonders such as we never see in Valhall the Great.'

At this he threw me Mollnir, and with rolled up sleeves I tossed the hammer up into the rafters and it didn't come down again. Instead, at intervals I plucked out of the air and passed to Donar a rose, a silk handkerchief, a couple of live pigeons, some horse-dung on a leaf which he passed to the minstrel, a gold cup of Honeydew, and an egg. When he had drunk the Honeydew he broke the egg into the cup, stirred it round with the point of his knife, and poured it over Baldur's head. And all that with never a pause in his flow of speech.

'Now the way that the sun goes round and round brings a snag you may not have noticed. Where the night is half a year long, there is only one night in the year. You eat when you're hungry, go to bed when you're … sleepy, and snore when you're dead beat. And better it is to sleep than to wake when the Earth Serpent walks. Aye, better it is to die without waking, to sleep and not see the Earth Serpent approaching, with great teeth for tearing and crunching the breast bone. His breath strikes cold, it is rank, and it stinks of the holes and the caves at the roots of the earth. There dwell the Scrawlings he kills in the Northlands, for any man who goes out in the snow, who goes out in the dark, to wander alone, the Earth Serpent takes him, to be, to exist, not to die, not to live, in anguish and misery down in his burrow under the roots of the earth.'

To rub in this point I passed Donar a human skull, which he stood fondling till it turned of a sudden into a sheep's stomach, stuffed and boiled, a dish of which the Germans are extremely

116

fond, and then he threw it to the minstrel who ate it all, even the casing.

'When morning was near, or spring, whichever you like, and once in a while for a space the sky would lighten and show us a morsel of twilight in the gloom, I heard once at dinner, as we often did, the howling and skirling and scream as the Serpent went by. I was full as an egg, I was oiled as an owl, I was drunk as a Lord, as a King, as an Aser, I said to the King, to old Jokuhai-inen, I'll go out today and I'll kill the Earth Serpent!

'I put on my boats and I went out in the snow, and all I took with me was my hammer, my own little Mollnir, my dear little Mollnir.'

I let him have it back, and it dropped from the rafters on to the table with a crash and he picked it up and brandished it in the most dangerous manner all the rest of the evening.

'They were all drunk or they'd never have let me go, and old Jokuhai-inen, well he was the drunkest of all. But of course, if you've got to stay and stew up there, in darkness from summer's end to summer's beginning, what else is there to do but drink to drown your dreams? So out I went, my hammer in my hand, my belly full of beer, to meet the Serpent and the terror that wanders in the winter woods.

'I walked through the pine wood, I walked through the fir wood, I walked through the scrub land of birches and alders, I met the hare and I met the fox, I met the wolf and the lynx and the stoat, I met the creatures that walk in the winter, but nowhere could I find the Serpent tracks, though I could hear his voice shrill in the air, and feel the snow tremble beneath my boats. The dark was thick about me, it filled my lungs, my eyes, and my mouth and my hands, it flowed like water or tar, and all I could hear was the noise of the Serpent as he hunted me, as I hunted him.

'Then sudden without warning, the Serpent was on me. He kicked away the earth itself from beneath me, and pulled me down. I felt the huge snake body, cold as death, all round and thick and long. I felt his long smooth teeth, and I smelt his breath, all foul and stinking of death and cold as the dead. I shouted, to cheer myself, all the war cries I knew, and I struck with the hammer again and again and again. I heard the bone crack and splinter, and the beast let me go, and flung me down on the ground – and by then I was sober.

'I saw a light far off across the snow, and I thought another demon was come against me, so I took up Mollnir again and I walked towards it. But it was King Jokuhai-inen, sword in hand, come out to find my body in the snow. And none of all his warriors would come with him, except a small boy who came out to carry the torch. His name was Leminkai-inen, remember it, and he was the bravest Scrawling you ever will see. This summer I will make him a sword, and send it back when Jokuhai-inen comes in the Autumn.

'We went back to the Hall, and I got drunk again as soon as I could, to forget the horrible smell of the Serpent and death. When I die, my brothers, do not lay me in Earth, for the Serpent to suck out my eyes and lick clean my bones. Let me go to water or ice, or even to air, or best of all, as a smith, let me go to fire. But not to the earth, my friends, not to the earth …

'When Spring, or morning, had come, and every day had morning and eve, and something in between we could call day, we went out, the King and I, to find the Earth Serpent again. Where a river ran down through the winter wood, and the banks steeped down to the water, there the Serpent had burst from the earth and there the bones were lying. The wolves and the weasels and all the other vermin that feed on the carrion their betters have killed for them, had stripped away the flesh and gone off with full round bellies.

'Only the tail remained, long, round and thick, and at the end an anus split into two passages for all the world like nostrils. There too the skull, the forehead stove in and shattered, where Mollnir had struck and broken through to the brain box. Greatest of all were the teeth that lay before the skull, and those I brought home to show that my tale is true.'

Then the Scrawlings and the Vandals and everybody shouted and beat on the tables, and Donar once again shouted all the war cries he knew.

But I for one never believed there was an Earth Serpent, but I did not dare say so lest I be accused of slandering Donar. I remembered what I had heard among the Polyani, and I am sure that Donar came on one of the Mamunts as it broke from the earth, and that even as he came on it, it was dying or already dead. And he wounded it badly enough to kill again, and what he took for its tail, that was too tough to eat, was in fact its trunk.

The evening came to an uproarious end, and we played all the games and we muttonboned the minstrel, who left next day. Somehow we had difficulty in keeping our minstrels and we usually had to make do with Blind Hod, who wasn't much good as a minstrel. Come to that, he wasn't really blind either, but could see a little. Loki once sold him a bean-shaped piece of glass, which he swore was the emerald his late Sainted Majesty Nero had looked through, and indeed Hod found it very useful, but in the end Freda begged it from him to mount in silver and hang on a chain round her neck.

When the feasting was over, the Scrawlings took the silver for all the walrus ivory, and sailed back. But that silver was not wholly lost, for I sent a man to Sigmund, who caught them and their ship off Bornholm. He kept the ship and the silver, but the men he sold off south through Loki, who sent me my share. For we all three agreed that personal disagreements should not stand in the way of honest trade.

9

When I reached my own hall, Freda's time was come. I took care not to be too much around, but not too near either, and while Freda's birth screams filled Asgard I sat at the gate and haggled for pots of wine and bolts of linen. When Skirmir's wife came out to tell me I had a son, I went and brought him out to show the Asers, not in my arms, but cradled in my great Goth shield. And that is why we called him Scyld, which is the Goth word for a shield. We placed a sword in his hand, a tiny sax that Donar had made ready, and then we put wealth in his fingers, and we rubbed his fingers with wine and oil and honey, and we made his shield cradle soft with silk and furs. But the first thing he touched was a weapon.

After that I was less in Asgard than ever, because there is nothing I like less than a crying baby at night, and I much preferred to sit up at feasts and earn my headaches that way, if I *had* to get them.

About that time, Donar made me a helmet. He remembered the great parade helmets he had seen south of the Danube – Aristarchos had a splendid one – and he made me the nearest he could to that. It was a cap of iron with a ridge from nose to nape. The neck piece came down to protect my spine, and side guard for my cheeks. It left plenty of room inside to pile my hair for padding, as was the custom. You could always tell a Vandal by his topknot in those days.

Then he made me a face piece, with a nose and moustaches. The eyebrows he worked with boars set with garnets, and the ends of the eyebrows were the boar's head. Bragi carved shallow on wood the scenes of my own real life, Apollo and Artemis, the death of Grude and the treaty with the kings, and he beat out plates of bronze, thin as vellum and moulded them over the carved wood, and fitted them to the helmet, and gilded them.

This he did in the smithy next to the black sheds where a hundred now watched the Honeydew. Snake swords we sold, the swords that would cut two bodies at one stroke. Honeydew we never sold. We gave it away.

Yes, we gave it away, free. The Germans would give their eyes for a smell of the stuff, so we let them have it free, as a gift, after a sale had gone through. In hope of a cup, a sip of Honeydew, a man would cut short his bargaining, bring down his price, forget to weigh his silver, measure the cloth, look for moth holes in the furs. We gave the liquor away, it was more profitable. But no Aser ever gave something for nothing.

Pictland

1

It was boring in Asgard that Spring. Freda was pregnant again, and I never got a chance to play with Scyld, Donar always had him. So when Cutha Cuthson came by and said I ought to go with him to the Saxons for some sea fishing, I went.

'It's not only the sea fishing,' he told me one evening on the way. 'It's my daughter.'

'The Queen?'

'The Queen. Mad on horses she is, and she leads the women in the dance, like her mother did after the old queen, Edwin's first wife, died. She wants Sleipnir for her mares, wants to improve the blood.'

I learnt more about the Saxons as we went on.

'Edwin's had bad luck. First of all there was his wife died giving birth to Harold, and he didn't take another. Well that's all right, there was always, let us say, the possibility of fertility that only a fertile king can give to a nation. But then Harold was going north to marry Gambara, and the Black Danes caught him in the Strait.

'Then we were able to persuade Edwin to get married again, and he married Edith, reasonable, I'm the richest Saxon there is, not to speak of being Edwin's cousin. But that was three years ago, and there's no sign of any heir. Some people are beginning to grumble. In the old days, of course, there would have been no hesitation, he'd have been ploughed in to make the barley grow the first barren spring, but now – well, we know there's a lot more to being a king besides the barley. There's the herring shoals to foretell, and the whales to call to shore, and treaties to make with the Friesians, and the price of salt to fix ... and besides,

Edith won't have it, and if she won't have it the women won't have it.'

The first few days at Edwin's hall on the edge of the salt beaches were taken up in games. Or at least in one game, the Head Game. There were two villages involved. They took a Batavian that had been shipwrecked, and that they had kept in a cage for the purpose, and someone cut off his head. The King threw the head up in the air, and the two villages fought for it. There were no weapons used, not even sticks, but three men died, two who burst when they were running, and one who got sat on by a couple of hundred men when he had the head in his hands. I had a busy week after that looking at sprains and bruises. The village that took the head within their own gates kept it and put it up on a stake and were proud of it.

This game lasted for three days. The two villages were unequally matched, which was why it took so short a time to finish.

Each night in hall we talked, and Edith sat with us at high table. I must say she was very taken up with her horses. She had grown up with horses – Cutha was the chief horse master of the Saxons – and she kept on bringing the conversation back to them, till at last I said to her,

'You shall have Sleipnir for your mares, tomorrow.'

It was two days later that we went, riding alone, the two of us, with a gelding led behind for my return. The mares were, of course, in the Grove where they worship the Mother.

When we came to the fence of living thorns that surround the Grove, we dismounted. I wondered already that she should take a stallion into such a place. We unsaddled Sleipnir outside, and turned him loose to run with the mares. Then to my surprise and horror Edith took my arm and led me toward the gate in the fence. I stood still.

'Come!' she cried. 'What are you afraid of? Little bears? I tell you, there is no woman here but me.'

'Except the Mother.'

'The Mother? I suppose you think there is no Mother, or that I am the Mother? I tell you, Votan, the Mother sleeps, and she shall sleep here till a man wakes her – a man, Votan, not a god, or a half-god, or an Aser.'

'The guilt is on you,' I told her, 'for you, that profane this place, are a queen.'

'A queen?' She looked at Sleipnir galloping toward the white mares. 'What is a queen? I am not a queen. I am only Cutha Cuthson's daughter. I've never been anything else. Married to Edwin I may be, but a queen, never.'

'But if you are the king's wife, then you are queen.'

'What is a king, then? A king is the luck of his people. It is the king who calls the fish to the shallows, or the ships to wreck. The king is the luck of his people. It is the king who charms away scabs and brings rain and makes the corn to grow. A fertile king makes fertile all the nation. And if he is not fertile?'

Ploughed in to make the grass grow, I thought. She read my mind.

'Would you have that happen to Edwin? Would you have it happen to the Saxons? Without him the whole nation would split up, some to be Danes and some Friesians and some Lombards. Or worse, dissolve into a thousand leaderless families like the Vandals, and serve foreigners for a crust of bread.'

We watched Sleipnir among the mares. She spoke again, bitterly. She was nineteen; she was Cutha Cuthson's daughter. She had grown up in a mist of riches. No bog woman, she had heard all the tales of the merchants, all the gossip of the trade roads, all the songs of the bards. She had led the women in the dance before the Mother, as her mother had done when there was no queen. She was bitter.

'What then, is a queen? She is the living proof of the king's luck. Her fertility shows forth his power. How can he crop the fields if he cannot crop her?'

She took my elbow. She sensed my reluctance, my fear.

'What's the matter, Votan? Do you think we will cut you in pieces, you who hung on the tree? Last night I burnt the blade bone and I watched the fat on the pot, and I know you will see lands the Riders never knew. I saw your life, Votan, and it will be long.'

We came to the cart, the Mother's cart. It was high built on man-high wheels of foot-thick elm. The frame was of ash, and the panels of lime, carved and painted with the rites of the

123

Mother. The roof was pointed, and thatched, with barley straw. There was a door in the end and steps to it.

Outside the thorn fence I had left my spear and my knife, the only iron things I had. Here before the cart I laid aside my bronze cloak fastener and my gold armlet. The foot of the steps must serve for the threshold, and there I did what else was necessary. Edith had chosen as wisely as she knew, a stranger, a wandering man without father and without a nation, yet a man of wealth and power, known to be potent, his wife with child again. Now by what I did at the steps she knew that I was no stranger to the Mother.

We paid our duties to the Mother. She was here carved, roughly, no not even carved, chopped with an adze out of the ash whose shape She still kept. Before Her was Her bed, down mattress and down quilt, covered with sheets of linen.

Later I asked Edith,

'Why a cart? Why, here, a cart?'

'Votan! That *you* should ask.' She laughed. All the tenseness and bitterness was gone. She stood naked and went to the door, and took from hands unseen cups, and a jug of barley beer, and barley bread, still warm, and deer meat, smoking hot.

'Long, long ago, the Women tilled the earth and worshipped the Mother. The horse gave us no more than the cow, meat and hide and hair. Then the Mother lived, as we did, in houses, or caves, and, in the heat, in groves and woods.

'The Riders came out of the east. They worshipped only the cruel sky that sends snow and sun to torment us. They swung their great iron swords from their high, high horses, and they took the poor Mother from her groves, and shut her in a cart to travel the roads of the world for ever.'

'So now it is the Mother, and not the king who makes the corn to grow?'

She giggled.

'So they say, so they say. What do the men know of what we do or whom we honour? Yet, the days of the kings who are kings because they make the crops are ending. Soon they will give way to kings who are kings because they are born of the Gods themselves.

'I tell you, Votan, from this day on, there is no man in all the Saxon tribes who will move to bring down Edwin. No woman will let her man depose Edith's husband. Yet the men will never know why the women are so much against civil war, when there have been other times ... Votan, you came when the Mother called.'

Late in the afternoon we went down the steps. I put on my bronze buckled shoes and someone had waxed them. I picked up my bronze fastened cloak, and someone had wiped the mud from it, and ironed it. I left the gold armband where it lay. We walked to the gap in the hedge, and I saw it was a hedge of thorned roses, and the buds that had been when we entered were now full flowers.

2

Eventually, I got my day of sea fishing. I went down to the jetty in the grey and chilly dawn and looked at the boat. It was quite big, about twenty paces long, clinker built, with overlapping planks, not nailed or dowelled together, but sewn, rib to keel and plank to rib with juniper withies. She was undecked and there was a rickety tabernacle for a mast, but no mast or sail in the boat. I asked Edward, the owner, if he were going to take them. He looked at the grey sky and spat.

'Good fishing day, and it'll be dead calm. No use taking mast or sail. You know the great rules up here for foretelling the weather?'

'No,' I said. 'Not up here.'

'Well, the first is this. The best forecast for tomorrow's weather is a description of today's, whatever that may be. The second is this: any change will be for the worse for your purpose, whatever that may be., Stands to reason, any change will mean an offshore wind, to make us row back against it, and what use will a sail be then? Unless, that is, you have any other ideas.'

It is sometimes embarrassing to be a manifestation, however imperfect, of a weather god. I declined to interfere, and we got in.

This was the only time I went anywhere without Gungnir.

I left it leaning behind Edwin's high table. I had good clothes on, too good to go fishing in Edith had said, with a gold chain and a couple of rings and a big morse of gold and garnets to fasten my grey cloak. I had no sword of any kind, only my knife.

There were twelve Saxons in the boat when we pushed off. There was the usual jumble of gear and fishing lines in the bottom of the boat, looking in complete confusion the way it always does at sea, till the time comes to do anything, and then you find how carefully it was all stowed. Ten men rowed, with light chopping strokes. The oldest man, Ethelbert, leaned over the bow and took us out over the shallows and the sandbanks to where we could expect fish.

I sat in the stern with Edward, who had the steering oar, of course, and we talked about the sea. After a while he grasped that I had handled ships before, though quite different ships in another sea, and he let me handle her for a bit. You couldn't tell in that flat calm, but the whole boat felt too limber by half. All the time I was in her, I was expecting those withies to wear through, all together, all at once, and leave us floundering in the water.

Now just when Ethelred had picked up the anchor, which was a courtesy term for a big stone with a rope tied to it, the wind came. It came just as when you tilt the jug and the liquid comes rushing out of it all at once. One moment there was no wind at all, just a flat calm; the next moment it was blowing from hard astern, just a little off the sirocco, south of south-east. It was howling and blowing, and we were going up and down enormous waves. I had never seen or heard anything like it, and neither had the Saxons. Edward and I laid on the steering oar.

'What about getting her head round?' I shouted. 'Aren't you afraid of being pooped?'

'No,' he bawled back. 'Pooped we may be this way, but if I come round we'll be swamped for sure broadside on.'

'Your boat,' I told him. 'You know how she handles,' and I hoped he did.

He was right. We found we could hold her fairly steady with two men on the steering oar. Ethelred came aft, and tied a line on a bucket and threw it overboard. We all gasped as we saw the way the line whisked out, and we never did get the bucket back. It was a good bucket, too.

After an hour we were out of sight of land. The sky was still overcast, not raining, but grey, and there was still that wind. A little later we could see a blue smudge to port. Edward waved his arms at it.

'That's the Holy Island. Nobody lives there. Past that and we're in the great sea.'

Nobody ever likes to be out of sight of land, certainly not on a strange sea. There were all kinds of tales about this sea, how it was solid with fish and so on, and by logic if you went across it you should reach Britain. But who wanted to go to Britain that way when all you needed to do was to go down the coast to Boulogne, slip across and then coast north or west to wherever you wanted to go?

But drifting out to sea had happened to other people before, always to other people. If it happened to you once and you ever came back, it usually put you off going to sea again. Therefore Edward had been careful to bring drinking water and a little food, sun-dried beef and twice-baked bread. The water casks were full; I had seen that done before we went aboard.

A little way outside the Holy Island we saw something horrible. We came to the crest of a wave and we saw another ship. She was about half a mile away. She had a sail set, and drawing, and she was making reasonable way, not fast, but enough, and right before the wind – her wind. For while our wind drove us west of north, she was making north of east. We went across her bows, our tracks at right angles.

Out of Richborough for the Saxon coast, the Saxons agreed, and they argued among themselves about her cargo, and all this to drown the thought that this was our own private wind, blowing for us alone. Only one man came aft, called Osbert, and he asked,

'Has any of you wronged a Scrawling?'

'No,' said Edward, and Osbert went on,

'Because the yellow Scrawlings in the east, they keep the winds in a bag, and when any one wrongs them they let out for him an evil wind.'

127

'And then?'

'He gets blown out to sea, and over the edge of the world. And that's the end.'

'Don't be stupid,' I said, in as superior a tone as I could manage. 'Why do you think I came fishing today?'

I leant back in the stern and looked as confident as I could and occasionally said things like,

'Hold her steady there,' or,

'That's fine, dead on course.'

I remembered how Jokuhai-inen could bring the winds to his whistle, and I remembered the Scrawlings that brought back Donar and that Loki had sold for me. I knew that if I let the Saxons think that this wind was sent against me I would be overboard in no time. I dared not, therefore, ask if they had any salt or garlic on board. If I had brought Gungnir I might have tried to cut the wind, I remembered the proper things to say, but I didn't want to try with only a knife. So I sat back and let them think, without my saying so, that the wind wasn't sent against us, but that I had brought it.

Toward evening, Edward issued a ration of water, not much. I had my old waterbottle, on its strap, full of hydromel, and we didn't dare let the men know about that, so Edward and I hid it under the nets and sat on it. Albert, who was a careful dresser, came aft and went on the oar.

For the night we tied ourselves to the thwarts, for the boat was rolling and pitching together in a most unpleasant spiral motion. Some of the Saxons were sick. At dawn we had water and dried meat, and at noon we had water and some fish we had caught, raw. During the nights we were kept awake all the time by men clambering over us to relieve the steersmen and to hold us end on, any end on, to the howling wind that blew out of nowhere. Yet no one suggested offering a sacrifice of what we had to Wude.

Toward noon on the third day we saw land, quite close, for the boat was very low in the water. It was a low green shore, with two or three strange green hills like upturned buckets, and an island a little offshore of the same shape. There was more land visible to starboard. We were in the mouth of a river. Suddenly the wind dropped, stopped, just like that. The Saxons left off arguing whether we were off Britain or Ireland or the Land of Norroway, and with one accord began to row for the nearer shore. I said nothing; I was sure our troubles weren't over.

When we were close in, the current changed, the tide began to tug at the boat, and we were carried out to sea again, the oarsmen crying and cursing as they heaved. It was no use. Out we went, north and east, out of sight of land. We spent another night at sea, still under that black blanket of cloud, with nothing to tell us even which way we were going.

By now the lashings that held the boat together were in a bad way. Edward and Ethelred had spent most of the voyage crawling about in the bottom finding frayed withies and replacing them from a supply that they carried, but now there were no more fresh withies left. We had had two men baling all the way, but now we had four. We were no longer rationed on water; we were more likely to drown than to die of thirst.

3

Now and then through the night we thought we heard waves on the beach. Once Albert said he saw a light, and we tried to believe him. When dawn came, we found we were in an estuary, but either further in or in a different one. Now we had flat land with sand dunes on either side. The clouds had changed into a thin haze through which we could see the rising sun.

It was the tide that was carrying us in, said the Saxons, though what these tides are or how they are produced I could never understand. They do not happen according to any regular rule of time. Anyway, this tide carried us in over the shoals and glad we were to be in water that at least we would be able to wade through, for at the first oar stroke the boat creaked and let in water at a dozen places.

We were now sitting up to our waists in water, and yet we were reluctant to get out of our boat while it would still carry us. When at last it grounded we got over the side and we were no wetter than we had been. We couldn't get the boat afloat again, for the tide had left her stranded on a sandbank. Once the support of the water was taken away she began to break up under her own weight. The wonder was that she had held together so long. I noticed that it was only now that she was dying that I began to think of the boat as she and not as it.

We took what was worth salvaging, knives and saxes and what food we had and my flask of hydromel. We had a long walk ashore, from ankle deep water to slushy mud, but it would have been much farther had we not come in at the highest point of the tide. When we reached the line of seaweed and wood chippings and rubbish on the high tide mark we looked back. Our boat was already in ruins. Farther out on the water there were half a dozen other boats, big ones, full of men. We could see the glint of metal.

In front of us, about half a mile away or less, there was a village, a cluster of huts. We could hear all the land noises we had not heard for days, dogs barking, children quarrelling, and the wonderful noise of women grinding corn. We could hear them at that distance, and that was a wonder seeing what lay in between. There stood a long line of spearmen, about a hundred of them, and on their flank, on our right flank, at right angles to their shield wall there was a long line of bowmen strung out to enfilade our charge on the shieldless side.

The weapons were the ones we were used to, spear, long sword, shield. The man who walked forward in front of his soldiers to address us was clad in familiar clothes, trousers, tunic, cloak, but his cloak came down almost to his heels, not to the hips like the German cloak. All his clothes were worked in an intricate pattern of red and yellow lines on a green ground. That much was strange, but his face was stranger still. As he came forward his face looked dark. At his nearest we saw it was blue!

A few yards from us he stopped and drew his sword while his little army stood stock still and waited, the spears at the ready and arrow feathers back to the shoulder. He placed the weapon carefully on the ground and drew back. The meaning was clear.

'Do it!' I said.

'May as well now as later,' grumbled Edward. He unbuckled his sword belt and laid it on the sand. We all followed suit. I laid down my knife. Then we stepped back a few paces. There seemed a general agreement among the Saxons to leave me nearest to the arrows.

Another man came forward and picked up all the swords and tucked them under his arm. Blue Face seemed to be keeping a tally, notching a piece of wood. They took the swords only, they even left the sheaths, some of them beautifully ornamented, and they left our knives, the kind of things you use for cutting your meat and trimming your toenails.

Blue Face came further forward. He spoke to us. He spoke at length with considerable eloquence. With fine gestures of his sensitive fingers, with exquisite modulations of tone, he went through a complex reasoned argument. It took some time. It was a pity none of us understood a word.

When he had finished I stepped forward. I told him in German that we were simple fishermen, shipwrecked by no fault of our own, and that we were men of substance at home, and I for one had enough gold on me to buy another boat.

He explained, unintelligibly, but perfectly clearly, that I was just as unintelligible to him. I tried in Greek, but this got no response. Then I spoke in Latin, and he brightened up. At least he recognised the language, even if he couldn't understand it.

He pointed inland and said,

'Rex, Rex. Venite. Tutti, venite.'

This I took to mean that he was going to take us to his King, and that we would be safe ... safe there, or safe till we got there? I didn't even bother to tell the Saxons, I just left them to trust me.

Then Blueface pointed to himself and said,

'Morien.'

I took this to be his name, and I answered in the same way.

'Votan.'

Morien thumped his own chest again and, as I found later, recited his pedigree which began 'Morien map Seissyllt map Kynedr Wyllt map Hettwn Glavyrawc map Llwch.' I only caught the first word, so when he finished I said again 'Votan'.

Morien Blueface, who all this time had not approached nearer than twenty paces, motioned us to sit down on the dry sand, which we did. Then he walked away, and so did his little army, back to the village. Only about thirty spearmen, young men, came and formed a circle around us. These men, all wearing cloaks of the same red and yellow and green pattern as Morien sat down, each man with his spear across his knees. Some of them had dogs, great ugly things, fit to tackle a wolf alone, two to settle a bear.

After an hour or so, some children came out with food for the guards. After a lot of giggling and encouragement from their big brothers, they brought some into the circle for us. There was beer, good beer, and plenty of boiled bacon, and big flat cakes of bread, hot, baked on stones, and not of wheat, but of some other corn, millet I thought.

It got warmer, and some of the Saxons went to sleep, and some of the spearmen looked as if they wanted to. One or two of the other Saxons were talking loudly about not being ordered about and one Saxon being worth ten Scrawlings. I spoke to them pretty sharply.

'Once outside this circle and I will no longer protect you. Stay here and do what I tell you, and you will be safe.'

That seemed to calm most of them down, but of course it had to be Albert who would keep on walking about and going up to the spearmen in an experimental way. None of them so much as looked at him. Then, all of a sudden he was out of the circle and running like a hare for the edge of the woods. The spearmen didn't follow him, they all came up to their feet and to the ready. The dogs moved, though, and before he had gone a hundred yards they had him down. A crowd came running out of the village, and we could hear Albert yelling. A man came out of the crowd carrying Albert's clothes. We realised that the rest of the crowd were all women. Suddenly the yelling stopped, and all the women came away. There was no sign of Albert. We remembered it was the first of May.

Our guards seemed as frightened as we were. The Saxons realised that these men were there to protect us, not to restrain us. The man came up and placed Albert's clothes in front of me. He seemed very concerned about the way the dog had torn the trousers. The belt and knife were there, and two rings and a neck

132

chain, and Albert's ear-rings that he always wore, with blood on them. We all sat down again. We didn't talk about it.

After another three hours or so, Morien came down from the village. He made a face as he passed the stain on the sand where we had last seen Albert. We all wondered what happened next. I remembered the shipwrecked sailors we had thrown into the bog.

When Morien came close to us, we saw that his face was not really blue. It was tattoed in a close and intricate pattern of blue lines so that little pink skin showed. On each cheek was a crescent moon, on its back, with a line that went up to each corner of his eyes. On each jaw bone, around each temple, writhed a snake with a horse's head. Eels wriggled up his arms, five headed eels, a head on each fingertip.

He took me by the arm.

'Rex, Rex,' he said. 'Ad Rex Venite.'

I went with him toward the water's edge. The Saxons and the spearmen followed. I wondered if we were going to ford the river, which looked a mile wide, when I saw men running down from the village carrying boats, big boats, two men to a boat as if they weighed nothing.

When we came to the water's edge and got in we found they did weigh nothing to speak of. They were made of a wicker frame covered with leather. Seal, I found, is the best leather for the purpose, which is why we hardly ever got any seal fur through Asgard. The boats were short and round, with two thwarts. This meant two Saxons and four spearmen in each boat, except that Edward and I each had five Saxons to look after us. Morien came in my boat. He tried to keep as far to windward of me as he could; I suppose he found the smell of my pig fat strange.

It was now clear that we had been waiting for the tide to turn. Villagers held bobbing boats for us to get in. They ballasted them with stones. Old millstones are the best, with no sharp corners. If a Briton tells you he sailed the seas on a millstone, that is what he means.

Yes, a Briton. I was already quite clear about that. Tattooed men, great brindled dogs, patterns like the Gauls wear, where else could we be? The only question was whether we were inside

133

or outside the Empire, going to a British puppet king or a real Pictish one?

With the tide and the paddles, for the rowers faced forward and scooped the boats along, we went up stream as fast as a man might walk and much more comfortably. We kept it up for hours, and at sunset we pulled in to a village. We had to; we were well out of the influence of the tide, and the stream was getting too shallow.

The headman came down to the shore and greeted Morien with great deference. A crowd of people and animals were turned out of a house to make way for us, and all the Saxons were ushered in. It was a big house. The spearmen turned paddlers turned back into spearmen again, and slept outside. If I am any judge, Morien had the headman's hut, and his supper and his wife into the bargain.

We got the same supper as our guards, and like them nobody's wife, though after what had happened to Albert we had no wish to meet any more British women. They gave us porridge, like the stuff the legionaries eat, but not wheat. It was a grain called oats, and they grow it in the Land of Norroway too, where the weather is always too wet for real corn to ripen.

The spearmen put salt on their porridge and ate it like that, but the Germans found it unpalatable. The spearmen laughed and brought pitchers of honey and warm milk which we mixed with it, and then the stuff was edible.

We curled up to sleep on the floor, wrapped up in our cloaks and what blankets had been left. There was more left than blankets, and we were soon scratching; new fleas came to avenge their comrades drowned at sea.

At dawn we were awakened with platters of bacon and a black greasy substance fried up with oatmeal. I wondered what it was, being so tasty, and in the end it turned out to be the boiled seaweed I had always refused to look at, let alone eat, at home in Valhall.

We got outside the house and mingled with our escort. The huts were round. German huts are square, or oblong, foursided anyway. In Britain the smaller houses are round. These particular houses looked flimsy and ramshackle as if they were only intended to last for a few weeks, and that was just the case. It was what they call a Havod, a summer place, where the young lads and girls lived looking after the cattle through the summer. The young men, the nobles of course I mean, go to spend three years at the king's court in his warband. There they learn to make war, and they ride the forest and guard the havods, and catch cattle thieves from other tribes, or perhaps steal a few cattle themselves. There is small difference between keeping and taking.

It was of course a party of these young men, from the king's family as they say, who had been ready to catch us on the shore, and now, under Morien the head of that village, were taking us to their King.

After breakfast, we were mounted on shaggy little ponies, smaller than the German horses. The Saxons kept on falling off; they are the worst horsemen I have ever seen, and proud of it. But we moved away from the river along a great ride cut through the wood, for cattle droving I suppose.

After a long day's ride, with a stop at another havod for a meal of oat cakes and cheese and cold bacon and warm milk, we came in sight of a city. Yes, a city! Not a city like Rome or Athens, but a city that Homer or Hesiod would have recognised. There were a hundred or so houses gathered around a market place, and above it on the hilltop were the walls of an Acropolis.

We reached the market place and stopped, and we took another step back to Homer. There was a blowing of horns, and Morien waved to us to dismount, and some of the Saxons slid off, and others fell off. Then we saw something that only lives for us in legends. We saw chariots!

These were not racing chariots like the ones you see at the games, those are only coachbuilders' fancy. These were real war chariots. I saw plenty in later years, but these were my first. They had wicker bodies, and bronze fittings, and six-foot wheels to go bounding over rough ground. Each had two horses harnessed to the pole. That, of course, is the trouble. You know you can never get cavalry to charge twice in one day; even if you can get them all back together again, they're blown. You're lucky if you can get chariots to charge once, certainly not if you have to cover more than two hundred yards. It chokes the horses. There's

135

absolutely no future in trying to use horses to pull vehicles, unless you can find some way of not tying the harness around their necks, and if nobody's thought of a way by now they never will.

Each of these was a three-man chariot. The first and the last were purely military, even if they had unshipped the long knives they fasten on the sides to discourage anyone getting too close. They each carried a very small driver, and two other men, bowmen, again very small.

The second was more ornate. The driver was very small. The other passengers were both quite big men, one old, one fairly young. Each of them was dressed in loose white clothes. They were clean-shaven and short-haired, both red-headed. Each wore on his head a garland of oak leaves. Each had on his breast a fresh sprig of mistletoe. These then were the priests of Britain I had heard of, the Druids, the Pythagoreans.

The third chariot, though, was the important one. The driver was a big middle-aged man, in patterned clothes, the same pattern as Morien. There were gold bracelets, gold chains, gold armbands enough to show that he was rich. The great gold collar above his neck and breast showed that he was royal, the gold diadem in his hair showed that he was a king. The brindled hounds that followed the chariot wore collars of gold. Spearmen pressed about him. If ever there were a king in Britain, this was a great king, and a Pictish king at that.

And with him there was a woman. She was small of build, neat and trim in all her movements. Her hair was black, yet not the same black as our Greek girls. Her eyes were a light, innocent cornflower blue. But what her skin was like or how old she was, how could I tell? Her face, like the king's, like Morien's, like everyone else's in the whole company, except the two Druids, was covered in blue tattooing. A procession of crabs went clockwise round her forehead. An oystershell was on each cheek, and on each finger a sea horse's head was joined into one neck that ran up her arm beneath her sleeve.

The king, and the lady, stopped and looked at us. I thanked heaven that I was wearing a good suit of clothes, even if it had been four days at sea, and some gold. I stepped forward ready to

136

act as spokesman for the whole crew, but the woman pointed at me, said a few words I couldn't understand, and they moved on. Still, I thought, it was something to catch the eye of royalty. I don't know how I'd have felt if I'd known then that what she said was,

'The one with white hair, he looks tasty. I'll have him.'

4

There was then a good deal of confusion in the market place, as is usual after the great have gone by. Somehow I got separated from the Saxons, but the noises I heard later that night showed that nothing very dreadful had happened to them. Morien took my arm, and a few spearmen jostled me from behind, and before I knew it I was inside a house, and that is more difficult than it may sound. For these houses were like none in Germany; they were of stone. They were round, and walls of unhewn stone fitted together without mortar rose to shoulder height, and a pointed roof of poles and thatch rose twice as high again. There was a hole at the peak, to let the smoke out and the light in. There was a fire of peat, and even in May we needed it in the evenings.

The spearmen crowded in too. There was a stone bench around the walls, and they sat on that. They kept on changing over, but there were always enough there to make sure I stayed.

After a while Morien came and they brought me food, porridge and bacon and baked meat and cheeses. I ate sucking pig, and lamb, and veal. I ate kid, and so I pushed aside one of the cheeses, which, by the smell, was goat. I left bear and goose. I ate duck. There was a dish of vegetables. I fished about in it with care, and I laid out eight beans on a plate, for the bean is sacred to the Pythagoreans and it would have been imprudent, at the least, to have eaten it with meat. Then I had another thought, and I went back to the dish, and I found another bean, and I laid them out on the plate in a square, three beans long and three beans wide and three beans from corner to corner, three and three and three, the perfect number in the perfect form. Morien watched every move, and I hoped that he knew no more of the Pythago-reans than I. But at least he learned that I knew something.

When Morien and the empty dishes, for there was not much difference between them in attractiveness, went away, and we were left with a big pot of beer, I began to get bored drinking with people I couldn't talk to. So I wandered about the room, and after a little I was sitting looking at three cups and a nut, and the spearmen were looking at me. I remembered having an argu-ment with a man in Alexandria as to whether you can do this if you haven't a chance to say anything. I found it is possible, but rather difficult; it even helps to talk away earnestly in a language your audience don't understand.

I did quite well at first. I got a new pair of shoes, for mine were ruined with the salt water, and some leg wrappings, and a bone comb, and a mirror, and an embroidered belt, and an arm-band, silver set with polished pebbles. Then we all lay down to sleep round the fire, though some of the lads stayed awake all night arguing over how it was done.

They woke me at dawn with lots of food, porridge and bacon and seaweed. Never confess to a liking for anything in a foreign country; they try to ensure you live on nothing else. After a little while for digestion I turned my attention to a young man who hadn't been at the session the night before and wanted to know what we had been playing. I showed him, and won his cloak fas-tening; I didn't want it really, except on principle, but he *would* wager it against mine, and I suppose he thought he was cleverer than the rest. Suddenly the laughter of the game stopped abruptly. Among the players there was the young Druid from the chariot. He reached out and touched the cups.

He was good. Quite quickly he won from me the cloak fas-tener, the armband, the belt, the comb and the mirror. With a pointed gesture he left me the shoes. I passed him the cups. With a little difficulty – I said he was good – I won back the cloak fastener, the armband, the belt and the mirror. With a pointed glance I left him the comb.

He combed his thick short red hair. He combed out of it a flea, a snail, a lizard, a mouse and a squirrel. They all sat on the table. I threw the end of my cloak over them, and they changed into a flock of pigeons which fluttered away through the chimney hole, leaving two eggs on the table. He stroked the comb, which turned into a centipede and wriggled off among the floor straw. I put the mirror on the coiled belt, and it turned into a frying pan full of sizzling fat over a crackling fire. I broke the two pigeons' eggs into the pan and had a second breakfast. I didn't offer the Druid any; I didn't think he deserved it.

None of this is very difficult if you know how, and so, having shown each other our professional credentials, we were free to talk. The Druid spoke first, in Latin, with a dreadful provincial accent and full of tricks of speech carried over from his own tongue.

'I am Taliesin. I am Himself, without Father, without Mother, born of the Oak, I live of the Oak. Photinus, Man without Kindred, are the Kindred that you are without the Kindred that I am without? Are you come of the tree I am come of? What then do you here? Man brought on the Wind, what did you there?'

'What does it matter to you what I have done, or what I will do?'

'Nothing, indeed, what you will do, for that is as much in our destinies as in yours, but it is out of interest and out of curiosity and out of inquisitiveness that I ask you what you did do, for you brought the Sun with you, and it is seldom enough that we see him, and three days running is unheard of. And it is known, and it is patent, and it is obvious, that the wind was your wind, for there was a singing in your praise all last night by your crew, and your shipmen, and your sailors.'

That I knew was an exaggeration, since the last thing I had heard Edward singing was a dreadful song called 'Knut, the Bastard King of Scania', and I will not trouble you with the words, except to say that even the Saxons will only sing it when they are out of earshot of land. Taliesin went on:

'They sing of how there was a leading of them out of the sea, and out of the weather and out of the wind, into a land of beef and bread and beer, a land of meat and milk and maidens, and there was a wishing and a desiring and a longing on me to see, and to perceive, and to observe this mighty man of marvels.'

I said no word till I had made the sign of the four in the air, and had plucked out of it the beans by one and three and five. Then I answered as proudly as I could:

'How can we talk, such as we are, under the turf of the roof, in the stench of the peat? Let us talk, let us walk, in the face of the day and the eye of the sun.'

And that was how he knew that I like himself was vowed to the unconquered sun, though I was no Pythagorean dedicated to the rule of numbers and harmony and abstinence from meat and from pleasures.

'Once there was a throwing,' said Taliesin, 'and a casting and a projecting of a spear into the face of the day, into the eye of the sun. No good came of that, no good will come of it, but what is that to me? Walk with me then, if you wish, in the face of the day, in the eye of the sun.'

And he motioned me before him, to go out through the low stone passage with an elbow in it to break the force of the winds. But I motioned him politely in front of me, for I did not want a golden knife in my ribs. And when we came to the doorway, I stood close to him, that no man with an axe or sword might strike me without hurting him. But I wronged him, for there was no one there.

We walked down through the city, and the people stood aside for the Druid. I saw Edward sitting on the step of a house holding his head in his hands while a girl washed his feet. There was no need to worry about my Saxons.

5

As we walked in the Grove, beneath the oaks coming into leaf, and the mistletoe with its leaves never old, never young, and the berries just ripening, Taliesin told me where I was.

'If you had gone from the river south-west as far as you have come north-east, you would have come to the walls, and the fortifications, and the ramparts, of the Romans. And if you were to stay here for five years, or ten, or maybe half a lifetime, you would perhaps once in a generation see the Romans march by on a raid, and an expedition, and a foray. And there it is proud they are of it,

140

but even when they are here they hold no more of the land than their boot soles cover. And Casnar whose dun it is on the hill and who is king of this place, even he does not try to stand against them in battle, but he and all his family and his kin and his cattle go into the wild places till the Romans are gone. Yet no Roman dare walk in this country unless a hundred more walk with him.

'Casnar who is the king of this place is a great man and a rich man, and above all he is a hard man. Tonight we dine with him in his hall in the dun. Listen to what he says, Photinus, and take what he offers, for he seldom offers much to anyone. And if you do not take what he offers, you will be soon left with nothing, no, not even your head. If you want him to offer you anything at all, even your life, come with me and wash, for you stink.'

And that was true, for I had still on me the pig fat of the winter. We went down to a bath house the king's young men had built for themselves by the river, and found there a number of young men oiling themselves after drill. They were all eager to copy Roman customs. They welcomed me as a sailor, and therefore as a fit person for soldiers to talk to, even if I sometimes had to depend for my life not on my strength alone, but on my knowledge of winds and currents and the balance of forces and the strength of pulleys.

They brought me hot water and soap and oil to wash off the pig fat and the salt and the road dust, and rough towels to dry myself and wrap myself in while they took away my clothes. Then I sat in a steam room where they dashed cold water on red hot stones, and I was more comfortable than I had been in Vindabonum, for many of these men spoke Latin, more or less, and they were all great talkers.

We sat on the river bank in the unwonted sunshine, and fished with long lines and bronze hooks, which small boys baited with a paste of bread and cheese. We ate more bread and cheese, and washed it down with beer, and made bets on the size and shape of our catch, though in fact we none of us caught anything, and I sang them, in Latin, the tale of how when I was recovering from the wound in my side I sat by the river in the forest and fished. They thought it a beautiful story, and indeed I have heard several versions of it since, with magical additions.

Then Taliesin recited, in Latin, in prose, the song he intended to sing that night, in his own tongue in Casnar's hall. It was all about how he began life as a poor boy, little Gwion, and about how he had escaped from his wicked stepmother and became a great bard, a Druid of the great line of bards, and a credit to his teacher Merlin, whom we had seen with him in the chariot the day before. Now Merlin had gone off to sponge on some other poor king, leaving Taliesin to squeeze Casnar.

Now, mark this, every bard in Britain has just such a tale of how he started life as a poor little Gwion or Gwynno or Ianto, and of how he rose to power by his own unequalled intelligence, and gained some such title as Taliesin, which means Radiant Brow, and indeed hair of that colour demands such a name. But this man had a tale to tell worth hearing, of all his transmigrations, and of how his unconquered soul went from one thing into another. For he had been a hare, and a fish, and a grain of wheat, and a sparrow, and a black hen, and at the last an egg, hatched of the black hen, from which there came at the long last little Gwion, already a half grown youth. And he had floated in from the sea in a leather boat and been cast up at the feet of his Master.

'And now I am left alone,' he told us. 'Now Merlin is gone into the cruel west, where there is neither bread nor light nor moderation nor true learning nor number nor respect for sacred things. Only I remain to sing, of all the Druids that once sang their hymns to the Sun in the Great Temple of the Isle of Britain. Raised it was, and built, and constructed, by the men of old, and their kings lie in a circle around it. Those were the kings that built the Temple at the beginning of time, at the foundation of the world, at the first going forth of the Chariot of the Sun. Stone are the pillars of it, and of unhewn rock are the columns and of the bones of the earth are the uprights. Of oak and of ash and of elm were the rafters that lay from pillar to pillar and from column to column and from lintel to lintel. Of reeds and of rushes and of barley straw was the thatch that they laid on the roof. Now all is departed, the rafters are burnt, the thatch is rotted away. The legions march by the roads of the men of old, and they go past the pillars of the House of the Sun, and they march by the Hill of the Sun, and they see them not.'

Now that is all true, for although a few Romans talk of the Temple, none claims to have seen it, nor has any one of them heard of the Hill of the Sun. But there is no need to believe the tale I have heard, that the Druids hide the Temple and the Hill in the mist, for why should a magician labour to raise mists in that island that is full of mists all day and all year long?

6

When the sun – for that was one of the rare days that we saw it – began to sink, they brought me my clothes, still a trifle damp in places, but clean and a few tears mended, and my boots new greased. Then we walked, Taliesin and I arm in arm, and a cloud of young soldiers behind us, and a bagpiper in front of us, and it was a wonderful thing to hear that civilised music in a savage land.

We climbed out of the village up a long flight of steps, each step made out of a single stone, to the great stone wall of the dun, unworked stones framed in timber. The side-posts of the gate were two great boulders, man high, with a stone lintel above them, and on each face of each boulder was grooved, incised, in one deep line, the figure of a bull, strong and proud, the head down to charge, the tail in motion. I wondered where I had seen before such a way of drawing with a chisel, why the bulls looked so familiar. Then I realised that the man who drew that bull on the rock had first drawn it on skin, had used the tattooist's needle before he brought his hands to the rock.

Njord lived in a warehouse. Edwin lived in a farmyard. Casnar lived in a city, and in that city he lived in a citadel, and in that citadel he lived in a palace, a palace of many rooms. True, each room was a separate house, and these houses were connected by low passages, shoulder height, and small courtyards.

The citadel, the dun they called it, was oval, and the palace took up scarcely a third of it. There was room enough within the walls for all Casnar's people and their cattle to take refuge.

I never found out how many rooms were in the palace, or how many people lived there. To the end I kept on bumping into strangers. The Great Hall, and it was a great hall, though, was built on the German fashion, and it stood at the front of the palace. It had the usual high table and sidetables, but inside it was the most hideous hall I have ever seen.

King Casnar was rich, richer than any king I had ever heard of. He was master of flocks of sheep and spinners and looms, of dyers and fullers without number. That pattern of red and yellow on green that Morien and the spearmen wore was King Casnar's pattern. In the hall I saw it everywhere. I mean quite literally everywhere. The walls were hung with it, and the rafters were hung with it, and the tables were not bare and polished but covered with patterned cloth. You could never rest your eyes in that hall.

There were a lot of men in the hall. Most of them were in King Casnar's pattern, but some of them were visitors and wore other colours. You'll never see anything like that among the Germans. Uniformity in dress is utterly foreign to their nature.

All were standing up. Taliesin led me to the high table, and we all waited till King Casnar entered. Then we remained standing, King and all, for a full hour by anyone's reckoning while Taliesin sang his song of Little Gwion's metamorphoses. *He* sat, of course, in a great chair that four other bardlets, apprentices I suppose, in blue, brought in for him, while we remained on our feet without food or drink or any chance to relieve ourselves or our feelings.

When Taliesin finished, he was not muttonboned as he so richly deserved, but he was loudly applauded and deigned to accept from the King's hand a gold oak-leaf wreath.

Then great bowls of steaming soup were brought in and set before the diners, who waited while the King made a speech, quite incomprehensible to me. The soup went cold, and the only comfort was that they hadn't even given me and the King that, only a glass of wine each.

When the King had finished he turned to me and bowed and tossed off his drink. While I was bowing back he vanished. I was still trying to work out what had happened when Taliesin seized my arm and steered me through a slit in the hangings into one of those low passages. I kept on bumping my head on the lintel, but after three courtyards and the intervening rooms, we came into the King's private dining-room. Somehow the bardlets had got there before us with Taliesin's chair, for this was the very symbol of his bardity.

It really was a cosy little party. We didn't go as far as couches, but we had chairs with padded leather cushions. The main dish, that night, after a first offering of mussels, was a pie, a wonderful pie, top and bottom crust full of suet, to soak up all the gravy from the filling of beef and oysters and onions. Such a pie I never saw in all Germany. The heavenly texture of it, the smell, seduced me from all thought of my predicament. I was drugged with food; I would have agreed to anything.

The servants who emerged from the stone passages whenever Casnar shouted for them brought Taliesin a silver plate with seven beans, boiled, pink, revolting, and a silver cup of cold water. When he had finished this, and we had finished the mussels, the servants took away his chair. This done he hung his oak leaves on an antler nailed to the wall, put his mistletoe on a side table, and, having thus gone off bardic duty, proceeded to make us fight him for every last scrap of the pie. I must say, I appreciate asceticism under those conditions. However, each time the servants came back, he would spring to lean against a pillar with an abstracted air.

This was much better than eating in a noisy hall with drunken retainers fighting at the bottom of the table, and the minstrel groaning on. Instead, there was a choir of men in the courtyard who kept up a Pythagorean harmony. It may have been churlish of me to notice that they only knew three songs, which they sang over and over again, but when I had heard one verse often enough to memorise it I asked Taliesin what it meant.

'It is,' he told me, 'a song, a most beautiful song, a most harmonious song, in praise of purity of heart. The particular line you asked me about means "The pure heart does nothing but sing, day and night".'

'And these singers?'

'Pure,' he answered, with his voice full of innocent candour and sincerity. 'All pure, very pure indeed.'

The singing went on while our gay little party conversed in

Latin. I noted that efforts were always made to give me companions who could speak Latin, thus preventing me from learning the British tongue. We got on quite well in Latin, we four, I and Taliesin and the King and the lady from the chariot, especially by the time we were dealing with a suety dish full of apples and served in a sauce of honey and milk and eggs.

Now, Casnar was reciting his pedigree, which meant that we three were at leisure to eat. He went into some detail over his immediate ancestors who had moved north, he said, after Caesar had come to the south. Here, in the north, they still kept up the ancient customs, like tattooing. I reflected that he was better paid for his ancestral piety than was Hoenir, the poor Lombard king. Then, as we were moving on to walnuts from Italy, and raisins, very expensive, Casnar put his arm around my shoulder and said,

'You are a man of wealth and power, power natural and power supernatural, and we learn from Taliesin that you are a priest of his own holy order.' I gave Taliesin a look which showed I held him responsible for anything that might happen.

'Here I sit, King of all the north. All the other painted kings owe me their allegiance.' Owed, indeed, but paid seldom. 'I receive rent and tribute from all around. Even the Romans pay me for the inestimable blessing of my good will. Yet I have no one left in my family to share my wealth with me. I have no kin but my little sister Bithig.'

I looked at little sister Bithig. I was wrong, it was seagulls, not crabs, that went in procession around her forehead. Casnar went on,

'Her son shall be king here when I am gone. Photinus, I give you my sister in marriage. You shall stay with us as long as you live.'

And little sister Bithig opened her thin lips for the first time that evening, and said in a small innocent voice,

'I am named after my great-aunt, whom you know as Boadicea, who sacked London and killed ten thousand Romans, beside many Syrians and Greek pedlars.'

She shut her little lips tight again, it was the only thing she said all the evening. I looked at Taliesin over the King's head. He smiled happily and drew the back of his hand over his throat. I made desperate choking noises, and they took this for acquiescence. All I could hear was Albert screaming, and then stopping screaming, while Taliesin stood on a stool and delivered a five hundred line epithalamion.

I decided that the only thing to do was to join the others and finish the Spanish wine. For them it was celebration, for me an anodyne. I determined to drink till the sea-gulls on Bithig's forehead started going around the other way. Long before that I was unconscious.

7

I woke up next morning in a room in the palace. I had a frightful headache. A young man called Annwas brought me some hot milk and boiled seaweed. I asked him in Latin if I could go into the fresh air, and he led me to the nearest courtyard. It was raining steadily. I stayed inside.

In the middle of the morning we went to the hall. It was full of warriors, but they crowded around me and asked me to recite to them in Latin, for they were all eager for learning even if none of them could read. I gave them nearly the whole of Book Four of the Aeneid. Just as I came to the death of Dido, as I whispered,

> The shears sever, the shining hair hangs down,
> No longer lingers life, Dido lies dead,

I found I had no audience, because the first servants had come in with midday drink and food. I tried to forget it all again, this time with cider.

The next I knew Annwas was calling me for dinner. This time we ate in the hall. Bithig wasn't there. Taliesin was furious and showed it in a thousand little hints. Etiquette forbade him to leave before his King, and as a result he was limited to his seven boiled beans and water. Casnar was amused, and told me so.

'We've got to have him pure overnight. Can't have him unclean in the morning, spoil it all.'

'All what?'

'The wedding, of course, Bithig is fasting too, and it always ruins her temper.'

I did a lot of drinking that night. I just hoped it would keep me fuddled through the day. It didn't of course, it just gave me another headache. Annwas woke me early with a colossal breakfast, all salty. Have you eaten salt herrings and salt bacon when you have a dry mouth and a nasty taste to start with?

Annwas and another man named Evrawc argued for hours about how to dress me for the occasion. I refused to wear the red and green pattern, or any gay colour, and they insisted, and they were quite right, that my grey was in no condition for a formal appearance. In the end they stole Taliesin's second best toga, and someone sewed a purple border on it, so that I went to my first bigamous wedding dressed as a Roman magistrate. But my long white hair was most un-Romanly dressed with goose grease.

We walked in a kind of rough procession down to the grove. The main part of the ceremony was my paying of a bride price, and the original intention was that this should have been a token offering, a small bag of gold supplied from the Royal treasury. However, my pride would not allow that, and I had had a hard day's work with the three cups and the dice the afternoon before. As a result, the bride price I paid was a wild mixture of collars and armbands and brooches, but all gold and of good quality. My escort, however, though they carried their weapons with an air, had a rather bare and poverty-stricken look. While I was in Casnar's kingdom, I got on to reasonable terms with the king, and I felt that by paying my gaming winnings into the family purse I was at least earning my keep.

After we had waited in the Grove for a very long time, so that Taliesin began to worry whether we should be able to start within the propitious hours, Bithig and her brother arrived in a chariot. She wore a veil. I was glad of that. I had spent most of the night dreaming of being married to Medusa, and I still had a headache. The ceremony was short and simple. We shared a cup of a rather horrid drink made out of dandelions, and paid the bride price: in fact the longest part of the whole proceedings was waiting for Casnar to finish counting and weighing it.

Then we got into the chariot, Bithig and I. She peeled off her

gloves and threw them into the crowd. She threw back her veil.
I nearly leapt out of the chariot, but there was a double line of
spearmen on each side. They *had* married me to Medusa. It was
not sea-gulls or crabs that ran around her forehead, but an
inverted crown of snakes' heads. Snakes wriggled up her arms
under her sleeves. And there was a dragon's head on each cheek,
that snapped at me each time she changed her expression. I tried
not to think of the night, when those snakes would twine around
me and throttle me.

Before us in the chariots marched bagpipers. It was wonderful
in that desert place to hear real civilised music again. The pipes
are the absolute peak of human achievement in music making.
They played, and the crowd sang, a song I had not heard before,
which, I was told, was a prayer to the Goose God to lead them
through the barren land. We rode to the open space below the
steps to the dun, and mounted a dais.

There, so near to civilisation were we, we watched a whole
day of ritual games. They raced chariots and they raced on foot,
and they had contests in throwing the javelin, and in throwing a
great stone, and something I had never seen before, in throwing
a tree. And they danced. These people do not dance as all other
nations dance, for rain or dry weather or victory in battle. They
danced for the sake of dancing, with no real religious feeling
behind it at all. It struck me as almost blasphemous. They danced
by ones and by twos and by fours, and by twos of fours and by
fours of eights. They danced till the dusk came.

Then when it began to get a little chilly, and the pedlars were
selling hot soup and mulled beer instead of cold boiled ham, we
went into the hall for the marriage feast. I was rather glad that
Taliesin took so long over his marriage song, and that he translated it line by line into Latin. After that, while we ate, the
competitions went on, but now they were competitions in the
composition of verse, and in singing and in playing the bagpipes
and in blowing the horn. It would have been glorious, at least the
pipes would have been, if I hadn't had such a dreadful headache.
Drinking did nothing to settle it.

Every time I looked at Bithig, the snakes flickered their
tongues, and the dragon mouths opened and closed at me. This

149

was no place to stay, but it was worse to go. The pipes played louder, and Bithig's lips grew more set and determined. It was a situation to turn a man's hair white. Mine was white already.

Bithig began tugging at my wrist, under the table. Later, she got me by the elbow and pulled, not caring who saw. I pretended to be affected by the music and beat time with my hands on the table. Bithig went on tugging. I went on tapping. The pipers went on playing. My head began to fragmentate. Taliesin was nudging me. I took no notice. Finally Casnar leaned across the table, picking his teeth with his knife, and said very loudly,

'This has been a long hard day for the pair of you. Especially for my poor little sister, always delicate she was. Feel like going to bed, now, don't you?'

Taliesin was jerking his head toward the private door. Morien was stropping his knife on the sole of his shoe. Those Picts have no doubts about the main purpose of a wedding.

I got up rather unsteadily, and Bithig gripped my wrist with a hand hard and strong after years at the hunt. She heaved me after her through the private door, and through half a dozen more doors, and each time I hit my head on the lintel. Nobody in the hall took the slightest notice of our disappearance; I felt that there the fun was only just beginning.

I was dragged stooping through that maze of passages for what seemed an hour. It would have been pleasanter in the Cretan Labyrinth, for Bithig went first, and the Minotaur would have eaten her before me.

She got me into her bedroom, a much more comfortable room than the one they'd given me. It was done up with very good Roman furniture, all fifty years out of fashion of course, but they tell me that kind of thing's coming back now. The whole room was ablaze in the light of at least two dozen candles.

'All right,' said Bithig. 'Bed!'

'Please,' I asked her. 'Can't we put the lights out first.'

'Who do you think I am? Psyche?' She'd had a good education, I'll say that. 'Don't you want to see what you're getting? I went to a lot of trouble over this.'

She slid out of her dress. Her short sleeved bodice in red flannel showed the snakes peering from a forest of convolvulus that

150

went up to her shoulders. She took off five more underskirts, red and yellow and green and blue and purple. Finally she flung the bodice and the last skirt, a black one, at my head, and I saw it!

Before and behind, snakes and dragons' heads and tails peeped out from the riot of intertwined briar and bindweed. Not an inch of space was wasted, not an inch. Out of the symmetrical cloud of blue patterns, beautifully designed if you like that formalised art, there crystallised a few close coarse spirals. One centred on her navel, one on each breast, one on each buttock, one on each knee cap. As I looked in horror, each spiral began to revolve, to open and shut, to expand and contract. The whole room shrank in on me, and swelled out to fill the Universe, and shrank again, and the candles flickered till you couldn't see for dancing shadows.

'I need a drink,' I said.

'Nonsense. You'll be all right, as long as you don't sit down.' She was a hard woman, all right. 'I don't want you going to sleep here. Stand there and listen.'

Outside the bagpipes were playing. For a moment Bithig stood poised. Then she began to dance. Perhaps the people at the games didn't dance anything in particular, but she did. They didn't dance rain or barley, but Bithig danced bed. Bithig danced sex.

The pipes droned and throbbed in rhythmic surges. The dragons and serpents crawled and chased their tails among the rustling leaves. The spirals expanded and contracted, in and out, in and out. I never knew when I started too. I danced my clothes to the four corners of the room, I danced my clothes to the four corners of the room, I danced my wits to the eight winds of heaven, I must have danced my headache somewhere because I never had one again in all my life. I danced Bithig into bed in the pressing bounding beat, and as we rolled to a climax, the pipes and the harps and every singer in the palace joined in that song about the need for purity of heart.

8

When day came, and the candles were burnt out, a woman came in with a jug of hot milk.

'There is a fine day it is,' she said brightly.

'Fine? You mean sunny?'

'No, no sun. But it has not been raining for, oh, half an hour at least.'

Good weather is a question of what you are used to. Two days without rain are a wonder in that country. Two days of sun are a miracle, and I had brought three.

I drank most of the hot milk. Bithig was snoring. I never had a wife like her for lying in bed in the mornings. I summoned up courage to look at her. I took a good look.

This was not the woman I had married. There were no snakes, no dragons, no crabs or butterflies either. She was just a blotchy mess of blue and white. Blue and white blots, smudges, smears, stripes all over. I looked down. I was in the same state, blue everywhere. I leaped out of the bed. There was a bowl of water in the room, and towels; I washed, I rubbed till the blood came. It only spread the blue.

There was laughter from the bed. Bithig was laughing at me. She lay there, all blue and white and blotchy, and she laughed at me, damn her.

'Water only makes it worse,' she got out at last. I went over and emptied the bowl over her head.

'Now get it off yourself,' I told her. I rolled her over and beat her on the buttocks till there must have been some genuine blue among the blotches. She wriggled out of bed, tripped me, and sat on my face to rub the stuff into my legs. I got my head round far enough to bite her in the bottom and as she sprang howling across the room she cannoned into the serving-woman, who showed no surprise at the yelling wrestling pair who bounced off her and covered the room with fried eggs and sausages.

'Get some more milk, Myfanwy,' said Bithig. 'This Mesopotamian idiot drank the last lot.'

'I'm not a Mesopotamian.'

'Greece, Mesopotamia, India, what's the difference?'

Myfanwy came back with more milk.

'Nothing else will take it off. Shall I do the gentleman's back, dear?'

'It's a wife's prerogative to wash her husband's back,' I insisted. After all, she ought to do something.

'And vice versa,' snapped Bithig. 'Have you got some butter for the hard bits, Myfanwy?'

'Two big pats, best salted. Dreadful it is when it gets wet. You have to scrape and scrape. Would you like some more egg and sausage?'

When she brought it, and we were both clean down to the navel, Bithig asked her again what the weather was.

'Well, it was quite fine first thing, but it's raining again now.'

'Heavy?'

'Pouring down, sweetheart.'

'Oh good, now we don't have to go out all day. Mackerel for lunch, and a few gobbets of everything for dinner. Now, back to bed.'

And that was how three days went by, in rain and bedding, in lechery and luxury, bigamous and entrancing. We once or twice came up for air and conversation.

'But I thought you were tattooed.'

'No, only men. Women used to be, but it's quite impossiblé. Just think of being saddled with the same face for life.'

'Or the same body.'

'That's only for special occasions. It takes so long to put on and off. It's very good for the milk trade, though. There's a limit to the amount of cheese we can find a market for.'

'What do you do it with?'

'What do you think? Woad and goose grease, of course.'

9

The fourth morning it had stopped raining. We spent a couple of hours putting on Bithig's tattoo, and then we went hunting.

153

We spent all the afternoon careering through the forest after a stupid hare that hadn't enough sense to climb a tree or dig a hole, and even then we never caught it.

We went hunting nearly every day. The days we didn't go for hare we hunted deer, which meant crawling about on your face in the wet woods trying to get a crossbow shot in. We never actually got a deer either.

None of this was very good for my grey suit. In the evenings I would cover it up with Taliesin's second best toga, but with the soup stains and the drips of beer that too was getting to look grey. I didn't dare get it washed, it would have taken two months to dry.

Then one evening, in hall – the royal family dined in hall once a week – I was moving around late in the evening trying to find someone to play dice with when I got into conversation with a stranger, who said he was a cloth merchant, and had a couple of suits in grey that would fit me without much alteration. He reminded me of Occa, somehow, his Latin was good, and he'd come up from south of the Wall.

'Those suits aren't much, but they *are* grey, and you only want them for a year and a day, don't you?'

'A year and a day? What do you mean?'

'Don't know much about the Picts, do you, boy. They're old-fashioned up here. They still pass the kingship down from uncle to nephew, you know, and they still choose fathers for their kings by chance. Any stranger passing by who's moderately royal, they marry him off to the king's sister, and after a year and a day, when they're sure he's done his duty, or not, off he goes.'

'Off he goes? Where?'

'Nobody knows. Some do say that he don't have no proper burial.'

'You mean …?'

'They eats him. Still, you never know, not with Picts.'

Well, I didn't take much notice of that, there are all kinds of strange things they say about the Picts, and I bought the two grey suits, that is, I played him dice for them, and they were both quite a good fit. But a few days later, we were having a quiet dinner in the king's diningroom, and I was trying to get out of them when there would be fair winds to get back to Germany, and

154

they were trying to wheedle out of me where the Amber came from, and Morien and Evrawc were there. Bithig got up to leave and I got up too, and she said,

'No, Photinus, not in my condition,' and she went! That's all she said, 'Not in my condition,' and I didn't see her again. Instead Morien and Evrawc stood very close to me, and Evrawc said,

'We've moved your things into another room.'

They took me there, and Annwas was already outside the door, with a big shield and a spear. It was a good room, better than the one I had had the first night. There was a great big bed, chairs, table, seal-oil lamps. For some reason the rafters were full of sealed jars. It was a good room, but it was quite clear I couldn't get out. I didn't try. I went to sleep.

In the morning, Evrawc woke me up with an enormous bowl of porridge, and enough fried food for three. I looked at it wanly.

'Come along,' he said. 'Eat up. How much do you weigh?'

'About a hundred and sixty pounds.'

'You'd better eat well. We're counting on at least two hundred dressed for the oven, by next spring. Morien won't be pleased if you fall short.'

'Why Morien?'

'Well, you came up on his land, and he gets paid by weight. There's only been a deposit put down on you yet, the King won't settle till after the feast. I think we'll have to be putting a German in to make it go round. This Edward of yours, is it royal he is being or only noble?'

'Just noble. Why?'

'Well, thinking of him for next year, Bithig was.'

I got worried.

'Is this all serious, about eating me?'

'Of course.' It was obvious that Evrawc could conceive of no other way of life. 'Of course most of us nobles don't really like the taste, but the peasants expect it.'

'But you can't do it to me. I won't have it!'

'Nobody's ever complained before.'

'I'm complaining now. Get Taliesin!'

'He won't help you. He gets the best bit, as a Druid, you know.'

'Tell him I want the consolations of my religion.'

Evrawc went off and left me to breakfast. How anyone could eat in such a situation, being fattened up like an ox! To treat me like this, Photinus, Votan Aser, to treat me as a piece of flotsam cast up on the beach and sell me off to the highest bidder, not even for cash but on some kind of credit arrangement. The porridge was better than usual, it had pats of butter floating in it. And sold for what? I was practically incandescent with rage. Not for the sake of my muscles which were in fair state. Not for the sake of my intellect, keener than any they had in the dun – the bacon had been too long on the grill – not for the sake of my store of priceless knowledge, or the dexterity of my fingers. Sold as a sexual chattel – the sausages were quite fair, why weren't there any more – solely for some lewd woman's pleasure. The night she danced, Bithig practically raped me. The indignity of it! Was that the last of the cheese? It should never happen to anybody. And when it was all over, to be thrown away, useless, missing all the fun, fit only for food …

10

Taliesin came with my lunch. It was quite a good one and would have been enough for two people if there hadn't been two people, and one of them an ascetic vegetarian Druid.

'Look here,' he said. 'You can't go breaking up traditions like this.'

'Your tradition,' I told him, 'not mine. Where I come from, royalty dies peacefully of old age and overeating.'

'General tradition, my boy. The King must die for the harvest, we've got a good king, let's have the next king's harvest instead. Break the chain, and the world will come to an end, all starve.'

'We won't. The world will end in fire, and not for a long time yet.'

'How do you know?'

'I had a vision.'

'Tell me.' Taliesin was all professional interest. I let him have as much as was good for him of my nine days in the tree.

'Now, if there won't be a cataclysm at once, and if we can have

156

enough pork in the pot, and one of the Germans too … I could get you as far as the grove tonight, and down south at the end of the week. But why should I? I mean, the festival is the only chance poor men like me have of tasting meat.'

'You great solar hypocrite, sitting there with a leg of hare in your hand, my hare, that ought to go into fattening me up … and anyway, you get the best bit.'

'I do not,' he was indignant. 'I only get the right thing, Merlin gets the right buttock, that's the best bit.'

'And Bithig? What does she get?'

'What do you think? Anyway, we keep your head, look, up there. That one was your predecessor, a man from the outer isles, called Fergus. A bit salty, I thought. When we first saw you, we were on our way back from the ceremony. First of May, you know. But still you haven't said, what's in it for me?'

'When I landed I had a waterbottle, on a strap.'

'I've got it.'

'Come round after dinner, and bring it.'

11

At least he did come after dinner, and gave me a chance to eat a meal for three men in peace. He gave me the bottle. I pulled out the bung, and offered it to Taliesin. He refused.

'You might be going to turn me into anything.'

'Then I shall.'

'No! Who knows what powers it might not give you. I'll call Morien. Any change there would be an improvement.'

I poured Morien four fingers of the Honeydew in a silver cup. He tossed it down, looked puzzled, and then stood up very straight and sang what I took to be several stanzas of the song about purity of heart. Taliesin looked interested.

'It is a great deal of good that it has been doing to his versification. But as for the matter – there has been a developing, and an expanding, and a flowering of his imagination. In his own verses he has touched depths of depravity I did not think he has as yet plumbed, and he has reached heights of obscenity of which any man might well be proud. At some convenient occasion I will tell you of how I was consecrated, and initiated, and made secure against all the temptations of gluttony and strong drink.'

'I've noticed the effects.' I poured Morien a second drink. He finished it, and with a happy expression lay down by the fire, and went to sleep.

'To think I had that, and wasted money on bribes,' said Taliesin. 'What does it taste like?'

I poured him some. He savoured it, and tried a few stanzas.

'The effect on the flow of ideas is very good, and on metre, but alliteration is only slightly improved. Still, you can't have everything. How do you make it?'

'You start off with a mash,' I began. 'This is honey, but barley or apples will do ...' I went through it all carefully, once. Taliesin's trade, mainly, was in memorising immense long poems, and he had the whole process of Honeydew off pat at one hearing. But I had no fear that he would ever be able to make it. Setting up the stills calls for a great deal of technical skill, and the most he had ever done was to cut mistletoe with a golden knife. He didn't realise the difficulties.

When he had memorised the recipe, he said,

'Let's make the grove.'

'Now you have the secret, how do I know I can trust you?'

'I give you my word as the priest of the Unconquered Sun—'

'Stop it,' I told him. 'We both know how much that word is worth.'

Silently he laid his hand on his mistletoe. That was good enough for anyone to believe.

I motioned Taliesin to leave the room before me. Before I went I took Morien's belt, and his cloak fastener, and a few other worth-while trinkets. Then I followed the Druid along the long stone passages and through the courtyards. When we were in the last corridor and I could feel the air on my face, I saw Taliesin straighten up in the doorway. There was rather a nasty sound, and he fell down. Hit his head on the lintel, I thought, but the body in front of me suddenly slid quietly to one side. There were voices in Latin. The first was native, sibilant and adenoidal, and I could swear it was the cloth merchant.

'Now look what you've done. It comes very expensive out here, killing a Druid.'

'Well, well, Gwalchmai, there's nothing you can do in this island that a couple of sheep for Cernunnos won't put right.' And this voice, too, was familiar.

'Well, now I look he is not dead at all. An ox to Mapon will be best, and I can introduce you to a very reliable dealer, my second cousin.'

'I'm sure that the transaction will be free of all trace of self interest. We can arrange it later. Now how do we find Photinus in this jumble of rooms?'

It was time to say something. I whispered very loudly in Greek,

'If you have quite finished your theological speculations, I'll show you where I live.'

I came out. It was the cloth merchant, and the other ... well, who else, it was Aristarchos, and he only said,

'I think you've met my troop sergeant-major. Now, Gwalchmai, what do we do with Taliesin?'

'Easy. I take this jug of beer, which I providentially happen to have with me, and I pour it over him ... so ... and the jug in his left hand ... so ... and in his right this half-gnawed ham bone, which I brought in case I might be hungry in the night. And there is your abstemious vegetarian Druid, dead drunk on his own doorstep, and no one will ever believe a word he says.'

'Back we go,' said Aristarchos. 'You ought to get away easy. I've got eight hundred men out here tonight, and by dawn every cow for twenty miles will be milling round in one enormous herd close to the Wall. It'll take the Picts the whole summer to sort them out, and a generation to settle the blood-feuds. Peace in the north for thirty years, and not a single silver coin to Casnar. That's where he got his wealth, subsidies not to attack the Wall. Let's see how rich he gets on farming when he's quarrelling with all his neighbours. By the way, there was no sentry on the gate of the dun, or in the village either.'

'Taliesin bribed them to go away so he could get me out. You would pick tonight. What are you doing here, anyway?'

'I've been raising a cavalry regiment. We're off to the Danube next month, this is my last training exercise for them. At least it's productive. Now, here's the beginning of a path. Keep south-east on this for a mile and a half, and you'll find something. Good luck.'

I made all the speed I could along the path. A mile and a half, I thought, and there'll be one of Aristarchos's patrols, or at least a horse holder, and then a night's ride and I'll be back in the Empire, safe. Nothing will ever tempt me to go back to the north again, good riddance to the lot. I didn't want to see a Briton again as long as I lived, or a German either – somebody jumped on me. He wasn't a very good wrestler and I was on top almost at once before I found he was swearing in Saxon; it was just in time to stop me putting Morien's knife into his ribs. I got off him. Osbert sat up, and the other Saxons came sheepishly to me.

'What are you doing here?' I asked them sternly. I'd had a severe shock.

'There was a man named Gwalchmai, cloth merchant he was …'

'Auxiliary sergeant-major, you mean.'

'Well he did seem to have things organised. He woke us up one by one, and said that if we went two nights' march to the south, and a night lying up in between, there'd be a boat to take. But when we got to these birches we'd better wait for something to happen. I suppose he meant you, but these Brits never say anything straightforward, and he couldn't speak German properly anyway.'

Off they'd gone, straight for the coast, never a thought for me. Just selfish, that's what, looking after their own skins, and never a thought for their brave leader who had brought them for his own purposes across the sea to this place of plenty and now had raised the whole Roman Army to send them safely on their way. I was shocked, and I told them so. They had the grace to look ashamed.

We lay up for a day on a hillside overlooking a valley with a cattle road. We'd found a havod, quite deserted, but everyone's belongings still scattered about, so as well as blankets for the day we all found some stray trinkets to remember Britain by. We watched through the morning as bands of angry men, armed, came through hurrying southwest.

'They look fierce enough to eat you, indeed,' said Edward.

'We did hear the nobles were going to eat you. The peasants don't do that kind of thing, they say it's too old-fashioned.'

No men came in the afternoon, so I started off before it was properly dark. We reached the shore, the banks of a big river really, about an hour after dark, with the moon coming up.

We were near a village. I took stock of the boats. There were a number of leather boats beached, two of them big enough to take us back to Germany, but I didn't mean to do any more rowing, it was too much work, and too chancy. I pointed out under the moon and said,

'We'll take her.'

She was anchored out in the stream, too far for a spear to carry, but not too far for swimming.

'The south-wester?' said Edward. 'Who's going to sail her?'

For this was one of the big ships from the west of Britain, the kind the Veneti used to sail that gave Caesar so much trouble. She wasn't a galley.

'You take her,' I said. 'I'll sail her.'

Oswy and Egbert were already stripped. They slid into the water and swam out without splashing. They might have been seals for all anyone could see. In a little while one of them was standing by the mast and waving. Osbert went around and slashed open most of the leather boats. We all got into the largest, and paddled our way out to the ship with our hands; of course all the paddles were hidden away. We were well afloat before anyone remembered the swimmers' clothes, and we had to go back for them, giggling.

We heaved over the bulwarks on to the deck, Osbert remembering to slash a hole in the last leather boat. This ship *had* a deck, too, and a high poop, with a shelter under it full of things. She was oak built, great thick timbers, iron bolted, and a big leather lug sail on a mast stepped well forward. She was big enough, and roomy, three times as long as she was broad. None of the Saxons had ever *seen* a ship like her, let alone sailed in one.

I picked out the brightest, and stood them with ropes' ends in their hands. The stupid ones I set to holding the standing rigging; they heaved away at the shrouds and backstays like mad and thought it was important, and it kept them out of mischief.

'Edward, take the steering oar. Now all of you, listen. Edward as well. Listen to me all the time. When I tell you to do anything, MOVE! If you don't hear your name called, stand still. Anyone who misses a call or pulls out of turn, I'll kill him, I tell you, I'll kill him. Now, listen while I call out what I'm doing.'

I was doing this for my own benefit as well as theirs. I couldn't afford to make a mistake.

'My sail is – lowered. My steering oar is – inboard. My wind is – light west-nor'-west. Now! My cable is – *cut*! Oswy – loose, my steering oar is – put her in, Edward – outboard, my sail is – pull, Edwy, let out the line, Egbert – set and ... drawing. My wind is on the ... port quarter, my heading is ... a little south of east.'

When I was satisfied that Edward and Ethelbert could hold her reasonably steady, I called Osbert, who was the stupidest.

'Hurry along there, you're at sea now, not on your farm. How much water in the well?'

'What's a well?'

The Gods gave me patience not to hit him on the spot.

'You remember about baling, I hope?'

'I baled all the flaming way over.'

'And you'll bale all the flaming way back if you aren't careful. There's the bucket and this is where you do it. Let's see. Not much there, keep it up till you have to use a sponge, and then tell me.'

'What's a sponge?' but I left him.

I called Oswy Karlsson, who had had enough sense to make the halyards fast.

'What else did you find – or miss?'

'She's in lead, big pigs with a mark on them.'

'I thought as much, from the way she's handling. Any food?'

'In the shelter deck. Monotonous, cheese and twice-baked bread, and a bit of bacon. Plenty of water, in two big casks.'

'Good. I was afraid we might have to raid for it. Anything else?'

'There was a watchman. We knocked him on the head and tied him up on the lead. Where's she from?'

'In lead? from south-west Britain. We'll find out for certain when the watchman wakes up.'

162

'If he speaks German.'

'But you speak Pictish, don't you?'

'No, why should I? All these Scrawlings understand German if you talk it loudly enough.'

And it was quite true. The King had taken great care that I should have no chance to learn Pictish. The Saxons had had every chance, and just never bothered.

12

By daylight, we were well out of the river mouth, and standing out to sea. Edward asked me when we would turn south-south-east to follow the coast, which, he pointed out, would bring us dead before the wind like a ship ought to go. I just told him to hold her steady.

There was a bit of grumbling among the crew as the coast slipped out of sight. I must admit that it is never very pleasant to be out of sight of land, but I had to take these men where they had no choice but to do what I told them.

First I had breakfast served, biscuit and cheese and a cup of water. When we had finished, I put Oswy at the steering oar, and brought her round almost due south. This brought smiles to everybody's faces. They soon vanished. I gave them a couple of hours of sail drill, tacking about a point on either beam of the wind. After that, even the stupid ones realised what we were about. Of course most of the Saxons were sick, the motion of that heavy ship wasn't very pleasant, but they'd all been sick on the way over and they expected it.

When I was satisfied, I stood half the men down, and gave the oar to Edward. We had a talk with the watchman. In spite of a night tied up on the lead with an aching head, he was still glowing with rage, a crabby old man. He was obviously cursing us up and down in his own language, so we threw a couple of buckets of water over him.

He talked then, grudgingly, in very bad Latin. He told me he did come from the south-west. He seemed to be saying, as far as I could follow, that he came from a town in the water underneath

163

a glass mountain, where the Druids supped from a sacred cup beside a tree that bloomed at the Yule. Serve you right, I thought, for hoping to get sense out of an angry man.

The wind held steady into the night. I felt enough confidence in Edward to let him steer in the dark, and I slept on the deck beside him. I dreamt again, of ghosts, ghosts of men who were yet to die. lots of men in great grey ships, in a lost battle launching themselves in a desperate charge to save a fleet. I woke out of a nightmare of smoke and steam and fire to find Edward shaking me and saying,

'There's something wrong with the ship.'

It was near dawn. There was nothing wrong with the ship, but the wind had come right round, it was the wind that had brought us to Pictland. It came from near the south, in the end; we watched it back all the way from west-nor'-west through west to a trifle west of south in an hour, but I waited till it steadied before I made up my mind.

'Right, Jokuhai-inen,' I thought, 'you did what you liked to poor Saxons in a rowing boat. Now try a real man in a real ship. You bar me the way to the south? South I will go.'

I turned to my crew.

'Duty watch,' I called. 'The rest of you get some sleep, you'll need it. I'll call you later. Duty watch! Now you'll learn what work is.'

They did, too. I know you'll never make a sailor out of any Saxon, but I did my best. I took my direction from the sun, and brought the ship's head round as near south-east as I could and held her there.

How close to the wind would she sail? Very close, I found. In the end I was able to make way with the wind a whole point forward of the beam. How? Well partly it was that great lug sail – I'd never seen a lug sail on such a big vessel before. Partly it was the way the steering oar was hung right at the stern, and partly it was just the way she was built.

The Saxons, of course, thought it was magic that I could sail against the wind. It was not magic that beat Jokuhaiinen's magic. It was the mind of man – or rather several minds, the mind that built the ship and gave her that deep keel, the mind that set out the sail plan and cut and sewed the leather, the mind that stowed and trimmed the lead, and the mind that held the whole picture of wind and sea and trim and draught and knew when to go about.

It took all day to beat Jokuhai-inen. By evening, the wind veered back to west of north, and at dark it dropped. So we threw out a sea anchor, and hove to for the night. In the morning we had a fair wind again. Now the crew were cheerful, but the day's work tacking and changing course had done them a lot of good. They had even got quite used to moving about on a heeling deck; most landsmen, or people who go out in rowing boats, think of a ship as a floating platform they must keep steady, not as a living thing that must swim and find her own attitude in the sea.

So we made another day toward Germany, and a night and another day. Edward felt a bit light-hearted, and he untied Caw. The time on the lead without food or water had calmed the old tiger down, and we gave him a bucket and set him swabbing under the poop where some of the Saxons had been sick.

The wind was gentle, and the day sunny, and the motion of the ship easy, and I was sitting on the poop telling Edward about some of the finer points of sailing into the wind, and he was not believing a word I was saying, and most of the others were dozing; there was a sudden commotion. I jumped up.

'Egfrith, get off Caw! Oswy, you fool, get back to the steering oar. Now what's up?'

'He chucked something big overboard. Then he was jumping in himself. I caught him in time.'

'It was the cheese sack,' said somebody. 'It went straight down, he must have put a pig of lead in it.'

'Let's see what else he's done.' I took Edward into the shelter deck.

'Yes, the cheese is gone. What about the biscuit barrel? Full of sea water. Now knock the water casks. That one shouldn't be full. He's topped it up with salt water. And the other one, too. No wonder he'd rather drown.'

I went back on deck. Two men were kicking Caw in the face.

'Stop that, it never does any good,' I told them, 'not in those soft shoes. Go for the groin, like this.'

When Caw had reached the vomiting stage, we tied him to the mast, and everybody who passed him had a go with a rope's end He was a reminder that we had no food and no water, and though we could have done without that reminder, there was no reason why he should die any quicker than we did, and if we didn't die, there was plenty we could do to him on shore.

We had a night and a day and a night more running before that drying wind. Then about noon, everybody was very low. Nobody had had the heart to hit Caw since dawn. Ethelbert, the oldest, was played out. Then Egfrith, who was holding on to the forestay, said he thought he'd seen land.

'All right,' I told him. 'Climb up the mast and make sure.'

'I'm not going to climb up that. It's impossible. Whoever heard of anyone climbing up a ship's mast? I might fall. It's dangerous.'

This was no time to lose my authority.

'Get up that flaming mast!'

'I can't climb it.'

'CLIMB IT!!!'

He climbed it. He called down from that dizzy height, fully ten feet above us,

'It's the Holy Island. I know the shape.'

At those words the wind dropped. The motion of the ship ceased. We wallowed. Caw, hanging from his ropes, opened his eyes and said, very clearly,

'You'll never sail this ship to a German shore.'

'We will yet,' I told him. I never spoke again in that ship.

13

For the rest of that day, and for two days more, we drifted about off the Holy Island. Carried about by the tides and the currents, sometimes we drifted to within a hundred yards of the shore, sometimes it was out of sight from the deck. I would send no other man to climb that mast.

Once I thought I could see someone on the beach, and I touched Edward. He knew what I meant, but he didn't even

166

bother to look. Nobody lived there. But it must be habitable, there must be water, it was green.

We sat and looked at the green land and we heard water splashing. We sat on the deck and we began to die of thirst. It was the second time in my life that I began to die of thirst, and it made it no better that I was not alone.

There was no sun to dry us up. There was just a cloudy grey sky. I think the cloud saved us. We died slower. They say a man can last three days without a drink. We lasted four.

There was that last night. I had no dreams, no visions. I did not sleep. I just sat and looked up. There were no stars, just a black sky.

After a time it was morning. The ship was dead. It took me a long time to notice that she no longer moved, that she no longer swam, that she was dead. She just lay, heeling over a little. I decided, and I remember how slowly I worked it out, that we must be aground.

A little later it occurred to me that it might be interesting too see if we were aground on a sandbank or on an island. It might even be worth the effort of turning my head. It was a great effort, worth thinking over.

When I did, I saw that we were close under the cliffs. We had come ashore on Holy Island. We had come in at the peak of the tide, stern first. Now the tide was running out and we were left.

It was running out. Running. It was running. It was running out of the cliff. It was running out where the rocks changed colour. It was running. What was running?

It was water that was running. How interesting. Water. Water for some. With almost a physical convulsion I grasped at the thought. Water. Perhaps water for me. Water for some. Water for me?

Over the bulwarks. Hang down. Can't hang long. What am I hanging for? Drop. Something still works, I land on my feet. Can't stay on them. Lie down. Must lie down. Don't lie down. Move. Pull. Hands and knees. It hurts my knees. Hands. Knees. Hands.

Choking noise. Not me. Oswy lying under the ship. Edward looking over the side.

Hands … Knees … Hands … Knees … pebbles hurt hands … Knees … feet … My feet. No, my feet behind me. Can't pass … feet in way. My feet have shoes on. Feet. Somebody's feet. Bare feet in way. Somebody's feet. Somebody else's feet.

Feet … legs … Man … Old Man … loincloth … cloak … Beard … Njord … not, not Njord, Beard … Beard-Njord, Beard-Njord, funny, Beard-Njord … not Njord … not Joy … Someone …

'No,' he said. His voice was rusty, a voice not often used. 'No, not Njord, Votan Aser. Not Joy, Votan Aser. Joy left us long ago, Votan Aser, half-Aser, false Aser, beggar from the south, robber of dead men's goods, stealer of women, digger of kings' graves. Don't know me, do you? You're too young, too insignificant, too poor, to know me. You've never even heard of me. Njord wouldn't tell you, he'd be ashamed, and nobody else would dare.'

My tongue was a piece of dry wood. I could hardly hear him. All this he was saying, it sounded so unimportant, so trivial. I just wished he would finish and let me reach the water. I said,

'Water. Water.'

'Water, you ask me for water? Great Votan Aser, asking me for water. Gold he has and bronze, furs and silk and Amber, and he asks *me* for water. He asks Mymir for Water. He doesn't even know who Mymir is. Long long ago, we built Asgard, Bergelmir and Bors and I. We were rich and proud and happy, the Great Asers. And then Bors died, and Njord Borsson elbowed us out. Only Bors could control Njord, and then Bors died. Ask Njord how Bors died, kicking his head with his heels. Ask who brought him the mushrooms. When Bors was gone, we were wormed out of Asgard. Ten years have I been on this island. And who brought Loki into Outgard, that drove out Bergelmir? And where is Bergelmir now? Tell me that.

'Njord drove out all the great Asers, the men of fine and royal blood. And in their stead he brought in this … this ordure, Baldur, Heimdall, Tyr … The only good thing that Njord ever brought into Asgard was Skazi, my sister Skazi. And what of the boy she bore to Vikar, before ever she went to Njord? And where are the two daughters she bore to Vikar again, when she left Njord and returned to him? Where are they now?

'Now to this comes the latest of the Asers. A snivelling white-haired boy, crawling on the ground from his stolen ship, crying for water like a baby, licking his cuts, weeping. No water shall you have but your own tears. Die of thirst, thief!'

I could not move. I was on the edge of night. As long as he stood there, I could not pass. I could not move while he stood still. Then he made his mistake. He kicked me in the face. It was undignified. It was unnecessary. Besides, it was fatal.

I caught at his ankle and I clung to it. He pulled away, he staggered and fell on top of me. I let go his ankle and I went for his throat, he caught my wrist, I could not get a fair grip. I grasped his other wrist and kept his thumb out of my eye.

Like that we lay for a long moment. Had I been well there would have been a short ending. I was dried up, burnt out. I could scarcely hold him off. Those bony wrists were strong as mine. A bony knee ground into my groin. Those horrible blue eyes said only 'Die, die, die!' I could feel myself going, slipping away. Even his little strength would outlast mine. I must finish it quickly. I must pay.

I let go his wrist. My knife came of itself to my hand, the knife Joy had spun on the tavern table. The iron knew what to do. It was thirsty. His thumb came to my eye. I struck and struck and we both writhed in pain. Blood ran, eye ran, all was black and red and fiery, all was pain, pain, eye and head and face, all pain, blood, pain, hate, pain, death, pain ...

14

It was dark for a long time. It was dark and painful and noisy and smelly and hard. There were rough hands trying to be gentle. There was food given in kindness and drink poured in solicitude that only nauseated. There was love that could not understand, and that hurt what it cherished. There were dreams and there were horrors that were not dreams.

After a million ages the world was still, the heaving stopped. There were hands that were gentle and smooth. There were cool things and soft things about me, and I knew it was bandages over my eyes, though I didn't know why. The voices were women's voices. There was warm milk and honey that the voices brought. At last I was able to understand what they were saying, to hear Edith …

'All right, my darling, you're all right now, just lie here, just be still.'

'I can't see you … hurts … hurts …'

'You're all right now … quick, that cup … You'll soon see me. Drink this. I'm holding you. Just press against me. Drink it all up, there's a good lad.'

Dark again. They drugged me before they cut away the clotted bandages from my face. When next I woke I could see something. One eye was still bandaged. With the other I could see Edith, Edwin, Cutha Cuthson … how many more … Ethelred, Oswy Karlsson and his father Karl Cuthbertson … all of them. Edward was on his knees by the bed holding my hands.

'I am your man for ever. All Saxons are your men for ever. For us you gave what you could, what no man can give and receive again. For us you gave all a God can give, no God can give his life. No God can die. For the water of life you gave the light of your life. For our lives you gave your light.' I hadn't known he was a bard. 'Hail to Votan the Saviour, the King of Mankind, who brought us the water of life from the edge of the sea, who bought at a price beyond measure the water of youth.'

'Mymir?' I asked. 'Mymir?'

'His body we burned, the ashes we cast on the sea. Your kinsman the Aser we bore with respect to his pyre on the beach.'

'The ship?'

'The ship we sold to the Friesians, let them try to sail her, she nearly had us all drowned. The lead we leave to the Asers. One-handed Tyr came to seek you and bring you home. Yet while he waited to gather a crew, and Starkadder Eightarms and Sweyn brought ships from the north to row to the west and raid till they found you again, he saw us sail in to shore in that heavy old tub.'

'Caw?'

'We sold him to Starkadder Eightarms, to be chained to an oar, and row for the rest of time he knows not where.'

170

That was just what did not happen. Starkadder had too much use for a man who could tell by the smell of the air or the taste of the mud on the tallowed lead where he was anywhere up the coast of Britain or down to the edge of Spain to keep him in chains. Of course at last there was a foggy night, and Caw went over the side in a skin boat, and heaven only knows how much silver and Amber with him out of Starkadder's chest, and he was never seen again. But when the fog lifted, there was Starkadder at the mouth of the Thames, and a dozen Imperial Galleys lying within a cable's length, and if he had not been readier to run than they to chase him, there would have been an end to Starkadder the Pirate. But his end was not fated for years to come.

Edith got the men out of the room at last, and even, after a few days, persuaded them it was needless for them to march around the house daily at noon nine times with the sun, shouting 'Long Life to Votan Aser' in chorus.

I made her get a mirror, she knew what one was all right, not like the Scrawlings, so that I could see my face. The local doctor, Aldhelm, had made a good job of the eye. I've seen too many of these cases not to be impressed by what he was able to do. Usually the wound goes rotten, and it spreads back into the head and you die. He'd stopped that, somehow.

No, on second thoughts, not somehow, I know exactly how. He took the most magical liquid he could think of, and that was Honeydew which Tyr had brought. He washed his knives and needles in it, and he washed the wound. I've tried it myself since, and it works. Not always, of course, but often enough the patient doesn't die. Not straight away, at least. As long as a patient lives to pay the bill, the doctor counts it a cure.

Later when I got back to the Old City, my father cleaned it up and padded it out, and I had a smooth gem of glass set in it, so that to the casual glance it never looked worse than half closed. But the eye was gone, and in the north I always wore a patch over it to keep out the wind.

Life is different with one eye. You stop taking risks, you don't do anything that might endanger the other. You always have a blind side. And you can't judge distances any more. Long distances are all right, you can tell if a ship is one mile out or two,

171

but under a bowshot it becomes very deceptive. Spear throwing is something you can't do any more either, and as for putting a horse at a fence, I never risked it again except on Sleipnir.

The penalty of virtue and a clear conscience is a short convalescence. Too soon I rode with Edith to the Grove, her last ride till after the baby came. I left the gelding, and I leaned Gungnir against the fence. Together we went to the cart. Before the Mother I spread the gifts I had brought her, polished pebbles from the brooches and armlets I had brought back from the Picts. I cast the mounts in the bog. Silver for the Gods above and Those Below. Stone for the Mother.

When that debt to the Mother was paid, I whistled Sleipnir, and he left the mares and came. I rode east to meet with my own Vandals who had come to see me home. The Saxons came with me to their borders, Edwin and Cutha and all my crew, and I embraced them all and so many Saxons more I cannot count.

After the Saxons there was a crowd of Danes to meet me, and with them Donar, who had gone to look for me in the Land of Norroway. To seek me, he said, but I believe he had still been in search of the land of fire, where a smith may live and beat out the iron, and never pay a penny for charcoal nor for carriage. Still, he seemed quite glad to see me back, and so did Tyr and Baldur who had come out with the Vandals.

They were all intrigued by the absurd song the Danes sang, about how Votan bought the water of youth of Mymir at the price of his eye, after he had driven about the seas in his magic ship, turning the wind to speed him which-ever-which way he wanted to go. I said nothing, I just pulled my grey hood down over my blind eye.

At the head of the causeway to Asgard, I dismounted. The Danes had gone back long ago, but there were still enough Vandals and Lombards to give the whole thing the look of a triumph, as if I had come back with all the pearls of Britain and all the gold of Ireland in my sacks, not drifted home hurt and broken and empty handed.

There at the end of the causeway Freda waited, all glorious in gold, and she threw her splendid arms around my neck. She took my arm to lead me into Asgard, and I felt that all the world was mine again, and that all would come right, and that no one had as much to boast of as I had.

And then, like any other woman, when her husband comes home tired out and all he wants is a little rest and quiet, she yammered and muttered and nattered and nittered and yappity-yapp-yapped as hard and as fast as she could. The harvest was good and Njord was keeping well except for his rheumatics and the maids were unreliable and she was short of hams and she didn't know how she'd have things ready for the Amber Feasts and Scyld was teething or whatever babies do ...

'The new baby,' I asked, 'did you have it all right?'

'Oh yes, it was the most beautiful baby girl, we called her Brunhilda, the loveliest blue eyes, I was keeping it a surprise, I was going to bring her to you in the hall ...'

'What? Didn't you expose it?'

I mean, what else do you do with girl babies, they're only an expense. But to my surprise, Freda burst into tears there in the courtyard, and called me brutal and heartless and a beast thinking of my own pleasures and several other choice things. As if she thought that losing an eye and risking death by drowning and thirst and by being eaten alive was pleasure. You never can tell with women, and she didn't quieten down till I gave her everything I'd taken from Morien, and half a dozen other brooches beside.

The Waste

1

It was a good thing I had come back to Asgard. The accounts were in a terrible state, and as for the warehouses. ... Everything was piled in hugger-mugger, fur and fish on top of Amber and bronzes, and no records kept. Skirmir's wife had a silk dress. One day I'd settle with him.

This year we'd got a lot of the fishing boats to come straight in to us, and with salt that came up from the Saxons we did the pickling and packing ourselves. This meant crowds of Vandal and Lombard women gutting and cleaning herrings. This needed supervision, and who was there?

Bragi said he was a carpenter and not a cooper, and so he refused to have anything to do with making casks. Besides, he also supervised the work in the black sheds where a hundred Scrawling slaves watched the Honeydew pots, gagged all the day that they might not steal a drop.

Donar and Tyr had spent the summer off looking for me, or so they said. A likely story. To judge by the tales they had to tell that winter, they had been enjoying themselves. Frederik was about as much use around the place as a wet scrubber.

Freda did what she could, but although she had a fine way of talking, the men only did what she told them in the hope it would keep her quiet. As soon as she wasn't there, they forgot all about her. Anyway, she had enough work, with her girls, making all the sausages and beer for the Amber Feasts. Njord and Heimdall were a fine pair of old dotards, not influencing the world any longer except by ornamenting it.

I soon had them all to work, and I was even able to introduce two new lines. All the fashionable kings in Germany we sold hunting dogs, that I got from Britain through a Friesian agent, and they were all eating that tart, thin British cheese.

Siggeir was the first king to come, and Jokuhai-inen with him. I tried to ignore the Scrawling King, but he came after me in the courtyard, and caught my arm and said in the awkward German he had learnt from Donar:

'Good winds, Votan, good winds, eh?' He pulled me round to face him, and for the first time he saw my ruined eye. He whistled.

'In the eye of the Sun, in the face of the day, was it? An eye pays for all, Votan, the light of man pays for all. When next you need a wind, whistle, and you shall have any wind you want, all the wind you want.'

2

There came with Jokuhai-inen in his ship a pair of little brown men, tinkers they said, tinsmiths or bronzesmiths, or even silversmiths if you would trust them with any silver, patchers of pots or botchers of bronze buckets, welders of broken slave-chains or sharpeners of goads. They stayed behind when the Scrawlings left. They built for themselves a little hut on the edge of the village, and they made themselves a nearly honest living by doing bits of metal work for Vandals or the men from the ships, any little job too small or too menial for Bragi or Donar.

They'd told poor Jokuhai-inen they were Romans, and he may have believed them, but they didn't try it on me. They would never own to being citizens of any one place, but my opinion was that they came from India, and this tale of their being Roman came from their being left over from Alexander's army.

Well they settled there, and they did their bits of tinkering, and the money piled up, silver at first, and then we found they were changing it for gold. I had a few words with Tyr, and we agreed that none of the bullion should go out of Asgard, and certainly none to Loki. We never could tell them apart either. One day I was wandering round the village, as usual, making sure there was no illicit selling of Honeydew, and that meant I had to

175

look twice as hard with my one eye, so it was no wonder I saw what I saw.

One of them had flung open the neck of his shirt as he worked over his fire, and round his neck was a necklace. It was made of that hard green stone I told you about, that I had in a ring, where a man could spend his life carving a thing as big as a cherry stone. But this wasn't one stone in a ring, this was a chain of thirty-six links. Each link was in the shape of a fish with its tail in its mouth, passing through the next rings on either side, so that the whole chain must have been carved out of one block of stone. And each fish was green, but its fins were white. One carver? This would have taken a score of men all their lives to make.

I stopped and I looked at the chain, and I knew that it was the one thing in all the world to give to Freda at the Yule Feast. She would give me no thanks for anything I had taken by force. I would have to buy it.

I knew better than to go for it myself. I found a Saxon trader, not a man of straw but a man who might well have wanted to buy it for himself. I sent him with a gold armlet, good stuff, dug out of a barrow, and a gold chain of twenty links, to use link by link if he had to. But he brought it back to me, and said they wouldn't sell.

'It's not even as if they want more than this,' he said. 'When I asked about it, they looked at me as if I were making an indecent suggestion, and me a respectable man as well you know, Allfather. They said it wasn't for sale.'

'We'll see about this,' I said, and a few days later, not to seem in too much of a hurry, I went down myself. Now you can't bargain with these Asiatics, you have to beat them down to size straight away, and I came straight to the point with these half-naked beggars.

'All right,' I told the one with the chain, and I couldn't tell whether it was the man I first saw with it. 'How much?'

'How much for what, Master?' he asked. 'Here I am mending a kettle for Tostig Gustasson, and for it he will give me a small horn of barley meal, though I will ask him for a large horn and let him beat me down and feel he is clever. And perhaps if he is drunk he will give me a large horn, or perhaps even two small horns, which is more, thought he will think it is less. But, Master, if you have a kettle to mend I will do it special for you, for a small horn half full of barley, and I will do a better job than I do for Tostig, special for you, Master, special for you.'

'I'm not employing, I'm buying.'

'Buying what, Master? We have nothing to sell but our sack of barley meal and a few clothes and our tools that are our life: And you are our father and our mother, you would not take those away?'

And how much silver besides all that, I thought.

'I want to buy that necklace.'

'Oh, no, no, no, Master, you would not want to buy this piece of rough native work. It is all we have to remind us of our homeland so far away. Look, Master, you buy this, a fine clasp, bronze and garnets, special price for you, only six links of that chain, for anyone else nine links, but special price for you, Master.'

And somehow, without my knowing how, I bought the clasp and went away without the necklace. I tried several times, and they still would not sell. When I got testy, they said,

'Oh, great Master, great rich proud Master, you are our father and our mother, we live under your shadow, do not be angry with poor men. We only wish to keep our little necklace, little piece of worthless stone. You would not wish to take it by force, Great Aser, all the north knows our little piece of stone, all would know if you took it from us, and who would trust Asgard then?'

That was true enough, and so disarming that somehow I sold them the cloak fastener back for one link of the gold chain. But there were other ways of changing their minds, and I passed the word, and no Vandal or anyone else brought them work. But they had enough furs to keep them warm that winter, and they could live if need be on a handful of barley meal a day, but even that they need not do. They knew the custom of the north, that they had only to walk into Valhall at dinner time and be fed. And so they did.

Of course Freda heard about it, and I told her that if she could buy it I would let her have the price. But with all her wheedling she could not make them put a price on it, though she even offered them the little yellow woman that Jokuhai-inen gave her.

177

And a good job they would not take her, for where could I have got another like her, unless I could have bought her back from the little brown men, and what a price they would have asked.

3

From the Amber Feast to Yule I had everybody at work taking stock, and trying to get some assessment of the year's profits. We had decided, that is, I had decided, to stop this business of the Asers living like one big family, and each one taking what he liked out of the stock whenever he needed it. We'd split the profit in equal shares this year, but next year we'd work out what each one had contributed toward the turnover and share out in proportion.

At that rate, some people would suffer. Heimdall, for instance, who just sat at the gate with Njord and checked stores in and out, he'd have to go on a fixed wage, and not a very high one, either. Baldur was a bit doubtful, too. He spent most of the summer playing about with Blind Hod, instead of getting out around the farms. Hod, too – there was another one who wasn't worth the food he ate. Maybe I could take the cost of his keep out of Baldur's share before we paid him.

One thing puzzled me that autumn. An awful lot of Vandals came in on the packtrains from the East. They were looking for work for the next summer, and for advances of pay to let them keep their families through the winter. Some of them looked familiar, so I asked, and sure enough, they had all been working for Loki. Now they hadn't a good word to say for him.

'He's getting rid of all us Vandals,' they told me. 'He's hiring Burgundians.'

Did this mean he was hiring Sigmund, I wondered. The Vandals told me.

'Sigmund's left Bornholm. His brother Synfiotli is holding it for him. He's afraid of Siggeir and the Goths in Scania, the cowardly squit. He's gone to hide with Loki in Outgard.'

178

4

It came to the Yule Feast, which is a few days after the winter equinox, when you can just notice that the days are getting longer again. The Feast began just as it had the year before, when Baldur put the great log on its bed of sand on the fire.

Freda lit the first candle, and we all went round and helped to light the rest. Soon all Valhall was ablaze with light, that shone off the gold-plated pillars and the bronze shields and the gleaming spears on the walls, and off the gold boar before Frederik and on the gilded helmet above my chair, and all served to light up the dull whetstone and the two black ravens.

Then when we were all sitting down, Loki walked in. He just came in, without any fuss, or any warning. He just came in and walked up the hall, leaving his Mistletoe Twig leaning against the door frame. The Vandals looked first horrified, then apprehensive, and then angry. The rest of us were just gloomy, except the little brown men.

Loki came up the Hall as cool as you please, and as he was still on the way to the top table Freda signed to some of the servants who came forward with a spare throne Bragi had made in the hope of selling it to any visiting king, but it proved too heavy to pack on a horse, which was a pity because we could have done well selling thrones. The men planted the seat down where Freda told them, on the far side of the top table, central, his face to Njord and his back to the fire. Loki sat in it. We all began to chat as if it were the most normal thing to have Loki in Valhall, as indeed it once had been.

I began to wonder if Loki could help me get the necklace. The two little brown men didn't know him, and he might do it, though I couldn't see how. They wouldn't gamble, and I doubted if even Loki could tempt them to get drunk on the Honeydew. I put it to him, in conversation, and he agreed to try.

When the meal was over, and the drinking had started in earnest and people were moving about, I saw him go over and speak to them, though what he said I couldn't hear; I was in the middle of a conversation with Donar and Tyr, and watching Baldur cuddling up to Blind Hod in the usual disgusting way. I

179

didn't know which was coming harder to Loki, to forget what Baldur said to him at the Feast of the Dead, or to forget that he and Baldur had lived together so long.

Now after dinner, as I said, we were all moving about, and we had the usual horseplay. There wasn't any real fighting, of course, not in Valhall, but we had a lot of pickaback riding, and the leg game where two of you lie down head to foot, and hook your legs and try to pull each other over. Then Baldur, who had been drinking, but not nearly as much as Hod, got a big shield from the wall, and he and some Vandals began to play the Spear Game. They had another shield, still hanging up, as a target, and Baldur stood with his back to it, a little to one side. The Vandals took it in turn to throw spears at the target, and Baldur would try to turn their spears aside with his shield. The spears, of course, were blunted, but it was quite a game of skill to stop them.

Now I was talking to Tyr, and I had my blind eye to the shield game, so I didn't see what was happening till too late. Loki, it seems, went to Hod and asked him why he wasn't playing. Hod, very flattered, said, of course, that he couldn't see the shield at that distance.

'Never mind that,' Loki told him. 'Just hold this spear the way I show you, keep it steady. Then when I call your name, throw. Baldur will look my way, and you'll hit the target before he knows anything about it.'

Hod thought it a huge joke. He held the spear carefully, and Loki edged round. Then Loki called out: 'Hod!' very loudly, and everyone turned to look at him, and Baldur dropped his shield to look at Loki, and Hod threw the spear, Loki's Mistletoe Twig.

Baldur took it in the side of the chest, on the left.

For a few moments everything was very quiet. Baldur was on his knees on the floor, the spear hanging out of him. There wasn't very much blood. Hod was peering at where Baldur had been, trying to make out what had happened. And then Loki began to laugh, to laugh.

I went over to Baldur, and I looked at Tyr, and we had both seen too many men like this. I held Baldur's shoulders. Tyr took the spear shaft and pulled. There was a lot of blood ... Baldur coughed and retched, and vomited more blood, and said,

'Loki ... Hod ... Hod ... Loki ...'

That was the end of Baldur.

Bragi cut up the shaft of the Mistletoe Twig and threw it on the Yule fire. Donar took the head and beat it out into a ball of rough iron, and later we threw it into a bog.

When we were quite sure that Baldur was dead, Heimdall went to the door of Valhall. Loki had gone long since. Heimdall put his hands about his mouth and shouted:

'Baldur is dead! Baldur is dead!'

Then all the slaves and the grooms and the sweepers of Asgard, who must miss the feast that they might rise early in the morning, knew. Heimdall walked to the gate of Asgard, to the head of the causeway, and looked out across the salt marsh to all the villages of Germany. He shouted:

'Baldur is dead! Baldur is dead! Killed by the Mistletoe Twig, Baldur is dead!'

For so it was the custom to announce the death of an Aser. As we stood around Heimdall at the gate, we saw lights on the ridge as the people came out of the village with torches lit from their Yule fires. And they called to each other across the snow, across the fields and the echoing snow:

'Baldur is dead, Baldur is dead, Baldur the Beautiful is dead, is dead, dead ...'

And as the news carried across the snow, the lights sprang up as far as we could see, to the edge of the Forest and beyond, and far beyond our sight, so that before morning Sweyn had heard it, and Edwin, and the Cheruscan King in the far south. Who told Sigmund I never knew.

All the women in Asgard stood by the body, and wept, and gashed their faces, and poured ashes on their heads, and swayed in groups with interlocked arms, and wailed:

'Baldur is dead, Baldur the Beautiful is dead.'

Njord and Frederik threw their arms round each other's necks, and wept. Heimdall, now his shouting was over, rolled on the floor and screamed and kicked like a baby. All was pandemonium and full of the sound of senseless sorrow. It was worse than a Mystery, without the hope and reason of a Mystery. I began to worry.

Soon the peasants would all be weeping for dead Baldur. I knew the influence he had over them, and how he had gone out on his spring rides, telling them what to plant and where and when, and when to reap and how to store, planning the harvests to bring most profit to the Asers. If the peasants grow so much wheat, say, for Asgard, that they have no room to plant flax, then they have to buy their linen from us, at Aser prices. And there are those who plant no wheat at all, and must buy it. If this system failed, if we could no longer guarantee food for all the packmen, clothes and iron and silver for all the villages, then our trade was over.

I caught hold of two of the biggest and soberest Vandals.

'Get my chair up on that table, there, over the body.' This much I had learned from Taliesin. I sat there above the noise, my gold helmet on my head, my sword across my knees, my ravens above my shoulders, my wolves beneath my hands.

'Listen to me, all ye Asers. Listen to me all ye traders and dealers, all men of war and people that till the soil, riders on roads and trappers of badgers and bees.'

They did listen. The voice that held a crew could fill a hall.

'Baldur the Beautiful is dead ... dead ... dead ... Baldur who brought you sun and rain in their season, giver of all good things, who sent you corn and bread and beef and beer and all that you wished. Baldur who showed to your men and your maids the way of the world, who made your bulls and your rams and your goats to bring you flocks beyond counting. Dead in the spring of his youth, in the bud of his life, Baldur the Beautiful is dead.

'Baldur is dead. There he lies at our feet. Baldur is dead. There he lies where he fell. There is no profit to dwell on the past, let the blame lie where it will, let Fate do its work. Evil will out and the murderer die at his time.

'Baldur the Beautiful is dead, is dead ... dead ... Yet Baldur shall live, shall rise, shall stand before us again. Again shall he bring us the bread and the ale at our call. Baldur returns to the earth whence he came, whence came we all. When winter is over, we shall see him before us anew. He will stand in the Spring, in the furrows, green and straight. In the pride of the grain, in

182

the glory of corn, in the green shoot and the golden ear, shall Baldur stand again before us all. Each year, each winter let us mourn for Baldur dead. Yet in the Spring shall we rejoice for Baldur risen again. Baldur will come in the hawthorn shoot, in the blossom that brings the fruit and the honeybees.'

Never before or since had I sung the Mystery of the Lord Adonis with more fervour or to a more willing audience.

'Go shout on the shore and say to the forest, call it from village to village and hill to hill, the glorious news that we shall never more despair. Baldur who died at our feet shall die no more. Baldur who died at the Yule shall live at the Spring. No more need we fear death for him who died. For ever shall we see him walk amid our fruitful woods and fertile fields. Baldur the Beautiful is dead, yet shall he live.'

All the crowd dissolved into paroxysms of joy mixed with their grief. Yet there were some who kept their composure. Bragi got together a handful of his apprentices.

'Snorri, get in there now and measure him. Length and breadth, and don't forget depth. I'll go over to the stores and get enough cowhides and linen for lining, and coffin handles, if we have any. The rest of you, fetch your adzes and get up to the timber yard. I don't care how cold it is. Get some pine billets for light, but be careful you don't set fire to the place. There are half a dozen elm logs in the north-east corner; elm's best, remember that, it takes the best polish. Pick out the two biggest, and start shaping, but don't overdo it till Snorri comes up with the measurements. Go on, get started!'

Freda was getting, beating, her kitchen maids together. She was more shaken than Bragi, but still capable.

'Get me a count of hams ... yes, *hams*, you can't have a funeral without ham, you always bury them with ham, why don't we ever have enough ham? Then we need to bake bread for ... let's see, yes ... Asers and kings, wheat bread for about a hundred and fifty ... peasants and suchlike, rye bread for about ... six thousand ... yes, and make that one-third ground acorn. Get every woman you can find on to grinding. No, I *don't* care if they have to grind all night. And ham, get me a count of hams ...'

I went to bed. They seemed to be doing well enough, to me,

working on the details. They knew how a German funeral went, and I didn't. So I slept. The next morning, of course, I was the only Aser fresh enough to receive the first Kings. Freda was furious, called me a lazy heartless brute, a shirker, callous. There were moments when I almost wished myself back with Bithig.

5

In the morning, of course, things were getting on famously, even though most of the Asers were dropping with fatigue. I sat at the gate with Heimdall, waiting for visitors and watching a party of Vandals hauling up on to the ridge a boat, called Ringhorn, in which Baldur had gone fishing several times that summer.

'Is that where they will have the pyre?'

'Pyre?' Heimdall answered. 'Why should there be a Pyre? We bury Baldur as an Aser.'

'I thought the dead were burnt in Germany.'

'Peasants are burnt. Kings and nobles and traders are burnt. Some are not burnt.'

'Who are they who are not burnt?'

'Who should know better than you? and yet how should you know? All who are sacrificed to the Gods, those who are hanged up between heaven and earth, those whose throats are cut to let their breath pass out to the air it came from, they are not burnt. Some are thrown into the mouths of the earth, into the bogs that suck and suck and are never satisfied. Some are left on the earth to rot away, open to the sky and the stars, and the beasts and the birds do not feed on them.'

'And the others?'

'Long, long ago, when the Mother ruled the land, before men had iron swords, the Great Kings of the North were buried in barrows. Wealth was wrought for the tomb, in gold and silver and in Amber. Then the King was a God, and the Amber shone as a sign of his Godhead.

'Yet every Aser shadows Godhead forth, and his whole life is a sacrifice to the God. Every Aser is himself a God, whether he knows or not of the Godhead in him. Truly you told us of

Baldur risen again, how he lives on. All the Asers shall live although we die.

'So an Aser is buried as a sacrifice. With treasure we fill the tombs, with gold the graves, in glory we go back to the dust we are made of.

'Each Aser must choose his grave. Baldur chose his. Do you see the smoke rise there beyond the hill? There they have swept away the snow, and they light great fires to thaw the ground, where they will dig the grave. Bragi is fitting runners to the boat. We will take Baldur to his grave across the snow.'

6

So the Kings came to Asgard across the snow and across the frozen sea. The Lombard Kings came, for the sake of the ham. Sweyn Halffoot leaned on Edwin's arm. Siggeir walked with Sigmund. Asers and Kings walked over the snow to Baldur's grave. Njord came out of Asgard, and passed the Standing Stone and never did it more.

Loki did not come.

Over the snow we went to Baldur's grave, across the forest to a meadow by a river. Feet had trampled the snow, and hands had swept it. The ground was black with charcoal, and the earth from the grave was spread about and trampled down into a hard floor. The smell of burnt wood hung in the air, though the fire had no part in what we did. Yet the memory of those great fires we lit to that the earth entered deeper into men's memories than the grave we dug.

Kings came and merchants came, Lords and Princes and Asers came. And the peasants came, men without surnames and without fathers, men who till the soil and are of no account. As a Danish King drives out a Saxon, and the Goth king drives out the Black Dane, so the peasant calls himself Saxon or Dane or Goth in turn, and copies their fashions of pots or clothes or speech. Yet the peasant lives always in one place, and the wars go over his head and over his land, and he has not the wit to change.

And the peasant thinks only of his crops and never of glory or

185

love or wisdom or change, he worships only the Mother. And that is why, of all the Asers, only Baldur who, two-sexed and gentle, was Mother and Father and God to them, was ever mourned by the peasants. They came to his grave and stood in rows about it.

When the boat Ringhorn was drawn by oxen to the side of the open grave, two coffins, Baldur's and an empty coffin, were placed at the edge of the pit. Then Skirmir's wife stood on a wagon and shouted:

'Baldur the Beautiful is dead, is dead. Alone he rides before us to Hell's Gate. Who rides with Baldur?'

Her voice streamed to nothing over the silent crowd and the frozen plain. A woman pushed her way to the front and said:

'I go.'

She was a fine woman, about twenty, and her name was Nanna. She lived in a village a little way from the grave field, and indeed it was because of this that Baldur had chosen it. It was to her house, where she lived alone, that Baldur came at the mid point of his every ride. For three years the country people had spoken of her as Baldur's wife, and for his sake, unasked they had brought her food and cloth and fuel enough and to give away to every beggar that passed. Now on that bitter day, Nanna stood out before the Kings and Asers and all the people and said:

'I go with Baldur to pour his beer and warm his bed as I have done these years past. Who else but I should go? Who has more right than I? Those who led him into evil ways?' She shot a bitter glance at Hod, who, blind, did not see it, and still stood looking dimly before him.

'I go with him where no one else dare follow.'

And she laid herself down in the empty coffin, and while she did so, and Skirmir's wife helped her, a Vandal packmaster named Hermod, whom we never thought of except as a hanger-on of Tyr's, stepped to the graveside and began a song he had made on Baldur.

Baldur the Beautiful is dead, is dead.
Baldur is stricken.
He lies on the floor of Valhall in his golden blood.
Down in the straw, where the rats rummage for the crumbs of
 the feast.

Baldur rises, he goes out of Valhall,
He mounts the horse that waits, the white mare of the dead.
He rides from Asgard, the hooves ring on the wood.
On the planks of the causeway, as he goes above the marsh.
The mist is about him, the smoke of the burnt reeds.
The eel and the frog, the worm and the toad await him.
He comes to the Standing Stone of the Men of Old.
He comes to the Gate of Hell, to the Door of the Dead.
He comes to the Threshold of those below.
He strikes the stone, he summons those below.
'Must I die?' asks Baldur. 'Must I die?'
'Must my mouldering bones be clad in rotten rags?
'Must my eyes fester from my head?
'Must my lips and my ears and my tongue rot from my face?
'Must I, blind, deaf and witless, gibber among the dead?
'Must I be a scarecrow to set the frightened girls giggling?
'Or startle the shepherd boys at the before-winter feast?
'Let me live again, let me walk on the dry earth.
'Let me feel the warm flesh on my bones, the warm sun in my
      blood.
'Let me sense and reason and think and love as a living man.'
Those Below answered, 'Aye, Baldur may live,
'Let him live if every live creature wants him to live,
'If nothing living on earth would wish him dead.'
The grain of wheat said, 'Let Baldur live,
'Though I am cut down and ground to powder,
'And thrust in the oven to roast, yet let him live.
'For if Baldur had not ploughed the land and limed it
'And fenced it to keep the cattle out,
'Would I ever have lived to cover the earth?'
The Ox said, 'Let Baldur live.
'He gelded me, and set me to draw plough and cart,
'Day through, year through.
'Yet all the winter I was fed,
'He gave me shelter from the winds.
'When I was young, no wolves took me.
'If when I die, he takes my horns for drinking,
'My flesh for food, my skin to wrap his feet

187

'Or wrap his corpse,
'What, then, is that to me? Baldur gave me Life.
'Let Baldur live.'
The very lice that crawled among his hair
Said 'Let Baldur live. He gave us his blood,
'He gave us food, to us he is our living,
'What use is he dead? Let Baldur live'
Then the old crone that lives under the mountain,
The bearded hag, that feasts on snails and slime,
Said, 'Let him die.
'I have no pleasure in life, nothing gives me joy
'Since Joy left us. Why should *he* have joy,
'Why should *he* walk as a man in the summer fields,
'When we must all go down to the place of the dark,
'And no man ever know what we were, that we were?
'He did the proper work of a man, he ploughed the earth.
'All things living had cause to bless him.
'He was all that I am not.
'Let him die!'
That was the bearded hag, that was Loki,
Two-faced, two-sexed, the back-and-front man,
He sent Baldur to die.
Those Below said, 'Come, Baldur, Come!
'Long have we waited for you here at our feast.
'We sit to feast on you … on you … on you …
'Out of your body we have drained the breath, the blood.
'Out of your mind we will suck the life.
'That is our food. On lives of men we feast,
'We feed, and are no better off than before,
'For we are still Below.
'Come down to us, Baldur,
'Come down,
'Baldur,
'Come!
'Remember, even Loki will come at the last.'
Baldur is dead.
Below the earth you go.
What though we give you gold and Amber,

Food and the kindly precious earth of our fields,
All memory of them will rot away.
As brain and heart rot, so will fade all thought,
All memory of what you are, what you have been,
Of what you have done.
Memory at last will fade that you were Baldur.
Only at last in the empty bones will linger,
Thought, suspicion that you were once a man.
What man is not recorded.
Only a man ...
And that at last will dwindle.
Baldur is dead.
We will not see him again
Urge on the plough team, walk the Corn Mother in,
Or hear him sing at the Feasts.
He *may* be with us in the bursting buds,
Or in the winds that blow across the cornfield,
Or even in the bubbling Barley mash,
But we will never see his face again.
Baldur is gone from us
Gone ...
Gone ...
Loki will follow!!

When this was over, Skirmir's wife, who was the only woman in all that crowd of men, stood over the coffins. She struck Nanna through the heart with a sharpened alder stake, and when the struggles were over, without another word she made straight the limbs. Tyr and Heimdall folded the cowhides over the two dead faces, Baldur cold and dead, Nanna not yet cold.

Peasants took the ropes and lowered the coffins into the grave. Then each of the great ones, Asers and Kings, came near and threw into the grave their gifts. Freda's gift was already on Baldur's finger. It was a great gold ring, too big for her, that some man had stolen from a barrow. It was well known in the north, its name was Draupnir, and I had won it from Siggeir at dice. Njord threw in a gold chain, Tyr a drinking horn, and Heimdall another, though these were not a pair. The Kings too brought

189

gifts; Hoenir I saw place very gently on the coffin a glass cup, the only piece of glass he then had ever owned. Cups, plates and rings they threw on the coffin, Kings and nobles. Then the richer farmers came with jugs of ale and loaves of bread, roast shoulders of mutton and legs of pork and ribs of beef.

After the rich, the poor threw in what they had. Each man had brought a handful of earth from his corn field, or a turf from his pasture, and there were enough to fill the grave and more than fill it; and the rest was spread over the field where we stood. They raised no grave mound, and the snow kept on falling and covering everything. In the spring they ploughed the field and planted it with corn, that no one might find the grave again and rob it. But ever after the barley grew taller above Baldur.

Baldur's chestnut horse we killed above the grave, and a black mare for Nanna, and the heads we left, but the bodies we roasted at the fire we made when we burnt the ship Ringhorn. We stood beside the fire, Kings and Asers and peasants, and we took our bread and beer and ham, and we ate our funeral feast. But do not think we had forgotten the main purpose of the Asers, and the cause for which Baldur had died, and Bors and Mymir before him. On each of the paths that led from the grave, about a mile from it, our Vandals had built booths of branches, and lit great fires.

By the time a man had walked or ridden a mile from the grave, then the heat of the fire and of the ale had worn off, and he was pleased at the chance to buy beer, or hot sausages, or even a heavier cloak or a blanket. Many of them were happy enough to spend a night in a hut by the fire safe from bears or wolves, and they paid for it; of course, the noise of our crowd had frightened all the beasts far away. Nor were there any bandits about, and men who would not have gone near a Vandal village slept happy enough guarded by Vandal swords.

It wasn't only food and clothes we sold them, but brooches in lead, Mendip lead, in a shape we said was sacred to Baldur, and plaits of straw that had touched his coffin. What man would go home to his wife without something of the kind? And by what we sold, you would have thought that corpse had lain an hour at a time in every hayrick in Germany. That spring Baldur dead brought us in more silver than ever did Baldur living.

It was a day and a night and half a day again from Baldur's grave to Asgard. The night we spent in a palisade where the pack-trains stopped, and the fleas thought summer had come again and swarmed out to feast on us. The night on the return was decidedly more cheerful than the night we had had there on the way out. Conversation had been difficult with that ox-wagon and its burden in the courtyard, with the frozen Vandals standing guard round it, changed every half hour. Still, one of them died of the cold, and so did fifty peasants coming to or from the grave, besides the four who succumbed to an excess of religious feeling during the burial. And it was at that cold graveside that Njord caught his death, months though it was in coming.

After dinner that night, Siggeir drew me aside and got very confidential.

'I've had enough of Sigmund. I can trust you, Allfather, I always could, you know how things work, no sham. Next spring I'm taking Bornholm, and I'll clear the shallow sea. After that, when I can, I'm coming ashore on this side. I'll not harm the trade, but I tell you this, I'll not deal with Outgard. Do you know what Loki did? Before he killed Baldur, not after?'

'Tell me.'

'He sent one of Sigmund's brothers to Jokuhai-inen to suggest that he lend the ships, and the Scrawlings the men, to raid Asgard.'

'And Jokuhai-inen answered ...?'

'He didn't. He asked my advice. He said he wouldn't mind killing Njord, or you, especially you, but he has some kind of blood bond with Donar. In the end I persuaded him it would be more profitable if he went for Sigmund when I attack Bornholm.'

Sweyn followed Siggeir.

'There's something you ought to know, Allfather. Starkadder Eightarms saw me before I came.'

'Indeed. Why didn't he come to the funeral?'

'And face Donar? Be serious. One of Sigmund's brothers came to him, and offered him land.'

'What land?'

'This land. Asgard, to be precise. He said if Asgard fell to Starkadder's pirates, he could keep it and no interference from Loki. Starkadder said he thought the land was a bit dear, but of course, Loki still thinks he may do it.'

'Won't he?'

'No, he was quite keen on tackling Donar, but he didn't want to hurt you. But look, if you want help in the summer, I'll be in the islands, and I'll always have ten ships ready to come down to you at a day's notice, and thirty more in three days.'

He moved away. Edwin came over. He was in a good humour generally these days, Edith was pregnant, he saw himself safe. But tonight he was particularly buoyant. He jerked his head at Sigmund.

'Look at that idiot Burgundian. There he is, so brave, so bold, so beautiful, a gift to the world. He hasn't heard yet, I killed his brother last week.'

'*You* did?'

'Oh, no, Allfather, not personally. We used him for the head game. A bit heavy, not like these Danish heads, they're empty. This one was Solar. He *was* a fool. He let Edward get to windward of him with three boats full of men, and then he couldn't sail away fast enough. We can't all sail against the wind, you know; in fact, none of *us* can. We heard he'd been down among the Friesians, trying to raise a fleet.'

'What for?' I knew, of course, it was monotonous.

'He wanted them to raid Asgard. The Friesians wouldn't come. They said us on the coast, and Starkadder in the strait, and Sweyn among the islands weren't serious, but you and Donar were more than they wanted to tackle. Listen, Allfather. You'll find there are a lot of Saxon packtrains on the roads this year. Lots of men and not very much to carry; except their saxes.'

I went away to think all this over. What did I need Ravens for? If Loki and Sigmund wanted to attack Asgard, then I would make them do it themselves, openly, and take the blame on their own backs.

8

The following night, in Valhall, we held our great Funeral Feast for Baldur, a private one for Kings and Asers. I sang again in Valhall, the song of Baldur-Adonis, not now as a desperate speech over a body, but as an entertainment. I sang loud to drown Njord's coughing. I sang long and loud, I stretched each line to a stanza, the patterns of alliteration growing wilder and wilder as I strove to make my mind too full for thought.

We had gone to table as usual. Boar and whetstone lay on the board. The Asers and the Kings stood in their places.

Then the curtains opened at the far end of the Hall. Freda entered. She was white clad and gleaming, golden haired and willowy, shining and splendid in the red and yellow torchlight. Gold rings were on her fingers, gold bracelets on her arms, a great gold brooch was at her shoulder. Behind her were her maidens in yellow or green or crimson. She sat between me and Njord. About her neck there hung a chain of stone. A chain it was of thirty-six rings, each ring was in the shape of a fish that held its own tail in its mouth, and each fish was green but its fins were white.

While the feast went on, while we ate and drank and made stilted conversation in rhythmic phrases, taking care of metre and alliteration as Kings and Asers must, I kept on thinking, Where did she get it? How did she get it? Yet all the time I knew, and I did not dare to know.

Njord went to bed early, coughing. I left with him. It was my turn, of all the Asers, to be up early next morning so that whenever a King might wish to depart, there would be one of us to see him go. I went round the gate and the wicket, spoke to all the guards, did much else. Tyr and Donar could look after the guests.

I went to my own house. Freda was sitting in the great bed, her golden hair loose over her bare shoulders, her bare arms, in the light of a dozen candles. We were the rich, the happy Asers.

'Come to bed, Votan. Do come to bed, darling.'

'How did you get it?'

'How did I get what? Don't stand there, darling, come into bed and tell me all about it.'

193

'Tell me how you got it. That necklace, tell me how you got it?'

'What, that old thing? I bought it, of course. Now, don't be silly, come into bed, do.'

'No! If you bought it, what did you pay for it?'

'Not much, I forget how much, a trifle.'

'Not much? I offered them gold, Amber, furs, garnets. I offered them a ship, free passage and safe conduct from here to India or anywhere else they pleased. I offered them free quarters here for life, horses, dogs, women, all of these things together. They would not sell. What more could you offer?'

'Perhaps I asked them nicely.'

I went rooting through the hall like a boar. I flung things about, I rummaged in chests and cupboards. I counted, I weighed.

'What did you give them? There's nothing gone here, you haven't had anything out of the store-houses. What did you give? What did you promise?'

'I promised them nothing. I gave them nothing you valued.'

'But something you gave.'

I pounded about the hall. The women scurried terrified into the night. I looked for my precious things, my shield, my sword, my helmet, my gold cuirass, the old leather bag that was the last Greek thing I had.

'What was it? What was it?'

I wouldn't come to it, I was afraid to come to it. I could hear Loki's voice at the Feast of the Dead: '… and if you had something really fine, and there wasn't anything else you really wanted, then you could have Freda herself …' All the Asers had heard it, all the Vandals, all Germany had heard it by now.

'What was it? What did you give them?'

She saw it in my eyes, she tried to boast of it.

'Something you didn't want, never wanted, always off riding around, worse than Baldur, after everything else that moves.'

'You slept with one of them.'

'All right, I slept with them, both of them.'

I slapped her face, back and fore, back and fore.

'Yes, both of them, two in one night, two in one night, little brown men.'

I hit her again.

194

'Slut! Bitch!'

'Little brown men, yes two in a night, cut and come again, what a night we had of it.' She sat naked in the bed and ranted at me. 'Better than you, you played-out satyr, better than you, young man, old man whatever you are. Look at yourself, white-haired, one-eyed wreck! Randy stallion of the Shallow Sea, *he* called you. Why shouldn't I have my fun too, why shouldn't I?'

'You're my wife, that's why, that's reason enough.'

'And what's it mean to you? A meal when you want it, a bed when you want it, a chance to make money and that you always want, all the wealth you can think of, all the wealth that's going – aye, and where's it going, tell me that, where's it all going? Aser silver, furs, Amber, and where's it all going? Nobody but you can understand the accounts, where's it all going?'

'I work for what I get.'

'Hard labour it must be, in bed with the Queen of the Saxons, rolling about with painted trollops – and what about Gambara?'

'All right, all right! I slept with Bithig to save my neck. I slept with Edith to save a good wise old man from being ploughed into the earth like dung. And I slept with Gambara out of pure lust, and that's something you never felt in all your life. All you want is pretty things. Never heard of desire, did you, you toad-in-the-bed, you sluggish cold snake. I never slept with anybody for greed, no not even with you!'

I paced up and down. There was a jug of wine on the table, I flung it over her as I passed, without thinking. I was frantic with rage and shame. I turned on her again,

'And how many more since we were married? How many more?'

She wasn't being brazen any more, she was terrified.

'This is the first time, the first time, I tell—'

'You lying whore! That boy, who's his father? Tell me that! Ginger-headed bastard, who's always got him, who's always fondling him, who's pushed me out, tell me that!'

'You can't say that!'

'I can say it, it's true, isn't it? Isn't it? Who was flitting around the forests before I came? I hear things, you know, other beings talk besides ravens. Who was always here, in and out, in and out?'

'It's not true.'

'Now we can see you squirm, now we hear you scream – too near the truth, is it, too near the bone? We'll go nearer to the bone yet.'

And at that point, when I had Gungnir at her throat, when I could have killed her, would have killed her, as custom and law allowed me to do, even commanded me to do, the noise outside our hall grew till even we could hear it. And still we might have taken no notice, if Skuldi, the oldest and the bravest of Freda's maidens – and maiden was a courtesy title at that – had not come back in to us, and stood at the door of the hall screaming.

'Allfather, Allfather, they're fighting in the hall, in Valhall, Donar is dead, the Kings have killed him.'

'Oh no,' I prayed. 'Oh no, don't let the Kings and Asers fight, don't let the peace be broken and the trade spoilt.'

I pulled my cloak about me, I went out of the hall across the courtyard in the bitter cold. Freda sat on the bed and screamed, she screeched and cursed after me as I went,

'Dedicated to yourself, yourself dedicated to yourself, that's what you are, always been, dedicated to yourself.'

I went from the clamour of her voice into the clamour of Valhall, all confusion and terror. Sweyn Halffoot, standing for once, was banging his face against a golden pillar, viciously, trying to hurt himself. Edwin was trying to hold back Siggeir, who had young Sigmund in a corner and was trying to brain him with a silver tray. Donar was lying over a table, face down, streaming blood, snorting like a pig.

'Quiet, everyone!' I shouted. 'Stand still where you are!' They did, too. Anyone would have stopped for white-haired Votan, furious, with the one blazing eye.

'Who's sober and capable? Idun, you look all right, get a bucket of hot water. And a jug of Honeydew, and some shears, and a knife. A sharp one, out of the kitchen. Tyr, help me get his legs on the table and turn him over. How did it all start?'

'He told him it was King Vikar's chain. Then he went for him.'

'Shears! we'll get rid of some of this hair. Now, slowly, who told who and who went for who?'

'Sigmund told Donar, the toad-brained turd. I'll kill him, só help me, I'll feed his guts to the rats, I'll cut his—'

'Let him be, Tyr, Siggeir will finish Sigmund for us. Save your curses for Loki. Idun, get some clean cloths. So Sigmund told Donar Sweyn had King Vikar's chain. Who went for who?'

'Donar rushed at Sweyn, had him by the throat. Sweyn had to hit him, he was being choked.'

'What with, for pity's sake? Pour some Honeydew over these tweezers, Idun, in this dish.'

'Fists first, and then a pot and it broke, and then a whetstone.'

'Njord's?'

'No, with his own.'

'Donar must have a skull as thick as the Mamunt's. Give me the tweezers. Look at the pieces of stone coming out, and the lumps of pot, right in the bone. Pour Honeydew over the wound. Go on, girl, don't skimp it. Keep all the pieces in that cup. He'll be proud of them when he comes round.'

'He will come round?'

'Of course he will.' I said. I hope he does, I thought, but I shall be miles away by then. 'Is this where – What's all that noise?'

'He's got away, Sigmund's got away, he's running like a louse.'

'Let him go. Stop there, Siggeir, he's not worth it, stop – Oh, what's the use, let them all go if they want to. Come over here Sweyn, feel this. There you are, only a bump, you've had worse yourself. Idun, thank heaven you're here, get a bed made up. And throw some water over this drunken Dane, there's nothing else to do when they start crying.'

Siggeir came back, swearing horribly and shaking snow off his clothes.

'Lost him, blast his eyes, blast him. I'd have got him too, if this Saxon hadn't hung on to my cloak, brought us both down in the marsh. I'd have got him if I'd been left alone. Off he went over the saltings and his men with him.'

'Well, you shouldn't have treated the poor old gentleman like that.' Idun had come a long way from the forest into Asgard, and now she was at her best, not caring whom she scolded or mothered. 'Come along, King Edwin, come along, sit by the brazier and have some hot beer. Get your wet shirt off – Bragi, get him a dry one – and wrap this cloak around you till it comes.'

Idun had learned, and I think she learned it from me, that if you talk as if you are going to be obeyed, then people will obey you. She was in charge now, I could trust her.

I stood by the high table, and looked over the wreck of Valhall, the remains of the feast, spilt wine and scattered food, broken pottery, and glass, even precious glass, broken. Silver cups squeezed flat, splintered horns, benches upset, and the hangings dragged to the floor, and the gold leaf scraped from the pillars here and there. I stood and I looked at it all, and I picked up a piece of the broken whetstone, I absent-mindedly took Gungnir from the wall, and began to hone him. I honed the edge of the long blade, and I looked at it, and I felt sick of all the riot. The long night was over and the light was coming back. What was I doing here?

'Saddle Sleipnir,' I told the Vandals, 'and a spare horse for my pack.'

Tyr watched me pull my grey cloak around me, and draw the hood over my head.

'Hunting Burgundians?' he asked. 'Or Loki?'

'Two little brown men. Tell your Vandals I shall need them.'

'Call for us when you want us.'

I went out of Asgard. It was close to dawn.

9

All that winter, from Yule to Easter, I rode the roads of Germany. I went from the Friesians to the Quadi, and from the Cherusci to the Black Danes. Once I came to the very gates of Outgard, and heard the Burgundians and their women shrilling inside.

I had not known there were so many of the little brown men on the cold plains. Did I find the two I sought? How should I know? The first five I saw I killed quickly, out of hand. After that they heard of me, and they began to hide from me, and to keep to the woods. I only got eight or nine more, besides women, by the time the snow began to melt. I learned myself how to melt into the earth, how to appear and disappear, never to be seen to come, or to go, but suddenly to be, or to be gone.

At intervals I would come into the palisades, and meet the Vandals of the packtrains. They always had news for me, and silver, and new clothes, and fresh horses, for I only rode Sleipnir when I went in to kill. They helped drive the brown vermin into my arms, though twice they nearly trapped me in the wild lands.

So, as I came into the palisades, I heard all the news of Asgard.

'Njord is sick, he lies on his bed, he coughs and drinks Honeydew, and sits no more at the gate.'

'Donar has begun to walk again, but slowly.'

'Freda now lives in Valhall and tends them both.'

Then when the hyacinths bloomed again beneath the trees:

'Njord is dying, Njord Borsson, Lord of the Asers, lies dead in Valhall.'

I rode back to Asgard. I stopped at Orm's place. He said:

'Only send Bragi back to me, and Idun. And let her bring the little girl, Brunhild. She looks after her now.'

I came to the place where Njord had chosen his grave. Ten paces west of the Standing Stone of the Men of Old, at the Gate of Hell, at the threshold of Those Below. There was no need of fire to thaw the ground. In the soft earth they dug. I saw that they threw up bits of burnt bone, and the ashes of men long dead, and pieces of broken pot. Yet I think I was the only one who saw this, the others were too busy digging, or thinking. I sat Sleipnir by the ash tree and I waited.

Out from Asgard, the blue-clad Vandals who had no King carried the body of Njord Borsson who was no King. What killed him?

'The cold,' Idun told me later. 'The cold he caught going up to Baldur's grave, he wasn't fit to go all that way, not at his age, and all that Honeydew he drank to cure the cold, and that Baldur was dead, and that Loki came no more, and that Blind Hod had gone off to live with Loki, and that Donar walked slowly and talked thickly and smiled always on one side of his face, and that Freda wept all day, and that you, Votan, were gone in wrath and without a word. That's what killed him, Allfather, that you were

199

gone, most of all, for he knew that without you, or against you, not even Asgard could stand.'

They carried him to the grave that he had asked for, leather lapped in his oak coffin. Who would go with Njord? Skirmir's wife did not cry her question, who would have answered? But he did not, in the end, go alone. For pity's sake, they caught the old woman who made pots at the end of the village, and knocked her on the head and threw her in. And is it not better to share the grave of a greater than a King, than to die in lonely misery, and rot unwashed, unwatched, on the floor of your hut till the roof falls in to be your grave mound?

No Kings came to Njord's funeral. Their agents came. No King would show his face in Asgard after Baldur's funeral feast. For their masters they threw into the grave their gifts, bronze, gold, bolts of cloth. From the kitchens of Asgard, they threw in roast meat, and sausages, and bread and stuffed salt fish. I saw someone throw in a handful of my olives. Njord never liked olives in life, why should he in death? What about the rest of the barrel, I kept thinking, what about the rest of the olives, as I watched the Asers come to the grave.

The Asers threw in their gifts. Heimdall in his fine Spanish boots I gave him, and he was so proud of. Donar, moving slowly on a stick. I looked across the heads of all the Asers. On the edge of the forest, beyond the village, he stood, in scarlet cloak.

Freda came forward. Into the grave she threw a chain, a chain of stone. A chain it was of thirty-six rings, each ring was in the shape of a fish that held its own tail in its mouth, and each fish was green but its fins were white.

I rode down from the ash tree to the Standing Stone, the only mounted man in all that throng. I rode past the Asers to the grave of Great Njord Borsson, Lord of the Asers. Into the grave I threw my golden armour, my cuirass of gilded leather. In that acid soil the hide would rot, the worms poke through the gold. All will rot, all will moulder away.

Then on the coffin I threw a clod of earth. As the peasants on Baldur's coffin, so I threw in Njord's grave a turf from my own field, that none but I would crop. From the centre of the Heath, I brought a turf stained with Varus's blood.

Then I rode on, past the Asers, past the peasants. Slowly I rode over the causeway. I walked Sleipnir to the Gates of Asgard, over the path where a man might lead a packhorse, but where no man had ridden before. I rode into the courtyard of Asgard where no man before had sat a horse. I looked at the Kingless Vandals who filled the courtyard, and I heard their shouts, and I knew that now I was Lord of the Amber Road, Ruler of all the Asers. I dismounted and I went into Valhall.

The thrones of the Asers were no longer as they had bèen. They were no longer as they had been even that morning, when Frederik went out to the grave. What did I have Vandals for?

I took my place at the centre of the high table of Valhall. Tyr sat at my right hand, Hermod at my left. Freda, Frederik, Donar, Bragi, sat at the sidetables. Heimdall entered. He laid before me on the table Njord's whetstone.

We ate Njord's Funeral Feast. There was enough ham for all the Vandals who came crowding into Valhall. Good honest men, they were serving me as they once served Loki, hating Loki now, hating the Burgundians who filled their old places. Who would now dare say a word against Votan Allfather? I spoke an oration fit for a Funeral Feast.

'Thus in wisdom spoke the great Asers at the first, that never should weapons go with them to the grave. The place for swords is in the bright dry air, not rusting with damp bones. Let all those swords hiss in the hands of men, who know how to fight for what they live by.

'An enemy comes at us from the east. Treacherously he tries to steal our trade. He undercuts us when we offer furs, he overbids us when we buy our Amber. Soon he will go further and take to arms, and bring the Burgundians about our ears.

'And so I call all loyal Vandals, and all the Lombards under both their Kings, about the Raven Flag of Votan, to fight for Freda, Frederik and Donar, led by farsighted Heimdall and wise Hermod, and by the bravest man of all, One-handed Tyr. This shall be the war to end all wars, to bring peace in the north for ten thousand years, the Aser Peace, Trade, Amber and Goodwill!'

The Amber War

1

So all the Asers, and all their allies, called for war on Loki. Yet I would not attack him. Let the blame lie at his door, that he marched upon us.

March he must. All through the winter we had planned, all through the spring we worked. We outbid Loki for Amber and furs, and we outbid him for all the wine and glass and cloth. Where men bought less than they sold, we promised them interest on what they left with us. When Loki too put up the prices he offered, we outbid him, and we lowered our selling prices. Even if for a whole year we barely doubled our outlay, cut our profits to the bone, still we could outbid Loki. We never sank to that low level. Soon we drained Loki's stores of silver, and never made the least impression on our own. Loki had nothing left to pay his Burgundians, nor could they be fed except from their farms. He must attack us if he wished to live. Beaten in trade, he must turn to war.

We had, I reckoned, till August, till the Burgundians had gathered their harvest. No army would march till the harvest was in. To make sure, at that time the Polyani would burst out of their forests, raid the Burgundian farms, burn the crops, so that Sigmund must march or starve. However the raids went, the Asers and their allies would not starve. We had great stores of food, in secret places in the forest.

When was easy. But where?

Loki must march on Asgard. Asgard with its stores of treasure, its furs and Amber and food, must draw him. It would give him enough to feed the Burgundians through a dozen campaigns. Asgard was the trap. I did not fortify Asgard. Why should I frighten the mouse away?

No need, though, to lose all the cheese. The reserves of Amber, and much of the silver, I got secretly out and packed them south where I knew they would be safe, train after train to the south.

I packed the gold out too, all together in one train. There were twenty packhorses, and half a dozen Scrawlings, as few as I could do with. From Orm's place we took the gold where it, too, would be safe. No one would go after it to the centre of the Heath. Nobody would ask dead Varus for it. The Scrawlings would never take it.

When they had piled the gold sacks on the ground beneath the ash, they turned and saw me with Gungnir in my hand, and knew. They didn't resist, they didn't even turn to run, they just waited. I laid the bodies on the sacks. I killed the horses too, and their breath mingled with the wind, and their blood flowed on the plain. Sleipnir stood still in all that smell of blood, and I rode him back.

We sat in Hoenir's hall, Tyr and I, and we planned the battle. We would not hold Asgard. We would concentrate our own army, nation by nation, on the Aser food stores in the forest. Then, when Sigmund came to the village before Asgard, he would find us waiting on the far side of the common where the villagers grazed their cows. There he must fight us, before ever he could think of taking Asgard. We explained all this to the Cheruscan King.

'First,' I told him, 'I think you've met Gand, one of our Vandals. He has a sister, that Synfiotli Volsungson has taken for his mistress. She has a way of getting messages back here, never mind how. The night that Loki makes Sigmund call his assembly for war, she will know. On the second day we will hear of it. By the fourth day, Hoenir will have all his levy here, and the Vandals will meet Tyr at Baldur's grave. The Saxons, and any Danes on our shores, and the Vandals who are out on packtrains, will meet us at Orm's place. We reckon Loki cannot be at Asgard before the morning of the seventh day. We fight him then. And here, in the very heart of the Lombards, where no one would expect to find them, we have three hundred young Vandals, and Lyngi Siggeirson teaching them to be soldiers.'

203

'This is a fine time,' said the Sergeant King, 'to be telling me Vandals can't fight.'

'I said making soldiers out of them. We're not going to fight this in the German way, two shield walls walking slowly up to each other and fighting a long line of single combats, all according to the rules. We're taking a legion as our model. I can't make them charge in line, but they understand what I mean by a wedge. They won't run, though, and they want to fight with their swords. Come over and watch Lyngi.'

We could hear his voice as we came near to the exercise ground.

'Fine soldier he'd have made if we'd got him young enough,' said the Cheruscan. 'Listen to him now, he's doing vital areas. Throat, groin, kidneys. Oh, to be young again.'

Lyngi had a squad waiting.

'Now, we've got important visitors today, you let them know what you've learnt already You, there, on the end, what's your shield? What do you use it for?'

'To stop him hitting me, of course.'

'You fish-brained little toad, what have you got between your ears? Horse-dung? You, next there, tell him.'

'My shield is my principal weapon of offence – SIR!'

'Next, you! What's your secondary weapon of offence?'

'My secondary weapon of offence is my spear – SIR!'

'And you, what's your shield rim for?'

'To turn the edge of his sword—'

'What? Where have you been all the week? You may have broken your mother's heart, you'll never break mine! You're on stables tonight, and for the next ten nights. Next man, what's the right answer?'

'For striking at the back of a neck – SIR!'

'And your shield boss?'

'For hitting him in the face – SIR!'

'Now we'll show that. Form … WEDGE! Now, that line of straw dummies over there is the Burgundians, and about as much use too, if only you remember all this. At a good trot, now … Charge!

'That's it, when you reach them just push at the man in front with your shield, stab at the man on your right. Never mind about the man in front any more, your left-hand man takes care of him. And a stab down as you go over, for your rear ranker's sake.'

Vidar took the squad over. Lyngi came over, holding his helmet in one hand, mopping his face with the other. He was enthusiastic, could talk of nothing else.

'The trouble we have getting these lads to go in at the run and use their weight. They all want to stand back and chop. They don't fancy the idea of fanning out when they're through the line and going for the backs. They think war's a game.'

'War's no game,' said the Cheruscan. He did well, for a sergeant in a regiment which had held the frontier for forty-two years and never been in action. 'That's because they've not been blooded. Kill them as you get over, kill them dead, or they'll only get up and stab your comrade as he passes.

'Now what do you want of me in your war, Votan? Do not remind me of my oaths. I was not sober when I swore, I send you no troops.'

It was hardly politic to accuse him of treachery, but my face showed my bitter feelings, so he went on,

'I give you better, I take away half your enemies and never shed a drop of blood. The Cat King has promised Loki that when he attacks Asgard, the Chatti will come against you too. But I will stand surety that the Cat King will never march when my war band roams his frontiers. I will keep your back, Allfather. Then, because I can count on the Cat King not fighting unless I actually cross his borders, I can let you have, let's see … yes … mail shirts, three hundred, on loan, I'll need them back. And to keep, heads, arrow, six thousand; heads, javelin, two thousand; heads, lance, six hundred; axes, throwing, six hundred.' What kind of a soldier he was I never knew, but he was a fine quartermaster. 'And for the kind of attack you're making, you'll need greaves. I'll lend you two hundred and fifty pairs. I'll withdraw them from my own bodyguard, and I'll want those back too.'

When we got back to the hall that day, Gambara met us with:

'There's another King come. I had to chase him out of my kitchen, or we wouldn't have had a cheese left in the palace. I made him go and wash – it can't have been much of a wash, here he comes now.'

Tawalz was no longer the only one of the Polyani to boast a sword, or even the only one to have a mail shirt and a helmet. Aser support had made him into a King indeed, head of five thousand families. He squeezed on to the high table with us and refused roast pork.

'Wheat bread and cheese and onions is a feast to me,' he told us, 'Meat, I can have all I want from the forest. I've got something awkward for you. Three things, to be precise, three heads.'

'Good man,' said Lyngi. 'How did you take them? Did you—'

Everybody kicked him. Tawalz went on,

'These were Burgundians. We caught them crossing our river. They told us why too, before they died. We gave them long enough. They were on their way to the Lesny who live beyond us. They were to persuade them to raid us when Loki marches on Asgard. Of course, we only got three, others may have got across. So I have sent to the Russ, who live farther east. The Russ will raid the Lesny, if they raid us. But I cannot trust them, and so only half my families will go against Sigmund when he marches.'

This was a blow. And Tawalz had not found out from his prisoners when the attack would come.

2

There was a night toward the middle of June, when we were sitting over Hoenir's ale, and talking of the autumn campaign, when there was a commotion at the bottom of the hall. To the high table there came a man called Adils, who was one of the few who knew of Gand's sister. He walked up to the table, and we knew from his face that there was trouble, and we made room for him, so that he could tell us quietly.

'Sigmund's out!' he said.

That was an end to all our planning.

'He's been out two days. He got a lot of his people in for the Midsummer feast ten days early, so that he had a sizeable war band ready. Then he just stood up at the end of dinner and said he was going to march at dawn with what he had, and pick up all his western families on the way. That's how Gand's sister wasn't able to warn us earlier.'

Everyone jumped up and argued and shouted and asked questions till I thumped my fist on the table for silence. I needed silence to think. I thought as fast as I could and that was not easy, I was as frightened as they were. Loki couldn't do this, he couldn't march before we were ready, he couldn't come before the harvest, nobody ever made war before the harvest. The truth was the Burgundians were starving, they couldn't even live till their own harvest, they had to march or starve, and in a way it was our fault. I pulled myself together, forced myself to think like a solid unemotional Greek, not like one of those volatile northerners. I asked:

'How many men has he?'

'Not as many as we expected. About half the nation, I should think, but of course the eastern families will soon be out after him.'

I called the ambassador from the Polyani.

'Olen, tell your uncle to raid. Tell him to raid at once, raid everywhere, burn crops, kill the women, destroy everything. Then the Burgundians that aren't out yet won't go, and the ones that have marched may want to go home. Off you go!' And Olen went.

'Then Asgard. Bragi, there's still a lot of Amber left, take all the pack horses you can find and get the lot out and away south. The other Asers? They can wait, we can go back for them. Anyway they're safe enough, we'll fight before Loki can get at them.' Later men would throw it up to me that I sacrificed the Asers for the Amber. Yet I did the will of my Father Paeon.

'Now, Adils, have you twenty men you can trust? Good men, like yourself, not squeamish?'

'Forty, if you like.'

'Twenty will do. Ride to Asgard. Clear the village on the ridge, send all the people to Orm's place, tell them to take their cattle, anything the Burgundians can eat.

'Then get over to the Black Sheds where they make the Honeydew. You'll find a half dozen Germans there, and about a hundred Scrawlings. Kill them, kill the lot. Don't let anybody get away, kill them all.'

'But they make the Honeydew.'

'Look, Adils, we can buy more Scrawlings. We can make more copper pipes, fire more pots, so smash all you can see. But if Loki catches the men who make the Honeydew, then our secret and our power are gone. Take all the Honeydew you can find, it's in big jars, and put it in the village. Put a jar in every house, and all the jars over, leave in the street. Don't let your own men get at it; leave it for the Burgundians, and watch what it does to them. Then burn the Black Sheds, and get into Asgard.'

Adils went. A man called Pybba took a group of archers off east to hold the Burgundians up. Nothing teaches you to walk warily so much as an arrow from nowhere in the ribs.

3

That was improvisation. Now for the plan and the army.

'Right,' said Tyr. 'I'll call out the Vandals.'

'Call them,' said Hoenir gloomily. 'They won't come. It stands to reason, you can't ask men to come out this time of year. It's the hay-making, and the barley's just beginning to turn. You'll never raise a host, and I'm not even going to try. Why not buy them off? There was never a King yet who couldn't be bought.'

'I'm not asking Vandals,' said Tyr. 'I'm telling them.'

'You can't, you'll never get them out. Mine aren't coming, anyway.'

'If there are no Vandals and no Lombards,' I said firmly, 'then I will meet them with Tyr, and the Saxons that are on the roads now. They came out to fight and fight they will.' Privately, I meant to do no such thing.

'Maybe, they're only lads, they don't know what war is. My men know. They won't come till after the harvest, and I'll not ask them.'

'Coward!' It was Gambara, she was furious, white with rage, in a flaming temper. 'Do you want me to go? Do you want to see the Lombard women fight because their men are afraid

208

to go to war? Too busy with the harvest? Who in heaven's name do you think actually *gets* the harvest in? Who do you think turns the hay and stacks it? What else is a man good for but to fight?

'And if you fight for no one else, you must fight for Votan! Whose fault is it you are still a King? Who gave you your wife? The very sword you are afraid to draw you gained through him. If you are afraid to use it, give it to me. If you have no blood, let me shed mine.'

And I think she would indeed have gone to war herself, for the men of the Land of Norroway are fierce and blood-thirsty, and their women no better if the tales Donar brought back are true. With such a choice between Sigmund in arms and Gambara in fury, Hoenir took the lesser evil. He went to war.

The Lombards came, of course. They came grumbling, and cursing, but it was Sigmund they cursed for fighting out of season. Every Lombard noble who came straggling in with his six or eight axemen was convinced that only he had answered the call, and each, prophesying massacre and disaster and a bad harvest, came prepared only to die beside his King. But a day or two on the Aser stores of bread and beef and beer put heart into them. Lombards, and Vandals too, went out to war.

4

We looked down from the edge of the wood across the common. No cows grazed there now. On the ridge opposite, the black ruin of the Honeydew sheds still smoked. Farther along we could see the roofs of the village. It was all very still. There was very little wind.

'Are they there?' Tyr wasn't the only one to ask. If Sigmund was in the village, he was looking at the wood and asking the same question. If Sigmund was in the village, then he was between us and Asgard. He might even be in Asgard.

'We'll have a look,' I said. Lyngi and I rode down on to the common. Suddenly the ridge was thronged with helmets. We were closer now, and we could hear a good deal of shouting.

209

There was singing too. We went nearer, and the men began to come down off the ridge and get into some kind of order. Synfi-otli seemed to be in charge, and having a hard task. We went closer still, and a few optimists loosed arrows at us. They couldn't reach us, but we took the hint, and went back a little.

'They're not very steady,' said Lyngi. 'Look at all those pots going round. Is that what Honeydew does?'

'In quantity, yes. I'd rather they had it than our men. How many do you make them?'

'Not enough. Only half what Pybba counted. The rest must be still in the village.'

Or in Asgard, I thought. Neither of us said it.

We sat and watched. The line was more or less straight now, and very quiet, the shields overlapping in the classical way.

'That's right,' said Lyngi. 'Keep those left arms up and tire them out for me. There must be more, they've left room for a second line before the top of the ridge.' He spat for luck. 'You want me to bring them down?'

'We'll have to break the line somehow before I let these raw levies at them,' I said. We had been over the possibilities so often, he knew just what he had to do. We rode back to the edge of the wood, and he dismounted.

'None of that going-in-naked nonsense,' I told him. 'Stick together. You'll have them all around you.'

'Do you have to remind me?' He called forward the Vandals, the first wave. They got into four wedges. This was the trad-itional Vandal formation, but in defence, not in attack. They pressed in, the rear-rank men ready to push their companions through. The front-rank men were the ones who owned mail shirts; the rear-rankers hoped to get them from dead Burgundi-ans. Lyngi went over and got in at the point of the leading wedge. Men were spitting and biting the rims of the shields, and looking for the snakes in their swords and all the other silly things men do for luck. Lyngi undid the soft leather bag that he usually had over the hilt of his sword to protect the gold and jewels.

I raised my spear.

'Go in, Vandals, and go right through them,' I shouted. I dropped the point. The wedges moved off.

210

Behind that leading wedge, the green grass had turned to blue. These were the Vandals who had served Loki, and had worn the cloaks made out of that job lot of blue cloth he had been unable to sell otherwise. Now, as he had cast them off, so they cast off his cloaks, they hoped in his sight. Every man in those four wedges was a Vandal seeking to kill Loki, except the leader, and he was a Goth looking for Sigmund.

They went forward across the common, at a trot. They didn't make much noise, they were saving their breath. The line opposite them was still steady, and there was a lot of shouting of 'Sigmund' or 'Volsungs for ever', and blowing of horns and beating on shields.

Of course, almost everyone on either side was badly frightened. Some had been in skirmishes or riots, or had gone to steal ships or horses, but this was the first time for two generations, the generations of the Asers, that two armies had met in the north.

I watched the meeting of the hosts. The rest of my army was still in the wood, and could neither see nor be seen. Hoenir and Tyr, and Oswy Karlsson the Saxon came forward to me to watch.

The wedges crossed the common, and slowed a little, as we had foreseen, as they came to the slope. Then with a splendid sense of timing, Sigmund brought his second line over the crest of the ridge and into position fifty yards behind his first. The sight should have unsettled the Vandals at the moment of impact. But this too we were expecting. The wedges cut into the Burgundian line in four places, and the broken ends of the line curled in, not giving the Vandals space to spread out. In a moment there were four solid masses of Vandals surrounded by Burgundians. The second line on the ridge stood rock steady.

'Come on,' shouted Tyr. 'Get Lyngi out of there.'

'Stand still,' I told him, not shouting, I didn't dare shout, everyone else was shouting. Oswy was moaning and screaming like a madman, which of course for that hour he was.

'Blood, out, out, blood!'

Hoenir took my mood and just said, in almost a whisper, 'They're murdering them down there.'

'Stand still.' I wasn't going to let these green Lombards and

211

unblooded Saxons loose on an unbroken shieldwall, even if it were only Burgundians. The only talent a general needs is success in his first battle. It is harder to hold an army back than to send it forward. I sat Sleipnir with my face to the enemy, my back to my own host. By sheer will I held my men back in the wood. On the ridge I could see Sigmund, his back to us, shouting at his men by the way his head was moving. Whose will was the stronger? Could I hold my second line longer than he could hold his?

My line stood still, held its form. I could see Lyngi hacking away at the press of Burgundians around him. Tyr was making my men sit down, stand up, tell dirty stories, count themselves, anything to take their minds off the fight they could hear and not see.

Sigmund was stretching his arms wide. Then his line broke, his will gave, he couldn't hold them any more. First one man ran down the hill toward the mêlée, and another, and then a group. Sigmund no longer had a shieldwall or an army, just a great shapeless mass running down to where Lyngi and his Vandals were still standing, living or dead, in their wedges.

I saw Sigmund's army dissolve. I saw Victory.

'Right,' I shouted. 'We'll go now.'

I walked Sleipnir forward. The rest of my army came on behind, in three lines. As they came out of the wood they saw the Burgundians streaming down the hill, and in that first sight they saw their enemies stagger and wilt as Pybba and his archers stood up and sent a shower of arrows into their flank. That much I had learnt from Morien.

I looked back from time to time. I shouted:

'Keep your dressing. Slow! Push, remember, push, push! Don't split up. Use your shields. Slow! Keep your lines locked!'

Tyr walked at one side of me, Hoenir at the other, their spears held out horizontally. I looked further back.

'Hermod, keep your line straight, don't let the flanks come forward. Slower, Bragi, you're overrunning Hermod.'

We could hear Lyngi now, shouting:

'Votan, help! Votan, help!'

He had done his part, he had gone in against odds to tempt

Sigmund's army down from its strong position, to break it up, destroy the shieldwall. We were almost to him, we were there.

'Votan,' Lyngi shouted, and 'Votan,' shouted the Lombards. 'Votan, help!' they shouted and 'Donar', as our flanks enveloped the Burgundians in turn, and pushed them back into a confused shouting mass, so that Lyngi and his survivors could burst out into line with us.

'Votan!' or 'Donar!' they shouted, and the Saxons shouted, 'Out, Out, Blood, Out,' and I pressed into the throng. I wore neither mail nor helm, and I laid Gungnir on my shoulder, and I struck at no one, the only mounted man on the whole field.

'Loki,' I shouted as I sought him. 'Loki? Find me Loki!!!' I came face to face with Synfiotli.

'Loki's in Asgard now!' he screamed at me. 'You're too late, Votan, Loki's in Asgard, and so's my blasted brother.' And as he shouted at me Gand came in at his elbow and cut him down and laughed. I pushed Sleipnir through the press, past that body and a score of other bodies, and I came through the battle and out of it and I was alone on the slope below the village, and alone in the village. I left the noise behind, 'Votan,' 'Donar,' 'Sigmund,' 'Out, Out.'

I went through the village. There were only dead men left there, there had been a fight, in the night probably, they were stiffening where they had been dragged into a heap and their jewels taken. That was Adils. And there, yes, it *was* Frederik. He was willing to fight, but as Loki had said, he couldn't. Easy to see what had happened, he had struck clumsily, and his spear had gone into that shield, the one with the dog on it. And while he leaned forward with the shock of the blow, someone had cut at the back of the neck. *His* body no one had moved.

I turned toward the causeway. The smoke wasn't only from the Honeydew Sheds. There was fire in Asgard. I was galloping toward the causeway now, but there was someone in front of me, running toward Asgard. When we reached the Standing Stone he turned to bar my way. Sigmund had a sword in his hand, the old Greek sword that I had given him.

'That's the end of you.' He screamed and slashed at me, and he missed.

'Stealer of women, breaker of the north, spoiler of trade—' and he struck at me again, and this would have done for me, but I used the only real parry, I stabbed with Gungnir at his eyes. He swayed away from the stroke, and he missed me and the sword struck the Standing Stone. The blade broke, and left him with only the hilt in his hand; it was a good hilt, but the iron was old and tired. He looked stupidly at the hilt for a moment, and then dropped it. Sigmund was incoherent with rage and terror and almost out of breath after the long run, and I heard him shouting:

'Kill me, yes go on, kill me, finish the job, ruin all the nations.'

I thrust him through. I saw no reason why he should die without pain, and less why he should live. I gave him in my heart to Apollo the Destroyer of Things, and I rode past Sigmund where he lay squirming like a crushed worm. I never killed a King before. This one lay to die on Njord's grave.

I rode on to the causeway. There were dead men lying everywhere. There was one living man. Skirmir was running toward me along the causeway. He too was shouting:

'All dead in Asgard, all dead in Asgard, all dead but Loki!'

I set Sleipnir at him and rode him down. He was still shouting when the hooves struck him in the face, still shouting:

'All dead but Loki! All dead but Loki!'

Then as Sleipnir recovered from the shock of hitting Skirmir, he jibbed at something else and came down. He screamed, and there is nothing so terrible as a horse's scream. I fell clear, and for a little while I couldn't get up, but lay winded, holding my stomach and retching. When I could move I looked as best I could at the thrashing beast, and there was a leg broken. There was nothing more to do. With Gungnir's edge I cut his throat, and his blood poured out to the ground and his breath hissed into the wind.

What had frightened him, after all that dreadful day? Whose body was it? By the Spanish boots it was Heimdall, dead on the causeway ten yards out of Asgard. The head was gone. There were more dead men about him.

There were others in the gate and in the courtyard, more Burgundians than Vandals. A brazier had been overturned and some of the houses near the gate were burning, but not badly yet, and what wind there was came from the sea. Then there was a gust, and flame and smoke with it, and I looked and the thatch of Valhall was on fire.

I held Gungnir before me, and I went forward into the smoke. At the door of my own house I found Donar. He was sitting there. There were four dead men in front of him, and Mollnir was dirty, with hair and blood and brains. As he struck, two-handed, someone had come in under his arm and stabbed him to the kidneys, deep. There was blood over his lap, and blood came from his mouth, but when I bent over him he knew me and said:

'Freda ... Loki ... sword ...'

I left him and I went to the door of burning Valhall. Just within the door sat Loki. He sat on a bench. His head was bowed on the table where he had eaten the Feast of the Dead and cursed us all to Death. Soon he would eat the Feast of the Dead in his own right. Someone had cut down hard on to his shoulder. The blade had shorn through mail and leather and cloth, through muscle and bone. The arm was almost severed, all around was drenched in blood. His other arm, the right, was on the table. His fingers touched Njord's whetstone. At each end were four faces under a red painted crown. Now all the stone was red with blood.

I looked up the hall, under the burning thatch. There were the thrones as always. There sat Freda. She was white clad and gleaming, golden-haired and willowy, shining and splendid in the red and yellow flames. Gold rings were on her fingers, gold bracelets on her arms, a great gold brooch was at her shoulder. Around her were her maidens, in yellow or green or crimson, four living maidens at her back and four oaken maidens on her chair. Across her knees she held a bloody sword. Donar's sword, I knew it by the copper and silver set in the blade.

I stood at the door of Valhall, burning Valhall. Freda stood up.

'Votan!' she cried. 'Votan! Why were you so long in coming?'

And all our quarrel was as if it had never been. And then the roof and all the wall of Valhall fell in upon her.

And that was the end of my wife Freda, Njord's daughter, Skazi's daughter, Goldlover. She died and all her maidens with her in the flames of Valhall. I took the whetstone from Loki's still living hand, and I left him to the flames.

I went into my own house. I thrust the whetstone through my belt. From the wall I took the helmet, my shield from the Goth king, the sword Donar made me. I looked around, and I found my old leather bag, the last Greek thing I had. I rummaged in the boxes, I stuffed wealth into the bag, all I could find, gold, silver, Amber.

As I turned to leave the hall I heard a movement on the bed. Wrapped in a bundle of furs was Scyld. He was asleep; by the looks of it, someone had given him a dose of Honeydew before the fight started. There was no reason why he should see the horrors.

I put my arm through the strap of the shield and held him against my body. It was the only time I was ever allowed to hold him in my arms without someone interfering.

I knelt by Donar. He looked at Scyld, and tried to smile with the side of his face that did not always smile.

'Sister's son,' he said. 'King's heir … sister's son … not King's son … sister's son …' He retched a little, we were both wrapped in the smoke of Valhall, the horrible smoke and smell from buildings that burn with men still in them.

'Hurts, Votan, Allfather, Allhealer, hurts …' he said and then very clearly,

'But not in the earth, my friends, no, not in the earth.'

So while he was looking at Scyld, I took the sword he made me that I had never used, and I struck at the back of the neck. Then I took the body into my own house, Donar, that was King Vikar's son of Norroway, Skazi's son, and Skazi was sister to Mymir the Oldest Aser, and to Bergelmir that was driven out. I kindled the thatch with a brand from burning Valhall.

I took Scyld and my arms and the bag, and I went down through the wicket to the jetty, where was still moored the boat Bragi had built for me, and rigged with a lug sail, though he did not understand what this tangle of mast and spar and ropes and leather was for. I laid Scyld in the boat and I took the steering oar. On this voyage I had no need of food or water. I hoisted the sail.

I looked back to the land. The battle was all up and down the sea shore, axes rose and fell on the edge of the marsh. All through the saltings the Saxons hunted down the last Burgundians. The fire had spread from the gate of Asgard along the causeway.

Heimdall and Sleipnir were both consumed. I cast off from the jetty and whistled, as Jokuhai-inen had taught me to do.

The wind came at once, a hard south wind, off the land. The smouldering houses at the gate of Asgard burst into a new flame. The wall of fire raced through Asgard, to meet the fire of Valhall, and sweep to the seaward end of the palisade. The well-tarred fence burnt, the old dry decking on which the houses were built flamed from end to end. The very piles on which all was carried flared down to the water's edge. Smoke rose from oil and cloth and wax and fur and wine. In that heat, gold would melt and run down the pillars, flesh and bone would char away to nothing.

The wind carried the great cloud of smoke over us. Our sail filled, and we stood out to sea. Behind us I could still hear the noise, the shouts of:

'Donar ... Loki ... Votan ... Sigmund ... Out ... Out ...'

At last the noise died. The wind was hard from the south. I held her a trifle west of north.

At dawn, we beached on the shore below Sweyn's hall. There were no ships there. They had gone south in the night. We had heard them pass in the dark, the rowers cursing the south wind that blew in their faces.

All night we had seen lights on the shore, among the islands. It was the night of the Midsummer fires. The men and the maidens leapt over the flames. Only the dead leapt the flames of Asgard.

Here by Sweyn Halffoot's house, all was still dead quiet in the dawn. Even the grinders of the corn had not yet started their daily task. I pushed the boat as far up the beach as I could move it.

I left Scyld still sleeping on the shield. When he awoke, I knew, he would have a headache. He was a strong and a determined child, the loudest baby I have ever heard. There was no chance, when he woke up hungry, that he would be overlooked.

On the leather of the shield, I scratched in Runes with Gungnir's point,

'I am Scyld, Votan-born.'

I left him there. My arms and my treasure I left to him. Only Gungnir, Joy's spear, I took.

I laid the spear on my shoulder and walked on. When I went from island to island, I took boats as I pleased. On the mainland I walked when I wished to walk, and when I wanted to ride, I took what horse I pleased. No man forbade me. No one denied me anything. I spoke to no one. They gave me food and drink and shelter, the peasants of the German plain, and told me all that went on.

'The Vandals,' they told me, 'have a King. After Tyr fell in the battle, and Adils, and Hermod, they followed a Marcoman, named Occa, that came into their country. Yet he is not their King, but his wife's son, Gerda's son, for the child is Votan-born.'

'The Lombards,' they said, 'have two Kings. One is rich and powerful, and he has wealth and gold beyond all telling, and his heirs are Votan-born. But the other Lombard King is poor, and wears his clothes patched, because he did not fight in the Battle.'

'In the Hall of the rich Lombard King,' I heard, 'lives Bragi, who may no longer be a smith or a carpenter now that he cannot bend his elbow, hurt in the Battle. But now he sings all the songs of Votan, of how he brought men the arts of writing and poetry, and how he gave them the magic Honeydew to drink, and how his ravens flew to bring him news of all that happened on the earth, and how his magic ship sailed where he wished whatever the wind.'

'The Burgundians,' they said, 'are destroyed, and their name will soon be forgotten. Those who did not go to the Battle are returned to their allegiance and call themselves the East Goths. Yet a few still cling to the House of the Volsungs, and they hide in the great forest, and their King is Sigurd Sigmundson who is a child.'

'The Cat King will not last long,' they told me. 'The Cheruscan King and the King of the Thuringians have allied against the Chatti, and the Cheruscan King has married the Thuringian King's sister, and his heir is her son, who is Votan-born. But it is that woman, the She-Bear, who rules over both nations already.'

'Edwin the King is dead,' they said, 'and Cutha is regent for his grandson Harald, for he is Votan-born. And the Saxons are ready to march to take back the salt beaches, and they say the Danes cannot be protected by the Treaty, for they did not come in time to the Battle; but the Danes say the Saxons cannot be protected by the Treaty, for their King did not come himself to the Battle while Sweyn sailed in his ships.'

So I went from farm to farm and from house to house, and never a prince or a noble did I see. The peasants gave me food and shelter, and I paid for my food with healing of sprains and bruises and broken bones and running sores and boils, and all the charms that I knew I taught to anyone without payment. And no one ever asked who I was that went one-eyed and grey-haired in a grey cloak.

6

At last, at the end of the summer, I came into a land where the rivers flowed south. One day, a little before sunset I came out of the wood, the scrubby patchy stuff you get near a river, into an open space. In the middle there was an oak, a very old oak, dead, blasted, and scarred by lightning. Around it were scattered horse skulls and bits of cloth held down by stones.

I went to the tree, and thrust Gungnir's point into a dead limb. I walked down to the river, and I washed my face.

When I looked up, the Most Holy One stood before me, as he stands in the Sanctuary. His cloak was of scarlet, and his hair hung about his shoulders. After a time I asked him,

'Father Apollo, Paeon, Joy, Bergelmir, which are you?'

He answered,

'I am all of these, and none of them. I sent you into the north, and my own spear I laid upon your shoulder that all men might know that you came from me.'

I asked,

'My Father, have I done your will?'

'All that I laid on you to do, as I laid my spear on you, you have done. Njord, that brought Loki to drive me out, is dead. Loki is dead. Mymir that watched me go is dead. Vikar that gave Mymir a ship to bring him to the Holy Island alive is dead, and his son, Skazi's son, is dead, and all Skazi's children that should have been my children are dead, but the one that shall bring misery to all the land of Italy in her own time. The Amber peace is broken, and the Amber road is closed, and the rule of the Asers, the Amber Lords, is over.

'Now I take my load from your shoulder, as I took the light from your eye. No one-eyed man, no man who lives in the flat world of half light, can serve the unconquered sun. From my worship for ever you are free.'

He held Gungnir in his hand. He walked away into the forest. I knelt by the river, and I cut short my hair and my beard with my knife, the knife that Joy spun on the tavern table, the knife that had killed the Catman beneath the tree, that had killed Mymir on the Holy Island. I left the knife embedded in the ground, and I threw the hair into the river, as a sign that henceforward I worshipped the Gods of Earth and Water, and not of Fire. And I walked toward the Danube.

7

I came to the ferry. I chatted to two cavalrymen. They were not very happy.

'We've got a new Cavalry Commander at Vindabonum,' they said. 'He's called Aristarchos. He's always getting us on stunts across the river, he keeps on talking about learning how to melt into the ground, how to move quietly. That's not what we joined the army for, that's how the barbarians fight. We joined to ride in line, with shields and plumes, the way the girls like to hear about it.

'He's brought a lot of Brits in, too. The sergeant-major's a terror, the killer type, and so fussy about his food, always wanting cheese …'

I wondered about the sentries at the landing stage. When I got off the ferry Gwalchmai took my arm and led me straight past.

'Taliesin's looking for you,' he said. 'He can't get the pots to work.'

'I'm not surprised. How's my bigamous wife?'

'That was an ill-advised thing that we did. Upset the whole social system of the Picts we have. Bithig's still married to you, she can't have another husband. But they gave the boy a new surname, Votadinus, to show whose son he is. Unusual, that is. Did you know your father's gone home? Amnesty, there was.'

I went round to Otho's house. The porter wouldn't let me in, but I made so much noise it woke the Spanish butler from his mid-morning nap, and he remembered me. He brought me in, and they gave me a bath, with plenty of oil. They scraped me down and got off all the pig fat of the year. The butler brought in clothes, my own clothes.

'Your father left them here when he went back, sir, to the south. He sold up all the slaves, we took one or two over, and we closed up the house.'

'What happened to Ursa?'

'Oh, her brothers came, just after you left, and wanted to buy her back, but your father let her go, for nothing. I heard that she was royal, whatever that may mean, among the Thuringians, but I don't know anything about that.'

I put on my own clothes. It was wonderful to walk with bare legs, like a real human being. I went down to Rudi's tavern. He had prospered, he now had three rooms, different prices, and the terrace outside was for the select customers only. His number five wife was serving. Otho was there, and Aristarchos, and Polycleites, and a young officer named Bion – he was killed the next year, trying to steal horses from Fenris Wolf. I sat down with them, as usual, no greeting. I asked Aristarchos,

'Were those Picts really going to eat me?'

'It was the possibility that mattered, and not the actuality,' he replied. Learning British had had a dreadful effect on his conversation. 'But it made you start moving out, didn't it?'

'What are Amber prices going to do?' asked Otho.

'Up.' I answered. 'There won't be any coming back this year, or for years to come. What you've got, hold on to.'

The girl came with beer and sausages, but I waved her away.

'It's never the same down here as it is out there. Bring me some stuffed olives and wine, real Chian with resin in it, while I make up my mind.'

'All that Amber you sent me back through Fenris in the Spring, I've never seen anything like it,' went on Otho. 'Wagon loads of Amber, worked and unworked, and furs, too. Where did you get it?'

I was ordering. A civilised meal, bread dipped in oil, thin slices of veal fried in oil, roast skylarks on a spit, green beans, fresh figs.

'Not too difficult. Just walk around the villages a bit, you can get it if you pay for it.'

'What are they like, the villages?' asked Bion. 'Are they like this?' He waved his arm at the orderly streets of Vindabonum's German quarter. They were clean, there were no dead dogs in the streets, no piles of manure at the very doors of the houses. I thought of the bustle of a palisade full of Vandals and Saxons and all their horses, of Edwin's hall with the fish nets always drying, of Asgard.

'Yes, just like that, more or less.'

I started on dormice in honey, something I had particularly missed. Aristarchos was silent. Otho went back to the Amber.

'What were prices like? Did you pay much for the Amber?'

I stared into my wine, real island stuff. I saw them all in the cup. I saw the Polyani pour out the beer before the tree. I saw Grude heaved across the bench. I saw the Goth ships row in, and I saw Jokuhai-inen dance the Bear Sacrifice, and I saw the Saxons play the head game. I saw a Vandal packtrain on the road, and I saw the Vandal wedges go up the ridge at the trot. I saw the painted Picts dance for no cause, and I saw the gagged Scrawlings make the Honeydew in the Black Sheds. I saw Edith in the Mother's Cart, and I saw Gambara, furious, seize Hoenir's sword. I saw Bithig in her chariot. I saw Loki at the Table of the Dead and I saw Donar stand between the teeth of the World Serpent.

And I saw Freda, Golden Freda, Freda Goldlover, sit among her maidens in the red and yellow firelight. The wine clouded before my eye, and I saw the smoke from burning Asgard roll foul across my life.

'A fair price,' I said. I closed my good eye too. 'A fair price. I paid it all.'

NOT FOR ALL THE
GOLD IN IRELAND

Gaul

Chapter One

Well, if you really want to know how it was I came to be in that lugger, on a fine reach south-west in a north-west gale, with the north coast of Ireland on my left hand, in company with a Druid, a Colonel of Thracian Cavalry (misemployed), the King and Queen of the Silurians, a Priestess of the Gods Below, to whom I may or may not have been married, and a handful of Brits who alleged they were sailors, then I will tell you.

It all started in my Uncle Euthyphro's house in Ostia, at dinner on a warm spring evening. It began with my Uncle Euthyphro saying:

'Someone will have to get it back. And he may even have to go to Britain to do it.'

I made a face at him. Go to Britain? He might as well have said go to the waters of Lethe. After all, what did any of us know about Britain in those days? It was difficult enough for the ordinary citizen to go there, almost as difficult as getting ashore in Egypt, though of course it was simple to arrange for members of a wealthy family of merchant-priests like mine. But so far nobody in the family had wanted to go there, although we did some trade, in dogs and wool and oysters and mussel pearls. We had an agent in Londinium, and so we didn't need to go ourselves.

Well, what did we know? It was an island where it rained a great deal of the time. A hundred years ago, now, His Sacred Majesty the Emperor Claudius had conquered the fertile southern quarter of the island, where the Brits live, and had left the Northern Desert, as huge as Africa, to the painted Picts, building a wall to keep them out. The Brits, we knew, were the same people as the Gauls, speaking the same language, and the Irish beyond the Empire were the same people also, Many of the nations of the Celts had been broken up long ago, and parts of them lived in both provinces. For instance, the Parisii lived around Lutetia in the north of Gaul, but another branch of them were spread all around the fortress at Eboracum.

The Brits were a strange people, we had heard. Of course we all knew that every third Briton was a magician, and that they had strange things to do with the dead, though quite what nobody was sure. Yet there were plenty of men in Rome who in their youth had served their time as tribunes in the legions in Britain, and they would always tell you how fond they were of their little Brits. You often find this among men who have to go and live among primitive races – they fall in love with their charges. Literally, too. There had even been a few who had talked wistfully of how they would like to live in the island permanently, farming for wool. Going native almost, if only they could find the daughter of some great landowner, once a noble and now a Citizen of Rome, as some were by great and rare good fortune, to marry.

But go to Britain myself? I thought, that evening, in Ostia. Not if I could help it. Somebody else could do that. But there, if you could learn to stand the taste of butter, you could stand anything, and I could eat it without turning a hair. Not that butter would have stood very long, in my uncle's house in Ostia that evening. Nor that it was really very hot, even for the first of May, but it was the last really comfortable evening I was going to have for a long time, though I didn't know it. So it wasn't the heat that made my cousin Philebus sweat. It was the talking-to that his father Euthyphro and I had just given him. All the names in my family follow the same pattern. It all started with my grandfather who had an obsession with philosophy, and believed that a thing partook of its name, that was part of its character. So he called all his sons and grandsons after dialogues of Plato, and I had uncles called Phaedo and Crito too. And if it had not been for my mother, who came from up in the hills and was half Galatian and so had a will of her own, and for the North Wind for whom she had a particular veneration and who therefore kept both my father and my grandfather mewed up in Alexandria for three weeks, I might well have been called Laws or Republic, or even Banquet. But even that might have been better than the name she gave me, Photinus. Neither good Greek nor good Latin, that name, and perhaps Grandfather may have been right in holding that the name governs the character of the thing. I seem to have spent half my life looking for better names. Votan I've been called, and Mannanan, and so many others, and each new name has brought me some kind of profit and some kind of loss, some gain in knowledge, some loss of innocence.

Well, it was quite hot that evening, and the dinner had been quite good, all except the goose liver which had been spoilt, and that was quite easily remedied: we just sold the cook and bought another which improved the general efficiency of the kitchen. I mean, it's not everybody who *wants* to go and work in the sulphur mines, is it? But my cousin Philebus wasn't thinking too much about the food: he had other torments on his mind. I had brought one of the family's ships in that morning, it being the easiest way from the Old City to Rome, where I had a good deal of business to discuss with my uncle. Clearing the port authorities and dealing with all the documents relating to the cargo had taken me well into the afternoon, and I had only got into the house just in time for dinner. I was very tired, and then I had been thrown into the middle of this first-class family quarrel. I felt that before I made any suggestions about future action, I wanted to hear it all again, quietly, this time. My uncle was one of those men who can never forget they aren't at sea.

'Now, Philebus, as I understand it, you bought some kind of monopoly from the Emperor, or rather from one of his Sacred Majesty's Chamberlains.'

'Yes. From Faustinus.'

'And you paid?' I knew it must have been expensive.

'Twenty-five thousand sestertia.' But not as expensive as that, twenty-five million copper sesterces.

'How much ...' I began to ask, and then thought, it was no use now asking how much of that was for Faustinus himself. 'You lost the deed gambling.'

'Three cups and a pea,' nodded Philebus miserably.

'The method is immaterial,' I said consolingly. 'I could take any man alive by that game if I held the cups, and even if I didn't I would never lose a game if only I could count my thumbs. But if you aren't up to my standard, you shouldn't play. Never stake anything of value unless you can cheat, or have enough influence to buy your way out again. But do you remember who it was you were playing with?'

'It was Gwawl. Everybody knows him, even though he's only been around the tables in Rome for a month. He'll play with anybody.'

'That's a strange name. Is he a Greek?'

'Sometimes he says he is, and sometimes he says he's not. Some people think he comes from a Lugdunum Greek family, and you know how Greek *they* are, been there for a couple of hundred years, and intermarried with the Gauls all the time. But if he is from Lugdunum, there's nobody here who knows his family. He might be anything, Gaul, Syrian, Spanish, anything.'

'But look here,' I protested, 'a Monopoly Deed like this isn't a bearer document, not usually. *He* can't use it.'

'He made me sign a transfer deed. He had it all written out ready, and the witnesses as well, waiting. The deed itself was in my name, personal to me. Now it's personal to him.'

'A lawyer, then, is he?'

'No. He lives by his wits, gambling on the Games, mostly.'

From this point on I ignored Philebus. He was grateful for that. I asked his father:

'You've tried to buy it back?'

'He wanted two hundred thousand sestertia.'

'And the monopoly is worth …?'

'I don't know.'

'What do you mean, Uncle, you don't know? You've spent enough of the family's money on it.' I felt I could speak like that to Uncle Euthyphro, I was on equal terms with him, not like Philebus. 'What about the man you took it over from?'

'Well, the truth of the matter is, we weren't taking it over from anybody.'

'Not from anybody? But someone must have had a monopoly of the Gold trade with Britain.'

'Not Britain.' My uncle was almost squirming. 'There's Gold in Ireland. That's what the monopoly was for. Everybody knows there's Gold in Ireland, whatever else they don't know about it.'

I looked so astonished at this that even my uncle noticed it and stopped talking while I got my breath back. I tried to remember what I did know about Ireland, and there wasn't much anybody knew. It is an island, not much smaller than Britain, and it lies thirty miles, or less, from the coast of Britain. It exports hunting dogs, now, and nothing more. Nothing at all. Certainly not Gold. And I had never met anybody who had ever been there. When I got my breath back, visibly, my uncle went on:

'Of course, any Gold you get from there will have to go through Britain, and it will have to come in legally, as there'll be too much to hide. There's no difficulty there. But there's been no Gold coming from Ireland that I can trace since the conquest of Britain. Even what used to come in was all worked up, and very old-fashioned too.'

'So you mean to re-open the trade with Ireland?'

'Well, I was chatting with Faustinus, and I thought it would be good for the lad.' He jerked his head at Philebus, who was trying to corner the world supply of Falernian into his own gullet, that being his best idea of a commercial operation. 'Every boy ought to have a chance to *do* something when he's young: it sets the tone to his own life. I had that long trip south of Leptis Magna, that set the tone for me. I've been thirsty all my life since, and I've passed that on to Philebus. And how long was it ... three years ... four ... you were away up on the Amber Coast? I know it made me, and look what it did for you.'

'Yes, look what it did for me,' I agreed, as he passed me the wine jar in a hurry while there was still some left. 'It turned my hair white in a night, and it took years for it to come back black again. And it gouged my eye out, and nothing will ever bring that back.'

'Nevertheless,' said my uncle, growing a little pompous as the wine jar emptied, 'you will not deny that it gave you a certain confidence in your manner, a certain *élan* in your dealing with the world ...'

'If you mean that I seem to think that the worst has happened to me, then I agree: I think it has. No calamity I precipitate on myself from now on can be as catastrophic as those I have gone through already ...'

'Not merely that. Surely you admit that you learned a great deal from what you experienced?'

'Well, yes. I admit, I did marry two queens, and seduce one, and that taught me to be very wary about Barbarian women. I'll never bother with another one as long as I live. I did reorganise a trading firm, and I sent half Germany money-mad. I made one king and I killed another, and that has taught me to be sceptical about the basis of authority. I led an army in battle, and won, and I made up at least four hundred songs about it that you may hear in any barracks in the Empire where there are German auxiliary cavalry. That taught me to be very wary of what the poets tell us. But on the whole, I think the effect was on the North, and not on me: I remained a Greek, nothing more, nothing less. You think it would have done Philebus some good?'

'Well, I did. I don't think so now. He could never stand the pace, you can see that. Here we are, only two hours at table, and he's out to the vomitorium already. Look what he's got to do now. He's got to get the Deed of Monopoly back first, and that's only the beginning. Someone will have to go to Ireland, and set up a system for getting the Gold over that we can leave an agent to work. The man we've got in Londinium now, for instance, he can do all that, once it's started, but as for the spadework – why, Leo Rufus couldn't organise an orgy in a wholesale slave warehouse. Someone responsible will have to go there.'

'But when you go,' I warned my uncle, 'you will have to leave someone just as responsible here in Rome. I wouldn't like to think of Philebus in charge.'

'Oh, I'm not going. I thought you might.'

I looked at him as bleakly as I could.

'I've done enough travelling up there. I've got a bigamous wife among the Picts, waiting for a chance to eat me the first step I take outside the Empire. And I've a real wife at home in the Old City, and a baby coming in the autumn.'

'You'll be back home by then.' My uncle was a good salesman.

'Well, I suppose … I might as well have a last fling while I have the chance.'

'You've had four last flings to my certain knowledge. This will have to be the very last.'

He blinked at me in a benign way, the look he used when he

232

was selling winded horses as racers. Philebus came back, his face the colour of the sea on a dull day. I asked him:

'Do you feel like going to Faustinus and asking him to cancel that deed and to issue another one?'

The green of his cheeks turned a little paler. He shook his head miserably.

'All right,' I told him, trying to sound kind. 'You can take the ship back instead of me. Have you been to sea before?'

'No.'

'Then there's no way to learn like being in command. The mate is a Galatian, and he's a good sailor, remember that. The supercargo knows what's what, he'll see you through. Then you can tell my father what's happened.'

'Oh no! I couldn't face him.'

'It's him or Faustinus, take your choice. When you've done your sea time, then perhaps we can let you loose on land.'

'But what shall I tell him?'

'Anything you like. Say it was a whim of mine, to go back to the North just once more. The whole voyage is fixed up. Troops to Byblos, cedarwood to Alexandria, corn to Corinth and statuary back here. And if you see my wife, smack her on the backside for me and tell her it had better be a boy, this time. Now, about my business. How's this Gwawl travelling?'

'There's a draft of Illyrians going up to join the Second Augusta in Isca. He's going with them as mule-train boss with the baggage as far as Bonnonia.'

'A man who has to work his passage across Gaul and you gamble with him for all the Gold in Ireland? What on earth was he staking against it – don't answer that! You thought it looked so easy there wasn't a chance of losing, and he probably put down an embroidered cloak or something. Now, Philebus, just you lose my ship like that, and I'll gut you alive, I will. *And* your father will sharpen the knife for me.' I never gave Philebus time to remember that he was only two years younger than I was. However, he might as well feel he could do something useful. I went on:

'You know Rome, you can help to get me started. First of all, send off a courier to our agents in Londinium and Bonnonia, and in all the towns on the way, to say I'm coming. Don't say why, just say I'm on my way, and they're to give me all the credit the family name will bear.

'Next, we'll have a night out in Rome. I want to see this Gwawl so that I recognise him in future, and so that he won't recognise me.

'Last of all, I want a litter and carriers arranged all the way from here to Bonnonia, starting, let's say, next Wednesday, and a bunch of reliable men as escort.'

'Wednesday? But he'll have two days' start then. You'll never catch him before he gets into the Province!'

'I don't want to. If you fancy tackling the baggage-master of a legionary draft when the troops are all around him, go ahead. Let *him* keep the Deed safe. If I can get to Bonnonia before him, I can catch him at sea – alone. Besides, I can have a few days in Lutetia on the way. People keep on telling me about the girls there. And that reminds me ...' a sudden thought had struck me. 'There's another last thing you can do. I want you, Philebus, to go and buy me a girl for the journey, as a parting gift. I bet you know where to go.'

'He does,' said Uncle Euthyphro coldly. 'And he'll pay out of his own money, not out of the family's. Will any woman do?'

'Of course not. Listen carefully, Philebus. I want a woman who doesn't weigh more than a hundred pounds, if she's going to come in the litter with me. For the same reason, she's got to be clean and decent and not too stupid. And the less Latin she speaks the better. You see, I want a Brit.'

That would be difficult, I thought. Nobody in their senses will buy a British slave. There are too many magicians in that island: you don't want to be bewitched overnight and wake up in an ass's head or something. I went on. 'She's got to be miserable and want to go home. If she does what I want, then I'll set her free in Britain when I get there. So make the bill of sale out to me, and put her age down as thirty-five, whatever it really is, or the manumission won't be legal.'

Philebus didn't object to this. He answered:

'I know the very thing. It's what Gwawl was wagering against the Monopoly Deed. And whatever he asks, it will be worth it if you can make him pay for what he did for me.'

Chapter Two

I had my night out in Rome, and another three after that, before I had my good look at Gwawl in a fashionable bathhouse, not at all the kind of place to expect to see the baggage-master, of a legionary mule train. If I'd been Gwawl, I thought, I'd have been a little more careful about the consistency of my disguises. Myself, I decided, I wasn't going to bother about any disguises or fancy dress in Britain.

No, I thought, time and again in those few days, I was going to be just Photinus and nobody else. No more was I going to do anything myself, either. I would have enough agents among the Brits for that. I would just stand aside and plan, and tell the others what to do. And least of all would I have anything more than necessary to do with British women. That was how I had got into trouble in Germany. First I had married a native, and then I had done other things, distilled drink, and organised trade, and even raised an army of my own. No, that personal dealing was over. What others wouldn't or couldn't do for me would remain undone.

My Uncle Euthyphro agreed.

'Just leave it in the hands of the Gods,' he told me. 'But what worries me, my boy, is what Gods? I know that the Unconquered Sun dismissed you from his service. Who do you worship now? The Moon and Stars?'

'No,' I replied, quietly, because it wasn't something I liked discussing. 'As far as I worship anything, I worship the Gods Below. Wherever you go, you find different Gods for this and that. But the Gods Below are the same everywhere.'

By dawn on that Wednesday morning I was glad enough to settle into the nice comfortable litter, and jog off with the curtains drawn against the sun. I hadn't been to bed on Tuesday night at all, and so I was glad of five hours' sleep. We moved at a steady trot, most soothing, with the litter bearers changing every quarter of an hour, so smooth I never noticed it. Our escort came close behind. Big hard men, they were, mule-drivers for the family most of the year, freedmen or freedmen's sons, and their leader was a nasty customer called Marco with a scar from eye to throat. I was glad he was on my side.

When I woke up, I had a good look at the girl Philebus had bought from Gwawl for me. She wasn't very young, she must have been eighteen at least, but she was small built and plump, nearly down to the limit I'd set, though she got fatter as we went. She couldn't have been anything but British with that dark brown hair, nearly black, and those blue eyes, not ice blue like the Germans so often have, but the blue of woodsmoke, soft, lazy but with the fire behind it all the time. She reminded me of my first bigamous wife, Bithig, who had been a queen among the Picts, and who was probably still looking for me. To get away from her, I remembered, we had had to steal a ship belonging to a crusty old man called Caw, whom we sold to Starkadder Eightarms the Pirate. Still I thought, I'll be quite safe, I won't be going within a hundred miles of the Wall.

I looked at the girl in my litter, who didn't really look like Bithig on closer inspection, and asked her what her name was.

'They call me Candida around here.'

'But your real name?'

'Cicva.'

'All right, Cicva. After this morning, we speak not one word of Latin together. Then, if when we land in Britain we find I can pass for a Brit, I shall set you free.'

She didn't like the word Brit, I could see it in her face: they none of them do. To outsiders they call themselves Britons, in full, but to themselves they call themselves Comrades, Cymry. But Brit is the old Army word and I used it when I wanted to. I was paying, wasn't I?

The best way to learn a language is in bed. That was the way I learnt German. I learnt the language of the Brits in a litter, which was almost as good, if not better. We watched the long coast swing by, and I learnt the words for sea and ship and for all

236

the fishes and shell-fish. We turned away from the sea, and I learnt the words for ox and plough and for all the plants that grew.

We turned north at Marseilles and up the Rhone. Coming south, it's much faster and more comfortable to take a boat, but not going north. This is a surprising thing. I saw a map once, hanging on a wall in Alexandria, and it showed quite clearly that Rome is in the centre of the world, and that Africa is at the top, and that Britain and the Land of Norroway are at the bottom, and that is why the greatest rivers of the world, the Nile and Rhine, flow downhill to the north. So going north ought to have been easier than it was, but if the Rhone flows in the face of nature, then perhaps the road does the same thing.

A little way before Lugdunum we caught up with the legionary draft. Of course they got off the road to let us through. It's wonderful what a show of money will do when you're travelling. I walked by the litter with Marco, and Cicva peeped out through the curtains. I pointed Gwawl out to them. Marco asked:

'Shall we kill him tonight?'

'No, no! I want him alive as far as Bonnonia. He's got something I want, and we'll let him worry about looking after it. We'll pass them and have a few days in Lutetia.'

I got back into the litter. I asked Cicva:

'Did you see him?'

'Of course. Why *can't* we kill him tonight? We could take all night over it.'

'You sound as if you want to kill him personally.'

'I do. If it weren't for him I wouldn't have been kidnapped and sold down here.' She wouldn't tell me anything more about it. She wouldn't say what part of the island she came from, or who her people were. This was unusual. Most of these girls are only too eager to assure you that they would be princesses if only they had their rights. But she wouldn't say a thing.

We stopped a little way further up, to have a midday snack at a tavern, and the handful of officers going up with the draft, and riding ahead of it to keep out of the dust, stopped there as well. I called them over to join us. We had various mutual acquaintances. I asked after Aristarchos the son of Demons. Last I heard of him, I told them, he'd been commanding a regiment of cavalry at Carnuntum.

'All Brits they were, too,' I remembered. 'What were they called? Hadrian's Own Danube Rangers?'

'Oh, the Wall-eyed Warriors,' said one of the centurions. The legions are always glad to make fun of the cavalry. 'But he's left those now. I don't know where, but I think it was a promotion.'

They asked after Philebus – I hadn't realised he was such a rake.

'He's well at sea by now,' I told them, and they all laughed again – they could afford to, I was paying for the wine.

'Better to travel like you with all home comforts,' someone said waving at Cicva, who had brought us some cheese she had been bargaining for in the village. Like all the Brits she was a connoisseur of cheese, and Gaulish was near enough to British, as even I could tell by now, to let her hold her own in the market.

'I've got to have someone to watch my blind side,' I told them – I had a quite tasteful false eye in that day, of jet, carved in concentric circles – and the officers hooted with laughter and tried to pinch her bottom without my seeing it, and they were in great good humour when the mule train came swinging up the road and Cicva ran off to hide her blushes in the kitchen.

I pointed to Gwawl. I said:

'Now there's a real old-fashioned mule-driver for you. Where did you find him?'

'Oh, that one,' they all said at once. 'He's a bad one, he is. Even his own family wouldn't own him, wherever they are. A Brit, you know, and one of the nastier ones. Good little fellows, but every now and again you find one like him. Usually, though, they have red hair. You've got to watch out for the red-haired ones.'

I looked again at Gwawl. His hair was black, and tight curled, and it bristled on his thick forearms, with the sinews knotted and corded under the skin. When I had seen him in the baths, I had only thought him gross, the kind of man who sits down in a tavern and then picks up his belly in his hands and puts it on the table. But now he had fined down with the long march, and he just looked big. He was as tall as I am, but he weighed at least

238

half as much again, I'm sure. I looked down at myself, and I took the hint.

After that, I used to get out of the litter for a part of each day and walk with Marco, much to the relief of the bearers. By the time we got to Lutetia I could walk the whole twelve hours of daylight, and that in the early summer, with my bag over my shoulder, and never want to stop once for a rest. We passed beneath the ruined walls of Alesia, that great fortress of the Gauls. Caesar had tumbled the ramparts and hacked the gates from their hinges. And the Lord of Alesia, that great king, who might have reigned as Emperor over all the Gauls of the world from Britain to Galatia, great Vercingetorix, long dead now, dead and thrown into the sewer. But there was no weeping, even for Cicva, over that old dream, no singing that old song again. There was no stopping till we reached Lutetia.

We had a few splendid days in Lutetia. We quartered ourselves on the family's agent, a man called Julius Macrinus, who had a very pleasant house on the south side of the island, looking on to the river. It was a really delightful time, and even today I occasionally meet people who remember it. The girls ... the drink ... the food ... surprising when you consider the reputation the place has for being a sad and strict town. There's no culture in Lutetia to speak of, no art or anything else to turn an honest penny over, which may be one reason why it's getting so prosperous.

Then one morning, while everyone else, muleteers and all, were sleeping off the last and most outrageous party, Marco and Cicva and I took horses and rode off to Bonnonia.

Chapter Three

We moved in on our agent in Bonnonia. He was even more embarrassed to see us than Macrinus had been. He was expecting an important Greek businessman, somebody used to dealing in millions and bargaining with the Governors of Provinces, and that of course he got. But he didn't expect me, with a variety of false eyes to suit my moods and hair all over – I had let it grow, beard and all, on the way up from Rome. And he got Marco, who had a scar across his face that turned his eye outwards, so that the milder he was feeling the more brutal he looked. Cicva was the most respectable of the three of us, to look at. I'd given her some money to get dressed up with in Lugdunum, and you know what Lugdunum fashions are. Then she'd had them altered to her own taste in Lutetia, and we all know the Parisii have no sense of how to dress. She ended up looking like an only moderately successful whore.

Marco was quite happy. He was anchor man, which suited him. He was to see that everyone was contented in Bonnonia after I left. He knew perfectly his place in my plan. The only trouble was that I hadn't got a plan. I had a vague idea that nothing would come right till I had a ship. I had to go and find one.

On the second night in Bonnonia I took out of my baggage an old grey cloak with a hood. I put it on, and went out. Marco followed me. He kept a few yards behind me, and when I went into a tavern he would stand by the door, just inside, making it clear that I wasn't alone.

The first tavern I went into – I was choosing the less reputable ones, the ones down by the quay, where the clientele would be sailors, and not the most respectable sailors either – well, the first one I went into, I called for drinks all round. While everybody was drinking my health – and after the long journey, and the nights in Lutetia, I needed some attention to my health – I stood

240

by the bar counter, and I drew idly in the sawdust of the floor with my toe. I drew a face, at least a circle with eyes and a mouth, and eight lines sticking out of it like arms, and to each arm I gave a hand holding some kind of weapon, an axe or a sword. Nobody took the slightest notice. I finished my beer and moved on.

I did precisely the same in the next tavern I came to. Again nobody seemed to take the slightest notice, except for the man next to me. He dipped his finger in a puddle of beer and drew a fish on the bar counter. He looked at me meaningly, which was difficult with the squint he had, and then quickly rubbed it out again. I didn't know anything about that, so I just said:

'And mackerel to you, brother,' in Gaulish, and moved on to the next tavern.

But when I got into the third tavern, I only had time to draw the circle, when someone took me by the elbow, and drew me away. I looked at him. He seemed familiar, somehow. Perhaps he had been in the other taverns and had run on in front of me. Perhaps I had met him before, sometime, on the Amber Road. He was a big man and yellow-haired, his face smeared with pig fat against the salt wind. He steered me across to a booth at the back of the room. Marco stayed by the door and watched.

The men at the back of the room were all sailors, and all dressed as Friesians. I turned back the edge of my hood, and let them see the patch over my eye. Nobody said anything. They put a big horn of beer in front of me, the kind of vessel you use in drinking matches. The beer was strong, dark and sweetish. I drained it at one long, slow draught. It nearly killed me. I was out of practice. Then one of the sailors asked in the Germans' tongue – he must have been a Dane from his dialect:

'You are looking for Starkadder Eightarms?'

'And if I were?' I lifted the eyepatch and let him have the full benefit of the emerald I was wearing in the empty socket. I had it carved by a man I know in the Piraeus. I will give you his name if you like. It showed, tiny but clear, the wolves dancing around a tree, a tree with a man in it. I listened to his reply.

'Then I would tell you, that he is at the other end of the Shallow Sea, harrying the Fenni.'

'And Alfhilda Vikarsdaughter, his wife?'

'With him. Where else should she be but with him?'

'And Caw? Where is Caw?'

'Gone, long gone. Who knows where?'

'Smuggling lead,' I told them. 'Let's have some more beer, and no half measures this time.'

And we did. Everybody got quite talkative in a secretive way. They were all painting ludicrous pictures of Caw swimming the Channel to Britain with a pig of lead under each arm in case he sank, and the whole atmosphere of the tavern became a good deal easier. We drank a good deal more. More Germans came in: soon there were about a score of them. By the time we started singing 'Sweyn, the Bastard King of Scania', the few respectable customers left. The landlord didn't object: he was singing too.

The Germans were all sorts. About half of them *were* Friesians or Batavians, but the rest were Saxons and Thuringians by their accents, and Goths, and even a Lombard. This last was rather stupid. He couldn't understand the subtleties of travelling incognito as quickly as the others, and once he called me 'All father' quite openly, and all the others shushed him. But every man was a sailor, just the kind you would expect with Starkadder.

I got into a corner with a few of the most prominent. The others were trying to make Marco drunk, and I could have told them they had little chance of succeeding. I asked the leader, who had first taken my arm, his name. He did his best to play the Friesian, but if his accent was anything to go by, he was a Goth. He said:

'Call me Bert.'

I asked the next man.

'I'm Bert too.'

'Just the same as him?'

'Just the same. We're all Bert, just call us Bert.'

Well, perhaps it's better not to have a name anyone can tell you by if you're in their trade. None of them asked my real name. They thought they knew it. Why should I know theirs? They only wanted to know my business that night, and whether it was the same as theirs was every night.

I was right. They *were* some of Starkadder's men, who had brought a prize down from the Shallow Sea, and now they were waiting for Starkadder to come back for them. Meanwhile, they were willing to try anything which would turn a profit and not make Roman ports too dangerous for them. After all, Starkadder had to have somewhere safe to winter in, and refit, and sell what he stole in the North. This was what I was looking for.

'There's a man coming here soon,' I told them. 'I want him—'

'Dead?' interrupted Lombard Bert, hopefully.

'No!' I answered, a little crossly. 'He wants to go to Britain. I want him to go to Britain – but òn my ship. And with me in it. And I want him to have a nice quiet game of dice or something on the way. But I haven't got a ship.'

'Anybody we know?' asked Goth Bert.

'A man called Gwawl.'

'Oh, him,' said Lombard Bert: I said he was rather stupid, and his talents, though considerable in their way, were limited in their scope. 'I can kill him easy. I haven't killed anybody for weeks.'

'If you don't keep quiet,' Goth Bert grumbled at him, 'I'll take that flaming axe of yours and throw it in the dock.' He turned back to me. 'So you want a ship?'

'And a crew I can rely on.'

'And one that Gwawl can't rely on.' Goth Bert followed my drift perfectly. A Batavian Bert came in with the crucial question:

'How much are you offering?'

'How much do you want? What's the regular rate around here?'

After that, it was only a matter of haggling. Hard cash for the crew; for the ship, I guaranteed a cargo both ways at four times the usual rates, wine out and hides back. That was to Londinium, but of course, I myself would leave the vessel when she cleared the customs at Rutupiae.

The Berts had two ships, prizes they'd not yet sold, and I went to look at them next day. One was very fine, a Gothship, sleek and beautiful and fast, twenty rowers a side. And the finish, wonderful! It made you open your eyes at the very thought of the kind of craftsmen they had up there in the North, doing everything, as I knew, with axe and adze and no other tools, no saws or chisels for them. I'd always wanted to have one of those ships under me. I didn't take her, quite unsuitable.

The other was a Friesian, comfortable and roomy, as broad as she was long, or at least she looked it. She was decked, and under the poop where there was enough headroom for a man to stand she had quite a cosy cabin. She set the one big square sail, and there were sweeps for the times when there was no wind, and that was rare enough up in the North. I took her, but that was the next day.

That first night, we had a real party. We had lots of singing and embracing and rubbing of cuts-together to mix blood, and I got Marco to join in that. One of the hardest things I had to do was to keep Marco feeling happy, since he couldn't understand a thing I said to the Germans. And then before the feast got too unruly, I bawled out:

'I'll give ten gold pieces for a sword!'

'Not on shore,' said Goth Bert. 'It's a hanging matter here to carry a sword, unless you have a licence, and I've never met a man yet who has.'

'Well I have,' I told him. 'A general licence, from the Emperor's Chancery, to carry a sword anywhere in the Empire, in defence of my goods.' And that's what a bit of influence does for you, that and a name for quite fair dealing all across the Mediterranean Sea.

'Even so,' went on Goth Bert, 'they're strict here. The Port Captain, he winks at what we've got in the ships, but we mustn't bring any weapons ashore. If you wait till we get aboard, I dare say we can fit you out.'

'I doubt it,' I told him. 'I want a Sax, a good one, well shaped, curved no more than the bow of a ship. A back edge thick as my thumb, the bone-breaker. The fore edge like a razor, the mailsplitter. Point like a needle, the heart-piecer. And I want an Ingelri.'

For Ingelri was the greatest swordsmith of all Germany, and his blades were like no others. They were all silent for a few moments, and one murmured, a fat man he was, that ten gold pieces wouldn't do it, no, nor twenty either, seeing it meant going across the Rhine. But in seven days he himself came to me with a Sax, a splendid one, but for one thing – he couldn't get an Ingelri in the time, he had had to make do with an Elfbert. Of course, to those who know their iron, this was almost as good, for Elfbert was Ingelri's apprentice, and if his swords had a fault

244

it was that he tended to make them a little heavier towards the point than need be.

There was no hilt to this sword, of course, just the blade and the tang with the iron pommel at the end. We took it to a sword-smith in the town, who did a lot of work for Officers of the Garrison. First he had to be satisfied I had a right to own the weapon, and then he looked at the quality of the iron, and his eyes glistened. He asked me if I had any preference in the form of the hilt. I said no, provided he made a showy job of it. And if he knew of a goldsmith, then he could melt down these coins, and set in it – and I took them out of my wallet – these stones, garnets and emeralds and a blue sapphire, and a here was a big ball of crystal.

It took him some days. He beat out the tang into ridges in the shape of an X, and instead of beechwood or horn, as is usual, he made the grip of walrus ivory, carved and weighted to fit my hand. Then, with the Gold, he ornamented the arms of the X to look like a man, spreadeagled, and the gems set in to point off his clothes, and the great ball of crystal where the head should be. A sword it was now fit for any of the great Kings of ancient Gaul, for Vercingetorix or for Dumnorix, or for Brennus himself to throw in a balance and make the insolent Romans pay.

But as for a scabbard, he told me to keep it in the plain wooden sheath, covered in leather, that Fat Bert brought it to me in. He insisted that he was the finest hilt-maker in the world – but his equal in the company of scabbard-makers lived in Londinium, and even if I were not going there, it would be worth the journey to have a scabbard made to match the hilt. He gave me the name.

I put the bill in to the family. So far this chase had cost about eleven thousand sestertia, what with buying Cicva (because I couldn't let Philebus pay for that, after all), the journey up, hir-ing the ship and crew, and all the expense of making sure that when Gwawl arrived in Bonnonia he would find no ship but mine willing to take him. This wasn't so expensive as you might think, because he had been in the town before, and everybody he had met on that occasion seemed to bear him a hearty dislike, though why I could not find out. Still, all this was a little cheaper than the two hundred thousand Gwawl had asked for in the first place. Or it would be, if I could catch him.

I asked Goth Bert where people usually went to ask about Channel passages, and he told me about a tavern called the Capricorn. We went there and arranged to take the whole place over the night Gwawl arrived in Bonnonia. At least, we told the landlord we were taking it over.

'And if you object,' Lombard Bert told him, 'I'll bash your bloody head in with my axe. I haven't killed anybody for days.' Even he had his moments of usefulness. The landlord agreed.

I spent a long time letting Cicva know exactly what she had to do.

'When he gets here, I want you to be ready and dressed up in the Capricorn. You'll want some of those clothes I bought you in Lutetia, that's just the right touch, ornate and flashy but a year or two behind the fashion. Now with your hair piled up on top and dyed yellow … No? All right, then, dress as you please as long as you think he won't know you. The most favourable thing is that he won't expect to see you. Are you quite sure, then, that you can handle Gwawl?'

'Yes, as long as I don't have to sleep with him. I don't *have* to sleep with him, do I?'

'That's up to you, dear. If you can manage without, so much the better. Don't let him have any profit or pleasure out of this that we can avoid.'

'I don't want to. I don't like him. I mean, as well as hating him. I don't like him either. I like you, Photinus. Why don't you try to sleep with me?'

'Because I don't do that sort of thing with every pretty girl I get hold of.'

'What will you do when you finish the hyena hair?' And that was a clever question. As you know, all you need do if you are a rake and worried about it is to take some hair of a hyena, and burn it to ash, and mix the ash with grease to form an ointment. Then you rub it in … that is … you rub it well in, anyway, and immediately your whole conduct changes. You stop running after women, you work harder, and get awfully staid, and everybody says what a reliable and respectable citizen you are now. Well, it may be good for trade, but who wants to live like that? And besides, the smell of the ointment – no wonder you can't get anyone to sleep with you in that state. So I said to Cicva:

'And why should I sleep with a pretty girl like you, with a wife and a baby at home?'

And that was more like the truth of it, that and my determination not to sleep with any more barbarian women, or even to speak to them more than was absolutely necessary, not like the last time I was in the North. It only gets you into the most appalling trouble.

Phryne was enough for me, I thought. I had come home from the Amber Road to find that my grandmother had arranged it all. I must admit she was not very exciting in her mild, submissive, Mediterranean way. And she had no mind at all, really, almost illiterate, and not the slightest inkling of what was going on anywhere outside her own kitchen. It made no difference to her whether I said I was off to Rhodes or to Gades or to Ultima Thule, they were all just the same to her, all vaguely somewhere 'away'. Still, she let me hold the little girl sometimes, and that was more than anyone had let me do before. And now there was another child on the way, in the early autumn, and this ought to be a boy – I had done all the right things, sprinkled the bed with the pollen of the male date flower, and turned it with the head to the North, and made Phryne eat parsnips and myself gorged on orchid roots till we were both sick.

Besides, though I flattered Cicva, she was not really very attractive to me, except in the face, for she was short, and heavy hipped. I like women that are tall and slender.

Anyway, I thought then, I ought to be back home by the autumn. The summer ought to see me into Ireland, to arrange terms of trade with whatever king controlled the Gold mines, and then at once back through Gaul to Ostia and a ship back home to the Old City. That's what I thought then. But first of all, I had to get the Deed of Monopoly back from Gwawl, and pass it on to the family's agent in Londinium.

Settling with Gwawl was all worked out in my mind now. It's fascinating how these problems solve themselves once you start to think about what resources you have and how they can be used. Now we had covered every possible variant. We knew how to deal with Gwawl loitering, Gwawl in a hurry, Gwawl early, Gwawl late, Gwawl drunk, Gwawl sober, Gwawl angry, Gwawl pleased. Marco and Goth Bert and I planned and planned, while Cicva looked for hours at a time into a mirror and tried on her wigs and painted her face in a thousand different ways. It kept us all happy while we waited for the draft to arrive.

One of Marco's Spaniards came into Bonnonia two hours ahead of Gwawl. There was another man following him, in case he changed his mind and went to another port. The legionaries had gone into a camp outside the town and cooled their feet a while. The mule-drivers cooled their throats, scorched raw by the language they had been using all the way from Rome on their treacherous beasts. But Gwawl came on into the town. You could spot him a mile off in his black and white shirt, striped from neck to hem. It was a Gaulish shirt. They like bright colours, and the more colours, and the more complex the pattern of stripes and checks, the better. And the Brits wear their shirts the same way, hanging down over their trousers loose to the buttocks, not down to the knees as a civilised man wears his tunic over his bare legs, or tucked short into the trousers at the waist as all the Germans do.

Gwawl just came straight into the Capricorn. It was the easiest thing and the simplest you could imagine. It was obvious he wasn't expecting to meet any danger at all, not as long as I kept out of sight. I wasn't in the bar, I watched from the kitchen – when you have only one eye, a very narrow crack is enough to look through.

In the bar, Gwawl found only a crowd of sailors very obviously having one for the Channel, and a blowsy woman with an empty basket. Cicva had done well with her face painting, and her wig – she could have passed for thirty easily, and did so in the dim lamplight. But you can never trust a woman – instead of the fine Roman dress I had got her in Lutetia, she wore a scarlet blouse in the British manner. And beneath that, she wore the ten or twelve petticoats the women up there delight in, each one a different colour and, if possible, a different material for each, cotton if you could afford it, and linen, and wool. Over the top one she had a linen apron, with lace frills at the edges, and over that a broad belt of red wool, embroidered with flowers, and fastened with a big bronze brooch. Her shawl, over her shoulders, had also cost a good deal of money, for it had a fringe of red tassels, and I thought then, from the little I knew, that Cicva had ideas about rank that were quite beyond her – only noblewomen among the Brits wore such elaborate shawls. And little, indeed, I knew. But if all this finery, justified or not, caught Gwawl's eye, it was worth the expense.

Gwawl bought something to drink, and then looked round. It was obvious that Goth Bert was the Captain: he was drinking two to his crew's one. Gwawl began to haggle for a passage. When they were nearly settled, Cicva put her arm around Gwawl's shoulder and said beerily:

'That's right, boy, you come in my little boat with me!'

'Clear off!' Gwawl shouted at her. 'Find your own bunk and someone else to pay for it!'

It was clear that he sensed some subtle double meaning in her words, that a respectable woman would never have intended. And Cicva resented that.

'You Syrian by-blow,' she told him, not loud or shrill, just quietly nasty. 'You big slob. Who do you think you're talking to?'

Cicva had a good vocabulary now in both Greek and Latin, as well as British and Gaulish, and a few choice phrases of doubtful provenance that Goth Bert had taught her, in every dialect of German from the Alps to the ends of the Shallow Sea. She used them all.

Here she was, she said between the profanity, sold her embroidery and trouble enough it was buying it up on her other side of the water to bring it across to peddle here, and not much profit she made on it either, not more than three or four hundred per cent, after all her expenses were paid, and now home it was she was going, with her passage paid and a purse full of money in her apron, and if Gwawl didn't appreciate her company he might as well wait for another boat, and the Gods only knew when that would be, the way trade was going in these days. And Gwawl heard Fat Bert say that that was right, and who did he think he was, talking like that to a decent woman who travelled with them every month punctual as the moon, and why should he bother about a casual stranger who had insulted an old-established customer. Lombard Bert said he hadn't killed anybody for weeks, and nobody told him to keep quiet.

Just as I began to think they might be overdoing it, Gwawl swallowed what was left of his beer and his words together, and bought three rounds, one after the other, for everyone in the place, Cicva included. Goth Bert put the passage money up by another half, and Gwawl agreed to it without any further argument, seeing himself at a distinct disadvantage and him in a hurry, too.

Lombard Bert picked up Gwawl's bag to take it down to the ship at once. I slipped out the back way and followed him. We whiled away the time of waiting by sitting on the forecastle and going through the bag, but there was nothing there of any interest to me, though the Berts earmarked several things for future distribution. When we finished I repacked the bag in something like the same order, and began rubbing pig fat in my face as a protection against the salt wind, which burns it otherwise. Lion fat is much better, but I couldn't find any in Bonnonia.

After we had arranged Gwawl's belongings to our satisfaction, I strolled on the quayside and looked at the ship. There is nothing as beautiful as a ship, even a clumsy broad-beamed tub like the *Gannet*, as the Berts had renamed her. When she was in the North I suppose she had been called something like 'Fleet Wind from the Ice', rather on my grandfather's principle that she would partake of the qualities of her name. She was a good ship, nothing remarkable, but reliable and sturdy. We would have to sweep her out of the harbour, but once we were clear of the land there was a wind from the south-west, just right for Britain.

Gwawl was a long time in coming. I went back into the ship, and I looked at Bonnonia. The full round moon flooded the shore with a bright pale light, so that the patches of shadow were as dark as a bottomless pit. I thought that it was like the good hard noonday sun of the South, that has no half measures. Either a thing is in the dark and cannot be known, or it is out in the pitiless light and cannot be hidden. I sat on the bulwark with my legs dangling and looked at Gaul, a familiar land of wine and olive, where everything was what it was, where a mule-driver was a mule-driver and a pirate was a pirate, and a slave girl only a slave girl. That was the last I knew for many a day of clarity and single-mindedness and fixity of meaning. For the wind was right for the misty island of Britain.

Chapter Four

It was an hour or so after sunset, then, on that evening at the end of May, when Goth Bert and Cicva brought Gwawl down to the quay – or, to be more accurate, before Cicva and Gwawl carried Goth Bert down to the quay. The delay had done us no harm, because we had to wait for the tide, but as it was we barely had time to take the three aboard and cast off. Gwawl and Cicva went into the cabin under the poop. I squatted on the deck above their heads, next to the steersman, and the crew rigged the sweeps. Goth Bert joined me. When I realised how much beer he had drunk I persuaded him to lie down while I took the ship out myself. It was a good thing the steersman knew the channel.

After a little while, when we were nearly clear, Goth Bert came to his senses again and I let him have his ship back. I lay down myself on the deck, with my ear to a knot-hole, and I could hear most of what went on in the cabin. I heard Cicva:

'It's a long trip. I always get bored. How about a little game to pass the time away?'

I didn't hear Gwawl answer for a while. He was still a bit drunk, and I hoped that he wouldn't be sea-sick: there wasn't much wind, really, and the ship was now doing that horrible motion like a screw. Then there was a slight scuffle in the cabin – that showed he wasn't *too* sick – and a bit of giggling and squeaking.

'Not *that* kind of game!' Cicva told him sharply, but not too sharply, not wishing to cut him short altogether. 'There are too many people about.'

There were, too. We had twenty-eight men in that ship, besides the two in the cabin, and it was a problem where to put them all. But at least they were sailors and didn't get in each others' way. Fat Bert suggested towing Lombard Bert behind on a line. This provoked a good deal of horseplay between the men

251

who weren't at the sweeps, and when I could listen again Gwawl was saying:

'… and then you guess which cup the pea is under.'

'Oh yes,' said Cicva, 'I have heard of it. Find-the-Lady, they do call it where I was brought up.'

Now, I never heard it called that before, which shows how limited even a Master's knowledge can be, and myself the greatest Lady-finder of them all. Gwawl added, deceptively offhand:

'Of course, you have to bet something on it to make it worth the while playing …'

And then I couldn't hear for quite a time, because Goth Bert had them ship the sweeps and set the sail, bringing her round into the breeze, which was beginning to freshen a little. When all the shouting and running had stopped, I could hear Cicva sounding clumsily coy and not being very good at it.

'We call it "Strip-Glyn-Naked". Every time you lose a turn, you take another garment off.'

Gwawl was very clever and played hard to persuade, but I could hear the prurient lust bubbling in his voice. For myself, I was getting a little worried, because I had planned for Cicva to do it all in one or two passes. But you can never trust a woman to stick to a plan. It was Gwawl, I thought, who needed the hyena hair, and Cicva played him like a fish when he thought he was playing her.

First of all, of course, he let her win. She had his cloak. Then, though he didn't realise it, she let him win. He won her apron, and her shawl, and her cap, a flat padded cap that the women there wear to carry tubs of shellfish on their heads. I was a little worried in case she took her wig off with her cap, but it all went well. She let him take all these with little squeaks of protest. Then she went to work.

All those weeks in the litter, Cicva had studied the game of the pea and the three cups with the greatest Master of the Art alive, the greatest Master of all time, that is to say, with myself. I had also got her to a fair stage of dexterity with the finger game, and she could palm and switch dice as if she were a magician born, and by this time I was beginning to wonder if that were not what she was. Now this was the first time that Cicva had played against

252

anyone but myself: it was, in fact, the first time she had played against anyone of inferior natural talent to herself.

She just cleaned him out. On each turn, she had him staking another garment against the ones he had already lost. By the local rules where Cicva came from, and to which she insisted on playing, talking Gwawl down in a shrill torrent, she nominated the garment. First of all she regained her own clothes. Then one by one she took tunic and shirt and trousers and shoes. When she pointed to his belt, which had a big pouch on it, I heard him cry in an anguished voice:

'No, no, you can't take that. A belt is not a garment. Who will recognise me without my belt? You can't make me gamble on that!'

We were prepared for trouble at this stage, and Bert Long-nose, who had looked in to see if they wanted any more beer, said:

'Do what the lady says. You started it.'

Bert Longnose was a very long thin man with a long thin evil face, and he had Lombard Bert's axe in his hand, by accident, it seemed. So Gwawl put the belt on the table, and did what he could with the look of a drowning man. When Cicva had won it – she was working the cups now – she flicked it onto the deck of the cabin, and Bert Longnose heeled it out behind him through the leather curtain that served as a door. In a moment I was looking through the great wad of vellum by the light of the forecastle lamp.

I had to read through the whole of the Monopoly Deed to make certain that all the pages were there, six of them, and to be sure there was no delicate knife-work and no clever alterations and improvements. The Deed of Transfer was on one sheet, with my cousin Philebus' signature at the bottom. There were also a number of other documents of interest, letters of introduction from bankers in Rome to bankers in London, and, quite intri-guing, some to the Commander of the Second Legion, who seemed to be in debt all over the place.

I took the Deed of Transfer into the waist, where one of the lesser Berts had a brazier alight on a sand tray, and we fried eggs and bacon over the parchment towards dawn. The moon had gone now, and so had the stars, and there was thick mist rolling around us. I was glad I had put on a pair of the Gaulish trousers I had bought in Lutetia: tunic and bare legs may be civilised and gentlemanly, but they're not for the sea in the North. Gaulish trousers – and British ones are the same – have wide bottoms to the legs, and they are easy to roll up when you're walking through the swamps of that rained-on land: in fact, in the far West, you may even see the old men, who do not care about fashion, walking about in trousers cut off a little below, or even above, the knee. German trousers, of course, you will know, are tapered to fit tight and snug around the ankle, and in my opinion are quite unsuited to a maritime life: but the Berts all wore them, however impractical.

When it was really light, Cicva came out of the cabin and sat with us eating, and peering through the mist trying to see the coast of Britain. Several times the Berts all agreed that they saw it, though I could have sworn it was just more mist. Gwawl didn't join us.

'Oooh! That *was* a night,' said Cicva, when she had finished her breakfast, licking the fat off her fingers in a lady-like way. She stretched and blinked. 'I hope that was what you wanted.'

'Perfect. I trust you didn't leave him anything.'

'Not a sausage. And I didn't give him what he was looking for, either. But I did give him an old apron to make him look decent. It was white, once, and I drew a black stripe on it with pitch, both sides, so he ought to be satisfied.'

'Can I kill him now?' asked Lombard Bert. 'I haven't killed anybody for – Hey! Come back! Bring it back!'

Goth Bert went up on the forecastle, and threw the axe with a splash into the water. Lombard Bert screamed things after him that even Cicva knew to be obscene.

'Waste of a good axe,' I observed.

'Oh, no,' Fat Bert assured me. 'It's on a line. We'll haul it out by dinner-time and sell it back. We often have to do it.'

Lombard Bert's curses were interrupted by some even more horrible cursing, and in a wider variety of languages. Gwawl had come out on to the poop, and was standing looking down at us in the waist. He was only wearing the apron for a breech clout, but he was by no means cold in the clammy air. He was aglow with rage.

'I ought to have known that your family was behind all this,' he shouted at me. 'Where's my clothes? Where's the money? Give me back my clothes! Give me back my letters!'

'Not likely!' Cicva was happy, taking off her wig and wiping the paint from her face with Gwawl's best shirt. 'I won it all, fair enough.'

'How much did she get?' asked Fat Bert in an innocent interested way.

'Every penny. She's cheated me out of every penny I had.'

'In that case,' ruled Goth Bert, who tried to sound like the captain sometimes, 'you can't pay your fare, can you? Chuck him over the side!'

And so they would have done, but Cicva asked, being soft-hearted, like all women:

'Have you got a spare boat? Cheap?'

Of course, they had, a round skin boat like the Picts use.

'How much?' she asked them.

'How much had he got?' they chorused. Cicva counted out all Gwawl's money, which only came to three denarii in silver and a few coppers.

'Just right,' they said, 'but a paddle is extra.'

So for a paddle she gave them his clothes to share out, and that was worth having, because he had bought a lot of good tunics in Rome, and he had also picked up several pairs of Gaulish trousers in Lutetia. His best cloak they very generously put aside to take back for Marco, Goth Bert insisting on that. Those two scoundrels were already on very intimate terms of understanding, and I was afraid it might eventually turn out to their mutual advantage, as long as neither of them was hanged.

We put Gwawl into the skin boat, and passed him down the paddle. Someone wanted to give him a knife, too, to cut his throat with, but when I pointed out that he couldn't pay for it they all remembered what a dreadfully unlucky thing it is to give a knife as a gift: a free gift of a knife always cuts friendship, they told him.

But we did give him a jar of beer, and a loaf of bread, and we left him the salmon mallet to scare the birds with. We gave him a lot of good advice, too, like, 'Britain's that way', or, 'A fortnight to Jutland if you paddled hard.'

We weren't so far from that elusive shore either. The Berts kept on pointing it out, but it all looked like mist to me, even though Cicva suddenly said that she could see a man holding a white shield. At that we pushed him off, and sailed away, leaving Gwawl sitting in his little boat, cursing us to the ends of all the world till we lost his voice far off in the mist.

Chapter Five

In fog there is no wind, or very little wind, and it was the drift of the waves and Gwawl's paddling that carried him out of sight of us. It got thicker. It is hard to tell at sea, but I do not think we could have seen anything fifty paces away, if there had been anything to see, or anything to pace on. We just sat there in the damp, soaking mist and waited for it to clear. We kept quiet. You never know who may not be about in fog.

About the middle of the morning we heard a ship. It went by close, but not close enough to be seen. It was a big one, I should have said by the noise, thirty oars a side. They were paddling and listening by turns, you know how. A long stroke, and then lie back on your oars while you count up to eight … nine … ten … and then the hammer falls for the next stroke. And in between the strokes the only noise is the hiss of the water under your forefoot, and you have time to listen for other oars in the mist, or men talking or laughing.

No one in the other ship talked or laughed. We only heard the oars. It might have been a Roman warship out looking for pirates, but Goth Bert thought it unlikely, and he ought to know. Cicva slipped into the cabin, and an awful lot of swords appeared from unlikely places. Someone gave Lombard Bert his axe back, free. We were safe enough, really. With twenty-nine of us altogether, counting Cicva with her cooking knife, in the old tub, there wasn't really room enough for a boarder to get on to the deck, let alone do any mischief. However I was glad nobody had tried it.

By the time the long-spaced oar-beats had died away into the wet mist, I had had enough.

'All right!' I shouted. 'Get the sweeps rigged.'

'Oh, no, not that again,' everyone said in horror, and someone suggested, 'Why don't *you* whistle for a wind?'

'That I won't. It's more trouble than it's worth, and I'm out of whistle. We'll sweep her – that is, you'll sweep her.' They still argued till I bellowed, loud as any wind, 'Who's chartered this barge, anyway?'

Then they got out the long sweeps, two a side, three men to an oar, and worked in ten-minute relays, grumbling that this wasn't what they had turned pirate for in the first place, and this was the penalty for descending to honest charter work. But they worked, all the same. We took a free vote on which way was north-east, and in that direction we made, I suppose, about half a Roman mile in the hour. I stood on the poop and gossiped with Goth Bert, who had made a study of his profession, about the general superiority of oars over sail, if only you can find enough men willing to row.

'But that's the trouble,' he told me. 'You can't get free men to do it, not in merchant ships. Has anyone tried using slaves? You must have done it, down there in the Mediterranean. You can always teach us a thing or two about the use of manpower.'

'It's not worth it,' I assured him. 'I've not seen it done in ships, but when you have a gang on a mill, pushing the windlass around all day, you have to keep them chained night and day, and you have the most dreadful trouble with sanitation. If you do that in a ship, you'll have the slaves dying off like flies.'

He agreed, and added: 'Besides, if you're boarded, with slaves you have fifty or sixty men you can't arm. Real rowers fight.' He changed his tone. 'Look! It's getting a bit thinner up there.'

It was, too. In another half-hour, it was quite clear and there we were, not half a mile out of Rutupiae. There was enough breeze to hoist the sail and start unshipping the sweeps – we had been rowing due south, as it happened – and so we slid in past the guardship. They shouted that we had been lucky to get in, that Starkadder Eightarms was cruising in the fog. The Berts murmured to each other that it wasn't him, that they knew the sound of his oars, they'd pulled them themselves often enough, he never took anything off this coast, he wanted always to be safe inside the Empire, this would be some Black Dane masquerading. One of the Berts said it had smelt more like Irishmen to him, but the others all laughed at him and asked who had ever heard of Irishmen so far east as this.

At least the guardship didn't think we were pirates.

'They know us well enough,' Fat Bert told me. 'There's many a time we've brought in merchant ships that we've rescued from wicked pirates that boarded them at sea, and an act of valour that is: half the value of ship and cargo is what the Port Captain's authorised to pay. Course, you have to be careful in the retaking that nobody gets hurt, and you've got to make sure that the merchant men don't capture any pirates in their enthusiasm, and you have to have two ships before you think of it, but a very virtuous way of dealing it is.'

We had the sweeps rigged again, to pull us round between Rutupiae Island and the mainland, so that we could lie off the jetty. The customs came off to us in a small boat, and had a cursory walk around. They were expecting me – there had been a clerk from our family's agent in London waiting for me for some days. They were very willing to take me ashore in their boat, while the Berts worked the *Gannet* round and into Londinium. I said a tearful farewell to them – they couldn't think how they would ever get such an enjoyable and profitable and wholly legal commission again.

Cicva and I took our bags and left. I don't know if you've ever been to Rutupiae. There's nothing to see on the island, only the customs post. Every ship going up into the Thames, or farther north up the east coast, had to come in there for clearance, otherwise they're not allowed to unload. There's no real town, except for the usual little cluster of small houses and a tavern or two outside the walls. Nothing to see? Yes, there is. Over everything is the great monument to the Emperor Claudius, marking where He first slept the night on British soil. His Sacred Majesty, three times life-size, stands on an eighty-foot arch of white marble, and out from under it leads the road that passes through Eboracum to the Wall. It is a beautiful gleaming sight. There's not a square foot of marble that is left plain. It is all covered with the most exquisite carving. There are episodes from the Conquest, and from the Triumph, with supplicant Britons and chariots and camels and troops in campaign dress on one side.

The other side has the full regimental titles and badges of all the units taking part, each with a group of various ranks in their dress uniforms. There's none of this monotonous white wall for you there, that's old-fashioned stuff. Just think, in two thousand years it will still be there, dominating the sea just as it does today.

I would have liked to spend an hour examining the details, even though Cicva obviously didn't like to see what to her must have been a symbol of national humiliation. However, the little clerk who had met us wanted to get us through the formalities of entering the province as quickly as possible. Of course, with him to vouch that I was who I was, and being who I was, it only took a few minutes to get past all the officials, and the main sensation was caused by the fact that I had a sword, and that I actually had a permit with me. The clerk was just explaining to me and to the officials that he had rooms ready for us in the village, when there was a sudden commotion in the doorway of the office, and there stood Gwawl, swearing in a mixture of Latin and Gaulish and British in a way which put me off wondering how he had got there so quickly. And there was the Port Duty Police Officer standing there listening to him as though he were being told the essential and total truth about the nature of the universe. Well, I know there's a lot to be said for equality under the Law, but there are limits, especially for people of my importance.

Gwawl swore at us so much that the Duty Police Officer told him to moderate his language. It's never good tactics to antagonise the Police over trifles. A serious offence it's easy to get away with, once you've established a price, but with a little disorderly conduct, where you can't easily conceal it, why, they have you at once.

Gwawl let off with a stream of accusations of how we'd tricked him into going on our ship, and then stolen all he had, clothes, money, everything, and set him adrift naked – 'No, not naked,' said Cicva. 'You had my apron on' – and that quite spoilt his flow. Anyway, he said, he'd been set adrift, in a skin boat, to die of thirst or be eaten by sharks or whales or sea-serpents. Was it our fault (and I agreed, privately, no it wasn't) that he had got ashore and been able to sell his boat for rags to cover his nakedness and then begged his way all along the road from Dubris to Rutupiae?

At this point he paused for breath, and I managed to start talking. I assured the Duty Police Officer that this fellow had been only the usual kind of trickster, with all his capital in flashy clothes. He had wiled his way into our ship with a promise to pay later, and then settled down to cheat the poor sailors out of all they had by indescribable manoeuvres with the dice. But in that he had failed, and unable to pay for his losses he had stolen a boat, a good one, and made off with it in the fog. So I demanded that the Port Authorities should immediately undertake criminal proceedings against him for boat stealing, and in any case, with such an important and valuable cargo clearing, and with one of the most important merchants of the Empire passing through, why weren't the Port Captain and the Officer Commanding the Garrison here as well?

The clerk wanted to go off to Durovernum, and warn our agent, who had a villa there and would be waiting for us, and bring *him* back to Rutupiae (in the morning, probably, I thought) to bail us out of jail where we would by then probably have spent the night. I told the clerk pretty sharply that he ought to be quiet, because if anyone was going to spend the night in a cell it was to be him as a surety for our answering any charges, and there was no likelihood I would hesitate to sacrifice my bail. In any case, why wasn't the legendary Leo Rufus here waiting for us, instead of wasting his time at Durovernum?

In any case, I insisted on the two officers being brought, and when they came, I saw that my luck was in. I would not even have to use family influence. Most of these officials at the ports are officers from regiments of native cavalry, themselves coming from outside the Empire, and now, too old to command a squadron any more, they are granted Citizenship and a peaceful retirement in a post like this. Of course, the really stupid ones don't get these jobs.

I'd begun to guess when I heard the Duty Officer speaking Latin, and when the two senior officers arrived I saw that I had been right. They were both Germans, born somewhere beyond the Rhine, Thuringians I should say, and I took it as a direct sign from Apollo that the Garrison Commander had his arm in a sling and a bandage about his wrist.

A gift from Apollo? But I no longer served the Unconquered Sun. Long, long ago now He had released me from His service, and I no longer practised the healing art, the art that I had learnt in the Temple in the days when I was a whole man and still had both my eyes. No, I had left His service, and in the years since I had healed no one. But here I stood to face the two senior officers, in my grey cloak with the hood thrown back a little to show my hair all crusted white with the salt, and my good eye flashing, and my bad one covered with a patch, as I always had it at sea, or on the road. I had little option, dressed thus, but to play the part I was cast for: but it was a great mistake, I know now, to deal thus in healing after I had been dismissed from Apollo's service, and I am sure that it was the cause of all the trouble I had later.

Gwawl stepped forward and began to make his complaints again, and Cicva interrupted and offered to buy his horse-blanket – at least, she said that if he had five more like it she would give him a copper sestertius for the half-dozen, and in any case where was the rest of the money he must have got for that valuable and well-built boat, made to last a thousand storms on the Western Sea, or had he been cheated out of it?

Meanwhile, I walked over to the two senior officers, and I undid the bandage on the Garrison Commander's wrist. When I felt that the bone was only pulled out and not broken, I tried to remember which way to jerk, and I said the charm I had so often said in the North long ago:

> Blood to blood,
> Bone to bone,
> Strength to the sinew,
> Skin strong as stone,
> Oak strong as ash,
> Elm at the end,
> Earth over all.

Nonsense, really, but it did the trick with those half-romanised German officers, looking so civilised, but savages at heart, and all the time worrying about whether their sons will pass for Romans born, or whether they'll always show that touch of the tow-brush. The charm did it, that and the smell of the pig fat that all good Germans remember from their mothers' faces, and that they play too clean to bother with when they come within the Empire to make their fortunes. And the quick twist of my hand on the bone of the wrist, and Apollo helping me, whatever he did afterwards. It set the bone to rights, and both senior officers looked at me, and the Port Captain said:

'What do you want of us, Allfather?'

'Allfather? I know of no Allfather' – for this was the name that the Germans gave me when I was in the North, and it had brought me enough trouble all along the Amber Road, I wanted no more of it. 'I am only a simple traveller, and men within the Empire call me Photinus.'

After that, they treated me like someone important, even more important than a leading member of one of the richest trading families of the Empire, travelling incognito. I was someone they shared a secret with. The Port Captain pointed at Gwawl and asked:

'What do you want us to do with him? Shall we charge him formally, or would you prefer us to kill him – privately, that is?'

'No,' I told them. 'Why should I hurt a poor, helpless, demented fool? You see, he even believes his own lies.'

I ordered our clerk to give Gwawl a silver denarius, one of the new kind, one-horse and half copper, and that he had in turn to borrow from Cicva. It was one she had palmed from Gwawl's purse before she had let the sailors have it in exchange for the boat: and he knew it by his own toothmarks, and it made him swear more. But plainly there was nothing more that he could do there, and so he went away. I thought, though, that we hadn't seen the last of him, and no more we had.

Then I told the clerk we were more than ready to go and see the rooms he had for us in the inn, and if they weren't the best in Rutupiae, he would be in trouble. The Garrison Commander, however, put in a word, rather diffidently:

'Excuse me, All – that is, Simple Traveller – but there is no need for you to go to an inn. If you would be so gracious as to be our guest for the evening, in our mess – there are fifteen of us here tonight, all men of honour and breeding, and you shall have good food, real German food that you'll like, not that Mediterranean stuff, all soaked in oil.'

I accepted, graciously of course. I told the clerk to escort Cicva to an inn, and see that she had room fit for a princess, or there would be no knowing what would happen to him in the morning. I drew the girl aside and told her:

'As far as I'm concerned, you're free now, but you'll have to stay with me for a few more days till we can find a magistrate and make it legal. So don't get into any trouble tonight, because your legal position, and mine for that matter, might be a little ambiguous.'

Off they went in a rowing boat, and off I went with the two senior officers, but I called in at the Port Chancery before I reached the baths, and I borrowed the services of a couple of the official copyists. They would have to work all night to do what I wanted. It's a wonderful thing to have influence – or credit; influence comes cheaper in the end.

I must say, that handful of officers lived well, even if there were only fifteen of them in a house built to hold thirty at least, and still staffed on that scale with cooks and waiters. The bath had all the normal amenities, and I went in to dinner with my body oiled and scented, and my hair and beard combed Greek fashion, but in a toga, as befitted a Citizen born.

All the officers were Germans, born outside the Empire, and with twenty or so years of service apiece. So we had a real German dinner, only we reclined in the comfortable Roman way. I hadn't had a real German meal for years, nor did I again for years. We had hot and cold sausages of all kinds, and rye bread, and strong dark barley beer. Then, after we had sung all the traditional songs like 'Cole, the Bastard King of Britain', the guardship captain stood on the table and recited the latest border poem – 'Pictish Nell', it was called. Well, I mean, one party is just like another wherever it is.

But these were all elderly gentlemen, and so there were no games or fighting after the drinking. The place to see that is where there are old men and young men together, where the old men push the young men into it, to break their heads and spoil their clothes. Old men are too wise to try it, and the young men think of the expense, but can't say no to their seniors. Instead,

here, the officers on early call went off to bed, and the duty officer went on his rounds, and only half a dozen of us were left to
talk a lot and drink a little.

I said I was surprised to find so many men of their age and
seniority living like this in a mess, not one of them married or
even keeping women in the town – the law on marriage for the
Army has got so complex in recent years that nobody is quite
sure what is illegal any more. They all laughed.

'We're all married, more or less,' one of them said. 'We've all
got families, legitimate or not, in Durovernum, and fine houses
there too. We do five days here, and then three off there. It's a
nice town, is Durovernum.'

It must be, I thought. It'll be worth spending a few days there
before I move on if it's full of neglected wives. Then I remembered Phryne – it was getting harder and harder to remember
Phryne – and I reminded myself that I was going to behave
properly in Britain, even without hyena's hair. I asked what the
Brits were like.

'Not too bad,' the Port Captain told me. 'If you don't mind
the taste of butter and the smell of goose grease. The ones down
here are not too bad, more like the Germans, but it's west of
Londinium you meet the real Brits. We never saw much of them,
in the Army. They look after themselves, with their own local
assemblies and senates, and as long as they pay the wheat tax and
do everything according to Roman laws, we don't interfere. The
worst thing they can do is take their law suits to the Druids, like
they used to before we came. That would really undermine our
system, so the order is strict – kill a Druid at sight, we're supposed to. There hasn't been a Druid seen down in the South, not
for twenty years.

'But they're not bad, the Brits, except the ginger ones. The
red-haired men are killers, and as for the women – why, I wouldn't
touch a red-haired woman, not for all the Gold in Ireland.'

'Much Gold in Ireland?' I asked, all innocence.

'Up among the Demetae you want to go for Gold. That's
where the mines are. But it's no place to go if you want to keep
alive. A lot of the Demetae still follow the old King, Pwyll, and
we've never caught him. I did four months up at the mines

there – no, don't laugh, it wasn't what you think. I had a turn as Guard Commander, and I didn't ask for another. Plenty of Gold up there, but what a place. I tell you, it rains four hundred days in the year. There's only one future for that country. They want to catch all the rain in buckets – they've got plenty of buckets, they worship a bucket. Then they can build an aqueduct across the channel, and across Gaul, and down into Africa, and they can pour all their rain into it and sell it down in Africa. And I tell you, if they thought it would show a profit, I think the Brits would do it. So mean they are up there, a man will walk five miles to have a look in your mirror to save wearing out his own.'

'But Ireland?' I pressed.

'Well, they talk about Irish Gold,' said another officer. 'But nobody's ever seen any. There may be copper, I've seen that come in. When I was supporting the Second Legion up there at Isca—'

'Supporting?' someone interrupted. 'Picking up, more likely!' It was lucky there was nobody from the Second in the room or there would have been some horseplay after all.

'When I was at Isca, I was telling you, we used to have Irish coming in in skin boats, selling dogs, mostly. I've never seen men as poor as the Irish.'

'Poor?' put in the unit accountant, who had been most helpful in getting the copyists to put everything aside to do my work. 'There are some Brits who are so poor, they can't afford charcoal or firewood to cook on. They burn the very stones out of the ground for fuel.'

'No!' I could believe a lot of things, I couldn't believe that.

'Yes, and the wheat won't ripen, they have to dry it in kilns. They won't eat wheat themselves, they only grow it to pay the taxes with. Themselves, they eat a kind of millet, oats they call it. But they make real beer, out of barley.'

'They're a cunning lot,' said someone else. 'Once when I was on outpost duty …'

And so they went on, telling tall stories of skirmishes on the hills north of the Wall, and weird tales of how other people, always other people, had been caught by magic. And so we talked our throats dry and our voices hoarse, and at last we all went to bed.

Chapter Six

Next morning, I finished my business in the Imperial Chancery, and saw several packets off by the Imperial Mails, here and there. Then I had a boat take me across to the village and met Cicva and the clerk. The latter said that he had a boat ready to take us up river to Sturry, where we would be met by a litter, but Cicva said:

'No, it's a lovely day. I'd rather ride.'

'Ride what?' I asked her. 'We haven't got any horses.'

'You haven't,' she told me. 'I have. I've got four: and a groom, too.'

'You hadn't got them yesterday,' I objected.

'Well, there were some people last night in the tavern who thought they knew which cup the pea was under.'

I looked at the horses, which were fine beasts, and at the groom, who was healthy enough on the surface. But then I saw that there were six more horsemen, cavalry troopers, armed.

'What about these?' I asked as sternly as I could.

'The port duty officer came into the inn on rounds last night. I remembered Gwawl, and I thought the most useful thing I could win from him was the use of half a dozen men for a day.'

The girl had some sense, I admitted that. But it was annoying. I had visions of every woman in the island able to handle the pea and the cups, and where would the men be then? I told her, with as much feeling as I could put into my voice:

'Surely you know that this game is forbidden to women in the ordinary way? If it were not for my continuous intercession with the Gods Below, for all my fasting and prayer through the dark, you would have been struck dead in your sleep. Cicva, by the Gods Below and Above, I forbid you ever to play this game again.'

She glared at me. Then she laughed.

'As you order. But I tell you, Photinus, for this prohibition, you shall play Find-the-Lady across all the Isle of Britain.'

I swallowed that. I might have brought a witch back to the island, but at least she hadn't red hair. Two days later, after we had been to the magistrates, and Cicva had been properly freed and had a bundle of parchment to prove it, I helped her to sell three of the horses and the groom. She got up on the fourth to ride away, all alone, with her bundle of clothes strapped on the saddle in front of her. I asked her:

'And where are you going now?'

'Home.'

'And where's that?'

'And would I be telling you? But I might, though, if it meant any good at all. You're a hard man, and a clever one, Photinus, but I think that I could trust you if I had to.'

Well, well, I thought, as I watched her ride away toward Londinium. Trustworthy? I learn new things about myself every day.

Londinium

Chapter One

Durovernum was indeed a pleasant town, with its large houses set apart in their big gardens. I would have been pleased to have spent a few weeks there, because with so many wives mourning their husbands detained at Rutupiae it offered opportunities to any young man with a love of pleasure and a strong constitution. Alas, I stayed too short a time.

Our agent in Londinium, Leo Rufus, had a house in Durovernum, as had several other well-to-do merchants from Londinium. It was the convention to pretend that there was a hot season in Britain, as in a civilised land, and to have a country house to spend it in, as an escape from the great city. It was a real Roman house that Leo had, with atrium, triclinium and all the other rooms you find in the textbooks on architecture. The feature that worked hardest was the impluvium.

Leo Rufus was just like his house. Even his name was a sham: I knew enough about the Brits' language now to know that he had started life as Llew Gough. He was not, in fact, a Citizen of Rome, but it took some time before he let that slip, and then only because he wanted to know how much it cost to become one. But he talked as if he had spent most of his life in Rome (where he had never been), and he had nothing but contempt for the 'natives', as he called his own kinsmen. He spoke Latin to me all the time, so I saw no reason to let him suspect that I knew any Barbarian language.

The first evening he and I had a little quiet dinner by ourselves, reclining, of course. We ate roasted skylarks, which a true Brit would never do, and we drank real Falernian. Everything was like that, the real thing with no expense spared, but, of course, much more meat than any Roman would eat at one meal. Leo said he always entertained like this for the sake of the prestige of the family, but I made a note that we would have to adjust the rate of commission we were paying him. Of course, every time he had a guest he would have a good meal like this himself, at the expense of the firm, and the privations of this existence were dreadful. But it was I, as one of the family, who was paying for all this, and so I made no bones about making myself at home. Not quite at home. We were alone in the house. Leo apologised for the fact that his wife had returned to Londinium the very morning I had left Rutupiae. Leo himself was left to do the best he could with a mere two dozen slaves.

Over the dessert I showed him the Deed of Monopoly. He read it through. Then he observed, with the air of someone making a great discovery:

'This is a copy.'

'Oh, yes,' I told him. 'Do you think I would travel with such a valuable document as this on my person? I had the Chancery at Rutupiae make eight copies. The original went on by Imperial Mail to the Procurator's Office, and others in the same way to the commanders of the legions at Eboracum and Deva and Isca. This is the copy for your own records. You will notice that it is certified by the Port Captain and the Garrison Commander at Rutupiae: they advised me on how many copies to make and where to send them.'

I left him to worry over who had the other copies. He didn't like the idea of any of the business going out of his hands, but what could he do? I added:

'I have made it quite clear in my accompanying letter how confidential this business is. Faustinus would be furious if it were to fall through because of any careless talk. He is waiting for his commission too.'

That made him even more disturbed in his mind. But I did not really expect what I said next to drive him so frantic.

'Go to Ireland yourself? You must be mad! It's quite impossible. No Greek could ever do it and return alive!'

'Why should it be impossible? I have been up the Amber Road: why should the Golden Road to Ireland be any different? I am used to long journeys in savage countries. I can rough it with anybody.'

'I am not thinking of your comfort.' It was a change for him to be so frank. 'Some Irish come here, a few, but all that nation knows what happened to Britain once the trade with the Empire developed. Therefore they have forbidden and prohibited and banned any Roman from setting foot in the island, and by Roman they mean any man from the mainland who talks any civilised language and wears boots and drinks wine. Wine, especially, they deny entry, for they believe that all the troubles of the Kings of Britain began with their thirst for wine, and indeed there is no denying that it happened so in Gaul, and in Gaul it all started with the Greeks of Massilia. So all the Kings of the Irish have agreed and compacted and decided that there shall be no trading nor bargaining nor intercourse of any kind between the people of the Island of the Blessed and us of the Island of the Mighty.'

Now these are the names that the Brits use in their language for the two islands of Ireland and of Britain, and I must say they sounded strange in Latin. Leo Rufus went on:

'And since this agreement, there have been horrible things and objects and relics that it is that have been returning. For I do not mean the stories and the rumours and the gossip, because there were always dreadful stories that came from the Island of the Blessed, and difficult to believe. But it is the actual bodies, and the heads, and the ships that we have been finding tied up to harbour walls in the dawn, with no living man aboard to say how they have come: but we all know why.'

'That is nothing to me,' I told him, scornfully. 'I once came alive out of the hands of the Picts, and out of the very teeth of their King.'

'And it is thinking then that it is you are, that it would be making it any easier for you to go to Ireland and to return again?' It was when you had him worried that you could hear the touch of the woad in his voice, in the adenoidal sibillants and in the collapse of all grammar into a continuous passive voice and a flood of impersonal verbs. The British tongue is one that is best spoken slowly by an old man, as Latin is by a middle-aged one in a court, and as Greek is made for the slangy arguments of the markets of Alexandria and Tyre. 'The less that it is that it is that it is being said about it, that is the better it is that it will be.'

I thought that I had better appear to take some notice of his warning, though I knew quite well that it was the excuse of a lazy man for taking no action. It was quite clear to me now that any merchant with a grain of enterprise would have opened up trade with Ireland long ago. There is nothing a Barbarian king will not do for his own profit, and if all the kings had made an agreement, then certainly they would not have the slightest hesitation in betraying each other wholesale for the treasures of civilisation, for silk and bronze and glass and wine. Especially wine. It *had* been their greed for Roman wines that had split the great confederation of the Gauls, and brought down the walls of Alesia on Vercingetorix's head, and laid the whole province open to Caesar's armies. After he failed to conquer Britain as well, it was left open to the wine merchants to trade for two generations. Then when the Emperor Claudius came, the whole drunken country fell into His Sacred Majesty's hands like a ripe apple.

'I can hardly go back to my uncle Euthyphro – you know what he is like in a fury – and tell him that I had this monopoly in my hand and that even then I went no nearer to Ireland than Durovernum. I must go at least as far as the port for Ireland, even if I go no farther, for I must satisfy him as well as myself that there is no possibility of going any farther.'

Leo went out to his vomitorium, the pride of his house, which he showed to every visitor, and he went there not because he needed to but because he thought it was the proper and civilised and Roman thing to do, and he left me slightly fuddled and thinking of everything in threes and triples and thirds like a Brit. It gave Leo time to think, and when he came back and started on mussels in honey, he said:

'Even if you are to go as far as that only, and to learn something that will sound convincing in Rome, it will do you no good to go as a man in the counsels of the Consuls, in the confidence of the Caesars, in league with the Legates of the legions. I think that I know a man who, it may be, will be able to take you as far as the port for Ireland, and speak for you to the Kings of the Irish, if only you will go with him and live as he does and do as he says, and trust him with your life. First, I will have to send and dispatch and instruct a messenger to find him, and bring him to meet us in Londinium, and it's lucky that it is not long since I talked with him, and I know that he is not in the Summer Country, nor at sea, where he is for a great part of the summer. So if we go to Londinium in a few days, then this man will come and meet us, and it may be that he will help us if he feels it satisfies a whim of his.'

I had two days' rest in Durovernum, and then, the third day, Leo and I set out for Londinium, which is two days' journey by road, though a messenger in a hurry, such as Leo had sent off immediately after dinner on the first night, may do it in summer between dawn and sunset. We had a dozen Pannonian troopers, borrowed from the garrison, as escort, although I felt safe enough. Surely Gwawl, about whom I had said nothing to Leo Rufus, was now in pursuit of Cicva. But then I remembered how she had ridden off, in her red and white checked shawl, with its long tassels, and a bronze chain about her waist instead of the embroidered belt, and I wondered.

Chapter Two

Leo Rufus had a house in Londinium which might have been a town house in Rome, six-storeyed and tiled-roofed. The ground floor was the warehouse. He had the entire first floor to live in, and he let out the upper floors for rent. Again he apologised, when we arrived, late in the evening, that his wife had taken it into her head to leave that morning for Durovernum. Perhaps I have a reputation.

That evening, on arriving in Londinium, I went to bed early. Leo promised that I should have at least one quiet empty day, and the following day again he would invite some of his trading colleagues to meet me, as probably the most influential and wealthy visitor to Londinium for some years. However, just as I woke, half-way between dawn and noon on that first day, Leo came into my bedroom and announced:

'You have a client.'

I thought he was being facetious, and I didn't like it. I am never at my best on waking. I snarled something like:

'If I'm a patrician, you're a Pharaoh,' but Leo stood back and the 'client' entered. This man did not really stand seven feet high. He only looked like it, in the undress uniform of his regiment, the Danube Rangers, Hadrian's Own. I leapt out of bed, and embraced Aristarchos, the son of Demons. Tall and lean, he was, and always walked like a horseman. His black hair, black as Gwawl's, and his cheerful black eyes, that charmed women everywhere, and his brown skin, telling of a sunnier home, were the best things I had seen for weeks.

'Why are you not still on the Danube?' I asked him. I remembered the regiment he had, patrolling the river frontier, and on the other side of it, usually. Horse-thieves and cattle-stealers they

276

were to a man, raised in Britain, and that is how he spoke the language like a native, though a rather disreputable native.

'All good things come to an end,' he replied. 'I'm having a period on the Procurator's staff. Oh Gods, I can't stand these cities in the summer.'

I agreed with him. He was, I thought, too clever for anyone to waste at a place like Rutupiae, however he might have liked it. I asked:

'What are you doing? I can't see you in an office, checking other people's claims for forage, though perhaps if you know all the dodges ...'

'That's more or less the kind of thing. All this administrative stuff about trade and finance – you'd understand it, but I never will. Not that there aren't some interesting cases on the Marine side. It's funny how the rewards paid for rescues from pirates always go to the same people. But how about you? I heard a rumour, inside the service from someone in the Second, that you were on the way, but nobody seems to know why.'

I hesitated a moment. For an instant, I was tempted to tell him that I was merely broadening my commercial education and Leo's as well; I was going to do that in any case. But then I relented. With an island full of people like Gwawl and Leo Rufus, it was as well to have somebody I could trust. I told him a little of what had been going on. He whistled.

'Trade with Ireland? Now, if you could start that, it would be useful. The Eagles follow Trade you know, and the Second and the Sixth and the Twentieth are just waiting for the chance. You ought to come and talk with the Procurator.'

I shook my head.

'I have my own troubles. I'll start talking to officials when I have some taxes to pay and clearances to do. Faustinus' name on the Deed ought to ensure that I can work undisturbed.'

'As you like. Still, if you want anything done ... or any entertainment, either ... I can get you into half a dozen gambling clubs.'

'Will I meet any influential Brits there?'

'Not very likely. A sad lot, the Brits. Either they are trying as

277

hard as they can to turn into Italians, in the hope of getting some kind of hereditary post in the administration, if they haven't got one already: or they've turned their backs on progress and are only interested in religion. And they are firmly convinced, most of them, that they are the favourites of the Gods, and that if they were conquered, then in itself it is a sign of the favour of the Gods. The reward of virtue is defeat. Odd, isn't it, what people will believe, if it makes them happy?'

'So all is quiet, except on the frontier?'

'Oh, there are a few who still don't believe the Empire is here to stay. They still pay taxes to the old kings. There's one, up in the rain hills, who is most troublesome.'

I remembered what the old men had said in the mess at Rutupiae.

'Pwyll?'

'Pwyll.' Aristarchos changed his tone, suddenly. 'But would you like to come out tonight?'

I shook my head.

'I have things to do. Later perhaps. Today, I have a little shopping.'

He laughed. 'You'll be soundly cheated, if you're not very careful. You ought to learn a few words of the language.'

'I'll try,' I assured him. He went out, off to the Office of the Procurator. I went in to the office of the family's agent.

It was a long and hard morning going through the books. In the middle of the afternoon I had a bite to eat, and then I unpacked my sword from my bag. I thought I could remember the name of the scabbard-maker I had been recommended in Bonnonia, and I even thought I could find my way, with directions from Leo. I refused his offer to come as a guide. I even refused to have a slave come with me. I wanted to see the town myself, with nobody to affect my judgements.

Londinium, of course, is just like any other provincial town, with the big buildings of marble in the official quarter contrasting with the low thatched houses where the natives live. Down there a civilised gentleman in his bare legs and his cloak is out of place among all the trousers and the jerkins and tunics of soft leather the Brits wear over their coloured shirts to keep out the

278

rain. There are no people like the Brits for wearing bright colours. They move about like a bed of walking flowers, with their shirts and blouses and shawls in stripes and checks and patches. In my drab grey I felt most conspicuous. Still, a Citizen and a Greek ought to be able to carry off anything. I found the scabbard-maker in his little shop, and I told him who had sent me. He looked at the blade, and then he stroked the ivory of the hilt as if he could feel the lock of hair that Cicva had insisted on binding up within it, or as if he could hear the things, unintelligible to me, that she had crooned over it.

'I am trusting,' he told me in a soft voice, 'that it is no firm idea that you have for the pattern of the scabbard.'

'An artist,' I replied, 'must choose his subject.'

The old man smiled slyly at me. He asked, of course, when I was born and what stars had shone over me, and then:

'What is the name of the sword?'

'Name? Now, you may think it stupid, but in spite of paying so much for the blade, and taking so much trouble over the hilt and the sheath, I had quite forgotten the barbarian custom of giving a weapon a name. I thought a moment. All I could think of was the Brits' word for a blow. I said:

'*Burn* is all I will call it.'

'Then a hard blow it will be to you,' he answered. 'It will be ready in a week.'

I left him, and wandered through the mean streets till I came out on the river bank. I strolled for a little, watching the men fishing for salmon. The salmon they catch above the bridge at Londinium are the best in the world. Here and there clouds of seagulls fought about the places where men cleaned the fish. And then suddenly, on that summer evening, with the sun below my shoulder when I could see it in the broken cloud, out of a cloud of seagulls I heard a voice singing.

I tell you, it was the most beautiful voice I have ever heard in all my life. In it I heard the humming of the bees and the rustle of wind over the summer grass, the ripple of fresh water over shallows and the lap of salt water against the side of an anchored ship. It was a voice of cream and a voice of silk, a voice of honey and a voice of wine. It was a voice that brought the scent of roses, and of honeysuckle on a sultry night. It was a voice that brought the feel of air heavy and hot before the thunderstorm.

I walked towards the gulls, towards the voice. Out of the flutter of white the words came clear, some old song of the Brits, from days of old.

> A handsome warrior rode down from Alesia;
> A lovely young maiden he chanced for to see:
> 'Oh, sir, take me up in your chariot behind you
> 'To dance at a wedding till sunrise,' asked she.

I walked towards the voice. The birds rose in a great flock. She stood there, tall and slim and stately, wrapped from head to feet in a cloak that shimmered in white and gold. I stepped nearer. She slipped her shawl from her head to her shoulders, the tassels and fringes hung long and thick, to her knees. She showed her hair, red in the late red sun, shining like a helmet of copper, coiled in great braids and pinned over her ears. And as I approached her she floated away, gliding and smooth, but bobbing a little up and down as she went like a boat upon the water, light as a skin boat, and gleaming. And as she floated away, she still sang:

> His mail it was gilded, his helm was of silver,
> His shield was of bronze, enamelled in red.
> Her blouse was of silk and her skirt was of linen,
> Her rich golden hair was piled high on her head.

I remembered all that I had been told. The redheads are the worst, they had said, everybody had said. I remembered all this, and yet I went forward. She bobbed away from the river, down an alley. I followed. The thatched roofs above us were covered with gulls. I pushed my way between people and pigs, following the Lady in the Cloak. I could still hear her voice.

> They rode to the wedding, they danced at the wedding,
> They danced to sweet music till daylight was near;
> At cockcrow, the palace, the dancers, the pipers,
> The maiden, all vanished: the warrior knew fear.

I knew no fear. I only knew that I must follow that voice through the crowds and through narrow streets, across court-yards and around corners. I wanted to find the Lady in the Cloak, the lady of the seagulls, Phryne or no Phryne, hyena hair or none.

His mail shirt was rusted, his helmet was tarnished,
His beard had grown long and his hair had turned grey.
The people around him wore strange-fashioned garments:
The walls of Alesia had crumbled away.

Now I was quite lost. I did not know the way back to the river or back to the official quarter. It was nearly dark. I did not know, I did not care, what would happen next if only I could reach the Lady. I suddenly came out into a kind of open square, sur-rounded with houses of a better sort. A lantern hung outside a door. She stood under it, the light on her hair. She had thrown open her cloak, and I could see the gleam of her belt of enam-elled bronze. I walked slowly towards her. I heard her:

So if you drive out on the road past Alesia
Take no young maid up, whate'er she may say:
For if you dance one night with the Princess of Darkness
It's all of your life you will dance clear away.

I was almost on her, I could smell the fragrance of her hair, I could feel her breath, I could hear the sound of her breathing in the silent, empty square. And as I almost touched her, the door opened behind her, she passed through, and it slammed in my face.

And then, as I stood a moment, dazed, it came. It is very clever to attack a one-eyed man. All you have to do is to come at him with his blind side. But it is advisable to be sure that you know which *is* his blind side, and this was a precaution that Gwawl had failed to take. He came rushing at me, and I stood still to the last instant, and then I leapt away, and he thudded with all his weight into the side of the house. He fell back on to the ground, winded, and his knife skidded away across the pavement like a flat stone across water, the water that the Lady had floated on, boatlike. Of course, if I had any sense, I ought to have run for my life; all I wanted to do was to stay and get into the house whose door had been closed against me, and I could not do that with Gwawl behind me. I flung myself on him, my knees into his black-and-white-striped stomach – or so I planned. But he was already recovering, and he rolled clear, and I nearly broke my kneecaps on the cobbles. He grabbed at my throat. I was worried about two things: I did not want him to get at another knife, least of all mine which was sticking in my belt, and I did not want to lose the other eye, so I gripped his wrists and hung on desperately trying to force them apart, the whiles we each tried to kick the other in the groin. As a result of this kicking, we rolled over and over in the dirt. At last I became conscious of a pair of feet close to my face. Next, I realised that the owner of the feet was waving a heavy stick, such as almost all the Brits carry, and he was obviously looking for an opportunity to strike. To strike whom? I had no friends in this country, and Gwawl had, I knew, at least two. And he had come prepared for this meeting, if he had not engineered it, and I braced myself for the blow. Of course, all this took scarcely enough time to repeat a line of Virgil. And then the blow came, and for all our mutual dodging it was Gwawl who was struck, and I rolled away and scrambled to my feet. I looked at my rescuer, idly swinging his cudgel and regarding the still figure of Gwawl with a satisfied air.

He was not a tall man or a heavily built one, rather spare and slender. He was about my own age. He wore shabby clothes of an indeterminate brown, but in the light of the lamp at the door I could see that he had round his neck a strip of coloured cloth, black streaked with yellow. As I looked at him and wondered what to say, the empty square suddenly filled with men, a score at least, and I realised that every one I could see near enough was wearing somewhere on his person a scrap of black and yellow. And it was then I began to wonder if those gay colours that Tacitus remarks on so idly had not some inner meaning. I had no chance to ask. One of the newcomers brought a bucket of water, and threw it over Gwawl, who began to stir. Another happened to be carrying a leather sack, and the first man took it, and when two others held Gwawl on his feet, the bag was pulled over his

282

head and tied down to bind his arms. Then the men formed a
circle and the leader pushed Gwawl across it, singing out:

> The badger's in the bag.
> The badger's in the bag.
> Heigh-o, heigh-o,
> The badger's in the bag.

And they pushed Gwawl across the circle, and every man he
bumped into hit him – hands only, though, no sticks or knives.
The more he staggered and cursed them from inside the bag, the
more they, no, *we* all laughed, till at last he bumped into someone who was laughing so hard that he just fell over, and Gwawl
escaped into an alley, running zigzag and bouncing from one
wall to another till he finally bounced around a corner and so out
of sight. We were all laughing after him.

Then I pulled myself together. There was no time to waste in
laughing. I turned to the door. I raised the latch and pulled it
open. I looked through the doorway to nothing. There was no
house. It was merely a facade. Before me an empty waste
stretched down to the river, strewn with all the rubbish of a city,
broken pots and oyster shells and the half-gnawed carcasses of
dead dogs and unwanted babies. No Lady. No one at all.

Chapter Three

My second evening in Londinium, Leo Rufus gave a dinner in my honour for a few of his friends, all men deeply involved in trade with him, and by what I had seen of his books, once a man got involved with Leo it was not easy to disengage nor cheap to remain involved. Still, they seemed to bear him no malice. They were all romanised Brits like himself, and they lay there, eating roast goose in a daring manner and making sly little jokes I could not understand over the roast songbirds on a spit, just to show how civilised they were.

All the same, they talked in the most atrocious Latin, with the accents vile and the vocabulary pedantic, and the slang at least a hundred years out of date, and while they even corrected my quantities, and corrected them wrong, I learnt quite a lot. They talked of how trade had fallen off since the old freebooting times before the conquest, which none of them could remember, and how heavy the customs were, and how the Army was interested in nothing but the silver they cupellated out of the lead they mined near the hot springs at Sulis. When at last they went, Leo said:

'Come you down into the warehouse. I have someone you ought to meet.'

I followed. The warehouse was a big place, and at this time it should have been deserted, since Leo was a very humane man and insisted that all his slaves should get at least five hours' sleep a night. But now there were lights burning at the back, and as we picked our way between the bales, I saw a man sitting, eating a cheese, slowly, deliberately, with the point of a knife.

He was wearing an old brown jerkin with a hood, patched with leather at the cuffs and elbows, but showing at the neck a flash of colour, of black striped with yellow. And he had a belt – I was beginning to learn, now. No Brit will be seen without a belt, man or woman. The poorer people will wear belts of plain leather, and women girdles of the best cloth they can afford. But a noble by blood will wear a belt of Spanish leather with embroidery in gold and silver wire, and his wife a network of bronze chains. The more noble a man, the more expensive his belt. This man's belt was of plates of bronze, the size of my palm, enamelled in bright red with strange patterns of stags and bulls, garnet-eyed, and joined with links of Gold – Irish Gold.

He stood up, this man of my own height, whom I had last seen swinging a cudgel in an empty square. His light brown eyes looked into my one black. He pushed aside his thick brown curls, and took my hand.

'I had hoped,' said Leo, 'that the Master of the Western Sea might have come himself to meet you, but he cannot because he is at sea, or because he is old, or ill, or at a wedding, or for some other great and pressing reason he has failed to specify. But you may speak as you will to Pryderi, and not be deceived by his dress.'

'So it's you, is it?' Pryderi asked. 'Any enemy of Gwawl's is a friend of mine.'

'I am not so much concerned with Gwawl,' I answered, 'as with Bithig the Pict.'

I do not know what it was that made Leo look so concerned, the mention of Gwawl or of Bithig, or his discovery that I could converse in the language of the Brits, and might have heard anything in his house. And I had too, but that is another story. Pryderi continued:

'Well, Bithig is far away, and will stay there. I remember seeing you at the wedding. Missed you we did, especially at the May Feast. A real gap you would have filled.'

'I suppose that I would.' I felt that the whole subject was rather distasteful to me, anyway, however Pryderi might look at it. 'How is the … er … lady?'

'Well, you know, well. A bit regretful, in a hungry sort of way. But it will give me a little personal satisfaction to keep you two apart. Now, the Master of the Western Sea has given me a little discretion to consider any propositions you may have in the way of trade. Tell me, what is it exactly you are wanting?'

I explained the whole situation to Pryderi more fully than I had to Leo, who looked gloomier and gloomier as he saw the road to ruin opening before him. We ignored him, and he was reduced to a mere putter-out of the fires that Pryderi caused by oversetting lamps with his eloquent swinging arms. Northerners need more room to talk than do we unemotional southerners. But at the last, he just sat still and quiet, thinking hard for some moments. At last he observed, sadly and quietly:

'Mad. Mad you are, Photinus, and I always said as much. This is no easy thing you are proposing to do, like sailing across the Narrow Sea and selling a few pots of wine. If it were anyone else, I would walk out now and leave you. But seeing it is you, and seeing that your marrying Bithig makes you Royal, and seeing that all us Royals are brothers at bottom, then it is help you a little I will.

'Listen to the situation. There are four kings in Ireland, of the four parts of the island, but there is always one of them is High King. Now, if it is trading you want, it is the High King that you must persuade. But at the moment, it is quite the wrong man who is High King. However, I can find you an Irishman to speak to …'

'I'll talk to the High King. I have had enough of middlemen.'

'Politics is full of middlemen, Photinus. And this one – will it satisfy you to know that he is nephew to the King of the North, who is not High King?'

It did satisfy me a little. The King's nephew might well be the King's heir. I asked:

'When can I see him?'

'At the moment, he is the mate of a grain ship running between Lindum and Londinium, coasting and up the canals. Exiles, you know, have to do strange things. But he will be here on Friday night, and we can see him then.'

That would have to do. The interview was at an end. But not quite. As Pryderi stood up, I asked him:

'And the Lady? Who was she? Where can I find her now?'

'What Lady?'

'The one who sang: the one I was following when Gwawl attacked me. The one who went through the door with the lamp.'

'I didn't see any Lady. I just came round the corner by chance, and there you were, the two of you, having a lovely fight. Pity it was to stop you, and if it had been anyone else but Gwawl I'd never have stopped it. But I saw nobody else. Friday at dusk, then – here.'

He picked another cheese off the shelf and went off with it into the dark street.

Chapter Four

For three days, I led an exemplary life. Each morning I spent going over the accounts, till even Leo Rufus had to admit that I knew more about business than he did. Each evening, I stayed at home, and dined quietly, not even going with Aristarchos to one of the gaming parties he was so fond of: it would have been tame fare to me. Besides, I wanted to be so retiring that nobody would question my presence in Londinium, or notice when I left.

But in the late afternoons, till a little after dusk, I would dress inconspicuously, like a Greek sailor, and there were plenty of those about, and I would walk about the river banks and the quays looking for the Lady who sang. Everywhere I saw a cloud of seagulls I hurried, everywhere I heard any voice raised I loitered to listen. I went into every tavern, I inspected the girls in a hundred brothels, I haggled with every bawd and pimp in Londinium, and there are more there than in any port I have seen, because you have to do something to keep warm in their long cool winters and their long cold summers. But I could not find her, although I penetrated into every group in society where women might be expected to walk the streets alone. Yet, no one had see her, no one recognised her description. She had vanished, and the more I looked for her, the more I threaded the narrow alleys, the more I lost count of the corners I turned, the more eager I was to find her, the more her face swam before my inner gaze.

On Friday night, I was waiting in the warehouse when Pryderi came for me. He was dressed, even more shabbily than before, with a plain leather belt. I wore a heavy hooded grey cloak, and I had a long knife in my belt, and a heavy stick in my hand, as had Pryderi: most Brits carry a cudgel all the time, swearing of course in case of trouble that they need it to drive their cattle or to beat off dogs.

Pryderi led me through narrow streets that even I had not dared to penetrate in daylight, down into the sailors' quarter, at the east of the town along the river bank. It was as dirty and crowded a place as you will find in any town, and Astolat, as this quarter was called, was full of sailors' taverns. It stank of poverty and corruption.

'The only thing to do with this end of the town is to burn it,' I murmured to Pryderi, not too loudly, in case anyone might overhear me who was proud of the place.

'We've done it often enough, from one end of Londinium to the other, and the last was in my father's time,' Pryderi replied. 'The Lily is all right, though. That's where our man is waiting for us.'

It *was* fairly clean, by waterfront standards, and not too crowded. Pryderi called for cider – I had to pay, of course – but I wanted beer. I mean, there's good wine, and there's bad wine, and in a miserable place like Londinium it's nearly always bad wine. But beer – why, there's no bad beer, only better beer and worse beer. When I think of the time when I didn't drink beer – but I was back in practice now, and I drained the first pot at one gulp and called for another.

A little man alongside me dipped his finger in his pot and wrote on the counter:

> R O T A S
> O P E R A
> T E N E T
> A R E P O
> S A T O R

It was clever enough, reading the same way up and down and back to front, but it didn't mean anything to me.

'And the same to you, Comrade,' I told him – I was feeling in a friendly mood. 'Weren't you drawing fish in every tavern in Bonnonia the other night?'

He squinted at me in alarm, and then rushed out into the night, like a frightened hare. I turned to Pryderi who was complaining about the cider to the landlord.

'Muck, this, proper muck. All you can say for it is that it is wet. I suppose it *is* cider – it must be, because it isn't beer or mead, and it doesn't taste good enough for ditch-water. How they have the face to bring it into the country I can't think. Not your fault, I suppose: you have to sell what you can get. You ought' – this to me – 'to try some of my grandmother's elderberry. You will, too, as soon as we get down into the Summer Country.'

He said this last sentence very loudly and distinctly, and the landlord, who had been standing with his back to the counter and taking no particular notice of his customers, so that I had had some trouble in getting my second pot of beer, now turned sharply round and snapped:

'If you don't like this, then go you back to the Summer Country where you belong.'

And I suppose this must have been some kind of password, because Pryderi immediately asked:

'And where is he now?'

'In bed with Elaine, the front-room barmaid. You can see him when – hey! You can't go up there now! a man's entitled to *some* privacy.'

'We're going up,' Pryderi told him, and went on muttering something about nobody spotting an old sweat from the Danube Rangers – Dredgers, the landlord told him, more likely – Hadrian's Own, that had seen more bloodshed than any man in the house. I slipped the patch off my eye and looked at the landlord with it. I had the garnet in, and somehow that carving always put people off, Hercules taking off the shirt of Nessus, delicate work, you could see the veins going into the kidneys and all the tubes of the lungs hanging out. And he saw the knife in my belt, and my stick, and Pryderi's, and so he stood back politely and let us go up the ladder to the top floor.

'Old sweat, indeed,' I said to Pryderi on the landing, 'and I know very well you've never been a soldier.'

'Indeed, and I was a regimental tailor for three months, and then they wanted to send the whole regiment back to the Danube, so I … left.'

'Deserted?'

'Well … not really. My cousin came back. I only took his place

290

for experience while he went off to see a man who had seduced his cousin. Lovely head it was, too, when he took it, and dried a treat, very decorative. You see, for all the way old Aristarchos used to talk, one Briton looked just like another to him. Now, this ought to be the door. Do you think we ought to knock, or would it spoil the surprise? Let's go straight in and see how he's feeling.'

So in we went without any warning, but Pryderi was disappointed, because either the Irishman had just got out of bed with the barmaid or he had not yet got in. He was ordering his supper, and when he saw me with Pryderi he made no other comment than:

'Make it three times, Elaine, and the same for yourself.'

She was a big slattern, and I couldn't see any man of taste going after her. I suppose that I must have shown my thoughts in my face as she went, because the Irishman said:

'And is it thinking you can be of a better way of getting a room to yourself for a few hours? She only costs six coppers a time, for the house, but of course I always tip her and she gets a meal out of it.'

He did not bother about greetings. It was obvious he was expecting us. He and Pryderi showed for each other neither affection nor dislike, merely the attitude of two men who find it advantageous to work together, but who have otherwise nothing in common. I looked long at him, the first Irishman I had seen, I thought, though I was wrong about that.

He was a big man. He had long hair, down to his shoulders in the Irish fashion. The Brits wear it that way too, but while Germans cut their hair short, except Vandals, and wear long beards not cut or curled but combed, the Irish wear their beards long and neither washed nor combed but matted; the Brits are quite different, because they are unique among men in shaving off their beards and letting their moustaches grow, hanging down as long as possible on either side of their mouths. Pryderi's moustache was very fine, almost to his collarbones.

But the Irishman not only wore his hair long, he had combed it back and plaited it up on top into a ridge like the mane of a horse all ready for a show or parade. He had stiffened his hair with grease, and before this he had dyed it a bright yellow so that no one could tell what the original colour had been. It would have been most distinctive in Rome, but here in Britain men dress so fantastically that no one gives it a second thought.

The Irishman was dressed *as* an Irishman, in a way I had not seen before. I know that if your life has been passed in the centre of culture, then you will believe that all Barbarians wear trousers and that to let your legs go bare is the mark of civilisation. This is not true. The Irish go bare-legged, but no one could call them cultured. This man had taken a length of cloth, about fifteen yards long and two wide. This he wound two or three times around his waist, and then he drew the end up over his left shoulder at the back and across the front of his body down to his waist again at the right. The cloth was fastened with two big cloak pins of silver set with pebbles, of good workmanship but too flamboyant in design for my taste.

This Irishman had, however, made some concessions both to fashion and to decency, not to mention the climate, and he had on a fairly good linen shirt under the cloth. He had not changed it for some weeks, that was plain, but under the dirt I could make out that it had once been the colour of a Spanish orange, if you know the fruit, embroidered with a variety of flower motifs in bright green. The cloth itself was all of one colour, a dirty saffron, but I saw later that some of the Irish in the far north were beginning to weave their cloths in complex patterns of many colours like the Picts, from whom I suppose they learnt the art. Elaine came back with the supper, big plates of food of all kinds fried in butter. The Brits do not use oil, professing not to like the taste of it or the smell, though I think this is a way of hiding the fact that they are too mean to pay for it. They fry things in butter instead, which to us seems disgusting, since it is plain the Gods intended it for use only as a cosmetic.

'Can't eat this at sea,' said the Irishman, with his mouth full. 'It turns my stomach.'

I knew just what he meant, and said so, and finding that I knew what I was talking about in discussing ships he became more communicative. Then Pryderi asked:

'Anybody like my black pudding? I can't eat it.'

'You don't like it? We'll share it.'

292

'No, I like it, but it's a question of religion. All my family are descended from the great Black Pudding of Gabalva. I'll tell you some time. My house began in a fever of lust and greed, with a tradition right from the start of filial neglect, and I cannot think of a better way to power.'

'And you?' I asked the Irishman. 'What can't you eat?'

'What no one is likely to offer me.' He grinned. 'Dog, I can't eat, because when I was a child I killed a big dog, and so I got my name.' He paused, as if expecting me to say something. I kept silent. After a little he went on. 'And it is very considerate of you, and shows that even if you are a Greek, you are a noble born, and makes me ready to trust you, that you do not ask me my name. For if you did, I would not tell you, and if you asked me a second time, then I would kill you.'

He smiled again, very engagingly. I have known several men in my time who would kill for nothing at all but the whim and the enjoyment of it, Aristarchos, for instance, and they all smiled that same dreamy smile.

'Can you tell me your Clan?' I asked.

'Oh, yes. I am of the Sons of Mil, the noblest of all the houses of the Kings of Ireland. And I am of the nation of the Setantii, and I myself am the bravest and the strongest and the cleverest of all the Setantii of Ireland and of Britain and of Gaul and of Galatia. So it is *the* Setanta that I am, and so you may call me till you hear my name called in victory on the holy soil of Ireland.'

Obviously, he could not risk anyone's using his real name while he was in the land of his enemies, because it would then be so easy to cast a spell on him. But he had said something interesting, and I went back to it.

'My mother is Galatian.'

'Why, useful that will be, indeed. For it is raising a fianna I must first be about. There is not a man will join me if it is thought I am in league with a Roman, and a Greek is not much better, though it is hating the Romans you must be as much as we are.' (I wondered where he had got that strange idea from.) 'But if it is a Galatian I am consorting with, then it might well be my own cousin within seventeen generations.'

I looked at the Setanta and dismissed that idea in horror.

293

'What is a fianna?' I asked him.

'Why, a band of brave fellows that will follow me to the over-throwing of the High King?'

'But why cannot you go back to Ireland and raise an army in Ulster?'

'For the same reason that I am in exile here in the Island of the Mighty. I could not bear to stay in an Ulster that the Con-naught men had ravaged from end to end, and disarmed utterly so that there is neither sword nor shield nor horse trained to war in the whole Kingdom. No, it is here. I must raise a fianna, and arm them, and find weapons enough to fit out an army. I have been thinking over it for a year, and I know the very day that I must land in Ireland again. Now, you with all your connections can find weapons enough for an army. And if it is only a little matter you want in recompense, like all the Gold in Ireland, then it will be easy enough to let you have it, I promise you that. But, meanwhile, there are arrangements to be made, while I spend the winter in the rainy hills with Howell, and they will cost something in silver. But it will only be a trifle.'

'I can arrange that through Pryderi,' I told him.

'But then there is the question,' the Setanta went on, 'of get-ting the arms, when you have them, into Ireland, and for that you will need a ship.'

'Pryderi will see to that too,' I told him.

'I cannot,' Pryderi put in. 'There is a limit to my discretion, and I cannot here and now divert a valuable ship from the honest and peaceful trade it is now engaged in. Besides, I would not like to see it lured ashore and looted and burnt on the coast of Ire-land, as has happened before.'

'But you promised—'

'To help. I will help all I can. You must come with me, Photi-nus, and ask the Master of the Western Sea yourself. I will help you all I can, but I cannot promise.'

'You give and then you take away again,' I said bitterly. 'If one of you does that, then the other—'

'I have my Gesa.' This was the Setanta in his pride.

'Your Gesa?'

'Every man of noble blood has his Gesa. It would not be just, or right, or morally praiseworthy, for a Son of Mil and a cousin of kings to exert his full strength against an ordinary man. It would be more honourable for me to contend with one hand tied behind my back. But that is undignified, and therefore I have taken on myself an obligation, that I must always obey, even if it be to my disadvantage. My Gesa is this, that I must never refuse to take what is offered to me, nor to give what is asked of me. And I have given what you asked for, all the Gold of Ireland. But if it is thinking you are that this is an easy burden to bear, then it is little you are knowing about it. And think, too, of the Gesa laid on my cousin and my enemy the King of Leinster. The Badger King may never refuse a wager, or a bargain, or a challenge once offered, however disadvantageous it may be.'

I hope, I thought, that one day I will meet this obliging monarch. But now I knew that the Irish were all mad, for no Greek would so bind himself. It was only necessary to find a man's Gesa, to see a way to destroy him. Pryderi snorted.

'Easy it is for them to take on a Gesa, and to think it so meritorious to accept odds. They are still a free people. If ever they are conquered, they will realise that victory is the only thing that matters. And then it will be too late. But come you down with me into the Summer Country, Photinus, and ask the Master yourself for a ship.'

I hesitated. Perhaps as far as that, but no farther. And quickly, so that I could get back to the Old City before the end of the summer, before the baby was born. And no farther. That was tempting. And I would not make myself any promises. I had told Uncle Euthyphro that I would see the trade started, and if it meant a month or two extra in Britain, then I would bear with it.

'Now, if it's there you're going,' warned the Setanta, 'it's not as a Roman you can go. You can be a Galatian if you wish, because you speak British with a strange accent.' This annoyed me: I was sure that no one could have guessed I was not born and bred in the island.

'With a new name,' Pryderi added.

'No, no,' corrected the Setanta. 'Clan first, name after.'

'All right, Clan then,' agreed Pryderi. 'Now, do you know your ancestry on your mother's side?'

'Not very far,' I warned them. 'Not more than twenty-one or twenty-three generations.' And I recited it, going back in the male line only but of course naming all my grandmothers as they came and inserting their fathers too. My two companions listened with care to my pronunciation of these outlandish names, now and again correcting me. And when I finished, the Setanta said:

'Plain, isn't it?'

'Obvious,' agreed Pryderi. 'Son of Lear, he is.'

'What does that mean?' I asked.

'Oh, a great house it was once,' Pryderi told me, 'and ruled all the island of Britain, but few are they and rarely met with.'

'But in the Isle of the Blessed,' added the Setanta, 'it is an O'Leary you will be, and plenty of them there are and eager to welcome any kinsman from over the sea, especially if he is rich.'

'But what is it I can't eat?'

'Swan, of course.' They both answered together. I felt rather disappointed, because there is nothing I like better than a nice roasted swan. It is nearly big enough to serve as a dish for two, but if you are giving a party I advise you to cater on the basis of one swan per guest, since this avoids disappointment. Then Pryderi, in a doleful voice:

'This is all nonsense. There is no possibility, Son of Lear or not, of taking you down into the Summer Country as if you were one of us. It would be better, Photinus son of Lear, if you stayed here in Londinium and let me do all the work for you in the Summer Country.'

And let you have all the money to control, I thought. Not on any account. But I could hardly sound as distrustful, so I answered as ceremonially as I could:

'I come of a great and ancient House. Beside it your House of Lear is young and of little account. And I have sworn to all the heads of the House that I would go as far as the port for Ireland and bring back the Gold of Ireland. You talk of a Gesa which binds you. I also am bound. I can no more turn back from this journey than you, Son of Mil, could refuse me your cloak if I asked you for it.'

'Asked for it you have,' said the Setanta. 'And have it you shall.'

He stood up. He was a head taller than Pryderi and me, and well built, though not gross or corpulent like Gwawl. He was, indeed, the kind of man I would have been pleased to have as Mate on any voyage. He went to the cupboard in the corner of the room, stepping gently over Elaine who had long since sunk into a drunken sleep. He turned to me again, his arms full of fur. 'Take my cloak, Photinus, that I cannot refuse you. And I will take what I think you have offered. You have offered me the head of the King of Connaught, to hang on the pole's end.'

I took the cloak, a splendid garment of blue-grey fur, strange to the touch and warm, lapping me from neck to heels, and hooded. This is what every sailor who can afford it wears in thunderstorms, for there is nothing that wards off lightning like seal fur. I turned to show Pryderi. He knew, as the Irishman knew, that I had no more suspected that such a cloak was in the room than I could fly. And that is why Pryderi looked at the cloak with open mouth.

'There is no further we need be looking for a name. Seal cloak asked unknowing shows that you are Mannanan.'

'But he is a god of the sea,' I objected.

'And is it not meeting him we all have been at some time or another?' asked the Irishman. 'And what is the loan of a name between kinsmen?'

For I had forgotten that it is the Brits alone among all the nations of the earth who are so bold as to take the names of their gods and goddesses to themselves, and you must always be careful in telling stories there to make it clear exactly who or what you are talking about. And I remembered too all my grandfather had always taught us about the essential nature of every name.

'Yes,' I agreed, 'I will be Mannanan the Son of Lear, on sea and on shore in this island and in the other.'

We talked on and on, and later when I lay in bed and remembered what we had said, I was horrified. I had agreed that somehow or other I would provide the means for a change of government in Ireland, which only could give us terms of trade. And what had I as working assets in this undertaking?

First, I had one man, and now, when I could no longer see him, and was no longer overborne by his personality and the air of power and menace in his stout arms and his massive fists, he did not seem such a great asset. I did not even know his real name.

And of Pryderi, my other asset, I knew nothing, except that he had found me the Setanta and that he only could help me to hire a ship that would face the winter on the Western Sea, for no Roman ship could float for long in the North except in the summer months, and then only in calm weather.

But, in the ship? We had talked of money, but in the end it was not money that the Setanta wanted, or at least not very much. But he did want what he could not buy, weapons. And it never struck him that I could not buy arms either. I had a permit for a sword, and one sword only.

I tossed in the darkness, and always in the night before me shone the Gold of Ireland, and I was frantic to think of it there, free for the taking, and not able to take it. And then, suddenly, I remembered something that Pryderi had said to the Setanta in one of the wrangles that had enlivened the evening. He had goaded the Irishman:

'Why, we in this island will have thrown off the Romans and will walk in freedom, when you in the Island of the Blessed still lie beneath their yoke.'

And it came to me then, that I had another asset. He did not stand seven feet tall, he only looked like it. And he had the ear of the Procurator.

Chapter Five

It took weeks of arranging, before Pryderi and I went off into the West. There was a lot of work, at the Office of the Procurator, because it was ruled that this was all a civil matter, and a financial one, and that the military were only there to obey. But whenever I could, at dusk, I would wander about in the streets by the river, looking for a cloud of seagulls and listening for a voice and yearning for a cloak of yellow and white and for a head of red hair.

There was, however, one day I went back to the scabbard-maker. I must say that he had done very well. He had covered the beechwood sheath with thin plates of bronze, patterned in scarlet enamel, and the bronze between the enamel plated with Gold. Not a scabbard for use, a scabbard for show, as I had asked. This was not now a weapon I would ever carry into battle, even though the blade was better than any you will find within the Empire, a blade to cut down elephants. This now was a sword to be borne before me, sheathed, point up, on that great day when I would come before the High King of all Ireland at Tara to tell him the terms on which my family would deign to trade with him.

I received the scabbard from the maker, and I looked at it. It was a real Brit pattern, all twisted lines and coils, but meaningless. I peered at it way and way about, and then I asked the maker:

'What is this pattern?'

'Why, bears. What else for you but bears?'

I looked again, and sure enough, if you knew, it was bears all right. And I looked again at the X-shaped hilt, and now it was less clear whether it was more like a man or more like a bear. But how should the scabbard-maker, or, more curious the blade-maker, have known that bears were so sacred to my family?

Of course, when we left Londinium, I didn't wear that sword, on the belt of soft leather from Cordoba all embroidered with flowers in gold and silver wire that I found in a dark corner of Leo Rufus's warehouse. I didn't tell him about it, I just took it over. I wrapped the sword in my sealskin cloak, because there was no wearing that in the summertime, even though Britain is always as they say, two tunics colder than civilised countries. I didn't wear a tunic either, but I was dressed as a Brit, in blue shirt and trousers, good boots of soft Spanish leather dyed blue, and a jerkin of soft brown sheepskin to keep out the rain. It *was* raining, of course.

We left Londinium at dawn, as soon as the city gates were open. I had been up early, shaving off my beard, or most of it. I was very careful about how much of it I did take off, and by judicious clipping of the hair either side of my mouth I was able to give myself a real British moustache which reached down to my nipples and made Pryderi so jealous he did nothing but grumble for miles.

We each had a horse to ride on and another to carry our baggage, done up in bundles. I had quite a lot, because I saw no reason why I should not turn an honest penny on the journey. The horses were native ponies, and the less said about them the better. They were small, and very strong: if you don't mind your legs hanging down so far that your spurs hurt your mother the Earth and not the beast, then you can ride one of these ponies all day without a stop. But not two days running. I would have preferred one of the cavalry horses the Army use, with the Parthian blood, but it would have been so conspicuous, and Pryderi was dreadfully concerned with not being conspicuous.

Of course, I am disenchanted now with horses. I had one once on the Amber road, and he was a *horse*. He was a horse that would carry you a hundred miles in one day, and then again the next day, and then into battle on the third day, and in the pursuit on the fourth. He was a horse that understood the speech of man, and the very thought of man he would know unspoken, and obey. He was not got by any mortal stallion, I tell you that; he was by Divinity out of the Platonic essence of all horses. I rode him for three years, and at the end – I weep when I think of it. I killed him myself. I will not think of it.

But we had our packhorses, and they would cover, if they had to, thirty miles in a day on the hard roads. We went out by the road on the north side of the river, which cuts out a great bight of the Thamesis. It was a very busy road. After we left the walls of the City, we found that we could count on meeting at least half a dozen travellers going the other way in every hour. Some of them were ox wagons full of vegetables, beans and carrots going in to the markets of the city, and looking at the poor innocent plants shrivelling away on the carts I began to understand why the food in Londinium was so bad. But we did come across one group that was different. It was a military convoy, the only troops we ever saw on the road. There were only a dozen of them, just enough to stop the Brits from stealing the oxen for meat at night, and to wait on the very junior centurion who was in charge. I recognised him, I had bought him wine at that inn north of Lugdunum, but he did not know me, hardly gave me a second glance, just another Brit on the road.

Pryderi, though, nudged me to look at what was in the wagons. They were light, you could tell that from the way the cattle moved, and so the big baskets, the fisces, in them were empty. I knew those baskets, all right.

'Silver?' I asked Pryderi.

'Party from the Second Legion, at Isca, going up for the salt money for the troops,' he told me. 'There'll be enough silver going back, all in coin, next week, to keep a kingdom going for a year, and no more escort than you see now.'

'Easy pickings for someone,' I hinted.

'When the time comes,' agreed Pryderi. 'You see, they know the south is quiet. There are no troops in the interior at all. Anybody who takes on a pay convoy risks having all the civil zone under military law again for years. It will have to be done at the right time and in the right place.'

I said nothing. Perhaps there were comments I ought not to make, things I ought not to know. We pushed on. The road crosses the river at a place called Pontes, and in the little town we stopped for the night. There was an inn where Pryderi was known well enough to be asked no questions. Nobody asked about me, either.

'It's the blue,' Pryderi assured me. 'Wearing that, you are known as a Bard, and whatever you do, however eccentric, like wearing a fancy eye, or a sword for that matter if you want to, people will pass over without a question, as being natural to the poetic mind. Respected you will be, and as a foreigner they will answer questions and tell stories that will astonish you, because they all know that the mind of the poet does thrive on marvels.'

I looked sideways at him. This is an island of deceit and duplicity and mists indeed, I thought, and if ever I hear the truth about anything, then it's lucky I'll be. It was easy already to fall into the Brits' manner of speech, and after speech comes thought, and after thought comes life, and love. If you talk in Latin and think in Latin, you must be dignified, and think in dignity, because there is no short or easy or comfortable way of saying anything in that language. But in Greek, as we speak it all along the coasts of Asia and into Alexandria, from Massilia to Trapezus in the Caucasus, everything is easy and full of slang and comfortable ways of thought. And yet, in this unconventional tongue, it is always possible to say what you mean, and to know that it will only have one meaning to anyone who listens. But while the Brit's tongue is also full of slang, it is vague and imprecise and soft at the edges, and behind the plain meaning of everything said you have to look for another hidden meaning. I decided to speak plain.

'If we are going to stay here all tomorrow,' I said, 'then I am not going to be idle, nor am I going to spend the day here at my own loss for the horses' comfort. Let us away to the hut that you have taken for us, and get to work.'

'Work?' Pryderi wondered as he followed me. 'Do not mention that word to me, that am a British gentleman. I do not mind a little usury, or profitable sharp practice, but not work.'

'And you a sailor?'

'Hauling at the rope, and straining at the oar, ten days together on the heaving sea, with not a drop of water nor a bite of bread to pass my lips, and often enough I have done it, why, that is not work. That is sport.'

'Indeed, then, it is not work that we will be employed in here, but sport, tomorrow, and art today.'

I unrolled one of the bundles that I had brought with me on the packhorse. Pryderi looked at it with interest.

'Leather?'

302

'Leather, soft leather. Guaranteed the best soft Spanish leather from fighting bulls of the plains.'

'Whose guarantee?' He fingered the sheets like a connoisseur. 'Not ten days ago this was baa-ing for its supper on the Rainy Mountains. You must realise, I have met Leo Rufus before.'

'And I have seen leather before,' I assured him. 'Now, as we came through this town, there was something that struck me, and it was this. I saw that there was a lack, and a scarcity, and a dearth, of one thing only, and that was – shoes. Boots I saw, of the kind you wear ploughing, and for fishing in the river, but no dainty shoes of quality on the feet of men or women. Come to that it did not seem to me that the feet were moving very quickly or that anyone was in a mood to dance through the streets.'

'And what did you expect?' Pryderi was a trifle impatient. 'Yesterday was the first of August, the day of the feast of Luggnasad, the end of shearing. There would have been a splendid time here, as indeed there was even in Londinium, if you knew where to go for it, and there is not a man, or a woman either in a country town like this who has not a headache.'

'Headache? I never have them, however much I drink.'

'Then lucky it is you are. But what you are going to do about this lack of shoes?'

'Why, we are going to make shoes.'

'Do we' – I was glad that Pryderi was counting himself in with me – 'do we know anything about that craft?'

'We can try.' I unrolled the leather. 'Hold out your foot. We'll do you a pair to measure first, and then some smaller and some bigger, as samples. Then tomorrow we'll sit in the market place and make them to order.'

I cut, and Pryderi sewed. He did it very well, and I remarked on this.

'Three months as regimental tailor to Aristarchos, and there is not much there is left to learn about clothing, or equipment, or how to make little economies which no one will notice till they have accepted the articles. Fit well enough, these do. Style is a bit odd, though?'

'That's the beauty of it. The women will all go for a new fashion.'

'A bit plain though, they are. They go a lot more for decoration, I tell you, around here.'

'I have thought about that.' I delved into another bag, in which I had brought a variety of oddments which I knew would be hard to get out in the West, like the gallstone of an ass, and an ounce of powdered unicorn horn, the ashes of a boar's pizzle, and the ground ankle-bones of a nanny-goat. Among all this were a few crystals of vitriol, which I dissolved in a cup of warm water. Then I added a few other trifles, and began to work with a piece of fairly clean rag. Soon the leather was a bright and striking blue.

'Will that do?'

'As long as it is fine tomorrow. But it is a foundation, and a ground, and a beginning. Allow me.'

Pryderi busied himself a moment with a few more of my little treasures. I was startled to see how much he knew. In a short while he had another cup full of a scarlet dye, thick, a paint rather. He took a hazel twig he had brought in from the hedgerow to clean his teeth with, and he dipped the frayed end in the paint. Then, in one clean flowing line, he drew on the toe of each shoe a fish.

We made many more pairs that night, and painted them in blue and in scarlet, and in a variety of other colours. I made the shoes, and dyed the leather, and it was Pryderi's task to paint on the designs. I only painted one pair. I did that when Pryderi had made up several colours, so that I could spread myself, and then, on the toe of each shoe, I painted Aphrodite rising from the sea. And when I had finished I looked at the Goddess, and somehow I could not think where I had got that face from, because it did look familiar and not only because I had drawn it.

In the end, when our oil lamp had burnt too low to see, we had to go to bed. I had to abandon the ways of civilised men, and so I could not go to bed in my day tunic, but in the fashion of the Brits I stripped and put on a clean pair of trousers. Pryderi had so made fun of the style and the cut, to say nothing of the workmanship, of the pairs I had bought in Lutetia that I had relegated them to this use, except for a few pairs I had given to Pryderi, and I was half annoyed, half amused to see that he did, after all, consider them good enough for wear during the day. But as I took off my shirt, Pryderi whistled and pointed to the great scar that runs under my arm on my right side.

'That's a bad one.'

'I got that a long time ago, on the Amber Road. It was with my own spear he did it, too, you know the way things get mixed up in a mêlée. But I killed him, before the night was out.'

'That was a head worth taking.'

'No, I left it. There was nobody to play the head game against.'

'Head game?'

'Yes. You know, you throw the head up between two villages, and then wrestle for it, all in on both sides.'

'The Germans do that?'

'Yes.'

'And a godless lot they must be, indeed. A head is too sacred a thing for that. Once you take a head, the thing is to carry it home, and vow it to the Goose God. And then if it is not an important head, or if it were easy enough to take, you may hang it up outside your house, but if it were the head of a great enemy or the result of a desperate deed, then it is to the Gods you give it, either hanging it up before a shrine, or casting it into some sacred place. When we get to the Summer Country, I shall show you some of mine. I have to keep a bit quiet about it here. The Romans don't like it.'

I began to feel that I was travelling with a different kind of human being from myself. This man would be a suitable companion for Aristarchos. And yet, I felt I could sleep easy in his company.

Chapter Six

Next morning it was a fine day. You may take it as given, that unless I tell you otherwise, every day I spent in that Island the sky was overcast, even if it did not rain. But that day it was fine. Pryderi went off and slipped a denarius to the man who allotted positions in the market place, and we settled down on quite a good pitch.

'You'll have to work hard to sell anything here,' Pryderi warned me. I answered:

'I've been selling all my life. There are plenty of men who can boast that in Alexandria they sold the Pharos to visiting Arab chiefs. I sold it there once to an Alexandrian.'

I stood up. Pryderi sat below me with a pile of half-finished shoes. I began to speak:

'My friends, my cousins, my kinsmen! Here am I, Mannanan the Galatian. I have come across the Empire, out of my own kindness and goodness of heart, simply and solely to benefit you. And that I will do. Listen all to me.'

And early as it was, there were already a number who did stop to listen to me. I had several advantages, like a foreign accent which will always disarm suspicion, and my great fur cloak, which looked rich enough to dispel any idea that I could be wanting to make money, since I had so much already, and my one black eye and one sapphire.

'You and I are brothers. We alone of all the world speak the language of the gods, who saw the foundation and the construction and the erection of the universe. And once, we were famous among all civilised nations for the quality, and the excellence, and the beauty, of our shoes, and our boots and our sandals.' I bowed my head, and swept my hand in a great circle, pointing to their feet.

'Those days, my brothers, are gone. Look at yourselves. Should we be proud of what we now wear? Should we want the

306

Romans to come and see us like this? How can you hold up your heads, unless it be not to see your feet?

'I have not come, my brothers, to tell you Galatian stories, though I have some that would make your flesh creep. No, I have come to benefit you. I have come on a mission of pure charity.

'Look at these shoes, ladies and gentlemen, especially you ladies, just look. Start off by inspecting the craftsmanship. Look at the cutting! Look at the stitching! Look at the patterns! Where ever did you see styles like these before? And no wonder. Here, my companion is one of the greatest Master Shoemakers of the Age.' Pryderi stood up, bowed silently and sat down again. 'Personal and private shoemaker he was to his late Sacred Majesty Himself. All the shoes of the Emperor's Household he made, for all the ladies of the Court, as well as for the Emperor Himself. Why, his late Sacred Majesty was cremated wearing a pair of my friend's slippers, and there in Olympus He walks today, wearing them, and it was His express wish. What better warrant of quality could you have but this? Who would like to wear the shoes of heaven?

'Now for shoes like these, what would you say was a fair price? What do I say? Twenty-five silver denarii a pair? would that not be fair? But am I asking twenty-five denarii for a pair? I, who only came here to benefit my kinsmen? I who only came here to make you remember, and remember kindly, your brethren in Galatia?

'Shall I ask you for twenty denarii a pair, then? Shall I even ask for ten denarii a pair? No!! I have come to invite you to share in my own good fortune, because I walk in such shoes every day of my life. Shall I ask for five denarii a pair, that would hardly cover the cost of the leather and the dye, and leave nothing over to reward us for our labour? No!!! All I need here is enough money in my hand to pay for the night's lodgings for myself and my friend, and for a handful of musty hay for our horses, who are religious and given to fasting. All I ask is two denarii, just two little horses, for a pair of the most durable, the most comfortable, the most distinctive shoes you will ever wear.'

They sold like water in a city under siege. Long before noon we had sold almost all our stock, and I was already beginning to

307

reckon up my profit – I estimated that I had made three pairs for less than one denarius. All kinds of people had come to buy, first the market people themselves, and then farmers and their wives, and our greatest sale had, as always, been among the local lads buying what they hoped would get their girls into the long grass with them. But then as I looked at my last pair, a different customer arrived. There was a sudden thinning out of the crowd in front of me, leaving a space, and as I looked it was covered with a swarm of sparrows, hopping about and quarrelling for the crumbs and the grains of oats they found in the horse-droppings. And as I looked down, there appeared among the birds the feet of a Lady. It was feet and shoes I was looking at that day, and by the shoes this was a great Lady, the litter trade if ever I saw it. They were fine and dainty feet, and that was real Spanish leather that covered them, and dyed it was in a dye that would stand up to all the weather of the world. Dressed she was like a woman of the country. Not like the women of Pontes, who wanted to show how sophisticated they were and walked Roman fashion in tunics with a pallium to throw over their shoulders if the weather required it, which it always does up there.

I saw beneath her skirt of wool, fine wool, all woven in a check of light blue and dark blue and grey, there were a dozen petticoats. Each one was of a different colour. I raised my eyes to her apron, of fine linen, white, and embroidered with the flowers of the flax. This linen I knew, it had come from Egypt. About her waist was her belt, and this if not the belt of a queen was the belt of a queen's daughter or of a queen to be, for it was of a dozen strands of chain, alternate links of Gold and silver, and at the front it was dastened by a buckle of silver, the size of both my palms, studded with garnets. I looked farther up, to the full bosom hidden, half hidden, by a blouse of silk, white silk, but embroidered in its turn with blue silk in a Pictish pattern of whorls and spirals. I looked up to her shawl, and this was of cotton, white again, and tasselled, and it was woven through and across with golden wire, and the wire ran out to stiffen the tassels. And under the shawl I saw hair of a light lively red, and it framed a face well known, well known indeed.

There she stood like a rich and splendid trireme, beating back from a voyage to the Seres, all laden with silk and Gold and pearls and diamonds. Rich enough she was to buy up all the ocean, strong enough to beat off all attack. She stood before me with her flags and banners flying, her birds sang about her like a cloud of sail full drawing. And she spoke, in a voice that I surely had heard singing:

'How much for shoes, Mannanan?'

At the sound of that voice, all my bones turned to water. Somewhere deep down inside me the merchant said, 'Go on, tell her the tale, how they are dyed by a secret recipe known only to the ancients of Galatia, and how they would be cheap at a hundred denarii, and how you will reduce them for her, special for her, to a mere twenty-five.' But I could not do it. I looked at that oval face, the straight nose and the firm lips, and I looked down to where it looked back at me from my own shoes, and all I could say was:

'For you, my Lady, there is no charge. They are a gift. Take them as an offering to your beauty from your brethren in Galatia.'

She stood still for a moment. Then she called over her shoulder:

'Pay him, Hueil.'

A man came forward from the crowd behind, and I saw that he was wearing trousers in the same blue and grey check as her skirt, and more, that he was one of a group, four or five. He came to me, and picked up the last pair of shoes, then shook his head and threw them back on the ground. Then he stooped to where I squatted cross-legged, and in one swift movement whipped the shoes off my feet, the shoes on which I had painted Aphrodite, and stuffed them into his bag. He tossed me, contemptuously, a coin, and followed his mistress into the crowd. I went livid, I felt it, and for a moment I almost threw the coin back after him, but the basic sanity that is the salvation of every merchant prevailed, and I bit it. It was Gold, all right, not lead. I looked at it more closely. This was not the head of any Emperor. Wafer thin, the coin was about the size of my thumbnail. On one side was a horse, with a human head. On the other was a name, in crude Greek lettering – the coiner, however well he could draw a horse on the face of the die, certainly could not read. With difficulty

I read it: Niros of the Treveri. Here, on a quarter of an ounce of Gold, this long-dead King of the Gauls still lived. But the coin, minted how many years, how many hundreds of years ago, was still new, and unclipped, and unworn. The outlines and the letters were as crisp as on the day when they were stamped out. This gold piece had never been carried in a purse to jostle its fellows and wear itself into dust. It was almost as if it had been carefully put aside against a day – against today.

The sight of the gold, Hueil's action, paralysed me for as long as a man might take to count to twenty. Then I sprang up, seizing Pryderi by the arm. All through my conversation with the Lady he had sat there, his back to us, huddled up, as if trying not to be noticed.

'Come on!' I cried to him. 'Follow the Lady! Find her!'

He looked up at me.

'Mad you are, Mannanan, I always said you were mad. There's no following her, not for a sane man.'

'Why? Do you know her? Who is she?'

'Know her? Of course I do, and so does every Briton who sees her go by. My own first cousin she is, daughter of my mother's sister, and named after my mother. Rhiannon of the Brigantes, she is, and a great Princess, and a wealthy one, because it is the Brigantes that have made their peace with Rome, and they get all kind of favours. But I would not have you talk with her, for that very reason.'

'Making your peace with the Emperor seems to be profitable,' I observed, holding out the gold coin.

'Ach-y-fi!' he said, which is the Brits' expression of disgust. 'And would I be touching that, knowing where it has come from?'

I thought this was a trifle extreme a way of showing that he was not on good terms with his cousin. I said as firmly as I could:

'Well, whoever she is, I must find her.'

I stood and I was about to make off into the crowd, where I could still see Hueil pushing along, when there was an interruption. Pryderi was gathering up the knives and needles and last and the rest of the shoemaker's tools, when two fat and scarlet men came puffing up to us like a pair of roosters in the spring.

'Look here,' said the redder and fatter of the two. 'And what do you think you've been doing?'

'And who do you think you are, when you have stood still long enough for your manners to catch up with you, and running hard they must be because they are so far behind.' Pryderi could be insolent when he chose, and I decided that as it was his language the men were speaking, I would leave him to carry on the conversation, which promised to become a little acrimonious.

'This is a formal complaint. We are the co-equal Chairmen of the Shoemakers' Guild of Pontes. We have been told, and informed, and warned, that you have been making shoes within the boundaries of the unincorporated Municipality of Pontes, contrary to the Charter agreed between the Guilds of the Town, and amended by, in particular, the by-law of the Fourth Year of Domitian, Chap Six, Clause Four, Para Two.'

'We were not making shoes. It was slippers we were making.'

'It is the same thing.'

'It is not at all the same thing.' By the light in Pryderi's eyes, it was clear that there was nothing he would like more than an argument at the end of his long silent day sitting at my feet in the market, his mouth full of waxed thread and needles, and if necessary, I could see, he would keep an argument of the type of 'You did' – 'I didn't' going for hours. The two men could see it too. The spokesman avoided the trap. He merely said:

'The terms "shoes" is general, and subsumes under it all slippers, boots and other footwear.'

'It does not,' Pryderi snapped back. 'Slippers are most clearly defined and distinguished and differentiated from shoes by a Law of Lud Son of Heli that was King of Londinium in the years before the Conquest. And it is known to every thinking man that it is precisely these laws treating of the definition of terms that are by the laws of the Empire and by the grace of the Caesars deemed to be the basis and the foundation and the substratum of all local municipalities and corporations, especially of unincorporated federations of Guilds.'

'Careful, you. It is our town you are in, unincorporated or not, and you will do what we say.'

'Force is it now? You can always tell if a man has a bad case that he would not argue in a court of law, when he begins to talk in terms of numbers and of possessions.'

'Another word, and you will be in front of the Magistrate, and there is little chance you will have in front of him, being as he is my brother-in-law, and treasurer of the Potters' Guild as well. Hand it over, we want every penny you have made by cheating this afternoon.'

'And there is not a single denarius we have made by cheating. That is defamatory, and it is before the Magistrate we will be arguing that, I tell you. I rely on the help of my friend here, who is familiar with the law and the Rescripts of the Empire covering this very point, and has the more important of them by heart, seeing he is a Citizen – of Rome, I mean, not of any little hamlet like Londinium or Pontes.'

There was a short pause. There is an advantage in having the kind of influence being a Citizen gives you out in the more distant provinces of the Empire, where Citizens born are rare outside the Army. The second of the co-equal Chairmen, seeing his chance, muttered something about 'never sue a Citizen, they've always got some pull somewhere,' which is true enough. The two officials of the Guild muttered more furiously after that, but so quietly they could only be heard by each other, and when Pryderi tried to put his head in between theirs they cursed him so roundly that even he stood back. At last the first Chairman said:

'All right, then. Keep what you've got, but clear out of town now. I mean now, straight away, this instant.'

Pryderi began to look fierce, but just in time the second co-equal Chairman said himself:

'No, not this afternoon, but tomorrow morning. We want to send a man ahead to warn all the other Shoemakers' Guilds ahead as far as Glevum.'

We didn't object to that. I was tired of making shoes. But the interlude had done the damage. The Lady had vanished, and try as I would, walking about the town, I could not find her again. I was able to do a little shopping, against the next town, investing the proceeds of the morning's work, the silver, that is. Not the Gold: I kept that.

It was dusk when I got back to the inn. Pryderi was in the

main room, drinking cider with a rather motley set of companions. I joined them.

'I think there's a story here you would like to hear,' was Pryderi's greeting. 'It's about Gold. You buy old Blino a mug of cider, and you shall hear it.'

I obeyed. It was a very old man who sat there, very old indeed. As soon as he was satisfied that I really was going to buy him cider, he drew me into the darkest corner of the taproom.

'Not everybody I would show this to, you understand,' he whispered, suffocating me with the foul wind from his decaying teeth. 'But since you are a friend of him, then I will.'

He fumbled in his pouch and brought out a twist of black and yellow cloth. He untwisted it, and showed a ring, a Golden ring. It was made of Gold wire, fine as a hair, twined into a sixteen-fold strand like rope, big enough to go on his now shrunken little finger.

'That's Irish Gold,' he told me.

'How do you know?'

'Why, that's where I got it.'

'From Ireland?'

'No! nobody alive goes to Ireland. I got it out of a grave. Dug it out with an iron spade, I did, so I was safe enough. They won't never come back from Ireland to find me that way.'

'Who won't?'

'The dead, of course. That's where the dead go, to Ireland. I'm keeping this, like they did, to pay my passage, where every labouring man is paid in Gold, where there is neither hunger nor thirst nor pain, nor cold nor the bitter sadness of defeat, where age rusts not away the spring of youth, where men and women are for ever young, far in the Golden Island of the Blessed.'

His voice died away. I wondered how the rest of the poem had gone. He was past asking now. Cider and age had done their sleepy work. I raised my eyes from the Gold in his hand, and I looked over his shoulder into the face of a man with a squint. He made the Sign of the Four, as the Druids do, on face and chest, and was gone in the flickering light. I put the ring back in the pouch, and the pouch firmly into the old man's hand. If he had nothing now, why should he not have his youth again?

Chapter Seven

Next morning we took the road again. Pryderi looked suspiciously at the big packages I loaded on my horses and on his, big and awkward, but light as a feather. However, he said nothing, probably thinking that anything I told him would only spoil his peace of mind, if he had any left.

The road from Pontes to Calleva soon leaves the river valley, and goes up on to higher ground, a long belt of barren sandy soil, sour and good for nothing but growing timber for charcoal. Where the country was more open it was covered with gorse and heather. Sometimes the sun shone, and then I felt at home. It was good adder country if ever I saw it.

Calleva we reached at sunset. It is quite a pleasant town, in a provincial way. The only trouble with it is that there is no reason at all why it should exist. Usually a city has some reason for being where it is. Either there is a bridge, or a ford, or two roads cross, or there is a good site to build a fort. But there Calleva stands in the middle of an oak forest, on the edge of that adder country, with not so much as a little stream close by to give it an excuse for being.

Why was it there? Well, there had been the day, back in old Claudius's time, when the Legion had first pounded along into the wilderness, laying down the road as it went. Now it so happened that in that month the King of the Atrebates was spending the time eating up his rents in that particular dirty shabby little village, as he had spent the month before in another shabby little village, and as he would move on to a third when the country around Calleva was eaten bare. If you have no roads, and your wealth is in food and cloth, then it is much easier to go where your wealth is to consume it than to have it brought to you. So with the great decisiveness an Empire expects from its commanders, the legate of the legion decided that this must be the capital of the Atrebates, and that the country of the Atrebates must be governed from a great city here on this spot.

The kingdom, therefore, became the country, and the King became the hereditary chairman of a local senate, and his nobles became hereditary senators. Nothing else was changed at first, only the names. But the country had to pay a corn tax, and in wheat, too, which up to now they only grew to make a kind of beer out of.

Then there came the development. Under the pressure of the Procurator and his staff, the local notables marked out wide boundaries for the new capital they hadn't realised they wanted. They built walls, of earth first, with a stake fence on top, and they put a gate in each of the four walls, just like a legionary camp. Then they laid out two straight roads across the town, from gate to gate, just as in a camp, and where the Praetorium of a camp should be they built a basilica to serve as a senate chamber and as a court. It was a mud-and-wattle hall at first, but when I came to Calleva they had just rebuilt it in stone, and they were very proud of their marble barn.

Now, if the nobles were going to sit in the local senate they would have to live in their capital for some months of the year, and so each one built himself a house in the town. Of course, each one thought he would not settle there, but he would still live most of the time in his own farm-house in the country, which gave him his income. But the nobles reckoned without their ladies. You know how women are when they get together. They soon find out the pleasures of gossiping, and they object when their husbands begin to suggest that it is now time to return to the country. That is an end to the free and lonely life. So now the nobles live in the town all the year round, and their stewards bring them in their rents by the fine new road. Now-adays the nobles never see their farms at all, and their people who would once have followed them into battle even against the legions forgot what they looked like or even who they were. Only in a few wild regions, where the kings had refused to sub-mit to Rome, or to live in towns, did the people still follow their ancient lords. But kingdoms were one thing. Clans were another, and even if a man forgot who was his king, he would remember who were his ancestors, and accept his relations, even to seventeen generations. And that, I thought, was why Pryderi was so careful about choosing his inns, and why he was so calm about leaving our property unguarded.

Very few people, however, would come and live in a town like Calleva, because there was nothing for them to do there, except to satisfy the demands of the nobles and their families, and of the lawyers who would come when the courts were sitting. There were a few craftsmen, protected by the nobles' insistence that there should be no market in the county except in Calleva itself, where they could easily collect the market dues and share them out equally. It was in the market place that we got into trouble. But that was on the third day there.

On the evening of the first day, we only put up our horses and carried our packs into the room we had been given. Then we went into the public room of the Inn, in the hope of supper. There were a number of people there, including the two middleaged men with the boy that I could remember from Pontes. They were sitting together in a corner playing Fichel. The rest of the clientele were discussing a particularly juicy rape case that was coming up the next day at the court. They went into a lot of circumstantial detail none of which had anything to do with the question of guilt or innocence, till I decided that the only possible verdict was an acquittal on the grounds of public entertainment. At last the landlady, who had been looking more and more uncomfortable as the discussion developed, said:

'I *do* wish you'd stop talking about it. You're all going on and on like so many querns, and it's a dreadful headache I've got with it.'

'Headache? I'll tell you what to do.' I must have been feeling a little drunk and very conceited, in my character of the wise and experienced traveller. 'You ought to take three walnuts and crush them together in a pestle, but you must begin by cracking them so carefully that the meat comes out unbroken in one piece. Now, you must use a pestle of oak and a mortar of elm to mash the meat of the nuts into a paste, and the paste you must then spread on a platter of wood and divide into five exactly equal parts with a sea-shell – an oyster shell will do. Now one of these parts you must offer to the Sun, and one to the Moon, and one to the Wind, because there you have the three greatest causes of headaches, namely walking too long in the Sun, sleeping where the Moon can shine on your face, and facing into the cold Wind. Of the remaining fifths, the fourth you must put on your head, and fasten it there with a bandage of linen, spun from flax sown at the waning, and not at the waxing, of the Moon. The last fifth you shall eat. And then you will find that the headache is gone.'

And this is in my experience an infallible cure, because by the time you have done all this most headaches will have worked themselves out, and the cares of making the spell will make you forget the sickness if any remains. Now that I had my audience, I thought I would impress them some more with my Galatian wisdom, especially the man in the corner with a squint, who merely sat there saying, 'That is all magic and nonsense and an invention of evil spirits.' I thought it would be worth my while silencing him, to show the difference between real medicine, which is founded on logic, and magic. I explained:

This is a most efficacious remedy which had never been known to fail. And why is it so effective, I hear you ask? I will explain it to you, I who am a philosopher who am used to examining the causes of things and the reasons behind the motion of the world, and in making things clear to even the meanest intellects, as I see here tonight. You are all aware that the ague springs from the marshy places, and is given off as a mist and as an effluvium from the stagnant waters. Now, I am sure that you all know that the surest way to cure the ague is to chew the bark of the willow that grows in marshy places. For every disease carries in itself the sign of its own cure, and every cure carries the signs of the disease proper to it, as if it were written thereon.' I am afraid that I allowed my language to become pompous, because the Brits are most impressed with this. 'If you ask me, doctors spend too much time examining the diseases they know, and then seeking cures to fit them. They would be better advised to find the cures first, and then to seek out the diseases against which they are effective.'

I drank some more wheat beer.

'Now, for any disease of the outside of the head, for the skull, for complaints of the scalp or for falling out of the hair, the best cures are made from the flesh of the Indian nut, which perhaps you have seen.' I was quite sure that nobody there would have seen one, for at that time I myself had only rarely set eyes on it. 'This nut is the size of a man's head, and it has hair that grows on it. Beneath the hair, you will find on the skin of the nut three marks that signify two eyes and a mouth, so that the nut is in every way the sign and symbol of the head of a man.

'But this nut is only good for ailments of the outside of the head, for if you open it, you will find inside a hollow filled with a little sickly juice, though I am sure that there are heads in this very room' (and I looked straight at the man with the squint) 'which are like the Indian nut in all respects.

'But for pains of the inside of the head, you must always use a cure made from the walnut. And why is this? If you crack a walnut as I have told you, so that the flesh comes out in one piece, then, as I would show you if the nut were in season and there were any walnuts here to be had, you would see that the surface of the unbroken nut within the shell is an exact copy, and simulacrum, and model, of the brain of a man when you have carefully removed the skull. Now, it is no wonder that you should not know that, because I doubt whether there is anyone here who has ever looked on the surface of the uninjured brain—'

And a man at a table in the corner murmured, not loud, but very clear:

'I have.'

I looked at him. I peered into the shadows where he sat, and I began to have my suspicions. I went over to him, and I raised a lamp and I looked close at him, in his shabby clothes, all spattered with the muck of the roads and the straw of the stables where he had been sleeping till the russet of the cloth hardly showed. He was a good deal taller than either me or Pryderi, but he was very slender, emaciated almost, as if he had been fasting a long time. He was clean shaven all over his face, and that in itself was strange in a land where all men wear moustaches. His hair was red. I knew him all right. I looked at his plate, grilled kidneys and boiled beans, and at his mug of cider, and I said:

'Come, come, Taliesin. Last time I met you, you would eat no

318

meat and drink no strong drink' – in public, I meant, and he knew it – 'and I wonder to myself, how it is, since it is a paying trade, you have given up being a Druid.'

And at once everyone in the room, Pryderi and the landlady and the middle-aged men and the youth and everyone else except the man with the squint said 'Sshh! Ssshhh!!'

The landlord, who had up to now left the running of the place to his wife, came over and pulled me down on to the bench between Taliesin and himself. He said to me:

'Fine times it must be you are having in Galatia, and a liberty far beyond what we enjoy. But here we must be careful. Do you not know that the Romans killed all the Druids they could find when they first came here? It is unlawful for any Druid to do his holy work of judgement and sacrifice and prayer, or even to be seen within the confines of the Empire, or to walk abroad in the sight of men in this unhappy part of the Island of the Mighty. And plenty there are who claim to be Britons born who yet would betray this sacred patronage to torture and to death for the sake of money and for the favour of the oil-soaked wolves that are now so powerful. Some of our young men do still go over the seas to learn the Holy Law from the Druids of Ireland, but I do not need to tell you that of these brave lads there are none that do return. So, if we do hear, and suspect, and surmise, that there is a Druid travelling about the roads, in whatsoever disguise he may present himself, then there is nothing we do say about it to anybody no, not even to the Holy Man himself. And we understand, and it is essential for you to understand, that it may be necessary for such a Holy One to defile himself in the sight of the ignorant so that he may live to carry out the will of the Great that are invisible.'

'Aye,' confirmed Taliesin. 'It is for the sake of the fulfilment of my most holy vows that I must undergo all kinds of pollution.' He stuffed his mouth again with kidney. The landlord filled the resulting gap in the conversation.

'A virtue it is, and rewarded in this life, and in the time of transmigration, to give charity to a Druid. Therefore, it is incumbent on us all to assist this Holy Man on his pilgrimage to the Summer Country.'

The landlord was so pointed about this that I hastened to order another pot of cider for Taliesin, and one for Pryderi who joined us, as well as wheat beer for myself. I ordered our three dinners – for Taliesin agreed that his first dish of kidneys, being interrupted, had been a false start – to be brought to us in the corner. The landlord took this for an index of my desire to attain virtue, because when I went to pay our bill some days later I found he had not only charged us all double, but had made me pay for Taliesin as well. When I protested, the rogue said it showed how virtuous he was himself, in allowing me to assume a burden of charity which would certainly assure me future bliss.

I looked again at Taliesin's dinner, his second. I remembered what we all hear, that the Druids of Britain, like those of Gaul, are Pythagoreans, believing in the transmigration of souls, and living on vegetables alone without the taste of meat. I therefore had great pleasure in telling him something it had been obvious he had not known at our previous meeting.

'I've found out something about the Pythagoreans,' I told him with relish. 'I got drunk with a lapsed one in Byblos the year before last, and he tells me that the Bean is not a sacred thing to them, but unclean, and therefore they never eat it, while you, as I remember, used to live on them. And those kidneys you are eating, besides being made of meat, good solid meat, are bean-shaped and therefore instead of reducing the sin, as you imagine, they are adding to it.'

'And whoever said I was a Pythagorean?' asked Taliesin innocently. 'Indeed the vile slander has been spread by the Romans, who know no more of either doctrine than does my grandmother's cat. But we have little in common with the Pythagoreans except one element in our doctrines, and that little I shall reveal to you as the night goes on, or at some other convenient time.'

'As the night goes on?' I asked him. 'And where do you think you are going to sleep tonight?'

'Why, with you two. And it is not possible that you should be worse company than the horses.'

I could do little about it. I had to let him sleep in our room. I wanted to make him lie on the floor, but Pryderi, full of a reverence that did him little credit, gave up his own pallet to the Druid.

'I don't know why I allow it,' I grumbled. 'The last time I saw you two together, you were both ready to eat me. Going to quarrel over the marrow bones, I shouldn't wonder.

'Appetising he looks, doesn't he, standing there without any trousers?' said Taliesin dreamily. Pryderi agreed.

'The right thigh, the champion's portion. Promised it I was.'

'But even so,' went on the Druid, 'I was not expecting such a welcome, seeing I came out of my way to travel with you.'

'Travel with us? Certainly not! It's too dangerous. Citizen or not, I'll be in real trouble if the Government find out I've been concealing a Druid.'

'And who is there to tell them but yourself?' asked Pryderi, logically. 'You will be safer by far travelling with him than if you were in the midst of a legion, in the country.'

I changed the subject.

'In any case, I don't believe you were trying to travel with us. How would you have known we were on the road together?'

Pryderi, not Taliesin, answered me, too readily for my liking:

'Shoemakers' talk. Of course, you can't understand half what they say, their mouths being full of nails all the time, but still – it gets around.'

'True,' agreed Taliesin – you might as well try to shout down a waterfall as to get a word in edgeways into a conversation with the two of them together. 'If it is hearing you are about one Pryderi the Ingenious, and a young man from far away with only one eye who sells slippers to shoemakers' wives when they don't want slippers, then there is easy it is to come to a conclusion. By the way, when it was knowing you I was, there were two eyes you were having. Caw told me you'd lost one. What's that you've got there? Amethyst?'

'Yes. There's a little man in Corinth who does them for me. I'll give you his name if ever you need it. Do you like the carving?' I slipped it out and put it on the palm of his hand.

'Oh, indeed, and lovely it is, too. Hercules cleaning the Augean Stables, isn't it? Oh, the detail in that heap of manure … poetry in stone, I call it. An original design, mind you, seeing what it is for.'

'Perhaps. I have several others, but I like to suit my eyes to the occasion. I put this one in today in case we met Rhiannon again.'

321

That meant something to Taliesin, and nothing that he liked. He sat straight up in bed.

'Not Rhiannon of the Brigantes? Is she on this road?'

'He sold her some slippers,' said Pryderi: he seemed to think it funny. 'Hueil the son of Caw told me that she was going south to Dubris to spend the winter in Gaul. But there, you know what his Gesa is? He may never receive a gift, nor give one, nor speak the truth except in jest.'

'Why,' I asked, 'do you know this Hueil?'

'My second cousin on my father's side,' said Pryderi contriving by his tone to imply that I had asked a stupid question, carrying in itself its own answer. I wondered. Caw was a common enough name ... But Taliesin was worried.

'Well, let's hope that he was jesting when he said it. Principal Chief Bard I have been to Casnar the Painted Pict King, and Bithig the Bitch. Trouble and tribulation and trial, shortage and scarcity and starvation I saw there, but ruddy Rhiannon is worse. I will say no more. It is not a subject I wish to pursue before I dream.'

Perhaps Taliesin dreamed. I did not. I lay awake for hours listening to the most tremendous snores. Kidneys were not his ideal supper.

In the morning Pryderi went down and brought us a breakfast of beer and oat bread. While he was about that I unpacked my bundles.

'Shield frames?' he asked. 'Where did you get those?'

'In the market at Pontes,' I replied. 'And finished shields they were selling, too, there, so plain it is that they will sell here. But what I did not understand was this, why men in a disarmed country, and women too I saw, should want to buy shields.'

'For decoration,' Pryderi told me. It didn't matter to me, of course, why people bought them as long as they would sell. 'It is hanging them up people are, inside their houses and outside them too. It is their family badges they are painting on them, to proclaim to all that pass their ancestry and their nobility, and the less noble they are, and the more obscure their ancestors, the more shields and the bigger and the gayer they will hang up, and the more they will pay. So I understand the thinking there has

322

been behind your purchase, but it is, indeed, the policy I am questioning. It would be more politic for us to travel with as little fuss as possible, and the fewer men that see us, and see us to know us, the better it will be.'

'Indeed, and that is nonsense,' I told him. 'There is nothing more suspicious than the traveller who has no reason for travelling. But who will notice or remember or think the worse of the travelling craftsman? No, the more things we make and sell, the fewer men will remember us.'

Pryderi grudgingly agreed to join in. I looked at the shield frames. They were great flat baskets, oval in shape, that would cover a man from shoulder to knee. How anyone would use such a thing in battle I could not think. I found out, later. But of course these shields were not meant for war, and so, instead of planks of lime and sheets of gilded bronze, they would just be covered with leather.

'Do we know anything about shield-making?' Pryderi asked me.

'We can try,' I told him.

'Well, the best thing we can do is to cover the frames with leather, dyed in a variety of colours. Then if we paint a sample pattern on one, we can paint the rest to order in the customers' own patterns.'

We set Taliesin to dyeing the leather, while Pryderi and I cut it out with our shoemakers' knives and stretched it on the frames and stitched it. By noon, all the frames were covered and the leather was drying. We ate a light midday meal of a sucking pig between us, and then I told the others that I would work on a sample. I took a blue shield, the same beautiful heavenly blue as the shoes, and I made up dyes and colours from the variety of substances I carried in my bag.

It was a beautiful picture, I must say. I chose as a subject the marriage of Thetis and Peleus. There they stood, their divine beauty scarcely veiled by their flimsy garments, but Thetis further hidden by the shimmering of her form as she changed from one shape to another. The muscles stood out on Peleus's arms as, still at this late moment, he clung to the wrist of his unwilling bride, while Chiron prompted him over his shoulder. In the background were all the gods and goddesses, with their emblems, and with only one exception. And She, too, was present in Her own way, for the Apples of Discord fell among the throng. It was, though I say it myself, a masterpiece of art, and it is a great pity that it has not survived to be handed down to all posterity as a supreme example of what the mind of one man can conceive in colour and form and balance and symmetry. And for sheer workmanship, too – there was not the space the size of a finger nail over the whole surface of that man-high shield that was not covered with some part of the story or other: here you might see the arms of Peleus, the gift of Zeus, there Thetis' Golden urn, and in one place, the size of a man's hand, I had drawn the city of Troy, and Golden Achilles in his chariot. And yet, as I looked at it, it seemed there were things that were not quite right, though I could not imagine what, in Peleus's moustaches, in Thetis' heart-shaped face and the swell of her lovely breasts. I looked and I looked, but I could not think what it was that should disturb me so.

This painting took me the latter half of the day, and when I finished, it was nearly dark. But there, in the twilight, Pryderi took another shield, and a tiny disc of scarlet paint, and a chewed hazel twig. He dipped the end of the twig in the paint, and on the azure surface of the shield he drew one line. It was a long sinuous line, and he drew it all in one movement, never lifting the brush from the leather. There we saw, when he finished, a great Pictish bull, head down, tail up, pawing the ground, ready to charge. I expected him now to fill in this outline with lights and shades and patches of colour, and to make the background rich with trees and grass and rocks. But no, instead he took the same brush and the same colour, and in the bottom half of the shield he drew a second bull, but this one facing the opposite way. Hideously bare and stark the whole shield looked, when he laid down his brush, just the two bulls in outline. Ah, I thought, tomorrow we shall see I will have to fill in that picture for you, when all the other shield blanks are sold and we want to get one off our hands. You will be coming to me, Pryderi, and asking for lessons in how civilised men paint pictures.

So in the morning he and I went into the market place. Taliesin excused himself, on the plea of business elsewhere. We two found a comfortable place at the base of a pillar, and a couple of denarii to the market warden made sure that the lack of early booking would be overlooked. And I stood there, with my great picture shield covering my body from neck to ankle, as we see painted on old vases, and I began to talk.

'Comrades and brothers, listen to what I say.' Of course they always listen, it doesn't cost anything, but once they listen they may, may perhaps, buy.

'Proud am I of my ancestry. Proud am I of those who came before me. Proud am I that I can recite the names of my progenitors, to the fortieth generation. And so should you be proud, that can do as much. But do you show your pride in your houses? Do you hang on the walls the signs of your noble birth and the deeds of the great kings from whom you are sprung? I know you do. I know that it is only the cost, and the dearth of men who are skilled in handling the brush that holds you back from honouring each several one of your immortal ancestors. But now all your problems are solved. Here we are before you, shield- and sign-painters by appointment to His late Sacred Majesty. Out of pure piety, and love for our kinsmen, and desire to improve the palaces of our native land, we have come to offer to you shields painted and decorated in any pattern your ancestral piety requires, and that merely for less than the cost of the materials. And such a small sum we only charge because it is well known that no one values a free gift. But do not delay, because we wish to be equal benefactors to all the nations of the Isle of Britain, as much to the Silures and to the Coritani as to the Cantii and to the Atrebates. Come now while there is still time, and while we have any shield blanks left to paint on.'

And they came – oh, Zeus, how they came. They pressed on us to buy. But to my chagrin, there was not a man who wanted to buy my shield of Peleus and Thetis, even though we swore that it showed Dylan the Son of the Waves, nor did anyone want anything in that style. In fact, they said bitterly that it was rubbish like that which was all one could buy nowadays, and that good honest old-fashioned art like Pryderi's bulls could not be bought for love or money. And indeed, when I thought of it, it *was* in pictures like his that the Brits embroidered their linen and painted the outsides of their houses, in bright lines on the whitewash. So I talked and sold and haggled, while Pryderi sat with bowed head and painted bulls and sea horses and chariots and the geese flying high.

So, with great profit, we came to the end of the morning, and Pryderi was painting the last shield blank with a wild boar, and I was even wondering whether it would not be good trading to wipe out my Thetis and let him spread his swine over it, if only it showed a profit, when I realised that the crowd that had thronged about me all the morning had fallen back, and that in front of me instead of people were a flock of pigeons, all cooing and coocoorooing and sweeping the ground with their amorous breasts. And even as I divined what it was, I heard a voice say:

'That's a pleasant daub. I would have preferred Eurydice, of course, but there's no choice.'

There was never a voice like Rhiannon's, singing or speaking. Smooth and clear it was, like cream pouring out of a jug, whatever language she used, whether Greek or Latin or the tongue of the Brits. Sweeter by far it was than the murmuring of the doves, that still swarmed about her feet like bees upon a lime branch. A voice it was to make your hair stand on end with love and lust and desire for beauty in the dark as well as in the light. I looked up to where she stood, Hueil and four other men behind her.

Oh, have you ever seen the Imperial pleasure galleys on the Lake of Trasimene? Splendid they are in scented cedarwood, with figureheads of ivory and rams of bronze. Each mast is a single fir tree from the groves about Olympus, and the yards from strange and secret woods, from the sources of the Nile. Of cloth of Gold are their single sails, the shrouds and stays of copper wire, the dead eyes are carved from ebony and the blocks from the wood of life. The handles of the oars are lapped in the hide of the gentle unicorn, and the rowers' benches cushioned with velvet stuffed with down. The tacks and sheets and braces they twist from the hair by virgins, vowed to the Great God Neptune in Colchis by the sea.

So I saw Rhiannon stand there in the market. The infrequent sun was shining on her Gold and copper hair. About her shoulders she had thrown, to hide her splendid bosom, and veil from the eye of covetous man her silk and cotton blouses, a cloak of strange and shining cloth, of the fine, close silk from Samos, the warp of white and shining thread, and all the wool of yellow. Thus in that fine and shimmering Gold and white, fastened by a morse as big as a man's two hands, of bronze inlaid with Gold and emeralds, Rhiannon bargained with me for my painting. So I began to talk, and I took my tune from some brown pedlers I once met, men from, I think, India. I told her:

'Aye, this is a masterpiece, Great Lady, a painting fit for the Gods. It is on work like this that I rely to keep my children from starving through all their long lives, without their doing any work themselves, because all they have to do is to say that it was their father that painted this shield, and in any civilised place a grateful Government will feed them at the common table and clothe them out of the public purse, out of sheer joy that a man could exist who could bring such beauty to birth.'

'That is as may be,' she interrupted, and at the sound of her words I would have given her anything. 'How much?'

But the inborn skill of a hundred generations of merchants was too strong in me at first. I answered, without thinking:

'How much? You ask how much, Great Princess, for the work of all my life, for all my stored-up skill, for all the knowledge that went into compounding the colours and priming the ground? How much is the wisdom of all mankind worth? Think of the great emotional experience that went into it, that was necessary before I could conceive of such a scene' – and looking at it dispassionately, I had to admit that I had given to Peleus a look of sheer lust that I would have given a great deal to have achieved: I mean, at my age it would have taken something pretty ripe to have aroused a response like that. I went on:

'But let us be looking, Great Lady, at the hypotheses of the matter. Supposing that such a painting were for sale, where should we start the bidding? At two hundred denarii of silver? At—'

She looked at me coldly and said:

'Three.'

'Glory be to all the Gods. At last, Lady, for the first time in all my life, I have found someone who would truly admire and value

327

great Art, who would start the bidding at a price higher than even I would deem proper, at a price which would almost cover the cost of the materials and the hire of the splendid studio where I did the work. Hear, all of you who stand round' – though it was painfully obvious that the only people within earshot were Rhiannon's bodyguard, their cloaks much streaked with bird-lime, for everyone else had retired to a safe distance, though whether to be safe from the men or the pigeons I did not inquire – 'hear, all the men of Britain, this Great Queen values my work at three hundred denarii!'

'Not three hundred, you fool. Three denarii. New ones.'

'Oy-oy-oy!! Do not mock a poor artist, Great Lady, do not make game of a humble man who labours with his hands day and night to bring beauty into the world, and has nothing in his purse but what will bring him a crust of bread tonight, and a dip at the common fountain, and leave to lie in the corner of a stable seeking the filth of the horses for warmth! Look, Lady, look at these nymphs' – and I traced the outlines of their bottoms lovingly, taking care, however, not to touch the surface in case the paint was still wet – 'see the warmth of affection I put into them, the delicacy of the brush strokes, the vibrating movement of their draperies ...' The draperies seemed to vibrate because while I was painting Thetis' attendants, Pryderi was telling dirty stories, and I laughed so much at the one about the Old Woman of the Bog and the Pedlar's Mule that I couldn't have drawn a straight line to save my life. 'How could you think of such a paltry sum in the same moment as seeing these little darlings? Let us say fifty. Great Lady, a mere fifty, to anybody else it would be a hundred, but special to you, Lady, special to you, I will charge only fifty.'

'I might pay twenty,' she said cuttingly, '*if* I were buying it in the dark, and there was no other picture in the market, and I were anxious to cover up a bad spot on the wall in a room never seen except by candlelight.'

'At twenty denarii you value it, my Lady? Then I will not ask you to pay twenty denarii for the great crowning glory of my life. I will not ask you ten, or even five. Lady, I grant it to you freely as a gift. I will take nothing for it. I say, I give it to you.

Take it away quickly before I repent and take it back again. I am already in tears at the very thought of losing it.' And I pulled the hood of my cloak down over my face, but not so far that I could not see, and I wept bitter tears, most convincingly, loud and wet.

Rhiannon picked up the shield. She put her arm through the strappings. It looked, in spite of the painting, very martial – I still wondered why the Brits liked shields of that size and shape. She called over her shoulder:

'Hueil! Pay him!'

Hueil came over. He looked me straight in the eye a moment. Then he flung a coin down into the dust. I felt outraged at this insult to my dignity, but I picked it up, all the same. I mean, Gold is Gold, and it can all be spent. Hueil walked away, brushing feathers from his cloak and all the pigeons flew off after Rhiannon in a swarm. I tied the coin in a corner of my shirt, and I looked around for Pryderi. He emerged from behind the pillar. I was about to start to discuss with him the disposition of the profits when a large and important-looking man came up to us.

'Are you the two who've been selling shields here?' he asked.

'And lovely shields they were too,' answered Pryderi, though I was pinching his arm as hard as I could, because this man had petty official written all over him. 'Now, if you want one like that, then just tell me your name, and your clan, and your nation, and the name of your father, and I will have one designed and painted and executed that will tell all the passers-by unmistakably and clearly and plainly how rich and great and powerful is your descent.'

'That is all I wanted to know,' the minor official replied. 'An obvious admission. I am the treasurer of the Guild of Shield-makers and Armourers of the County of the Atrebates, and though it is disarmed we are, and have been for many years, and there is no making of weapons allowed, so that the main concern of our members is with the welfare of the poor and sick among us, yet still we have the monopoly of the making of shields in this Country, under the provisions of the municipal by-law "What-soever person" of the seventh year of the Emperor Hadrian. And this Country, which extends from the southern edge of the Oak Forest to the banks of the Thames, has for its centre and chief place this town of Calleva. And I have not seen any record that you have paid a contribution into our common fund, as is good and right and proper.'

Now the last thing that I was willing to do was to pay for what by now amounted to a burial club of well-to-do tradesmen to eat an extra dish at their annual feast if there was any way out of it, but for the moment even I could see no way out. But Pryderi caught on something.

'The making of shields.' He rolled the words around his tongue. 'There is a fine phrase for you. There is a fine legal phrase. It insinuates the activity of a trained man, who has passed through all the stages of his apprenticeship, and who can cut the wattles and plait them into a basket, who can plane the seasoned lime planks, who can tan leather and dye it, who can beat out sheets of the red bronze and emboss it and enamel it. All this is comprehended in the phrase "the making of shields". No, there is no ambiguity there. "The making of shields". A splendid craft.' Pryderi looked sideways at the official, like a cat at a mouse it wants to make a move to escape. Then he struck, fast and accurate as a shark. 'But we have not been *making* shields. We have been supplying them, and we have been assembling them from materials made for us by other trained and skilled shieldmakers in other towns: and it has been for citizens and councillors and senators and noblemen of your town and of all the County of the Atrebates that we have been doing it, and I can recite to you all their names, and their attributes that I painted on the shields which we *assembled*. So it will be all these gentlemen as well as us you will be having to prosecute if this comes to anything, if it is that there was an offence which it is not saying that there was I am there was.'

The official spent a little time disentangling Pryderi's meaning from his syntax, which had grown a little wild, and that not by chance. Then he said:

'Deceived it was they were, all these respectable people. They could not know that you were not members of our Guild nor of any Guild affiliated thereto nor licensed to act as if you were being members of our Guild, and they will so testify.'

There was a point there that Pryderi could have kept the pot a-boiling on for hours if he had felt so inclined, but he was tired, and hungry, and, especially, thirsty, as he confessed later, and so he returned to an earlier point of attack.

'It is showing, you will have to be, that your by-laws have been infringed by our making and supplying shields. Now in the first place, it is showing you will have to be that either of us both made and supplied shields, and that is difficult, because although you may be able to prove that one of us sold shields, you will not be able to show that he made or painted shields, or that the other, though it may be he painted shields, ever supplied or sold or even presented any shields. And it is then showing you will have to be that the painting of shields, which is all you will have any evidence for, is covered by that clause, and sentence, and phrase of your by-laws that concerns the making of shields, and it is tolerably certain I am that it is not, and that if you appeal to the by-laws of other towns on this point, then there is no parallel you will find. Now my friend here is of that opinion, and he has had experience of all manner of courts throughout the Empire, though it was always Not Guilty it was they were finding him, the Gods be glorified, and it is easy enough we will find it to hire lawyers, better than any that usually find it worth their while to practise in a hole like this. Now, is it willing you are, and only the hired treasurer and all, to commit the members of your guild to an expensive lawsuit when it is plain that it is not the by-laws of your own Guild you are knowing yourself?'

Well, the official, poor man, hummed and hawed to make a brave face of it, but of course in the end he agreed not to begin a prosecution, as long as we promised him not to do it again, and that we could easily do as we had used all the shield frames, though not all the leather and the dyes. And on top of that, Pryderi terrorised and browbeat him, by threatening to blacken his name to the Guild members, into giving us a silver denarius to pay for our dinner at the inn, to which we merrily returned, but not till I had myself made a few purchases in the market.

At the inn, we found Taliesin already waiting at a table for us. We called for our supper – the argument with the treasurer and my bargaining had taken more time than you might imagine. The inn was unusually luxurious for Britain. There was a real choice of dishes for the meal. I could have sheep's head, breast of lamb, shoulder of mutton, or a sheep's stomach stuffed with mutton offal minced, and then boiled. I began to realise that by leaving Londinium I had entered into the land of the Sheep. It is mutton that the Brits mostly live on. Cattle they keep, but only for milk, and to boast about how rich they are. Their real life is based on sheep, which clothe them and feed them, although they will deign to eat pork when it seems appropriate. I remembered bitterly that at Pontes I had a choice of leg of lamb or stewed beef, and I had chosen the lamb as being more of a rarity in my life. Alas, alas, what we miss through ignorance.

However, I chose a dish of sheep's brains, and beer with it, and we chatted on this and that, till suddenly, apropos of nothing at all, Taliesin said:

'And if it is Ireland you are thinking of, then I am thinking it would not be a wise place for any man of this island or from farther east to be going to. For the Irish to come here is one thing. But for a human being to go there is another, because it is doubtful it is, I am telling you, whether the Irish are human in the sense in which we use the word.'

'What do you mean?' I asked him.

For answer, he turned towards the door, where looking timidly into the room were two people, an old blind man with a kind of lyre which is popular in those parts of the world, and an older woman. He beckoned them over.

'Now, Tannwen, my daughter,' he said with all the assurance of Priesthood and thirty years (or less – I was never quite sure), 'sing us your old song about the Western Ferrymen.'

The blind man struck a few chords on the lyre – it was soon obvious that he knew nothing about music, but merely beat a rhythm and was there simply out of charity on Tannwen's part – and the old woman sang, in a kind of monotonous repetitive melody:

The people down in Menevia that live by the edge of the waves,
The fish and the weed are their portion, for they are the Dead
    Gods' slaves.

They shut themselves in their houses on the night of the
    Samain Feast;
They sit with their eyes to the water, they sleep with their
    backs to the east.

There comes a knock on the lintel, and the Fisherman walks
    to the sand.
He sets his boat on the wave tops, and he paddles away
    from the land.
The boat sits low in the water, the Fisherman hard strains he,
For heavy it is as if packed with men, though no man does he
    see.

When they come to the Isle of the Blessed, where the Green
    runs down to the Grey
The boat grows light and the dead go ashore, before
    the beginning of day.
But the Fisherman waits till he is paid, as he waited in
    days of old;
For every Blessed Soul he bears leaves him a scrap of Gold.

Oh, that is the Gold of Ireland, treasure that floats on the
    waves,
Collars and bracelets and cloak-pins, that the dead bring from
    their graves,
Though live men may go to Ireland, no living souls
    come again.
From the Isle of the Dead and the Blessed, the island
    beyond the rain.

Nonsense, I thought, just nonsense, as sensible as the doggerel metre it was sung in. But I wouldn't be going to Ireland,
not till the land was safe and settled and merely another good
place for the family to have an agent. Then I might, *might*, go
across and choose the agent. That could wait.

333

Chapter Eight

The next day we rode from Calleva to Spinae. There is, at least, some reason for Spinae's being where it is. It is the place where the road to Corinium and Glevum leaves the road to Sulis and the Lead Hills, on the high ground above the crossing of the Kennet. But there is no real town there, although it would have made a much better place for one than Calleva. There are two inns, and a few small houses, and, where the roads part there is a kind of permanent market, where the peasants sit and sell off odds and ends of country produce to people who pass by. There is quite a good clientele, as a number of the travellers to Sulis are wealthy.

We clattered down into the village, Taliesin on his rather horrible horse, which kicked and bit everything and everybody in sight, and all of us loaded with the light bulky packages I had had so much trouble in picking up in Calleva, but which were, Pryderi noted with relief, the wrong shape for shield frames. We had an argument about which inn to stay at, and my two companions insisted for reasons of their own on our stopping at the dirtier and smaller of the two, even though I was paying. We unloaded the horses into a hut where we could all sleep on straw pallets on the floor. I stroked my parcels lovingly before I opened them.

'These ought to sell well at the Forks,' I said. 'All we need is a few hours' dry weather to sit out.'

'What are you going to sell this time?' Pryderi's voice betrayed a certain loss of patience and confidence.

'Saddles. We're going to make some saddles tonight.'

'Do we know anything about making saddles?'

'We can try.' I unwrapped a package. 'I've got some saddle frames here, best second-quality beech, warranted well seasoned, at least three weeks since they were cut. Never mind, this leather will cover it all. It's a good thing I brought so much of it – I wonder why Leo Rufus couldn't sell it. Now, if we can make up some of the blue dye, we can have a fair stock by the end of the evening.'

'But you can't sit on leather and beechwood,' Pryderi objected. 'What about the horsehair for stuffing?'

'Horsehair? No need for that. Why do you think I cut all those rushes when we crossed the Kennet? Now, we can all start by cutting out, and then stuff later.'

'No,' said Pryderi. 'Taliesin can do all the stuffing. I can cut and sew, but he can't handle iron.'

I hadn't noticed it before, but now I came to think about it, Taliesin always ate with a bronze knife and he always shaved with a sliver of flint, and otherwise he never did touch iron. But while he worked on the saddles by lamplight I asked:

'Are we likely to have any more trouble with the local guilds?'

'Am I going to have trouble, you mean. The answer is, no. Spinae isn't any kind of municipality, incorporated or unincorporated.'

'If it comes to that,' I went on, 'could we really have argued our way through a court on those charges? Were the charters as specific as you said they were?'

'How should I know, boy?' Pryderi laughed all over his fat face. 'I can't read.'

Luckily there was no one in the inn that night who could read or tell a story. I should have slept peacefully, but instead I dreamed. I had not dreamed in Calleva, and that is why I know that nothing will ever happen there, but in Londinium I had dreamed of fire, and here on the road to Sulis I dreamed of battle. I remember a little. All through a day, I dreamed, we had stood against an army that came at us from the East, and towards evening they had fallen back, exhausted, and left us holding the field. And yet at that moment, a new army came at us from the West, along the road, and though they were as many as we were, yet we laughed, because they were too late. And I woke from that jumble of weary men and dead horses to find the dawn breaking bright and clear on a fine day for sitting by the roadside and selling whatever we wanted.

Pryderi and I sat there at the Forks, and the first four saddles we had made, and that Pryderi had painted, went very quickly and easily. But the last saddle stuck, and nothing I could say would persuade anyone to buy it. Of course, it was the old story you find all over Britain. Nobody will try anything new. This saddle was entirely my own work. I had painted it in the latest civilised style as I had the shield, with splendid details and gorgeous colours of the battle between the Lapiths and the Centaurs. This was much superior to the simple line patterns Pryderi used, and I'm quite sure that it wasn't the art that people didn't like. No, I know what it was. I had fitted the saddle out with an innovation just coming in then from Scythia. I had put two straps hanging down from the saddle, one on each side, and a loop on the end of each to put your big toe in. It was supposed to hold you on the saddle and let you use your hands more and give your knees and thighs a rest. Myself, I think it is a mistake in technology. I have tried it myself, and I didn't like it at all. It took twice as much effort to stay on, and you couldn't get off in a hurry if the horse fell or anything. Besides, there was all the trouble of riding barefoot.

Anyway, whatever the reason, nobody wanted to buy it. I began to think that I would never get rid of the thing, and that perhaps we would have to carry it on, or even use it ourselves. Besides, it was getting late, and I began to see us spending another night in Spinae. Then I noticed a scattering of birds among the sheep droppings. Even Calleva was a decently clean and cultured town, and they kept the streets quite tidy in a civilised way with pigs, who foraged everywhere and got rid of all the garbage people threw out of doors, just as they do in Londinium and Rome. But in Spinae, and in all the other little hamlets we came to after this, it was sheep they used, and the horrid things would come up and take the bread out of their mouths if people weren't careful. I began to see why the Brits ate so much mutton – it was a way of getting their own back. But when there was a chattering of starlings among the droppings, I didn't have to look up, nor listen for the chink of money bags. I began, automatically:

'Great Lady, Great Lady, look here at this saddle. A masterpiece it is, a marvel of the saddler's art, brand new and incorporating all the latest improvements and innovations brought straight from

Rome. This is the way to be in the fashion, Great Lady, to be the envy of all your peers. Buy a Scythian saddle, made for the men who ride the great plains of grass not only all day but all the year. On their horses they eat, and they sleep and do all that they wish to do, and that without fatigue, and it is all due to these straps which they use to stay on their steeds while their hands do other things ...'

'Let's see a two-seat saddle, then,' said Hueil with a snigger. 'For otherwise one generation of Scyths will have to last the life of all the world.'

I ignored him.

'Now, Lady, just look at this decoration, at this painting,' and I looked at it myself and the more I looked at it the more I real- ised that the side of the saddle I had facing me showed the rape of a mare-centaur by a one-eyed lapith, and the centaur's anguished face, turned back over her shoulder as she tried to unseat the unwelcome Greek who tried to mount her, was that of Rhiannon. I could not remember consciously trying to do this, and yet, how our actions betray our thoughts. I could not for the life of me remember what was on the other side, so great was my confusion now as on every occasion I had seen Rhian- non, but I hoped that it was nothing to give offence, as Hueil was bigger and nastier-looking than I was, and there were the four other men, and Pryderi and Taliesin had run away. I went on:

'Here we have the peak of the painter's art, born of a skill built up over years of practice and hard study. Twelve hours a day this painter worked, Great Lady, all the days of his life, for forty years and more, till he was able to produce such a scene as you can see here. And look at the leather, Lady, look at the leather, feel the quality, genuine Cordoban, double-tanned for durability, dou- ble-stitched for strength, double-stuffed for comfort, the ground just the right colour to match your shoes. Most Mighty Princess, how could you ever forgive yourself if ever you missed an oppor- tunity like this, a chance to buy his gem, and at such a price, too. And what is the price? What am I asking for it? Do I ask—'

She cut me short.

'Why do you talk so much, Mannanan? You know that you could sell me anything, even yourself.'

I looked up at her, for the first time at the Forks. Have you seen the fishing-boats come in to sunny Naxos, the low sun glinting on the white and purple sails, loaded down with tunny, octopus and cuttlefish, oysters and mussels and sponges from the deep? As you see the skipper, leaning on the steering oar, smiling in joy for wealth and hope to live another day, so I saw Rhiannon, smiling as she bent above me, as a spear-fisher smiles looking down upon his prey. There was a necklace about her neck, of mussel pearls on golden wires, and her head piled with its copper hair was bound in a coral wreath. Her white and yellow silken cloak parted to show her linen blouse, embroidered with sea anemones and the weeds of the shore. She was a sight to drive any man mad. But I remembered, I was a Greek, I know logic and how to think and all the rules of Nature, and I drew myself up and I told her:

'I am a Citizen of Rome, and of another city older than Rome, and I am no man's slave. I am not bought or sold.' I shifted back the folds of my sealskin cloak, which I was wearing that day to look more the great and rich merchant which I told the passers-by I was, and which indeed I am, greater and richer than any in Britain, and I showed the jewelled hilt and the bronze scabbard of the sword Burn, so that Hueil could see it. 'I give myself where I please, and for no price that anyone can pay. I do not give myself to anyone who asks for me. But I will give you, Rhiannon of the Brigantes, this saddle.'

And that was the first time I spoke her name. Hearing it in my voice changed her temper. She turned and spoke sharply:

'Hueil!'

He bent and picked up the saddle, and threw a gold piece in the dust before me. I picked it up, and bit it, ostentatiously. Then I told them:

'Beware, Lady. A gift thrice refused brings bad luck.'

She had the last word, of course. She called:

'Tell me that again, in the Summer Country.'

And off she walked, her cloak billowing out in the wind like a sail, but her shoulders beneath it were shaking with – what? Rage? Shame? Laughter?

I went back to the inn, where I found Pryderi and Taliesin

already saddling up the horses. I tossed the gold piece in the air before them.

'A fair rate of profit,' I told them.

'Count your money with care,' Taliesin advised me. I looked at the coins. The first was struck by that old King in Gaul. The second – on the reverse was a tangle, dots and squiggles, not intelligible to any human being, not even to a Brit: it was just the pattern they always put on coins. But on the obverse was a head, crude, but recognisable: it was an attempt to draw a real man, someone who once walked the earth, and the artist had seen him, had known him. And above his head, some letters. With difficulty I read them: *Tascio Ricon*.

'Tasciovanus, you would have called him,' said Taliesin. 'My ancestor, and Rhiannon's, and even Pryderi's. It was he, the great King, who defeated Caesar, and drove him back into the sea, never again to see Britain. That was in the days of glory.'

Like the first, it was new, crisp, unworn, unclipped, a marvel in a coin twenty years old, let alone nearly two hundred. But that the third coin, that I had received that day, should be in such a state was even a greater marvel. For a stater it was, a gold stater of Alexander, the Greek who conquered the world, and had he lived there would have been no need to call myself so often a Citizen of Rome as well as of my own city. And Alexander, remember, was not a Greek of those outworn cities of Attica, but a Macedonian, as far from the line of Themistocles or Solon as we of the old towns of Asia. But this stater – I looked at it. I knew the die well. This had been struck in the Old City, in my home, in my very house, by my own ancestor. These coins showed common ground between Rhiannon and myself. They were not choosen foolishly. I would not spend them easily.

Chapter Nine

We rode out of Spinae immediately, keeping our faces hidden as we went past the other inn, the one with a fine modern bath, for there, it was clear, Rhiannon would be staying. Beyond the Forks, we soon entered the Forest, and I began to wonder where we would sleep, because it was getting towards dark. But an hour's ride west, Pryderi suddenly turned his horse off the road, and we followed him along a half-hidden path till we came to a hut, built, I suppose, long ago by some charcoal-burner. While I unsaddled the horses and hobbled them, and Taliesin fetched bundles of green bracken for our beds, Pryderi went into the hut. He came out again with, to my surprise, a hunting bow and a boar spear.

'I feel like a taste of decent meat,' he grunted and slipped into the woods. By the time I had lit a fire he was back, calling me, and I brought a packhorse and followed him to where he had killed a great stag. We got it back to the hut fairly easily, slung across the horse's back, and there we did all the real butchering, burying the offal and hanging up the joints and the hide. We ate well on venison steaks broiled on sticks over the fire, and mush-rooms Taliesin collected, of several different kinds which I had not seen before, but which he swore were harmless, and so they were, except that it was them, I suppose, that made me sleep so sound in the open air till Pryderi woke me to stand the last watch by the fire against wolves. Or perhaps it was the cider. Up till now I had drunk beer among the Brits, but my two companions had brought with them no beer but only a jar of cider, and then I began to realise what real ecstasy was. I will not hear a word said against beer, if that is what all around you are drinking. But if you have the choice, then cider is a drink for kings. I tell you this, once the Germans begin to taste cider, they will soon forsake beer utterly and plant apple orchards where once they grew barley.

But it was cider and venison again for breakfast, and then we travelled on to a village a little way from Cunetio. We stopped eventually outside an inn, and this at last was a real Brits' stopping place. The other inns where we had slept had all been possible, just possible stopping places for civilised men who weren't too particular, but this was no place for anyone who was not native born. We had stopped in the middle of the day for a bite of cold roast venison and an oatcake we bought from a girl at a farmhouse by the way. All alone she was, and baking like a mad thing, for every other soul was in the fields at the last of the wheat harvest.

I remarked that I had already tasted enough of that stag to see me through a lifetime. Pryderi laughed.

'And it's more of him you'll be having for your supper, but it's depending I am on him to pay for our beds too.'

Sure enough, he was able to persuade the innkeeper that it would be just to take the carcase of the deer, and the hide and horns, to pay our bill.

Now, this was the first British house I had stayed in, that is to say, the first built in the British way. For all the nations of the earth build their houses with straight walls, and it is only the houses of their gods and their graves that they make round. But your Brit likes to build himself a round house, and simple it is to do. First of all you mark out a circle on the ground, and around this circle you dig holes two or three paces apart. In each hole you set an upright post, twice the height of a man. Then you join the timbers together with light rafters, and this you can thatch, leaving a hole in the middle of the roof for the smoke of the fire. Perhaps the house is not big enough for you. All right, then you draw another circle outside the first, and set there another ring of uprights, and thatch the roof between the inner and outer rings, and if you feel so inclined there is always room for another circle, because you have all the island to cover if you have a mind to. The walls you then fill in with basketwork well caulked with mud, or even with a few courses of stone. If for any reason you are not satisfied with one open hall to live in, then you can join uprights together to make booths, and so this inn consisted of a great round house, with an open hall at the door, and a ring of booths at the farther circumference.

We exchanged our deer, then, for the use of a booth for a night, and glad we were to get into it, because the luck that had brought us dry, if not fine weather now deserted us. The cloud got lower as the morning wore on. The girl who sold us the oatcake was looking anxiously at the first few drops showing on the flagstone at her door, and awaiting the rush home from the fields. By the time we reached the inn, three hours after noon, the rain was falling steadily in a monotonous drizzle, not heavily, but thoroughly. I was tolerably dry myself, because I put on my sealskin cloak, and that shed the water like – well, have you ever seen a seal? The other two had their soft leather jerkins, but all the same we were all glad to get indoors.

The innkeeper seemed almost to expect us, or perhaps it was my fancy, and he gave Taliesin the same exaggerated respect as had the man in Calleva. Of course, beside the inn he had a farm, and his stacks of oat and wheat stood behind the house. He was ready enough to talk about the weather and the prospects of the harvest while his wife and servants bustled about, as if they were expecting a busy evening. Other travellers came in. There were the two middle-aged men and the youth I had seen in Pontes, and then a little man with a squint leaned over me, too close for my liking, and said:

'There is one flock, and one shepherd: one vineyard and one true husbandman.'

What that meant I had no idea, and so I only said back:

'And a pretty small farm that must be, brother.'

It seemed to satisfy him; at least, he didn't speak to me again that evening.

The dinner was good, nine-year-old mutton since the venison hadn't hung long enough for the landlord's taste, stewed, with onions and leeks and turnips and oat bread, and oat dumplings in the stew. We ate as only men can who have ridden all day in the summer rain. It was a warm evening, in spite of the rain, and as the inn filled with people, men and women, all in their dripping cloaks and sweating under them, the room turned into a

342

good imitation of a steam bath, except for the smell, which was of bodies and not predominantly of scented oil.

All the people present were Brits. Any Greek or Roman on the road would have taken one look and preferred the open road, which would in any case have taken him to a civilised tavern at Cunetio, where they would use oil to cook with. There were all sorts in the inn, and all free men and women, no slaves. If you go outside the Empire, or to these hardly settled places, whether among Brits or Germans, you find that there are very few slaves. A rich man may have a few women captured in battle or kidnapped by pirates, who are used for grinding corn and other heavy work in the house, but apart from that a free man, or woman for that, does everything for himself. That, of course, is just why these areas are so backward. A civilised man, if he is to live a full life, has to be backed by power not only to grind corn, but to cut and carry fuel and mine metals and smelt them. But the Brits, if they will not use slaves outside the household, are doomed to barbarism for ever.

The room, as I said, became very full, but you can drown any discomfort in cider. We were busy denying any virtue to lifesavers, and singing a song popular in the neighbourhood called 'Bran, the Bastard King of Mona' – I noticed that Pryderi was not showing a single trace of black-and-yellow – when in at the leather door, out of the rain, there came six people, dripping wet, sodden, half-drowned, squeezing, water out of their hair, out of their shoes, out of their cloaks, weeping with relief to be inside, the tears running out of their wet eyes over their red chapped cheeks. Rhiannon it was standing there, like a wrecked barge, swamped, mast and spar sagging forward in a tangle of rope and splinters, and floating she was in her own private lake of fresh water that she had brought in with her.

Her five followers, Hueil first, wetter even than she was, pressed behind her to help her off with her leather cloak and the leather overskirt in which she had ridden. She flung the garments behind her without looking, and scattered the flock of ducks which had waddled in after the Lady.

The landlord went towards her, his eyes on her belt of hexagonal plates of gilded bronze, but whether he wanted to assure her most humbly that this was no place for such a great Princess as she, or whether he wanted to tell the five of them to go and hang themselves on lines till they had drained enough to mix with decent folk, I never knew. Rhiannon pushed him aside, and looked around the room.

Her eyes fell on my face. She walked towards me as I sat in that booth behind the table. She walked like – have you ever seen a bireme of the Imperial Navy bear down on you all cleared for action? Cruel glitters the ram of iron as it cuts the swell, cruel beat the oars in time, cruel fly the flags. The sail is furled, that it shall neither take fire nor press the rowers. The gilding and the carving is stripped away, and black she is painted and not a man who is to be seen but has hidden his face behind a mask of brass. So Rhiannon came to me, her face a mask of anger, terrifying and awful. I looked about me in terror. On my right sat Pryderi, still as a corpse, his stern face held steady by an effort of his will. But on my left – Taliesin was no longer there.

Before I could ask Pryderi, or even ask myself, where the Druid had gone, or where we could go, Rhiannon stood in front of us. I could have sworn that her red hair was itself on fire, sending as it was great clouds of steam to the roof. She bent down and wrenched off her shoes. She flung them down on the table in front of me with a bang. Shoes? You have never seen shoes in such a state. The blue colour had run and the Gold leaf had floated off. The threads that stitched the uppers to the soles had broken in some places, and in other places had torn through the leather to run three or four awl holes into one. The soles themselves were worn into holes the size of oyster shells.

'Shoes,' she said, spat, rather. She beckoned to Hueil.

'Shield!'

He held it up. It had been a good shield, once. The limewood panel had warped. The leather cover had split in some places and was peeling away from the curling wood, and in others it had blown up into great hollow blisters. And where, oh where, were my Thetis and my Peleus, my nymphs and gods and goddesses? All had run into one horrid brown-purple splodge, which even as I watched dripped dye onto the clean floor straw. It is a dreadful thing to see the work of a man's hands spoiled by a woman's stupidity in riding in the rain.

Then 'Saddle!' she said.

Hueil threw it at Pryderi, who was too terrified, or too digni-fied, to duck, and it bounced off his face and fell back on to the table in front of me. It was the worst of all. I could now remem-ber what I had painted on the side which faced me. I had shown the lapith leading the she-centaur away captive, a rope around her neck. But it now existed only in my mind, and in Rhiannon's. The wet, and the stress between horse and rider, had twisted the frame. And then with the heat between saddle and horse's back, or between saddle and that lovely bottom, even through nine layers of skirts, the ripe seed heads of the rushes had germinated, and sprouted, and thrust through to cover all the surface of the leather with a dense green fuzz.

Everybody in the room crowded round to see. I could hardly hear my own teeth chattering, as they did in face of Rhiannon's fury, for the 'Oohs' and 'Aahs' of horror and disgust. Pryderi's nose was bleeding, and though his dignity forbade him to move his hands he kept on trying to wipe his face on my shoulder, so I told him what I thought of that and it hardly helped to calm me. Rhiannon, having thus gained an advantage, proceeded to use it, and addressed the crowd in that lovely creamy voice of hers, and indeed it was the first time I had heard it properly without the twittering of birds, and now there was no other noise at all, because all the people were silent clustered in a semi-circle behind her and glaring with her at us.

'Men of Britain!' she said, and that miserable raggle-taggle of batteners on travellers and sellers of watered beer and tough mutton and of shelter under leaky thatch all straightened up as if the words meant something.

'Men of the Isle of the Mighty! How long, I ask you, how long? How long will we allow foreigners to cheat us? How long will we be carried away by a curious accent, by charming infelici-ties of phrase? How long will we be put off our never-ending search for quality and true value and honest dealing by strange tales of the impossible and by the enchantments of Syrians and Greek pedlars? Are we always to be dupes? I call on you all to be witness.

'These men have sold me at different times shoes, and a

shield, and a saddle. The price was high, but the price they asked was higher. What profit they have twisted out of our brothers and sisters down the road I can only guess, but believe you me, their saddle-bags are heavy with Gold. Aye, I know what the law is now, "Let the buyer beware," but I call on you to witness that there is an older law than that, a law of the Gods and not of the Romans. Even a merchant must speak truth, and the meanest and poorest buyer must know what to believe. Remember the great motto of the Blessed Ones who are now gone from us, driven from us. "The truth against the world," is what they said. I call on you all at the last to stand for truth.'

This was a new approach to business morality. How on earth can you proceed in the way of trade except on the assumption that the man you are dealing with is a liar, and that he is stating a case that appears to give you the maximum benefit while in reality it is himself that it profits the most? To suggest that a trader should ever speak the truth betrays ignorance of the whole basis of a merchant's thought. In any case, it is obvious that the innkeeper, and indeed everybody else who tried to sell me anything in the whole Isle of Britain, would disagree violently with Rhiannon in practice whatever they might say aloud in her presence. But I was unable to break into the flow of her speech to put my point of view, because she never drew breath.

'A saddle, and a shield, and shoes, they sold me. Warranted to last till the day of the transmigration of the whole earth they were. The colours were warranted fast and the workmanship good, and now look how much their word is worth. See what has happened to this costly merchandise after one shower of rain! See what they think to foist on us here in this land where rain is our daily portion!

'My brethren!' Her voice rose, and even I felt a surge of indignation against all dishonest traders, so persuasive was her speech, in manner if not entirely in content. 'My brethren! What shall we do with these men who cheat us? What did we do by the old law?'

Some of the people shouted, 'Hang them,' and others shouted, 'Burn them living,' and these last included Pryderi who prudently supported the larger party till I reminded him that it was likely to be himself who would be the first sufferer. They would, I was sure, keep the best bit to the last. He urged me:

'Say who you are. Are you not a Citizen of Rome? Appeal to Caesar. Demand to be tried by a Roman magistrate. Such an appeal they will not resist, even in their anger. And once in front of a civilised court, as you call it, you are safe, for who would think of preferring the word of a pack of us miserable Brits.'

And I ought to have done it, I should have done it, but there was something held me back. I said:

'No. I have come into this country dressed as a Briton, and as a true Briton I will endure what must be. I will depend on my own unequalled skill and power.'

'Then it is a Gesa you have taken on yourself,' replied Pryderi. 'A vow it is you have made on the presence of death that it is not on legerdemain nor on trickery nor on fine words that you will rely while you are in our country, but that what you have undertaken to do, that you will do yourself.'

It was, I agreed, one way of looking at it. After all, I do trace my ancestry back through sixty noble warlike generations. And as we spoke, Rhiannon went on:

'Thieves! Liars! Cheats! Men of the island of Britain, men of the Isle of the Mighty! Rise up, great nation in your wisdom. Judge these men for yourselves, judge them for me, judge them and execute judgement.'

For a moment I would have thrown myself on the floor at Rhiannon's feet, begging for mercy, but then I glimpsed Pryderi sitting there, arms folded, bleeding, and I caught my courage together and I stood up and I said:

'Let no man be judged unheard, men of the Isle of the Mighty, descendants of Brennus. Here I stand, a Son of Lear, and I demand to know two things. By what law am I judged, and what is the penalty?'

The landlord stepped forward as spokesman.

'As for the penalty, that is simple. If a man sell short measure or worthless goods, then he is the property of the buyer, for the buyer to sell or to keep, to let live or to die, as it pleases him – or her. In olden days it was thought most fitting for the buyer to give such a man to be burnt as a pleasing offering to the Gods.

347

But as for the law, why, we will go by the law of the country as it always was, and as it always will be when the Romans are gone. It is the nobles and the princes and the kings who administer it, and it is the most noble person in the room who shall pronounce judgement. And there is no denying who is the most noble person here, for who is more noble than a princess of the Brigantes, and even here among the Belgi we acknowledge that. As indeed we would acknowledge any prince or king, aye, even a king of Demetae. There is no judge greater than a king of the old line, except it be a Druid.'

'Yes,' said a clear tenor voice from the doorway. 'Except a Druid.'

Taliesin stood in the entrance. But not the Taliesin who had come with us, the ragged man in dirty brown, with muddy face and matted hair. Now he was wrapped in a robe of fine white linen that hid him from shoulder to foot, and I will swear that he had grown a head taller. His hair, red as Rhiannon's, was clean and combed and sleeked down with water. Upon his head he wore a wreath of oak leaves. The leaves were fresh, and the broken ends of the twigs were oozing sap, but the acorns, now in early August, were already hard and dry and brown-shelled and ripe. In his left hand, thrust from beneath his linen shirt, he held an apple, and in his right hand he held a sickle of the rich Gold of Ireland. And on his breast, held by a Golden pin, were a pair of bright green leaves and between them on the stem two fresh white berries. Whenever did you see the berries of the mistletoe ripe and smooth and plump in August?

It was late in the evening of a summer's day. It was still light enough to ride, but in the inn the servants had long lit the torches. The rain had stopped, but we could not see the setting sun for the low grey cloud. The air was misty. The whole land smelt of the warm steam. The birds were silent. Outside even the rooks and the pigeons of the woods had ceased to call.

In all that stillness, Taliesin the Druid walked through the filthy inn room. The floor was covered with straw littered with the bones and refuse of years of feasting. And I swear that I saw the straw move itself aside that his feet might touch only the sacred earth. The oak tables were stained with the spilt drink and gravy and littered with the fragments of the evening's dinners,

348

and I saw the table legs bend back as the wood shrank least Taliesin be defiled by the touch.

The old men in the room knelt before Taliesin, and the young men held their hands before their eyes that they might not be blinded by the radiance of his brow and the glory of his face, for they had not seen a Druid before in all their lives. He came to Rhiannon, and she went down on one knee before him, her skirts spread about her feet. She drew her shawl over her glorious hair, for respect, and the fringes of her shawl before her face, for modesty.

There stood Taliesin, walking as a Druid in a land where no Druid might walk abroad in freedom. He faced the rack and the cross and the fire, the lash and the salt mine and the beasts, and that for the sake – no, not for the sake of my life, nor of Pryderi's, nor for that of friendship in the abstract. He came for the sake of truth. Courage is a kind of holiness. I knelt before Taliesin.

He looked at Hueil. Hueil scurried around the room, and found the biggest chair in the place, one that stood in a corner, with arms and a high back. He lifted it on to a table, the highest in the room, and stood back. Taliesin still looked at him. Hueil looked puzzled, and then he began to burrow into one of Rhiannon's saddle-bags. Out of it he brought my Lady's cloak, that enormous garment of silk, shot yellow and white, shimmering Samite of Gold and silver. This cloak he spread over the chair, which thus became a glittering throne.

In an instant, without seeming to move, and certainly not making any jump or violent movement, Taliesin was seated on his throne, his arms crossed on his breast, the apple at one shoulder, the sickle at the other, so that he looked like some ancient Egyptian King, carved in the red rocks of the Nile. And then in the silence of that crowded room – for the alley that had opened to let him through had closed up again and it was plain that every Briton for twenty miles had come to hear him and see the Druid – Taliesin spoke:

'The truth,' he said. 'The truth against the world.'

Rhiannon rose and stepped forward. I too moved and stood beside her. I was her equal in this trial, as I had not been before. I never doubted an instant that I should subject myself to Taliesin's

349

judgement, nor did I remember that he was my companion on the road. I never hoped for an instant that he would bend his rule to favour me. I only saw a Druid, and I bowed before my Judge. Rhiannon spoke first, as the plaintiff.

'Master of Light,' she said. 'It is for truth I call, for truth and justice. From this man I have bought three things.' And I accepted this new state of affairs, that the case was brought against me alone and not against Pryderi. 'My Master, I bought of him a shield, and a saddle, and shoes. Not for a shower of rain did any of these last. I ask you for justice by our ancient laws. This man has said in my presence that he is not bought or sold. He says that he belongs to no one. Let him then, my Master, be given to me. Let him neither be bought nor sold, but confiscated and devoted to compensation.'

She stopped. Taliesin did not look at her. Neither did he look at me, but I knew it was my turn to speak. I said:

'My Master, I have sold this woman nothing. Thrice I offered her gifts, and thrice she refused my gifts. But the goods she took, and Gold she flung in my face. I have not spent it, the coins I have here still. I give them back.'

I took the three old pieces of Gold from the fold of my shirt where I had twisted them. I tossed them gently across the room, one by one, and all present saw them shine in the air, saw Rhiannon catch them. And she opened her hand, and we all saw there, not three pieces of Gold, but three cockleshells. Easy enough to do, you will say, if you know how: but who did it?

Taliesin looked down at us from his throne. He had called on truth, and the truth was come upon him. I knew the signs. The God had come upon him, the Muse, the Awen the Britons call it, though whether the Awen is to them a separate God, to be worshipped, or merely the abstract epiphany of divinity in its essence I never found out.

When the Awen comes on a Bard you cannot mistake it. The Bard does not go into a trance. He is conscious all the time of what he is saying, and indeed it seems to him that he sees suddenly of his own unaided intellect the reason and above all the truth behind all things, and he realises at once how he can express what he knows so that all can understand. So now we heard, as Taliesin's voice deepened in pitch and changed in tone, not the even measured speech of the impartial judge, but a strange chant, the song of truth.

'In all the world is like and unlike, like married to unlike, equal and opposite, completing and complementing. East there is and West, dawning there is and sunset. North is there, and South, heat is there and cold. Being is there and extinction, life and death, seeing and unseeing, seen and unseen. Those who are vowed to the truth must walk in the midst of lies, and the Sacred One of the Sun must call on the Gods Below.

'So Rhiannon and Mannanan, equal and equal, opposite and opposite, hear you me. To you Mannanan of the House of Lear, who may no longer call on the Unconquered Sun because so long ago you did the will of the Unconquered Sun, to you I give Rhiannon, Queen of Those Below, to keep to the ages of ages, to serve you and to serve, through life to death and beyond death.

'Rhiannon, Princess of the North, Lady of those that are gone, I give you Mannanan, Photinus the Greek, man of many names and many lives, last Lord of the Amber Road. He who is no man's slave shall be your slave for ever.'

He stood up, and out of his oak-leaf wreath there rose a wren, ticking loudly. Three times it flew around the room and then fluttered out into the open air. It was the only bird I ever saw that took no notice of Rhiannon. It flew away. I did not know it then, but it was at sunset on that very day that my son was born and Phryne died.

Ours was the first case of the evening, but to my surprise it was not the last, and indeed it was the only summary hearing, the only dispute that belonged to a court of first instance. There came up to stand before Taliesin a long series of pairs of men, each with a dispute to settle, one already judged by a village gathering, and appealed from there to a nobleman or a prince, and now referred at the last to a Druid for final solution. It was clear, too, that Taliesin had been warned of each case long before and was ready with his judgement, with all its references to times of old and the decisions of kings long gone. And it was intriguing to hear how each pair of adversaries, especially where the case concerned land, made their arrangements to have the case heard in a Roman court, so that the decision could be ratified and made safe against any desire of the Government to overthrow it, and so presented that only one Roman verdict would be possible and that the same as Taliesin's. Indeed, I wondered, who rules this land?

Fifteen of these cases there were. Fifteen times the Druid fulfilled his function, which is nothing to do, I found with sacrifices and rites as Caesar imagined, but is a business of preserving the laws, which in a society where no man can write or read is a more difficult matter than you may imagine.

And then at the end, after the fifteenth case, and I can guess how it happened, since I have done the same myself, there was suddenly a red glow from the brazier in the centre of the inn, and the whole room was filled with a cloud of choking smoke. When it cleared, of course, there was no Druid but a dirty-faced man in ragged brown clothes was sitting at my side.

And then the feasting began. All the local people were trying to nerve themselves to go out and home in the dark, and that of course uses up a great deal of cider. And Rhiannon came and sat down opposite me, as if nothing had happened at all – her retainers found themselves somewhere else to sit and drink – and everything was quite ordinary, except that a crowd of Britons in a corner were singing a cauldron song, the first time I had heard such a thing:

Oh, the cauldron on the fire is a pot that some adore,
But the cauldron that we worship is the little one on the floor.
Yes, the little one –

and they all thumped their drinking cups on the tables, bang-bang-bang-bang:

Oh, the little one on the floor.

I leaned across and I said to Rhiannon who sat opposite me, as Taliesin had now moved to be next to her and opposite to Pryderi:

'Now, I am your master, and you must leave your journey to Sulis or wherever else it has struck your fancy to go, and come with me wherever *I* wish.'

'Indeed,' she answered, not angrily, but half laughing, and

there is little I like less than being laughed at. 'It is you that must go wherever your mistress tells you, and follow *me* you must if it is your mistress I am.'

Taliesin, now recovered from his Awen and as stupid as the rest of us, opened his mouth to speak, but I felt Pryderi kick him under the table as he said:

'A cock there is to every hen, and a bull to every cow, and a dog to every cat. Fight they will and must till one has the dominion, and evenly matched this pair are for cleverness and wit and for mischief and for stubbornness, and it is patiently I am waiting to see which it is will take the other along.'

'And there is true it is what you are saying,' Taliesin agreed, now all innocence of face and voice. 'But interesting and informative and inspiring it would be to hear where she *is* going.'

The crowd in the corner were still singing:

Pots of bronze and pots of iron on the charcoal flames are stood:
But who would light a fire 'neath a cauldron made of wood?
'Neath a little one (*bang-bang-bang*) 'neath a little one
    made of wood?

Some kind of riddle, I thought. In the middle of this nonsense I felt a little more intelligent approach to the problem would be helpful, so:

'And to where might you be going, Lady, if I may be so bold to ask?'

'Boldness is it now?' and her blue eyes flashed, and her cheeks glowed with pure enjoyment of a quarrel, because she was one of those people, and there are men as well as women, who enjoy nothing more in life than a dispute with an opponent fairly matched, and I am not saying that I am not one of them. 'And how far is it you are meaning your boldness to go? There are limits, and I hope you know them, to your impudence in the face of your mistress.'

'My boldness will go as far as I like with my own,' I replied, 'but your boldness itself goes too far. Wherever you may be going, or think you may be going, it is leaving it you will be and coming down with me into the Summer Country.'

'And where else is it thinking you are that I am going? I am bound to the Summer Country for the winter, and it is there I will go whether you come with me or not.'

And for some reason Taliesin leaned back on his stool with a look of relief on his face, and nearly overbalanced, and we very nearly deafened with the singing behind us and the banging of pots and fists and even of feet on the tables.

Let the Romans sip Falernian, and the Germans swill
    their beer,
While we Brits taste life immortal from the cauldron in
    the Mere.
From the little one (*bang-bang-bang*) from the little one
    in the Mere.

'*Yes*,' she hammered bang-bang-bang back at me. 'I will go there if I please.'

If she pleased, indeed. I glared at her. The party was nearly over, there was no one left in the inn room except the few who would be staying for the night. I felt I had drunk too much, and I decided, while the others arranged who was going to sleep in which booth, I would go out and dispose of some of the cider. It was so hot inside that I pulled my sealskin cloak around me, and in doing that of course my sword fell out of the pack, and I was slightly drunk so that it seemed less trouble to pick it up and take it out with me. I felt better out in the open air, and I tried to recover myself and understand precisely what was happening, and though it had all seemed quite clear and, indeed, welcome in the fury of the opening of the trial, when the mob were gathered round me and behind Rhiannon, with axes and cudgels and all kinds of intricate agricultural implements like gelding shears and branding irons, I failed to see now how the situation had changed in any way, for though I had found the Lady – my thoughts rambled on and on. I breathed deeply and groped my way round the inn and into the rickyard.

Everything had now grown quiet. I wondered if the other three had noticed that I had gone. I leaned against the stack of oats, and considered improving the taste of their bread for them.

When I had finished, I stood still again. I listened. I could hear someone moving. Now, that was strange. There were men moving about, a lot of them. And they were taking care to be quiet. That was the strange thing. If they had been about normal business, as might just possibly happen around a farm or an inn, then they would be moderately careful to be quiet, but only so far as to escape things thrown at them by sleepers awoken out of turn. But these men were trying to be quiet as the grave, hoping to wake no one. I clutched the sword hilt under my cloak.

Well, there's a thing, I thought. If I shout I don't know what will happen, and it's up to no good they are. So I pulled up my hood about my face and stood closer to the stack and listened to the feet squelching in the mud.

Then all of a sudden, people started shouting, lots of people, men and women, and I began to feel glad I had something behind me, and of the way I was standing in the angle between two stacks, to shield my blind eye too. While all the shouting went on round the inn I heard someone coming, very quietly, around the side of the stack. I sensed him rather, just smelt him and heard the half-breathing, and when he came round the corner, backwards as if he were watching something I caught him across the side of the head with my sword, still in its scabbard – I didn't want to do any damage we couldn't repair just in case it was a friend. Down, of course, he went, and I knew that he wouldn't move for a little time, at least. But after that there was a sound of shouting and running my way, so I pulled a mass of oat sheaves down over the pair of us. I'd had time to look at his face in the glow from something that had been set afire, a stable or something, and I knew him now all right. It was the lad I had seen in the successive inns, the one who was travelling with the two middle-aged men.

I lay there where I was safe and listened to the rumpus. I could hear Rhiannon screaming, but it was anger in that voice, not pain or even fear – she could look after herself and certainly nobody was doing anything drastic there. Pryderi was holding forth in a fine flow of language, and then his voice died away in an unmistakable grunting as someone gagged him. And then, quite near, there was a voice I knew.

'What? Do you mean to say you haven't found him?'

355

'No. He isn't in the inn, or in any of the huts.'

'Flaming Greek! You never can rely on them,' said Gwawl. I would have recognised that voice even through a gag, and that was how I wanted to hear it. The other voice, too – it was one of the middle-aged men who had been with the lad. Gwawl went on:

'Have you seen Lhygod?'

'No, not since you came. Must have gone ahead. Shall we look for Mannanan? If we set the place afire we'll smoke him out.'

'No. It will attract too much attention, and it won't be any good if he's gone off into the woods already. But if we take these three away he's bound to come looking for them. We can leave a few men in the inn till dawn, though, in case he comes back. Right. Off we go.'

I lay still till I heard the sound of horses. The lad was beginning to stir. I felt that, as Gwawl said, the woods would be safer for me. I took some of the straw ropes from the oat sheaves and bound Lhygod's arms, and with a shorter length I gagged him. Then I woke him up by rubbing his face in a puddle and pulled him after me, leading him by the neck like a horse. We plunged into the darkness of the forest.

Chapter Ten

We walked through the dripping woods in the dark. I heard the shambling rush of the frightened badger, and the hoot of the owl. Once there was a heavier noise, and I knew the bear was near. The wolves, at this time, might come by ones or twos, but, I remarked loudly, I would be all right because I could leave them Lhygod to eat. I was satisfied to hear him add a muffled terrified grunting to the slight noises of the night.

Where was I going? I had not the slightest idea. I was making, roughly west. I knew that it would do me no good to ask help from the local farmers, who were all Belgi. Pryderi's people lay farther west, I knew that much, how far I had never asked, but not far, to judge from odd remarks he had passed about the ability of Taliesin's brown horse to stand up to the journey. It might be only a day or two.

The grey dawn came on us slowly, through the rainclouds, and it was at about the moment when one can tell a white thread from a black one at arm's length that we came into a clearing. In it was a hut, like the one where Pryderi had found the bow – had earlier hidden the bow, he or someone like him. I wondered if there might be something useful here. I quickly tied my prisoner to a tree and went forward. I peered cautiously round the leather curtain that closed the door of the hut. There was the sound of snoring. I drew my sword, and with one swift slash cut away the door. Then I shouted:

'Come on out.'

There was a moment of confusion. Then there crawled from the hut, blinking in the daylight, such as it was, three men. I looked them up and down as they stood in some kind of line. They looked miserable and half-starved, but that was nothing: on each of them, one on his belt, one around his neck, one peeping out of his sleeve, I saw the welcome sight of yellow and black.

'I am a friend of Pryderi,' I said, risking being mistaken in that light about the colours.

'Then let us have a good look at you,' said one of them. 'Because it is a rare and strange being you are in these parts.'

'And who are you, and what are you doing here?' I asked them.

'We are Duach—'

'And Nerthach—'

'And Grathach.'

'We are the Sons of the Hard Dawn.'

'We are the men who come from the confines of Hell.'

'And we are lost.'

I looked at them. Three big savage-looking men like that, and lost.

'Where then are you trying to go?' I asked.

'To say we are lost,' Grathach explained, 'is a figure of speech. We know where we are, but we do not know where we ought to be. For it is meeting Pryderi we should be today, but where he is now we do not know. So as we are his men and all our life revolves around him, it is lost we are till we find him.'

'In that case, I can help you a little. Gwawl has captured him.'

Grathach looked worried. 'There is bad, that is. Late he'll be for the wedding, too, I wouldn't wonder.'

'What wedding?'

'His wedding, of course. He's getting married on the thirtieth day after Luggnasad.'

'He didn't tell me.'

'I don't suppose anybody told him, either. It's only just been arranged. Enough trouble we had finding her, too.'

I felt that it would be too confusing to inquire further. I merely said:

'Well, if you want him to be any use at the nuptial feast, or after it, you had better help me. We want him back.'

'If we could wait a week,' volunteered Duach, 'I could ride back to the Summer Country and raise a party from old Caw. It's his niece Pryderi's marrying.'

358

'We might have to fight Romans as well,' pointed out Nerthach.

'There'll be no fighting.' I was firm about it. I went over and led Lhygod out. 'This is one of Gwawl's party. We've got capital.'

'Now, we can soon find out where Pryderi is,' said Grathach. 'There's always the old red-hot poker up the backside to make a man talk.' I was gratified to notice that Lhygod went a pale green colour and made choking noises. I insisted:

'No torture. Just a straight clean death. Now, is there anywhere around here that is fairly easy to see and good for a public hanging, because I think that will be the best.'

'Oh, yes. The mound of Arberth.'

'How long will it take us to walk there?'

'Why walk? We have horses.'

And so they had. We four rode, but Lhygod, hands and feet tied, we threw over the horse's back like a sack. We went west and north, till we met the road, and then we kept west over the flank of a chalk hill, past a line of barrows that marked the path of the Green Road, the Ridgway. And then, coming down from the Ridgway, down around the shoulder of the hill, we saw in front of us a great mound, an enormous barrow hundreds of feet high. It was more like one of the Pyramids of Egypt than anything else, and like them it had been built of great lumps of chalk, carefully cut and squared. But that had been long ago, and now the blocks had been weathered and rounded and the cracks between them filled in with dust and mud, and green moss and even grass now grew on what had once been white and shining walls. There was a path that led up to the top of the mound, but now one could only with difficulty see that it had once been a spiral staircase to a flat platform.

'Is it a burial mound?' I asked Grathach.

'Who knows?' he answered. 'It has many names, and most people call it the Hill of the Sun, or the Hill of Sul, who is our Goddess of the Sun. But what we used to use it for, and have done since time immemorial, was something quite ordinary. It used to be the Hill of Judgement of the kings of the Isle of the Mighty, and on top the High Kings of all the island, for we had High Kings once, would sit to give judgements in all manner of cases, their crowns on their heads and their Druids sitting at their feet to guide them in the law. But it is also called the Hill in Arberth, for Arberth is this land, and Arberth is the name of the village that lies to the north.'

'It will do me very nicely,' I told them, making my voice sound as off-handedly evil as I could for Lhygod's benefit. 'First we will take this wretch up to the top, and then I want you to go to the village and find me three beams, strong enough to bear the weight of a ... lad, and a hammer, and nails.'

This they did, and Grathach, who only looked stupid, remembered the spade I had not mentioned, and also brought a chair for me to sit on.

'What shall we do?' he asked me in a loud voice, so that all the passers-by on the road, and all the people of the village of Arberth who had come out to watch, could hear. And I answered him in the same way:

'Build me a gallows. Build it high and build it strong, that it may stand here for a hundred years to show what happens to those who steal Mannanan's property. Dig holes into the hill, and set the uprights well into the soil. Nail the crossbar firmly so that it will not give, and throw the rope over. Then we will set the noose about this young rat's neck and pull ... pull ... pull ... slowly and watch him kick. But do not work too fast, because it would be a pity if there might be anyone who would have too little time to see the justice of Mannanan.'

It was still only the middle of the morning. I looked about me as Nerthach and Duach took turns with the spade to sink the holes. To the east of us wound the Roman Road, and to the west of us, and in both directions it disappeared into the forest. To the north I could see the village of Arberth, and it was surrounded, I could see, by a circle of stones of the men of old, and another line of stones ran away to the east. But to the south, crossing me from left to right, I could see the line of the Green Road.

It was when the lads had finished sinking the holes and we were about to put up the first post that I heard scuffling on the path, and the grunting and blowing of a man out of condition, almost drowning Lhygod's sobs which grew louder as the holes were dug deeper. Then round the corner of the path the face of a man appeared and spiralled up to the top of the mound. He was a big, stocky man, very thick built indeed, with linen tunic and fine wool trousers, boots of Spanish leather, and a Gold chain around his neck. He looked the part of a merchant. He looked at the poles, and he looked at Lhygod, and he asked:

'Why sir, what are you doing here? Why are you putting up these timbers on this mound?'

'Simple enough it is,' I replied. 'Last night, I was walking hither and thither among my oatstacks, and necessary it was, because the mice have been at them lately. But of course when I came they all ran, and all I was able to catch was this one little mouse.' For that is the meaning of Lhygod, which I took to be some kind of a pet name. 'Therefore, I am going to hang this mouse by the neck till it be dead, for a warning to all the big rats of the Isle of the Mighty, and indeed of the Isle of the Blessed also, that I will have mercy on neither great nor small till what has been taken from me is returned.'

'Oh, but come now,' and his voice was smooth and silky as if he were trying to sell me something no sane man would take as a gift. 'Surely vengeance like this is beneath a great lord like yourself. The death of so little a mouse will not help you. I have always wanted a little mouse to play with, as a pet. Come, sir, sell it to me for five pieces of Gold ... or should I offer ten? It is only a whim of mine ... Oh, yes, I can pay, I can pay, I am a trader of some repute in these parts.'

'I will ask you something.' Never, I thought, fight an enemy on his own ground. 'If I take five Gold pieces, new minted and not yet clipped, and I buy a hundred amphorae of Gaulish wine, and I sell them for two hundred two-horse denarii, and with that I buy one thousand cheeses and I sell those for forty thousand copper sesterces, then have I made a profit or a loss?'

'Now, if you will repeat that slowly,' he stammered, 'and let me send for my abacus and my tablets and let me inquire the price of cheese and how many sesterces there are in a sestertia—'

'Any merchant carries all these things at his fingers' ends, and would have answered me in a moment,' I said sternly. 'No merchant you.'

And Nerthach and Duach took him by the shoulders and the

ankles and rolled him down the sides of the mound, and he scrambled up on to the road and ran as fast as he could towards the wood from which he had come.

Then the lads got the cross-beam up on to the gallows, and they made a great deal of fuss about it, banging away with the nails fit to wake the dead in the long grave mound I could see, and at every bang Lhygod sobbed the more. But when they had finished, a head appeared over the edge of the mound as a man strode up the spiral path as easily as if it were the level ground. He was dressed as an officer of an Auxiliary Regiment of Cavalry, in the German fashion, with his shirt tucked into his trousers and his trouser legs tapered to his boots. His breastplate was polished, and his helmet shone, with a yellow plume set crosswise. I wondered idly what regiment he thought he was in. Before I could ask him, he began to ask me, in a Latin thickened with an accent that might have been that of Friesia or Pannonia:

'Now, sir!! What are you doing here? Do you not know that the administration of justice in this country is the task of Caesar's officers? Are you indeed preparing to carry out a hanging? Hand your prisoner over to me at once!'

I shifted my position in my chair so that the handle of my sword came before his eyes, and I answered him mildly enough:

'I am merely ridding my land of vermin. Last night I was taking the air in the rickyard, hoping to catch the mice that have been eating up all my grain. But they saw me coming and ran away, and I was only able to catch this little one. Therefore I am setting up this high gallows, and here I will hang this mouse, as a warning to all the big rats within the Empire and outside it that I will have mercy neither on great nor small till what they have stolen is returned to me.'

'A mouse, is it?' he mused, twirling his moustache between finger and thumb, and I felt pity for a man whose chin had been so recently scraped clean. 'Now, if, as I see, you have a large performing mouse, I would be glad to buy it as a regimental mascot. Expense is no object. I will reclaim it from the regimental funds. Will you take twenty Gold pieces ... forty ...?'

'All right, German cavalryman,' I answered him. 'Tell me this – is the World Tree an oak, or an ash, or an elm?'

He looked at me a moment in confusion.

'Why,' he stammered at last, 'the most sacred tree of all must be an oak tree.'

'You are no German Cavalryman,' I told him, and Grathach and Duach took him by the shoulders and the ankles, and rolled him down the slope, and pelted him with lumps of chalk as he ran back into the woods from which he had come.

It was now half-way through the afternoon. The men from the Confines of Hell threw the end of the rope over the cross-bar, and began to make a noose, trying it on Lhygod's neck for size and remaking it several times because it was too large, or too small, or not tidy enough. And while they were laughing over this, the head of a man appeared as he walked slowly up the spiral path. And this was not a merchant nor a soldier, but a Druid. His clean-shaven face peered out from his white headcloth, and his white tunic brushed the ground before his feet. On his breast was a shrivelled leaf, which might have been mistletoe, and on his head was a wreath of oak-leaves, the ends of the twigs fresh broken and oozing sap, and the acorns, since it was mid-August, still unripe and green-cased. He came to me and he said:

'What are you doing here, my son? If you wish to offer sacrifice, it is not for you to carry it out, and there is no law in this isle that allows you to hang an offering to the Gods. Let me have this man, so that at Beltain I may shut him in a basket and burn him alive.'

'Why, this is no man,' I told him, 'but a little mouse. I was taking my ease last night in the rickyard, where the mice have been troublesome, but when they heard me coming they fled, all except this one, which I caught. And I propose to hang it from this high gallows, so that all this vermin, of this world and the world that is to come and the world of the Dead, shall know that I will have mercy on neither great nor small till all that I have lost is returned to me.'

'Then if it is a mouse, my son,' said the Druid, and I was full of admiration for a man who could talk thus so soon after his moustaches had been scraped from his upper lip, 'I would indeed like to possess it, because it is foretold that when I die I shall be transmigrated into a mouse, and so it would be unworthy of me to allow anyone to kill what may, in time, become my own wife. Therefore, let me buy it from you as an act of piety, and though I have no money of my own, yet I am entrusted with certain funds to be disbursed in charity, and therefore I could offer you for this mouse sixty pieces of silver … of Gold … eight pieces of Gold …'

'Druid!' I spoke to him without reverence. 'Tell me this. What is white and black, of the sky and not of the sky, of the earth and not of the earth?'

He looked puzzled. Then he said, 'I must have some time to consult my sacred books.'

'You are no Druid,' I told him, and Nerthach and Duach were ready to roll him down the slope again, but I merely said to them:

'*Pull*!'

With relish they began to take in the slack of the rope, but as the rope tightened Gwawl shouted in his proper voice:

'Stop it! Stop!'

We looked at him., He had thrown off the Druid's robe, which was only a bed sheet he had stolen from the inn the night before, and he stood there in his black and white shirt, but clean-shaven now.

'What is there I can give you for this mouse? Name anything you want, even to the half of my Kingdom.'

'First,' I said, 'tell me who is this mouse.'

'This is my wife,' said Gwawl, 'new married, and this was the only way I thought she could travel safely from her own Iceni across a land full of desperate men like yourself, and at the same time have my two men keep an eye on you. And treat her carefully, I beg of you, because she has just found out that she is pregnant.'

'Then if you want her back,' I told him, 'you will have to pay for her, and sorry I would be to have to hang her, for I like her as well as any woman I ever met who did not speak a word to me.'

'Yes, yes,' gasped Gwawl, sweating with worry. 'I will exchange her for Rhiannon.'

'And besides Rhiannon?'

'Yes, then – you may have Taliesin too.'

'And besides Taliesin?'

364

'No, no: you cannot ask me to give up my real prize, my ancient enemy.'

Grathach gave a playful tug at the rope, and the mouse stood on tiptoe, gurgling.

'All right, then. I will send back Pryderi also.'

'And besides Pryderi?'

'What? Will you give me no profit at all from this night?'

'None at all. Let us have back also Hueil and his four men, or their weight in Gold if they are dead, and our horses and all our baggage unrobbed and untouched.'

'All that I will do, only let me have my little mousey back.'

'And bring them before the sun is set, to the road below this mound. And then let us see you go, vowing not to molest us again on this journey, as we will not molest you.'

And so we agreed.

The Mere

Chapter One

How far from the Mound of Arberth to the Summer Country? Far enough, with five men wounded. Hueil had an arm broken, and his four comrades were hurt each in a different measure – this one had his jaw broken and most of his teeth knocked out, that one had been struck in the face with a burning log, and so on. Pryderi had merely been kicked many times in the ribs, so that he found it painful to ride far in a day. Taliesin had been tied up, no one daring to offer any more violence to a Druid, and indeed that violence had been enough.

'For the first time in my life,' he told us, 'I regretted that the laws of my holy order forbid me to curse any man. But I did as well in my own way.'

'How?' we asked.

'Why, I drew in the dust with my foot, and I told each man his fate, and how he would die. And there is not a man there who will not die a dreadful death, violent and horrible beyond belief.'

Now whether he truly divined this or not I do not know, but I have no doubt that his prophecies will all come true, because there is no surer way to drive a man to court disaster than to foretell it for him. What we believe, happens.

Rhiannon they had kept apart, and she told us that Gwawl had made sure that she was treated like a perfect lady. It would, of course, have been easy to trace her, had I let Duach go to fetch a band of men, by the hawk that hovered above her all the day.

We moved along the old Green Roads, crossing the new stone roads of the Romans, but not using them. This was for ease, not for necessity: no troops march along the new roads any more, except once a year the Pioneers, replacing cobbles and clearing out the ditches, in case it should be ever necessary to hurry the legions down into the West again.

We stayed in farms at night. The people knew that we were coming. These were big farms, set well apart, because the Britons live thus and not in villages. Often the farms would belong to nobles, who now lived all the year round in the County Town, like Calleva or Sulis. Of course, a noble would never now go near his farm, but he liked at least to think that he had a house in the country where he could, if he ever wanted to, entertain his important friends if he ever made any. And it was at least a good thing, 'my house' and 'my estate' and 'my tenants', to talk and exaggerate about.

A number of these houses were quite comfortable, by provincial standards. Usually they had changed from a cluster of round huts into a series of straight-walled rooms, like the rest of mankind build, and the farmyard had changed into a paved courtyard. Sometimes the owners had gone as far as building the walls of stone, or even brick, and in a few cases they had put on a layer of plaster in the slim hope that some day they would find someone to come and paint them with some civilised scene. And in one case, the floor had been made ready in the dining-room in case the owner could ever afford to have a ready-made mosaic put down.

Heating, of course, was still primitive, charcoal braziers set wherever it was convenient. Still, they were somewhere to stay, since the stewards or bailiffs or what you like to call them were always eager to take us in, and as far as I could see never charged a denarius, or complained about the bird droppings in the room where Rhiannon slept.

We went west, and then south, and after that west again, to skirt the Lead Hills. You could, on clear days, make out the haze of smoke from the smelting furnaces at the mines. There were the nearest Roman soldiers, and not many of them: they would be little interested in the surrounding country, but would only be wondering how long it might be before they were relieved. And these men, and their lead, came and went by the new road, north of the Hills, that went through Sulis to Londinium.

All the hills were quiet now. The Army had gone from village to village and from house to house a hundred times, in the few years after the conquest, and seized every sword and helmet and mail coat. The chariots, too, belonged to the nobles, and they had also been brought in. You never saw so much as a real shield now, not the stout lime-wood panels, three-layered, bronze-faced and iron-rimmed: only the flimsy painted leather screens that Rhiannon's escort still carried. This was an old-fashioned area, but, even so, you never saw a Roman here either. Only, once every seven years or so, the surveyor came through, re-assessing for the wheat tax. Now *he* needed an escort. Otherwise, the peas-ants obeyed their lords as they had done before the conquest, or rather they obeyed their lords' stewards, because their lords never came any more.

Still, there was no need to go inviting trouble, in such a big party of ours, and that was why we travelled by the old Green Road, and spread out into small groups between farms, coming together for the night. We met few other travellers, and most of them were rather curious. We so often overtook or met single men with packhorses, two horses to a man, and each horse with two baskets, not big so they must have been heavy, or so I thought. What was striking was that always horse and man were black from head to foot: not black by nature which would have been understandable, but black with some dirt or other, grimed into white skin and brown hair beyond any hope of washing. The baskets were black, too. I took them for charcoal-burners, and I said so to Pryderi, one day. At this, he laughed, and the next time we met one of these men, he stopped and called him over.

He was a short man, and close to you could see the sweat run-ning channels in the dirt, and the hands and arms covered with the scars of labour filled with the black and looking blue under-neath the skin. The man came to us, and we got down to talk, as is only polite, while he sat down, balancing himself delicately on the heels of his feet, and doubling the backs of his thighs against his calves, so that only his feet and not his back side touched the ground. It was the art of a man who works hard, and does not spend his strength unnecessarily on standing up.

'Go on, ask him what it is he carries,' said Pryderi. Hueil and Nerthach, riding ahead, reined back and waited for us. The Dirty Man looked at my blue clothes, and nodded to them, not to me, politely, but respectfully, as though granting through good will and not through obligation, some slight deference to a social superior. I asked him:

'Is this charcoal?'

'Charcoal? Wood coal? Would I be selling you the worn-out ashes of other men's second-hand fires? No, this is earth coal, the best.'

'Earth coal?'

'Easy it is to be hearing, and understanding, and knowing, from your question, though it is very well you are speaking the language of the Gods, and only making a few mistakes in the grammar, and in the order of the tenses and in the mutations, and sometimes being indistinct in your appreciation of the fine gradations of meaning, that it is from far away and from foreign parts and from a distant land that you have come, and travelled, and ridden.' He spoke in a thick accent that I could hardly follow, but he had that easy flow of language and wide vocabulary and subtle sense of rhythm which are common to all Britons. 'No, it is not charcoal, it is the earth coal.'

'Let me see it.'

'Aye, I will let you,' he began, and it was obvious that he was about to launch out again into one of his interminable sentences, the only saving quality of which was that like all the Britons he was careful to begin each one with the main verb, but Pryderi passed him a leather-bound flagon of mead. The Dirty Man took a long, long swig. When he lowered the bottle from his mouth, he began to undo the basket with his free hand, saying as he did so:

'Aye, sweet it is, the mead of the bees, sweeter than water, sweeter than death. But not so good it is as water to quench thirst. There is nothing like pure water from the spring to wash out the dust of the tunnels and the grit of the caves. In return for this, I will even let you have a piece of the earth coal. For it would not be right, nor fitting, nor lawful to give you a piece without payment and without price and without exchange. Into the very guts of the earth we go to gain it, and we cut it out from the roots of the hills. Into the heart of the rock and into the liver of the world we make our tunnels to find it, and there we hear the friendly spirits of the earth our mother. They warn us, when it is time to close our tunnels, and when they wish to bring down

372

the roof so that the earth may rest fallow. And it is only the foolish man who stays when the spirits warn.' He took another long draft at the mead. 'Aye, here is a lovely piece for you, and worth the buying.'

Now, what he said about it being wrong to give the stuff away I could well understand, having once been a doctor myself. When you have some skill or access to some commodity, and this has cost you a great deal of work in the past, then it is an act of impiety to the God who gave it to you not to show how much you value it by asking for it the highest price you can get. And if a man will not pay the price you demand, then he must go without. If he cannot pay for a fire or for food or for a doctor's knowledge, then let him die of cold or hunger or disease. It is blasphemy for him to ask for food or firing or treatment free, and it is blasphemy for anyone to have pity on him and help him for nothing. This is the basic law of all religion, and the foundation of the science of medicine: no man is entitled to life unless he can pay for it.

Anyway, this man looked into his pannier, and brought out a lump of something, I couldn't see what at first, it was only a small piece and he hid it in his closed hands. With a look of complicity in some dark deed he put it into my hand. It was, to all appearances, a piece of stone, black, and sharp in contour, newly broken or quarried. It was soft, though, as stone goes. I could break it into little splintery pieces with my thumb-nail, pushing along straight cracks to split it into layers. It stained my fingers with black. When I split it along the cracks, the fresh surfaces caught the light. I was puzzled.

'What is it?' I asked.

'If it is not knowing that you are,' the Dirty Man replied, 'then it is guessing you will have to be.'

I turned it over and over.

'It is too friable to be building stone. Likewise it would never serve for paving, even as occasional black pieces in a mosaic. It might, however, do for the black in a wall mosaic. Instead of using it as it is, perhaps you grind it down and use it to colour plaster black for wall designs. Or is it a dye?' I spat on it. 'Probably not, since it doesn't dissolve in moisture. It might, though in

373

oil, though I haven't any and I can't try it. I know it isn't jet, since it is much too brittle to turn on a wheel. So, I suppose it must be an ore of some kind. What kind? Not iron, or lead, it is not heavy enough. But … tin is light. That's it, I have it. It's tin ore.'

It was rather humiliating, I must say, to show a fine example of the methods of the sophists as I did then, and to be laughed at, but all the same Pryderi and the Dirty Man did laugh at me. Pryderi said, when he could.

'Not to worry, you weren't to know. I'll show you tonight, you won't believe me otherwise.'

At that moment, the next section of our party came round the bend in the road behind us. The Dirty Man looked at them, moving on with the clusters of birds singing in the bushes at either side, and he asked sharply:

'Who's that?'

'Well, boy,' Pryderi seemed to be ready to settle down for one of those irritating riddling chats the Britons are so fond of, and he was using his peasant voice to do it in, 'that one in front, well, Taliesin that is, Taliesin of Mediometon.'

'Oh, aye,' said the Dirty Man, unimpressed. 'The Druid. I seen him before, I did, and not much to look at now, is he? But her – who's she?'

'Her? Oh, well now, that is …' Pryderi paused, savouring it. 'Her, well she's …' and then it came in a rush – 'Rhiannon of the Brigantes, Rhiannon herself, that is.'

'Rhiannon herself? Herself? Here? Already here?'

The Dirty Man was of a sudden out of breath. Rhiannon clearly was a different kind of being from us, or from Taliesin. He stared as she came nearer. As she approached, the wood on either side of the path was full of the scurrying of wood-pigeons, and jays, and tree creepers, and the songs of the thrushes and the warblers. The Dirty Man had pulled his old horse to the side of the road, and now he stood beside it, his hands raised level with his face, spread out, palms forward, his head bowed, the universal attitude of prayer. Rhiannon came level with us and reined in her horse. The birds fell silent.

'What is it, my son?' She gazed down at the Dirty Man, who did not dare to look her in the face. Rhiannon at this time was, perhaps, twenty-two or twenty-three, in the grand flush of her beauty. The Dirty Man was at least forty, nearing the end of a hard life. His drooping moustache was flecked with grey.

'Bless me, my Mother, Mother of Those Below,' he asked her. 'Give me good fortune. Let me find the seams below, fat thick seams, rich and good, that will kindle and burn and give warmth to make men live and cook good food. Keep the choking mist from my lungs a few more years, and let me not be burnt in the great floods of flame, nor drowned in the blaze of waters. Let me not be caught behind the falls, and let your messengers tell me when the roof comes down. Only for a few years, my Mother, only for a few years, till the boy is old enough to come into the seam and feed himself, and his mother if need be.'

'Be content my son,' answered Rhiannon, speaking slowly and with ceremony. 'Those who toil below are not forgotten by those who dwell below. You shall not come to your end till the boy can dig for himself. And this you have not asked aloud, but only in your heart and I will grant it you. You shall not die like the common run, standing or lying and in the light of sun and moon. You shall die like a man, crouching amid the falling stones and in the dark. When it is your time, I shall take you to myself in the bursting roof, quickly in noise and fury and in the blackness. This I grant you, my son.'

Pryderi and I mounted. We all passed on. At the next bend in the road, I looked back. The Dirty Man still stood by the wayside, his hands still held before his face. His horse patiently cropped the grass behind him. The birds sang again about Rhiannon.

Soon after that day we came to the crest of a hill. The sun shone almost level from a little west of south. In line with it, out of a great stretch of open country, a hill stood up, a tall round hill the shape of an upturned bucket, an echo of the mound of Arberth, but taller, much taller. Pryderi pointed.

'See that? Once we're past that, we're in the Summer Country. That's the place to be, for the winter. Spending winter in the Summer Country, there's lucky you are.' He spoke like a peasant, laughing like a simple man at the play on words, 'Just let's get past the Glass Mountain and then we'll be right till the spring.'

I took little notice of his Glass Mountain or any other strange names. Far, far away, something shone. It might be, it might not be, but I was sure, too, that I could smell it, faintly, faintly … it gave me life. Somewhere within a day's ride was the sea.

A mile or two down the forward face of the hill we came to another farm, and we were greeted by rooms ready for us, and stabling for the horses, and food ready in the pot. But this time it was no Steward who stood to welcome us. Hueil dismounted, his arm still bandaged, and stood to receive us at his own door. It was a fine evening, almost warm by our standards, overpoweringly hot to the Britons, and we sat to eat in the courtyard, around a brazier set there for comfort and light and not for heat, and we sang, quietly and in harmony, out of joy at being surrounded now, not by mere friends, but, most of us, by our own kinsmen.

'Where's your keepsake?' Pryderi asked me of a sudden. At first I couldn't understand what he meant, but then I remembered, and out of my wallet I took my little piece of black stone. Pryderi took it, and fingered it for a while. Then he leaned forward and put it into the fire.

'Watch!' he told me. For a little while nothing happened, it just sat there black and dead. Then the stone began to glow at the edges, and little blue flames started from it. I remembered the officer at Rutupiae who had said, 'They're so poor, they burn the very stones of the earth for want of wood.' Pryderi explained:

'The people near here dig it out of the earth and peddle it about the country. It is good for fires. The Romans buy a lot of it for smelting the lead.'

'It is the gift of the Gods Below,' said Rhiannon. 'It will be the salvation of the Isle of the Mighty.'

Well, you know how women prattle. I saw a lot of it used later, and it does indeed burn very well, once you can get it to light, and that's the problem: you have to get a good wood fire going first to kindle the stone, and of course if you can do that, what's the use of looking for anything else. So who on earth would want it? It's so heavy to carry, and takes so much trouble to dig out, that it will never replace the charcoal. No, there's no future for earth coal.

Chapter Two

It is a strange place, the Summer Country. It stretches between the Glass Mountain and the sea, from south to north. On the east, the boundary is the bluff edge of the Lead Hills. On the west is the ridge that marks the edge of the Deer Moor, a desolate bare country where only the wild beasts live in winter, and where the sheep graze in summer. Between them is a low ridge that men call the Apple Land. I will tell you why.

On either side of the Apple Land a river flows to the sea. And each river is ponded back by the tides into a marsh, so that swamps stretch from the edges of the Apple Land, east to the Lead Hills and west to the Deer Moor. That low land is covered in alders and willows, and little humps of land stand out of the swamp, which in winter are islands in the floods. And on a clear day you can stand below Hueil's farm, and look over the Summer Country, and count a hundred little smudges of smoke, and every one is a farm in the marshes.

We came down from Hueil's farm and we entered the marsh, the horses following a firm path. We skirted the base of the Glass Mountain. I suddenly realised, at the foot, that we were passing through where once a village had been. The ruined houses, deserted these fifty years, were overgrown with weeds. There were only two farms still occupied. One of them had a farmyard, fenced in on three sides, and on the fourth butting against a rock-face, and within that a barn against the rock. The people of the place looked incuriously at us as we passed. We said nothing. We did not talk to each other on the long road into the marsh.

The horses went well, carrying us down into the Mere. They stepped delicately along the track beaten out by the hooves of countless cattle. We passed into the meadows of long sweet grass, dotted with clumps of trees, and the ground about the track grew softer and wetter, and the grass longer and coarser, and the trees grew thicker and closer together. I realised that we were now riding along a made road, of logs laid crosswise in the way, covered with layers of gravel. It was a firm road, wide enough for two packhorses to walk abreast with a man between to lead them. It might well have supported even a wagon.

In some places about us the ground was firm and in the bright meadows, too wet for sheep, grazed the little black cows you find everywhere in Britain. In other places you could see the water gleaming around the roots of the grass. Soon there were open pools, and wider lagoons, between ridges and tussocks of stiff reeds and bulrushes. There was no riding here, or walking either, off the track, but there was not enough water for a boat. In some places the lagoons were shallow, mere low-lying fields filled by the summer rains; but some of the pools were deep and black, good places, I thought, for pike. Now instead of scattered clumps of big trees, there were willows and alders on the edges of the pools, and between patches of scrub, too dense for a man to push his way through quickly on horseback, or even to think of entering on foot. There was no choice but to follow the track.

Deeper and deeper we went into the marsh. The water looked like lead under the cloudy sky. There was now no sound but the scuffling of hooves, and the occasional twittering of birds following Rhiannon. Pryderi rode with me, and behind Taliesin went with Rhiannon. Nerthach and Duach brought up the rear. Both Rhiannon and Taliesin looked straight ahead, with faces emptied of fear or joy. Only, from time to time, Grathach far ahead broke the silence with a sad and shapeless song, too faint for me to hear the words. I did not know where we were going, or what we would find in the Summer Country. I tried not to guess.

We saw no people. There *were* people living in the marsh, sometimes so close to our road that we could smell their fires, but we never saw them. There were piles of willow withies cut and stacked by the side of the log road, and stacks of logs, too, sometimes, ready for the charcoal-burners. There were boats on the lagoons, crude things carved each out of a single log, blunt-ended, just enough to keep a man afloat while he fished. We still saw cows where the ground was firm enough: they must have belonged to somebody, I thought. There was nobody to talk to us, or to watch us, that we could see. But I was sure that we were seen, and watched.

Now we had been moving for half the day, with never a stop for food or rest. There was very little open land now, only the thicket and the marsh and the narrow road. It was now too narrow for two horses abreast, and I followed Pryderi. The willows hid the hills on either side. The Glass Mountain had long since vanished. There was nothing to be seen at all but the thicket, either within arm's reach on either side, or a spear's throw away across black stagnant water, covered sometimes with green slime. Beavers fled from before us into their lodges, and otters, water dogs, as the Britons call them, looked up from their fresh-captured fish on the far banks and watched us without fear. Herons stood in the reeds to see us pass. Moorhens and duck went about their business unheeding. This was no place for men.

I felt lost. I was lost. We were far from any human contact. There was an end now of houses and wine, of fires and the friendly talk of wise men. There was nothing but thornbush and grey cloud and water. There were no hills, no firm ground, nothing to which a man could cling, nothing real, nothing definite, only infinite marsh. All was lost. I knew that this was the end of the world, that all that lay before me was delusion and disaster.

I had vowed myself to the Gods Below, and now it was the Mother of the Gods Below who rode behind me, displacing the Priest of the Unconquered Sun, on whom I might no more call for help. I knew now that I would never return to the real world, that there was no real world, that whatever I might see in future would not be the world. I had passed through the Gates of the Dead. I would never return. I was alone. I was dead.

The scrub grew denser. It closed in on both sides of the path. There was only a narrow gash in the green wall ahead. Grathach, in his cloak of striped black and yellow, moved his pony through the gap, and was gone. Pryderi checked his horse a little. I touched his shoulder:

'Forward?' I asked.

'Forward,' he replied. 'There is no other way.'

The path wound through the wood. The green waterfalls of

the willows curtained me in on every side. I turned left and then right with the path, and left again, I moved here and there, twisting around the trees, turning in my horse's length. Pryderi was too far ahead to be seen. The twists of the path became more and more violent, more frequent. I became dizzy clinging with knees and heels and arms to the horse as he scrambled among the soggy tufts and the fallen branches, black with rot and speckled with red. I was lost and alone in this wilderness, it was death, it was Hell, this *was* Hell, to wander for ever with no hope of ever arriving, no hope of any rest or any end.

And then I came to, not an end, but a beginning, a choice. The path forked. One way went to the right, the other to the left. There was no telling which way to take. I sat still and listened. There was no sound, no sound of horses' hooves, no sound of feet. There was no voice to be heard, not even Grathach's song, nor the songs of the birds. There was no one in the marsh, no one on the path, no one before me or behind. I was alone. I had no help. I must decide. And yet, I was sure that I was not alone, that eyes watched me, alive or dead, that nothing I did but was known. And I understood that whatever I did now I must do alone, that there would be no help from any being.

Which way to go? I sat, and I listened to the silence, and I sniffed at the air. There was no sound, nor the smell of fire, nor fresh tracks on the path, nor horse droppings nor broken twigs. But somewhere, along one path or another, I would find the Master of the Western Sea. And where would he be but by the sea?

I put my hand into my wallet. I took from it a shell, one of those rare Indian shells, glossy and striped in cream and brown, and speckled over with black. The mouth of this shell is a slit, all set along with teeth that never move or grind together, and if a man puts his ear to the mouth, then he can hear the sea, however far he may be from it. And that I tell you is true, for by such a means I have heard the sea in the middle of a desert, and on the top of a great mountain. And there in the marsh I put the shell to my ear, spitting first on the ground, because I had no other offering to make to the gods of the place, whoever they were. I turned to my right, and I listened, and I heard the patter of little waves on a beach, rattling the stones in the undertow, and so faint that it could hardly be heard. And then I turned to the left, and I heard the great waves of the ocean, driven by the west wind, tumbling and crashing in ruins of foam, seas to crush ships and drown whales and take up great stone jetties and cast them into the market-places of towns. If there were ever a sea worth the Mastery, then this was it. I turned to the left.

I followed the twists and turns of the path, and whenever it forked, as it did every hundred paces, I listened to the sound of the sea, and I went where the storm was loudest, though never a breath of wind touched my face, there in the prison of the Green Marsh. I forded little streams and splashed through shallow pools, and even my weary horse began to scent some hope ahead, and himself to sniff the air. And then, of a sudden, there was a wind, a wind in my face, and I sniffed it like the horse, and what meant nothing to him was the smell of nectar to me, the smell of the salt sea. And now I had no need of the shell, I faced always into the wind, and when it veered, as winds will, I veered with it, heading into it, so that the evil spirits of the place should not swamp me. And at last on the wind I smelt smoke, the smoke of a peat fire, and sometimes I thought I could hear the sound of voices. The thickets became sparser and the meadows more open, and the ground about the path was firmer. Instead of the otter's half-gnawed fish among the rushes, I saw the padmarks of the fox, and instead of the beaver's dam, my horse avoided the molehills among the buttercups. There were cows again, and it felt to me as if the path were slightly, very slightly, up hill. And then it was not a path but a road, the gravel beaten down into the spaces between the logs, and through the trees I could see hills ahead. The wind blew strongly, and the grey cloud thinned above me and cleared from before me, and by the height of the sun as I rode into it I saw that I was travelling to the West.

And then in a sudden I was clear. In a marsh I had once left all I loved. Now I had come out of the marsh again, and I was a new man. I reined in my horse, and I dismounted because where I had come I must go on my own feet. I threw back the borders of my sealskin cloak, and I laid my right hand on the jewelled hilt of my sword. I flaunted my boots of cordoban leather, and my trousers of blue wool of the first shearing of the virgin ewe. I let

381

all men see my shirt of silk, blue silk from a world away, and the Gold chain about my neck from which hung an Amber globe, and the Gold morse that fastened my cloak, set with Amber, and my belt, plates of ivory engraved with strange scenes of the chase and sewn to elephant skin. Wealth I showed all who cared to see, the most precious things in the world, Gold and Silk, Amber and Ivory. And so I walked to meet the Master of the Western Seas.

I came across the open meadow towards him. We were under the bluff edge of the hills on the Western side of the Summer Country. The scarp sheltered houses scattered along the side of the marsh, above the flood level. Three hundred paces from the place where the path came from the woods stood a crowd of people, men, women and children, not in a shapeless mass, but ranked in order. And in the centre of the line Pryderi stood at the right hand of the Master of the Western Sea.

For who else could it be, seated there on a throne made out of the beak of a ship. The jutting forefoot was heaped with cushions, and the figurehead, a flying goose, spread its wings above him. He answered my belt of elephant Ivory with one of plates of the walrus's teeth. His boots were not of soft leather of the cow, but of the hide of the whale. The Gold chain about his neck suspended on his breast a pearl the like of which no man has ever seen, for it was as big as his fist. Instead of a sword, he held in his right hand a grapnel, three-pronged, of silver, the handle set with sheets of mother of pearl, and in his left hand he had the horn of a wild ox mounted in Gold. And his hair and moustaches were as white as the skin of the great white bear he wore for a cloak. But in all his splendour, I knew him, and he knew me. I walked steady and straight towards him, not looking round though I knew that a score of men had followed me in the marsh and were now behind me in the meadow. I halted three paces from him. He spoke first:

'Photinus-Votan-Mannanan, whoever you are. What is it you want of me?'

I knew I must stand up to him now, or never again.

'Caw!' I addressed him. 'Caw! Master of the Western Sea I know you. I stole your ship once, and I stole its cargo, and I even

382

stole you. Now I have come again to you for a ship, and this time I am willing to pay.'

'And I tried to kill you myself,' he answered calmly. 'I spoilt your water and your food. These things happen at sea, where there is no law except that a man may live if he is strong, and must live if he is wise. But are you indeed the man I knew then?' He turned to Pryderi. 'What kind of man is he?'

Pryderi looked at me dispassionately.

'On land, I grant you, he is a man of skill and resource, a man who is not too proud to work with his hands, and to produce works of art according to his lights. And he is a keen bargainer in the market-place, and able to turn anything into money, even rotten rags and green rushes.'

'What else do you expect?' asked Caw. 'He is a merchant. Is he nothing more?'

'He is a man who will take a Gesa upon himself, and will keep it, even when he is in danger of his life.'

'Any man may keep his Gesa, for fear of the Gods, or even for fear of the vengeance of men,' said Caw.

'He is a man who will keep his word when there is no profit in it,' said another voice. I knew this voice. I turned to it. There was a wreath of coral in her hair, and about her waist was a belt of silver chains, the equal of Rhiannon's, linked as it was and buckled with Gold. But even today she wore above her nineteen petticoats, an apron I had bought her. 'He kept his promise and he set me free, though he did not know who I was or where I came from or what vengeance he was giving me. Hey, Photinus,' cried Cicva. 'Have you finished the hyena's hair?'

'But that was a little thing,' said Caw.

'There is more,' Pryderi told him. 'When he was tempted to follow the love of his life, he did not, but he still pressed to the West, wherever she might go.'

'And so might any man for money,' objected Caw again.

'But time was when he was offered all he has worked for, and that he refused, to redeem his love. And he did not redeem her only, but his friends too.'

What he meant by that I could not think, because I could not remember I had refused anything of importance. But Caw asked:

'Where is the man I used to know? He was one who would do nothing except for profit, and who would run after any woman in sight, aye, and catch her too. What has happened to you, Photinus? Is it only that you have grown old like me?'

I thought a little. Perhaps I had changed. I was not conscious of it. But perhaps in the old days I would not have left Pryderi to chase Rhiannon, I would have redeemed her alone and never thought of Taliesin, I would never have left Cicva, or Lhygod for that matter, unviolated. Was I becoming more temperate, less realistic in my prime? There was more than that. I answered:

'When I first went into the North, I went for no reason but to save my skin, and I had no one but myself to please and no one to answer to. That I gained great profit from it was an accident. Then I did not know it, but I followed the great plan of others, and I was a tool in the hands of the Gods. But now, I have come into the West to carry out my own great plan, and I will do only what I will. And I do not will that for my own sake, but I am doing it for the sake of my family, and to them I am responsible. I may not follow my own desires, no matter how attractive they are. I am not my own master, but I tell you this, I am master of my own grand design, and that I will carry out, though thrones fall and kings die, yes, even though I die.'

'And what is my place in this grand design, Photinus-Mannanan? What do you want of me?'

'I told you. I want a ship, and for it I can pay.'

'No, Mannanan. You want of me more than a ship, and for what you want, no man can pay enough. Sit here, and watch, stay with me a winter, and see what it is you are asking.'

Men brought a chair, with arms carved in the shape of swans, and placed it at Caw's left hand, and there I sat, and looked across the meadow to the edge of the wood. And from the wood I saw Taliesin come.

Now he was dressed again as a Druid, in white from head to foot. His oak-leaf crown was on his head, and the sickle and the apple were in his hands. In stout shoes he came across the grass, and I looked at the people expecting them to kneel before him, but they did not. They cheered, they waved their arms and shouted:

384

'Taliesin! Taliesin the Blessed, the Radiant Brow.' The women sighed and whispered and oohed and ahed and said:

'Oh, the Holy One, how beautiful he is, oh, there's lovely he is.'

The little children ran forward to touch the edge of his white garment, while their mothers warned them not to dirty it, and there was small danger of that, because their hands had been washed a dozen times that morning in readiness. And the men, oh, the men, they began to sing, intricately lacing together their Pythagorean patterns of sound, they sang the cauldron hymn I had heard before, and why it was appropriate to a Druid I could not think.

Some people praise a cauldron on a fire of flashing flame,
But a cauldron on a cold cold hearth brings the Brits
    immortal fame:
On cold ashes (*bang-bang-bang*) brings the Marsh undying fame.

That was the song they sang as I watched Taliesin come to us, and sit on the chair prepared for him on Caw's right hand, a great throne all carved with dragons and sea-horses, and painted and gilded. The voices rose to a fortissimo, and then stopped, suddenly, cut off. Out of the wood came Rhiannon.

Had you ever seen, even in your dreams, the ship of Theseus beating back to Athens from flaming Cnossus, you would know how she looked. For on that voyage, you will remember, the Athenians failed to change the black sails for silver. When Aegeus saw that black ship of mourning, he flung himself from the rocks for sorrow. And it would have been understandable for any man to have died for the love of Rhiannon as I saw her that day. She came to us, barefoot across the grass, wrapped in her splendid cloak of white and Gold; and in the midst of the space, as Theseus should have struck his black sails, so she threw down her cloak, and we saw her clad from head to foot in black; her blouse, long-sleeved, was of black linen, and her skirts sweeping the ground were of black wool. Her shawl about her shoulders was of black silk, and she lifted her arms and arranged it about her head to hide her glowing hair.

She came to us, and Caw stood to let her pass. Taliesin and I remained seated. She came to us, and as she came, all the men knelt. Caw knelt. Pryderi knelt, Grathach and Duach and Hueil knelt. I slipped from my chair and I knelt. And most wonderful of all, Taliesin knelt. The great Druid, the Most Holy One of all, he knelt. Here amid the men and boys of the Summer Country, the great priest of the Unconquered Sun knelt before the Mother of Those Below.

The men knelt. The women stood. They closed about Rhiannon as she went towards the house prepared for her.

Chapter Three

Now you may think that I had had enough incident for one day, and that it was by now too near dark for anything else to happen, and so did I, but to my surprise, no sooner had Rhiannon vanished than someone brought me a fresh horse.

'What for?' I asked.

'Wedding, of course,' answered Grathach, laughing so evilly that I was afraid for a moment that it was to be mine, since the Britons as a whole, Picts or not, are wont to make such arrangements without consulting the main actors. However, it was Pryderi's wedding, to Cicva, and I was honoured by being allowed to take part in the chase. For the Britons maintain the fiction, and fiction I assure you it is, that every woman is averse to marriage, and will flee from it as from a wolf. Therefore, Cicva mounted a horse of her own, a white one to be the more easily visible, and rode three times around her own house, while Pryderi and a dozen of us rode after her, whooping and screaming, till at the end of the third circuit, Pryderi rode up alongside his bride and struck her on the shoulder with a twig at which she collapsed into his arms. I must say that running your wife to earth is a good deal less dignified than buying her.

At the ensuing banquet I sat on Caw's right, the happy couple, as I hoped that they would be, having the top table to themselves. Now one expects a wedding feast to be lavish, with imported delicacies, like chestnuts and olives, and enormous quantities of staple foods like mutton and oatbread, and enough drink, cider and beer and mead, to bath in. But there was more to the feast than that, held as it was in Caw's great roundhouse. And I don't mean Taliesin, who ate only boiled beans and drank only water, for now he was among friends and no concealment was necessary.

I lay back and belched towards the end of the meal, for it was the first food I had had since dawn, and I had had a long hard ride, and then a rousing gallop to give me an appetite. And I wiped the sweat off my face with my napkin, and then I looked at the napkin. Fine linen, it was, and there were enough of them matched to give every guest the same, not merely to use but to take away afterwards. Egyptian they were, but not fancy, nothing to look at till you did look at them. They were expensive, and I ought to know, because I had handled them myself, or a batch very like them, the year before, and I remembered thinking that I couldn't afford them for my house, and I am not a poor man. Caw's clothes, too, were very good, not only the furs but the linen and wool, and Cicva's; and the old lady who bustled round and waited on them was using the remains of a silk dress for a duster, and in most places I knew, if a silk dress had gone that far it would still have been worth while to unravel it, thread by thread and weave it up again into something else. It puzzled me.

I looked at the plates we ate from, and the cups we drank out of. They were not silver, they were only pottery, but when you looked again, what pottery! No Briton ever threw those pots. They were made in Gaul, or perhaps even in Italy – I was too polite to turn them over to see the potter's mark, but I could see they were expensive, and yet nobody was upset when a cup was broken. It costs a mint of money just to transport the stuff, mostly on the packaging. The hangings on the wall were in good heavy wool, thick enough for blankets, woven in the spiral patterns I was used to now, and I know well how much time it takes to set up a loom to weave it – dearer than embroidered. And the tables were painted too, and the chairs, in those patterns, and not amateur work.

And yet there was a lot missing. All the things that strike the careless eye as signs of wealth were absent. There was no silver on the table, and no bronze either except a few spoons and a wine strainer, which was merely an ornament as there was no wine, and no pile of broken empty amphorae outside either. There was none of the rich and splendid enamel work that I had been seeing so much of, except for personal pieces like the belts that more important people wore. No, the casual eye, for instance that of the ill-trained and well-bribed local tax-collector, would not have seen any indication that this was not the house of an ordinary marsh farmer.

I said nothing about this. I would have liked to know but the easiest way to find out was just to say nothing. So I said nothing. That is the only way with Barbarians, just don't ask. Ask them anything and they freeze up and don't say a thing, or else they take pleasure in telling you the biggest lies they can imagine. But, of course, they *do* want, really, to tell you about how wonderful they are, and how clever, and if you don't ask them anything they finally burst, and they are so put off by this display of non-curiosity that they will often tell you the plain and simple truth. So I asked nothing, and at last, when everyone else was singing dismal cauldron songs, Caw, that tough old man, broke, and began to tell me the tale of the people who lived in the Mere.

'You will be wondering, doubtless, as so many do, how it is we live out here on the edge of the world. Pleasant and happy is life, and decent is death, though far we are from our homes and the graves of our kin. In Gaul once we lived, our fathers were men of power, on the edge of the Ocean that nobody ruled but we. We sailed our ships up and down the rim of the world, from Spain to the Scillies, to Ireland and Anglesey, and up to the land of fire on the edge of the ice. Great were the ships we built, and stout were their sides, of oak beams dowelled together with pegs of elm. Never use iron in ships or your end will come soon. The oak and the iron are foes, that fight to the death, and we who worship the oak would never dare to take an iron knife with us into the grove. See how the Holy Man, who is priest of the oak, never touches iron, though he may hold Gold or bronze.

'So our fathers were Lords of the Sea, and carried their cargoes of tin and of copper, of corn and wine and Gold, and all the nations knew that they were proud and rich. But then *he* came, the bald old man of the South, eager and grasping to steal the whole of the world. He did not know the meaning of decency, no not he, and he did not even dare to meet us fairly. He came at us in rowing boats, whatever the wind. His men tied sickles on their long poles, and then whenever they got close to one of our ships, they would cut the halliards and bring down the great leather sail and if they could cut the stays the mast would go too.

'Conquered were the proud Venetii, beaten was the hope of the world, bankrupt and ruined and broken the kings of our nation. Those who were willing could stay and pay homage to bald-headed Caesar, the stinking oil-eater. But some of us said we could not abide it, we would go out and find a new country. We sailed to the north and we came to the marshes, a desolate land that no nation governed, and we built a town beneath the Glass Mountain. When we thought that all was recovered, Claudius came to conquer the island. How could we live in a settled city, where tax-gatherers might come to count and to number us? We left our town, we left our temple, we moved a few miles to live in the marshes. Here are we safe to live out our days, in hunger and hardship and bitter poverty. We are too poor and too insignificant for noble or tribune or quaestor to see us.'

'Yes,' I agreed, spitting out the stone from a dried plum from Dalmatia. 'Poverty is a dreadful thing.' I remembered the talk I had heard in Londinium. It was not conquest that hurt the Venetii – it had harmed, say, the Atrebates little. No, it was the Roman fiscal policy which insisted that all trade with Britain should go through the Channel ports, where it could be taxed, and the dreadful penalties inflicted not only on any Britons who dealt with smugglers but also on any merchants who might try, in Gaul, to hire a ship in the West and trade any other way. The Venetii had seen their ships destroyed, and even if they had been able to rebuild there would have been no further employment for them. But some of those ships still remained – I knew, I had once stolen one from Caw himself, and there might be others. If there were no others, what was I doing here? Oak-planked they were indeed, and pegged with elm, but on to frames of ash, and elm-decked, and these two woods had no quarrel with iron: and they were not rowed, but driven by a great lugsail of leather, that would let them beat into the wind. Were there indeed any left? And if not, where did Caw's wealth come from?

I wondered about that all through the evening. We were all very merry. At the end of the evening, Grathach and Nerthach complained, as we made our way to the house where we were to sleep, that I was very drunk: I must have been – they dropped me twice.

Chapter Four

I must say that Caw stood up to the drinking very well for his age. We drank till two hours before dawn, and the sun was scarcely beginning to rise when he woke me and hurried me out into the thin rain, clutching my cloak and sword.

Silently he led me along past the sleeping houses, set far apart, because it is a characteristic of the Britons that they hate their kinsmen and each man's ambition is to live where he cannot see his neighbour's smoke. We did not walk far, only to an arm of the marsh where there was a small boat, hollowed out of a single log, hidden under the branches of a willow. We got in and paddled away from the houses, north-west. I had the choice of either wearing my cloak and being hot and wet, or of taking it off and being cold and wet, in the strong west wind and driving rain. I was dead weary from lack of sleep. I soon had corns over my bottom from sitting on quite different places from the ones you use to ride a horse, and all the rest of me was stiff – there were so many muscles I had not used since I sailed into Ostia. After hours, all I wanted to do was to lie on the bank and die, but Caw hurried me on.

When we cleared the north edge of the Apple Hills, we could see the edge of the Lead Hills east of us, like a long cliff, and the column of smoke from the Mines, but only when we came, as sometimes we did, out of the patches of willow and alder that stood up out of the waters. Well after noon I was ready to refuse to go any farther, and the only thing that gave me any hope was the strong smell of the salt sea.

Neither of us spoke much, except what was necessary to keep her head the right way, and among the willows it was more like choosing roads in a city than steering a boat. But at last, of a sudden, Caw barked:

391

'Up there, left, up that backwater!'

We came left, into a narrow channel, which widened out as such inlets often do, into a broad expanse of shining mud. And there, beached, was a ship. A real ship, I tell you, not a skin boat or a single log, but a ship. This was one of the Venetii, all right. High she stood out of the water, or would stand when she was afloat, with sides of oak planks, and decks of elm, and a high poop to help her ride a following sea. She had a single mast stepped a little forward of amidships, and the yard was down on the deck, but there was no mistaking it – she was rigged with lugsail.

There she lay among the leafy willows, with a couple of men scraping the barnacles off her timbers. We pulled ourselves up a rope on to her deck. A man sitting at his ease in a shelter under the poop got up to meet Caw, bowing to him. He had First Mate written all over him, mainly in his attitude of extreme indolence while his men worked. Caw said to him:

'Keeping well is it you are, Madoc? This is him.'

'Oh, you, is it?' said Madoc to me. 'Here, have something to eat.'

He held out a plate, full of gobbets of some anonymous meat. On the bank, someone had a charcoal brazier and was frying some more. I looked at the food cautiously. You never know what Barbarians may, or may not, give you. They might well have been trying me with Swan, just for the fun of it. I asked:

'What is it?'

'If it's wearing it you are, then it's eating it you can be,' Madoc told me. 'Seal this is. Fresh, too – only killed three weeks ago.'

So I ate it. I looked around. The hatches were off, and there were a couple of men in the hold, trimming cargo, for the ship was obviously ready for sea, though where the water was that could float her was a mystery. On the bank, men were loading panniers on to packhorses. The strange thing was, that the cargo being trimmed in the hold and the cargo in the panniers was the same – dull grey bricks. Lead, I thought. I asked Caw:

'Where do you get it?'

He knew what I meant. He grinned.

'From up there.' He pointed to the smoke on the Lead Hills. 'Buy it?'

392

'Aye … in a way. You see, there are men we know who go in and out of the mines, and carry in the earth coal they use to smelt the ore. And there are other men there, in the mines and in the melting shops, who will do a great deal for very little, because it is very little they have, nothing at all, you might say, except their lives, and a twist of rag about their loins. So they will do, you understand, anything for a bite of decent food, or a jug, or even a sip, of cider. And there was once we even smuggled a woman in, and she stayed a week, and made her fortune, but she said she wouldn't do it again – too tiring.

'So men who carry earth coal in carry lead out, and lead in again. I suppose you know, there is more in lead than lead.'

'Silver,' I breathed. 'There is always silver in lead.'

'Aye, silver, and that is why the legions work the lead here and farther north, and if it were not for the silver they get out of it they would not stay in this island at all. So we take, let us say, perhaps one ingot of new smelted lead in five, and north we go to the Picts, and there it is arrangements I have with men, kings mostly, who will cupellate it for me. But we have to cover it over somehow, because book-keepers and centurions would come very expensive to bribe, as you may imagine, so it is pure lead we bring back, and send it in with the coal.'

'No wonder you live so well in the Mere,' I told Caw. 'A very pretty scheme. It does you credit.'

'As long as no one finds out. The tax-collectors don't notice what you have if there isn't Gold or silver on the table. And why shouldn't we live well? It is our land, and our hills, and our silver, and our lead. Why should we not charge a little rent?'

Then he drifted off into conversation with Madoc, and I sat down a little against the bulwarks, and somehow or other I fell asleep. When I woke up, my head now thoughtfully pillowed on a cushion of swansdown, we were, where I most love to be in ordinary times, at sea!

I leapt up, reaching for my sword, and cursing at Madoc, who was at the steering oar, and at Caw, who was conning us between the mudbanks, and this was difficult because we were, in general, working in the opposite direction to the one where the wind came from.

'What are you doing with me?' I demanded. It was clear that they were still on speaking terms because they had left me my sword. Caw answered, in his careful way, between orders to Madoc:

'It was thinking, I was, that if it is proposing you are to trade on the Northern Seas, then it is the realities of the situation you should be knowing, before it is any obligations you are taking on yourself and on your family.'

'Whatever the realities,' I replied, 'I am in too deep now to draw back.'

'But I am not,' said Caw, flatly. 'I have not yet decided whether I will entrust a ship of mine to you, and it is more I am wanting to know about how you behave at sea. And so I thought a short voyage would be a fine experience for you.'

'A short voyage? And what good will a short voyage do?' For I thought he meant a day and a night aboard. But he answered:

'We will be back for Samain. Seven weeks let us say.'

'Seven weeks? Seven *weeks! No!* Take me back! I have traced Rhiannon all this way, and now I have found the Lady, then I will not lose her again for you.'

'Quiet, boy,' said Madoc. 'It is in the Mere that Rhiannon must stay now, till Samain and past Samain to midwinter.'

'And there is no going back now, Mannanan,' added Caw, 'either for you or for us, because we held the ship a week to wait for you, and if we stay another day the weather will be too bad for us to return.'

There was nothing for it. A-voyaging I went, and if I were to tell you the whole story of the voyage, you would hear only the usual travellers' tales. We went to the land of the Western Picts in lead, and from there in wool and tanned leather to the Land of Norroway, and brought back walrus ivory and the hides of the tame deer to the land of the Picts where we loaded again with lead and silver, now separate. And I found, and it is true, that in these parts of Ocean, the waves at the end of the summer are as high, and the winds as wild, as anywhere in the Mediterranean in the depths of winter, when we prudent captains will not leave harbour. And more, I found that it is a common thing for the ships there to go altogether out of sight of land, not merely for a day or half a day, as we often may to cut across between two capes with a perishable cargo and an expensive crew, but for four or five days together between one island and another. And at the end, beating home south into a south-west gale, it took even all my strength and skill to hold her steady.

And you would not believe even the most ordinary stories I could tell, how we married Madoc to a mermaid when he was drunk, and how Caw won the crown for telling the saltiest story at the Salmon Feast of the Picts, and how we moored at an island so that Coth the son of Caw could cook for us, and it sank beneath him and left him floating, spouting out a cloud – oh, I could tell you tales for seven weeks of what we did in those seven weeks, and of each of them you would say, 'Oh yes, but I heard that tale of so-and-so.' So I will not bother.

But in seven weeks' time, we returned to the Mere, and we beached the ship where no man would find her. Then, in a skin boat, Caw and Madoc and I paddled back to Caw's house. And it was two days before the Samain Feast.

Chapter Five

My bad luck came at the Samain feast. It had to come, because there is no good luck lasts for ever. Samain is the feast at the beginning of November, when the Britons bring in their sheep from the hills to fold them in close to the farmhouse, safe from wolf and bear. And just as the animals are folded in, so the family and the nation are folded in, and the house is full not only of the living but also of the dead and those who are yet unborn.

Most people believe that the dead go down to Hades. There they exist for ever in dirt and rottenness, envious of the living, and therefore most people fear the dead. But not the Britons. Why, they say, should a man be afraid of the mother who bore him, and the father who fondled him and taught him to live? Why should he fear the grandmother who nursed him to sleep as a toddler and wiped away his tears when he fell over his own feet and kept for him the best titbits of the kitchen and the sweetest apples? Why should a man fear the comrades who fell at his side in battle or slipped from his outstretched hands into the waves, or the loved ones who died in his arms of fever or dysentery?

No, the Britons know better. Their Samain Feast is a feast indeed, and the Happy Dead are welcome. And so are all wayfarers. That is why I sat at the feast next to Caw, who as befits the head of the house sat with blackened face upon a ploughshare. And next to me, coming out of the mists the day before, only a day after we had landed from the northern seas, was the Setanta.

Towards dawn, when we had drunk and eaten everything in sight and were too full to go to the larder for more, the Irishman turned to business, as was his custom, always optimistic that other people would be more fuddled than he was and easier to do business against, and always wrong. He said:

396

'I am ready. I have a fianna in the Hills. I could move now, if you had the arms, but I would rather you waited till the spring.'

'I must wait till the spring,' I told him. 'The arms will not be ready till then.'

'But have you a ship?'

I looked at Caw. I waited to hear. It might all have been in vain. The Master of the Western Seas said:

'You have a ship. You have a ship for this trade, and for all trade you may wish to do across the Irish Sea.'

Far in the east, the dawn had begun, over the Lead Hills. In my impiety and joy and pride I forgot the Gods Below that all in Britain worship, and I forgot that Apollo had bade me worship him no more. I stood up on the bale of straw that had been my seat, and I lifted my hands to the advancing Chariot, and I called as I had done all my two-eyed life:

'All Hail and Blessing to the Unconquered Sun!'

And fate came on me, and I slipped from the edge of the bale. The hilt of my sword tore at my side, and I knew that the old wound was opened. I felt the blood run down, and I screamed, and I fainted with the pain.

Chapter Six

That day after Samain, they took me to Caw's house, where he lived now alone, a widower. I lay on a bed, my shirt off, while everybody who had any pretensions to medical skill or knowledge – and the two do not always go together – fussed around me like so many broody hens.

Taliesin had the first try. He looked wisely at the nasty gash, oozing blood and yellow pus through the bandages.

'The sword is no use. I suppose the weapon that did the original wound—'

'Lost long ago, on the Amber Road,' I groaned. It hurt me to breathe deeply.

'Then I am sure you will not be having the gallstone of a male ass, which is a sure cure for such afflictions.'

'In my wallet.'

Taliesin looked a little disappointed. However, he picked it out, and examined it for a while. I said:

'Have you used it before?'

'I know all about it.'

'Perhaps you do, but have you used it?'

'Well, no, not in the ... well, it isn't flesh, is it. Should we say in the lava? Rub with it, don't I?'

'And not too hard. It's got a surface like pumice stone. *Aaaaah*!' It hurt, too.

'I'd better put something soothing on it. I don't suppose you've got any lion fat ...'

'The yellow pot.'

'Oh. Powdered ostrich egg-shell?'

'In that twist of parchment – the one with the green lines on it.'

'Ground mummies' testicles?'

'In the small phial. Be careful, it's hard to come by.'

'Do you think I don't know that? And Phoenix ash?'

'The vulture-skin bag.'

'At least, I've got a pestle and mortar. I think I know the right proportions.'

He beat together the ointment in fury, using some very appropriate incantations. He laid across the wound two hairs from the head of a blonde virgin, and that is something very hard to find in the Summer Country, smeared on the ointment with nine strokes of a swan's feather, being the proper instrument to my clan, and bound it up with a strip of the horseblanket last laid on the back of a white gelding. I must say that in their knowledge of medical science the Britons do not lag behind doctors in more civilised countries: they only suffer a great deal from shortage of quite elementary necessities, like bottled moondust and salamander skin. I made a mental note that the family might as well begin business in this field in the islands.

For about two days, the wound seemed to mend, and at last I was so bold as to get out of bed and walk about. Nothing went wrong for at least an hour, and then I coughed, and the whole scar opened again. It hurt dreadfully. Now Caw came to look at it, and he had a remedy which was beautiful in its simplicity. He merely clapped on to my side a hunk of whale's fat, blubber they call it, and tied it there with a length of whale skin, reasoning that the strength of the whale would pass into me and give me energy to resist all strains. The blubber was strong enough, all right. The fish had been dead for three months, and when at last I got up and went out of doors, people could smell me coming half a mile away, and all the dogs of the Summer Country came to the point of interest, and some even from farther away. And I did well enough, since the smell meant that I could endure to breathe only in the most gentle fashion, but at last, through sheer boredom, I yawned, and it was all to do again.

Then Cicva decided she would take a hand. First she washed off the whale blubber, much to Caw's annoyance, but she pooh-poohed him away.

'Men!' she said. 'They think that they know everything.'

'But instead, *you* know everything, my girl,' I teased her, but of course she didn't see it and answered:

399

'The only things I didn't know, you taught me.'

'Thank you. Now what are you going to use?'

'First of all, spider's web, because although it is so thin it holds the weight of the spider, which is a great beast in comparison.' So a whole web, taken with the dew on it, and lifted from the bush and brought in whole and unbroken – and how many webs the children of the place spoiled entirely I have no knowing, but there must have been mourning throughout the halls of Ariadne – she laid across the wound.

'And now some soothing ointment we use a great deal where I come from, up in the Silures. Most of it is goose grease, and that provides the softening. But there are other things my grandmother taught me to use, such as meadow saffron and foxglove, and they will stop the pain and the itching. Now, we have that on thick, and then I will tie it up in a strip of linen – here, one of Caw's napkins will do, if I tear it up like this …'

I said that there was no evidence of poverty in the houses in the Mere, and no expense would have been spared if there had been anything to spend on. However, it was plain that the Britons here were doing as well as any civilised doctor.

'Now, what I really would like to do, and what would do you good,' said Cicva, 'would be to tie up both your arms so that you can't scratch. It's scratching that opens it every time, whatever we do.'

'I don't scratch.'

'Indeed you do, you scratch like half a dog with two dog's fleas.'

'Well, and how do you expect me to behave with this itching like it does as long as I lie still? And as soon as I move it tears, and then I can't feel it itching for pain and bleeding.'

'Then shall I tie your hands? There's not much you can do with them, lying here.'

'No, you may not tie my hands. I refuse to have anyone tie my hands.'

'All right,' she said crossly. 'There's no need to make such a fuss about it. It's not good for you – or for me, either.'

Well, I know that it is quite common for a doctor to prescribe restraint for a patient, but I wasn't an ordinary patient, I knew

400

too much for that. Besides, I knew very well that no human means could heal the wound. I had offended the Sun Above and the Gods Below. Only those Gods together could heal me.

All the human attempts followed the same pattern. First the side felt better, the pain subsided, and then the itch. Next, there would be a firm clean scab over the wound. All would be going well. Then I would get up to walk. And in a moment, all would be undone, the wound would be open, and the blood run down.

'Nothing there is for it now,' said Pryderi, after two weeks of this, 'but seeing Rhiannon.'

'If it comes to that?' I asked angrily, 'why isn't she here? Either she belongs to me, or I belong to her, as Taliesin said, and in either case she ought to show a little interest.'

'And is it not for you to be showing a little interest in her!' countered Taliesin. 'It's carrying you we'll be doing.'

Hueil and his brother Coth the Cook took the ends of the bed on which I lay, and moved out of the house into the rain. Cicva threw my sealskin cloak over me. I could not remember now how long it had been raining; I could not remember when it had not been raining. The edge of the Mere was now nearer to the houses. My bearers' feet splashed through what had been firm meadows. We took a narrow path between the flooded fields, between clusters of willows that stood leafless out of the water. We came to the Deep Pool of the Mere.

Many are the gates to the World Below. Out on the green sea there are whirlpools, that engulf ships and men, and spin them down into the green dark, and these are the least known, and the greatest and the most powerful, because there is no return. But on land, there are the mouths of volcanoes, spouting fire and lava, and into these men had leapt to seek those who have gone before. There are caves both in the mountains and on the sea-shore, and it is in these that men have buried their dead, and it is into these that wise women have gone to speak with those who have left us and who now speak with the wise of all the ages. Out on the level plains there are marshes and bogs and places of Green Moss, and on the level shore there are sinking sands and into all these men have thrown their sacrifices to those who rule our deaths, believing, as some do, that no ordeal is as grim as death, and that those who rule our lives may hurt us as they wish, if so be they do not kill us. Life, say some, is worth the clinging to in spite of all indignities. I do not agree. I have lived long and I have travelled far, and I have seen men suffer things to which death is a feast. But whatever one's opinions on this, who can doubt the wisdom of making offerings by casting booty into a bog?

Of all the gates into the World Below, the surest and the deepest and the swiftest are the Black Pools in rivers and lakes and marshes. Bottomless beyond reach of plumb-line, their surface smooth and unruffled by storm or rain, they lie beneath steep cliffs or smooth banks, and there for many generations wise men have come to make their offerings.

Such a pool there was in the Mere, where the river flowed against a bluff. In a backwater, the water gleamed no more than lead, the surface stirred no more than does a mirror. Only sometimes the great pike moved, hunting for what he could catch, and there was enough, for it was to the hungry Gods Below that the Britons of the Mere gave the scraps of food that even the dogs left. And here, on the bluff above the Deep Pool, Rhiannon sat.

She sat on a tripod, looking to the east, over the dark water. Above her head they had built a booth of alder boughs, thatched with the rushes of the Mere. Her food was the broth of nettles, and a fungus that grows on the trunks of trees, thrusting out in a fleshy shelf. I knew it as a boy: we called it Dead Men's Ears.

Rhiannon looked out across the flooded, sodden Mere. Little pools were become great lakes. Lagoons where in summer a man might wade a mile and never wet his knees would now float a trireme. The river, in the dry of the year a faint drift of leaves and twigs across the marsh, was now a strong current, sweeping whole trees to the sea, faster than a man might run. As a galley of pleasure is beached for the winter, her mast unstepped, her oars unshipped and stacked against the eaves of the boathouse, her sail of scarlet linen furled and carried under shelter, her cushions of velvet and of cloth of gold taken to grace my lady's boudoir, gilt flaking and paint peeling from her sides – so sat Rhiannon above the Mere. She was dressed in rough sacking, black, all black. She wore no jewels. Her hair had ceased to shine. Her hands, through hunger, were transparent, only the blue veins opaque. Above the waste, hardly sheltered from the rain, unwashed, uncombed, her nails uncut, she fasted for …? She waited for …?

Only the birds did not forsake her. The rooks cawed in the trees across the pool, the heron stood and watched. The king-fisher dived as if to seek out the sleeping swallows. Starlings hungrily combed the grass.

The sons of Caw put down the bed. They went away. I spoke: 'Help me, my Mother.'

Rhiannon did not answer. She sat and looked across the marshes. I asked her again:

'Help me, my Mother, for your birds' sake.'

Still, she did not reply. I waited a very long time, an hour or more. Then, I took courage.

'Rhiannon, my Rhiannon. By him that gave you to me, I challenge you. Speak to me. Who are your birds?'

Still, for a moment she said nothing. Then we heard the sound of wings in the east, and we both watched as the great birds went over us as an arrow. And after that, she sang: at last I heard that splendid voice again.

> Spirits now wending
> At full life's ending
> As Wild Geese flying
> Not regretting, sighing,
> In trust advancing
> Through low clouds dancing
> Faint like stars glowing
> To new lives going
> Passing and fleeting
> Sounds of wings beating
> Living, not dying
> As Wild Geese flying.

That was all she sang, and she sang it only once. Yet it was not an hour after dawn when we heard the wings, and when she

403

finished singing it was the grey twilight of a December afternoon under the clouds of Britain. Then she spoke, not sang:

'Tell Pryderi: the goose has flown.'

'Have you no word for me? Can I not be healed?'

'Oh, Mannanan, my son, my father, my brother, my husband! Come to me at midwinter. Come when the Thorn flowers.'

Uncalled, Hueil the son of Caw and Coth the son of Caw came forward. They picked up my bed, and they carried me back to the house.

I spoke first to Pryderi.

'The goose has flown, Pryderi. Rhiannon said, the goose has flown.'

He bent down, and he took ashes from the fire and threw them on his head. He smashed a pot that stood by, and with the sharp edge of a broken fragment he slit open the front of his shirt. He said:

'I am going to the Demetae.'

Madoc, who stood by, spoke:

'You cannot face the winter seas alone.'

They went out. Cicva, silent, threw the end of her shawl over her face, and followed. Caw watched them go, then:

'It is no kin of mine. They will lay him in his house, new built, on his bed new made. Every man who comes will bring a stone, and they will fill the house about him with stones and earth, and they will build the house about outside with walls of cut stone and they will whiten it. And that is an end of him. And an end of much more, too.'

'An end of whom?' I asked. Caw did not answer. Suddenly, with the air of a man throwing off unpleasant thoughts, he asked:

'And Rhiannon – did she say nothing to you?'

'She sang one short song, that lasted a day. And she showed me the birds, and what they are.'

'But for yourself?'

'Caw – when do the thorn trees blossom in this country?'

'If Rhiannon told you – well, then, it is a secret thing above all the other secrets of the Mere, and there is not a Roman who knows of it. Listen to me.

'Below the Glass Mountain there is a tree, and to look at it,

you would think it no different from any other thorn tree, growing where it do on the firm ground on the edge of the Mere. But
every seventh year, something strange do happen, and every
seventh seventh year, it is something wonderful that happens.
Because, every seventh year, the thorn do bloom, and blossom,
and come into flower, and that not in the spring, but at the
middle of winter, and strange that is because there is no reason
for any feast or worship of the Gods at midwinter which is a
dreadful and bitter time. Now every seventh year, it is one branch
or another only that flowers, and anyone may come and see the
tree, and the tree alone. But every seventh seventh year, then it
is the tree that blossoms, every branch, and it is then that the
other holy things are shown, if the right people are there to
show them.'

'And the right people are …?'

'Think, boy. They must all come by land, because the thorn
came to us from the sea. And the people are a virgin princess of
the days of long ago, and a priest of the days that are lately gone,
and a pregnant queen of the times that are.'

'And this year is a …?'

'A seventh seventh year, and then the thorn is given great
power over all those who come to it. And come to it you shall,
Mannanan, though it was some pretext we were going to find to
send you away for the midwinter. But if it is bidden you are, then
bidden you are. Lie still, boy, lie still in my house till midwinter,
because it is no more than twenty nights to go.'

The Britons, unlike all the rest of mankind, count their time
not by days but by nights, and all their feasts are feasts of nights
and not of days. And in the winter it is understandable, because
the night is longer than the day. So I lived in Caw's house, and in
the days, Hueil and Coth took me out, on my bed, to the lakeside,
and I fished for pike, and never caught one. And in the evenings,
Cicva would come from her empty home and sup with her grandfather and me, and she taught me to play the games of Fichel,
that the Britons play in preference to all games of dice. And in
truth I did not really enjoy Fichel, because there is no chance in
it at all, or delightful uncertainty, but a game of Fichel is played
on a board with men, and is entirely a matter of skill and wit.

405

There are a hundred different kinds of Fichel, and Cicva taught me to play them all, in return, she said, for my teaching her to palm dice and lose the pea under the three cups. And again and again she said to me:

'Be careful, Mannanan: you think that you have found your Lady, but watch in case someone does not move the cups again.'

Chapter Seven

The solstice came and went, and the lengthening of the days became noticeable, just. Before the solstice, the rains stopped, and the wind came round slowly through north to north-east. This wind blew cold, and there were one or two clear nights, and in the mornings the frost was thick on the grass, and there was a thin film of ice on the little pools. And yet, the time of year being what it was, it was mild, compared with the winters we had up on the Amber Road. Then, on the solstice, the sky covered over with low grey clouds, and the wind dropped, and all was very still and quiet, and I wondered how Rhiannon could still live there in her house, open towards the east, above the Dark Pool.

Towards evening, the snow started to fall. It fell steadily, in great light flakes, like the feathers of the wild geese. It covered everything, and made the grey light of the morning look dimmer still. In Britain, you get used to living in a perpetual twilight: but the white snow makes it less bearable. It fell all through a night and a day and the night after, till it was, as Caw said, the depth of a chariot wheel, or as I saw, up to the top of a man's thigh, if he cared to step into it.

Then we had a day without snow, and the sky was blue and it was bitter cold again, so that although the sunshine melted the snow on the surface, at night the moisture froze to leave a layer of ice over it. We lay close around the fire that night, with all the blankets and furs and sheepskins we could find heaped over us, and yet we were all cold.

In the first light, Madoc wakened me. He had a lamp, and I looked round to see that I was in an empty house. Madoc had been the last to try to treat my side, and he had merely made me lie still, and told me to wash it well each day with warm water. Then he had gone out into the winter sea, and I had not seen

407

him nor heard that he had returned. But here he was, making me take my shirt off so that he could see the healthy scab forming.

'That will do,' he said. 'You will just be able to walk to the Glass Mountain.'

'I am not in any fit condition to walk,' I told him. 'You can say what you like, but do you know what it feels like when that place tears open? If I'm going that far, I'll have a horse, or there ought to be enough water now to float a boat almost up to it.'

'Everybody walks to the Glass Mountain at midwinter.' He was firm on that, and as it seemed to be matter of religion, I agreed to try.

'I'll come when I've had my breakfast,' I told him.

'Decent people go to this rite fasting,' and as he seemed as ready to insist on that, I pulled on all the clothes I could find, with my sealskin cloak over everything and my sword handy under it, and I began to walk. At least we didn't have to go bare-foot, as some mysteries would have had us do.

We crunched across the icy surface of the snow, watching our breaths before our faces. Then, into the marsh. We pushed by willows, and the icy twigs cut across our faces like iron wires. The log road beneath our feet was covered in a layer of glass, and I feared to slip and tear my side again. The streams and pools were edged with ice, but never fully covered in, or strong enough to take a man's weight. Most of the paths we had used to come from the Glass Mountain were under running water, and we had to take awkward twisting ways, known only to the cattle and the deer, and the badger even, who made them. To push through a maze in twilight, with never a firm footing, with noth-ing dry, with the clouds threatening new snow, oh, there are better ways of spending a day in midwinter. Even when, at noon, the clouds cleared, it became no pleasanter, because it got even colder.

Sometimes, now, we could even see the Glass Mountain standing up in front of us beyond its screen of bare branches. A little column of smoke rose from before it, vertical in the still air, white against the blue sky. We walked in silence.

We were not the only people on the road. There was no one before us, but here and there, at forks in the way, we would find little bunches of men, and women and children, waiting to fall in behind us. They were all laden with bundles of wood, and with bags. They too went in silence, except that now and then, from behind us, we would hear voices raised in a melancholy hymn to the Cauldron:

> Cauldron our hope, in frost and snow,
> Bring warmth in plenty from below.
> O'er flowing panniers, laden carts,
> Flame out of blackness warm our hearts.

I could not have sung. My face was so stiff with the cold that I could not move my lips. I could feel that the end of my nose was dead. My moustaches froze to my cloak so that to turn my head hurt. My side was throbbing and hot: I waited for the tearing pain, the warm that I now knew so well. Let no one say that what I won on this journey I won without pain.

At last, at last, we came out of the Mere, we climbed the sides of the Glass Mountain. We came close to the farm built against the rock. Now, I noticed what I must have seen before, that the branches of a tree showed above the fence. Leafless they were and winter-barren, but, plainly, a thorn. There were people standing about outside the closed gates. Closest of all, I saw Pryderi sitting on the snow by a brazier in which a fire of earth coal was burning. Hueil was with him. I came to them and sat down. It was nearly evening, and I was hungry and tired, sweating from the walk and yet freezing with the cold.

More groups of people sat down around and behind us, each group with its brazier, or lighting a fire of wood on the bare ground, sweeping up the snow into windbreaks. They sat, quietly, waiting. Even the children were silent, and did not run about or play. When I was a little warmer, I stood up and looked the way we had come. All the side of the hill, all the firm ground around it, all the road by which we had come, was speckled with fires, mirroring in the cold clear air the stars above us. It was now quite dark. There was a constant murmur from the people. Not the angry shouting you hear from a mob in riot, not the cheerful turbulence you hear from the crowd waiting in an arena for the

409

Games to start, not the hubbub you hear from a market crowd: it was the gentle hum of voices lowered in reverence, saying meaningless things simply because the burden of keeping silent was too much.

Neither could I keep silent. I asked Pryderi: 'Who guards the shrine? Is it Druids?'

He turned to me. It was the first time I had spoken to him since he had heard me tell him Rhiannon's message. Now, as his cloak opened, I saw he wore a new belt, a simple one, only a threefold chain of Gold. Only that, only Golden links that would have held a bull, only the price of half a province. He answered me seriously. Gone now was his usual air of bantering superiority:

'No, boy. The Holy Ones are gone. Do you think we would have made poor Taliesin trudge all the way down from the other side of the Wall if there had been a Druid anywhere nearer in the island?'

'And why Rhiannon?'

'Family tradition. And once this is over, she won't have to do it again, unless she's still alive and a virgin in another forty-nine years.'

'Do what?'

'Very little. You shall see soon enough.'

'And where did you find a queen?'

'It is the wife of the King of the Demetae, that is Queen among the Silures in her own right, if she had her rights.'

There were too many people there, and too many people missing, for me to understand. I sat down and watched the stars go round. Sometimes people sang. Others came past us, seeking their places to wait. One man, squint-eyed, recognised me, and bent down to whisper into my ear, in Greek:

'It began with a word.'

I was in no mood for riddles or mysteries, and I thought his accent vile, so I told him sharply enough, but again in a whisper:

'The only word for you, brother, is *off*!!'

He went on. It was close to midnight. I looked across the eastern sky, from the Bear to Orion. They had reached their summit, they hung poised for the descent into morning. Others looked too. Everywhere, men and women were getting up, and looking

410

towards the farmyard. There was a smell in the air, a smell of anticipation, of excitement, as strong as woodsmoke, as distinctive as a mask. Pryderi stood, and I stood too. There was a sound of rattling at the gate. Everybody heard it. Now nobody was seated. We stood, Pryderi and I, in the very front of the crowd, and we saw the gate open.

Taliesin opened the gate. He shone there as he had shone in the temple in the Mere, but now he shone more splendidly. He wore his mistletoe, fastened by a brooch of Gold wire a span long. Above it he wore a collar, a Golden half-moon that covered all his breast. On his left arm he wore an archer's wristguard, as if to take the blow of the returning bowstring when he had loosed the arrows of the sun, and this too was of Gold, and it covered his arm from wrist to elbow. His Golden sickle hung from a belt of a sevenfold Golden chain. The buckles of his sandals were of Gold. And on his head the oak-leaves were beaten of Gold.

He flung wide the gate. We saw into a farmyard. The ground was frozen, ridged with the coming and going of cattle, but cleared of snow. There were piles of hay and straw. The barn, built at one side of the yard, against the rock, was wattle sided and roofed with thatch, like any other barn. But there was another gate, in the opposite fence, and this too was opened. As Taliesin guarded one gate, so did Caw guard the other, dressed in his whaleskin and white bear fur, ivory-belted and ivory-crowned. But he, too, wore a collar, a half-moon of Gold. For tonight, then, he was divine, for this night, once in forty-nine years, he was, surely, Dylan, the Son of the Wave, that ruled all the seas of Britain. But if so, then tonight who was Taliesin? I did not ask, but Pryderi breathed the answer:

'Mabon.'

I should have known. This was indeed the Glorious Youth.

In the middle of the yard was the tree, not a tall one, just an ordinary thorn. Somehow it all seemed full of a coming and going of people, though if you tried to look it was impossible actually to see anyone, only the general impression of movement. Then from Pryderi came the spark of light, struck from flint with an iron blade. He kindled a torch, and soon others were lighting torches, fresh, not from their fires. The space where we stood, and somehow the farmyard itself, was now as bright as day.

And then, there was movement. Not in the yard, but above it. There was a breath of the east wind. The branches swayed. And even as we watched, the whole tree burst into blossom. We saw the buds open before our very eyes. In the time it takes a man to count up to a hundred, we saw the branches covered with flowers, white they must have been, but in the glare of the red torchlight they looked pink.

The two people came from the barn and stood before the tree. Taliesin stood back from the gate. Pryderi took me by the arm and led me through into the farmyard. We bowed to Mabon, but he was not the one we had come to see, nor Dylan-Caw, leaning on his eight-foot steering oar. We passed towards the tree.

The women stood on either side of the tree. First, I saw Cicva. She was dressed as a Roman matron, richly and splendidly, if a trifle out of fashion, and even there I found space to wonder, irreverently, whether the clothes had been stored away for forty-nine years. Her tunic was of white silk, with a Gold-embroidered hem and girdle to match, shining in the torchlight. Her shawl was of Indian cotton, trailing to her heels. Her hair was piled on her head, built up on a pad, adding half a foot to her height, and capped with a gleaming diadem set with emeralds and Amber. Her hands were loaded with rings set with the rubies and diamonds of India. Three months pregnant, she stood proudly there, and in her hands she carried a spear, a great long iron spear on an ash shaft. For a moment I had hope, but then I saw this was no spear I had ever handled. Just an ordinary legionary pilum.

But beyond her stood Rhiannon, all in black. Her clothes were of wool, not the fine wool of the fat sheep the Romans brought to the island, but the coarsest of coarse wool from the little native sheep that you don't see any more except up in the wildest hills. Coarse as sacking it was, and not even dyed black, but shorn from black lambs, black as the earth coal. About her neck was a necklace of jet beads, strung on a thong of deer hide, and another of mussel shells. Her hair hung unbound, uncombed, on her shoulders. On her left wrist, where her gown, rough cut, unhemmed, sewn of one piece, left her arms bare, she wore an archer's wristguard, but this was of polished stone, of polished flint. And in her hands she held ... what? A cauldron ...? a dish ...? a cup ...?

Pryderi led me forward to the tree. I knew now, untold, what to do. I rolled up my shirt, tore off the bandage, hurt though it may, to show the bleeding, festering wound. Cicva reached forward the point of the spear and touched the wound. Rhiannon reached forward the cup, made, I saw, of turned olive-wood; I thought, a strange thing to find here, though common enough in Syria. She held it to my lips, and I drank the wine, sour as vinegar, bitter as defeat, sweet as death. I felt weak and faint. I wished to go out through the farther gate, but Pryderi guided me to lean against the wall behind the tree.

There I sat, for hours and watched the crowds go by. I saw the colours of every kingdom in Britain, and outside it. I saw the shields and badges of every clan and every family. There were lead-miners and copper-miners and diggers of the earth coal, and smiths in iron and bronze and Gold. There were fishermen of salmon, and men who went out on to the wide ocean to catch whales and men who dived to take oysters for their pearls and men who dredged limpets and mussels for food. I saw the old women who dig for cockles, and glean in the fields, I saw men who earn their bread as shepherds, and those who spend their lives hunting bear and wolf and the tall deer. There were men who break horses, and men who drive cattle along the Green Roads to feed the cities. There were merchants and innkeepers and brothel-keepers from the towns, and men who had sold themselves to the Romans to collect taxes, and men who hid in the hills rather than pay them, weavers and dyers and fullers, money-lenders and bankers. And above all there were the peasants, men who grew oats for themselves and wheat for the Army, and wore themselves into the grave trying to satisfy tax-collector and rent-collector and wife and child.

They were of all ranks. I saw King Casnar the painted Pict go by, in his red and green, and I thought that there were Romans enough who would give a year's pay to take him alive inside the Wall. I saw Leo Rufus, who had been so proud of being almost a Roman, yes, he came. I saw Gwawl go by, in his black and white

413

shirt, and he saw me, and did nothing. Each came past, and drank of the cup, and if he was ill or hurt or deformed or maimed, there he was touched with the spear. And all came in silence, and – this I have never seen in any temple or at any rite before – no man was asked to pay. You may believe that or not as you wish, because it is the greatest wonder I ever saw, but it is true.

Only one man broke the silence. He was a short man with a squint. He saw the cup and touched it – and then he did not drink, but shouted in his barbarous Greek:

'False! False and unclean! Be not yoked with unbelievers.'

And he ran out into the night, but as he went Cicva lunged at his eyes with her spear, and he never squinted after that.

At last, the sky in the east grew pink, beyond the hill. Still the column pressed on, hurrying now. Then, of a sudden, the cock crew. Taliesin stepped forward and bolted the gate in the face of the men next in line. From the crowd outside there came a low moan of disappointment: nothing more. The ceremony was over, that was all. Anyone else could now wait for forty-nine years more. The last of the crowd passed through the far gate. Caw shut it after them.

The cock crew again. The Epiphanies of the Gods passed into the barn. After a little, the cock crew a third time. The two woman came out into the farmyard again, and the birds burst into a song in the winter morning. Now the two were dressed as I had always seen them. Cicva was in a plain blouse and skirt, but now, she too wore a belt of threefold Gold, Rhiannon hid her splendid clothes beneath her even more splendid cloak of white and yellow silk.

The women came to where I sat. Caw and Taliesin, themselves again, followed. They all sat down. We huddled together for warmth, pulling the sealskin cloak over us, shivering for weariness. We slept beneath the dying torches.

Suddenly, we all came awake together. The sun was not high, we could not have slept more than an hour at most. We all stood up, rubbing the sleep from our eyes and remembering how long it was since we had eaten, and shivering in the cold winter air and eyeing the grey cloud that was beginning to drift in again from the sea, for the wind was now from the north-west. The

414

wind has changed, I thought, The world has changed. There is something strange and new about me.

I turned to look down at Rhiannon. She was on her knees. I reached down and drew her to me, to her feet. I made her lean on my left arm: she was frail as a bird from her long fast. Then I realised what was strange about my world. Half a day before I could have supported nobody. I held her a little way from me. With my other hand I rolled up my shirt. I looked at my side. The running sore was healed, and my side showed the old scar as it had been when I first came into the Mere.

I let Taliesin help Rhiannon. I drew my sword and cut off the hem of the long silk cloak. I sheathed the sword and went into the barn.

Inside, it was just like any other barn, bare-walled, with bales of hay and straw lying about. I looked up into the rafters, and there I could just see the shaft of the spear. The wooden cup stood on the floor in the corner. I went to the rock face. I looked for the signs, for the stains of libations of wine and fat. I pushed aside the hay, and found the sacred place, a crack in the rock, a deep dark hole. I greased the blade with goose grease and lions's fat from my wallet. I sheathed it again, and I wrapped the scabbard in the gleaming silk. I thrust the weapon, point down into the hole. It went well down, but when it grated on the bottom I could still touch the hilt. The crevice was narrower at the mouth than inside. I could curl my hand around the hilt, but I could not then draw the blade out. The sword would stay there till the Gods willed someone should take it. At least, *I* had left some offering for my cure.

I went out again into the open air. Caw opened the gate, and we left the farmyard. The hillside was still full of people, all the people who had been there the night before. Every group had lit fires. We joined Madoc and Hueil, who were cooking, with a group of people from the houses in the Mere. There must have been a hundred fires close by, and from each of them came the smell of cooking, and a smell that I never thought to meet in all the Isle of Britain. Everywhere I could smell roast goose!

I sat down beside Pryderi, who had a black pudding in his fist. Everyone was handed a platter of roast goose, everyone except

415

me. They brought me something else, that looked like goose indeed, but when I tasted it, I knew it – I was eating swan.

Everyone was laughing and blaspheming as they ate the sacred foods of their clans. Caw was telling Rhiannon, without shame, the story that had won him the crown among the Western Picts. It was like Saturnalia, that I knew well all my friends in Rome would be keeping that day. After the rite comes the time of laughter; when the strain of piety and sacrifice and of touching holy things that may blast and obliterate the unclean, is past, then forbidden acts are lawful and the topsy-turvy feast begins. We in the south have forgotten the rite, and keep only the topsy-turvy time. I leaned across Rhiannon, who was eating roasted skylarks on a spit, and I asked Caw, when he had finished:

'What does the rite mean? To whom are the spear and the cup sacred?'

He replied, 'We haven't the least idea.'

'What, you don't know?' I looked incredulously at Taliesin. He belched – his platter had been full of all kinds of meat and he was now sucking the marrow bone of a sheep – and told me:

'No, not these in particular. All cups and bowls and cauldrons are all weapons, especially spears, are or may be sacred here. Many places had their sacred cauldrons before the Romans came. But until, oh, just ninety-eight years ago, there was no cauldron here on the Glass Mountain, and even if there were there would have been no such great ceremony made, because there were so many at other shrines, and this place is inconvenient to get to. But, of course, the Romans have destroyed the other shrines, and that is why we hide this last vessel and worship it only in secrecy, and we pay it the same respect as we would to any other cauldron of life. That is the meaning of this rite, of the Druid, and the pregnant queen and the virgin princess.'

He paused to suck his bone, and Caw took up the tale:

'But as to how this cup and the spear came here, it is a strange story. Soon after the Venetii my fathers came here, not long before the Roman conquest, there came here by sea an old man, a Syrian, I think, who said he wanted to find a place where he could settle and fast and pray till he died. Now that is just the kind of thing a Druid will often do, and so they let him build a little house under the rock, where the barn is now. He brought with him three things: he had the spear, and he had the cup, and he had a sprig of the thorn. He said they were precious and holy, and there is no reason why we should not take his word for it. And he worshipped them till he died, and that was not very long, and now so do we. But he never told us why they were holy.'

So that was all, I thought. They were not even very old, or anything to do with the spot, or even with the ceremony. But I was certainly healed.

Chapter Eight

When we went back to the houses in the Mere, life was quiet for a few weeks more. Rhiannon lived in Cicva's house, because she had been much weakened by her long fast and the emotional ordeal of the midwinter night. I lived with Caw still, and I went to see Rhiannon frequently, and heard her tales of the great days of the kings of the Isle of Britain, such as how the Great King Lear had two good daughters who cherished him in his old age, and how he was set against them and tempted to his death by his youngest daughter, and how she came herself to a violent and well-deserved end. But while I listened and tried to put these tales in poetry in their own language, I wondered what I was to do with Rhiannon when she was well. I could hardly take her home to the Old City, even if she had been granted to me, and in return I had been granted to her, and I could not be hers, I was Phryne's and I had sworn to Phryne, jocularly, but validly enough, in parting, that I would sleep with no stranger till I saw her again.

But in less than a month after the Midwinter Feast, Pryderi came to me and said:

'Is it not seeing your other friends you ought to be?'

'There's no hurry,' I told him. 'It can wait until the spring comes.'

'It is necessary for me to go to that region,' he replied, 'and there may be no other chance, and true it is, and you know it, that unless I take you there is no finding the way.'

That was true. I looked at the black winter and I shuddered, but go I had to, saying goodbye to Rhiannon. First, Pryderi took a log boat, and we slipped down through the Mere towards the sea. The snows had melted – Britain is not like Germany, where the snow comes and lies for months. The Mere now was full, all the lagoons were great lakes where a man might drown a dozen times before he reached the bottom. The currents ran strong, and tree trunks and branches and dead sheep and all the other rubbish bobbed around us. We paddled hard into the north-west wind all the short day till we came near the mouth of the river, and there we found an empty hut on the shore where we slept the night.

Pryderi knew where to look for a skin boat. At the dawn we set off again in this, and I now realised that he proposed to paddle it across the Severn Sea. A man well may think hard before he sets out to sea anywhere in February: to go out on to the Severn Sea, and to do it in such a frail vessel – well, I kept on thinking that we must be both mad. But Pryderi kept on telling me that the skin boat was the only craft that would stay afloat.

I could never understand why a skin boat did float at all. It is a companionable way to travel, as the Britons' boats are nearly round, and the two men sit side by side on the single thwart. But how do they float? Everyone knows that a ship floats because the weight of the timbers press down on the water and the heavier the ship the better she will float, which is why you must make the keel of a ship out of the biggest and thickest tree trunk that you can find. And skin boats really have no weight to press down on the water, being made out of wicker and leather only.

We went down towards the smell of the salt water, past the backwater where the ship was hidden, or had been hidden, and between the high banks of the river. Soon, perhaps we were at sea, because the water was brackish, but in a maze of channels among wide banks of mud. It was the tides, of course. There is no rational explanation for them. It is quite untrue that, as some say, they are governed by the moon, because in that case they would always happen a definite time after the rising of the moon, and they do not; they vary in time from place to place. In some places, too, the sea goes away only a little between the high and low tides, but in the Severn Sea we must have been near to whatever is the source of the tides, because the sea receded about four and a half miles.

We paddled out cross wind, over the sullen waves, bobbing about like a sea bird. We were more than a mile past the last green growing thing and I thought the water was deep, when we met two men walking up to their ankles only in the water. They had come out across the mud, with boards tied to their feet to stop them sinking, and they were pulling a sled behind them: they had stakes set in the mud even further out, to stretch nets between, and they were taking the night's catch back to the land. We left them behind, and in the slackening wind we paddled out into mist. After a while, when the grey water all round melted into the grey sky, I begun to feel even more depressed than I had felt alone in the Mere. We were now well away from the mud. I was completely dependent on Pryderi.

The tide now set strongly and carried us to the northeast, so that we had to paddle very little to keep way on her, but only to hold her head the way Pryderi wanted it. *He* seemed happy. He sang to himself in a tuneless, wordless song. I just paddled.

I looked into the grey mist. It swirled round us in curtains, our clothes were soaked with it, there was nothing to see except each other. Pryderi insisted that it was northeast we *were* heading, taking his bearings, I thought, from the colour of the water and the smell of the fog. I was completely in his hands, more at his mercy than at any time before.

Suddenly I saw something in the mist.

'Look!' I called. 'Dead ahead – it's land.'

'Too far left,' Pryderi grunted. 'Bring her round a bit. There's still enough wind to throw us off.'

Oddly enough, it was a comfort to find that he did not know *exactly* where he was. We came round a little, to the north I supposed, and passed under an island. It was long and flat and very low-lying. We came further right, and suddenly we were under the savage cliffs of another island, towering steep out of the water. The cliffs were covered with sea-gulls, which rose screaming when I shouted. But even so, my shout sounded so feeble in the empty mist that I was frightened then in case I might have offended some sea god.

Then I gained my courage. I had not been afraid in the fog, with the Berts, who were more dangerous than Pryderi, and that other silent ship going by. I need not be afraid here. I need not even paddle.

'What way are we heading?' I asked.

'North today: north of east tomorrow,' Pryderi answered.

I knew a king of wizards once: he taught me to whistle; and I whistled. We must have been a long way from the cradle of the winds, but at last the mist began to thin, and the breeze was on our backs, even though the tide was now against us. The early night fell, but at least now we could see the stars, and head towards the Dog Star, and hold it till we were suddenly unable to see it for the great cliffs that towered over us.

We landed on a shingle beach, and carried the boat up beyond the line of seaweed which Pryderi told me marked the limit of the tide. I was rather uneasy, because there is no knowing that the sea will stop today where it stopped yesterday, but I could not over-rule him without appearing discourteous. I groped along the water's edge in the starlight, and picked up enough scraps of wood to light a fire, and keep it going through the night. We took it in turns to watch the fire and to sleep under the upturned boat.

At dawn we ate our morsel of cold mutton and drank a little cider, and set off again, with the tide. I was in a better mood for whistling that morning, and we had a wind to help us too, moving east of north along a coastline where the cliffs abruptly stopped and we had on our left hand a low shore and flats of mud. We passed the mouths of one big river, big for that island, though anywhere else in the world it would have been a trickle, and a narrower creek, and a long way after that the mouth of another wide river.

We turned into this mouth, trusting to the tide – we had sat out an hour of the turn staked on the mudflats and then paddled against the ebb and through to the flow again – to carry us up between the high banks of mud, mud, always mud, north to where we could see a long line of flat topped hills.

But it was some time before dusk, and much nearer to the sea than to the hills, that we came under the walls of Isca Silurum. We could see the walls, and the sentries at the gates, all wrapped up in winter order, which is nothing like any uniform the legions wear farther south. We came in to the wood frames of the quay, and someone threw us a line and helped us to scramble on to the bank.

There were the usual crowd of idle hangers-on by the water's edge, and Pryderi stood there in his black-and-yellow-checked cloak and looked at them. The front of his cloak fell open a little to show his belt of Gold chain. The loiterers all stood up from where they were lounging on stones and walls and bales, and I realised that those of them who weren't showing somewhere a trace of black and yellow were wearing the red with a thin white stripe that Cicva was so proud of. Pryderi didn't say anything, he just motioned with his left hand, and there was a rush to carry our bags and lift the boat out and stow it dry.

There were a number of more or less clean-looking houses between the gates of the fort and the river – not a city or anything like it, just an unplanned village. Pryderi walked up the street, and stopped at the largest house. I followed him. One of the men from the river bank went inside, and in a moment a whole family, men and women, young and old, children of all ages and hens and the pig all came tumbling out into the street.

Pryderi led me inside. There was a rush of people to bring us hot water to wash after our long journey, and also soap which the Gauls and Britons make out of fat and wood ash. It is very good for cleaning yourself, and I have often thought it would sell very well in Rome if only scented oils didn't have such a hold on men's habits. Someone gave me a razor – really gave, I kept it – and I sacrificed my fine moustache, consoling myself that I could grow it in a few months as long as ever. When we were clean, I changed. Pryderi handed over his belt to one of his new friends, which surprised me, and I threw on my sealskin cloak again.

Pryderi carried my bag after me up to the walls of the fort. The sentry seemed at first a little doubtful about letting me pass. I told him I was going to see the Legate – not wanted to, was *going* to. He called the Sergeant of the Guard, who turned out to be a Standard-bearer and so senior enough to take decisions. This man could read, not very well, but he knew the seal of the Office of the Procurator in Londinium and he let us through with a legionary to lead us.

The main street of the fortress was in the usual confusion of builder's rubble. I don't know what it is about soldiers. They spend years building a fortress and making it a safe and comfortable place to live and work in. Then as soon as it's finished, they think up some new regulation which will allow them to tear it down and live in squalor again. They now seemed doing nothing more drastic than turning the whole fort round to face the other way. At least, they had left the Headquarters in the usual place, and we picked our way towards it, Pryderi looking round him like a provincial in the Forum.

At the door of the Praetorium, I slipped off my cloak and let Pryderi carry it with my bag, and when the Tribunes of the Staff saw me in my toga, all gleaming white, as if I were in Rome itself nobody thought of challenging my right to be there or to see whom I wanted. At that time, Citizens were scarce enough in Britain outside the Army, and here in the far West they were completely unknown. So I went straight in past the sentry and turned along the corridor – all these Praetorium buildings are exactly alike inside – and I walked into the office of the Junior Tribune without knocking or any other warning. I tossed the Procurator's letter on his desk and said firmly:

'I am ready to see the Legate. Now. Announce me.'

And of course the young fop was too impressed to do anything else but usher me at once into the Legate's office, where the great man was having a nap and wishing it were late enough for him to leave decently and go home without setting a bad example to his junior officers.

The Legate, however, refused to be impressed. He refused very hard. He told me, quite curtly, that he had received orders from Rome itself to offer me every assistance, and he had heard from the Office of the Procurator what assistance I was likely to require. He did not think it at all proper for the Civil Department to presume to tell him how to dispose of the Army's property and resources, and he himself was in fundamental disagreement with the policy, but there was nothing now he could do. Therefore, would I go along to the Primus Pilus and get what I wanted. And he hoped that I would not make any special effort to come and bid him farewell if I were in a hurry to leave, as he knew that I must be.

I went along to the office of the Senior Centurion, the Primus Pilus. I was furious. You keep on meeting this kind of treatment from Latins. Just because they're born in Italy, and Patricians, they think they own the world, and they are a close little clique of the 'right people' who keep all these ornate and profitable offices among themselves. It's people like our family, Greeks and Syrians and Africans, who really have the money and control all the trade and the real business of the Empire. *They* control the details of government. So they take no notice of us. They treat us like dirt.

But their days are numbered. Who do they think they are? Who do they imagine really runs the Empire now? It's the long-service soldiers, the centurions, who know what the legions think, and what the legionary thinks about is who's going to be Emperor and how much he's going to pay for it. And who looks round and takes the opinion of the meeting? The centurions, not the legates and the tribunes. These Patricians, once they *were* rulers, and they can't forget it now. They have not yet woken up to the fact that we have an Empire, not their cosy old Republic, and they're only officials now and not very well-paid ones either.

After that treatment I was steaming with anger. I don't like being treated as if I were a slave, by a man I can buy up twenty times over and out of my own money too, without calling on the family's funds. I went into the Senior Centurion ready for a quarrel if he offered it. But, of course, he was quite different, a man from just outside Carthage named, or perhaps called is a more precise term, Caius Julius Africanus. He was much more inclined to treat a Citizen with respect, being a Citizen born himself, even though he was a provincial too. He did not trust Italians any more than I did. Oh, yes, Africanus knew all about my business, and all about me, which was more than the Legate did.

'Just look at this,' he said, as one harassed man to another. 'Here's the letter from the Procurator. The Legate just passed it over to me with "see to it" scrawled in the corner. That's what he always does.'

'At least it shows he trusts you,' I offered. The Senior Centurion looked at me. Then he described the Legate in detail, in a small vehement voice. I was impressed. I've heard many a sea captain do worse, and the delicate conjunction of epithets brought joy to my poet's heart. At the end I asked:

'But you *have* done it?'

'It's all ready when you want it. Tell me where you want it sent, and exactly when, and I'll do it. There'll be no questions asked about the ship. Don't tell me anything about it, either, I don't want to know.'

'There's another party supplying her.'

'I don't think we dare have you bring it up here. There are too many eyes to see. I tell you what, we have a signal station at the mouth of the next river, but there's a creek a couple of miles nearer here. We'll set off in a wagon train as if we were going to the signal station, and meet you in the creek.'

'No escort,' I warned him. 'Just hire wagon-drivers around here. You'll find a few ready and waiting.'

'Don't tempt me – I won't ask. But when?'

'I will set sail on the day the first shooting stars fall from the Lyre. It will take two days to get to the creek. Can you meet us then?'

'By the Calendar, that will be the end of April. I will watch for the stars.'

'I will expect you.'

'I will be there.' He looked at me. 'Where are you going to sleep tonight?'

'I think my man has found somewhere in the village.' Pryderi was, I supposed, sitting where I had left him, on the step of the Praetorium, looking around him curiously.

'Nonsense. Aristarchos said I was to look out for you, Photinus. You won't be safe in the village tonight, it's Imbolc. Would you like to come and dine tonight with the centurions? It's regimental feast. You can sleep in my house.'

It was wonderful to be addressed by my own name again. I accepted.

'But your man will have to sleep in the village,' Africanus continued. 'We can't have any Brits in here tonight. It's not etiquette, not in the Second. I'll send an orderly to take you down to the baths. He can have your man take your bag down there for you, and he'll carry it back for you himself.'

425

That was what I did. I went to the baths, outside the fortress, and I went through the hot rooms and the cold rooms, and I lay and luxuriated while they scraped me down and oiled me well till I smelt like a civilised man again. Then I put on a clean tunic and it took nearly half an hour to get shaved, the barber was so good and careful. Then back into my toga, and into the fortress again.

The Primus Pilus has a house of his own, while the junior officers live in little apartments at the ends of the huts where their men sleep. Thus it is very seldom that all the centurions of a legion meet together except on the parade ground. This was one of the occasions, and the feast was held in the Regimental Burial Club House, which alone in the fortress had a room big enough to hold us all with a kitchen near by. The room was warm, with real under-the-floor heating. I remarked on this to Africanus, as I stood at his right hand, receiving his Centurions as they saluted him, and introducing me.

'Yes, that's what makes these big forts almost untenable here in the North. We can never get enough fuel. I have something like three hundred men permanently at work all the summer cutting wood and piling it for the winter, and it takes over a hundred wagons because we are cutting it so far away.'

'Why don't you use earth coal like they do at the mines?'

'Impossible. It's too heavy. It would cost too much to bring all the way, on packhorse.'

Africanus greeted his Centurions as they arrived, one by one. This one, he said, was from Byblos, this one from Lutetia, one from Carnuntum, one from Bordigala, this one from Bonnonia even – all Citizens born, from all over the Empire except Britain, and except Italy. I was glad to see that, no Italians. More than half of them, though, were from Gaul and not so different from the Britons. It would be legions down in Egypt that would have British officers. It was the usual kind of regimental dinner, but notable for the absence of the Tribunes and the Legate, and for the presence of every Centurion in the fortress. That did not, of course, mean every officer in the legion, because about twenty of them were away on duty, on detachment at smaller stations. Still, we made four tables when we lay down to eat.

First, of course, we burned incense to His Sacred Majesty.

Then, still in silence, we were served with the traditional bowls of wheat porridge, and each of us took his ritual three spoonfuls and his three sips of ration red, that horrid bitter wine. And that one dish, in theory, *was* the meal. Then we were free to talk, and to eat a real civilised meal all cooked in oil, and drink good Grecian wine, with resin in it. After a few glasses, I asked Africanus:

'I know that every legion has its own feast. Why does the Second have a feast on the Kalends of February? Do you celebrate a victory?'

I asked that partly because I wanted to know, and partly because I knew that a stranger, if present, must ask such a question, otherwise one of those present must lay aside his military cloak and pretend to be a stranger asking. Prompt to his cue, the most junior Centurion stood and began to recite a lesson learned by heart.

'Think, brethren, why we are here. Tonight is the night of Imbolc. Tomorrow night, and for weeks to come, the Brits will watch every night beside their flocks as the lambs are born. Therefore they feast to cheer themselves for the long vigils ahead, waking in the cold lambing shed. Now on this last night of freedom from care they drink and sing in every village throughout the land. If ever we are to expect rebellion, it is on such a night, when men are drunk and tempers are hot. Therefore, it being a feast of the Brits, the Legion stands at its post, every centurion watching throughout the night, neither any soldier venturing out where he might cause offence and begin a riot. For from a riot may begin a war. On this night, brothers, let us watch, being armed, all through the night, knowing that our comrades of the Sixth and Twentieth watch also. Therefore we sit here together, ready to take our places on the parade ground, with the Standard-bearers and the trumpeters at the door.'

He sat down, sweating with the anxiety of remembering the whole thing. It was quite obvious that with what he had already drunk, it would not have been much use sending him on to the parade ground, nor any of the other officers either. I was glad the Standard-bearers were sober, being the senior under-officers. At that moment, the Night Duty Centurion appeared. He stamped up and saluted the Primus Pilus in a stilted tone:

427

'All quiet in the town – *sir*!'

'Take a glass of wine after your labours,' answered Africanus, this obviously being part of the ceremonial. The Duty Centurion drained it at one ceremonial gulp, and then less formally held it out for more. I asked:

'Is it really all quiet in the town?' I thought I could hear something far away.

'Quiet at Imbolc? There's never been such a thing.' The Duty Centurion took a third glass. 'I need this. I've never heard so much uproar. Half the hills seem to have come down for the feast, and they've burnt a couple of houses. And do you know what they've been shouting? They're shouting for Pryderi!'

Some of the drunker centurions laughed, but the soberer ones sat up and asked for the words to be repeated. I asked, as innocently as I could:

'Who is Pryderi?'

'Pryderi?' said Africanus. 'Why, he's a thorn in our flesh and no mistake. Down in the far West, there's the Demetae, and they've never submitted to Rome, they haven't, though nobody would mind if only they kept quiet, as most of them do. But the King there is called Pwyll, and it's his son Pryderi who does a lot of damage, cutting up wagon-trains and burning small posts. Then the nation here are the Silures, and they submitted all right, and we built them a city a few miles east, at Venta. But now some of them have quarrelled with the ones who submitted, and they follow another branch of their Royal House, and there has been a rumour that Pryderi has married into that family. If that's so, then there'll be trouble around here next. He has done us a lot of harm already; I swear, if ever I have him inside this post, then Pryderi will take a long time to die.'

'Do you think it's true?' asked one of the younger officers, who was itching for promotion as was clear from the way he had been flattering Africanus – he thought Africanus couldn't see what was going on, but the Primus Pilus was an old hand. 'I could take a century down there and find out.'

'True or not, they're shouting so loud you can make out the words, "Pryderi, kindle the fire,"' said the Duty Centurion, and one of the Gaulish Centurions opened his eyes wide and told us:

'Sounds like the old man is dead. It's the head of the family kindles the fire on Imbolc night.'

The ambitious young man still pressed:

'I could go down there at the run, and we'd have him in half an hour.'

'No, stay here,' said Africanus. 'If you did go out now, you'd want half a cohort at least, and all you'd do would be start a riot, if not a revolt. This is how it usually begins, and we're not here to start risings, we're here to prevent them. If that means staying in here and not giving offence even if the Brits call us cowards, then that's what we'll do. If it's fighting you want, there'll be enough of that by the summer's end.'

I thought it better to change the subject. I asked:

'Is it your custom not to ask the Legate to your feast?'

Everyone laughed. The Centurion from the borders of Armenia explained:

'We never ask tribunes, not since Carantorius insisted on billeting half a cohort in a village for Imbolc, about forty miles west of here, where the Via Julia meets the sea, and they were slaughtered in their beds. "Making them realise the Army are their friends," was what he used to say, but they weren't friends of the Army. We gave him a good tombstone, but there were two hundred and odd other good men dead as well. Forty years ago that was, but still ... And we would normally ask the Legate, but this one ...'

'Useless,' put in Africanus shortly. 'Perfectly useless. What does he, or any of the Tribunes either, know about this legion, or how to handle men? Look at old sourpuss up there. Fifteen years ago he did a year as tribune with ... the Seventeenth, wasn't it, and everybody knows the Seventeenth. Since then he's been wearing out his toga in one office after another in Rome, counting the obols for cleaning the drains. Now, here he is, just because he's from a Senatorial family he finds himself a Legate, with a legion, and four regiments of cavalry, and the government of a quarter of the Province. That's all he's interested in, feathering his nest to pay his debts so that he can go back to Rome and have his year as Consul.'

'It's not as if he even *tries* to be a good general,' added the

Duty Centurion. 'We've only had him out on an exercise once since he came to us. We took two cohorts on a long march up the valley. End of the first day, what happens? We halt, and I'm Senior Centurion, and I get on with my job, digging in, and you want to, up there, with Pryderi about. Then I look round. Where's his nibs, and the young Tribune he had with him, you know, little Peach-bottom? Are they placing pickets, noting routes of attack? Not a bit of it. They're finding a pretty place by the stream to pitch their mutual tent, where the rude dirty soldiery won't disturb their idyllic night out. Sets the troops a bad example, too. I hope he's not with us if ever we have to go into action.'

'If ever we go.' Africanus stood up. The rest of us who had been wandering about and chattering now the serious eating was over, resumed our places, and lay down properly. The Standard-bearers and their escort had returned to the chapel, and the slaves left the room. The most junior Centurion shut the doors. Africanus went on:

'My comrades, honoured guest, it is time for the toast. Remember, as you drink it, that our brothers of the Twentieth at Deva, a hundred miles away, are drinking it with us. A hundred years ago, we two legions came into this savage land. For forty years we fought against the savages, till at last we made peace and brought all this fertile quarter of the island into the Empire, and the great northern desert we left to the Picts. The Sixth at Eboracum can hold the Wall.

'All this time, we two legions have waited for the word to move forward to add the next province to the Empire. Here on the shore of the Ocean we have built our fortresses and amassed our stores, ready for the last great invasion to carry us to the edge of the Ocean. We have waited long for the word to march. It has always been our pride that whenever the word would come, we would be ready, if need be, to *march* into the very sea itself. If this winter we are cold, we must cheer ourselves that we need not march into the water, and we may warm ourselves by going into the saw mills to work and turn the wood that should have been our fuel into ships that will keep us dry. For I can tell you now, the word has come at last. Soon we *will* march. Gentle-

430

men, I give you, in greater hope than formerly, the annual toast. I hope that I now give it for the last time, and with it I couple the name of our guest, Photinus the son of Protagoras. Gentlemen, I give you – Next Year in Tara!'

I felt a tear in my one eye as I looked around. There they were, thirty-five centurions, from rear rank to front, of all ages, of all levels, and all men of action, hard and ready to fight. The lamps flickered on the brackets on the walls, and showed off the splendour of the plate. The officers were in their dress uniforms, each man in a cuirass made not of iron and boiled leather, but of scarlet velvet, padded to look like armour and trimmed and faced with Gold thread. Because it was Imbolc, and they were ready, each man reclined on his scarlet military cloak, and on the floor behind him each had laid his dress sword, and his parade helmet, and these last were gorgeous things, with face masks like you see gladiators wearing in the parade before the Games, gilded all over and each waving its plume of scarlet horse-hair. Several of them wore Phalerae, those medals of silver and Gold given only for bravery in the field, fighting against savage Britons, or the more savage weather.

They all stood, and I sat. All these brave men, to whom honour and the eagles meant more than Gold or power, men who knew what it was to endure, they all stood, and they drank to me, to Photinus, who was granting to them the prize they had always sought. They lifted their wine cups and they shouted:

'Next Year in Tara! Long live Photinus!'

And then they cheered and called for a speech. When there was some kind of order, I stood and said:

'Gentlemen, I am making you a bridge across the Sea. I have made the way clear for you, and I have done that without going there. But I want to come to Ireland in the end. You have invited me to one feast, gentlemen. May I now invite myself to another? Next Imbolc, I will feast with you in Tara!'

'Never, with old Pig's Bladder in command,' hissed the Duty Centurion, who was rather coarse-mouthed, being an Illyrian.

I turned on him.

'When you go, you shall have a real general.'

I saw to that next morning. I went back to the Praetorium,

431

and wrote a letter to Uncle Phaedo, sending it off with the military mail, partly for safety, partly for speed. It was short. I said: *Rejoice. Foreclose.*

I had sent him the contents of Gwawl's wallet. Already my uncle would have bought up all the Legate's debts. Within two weeks, now, the Legate would be broken.

While I was about that, Africanus suddenly came into the Registry saying:

'I'm very sorry, I quite forgot this. Aristarchos left this letter for you when he came through.'

'What was Aristarchos doing here?' I asked.

'What does Aristarchos ever do? He just passed by. It is my belief he was going native again. He's done it before. All I know is, he borrowed a Standard-bearer and five other good men – all Gauls, and, come to that, all from the same nation. All Setantii. After Pryderi, perhaps? With Aristarchos, you never know, and you don't ask. Here it is.'

I took the letter, and I went aside a little where no one could hear me read it. It was from my father. He had sent it to Uncle Euthyphro, and he to Leo Rufus, and he sent it on through Aristarchos, as he had no idea where I had gone, only a suspicion, and Aristarchos knew. It was quite short. I read it through twice. Then I threw the end of my toga over my face and stood silent for a while.

Africanus watched me, also silent. When I uncovered my face again, he asked:

'Is there anything I can do?'

I stood there, mechanically cleaning the vellum with a piece of pumice, to use again. When I could speak, I answered him:

'I have a son. My wife died in August.'

Chapter Nine

I went from the fortress gate alone. As Africanus said, it was better that he should not know where I went or to whom. I walked out of sight of the sentries among the houses of the British village. True it was that some had been burnt the night before, but not the one where I had changed and left my British clothes.

Pryderi was waiting for me. We went in silence, as soon as I had changed, down to the riverside. There were a number of men to see us off. I had not met them before, but I could tell their rank. After a winter in the Mere I knew the subtle differences of dress, and I would no longer confuse a noble in his hunting clothes with a peasant in his market-day best. Not since I had seven kings at my marriage have I had such august helpers to steady me into a boat. Nor did they speak to us. Anything they had to say to Pryderi, any agreements, any plans and policies, they were the work of the night before. They were committed.

We paddled all that day in silence, and in silence we spent the night on a beach as before. We had no breath to spare, trying to make the most of tide and current as we crossed to the south side of the water. Besides, I mourned a wife: Pryderi had taken possession of … a patrimony? … a dowry? … both?

On the morning of the second day, however, we felt less numb. We paddled with the shore close on our left hand, and we were caught by the current of a great river, wider and stronger than any river of Italy or Spain, wide almost as Nile itself, and I was glad we had cider enough to pour a libation to Sabrina. And then, as we paddled, Pryderi began to sing, a sad and lovely melody, and the words were old, but there was little doubt that he had chosen them carefully:

433

We listened in the sedges to the song of the birds of Rhiannon,
The song of the thrush and the nightingale, and the
    ever-ascending lark:
Yet there is no living bird on the wing that sings like the birds
    of Rhiannon,
The songs of our loves who died long ago, who wait for us yet
    in the dark.
Blackbird and finch still sing to us on the banks of the
    Summer River,
But the song of the dead who loved us will never be heard again.
Love that is given for no return will return to the giver, Love
    that demands love in return earns no return but pain.

We paddled ever south-west on the lead-dull waters. We heard the cries of the gulls and the slap of the water against the paddles and against the side of the boat, and we panted in our haste to drive the craft with the current and against the tide. I thought of Phryne, now dead, and I wept till fresh Sabrina merged into the sea. Perhaps she was no Helen, no Juno, but she was – I found it impossible to be coherent. Flung innocent into marriage with a man who knew worlds, who knew Hells she could not imagine, a man who at first had thought of nothing but his dead love in the North, she had been quiet and peaceful and forgiving and tolerant, and obedient, not as a slave, but as a partner. And she had always been there. There had never been a moment while I was in Britain when I had not known that Phryne would be still there waiting for me. I knew all the time that the moment I walked up the quay from the ship and came into my house she would be offering me her bread and oil. Nobody baked bread like Phryne, she always baked her own bread; she even ground the meal herself if it was for me. She said slave girls never would, no not could, would, grind the wheat flour fine enough for me. And it would be ready when I came home, however long I was away, a month, three months, two years … Now it would never be ready again.

And what of my children? My sister Xanthippe – my grand-father had won there – would take little Euphrosyne fiercely, proudly, to her own house, defying any claim by Phryne's parents:

Xanthippe had five sons. But the baby – how could he survive? My grandmother would scour through the houses of all our friends and through the markets to find a newly delivered slave who could suckle him, even if her own child died: they would try to make him suck goat's milk on the end of a rag. But there was little hope. I am cursed in my children. I have two sons, and a daughter in the North whom I will never see again: and no son in my own home.

And no wife. There was no one now to wait for my return. I need never return. Only as long as the Gold came back, I might stay here for ever, or go where I pleased, might live or die. Now, I might please myself.

The grey waters, the grey sky, the colourless gulls that swooped and passed, all made my mood. I dug my paddle with fury into the swirling tide, keeping her steady in the wilderness of currents. I cursed the useless birds that jeered at us. Now I was at the deep point of the mood that had possessed me all through the grey and misty land of Britain, the land of twilight and soft shadows, the land of deception and melting form, the land where nothing is what it seems to be or claims to be. Now it had struck me down when I seemed to be most successful, most secure. The Army was at my disposal, I could dismiss a Legate who was more powerful than any Barbarian king, and I would soon bring down not one but four Barbarian kings. I had a ship that would live on that stormy sea even in the spring when no skin boat, no galley, could keep it, or carry an army. And my enemy, Gwawl, was defeated, dismissed, made harmless as he had been on the night of the thorn. All the Gold in Ireland was in my hands. There was nothing more I need do. I could rest here, or wherever I liked, and wait for the treasure to come to me, and I could do what I wished with what I had.

In the grey dark that succeeded the grey day we came to a landing place in the reeds, and climbed a gentle slope to a hut. It was not empty. Three men sat there, waiting for the hard dawn that should come, men that came from the confines of Hell. They had fire for us, and food. We ate and ate in silence. At last Grathach asked:

'Will they come, my Lord?'

'Some,' answered Pryderi. 'Not many. Enough.'

435

'Silurians?' I asked. I did not know how far I might go, I was overbold, I thought.

'They are beginning to see now,' Pryderi told me, 'how they have been cheated. They submitted, and that not after a hard fight, on a promise. The Romans said they would protect them from the Irish. And that they have not done. The Irish still raid. Last year they came under the walls of Venta itself. All along the coasts of the Severn Sea they come, except in the Mere. They do not come along the shores of the Irish Sea, either. We Dematae are not disarmed, and north of us, in the Rainy Hills, they dare not face Howell. But the other coasts – they raid as they please, and the Romans can't stop them. Now, Mannanan, see if you are more powerful than a legion. They are yours, now.'

'Who?'

'The Leinster men who raid, from the south-east of the island, they are the men you want. It is in their country, in Wicklow, that the Gold was found. They have the streams rich in metal. Turn them back to mining Gold, and they will be too busy to bother us.'

'And then, Pryderi, you will submit, and go to live in Venta, or build a city just like it far in the West, or in the Mere?'

'I will never submit to the Romans.'

'The future lies in the towns, Pryderi. It is the Guild of Shoemakers and the men who peddle earth coal who will rule this land in the end. Submit, Pryderi. There is no other way to power.'

'I will never submit. I am a king.'

'I know what it is. You are jealous of the Irishman, the King's nephew, the Setanta. You want to be like him, to lead a fianna, to ride into great battles, to topple monarchs and empty thrones. It is too late, Pryderi. Submit and be rich and happy and have power.'

'I might be richer than I am, and have more power, but I would not be happy.'

'Is it only the luxury of your pride, then, Pryderi, that keeps you in rebellion? Is it the mere pleasure of knowing that you are doing what you like?'

'Here my Gesa, Mannanan, to which I have been obedient since I was a child. It is this: it is never to forsake a friend, or forget a wrong, or forgive a Roman.'

436

He said no more: he rolled himself in his cloak and lay on his bed of dry bracken. There was no more to be said. I too slept.

They woke me a little before dawn. Grathach brought me hot mutton soup and bread, and as I scoured my bowl he said.

'Up the slope straight, and there is a path. Follow it to the end, not turning to the left nor to the right—'

'Will you now forsake me?' I asked.

'No, you cannot be forsaken here.' Pryderi on his bed was calm, not offended. 'Do you not know where you are? You are at the south end of the Apple Country. When you reach the north end of the ridge, turn to the west, and in the reeds by the huts at the end of the path, you will find boats moored. Then you can cross the marsh to Caw's house. As for us, we have no time to take you, and we trust you enough to let you go alone wherever you wish. We have other business that will not wait.'

I made west along the path, among the orchards of cider apples. And now I knew why the Apple ridge was sacred, for though every tree was bare of leaf, yet each in the winter dark shone golden green and silver dotted. On every tree the mistletoe hung down.

I came in mid-afternoon to the edge of the ridge, where the Mere in winter flooded round on all sides. There I did find a boat, though I had to look for it, and in the end pick the smallest and lightest from a cluster cleverly hidden under a willow. The rain came down on me, and splashed in great circles into the marsh, as I pointed the bows up stream and paddled hard against the current in order only to make track straight across it. I waded to push the boat through shallows and lay flat to creep under low branches Where we had walked in the summer the flood would now drown a man. At last, I came to the edge of the main stream, rushing down from the hills inland with the force of a herd of frightened cattle, roaring and tossing. I struggled to hold her head, I saw lost all the way I had so painfully made north along the ridge. All the knowledge I had ever had of the sea, all the skills I had learnt in ships, all were useless against this sweet fresh water, whirling me back to the sea. I strained down to my heart, my back cracked, handsbreadth by handsbreadth I moved towards the opposite bank, taking first one mark to head for, and then losing it far up stream, and then another, and losing that too. And suddenly, as I thrust away a log that playfully butted me and almost turned me over, I was in calm water, and close under the opposite shore, under the west bank, on the surface of a calm black pool, a backwater where the water did not stir. I had lost my paddle in that last struggle with the ash tree. Now I splashed with my hands till I came near, and grounded on the mud beach. I did not think, I just pulled the boat up far from the water, as one always does. Once a sailor, you never forget. Then I climbed, foot by foot, ledge by ledge, up the bluff till I came where Rhiannon's hut had been, where she had sat for so long fasting and gazing out over the marsh. I sloshed soaking down the hill and by the last path to Caw's house.

Later, fed and warm and full of cider in the lamplight, I said to Caw:

'But would not cider pay you better than silver? There is no cider even in Britain like the cider of the Summer Country. You could sell it from here to Londinium, to Rome itself. I could arrange it all, act as your agent, and once it came into fashion at the Imperial Court, it is Gold you would be handling and not silver, and it would not take too much influence then to free you from the wheat tax. And it would be safer, too.'

'Attractive you make it sound, don't you?' He laughed. 'No wonder it is rich you do get by buying and selling. No, boy, it's the sea that is my real love.'

I changed my tack.

'How many of those great ships have you left now, Caw?'

'Well, there was another, but that one you stole from me. Now – to tell the truth, we only have the one.'

'After this one voyage for which you have promised her to me?'

'Back to the silver.'

'Why don't you build another?'

'It takes time to build a ship, time and space and skill. We could never do it, even in the Mere, with no one knowing. And what would we use another one for now? We cannot trade except as I do.'

'But if I were to trade with Ireland, then would you not think of building more? And then, you would not be a hunted pirate in the Mere, but you would have a style and a title and a place in the Empire, and under the Emperor it is you only would be the Master of the Western Sea.'

Caw sat silent, cracking walnuts with his teeth – fancy, a man at his age with his own teeth! Finally he said:

'I'll think about it.'

We went to bed. I was almost there, I thought, almost there. Soon I would be able to trade across the Irish Sea in all weathers and all the year, with an Ireland peaceful and settled and pouring Gold, rich Gold into my hands.

All I wanted in the Mere, almost all I wanted, was in my hands. Now there was no thought of home, no obligation, no loyalty, no promise to keep me back. I was free to take what I wanted out of all the island, to take what was mine, what had been given me and what had been promised me.

I walked along the edge of the Mere in the grey morning. I came to Pryderi's house, where Cicva sat grinding at her door, grinding flour fine enough for Pryderi, and Rhiannon with her.

'Where is Taliesin?' I asked.

'Gone,' replied Cicva. 'He is walking back alone through the land as he came, from nation to nation, judging the people and telling them what is right and just to do, whether it please the oil-eaters or not. Why should you want him now?'

'I wanted a witness,' I told her. 'I have come to claim what is mine.'

'And what is yours?' asked Rhiannon. 'I too may claim what is mine, what I too have been given.'

'You are mine, Rhiannon. I will take you now. You can plead neither sanctity nor weakness nor strength. I will take you with me back, through Rome and through Ostia, past Brundisium and Athens, through Alexandria and Byblos to my own home in the Old City. Come, Rhiannon, I have children there who need a mother, and I have slaves who need a mistress. I have a great house in the town, Rhiannon, with a hundred rooms, tables of ivory and beds of ebony, laid with all the silks of India and scented with the strange woods the Arabs bring out of the Desert. There we eat well, Rhiannon, of bread and meat, and fruits and nuts you have never seen and have never heard of, and that not at feasts

439

but every day. And wine, Rhiannon – we can drink a different wine every day for a year, and not exhaust my cellar. I have the wealth of ten kings in the Isle of the Mighty, Rhiannon, and in my own town I have the honour of a king. Roman Governors treat me as a man of importance, and merchants from all over the world bow low to me. And they will all bow low to you, Rhiannon, and bring you presents, because you are mine. I have an empty house that waits for you, Rhiannon, and an empty bed that waits for you. I will take you now, Rhiannon, back out of this land of mists and shadows into the real world.'

'And would that honour me, that am a princess already?' she asked. 'Mannanan, you are mine, given to me. Now I will take what is mine. Come with me to the North, Mannanan, to my own people of the Brigantes. Come and live there with me, and all will honour you as a king, because I bring you. You will have mutton to eat all the days of your life, and oat bread, the fine fruits of the forest, blackberries and elderberries, cobnuts and blewits. You will have wool to wear and to sleep on, pure clean wool, through the hot summer days up on the heather hills, through the long winters in the dry cold air.'

'I have a farm also,' I told her, 'up in the hot dry hills. I too have my herds of sheep, and I wear wool of my own breeding, that my own husbandmen have sheared, that the women of my own household have combed and spun and woven and sewn into cloaks and tunics, and into blankets for the winter nights when we shall lie warm together and listen to the wolves outside. There we shall smell the wood smoke, and drink the resined wine that we ourselves have trodden out, and on the bread baked of our own wheat we shall sprinkle oil we have pressed from our own olives. If you wish, Rhiannon, you shall never see a town again.'

'If you spurn the throne of the Brigantes,' she told me, 'and will not be turned from trade, then stay here with me in the marsh. Here we will eat and drink in plenty, since it seems there is nothing you think of except eating and drinking. We shall have venison and hare, wild duck and moorhen, carp and salmon, oysters and mussels, snails and milk-caps and horns-of-plenty, And I will be kinder to you than you to me. I will let you go out and trade, wherever you will, up to the Picts and across to the Land of Norroway, anywhere.'

I looked narrowly at her.

'But not to Ireland?'

'And what cause is there for you to go to Ireland? You have no need of trading there.'

'I have no need to go to Ireland. All I want done is done by others. I have used the weapons that I know, money and persuasion and planning, to make a hundred men each work at what he thinks he wants the most, and none of them even knowing the others exist, and by all that to bring about my desire. My work is done. All will now come about whether I go or not. I will only be an encumbrance. I need not go. We can leave now, Rhiannon, we will be home by the end of the spring, by the hot blue sea, listening to the first cicadas among the flowers in the grass, listening to the shepherded boys piping. Come, Rhiannon, let me take my own.'

'You are not going to Ireland?'

'There is no reason why I should go to Ireland?'

'There is no reason why you should seek the Gold in Ireland. You have been telling me of all the wealth you have. What more can you add to that?'

'I must bring it back. I told my family that I would bring it. You will understand this, Rhiannon. This is my Gesa, that what I have said I will do, that I will do, and neither the love of women nor the fear of men will deflect me; no, not for all the Gold in Ireland will I break my word.'

And then Cicva spoke:

'And it would have been well if there were Brigantes who had taken that Gesa, for it was the Brigantes who said they would not submit, and then they submitted and the great castle of Stanwyck they surrendered without a blow struck.'

She spoke with venom. I had not realised that Cicva hated Rhiannon so much, that she envied, from here in the Mere, hiding from Roman eyes, this princess of a surrendered house. Rhiannon at least could ride across all the island unchallenged. But Rhiannon did not hear her. Staring at me, she shouted:

'Then take their Gold back to them,' and at my feet she threw

441

three coins, three coins I knew well. I stopped to pick them up as she went by me, and then I followed her out.

She ran across the grass, round Cicva's house, towards the fence of the paddock. Hueil was there, acting as guardian of the Mere in Pryderi's absence, and he was preparing to go boar-hunting in the thickets of the Deer Moors. He had two horses saddled there, and Rhiannon ran past him and swung up on to the one saddled for her. I could not think where she was going. Half I remembered the ritual chase when we had caught Cicva four months before: half I hazarded that in fact she had nowhere to go, she just wanted to run away, to escape, to flee from me anywhere.

I rushed to the fence and swung up on to the other horse. Hueil, who had only just fastened the girths, looked at me in surprise. Then he grunted:

'You never know,' and before he slapped the horse on the rump he handed me up the boar spear.

The horse twisted to bite me, and I recognised him. It was Taliesin's evil-tempered brown again, a horse I hated. But it was the only one ready, and I belaboured his flanks with the butt of the boar spear and prepared to see if he would go.

Go? Oh, yes, that brown horse would go. You can forgive anything to a horse that *will* go, that will run his heart out the day, the one and only day, when he must. There was only one horse I ever had that went better, and he was dead, long dead. Rhiannon looked back and saw me following.

At first she thought she could play the old game, and keep just out of reach till my horse tired, while hers was still fresh but it was hardly a furlong before she saw that if once she hesitated, if once her horse pecked or stumbled, then I had her. She set her horse at the paddock fence and cleared it. Jumping is not something you do lightly if you have only one eye, but by now I was in such a state of suppressed anger and excitement and general rage with the whole world that I just pointed the brown at the fence and let him go, shutting my eye in case I lost courage. Every fence and hedge we came to the black jumped, but the brown, stupid blundering, marvellous brute, went through as often as over, and where the black cleared a stream, the brown went in and I was soaked. And this did not soothe me.

442

We left the edge of the Mere, and climbed the hill up on to the open moor, where there were no sheep at this time of year, but only deer and wolf, and the chance of bear or boar in the woods. It was into the woods Rhiannon went, seeking a twisting path. The brown did not care for paths. He went into the scrub all right, but he galloped straight as an arrow. Very soon my clothes were torn to pieces by the thorns, and I was glad that I had flung my sealskin cloak to Hueil as I mounted. It was a wonder that the horse did not run head first into a tree, or that I was not brained on a low branch, but by cutting corners we stayed with Rhiannon as she went, went north-west towards the sea, away from the Mere. Did she choose the way on purpose, or by the accident of its giving us a firm path? I did not know. I followed. We were in sight of the sea now, a paler grey line under the line of the grey clouds. There was a thicket ahead of us, and Rhiannon made for it. I saw a disturbance there, and I thought 'boar' and then I saw men and I still thought 'hunting party'. Rhiannon vanished into the thicket, and the nearest man was close to me, running towards me with a spear. I had scarcely time to think, 'Funny kind of spear to go after boar with,' when I was close to him, and I knew him. It was one of Gwawl's friends, the older of the two middle-aged men who had escorted the Mouse from inn to inn. He came at me with his spear, and as he lunged, I pulled the brown horse round and down we came, knocking the middle-aged man flying. I fell clear: I wouldn't have done that if I had been using one of my own saddles with a strap for the toes.

I rolled away from the threshing horse, still holding the boar spear, and got up just in time to receive the charge. I sidestepped the spear point, and the shafts crossed as we pushed against each other, sweating and straining for the advantage. Suddenly, we both gave together and each went staggering back. He was quicker on his feet, for all his age, and came back at me with the spear levelled. There was only the one thing to do, and if it did not succeed I would never know it. I poised the boar spear, regretted briefly that it was not very well balanced for the job, and that I had no chance to find another, and threw it, with all my might, when he was barely two yards away.

His run carried him past me. He fell on his side. The point of the spear stood out two fingers from his back. That, I thought, is the end of you, and who knows …? I bent to take his spear from his hands, and someone jumped on to my back from behind. There were a number of them, filthy men, smelling of dirt and fat, but of salt and the sea beside. They held my arms and turned me round to face the thicket.

Gwawl stood before me. He wore still his black and white shirt, and a pair of trousers he had bought in Lutetia and Cicva had won from him and given to me, cheating the Berts, and I had given Pryderi and Gwawl had stolen back. He stood there and laughed in my face.

'That was fair,' he said, jerking his head to the body on the ground. 'When a man armed meets a man armed, then there is neither blame on either for seeking blood, nor on the victor for drawing it. There is no call for vengeance here.'

'Where is Rhiannon?' I asked him.

He ignored the question. He went on:

'By every law of my people, I ought to kill you now, and save all the trouble that will come. But there was an oath I swore, and a bargain, and I must keep them. I may not kill you, Mannanan, in this land I may not kill you. So I must leave you.'

Someone had unsaddled the sweaty brown horse, which had remained standing cropping the grass and watching the fight unconcerned. After all, what concern was it of his? They flung the filthy saddlecloth over my head, and wrapped me in it, and tied my arms to my sides under it. Then they spun me around, and someone, Gwawl I think, struck me half a dozen blows across the face, not hard, but sharp, contemptuous.

I staggered about, trying to wrestle my arms free, trying not to breathe the sweat on the blanket, hoping that I would not step badly and break my ankle. I wrestled and struggled as if it were Gwawl himself I was fighting, and in a way it was. I wrestled as if it were Hercules I was faced with. Then suddenly, dimly through the blanket, I heard more hooves and shouting, familiar British voices, and in a few moments, someone was cutting through the rope and letting me breathe again.

Madoc asked:

'Who were they?'

444

I rinsed out my mouth with the cider someone gave me. I said:

'I don't know, except that it was Gwawl.'

Hueil was kneeling over the body.

'Irish,' he called. 'Wicklow man here, I think. Nothing of value, though, except his knife.'

They brought me the brown horse again, and handed me my bloody boar spear. Someone asked:

'What, doesn't he want the head?' but I ignored that. We set off again, through the thicket, where we found Rhiannon's cloak, of thick yellow wool, on the ground, and then down a steep narrow valley onto the coastal flats. The way was clear, with the marks of hooves and broken branches. The beach here, I knew, was shingle, with a bank above the sea. We could see a group of something on the bank and made for it. When we came closer, it was a group of horses. We reached them and went up the bank into sight of the water.

Far out across the bobbing waves we could see the skin boats, a dozen of them, big ones, already setting the lug sails that they too used, all paddling hard.

'Too late,' said Hueil.

'Wicklow men,' said Madoc. 'If you wish, we can be at sea in six hours. I will find a crew here, and we will pick up warriors in Pryderi's country. Or we could wait for Pryderi, but I do not know how long he will be. Then we can raid the coasts of Wicklow till we find her.'

I looked into the setting sun. Somewhere out there, on the leaden water, being carried across the February sea in a basket covered with a little leather, was Rhiannon, the glorious Rhiannon, that was worth the greatest ship that ever was just to carry her across a little stream.

'No,' I said. 'No, I will see to it myself. I *will* go to Ireland and find her, at the proper time.'

Chapter Ten

Two mornings later, I stood on the bluff above the Dark Pool, where Rhiannon's hut lay in ruins. I stood looking into the waters. To whoever dwelt there, to Those Below, I vowed, in bitterness, the whole of the Island of the Blessed. And as an earnest, to Those Below I gave, first, Gold. Three Gold coins, ancient but unmarked, I threw into the water, one by one, in order of age. And then I plucked the eye from my head and cast that in too. Not my real eye, you must understand, but my most expensive one, of diamond, carved with a scene of the judgement of Paris.

And then, quietly, Pryderi too came to the waterside. I had never seen him like this before. He was armed. He had on a short mail coat, to the waist, and an old-fashioned helmet, plain and unornamented, round and setting close to the head. The long sword, too, at his side, so long that he almost tripped over it, was plain-hilted and in a plain leather scabbard. A man who goes into battle wears no Gold or jewels. And Pryderi had been in battle. His forearm was caked with clotted blood.

He carried a big leather bag. He put it on the grass. From it he took a cloak of scarlet wool. Next, he took out handfuls of silver, dozens, hundreds of silver denarii, and piled them on the cloak. Plainly, though, there was more, much more, in the bag. Last, he brought out a head. His fingers sank deep into the close cropped black hair. The face was that of a man in his late twenties. He had had neither beard nor moustache: I thought it was a Thracian face if ever I saw one, but it was, I was glad to see, no one I knew. The look on the face was of surprise, nothing more, just surprise.

Pryderi laid the head on the cloak among the silver coins. He turned up the ends of the scarlet cloth to form a bag, and tied the mouth with a leather strap. Then he swung the bag backwards

446

and forwards once ... twice ... and the third time, he let it go and it sailed out and fell into the deepest centre of the pool. Weighted with silver, the head went straight down to Those Below. And I have no doubt it pleased them more than Gold or diamonds.

Ireland

Ireland

Chapter One

When the time came, Caw and Pryderi saw me into Madoc's ship at the river mouth.

'Don't lose the ship, whatever you do,' Caw warned me. 'We won't ever be able to build another without a pattern.' So that was settled in his mind, I thought. He had never said anything about it before. But all Pryderi told me was:

'If Cicva has a boy, I'll name him after you.'

Which name of the many, I thought, as we swept her out through the channel and into the shallow Severn Sea. We came between the islands and made the mouth of the creek at dawn on the second day.

There was someone on the wharf waving a red cloak. We tied up and Madoc's crew put down a gangplank. I went ashore and greeted Africanus. He had come himself, he said, to be sure that there was no treachery. Talking of that, I asked after the Legate. Africanus laughed:

'He's gone. There's a rumour he went bankrupt soon after you were here. True or not, he went back to Rome in a hurry last week, and he took young Peach-bottom with him. I'm glad of that, too – sets a bad example to the Brits. We haven't had a replacement yet, and with luck we'll be without one for the rest of the year. Of course, old ox-head would have commanded both legions when we go, but now it'll be the Legate of the Twentieth. He'll be all right. You can put too much store on regimental loyalties.'

I agreed. The thought of two legions going ashore in Ireland under a general that none of the senior officers trusted was chilling. But if the troops trusted the commander, then the battle, if there were so much as a battle, was won already. Africanus and I stood there in complete accord and watched the wagons unloaded into the ship.

451

'I'm depending on you, coming down with all this material and only twenty men,' Africanus went on. 'We lost the half-yearly pay convoy a few weeks ago. Nobody's attacked that for twenty years – we just didn't expect it. There were only fifteen men, and a very junior Centurion. Pryderi ambushed them on the steep hill east of Glevum, and took the lot. Half a year's pay for nine thousand men, all in silver. All the escort killed. As for the Centurion, Pryderi cut his head off and took it away. Horrible thing. Not been anything like that as far east as this for … no, not for fifty years.'

'You are sure that it was Pryderi?'

'He told the carters before he let them go. He boasted about it. "I'm Pryderi, King of the Demetae and of the Silures," he said. "Tell Caesar to think again what he rules." Now we can't move anything along these roads without an escort. Pryderi! When I catch him …' He changed the subject. 'Are you keeping a count of this?'

'No. I assume that you're giving me all you've got.'

All he'd got? I'd never seen anything like the arms we were loading. For a hundred years, the Second Legion had been disarming the country. Swords and shields by the hundred they had confiscated and stored in the Fortress of Isca. They had stored them, and kept fifty men busy looking after them and greasing them and counting them every year, while the quartermaster grumbled about the work and how long it was taking Rome to make up its mind about them. Now Rome *had* made up its mind, and I had them.

You see, you cannot teach Barbarians to use Roman weapons, and on the other hand, you cannot ask Roman troops to use Barbarian weapons. These were Barbarian swords, not even German which the cavalry could use, but British. They were very long, three and a half or four feet from hilt to point, double-edged, and a palm's width at the hilt. Why were they so long? You shall learn, in good time.

There were shields, too, of two kinds. Some of them were like the ones Pryderi and I had made. Roman shields are oblong and convex. German shields are round. These were big, almost as long as the swords, and oval. They were flat and very light, a thin

452

wood frame with a layer of boiled leather over, often covered again in the thinnest of bronze sheets. They had been, once, enamelled and set with jewels, like the scabbards and the hilts of the swords. But now all you could see were the holes where the Roman soldiers had wrenched out the gems. Who on earth would carry these into action I could not think: they were far too big to run with, and too light to stop a sword cut.

There were, however, a lot of smaller shields, round and a foot or a foot and a half across, just the thing for a swordsman. There was armour, too, mail shirts of iron rings sewn on leather, and other shirts of boiled leather which are almost as good as mail unless you are unlucky and get the full force of a cut with a really sharp blade. There were throwing spears, and a few pikes and axes. Besides this, we had helmets, almost laughably old-fashioned. Some of them were tall and pointed, others round like kettles, and many of them with horns or ridge crests of thin bronze.

And last of all came the things that made sense of the long swords and the big shields and the throwing spears. The wheels were about waist-high to a man, iron tyred, and light. There were great tangles of leather harness, and poles, and basketwork. All this we took aboard and stowed in the hold.

When we were loaded, the ebb tide was ready to take the ship out. I embraced Africanus.

'Why!' he said in surprise. 'I thought you were coming ashore with me. I have a room ready for you.'

'I've changed my mind,' I told him. 'Someone has to do the thinking.' I did not mention Rhiannon: how could I have explained?

'Well, then,' he warned me, 'don't get pricked with any of that sharp stuff. I want to see you there waiting for me on the beach on the first of August. And keep a few Irish wenches waiting for me.'

He stood on the wharf, waving his vinewood staff at us as we dropped out into the Channel. He was a good reliable man, was Africanus, and I wish I could have taken him with me on that voyage. But, of course, a Negro would have been *too* conspicuous on that expedition.

Chapter Two

We beat down the Channel, against the wind that blew from the south-west. First we had a low marshy coast on our right hand, then high cliffs, and then sand dunes with great mountains close inland, their heads high in the clouds. The Alps are fifty miles high, we know that because Pliny has measured them, and I think that these mountains west of Isca must have been at least ten miles to the tops.

I took watch and watch with Madoc, heaving on the steering oar and bellowing at the men who handled the leather sail, a great lug fifteen feet square. Oh, there's nothing like being in a ship of your own, handling the winds as if they too were your subjects. You have to woo a ship when you first have her, finding out her little ways and fads, discovering what will make her yield, what will best satisfy you. And at last she lies open to your every desire, your slightest whim is her command, you no longer have to show what you want her to do, she anticipates your demands before you make them. And the weariness that comes after a long trick at the helm, the fatigue that lets you sleep on the hard deck, although the spray drenches you and a battle rages over the bulwarks – the lion too, they say, the lion too.

But there is no joy in a whore you hire or a slave girl you buy for your bed. If you spend no effort, do not venture your pride, then what pleasure is there? Likewise, there is no satisfaction in steering another man's course or carrying someone else's mer-chandise, what you do not know. But as on that day in the Channel, steering a ship you have hired for yourself, carrying your own goods to make your own fortune, oh, that is joy, that is happiness indeed.

At noon on the second day we had the sun at our backs, when we saw it, and on our right hands we still had savage cliffs, that soon gave way to a land of high mountains. And on the third day, the mountains were highest of all, higher than the Alps, though we never saw the tops, being wreathed in cloud.

We were near the estuary of a river, with wide sandbanks at low tide. We worked our way in to the south-east side, where a great rock rose sheer out of the water, the waves breaking at its foot. We would come in close, though, near enough to see people on the top of the rock and hear them shouting to us.

'The Rock of Harlech,' Madoc told me. We watched a crowd of skin boats put out from the shore, full of men. They reached us and swarmed aboard, shouting. I felt glad that I had taken the pick of the arms from the cargo for myself, a light mail coat and a helm, a small shield and an axe. No more swords for me. The men who came aboard were all Irish by their dress. I would have let Madoc push them back into the sea again if I had not recognised the patchy hair of the first Irishman, the Setanta, in the last boat to leave the shore.

As soon as they were all aboard, we made sail for the west. Madoc took her, tacking among the shoals. I stood on the poop and watched the Setanta as he handed out the first of our arms to his men. There was one man there the others called Heilyn, who took a tall spiked helmet with a ring on top, through which he threaded some red rags. He was not really seven feet high when he wore it, he only looked like it. I tried to hear what the Setanta was saying to him and then what the others were talking about. I listened hard. I received my worst shock of the whole voyage. I couldn't understand a word they were saying.

For a moment, wild thoughts raced through my head. Were they drunk? Were they perhaps not Irish after all? They sat about in the waist, delousing each other and relieving themselves in the scuppers and chattering away, and I couldn't make out a word of it. I turned to Madoc.

'What language are they talking?'

'Language?' he asked in turn. 'What language do you think? Irish of course.'

'Irish? Have they got a different language?'

'Of course they have!'

'Not like yours?'

455

'Not a bit. Quite different. I can't manage a word of it.'

Different? Different! All these months wasted! I was going to land in Ireland, in a hostile Ireland, not speaking a word of their language. I might as well be deaf and dumb. I nearly wept. Cheated! Why had nobody told me? This was just the thing those accursed Brits would think was a huge joke. All those weary weeks learning British just so that I could talk with the Kings of the Irish, and now to find that they could not understand me! There was nothing to do but to whelm my sorrows in food. I ate myself to sleep.

Before dawn, Madoc woke me – I was sleeping curled up under a skin boat on the deck.

'Wake up, boy. It is happy enough you ought to be, seeing it is a Holy Day that it is. Let's make it a bright one and a happy one, for it's standing away by noon that I would like to be.'

It was a Holy Day indeed. This was the first day of May, on which the British and the Gauls, and I supposed the Irish too, drive out from the farms the beasts that they have kept folded in close all the winter, out to the summer pastures on the hills. And this, being the end-of-winter feast, is the fire feast for them, when they build their bonfires on the hills and jump through them and wish. Beltain they call it.

Now, it was with a fire feast that I had come into the North before, and I had gained wealth from it, and ever after I had counted such a feast as a lucky day for myself. I stood there in the cold wind of early dawn, and I looked at the sky, the first time since the year before that I had looked up at all the stars, all of them shining through clear air with never a wisp of mist nor any haze to hide them. There was a clarity here I had not known in Britain. All the winter I had groped in the mists of double meaning, till I had myself begun to think not in logic but in riddles. But here, now, I knew, I would be myself again. Here I would think and reason as a man, coldly and economically, and *know*, not guess, what I was about. Here at last, I would not be at the mercy of others. I would be my own master – no, I would be master of all around, I would be master of all Ireland before I finished.

In the shelter of a tongue of land, we dropped anchor, still on salt water, though near a river mouth. The Irish, and there were twenty-seven of them altogether, all armed, launched their skin boats and got down into them gingerly, weighted down as they were with mail. Armour does not float very well, in my experience. The Setanta tapped me on the arm.

'Is it the courage to come with us you are having, or is it staying where you are safe that you will be?' Of course he spoke to me in British, and as we had both had to learn the language deliberately, we understood each other perfectly.

'Naturally,' I told him, 'I must be at hand to protect my investment.' I was full of the confidence of the first flush of day. I went down into a skin boat with the Setanta and Heilyn and another smelly ruffian, a very hairy man called, it seemed, Callum, and we paddled towards the shore. At least they paddled. I lay back with an air of civilised polish. I had finished with manual work, I told myself. From now on it would be the Barbarians who did all the work.

Some way off the shore, the other boats stopped; that is they stayed in the same place while their occupants paddled like mad to save themselves from being carried out by the tide. We, however, went closer in till there was hardly room for a skin boat even to float.

As we paddled in, we could see three figures on the beach, and as we drew near to the shore, so they walked down to the line of seaweed and driftwood that marked the water's limit. As we came in so that we would have been better advised to get out into the water and wade, I saw that they were three old women, tall and gaunt, hooded and cloaked in dusty grey. They threw back their hoods, and while the wind dropped to nothing, their hair streamed back horizontal from their heads, streamed grey and dusty as their cloaks. We bobbed up and down, not ten feet from them, and we looked at them and they looked at us.

Their faces were lined and old and lifeless. They might well have walked out from the houses of the Dead. They pointed their fingers at us, their left forefingers, bony and fleshless, and they began to sing. In a high wailing voice they sang, a mournful wailing tune, a tune full of sadness and foreboding and warning. I have heard sounds in my time that few men have heard and lived. I have heard the scream of the wounded mermaid, and the cough of the crocodile in the night. I have heard the women wail for Osiris in the Sanctuary, and I have heard the rustle of the poison spider on my pillow. And nothing have I ever heard that chilled my flesh and raised my hair as did the sound of those three women, tiny, singing on the empty beach of Ireland. We sat there on the sea on the edge of the world, and in that song I heard all the gulf at the end of the Ocean open to swallow us.

I looked at the Irishmen. The Setanta was quite unconcerned. He explained to me: 'It is the Morrigan.'

I knew a little about this, as much as any Greek does, and that was not much. The Morrigan is what the Irish call the Mother, but there in that wild land on the edge of Ocean, the Mother is still a conquered goddess, wild and unforgiving and hostile to all living men. The Morrigan is the wild spirit of all the women of the land, and the farther you go from the warm countries where kindly men rule, the more clear it is that men and women are two different kinds of being, as different from each other as dog from cat or horse from cow, and the fact that they can breed together, and that they both feel an unsuperable need for each other and a bitter hatred and rivalry, is as accidental and irrational as the tide. It was in answer to this impossible bond that I was coming myself to the land of Ireland, and here stood the Morrigan, the spirit of woman, to bar my way.

The Morrigan may come upon any woman at any time, or on more women than one. Here she had come on three women, which is right, because anyone who has an upbringing like mine knows that three is the number for women, and seven for men, whatever the Pythagoreans may say.

'What are they singing?' I asked. It was clear enough, really, but after all the shadows and double meanings of the magical Isle of Britain, I was not ready to accept anything as simple and plain in its meaning.

'They are forbidding us to land,' he answered. He spoke to the other men, and they began to paddle us away from the shore. I had to take a paddle too, because it is very difficult to make way against the tide and the breaking waves. I looked a question at the Setanta, because I had no breath to speak.

'We cannot land where the Morrigan has forbidden it. We must go back out to sea.'

'Are you going to abandon your invasion because they tell you to?' I was incredulous. Religion is one thing, but money is another, and I had invested a lot in this expedition. It was worth a curse, I thought. There is no curse that cannot be lifted for some appropriate payment. If Gold will not do it then blood will.

'I will not abandon this,' the Setanta answered, short of breath.

'Go somewhere else?' I panted.

'No, we must land here.'

'When?'

'When we have made a new voyage.'

I liked that idea even less. We had now reached the cluster of skin boats, half-way between Madoc's ship and the shore. We looked back to the beach.

'Now,' said the Setanta. 'You may count the waves. We are out beyond the ninth wave.'

I counted. 'So we are. If we return, it will be a new voyage?'

'It will that.'

'But if we make a new voyage, will not the Morrigan forbid us again?'

'Now it is the witches of the Queen of the West that they are, and it is paying them well she had been to forbid us to land. It is earning their money they have been. Now it is earning their other money they will be, and it is not seeing us that they will be intent on. Witches are very expensive. The Queen cannot afford to hire them for more than one cursing in the day, and we can only hire them for the one abstention, but praise be to the Gods, abstention is a longer act than cursing, and it is good value we will be getting for our money.'

'My money, you mean.'

'If it is pedantic you are meaning to be – yes.'

'So it is all a paid performance, and not the Morrigan at all?'

'No. It is here they are coming to curse because they are paid, but it *is* the Morrigan that is on them, and she is my fierce enemy.'

I did not ask further after the habits of the Morrigan. I was too busy digging in my paddle and heaving the boat shorewards against the tide and the wind. The other boats came with us, holding back

459

a little out of politeness, so that we should be the first to land. Above us, the cloud began to break. The sun shone on us, clear and bright. At last I saw the colours of Ireland, and I saw them true and clear. In Britain I had lived half a year and more in twilight and in mist. There you will see no clear colours. Even the bright yellow of Rhiannon's cloak, the scarlet of a centurion's plume, everything in the Island of the Mighty, was seen as through a mist, the hues degraded, unsaturated, the outlines blurred, all hard edges softened. But now, as we came to the Island of the Blessed, everything was flooded in a clear hard light that took me home. The saffron cloaks and the green trees beyond the strand glowed bright and definite. I shook myself. I began to throw off the languors and the uncertainties of the Island of Britain, where nothing is as it seems, where every meaning is both doubtful and double, and I prepared to return to a life of logic and certainty and simplicity.

We beached the boat. The Setanta sprang first ashore, drawing his sword. I followed, waving my axe, and the other men from the ship, as soon as they had carried the boats up above the tidemark of seaweed, also brandished their weapons and shouted dreadful oaths in their own language, describing perfectly intelligibly what they would do to anyone who tried to bar their path. The Three Witches of the Queen of the West drew their hoods over their faces, and ostentatiously did not see us, only grunting a little when Heilyn went over and pressed purses into their hands.

We walked up the beach in a long line. The Setanta was in the centre with Callum on his left and myself on his right, and Heilyn came on my other side, and I was glad of someone to keep my back, being the first emissary of the Empire to set foot in the country, even if no one knew about it. We were ready to form a shield wall, but we were not attacked as I, at least, half expected. Instead, as we breasted the dunes at the edge of the beach, with the low sun at our backs, there was a great noise and a crowd of unarmed men came running to us out of the scrub ahead.

There must have been two hundred of them. This was why the Setanta had been so positive that we must land here, and now. They thronged around us, shouting and cheering, the weaponless men of the disarmed kingdom of the North. They offered us hunks of steaming meat, and barley bread and jugs of beer, but we followed the Setanta in refusing them with flamboyant ritual gestures of abstention. And of course, we had had a hearty breakfast of cold mutton and oat cakes and mead in the ship. Still, we came ashore fasting till the time should be ripe for us to eat.

The Setanta stopped in the middle of an open space, and someone brought him a bundle of dry sticks and a bow. He tore off the edge of his garment for tinder, and twisting a stick in the bowstring, he made fire just as we do in the Temple at home on great occasions. In Ireland, if not in Britain, the meaning of every rite was plain to see. When the tinder smoked, nine naked men brought him each nine sticks from nine different trees – oak and elm and ash, willow and alder and yew, hazel and apple and rowan. They piled the sticks in a cone, and with a good deal of blowing by the Setanta they were able to start a real fire. Then all the men rushed to pile on the wood, so that they all had a hand in the blaze. When there was a good roaring pyre, the Setanta added a handful of straw, and immediately the Northern men piled on damp straw and green leaves, until a pillar of white smoke rose high in the air, to tell all Ireland that there was a new champion come to challenge the High King at Tara, and that he had kindled his own Beltain Fire.

Then, and only then, did the Setanta accept food and we ate too. Madoc, seeing the smoke, brought the ship in and beached her, and his crew rigged tackle to swing out the bundles of weapons. Then the Northern men came around and received their arms from the Setanta himself, to each man a sword, and to the more favoured a helmet or a mail coat or a shield, and to the luckiest all three.

But while this was going on, other things were being hoisted out, wheels and chariot bodies and poles. For this was the ruler of the battlefield in the Island of the Blessed, and if the King of the North had none of these, then he could not hope to face any other king in battle. Heilyn called round him the smiths and the carpenters among the Northern men, and set them to work assembling the chariots. I watched. The wheels were as high as a man's waist, not the high frail wheels you see on the chariots in the Games. And while we fix tyres on our wheels in sections, nailed on to the rim, the tyres of these wheels were made in one piece of iron, jointless, and shrunk in some magical fashion which nobody would explain to me, so that they hold hard to the rim without nail or rivet or any other fastening.

They fixed a pair of wheels on to the first axle to hand, and drove the lynch pins into the felloes. Then they lowered a body on to the axle and joined body and axle with leather straps. The pole, likewise, was hooked on to the front of the body, so that the whole vehicle was most alarmingly flexible. I asked Heilyn, who spoke the British tongue, but with a vile accent, as did a number of the other men with him, who appeared to be Gauls, of the nation of the Sentantii:

'How many have we?'

He answered, without looking up from his task of fixing a pole into the first body:

'Well, there's nearly a hundred wheels, but mostly not in pairs, and forty-two bodies, and some in a dreadful state, and only twenty-six poles, but poles are easy to make, and I haven't counted the harness – I should say we will be lucky to have more than thirty when we finish. And the work in putting them together – you know, they were all made originally by a group of double-jointed Scythian dwarves that old King Brutus bought specially for the job, and unless we can find some more of the same breed, and it's expensive they come too, in any slave market, then it's not much of a success we will be making of this.'

I left him, and returned to the Setanta, who had paused in his rearmament programme.

'What will we do for horses? I can't see any.'

'Indeed, and isn't it getting them we will be now? Wasn't it in skin boats that those fine boys were coming down from the North, and how would you be carrying a horse in one of them?'

It was true enough, and now that everyone was armed, and it left great heaps of weapons and armour over, little groups of the Northern men were drifting off in all directions. Heilyn went on assembling his chariots, and all the day long more parties of unarmed men came straggling in asking for swords. Before noon, we could see other columns of smoke to answer ours, for we were on the seaward edge of a great plain.

By evening, the men were returning in their little groups, not just men, now, but warriors, for their new swords were blooded and some of them were wounded. One or two were left behind dead and many more dead drunk, and these also were dead in truth before the dawn.

They brought us back the horses, all right, plenty of them, because we had landed on the horse pastures of the High King, and we were able to take the pick of his herds where they grazed. Not that the pick was very wonderful. None of them was big enough to carry a man. This is why the Irish have to use them in chariots, because any beast, however puny, will pull a cart. There is something in the air of Ireland which prevents any horse from growing to its full size. They will never be able to breed a horse in all Ireland that will carry a man on its back.

They didn't only bring the horses. They had cattle, dozens of them, to be roasted at the fire that the Setanta had kindled, and others we had lit from it. We must have cut down half the woods of the province before we moved on. And they had mead, too, by the gallon, because they had robbed the village where the High King's horse-herders lived, and burnt it, and thus lit the whole land in a Beltain fire such as no one had expected.

Yes, that was a Beltain night to be remembered. The Setanta had returned after … how many years of exile? One year, said some of the Barbarians, and three years, said others. Before I left Ireland I heard songs that put it at seven years. However long it had been, the Northerners were glad to see him again, and made it clear that he was even more welcome than their brothers and cousins who had gone to join him overseas and were now returned with him. Now I could see that about half the Fianna were real Irishmen, out of Ulster, but the rest were strangers, Gauls it seemed. They, and I, received dark and suspicious looks from the newly arrived Irish, straggling in by threes and fours to demand their weapons.

This is what Pryderi would like, I thought. Instead of creeping from a little boat in the very shadow of his conquerors, to land from a great ship on a beach, and be surrounded by stalwart, obedient, faithful warriors, so that he could give each one his arms with a lordly gesture. No wonder Pryderi was jealous of the Setanta. This, to him, was the true place of a king, and his true work, raising an army for a great battle.

All through the night, the Northerners came streaming in, drawn by the light of the fires and by the smell of the meat as much as by the glint of the iron and the skirl of the whetstones, and by the screams of the women dragged from the horse-herders' village as they were mauled and raped and passed from man to man. Other women came in, too, of their own accord, as they always do when an army camps for the night. The Setanta, always a gentleman, had four of the younger ones passed in to the ship as a gesture of appreciation.

All in all, I thought at sunset, it was not a bad day's work. Five or six hundred men, all armed, and thirteen chariots ready to use, and horses for them, and food for us all for a month if anyone would take the trouble to store it and issue it, not bad, I thought, not bad at all, for one day. For one day, the day that the Setanta began his war of conquest of the Queen of the West and of the High King of all Ireland, that would set all Ireland in a blaze of quarrels and disunity. Not bad, even if no one in the island knew it yet, for the first day of the Roman Conquest of Ireland. Two months now to set the pot a-boiling, and then the seas would be calm enough for the clumsy galleys the legions built, calm enough even for those to bring the Army across the wide salt sea, first the Second, and then the Twentieth in support, and four regiments of cavalry, big men sitting on big horses, that would settle the business of any chariots that survived the coming battles of Irish against Irish. But this would be later. Let the war come first.

When it was dawn, I saw we had the beginnings of a real army, two thousand men or more. The supply of swords and shields had long given out: the latest comers were given spear heads and told to go away and cut their own shafts. When the tide rose and the ship floated, I waved Madoc out to sea. Now, I was alone in Ireland, as far as anyone to talk to was concerned, alone amid these howling savages. In Londinium, the Setanta had merely looked a bit wild. Here, in the middle of a great crowd of men dressed exactly like him, and he now as dirty, with a winter in the hills, as the worst of them, he looked at once both horrifying and commonplace. Looking around, I could believe all the tales I had heard in Britain of the Irish cooking their enemies in cauldrons to suck their valour from their marrow bones, and carrying the heads around their necks for years, till they rotted on the string.

Of course, the lack of communication could soon be remedied. I went to the Setanta.

'I want a woman. Next girl you catch, a young one, I want her.'

'Have one of these,' he said, magnanimously. 'Why didn't you join in last night?'

I looked at the huddle of weeping, bleeding, naked bodies. This, I thought, is what Pryderi would want, this is what the other island was like before the conquest, when every king was as good as any other king, and any man as good as his master if only he were strong enough. But the legions would settle that; as brutal perhaps in the first months, but in five years there would be roads all across the land, and inns by them, and even Rhiannon could ride unguarded and unharmed wherever she liked. And, I swore it, if Rhiannon had been treated one-tenth as badly as these women, then there was not a man in the south that I would leave alive, I would not grant one his life, no, not for all the Gold in Ireland. But now I replied to the Setanta, as casually as I could:

'No, thank *you*. They've been well used, too well used, over-used I should say. Anybody may have been tramping about there. I want something ... how shall I put it? I want something a bit cleaner and fresher.'

The Setanta called over our boat companion, Callum, who seemed to have a great following of his own, and translated to him, and I dangled a few links of Gold chain before his eyes. He was going off to forage anyway, and even if he had farther to go than the day before he was back not long after noon with horses and cattle, and half a dozen likely wenches to choose from. I picked the cleanest, to the accompaniment of a good deal of cheering and jeering from the warriors, and after a few days' hard work – and it went as hard for me as for her – I could make out a great deal of what they were talking about, though I never got as far as being able to make poetry in Irish, as I had almost done in the British tongue. The two languages were not all that different, after all. The grammar was almost the same, only most of the words were strange. When I could understand what the warriors were jeering and could jeer back, I was satisfied, and I let her go off to some of the best jeerers, and she could assure them that at least some of what they said was true, and the rest false.

After we had been there a week I began to get impatient. I had nothing to do, except sit still and learn Irish and watch them put together more chariots – we had nearly forty in the end. I also watched them training the horses. They had to be taught to run when they were told, and stop when they were told, and stand still whatever happened around them. One advantage of where we had landed was that some of the horses had been trained already. But there weren't many of the men who had been in a chariot before, and so we had to find a number of the lightest who could learn to drive. This was a thankless task, because you had one driver and one warrior in the chariot. The driver had to control the horses and satisfy his master, and if anything went wrong it was the driver's fault, and if there was success it was due to the warrior. And the driver had no way of defending himself. I thought that killing the driver was the easiest way of stopping a chariot, but the Irishmen assured me that wasn't the way to go to war at all. Noblemen fought noblemen, and left the drivers out of it.

We had to train a dozen horses, at least, for each chariot, since no horse could charge more than once in a day. And a number of the younger men were as unskilled as the horses, and had to learn how to hold a sword or a spear or an axe or whatever else they had been lucky enough to get. But apart from this, we did, effectively, nothing, except to eat up the country. After a week I went to the Setanta and asked him:

'What are we waiting for?'

'We are waiting for the High King. What else would we be waiting for?'

'Waiting for the High King to do what?'

'To come to Tara, of course.'

'What? Isn't he at Tara?'

'And why should he be now at Tara, seeing that it is neither the Feast of Tara, that they hold every seventh year at Samain, and it will be held again this winter. Nor is it the feast of his consecration as High King, for that was years ago, and it is ourselves will hold it, I am telling you.'

'How far are we from Tara?'

'Perhaps twenty Roman miles.'

'Then – if the High King is not at Tara, why do we not just march there?'

'What? Without a battle?'

I looked at him. I could not help saying what I did. It was in my interest to see a battle, to see as many battles as possible in the coming two months, and yet – something in me made me speak, made me want to show him how wrong his actions were, how absurd his manner of thinking, how – I could not contain myself.

'Battle? Why do you Barbarians always want to fight battles? Battle is the last resort of politics, to use when all other ways are barred. Battle is waste: waste is effort, waste of health, waste of blood. Why fight at all if you can get what you want by any other means? Speed is all we have. We could make a quick rush to Tara now, could have done any time the last week, and make you High King, or your uncle, or anyone you choose. As for the present High King, we can send one or two of your Northerners to assassinate him under pretence of making their surrender, or better still, we could bribe his bodyguard to murder him privately. So all the waste could be saved.'

The Setanta looked at me as if I were a child.

'Oh, you merchants. Why is it always only the end you look at, and never the means? It is how a thing is done that is important, not only what is done. Whoever is to be High King, he must show it, not by walking into Tara in the dark, but by killing his rival before the eyes of all the Island. If we shed no blood, no one will believe we rule.'

This is the way of the Barbarians. I knew he would never rule, not with all the four armies of Ireland broken against each other, and the legions wading ashore and the Eagles flying over Tara. That he did not know. He went on:

'But if it is any comfort to you, tomorrow the High King will indeed be at Tara, and we will be going that way too, and the day after that we will fight him, and the armies of the West and of the South.'

You'll fight him, I thought, not me. I'm not going into any mélée with only one eye. Nevertheless, while the others sharpened their swords, I honed the edge of my axe. You never know.

Chapter Three

Next day the Army marched. Our troops had come down from the North in skin boats, or by foot along paths that clung close to the sound of the breaking wave, to steal the well-broken horses and come at the High King from a direction he did not expect. Now, therefore, we marched north of west, to Tara.

We must have been five thousand strong, all told, and we covered a great square of country. For besides the men, we had the cattle we had stolen in the country round about, and the horses, and droves of swine, and all the women we had stolen as well, and who now wouldn't be left behind, after the way of women in a land at war, and their children came, and children who didn't belong to anyone who would own them now, but who had to come with the Army because there was no other way for them to beg a few scraps to eat.

We trampled over the grass of May and left it a great scar of mud, because it rained the day we marched, as one might expect, after weeks of dry weather. We strewed the countryside with half-gnawed bones and worn-out shoes, piles of ordure and dead babies and all the other litter an army leaves behind. This, I thought, is what Pryderi would like to see again in the Island of the Mighty: I wish he were here to see it now.

The chariots had been painted in gaudy colours, and hung about with bronze and silver bells, and charms of all kinds, in place of what they usually hung on them. For the journey, the colours were covered against the dust with sheets of coarse cloth. And men pulled them, because it was important that the precious horses should not be tired out or cast shoes or break legs before the battle.

We covered about fifteen miles in the day, and when we halted we were, they told me, in sight of Tara, but there was never a city

I could see where they pointed, only a few scattered huts between me and the distant hills where the sun was setting. But what I could see only too well, and see better in the dark, was the long line of fires that answered our own. From our farthest right to our farthest left the fires shone hard and bright in the clear dry air, for the hard east wind now blew the rain away. I could see clear and harsh the figures of men who passed between us and the flames. So we lit our own fires, and we made our force look bigger, as I was sure the High King had done, by lighting two fires for every man and a fire for every woman.

We cut down a forest to feed our fires, and we slaughtered all our cattle, so that every man could have the hero's portion, the thigh, to eat, and the rest we threw away as not juicy enough. The women stuffed themselves on what was left and then the straggling children, and the dogs quarrelled over the bones, and the mangy wolves crept out of the thickets and scavenged at the edges of the camp, and wished it were the next evening, because they knew, they knew.

There was mead enough for every man to get drunk, and stay drunk till Doomsday, as indeed a man will if he thinks Doomsday is tomorrow. So get drunk they did, all of them, before midnight. I went to the Setanta, who was still sober enough to speak, and I suggested that he should get a line of pickets out, in case the High King tried to rush us in the dark. He laughed at me. The Irish never do such things, he told me. They have no sense of prudence at all. Now you or I, if we had an enemy, would have used some intelligence when he left himself vulnerable, would ambush him with a knife in the dark, or put an arrow in his back in a narrow way, or burn his house over his head – or safer, when he was out of it. But the Irish believe in meeting their foes face to face. No, said the Setanta, there was no need to be afraid of anything.

I did not agree. I looked for Heilyn, or Callum, or any of the men who had come with us in the ship, but they were not to be found. Drunk, somewhere, I thought. Will there be no sentry in the night over all this army of the North? No, none but I.

I remembered how our army lay. Before us there was a wide level plain. It is only on such ground that you can fight in chariots.

469

About midway along our front was a mound, a burial mound of the men of old. On our right, there was a thicket, and between the mound and the thicket was an area of scrub willow, knee high or higher. Our left flank was quite open.

I moved through the host, my sealskin cloak open to show my mail coat, one eye black and one glowing red, ruby red. Nobody was sober enough to ask what I was doing, or to deny me anything. From one group I took a jug of bull's blood, hot and steaming from the heart, and from another I had a jar of mead. In a bowl I put the fat from around a bull's kidneys, and the thigh of a porker. These I balanced on my shield, a round bronze shield, enamelled, once set with garnets. I balanced the shield on one hand, and in the other I had a black cock.

I turned my back on the host of Ulster, and I walked towards the host of the High King. I went over the open ground in the dark, and there was not the least silver of moon nor any star to be seen; yet I did not step into a molehill, nor trip over a drunken sleeper nor an amorous one.

I came to the top of the mound, a low mound raised perhaps five or six feet above the level of the plain. I set down the tray. I took from my bag a knife, a bronze knife, broad of blade, and I began to dig. I knew where. It was an old grave and much honoured, the grave of one of the long dead kings of the country, and full, if only I had had the courage to open it, of Gold and jewels. But I found the funnel between the stones that led down to the mouth of the King. First into the funnel I poured the bull's blood, hot and still steaming, full of life and strength, and after that the mead, full of the warmth of the sun and the busy stirring of the bees. Then I offered the fat and the meat, and I put them into the hole, that the waking Dead might eat and be filled, and not hunger after me. Last of all I took the morse that fastened my cloak, a Golden pin, Indian Gold, not Irish, and I threw it into the hole. Phryne gave it to me. Phryne was dead. I gave it back to the dead. I did not fill in the hole.

I stood on the mound that led to the land of the dead, the grave mound that all the British and all the Irish believe is a gate to the Land Below, where we who live may meet those who are dead and those who yet may live. I had paid my private debt to

Those Below. That would have whetted their appetites. Now I would show them how to feast, now I would draw out life for them. Now they would have a feast indeed.

I stood on the mound in the blackness, and I looked toward the host of the High King, where the fires died uncovered and the filth of men was poured out on the earth, and I saw that they were ready. And I took the High King and all his host, and I devoted them to the Gods Below, I sacrificed them to the dead who sought their lives. I sang in the ancient tongue the rite of the Gods Below, that our ancestors first brought over the mountains out of the plain, when Greek and Trojan, Persian and Egyptian were one nation. I asked the questions, and I answered them too, for want of anyone to answer them to me.

'And you came to the crossing of the river, and what found you there?' I asked myself, and I answered in the dark:

'Waters swift to the knee, waters cold to the belly, waters bitter over the head.'

The fires opposite me guttered and died as if the waters indeed rose over them. The host of the High King lay down drunk to sleep, and they dreamed: oh, yes, they dreamed. Their dreams did them no good.

'And you came to the crest of the mountain, and what found you there?' I chanted, as I have chanted it before in the Temple of the Old city. And I sang the response, as I have sung it to my Father, and as my nephews have, and my son will sing to me:

'I found the heart out of the chest, and the liver out of the trunk.'

The darkness was thick enough to touch, thick enough to feel. This was a darkness that I called upon myself, a darkness that felt and thought and knew. With this darkness I cursed the host of the High King. The black cock lay still at my feet looking at the Holy Line. I asked:

'And you came to the gate of the pass, and what found you there?'

And who was it, then, that answered:

'I found the flesh of a thigh, and the marrow of a bone.'

For Those Below now stood beside me on the mound. First came those who had gone below and returned, before they died for ever. Ulysses and Aeneas, who spoke with the dead across the stream, my kinsmen both – the same blood ran in our veins and one flesh, living and dead, we stood upon the mound.

Next, but farther off, stood Orpheus who went below to seek his love, and lost her again, through love, and Gilgamesh, who was before him, and Persephone who stands half of every year before the throne below, and Pwyll the Old, Pryderi's forefather, who ruled a year in Hell in Arawn's place. They all came, and stood beside me on the mound. They held up my arms, and with me cursed the host of the High King.

To bring the friendly dead was one thing. To bring the just Gods was another, those who favour no man, who cannot be persuaded. Thoth and Adeimantus. But all the night I stood upon the mound in the cold dark, the worst May frost in a man's life, and the sweat upon my skin froze within my clothes. I sang the words I may not here repeat in the language none may know I speak, and at last the great Judges of the Dead stood beside me to judge the High King and all the host and condemn them for all the evil they had done. But they judged the host of the North, also, and they judged me. But that I did not know.

Last I sang up the named and the nameless Gods Below, the gods who do not care for justice or for right or for any man, and it is these gods above all who rule the world from their place below, rule the Sun and the Earth and all the other gods. They hate all things living, and they seek only to draw us down to themselves and suck out our life. These are the gods that no man worships, but the gods do: that men and gods fear, and will never tell their fear. They feed on souls. I promised them food in plenty.

And at last, they too came to me on the mound, and the ice crackled in my eyebrows as they came past. It was the last frost of a mild winter, and it blasted all the fruit blossom throughout Ireland, so that there was no cider pressed that year. And who ever before knew of frost out of a starless sky?

There came a gleam of light over my right shoulder, and I heard a rustling and a scraping before me. The light became stronger, and the cloud faded from the sky, and at last the sun shone full over the horizon behind me, and all the cocks of Ireland crew, as they had done under the Glass Mountain on Mid-winter's eve. Before the cock at my feet could crow, I bit off his head with my teeth, and I tossed the struggling body into the hole in the mound. And then those in front of me saw and heard the head in my hands crow louder than ever a whole bird sang. And then the head too I threw into the hole, and I pushed the earth back over it with my feet.

Behind me, I knew, there lay the host of the North in a drunken sleep. They would not stir for all the ghosts of the world. But in front of me, men came gently forward over the frost-white grass. The High King was a wise man, wise as I, and a worthy enemy, for he knew what war was about. He had thought, as I thought, that a determined rush by a few determined men would settle the matter for good and all, and so it would have done. If the Setanta were to die, who would stand here?

There were about two hundred of them, young men and strong, the High King's household troops. They came steadily and stealthily on, looking up at me as I stood before them on the mound, my arms stretched in prayer, so that they knew well enough what I was about. I sang my hymns to the Gods Below as loudly as I had done throughout the night, and yet they took no notice of me, they did not so much as throw a spear. They would see to me later.

But when they were well within a spear's cast from me, when their line stretched out to lap round the mound on both sides – then I stopped singing, and I dropped my arms. Their whole line stopped as if they saw another line rise up from the ground to meet them. And so they did. Had I not worked all night for it?

Each man of the household looked at the line that rose before him, and each man cowered behind his painted shield. Each man looked into the face of the man who stood against him, a sword's reach before him, shield to shield. And each man saw himself not as he was, as he might see his image in a pool, or even in a mirror if any man could cast and polish a sheet of bronze large enough to reflect a whole man. No, each man saw himself as he would end. This man saw his own ribs thrust up and out from a spear stabbing from the ground, and that one saw his own gut pour out on the earth from a slashing sword. Men saw their own skulls smashed by axe blows, their eyeballs hanging down on their cheeks, and their brains grey in their hair. They saw their faces shorn away, they saw severed arms held in good arms, they saw themselves try to hop on one leg and the stump of a thigh.

Now many a man, and a brave man too, is sickened by the sight and smell of his own blood steaming on his arm, or at seeing a limb of his, or even a finger, warm on the ground. But hot blood is one thing. Stale blood is another. The High King's household did not see themselves as they would be that night, fresh dead. They saw themselves as they would be in a week ahead. The clay of the grave clotted on their rusted mail, those that had not been rudely stripped. Their rings were torn from their fingers and their ears. Their clothing hung in stinking rags. Maggots teemed in their gaping wounds. Worms writhed in their empty eye-sockets, those that still had their heads. Their bellies swelled, and their navels showed the green spot of corruption. The stench of the grave hung like a curtain before them. And worst of all, it was not only the edge of the iron that had emptied those eye-sockets or laid bare the teeth within the cheek, or cracked the marrowbones. The wolves howled in the woods, and the crows hung in great cawing crowds above us and filled the trees. The household of the High King looked at themselves, and they knew themselves by their painted shields, and by their garments, what was left, and by the scars on their bodies. They looked at themselves, and they did not stay to look twice.

If I then had had a hundred men ready to follow, there would have been no battle that day. The household rushed back through the ranks of their own army, and spread the tale of terror, and not a man of them struck a blow in the battle that day, though all of them died before the sun set.

Then the crows rose from the grass and circled above us, and from the South and the East there came in the kite and the buzzard, the souls of those who have done evil and are condemned now to live on carrion. And there was only one who could have sent the birds, and it was for her that I did battle. I would not have raised Those Below on the mound for all the Gold in Ireland: I did it because only thus could I conquer all the land and find the mistress of the birds, the Lady of Those Below. And with Rhiannon's birds, my own wolves came howling on the

474

flanks. All the birds and beasts were working their way towards the rear of the High King's army, so as to have a shorter way to go for their dinner. And the host of the West saw this, and it did not make them more eager to fight.

The noise and clatter of all this, the cawing of the birds, the shouts of terrified men, a dawn chorus of a kind we seldom hear, woke all our army as nothing else could have done. There was a great shouting and blowing of horns, and in less time that it would take a stammering man who was not very sure of his arithmetic to count to a couple of thousand or so, they had formed a line of sorts, but well behind me, leaving me alone on the mound. And there I stayed.

Our warriors did not look very well, most of them. That is one reason why Barbarians fight so savagely. Usually they have been drunk the night before, and there is nothing like a raging headache to put venom into your sword strokes. Or so they tell me. I don't have headaches. Going into a fight drunk is quite another thing. I'll fight a drunken man any day, but a man who is sobering up – never!

The line of foot soldiers was not very straight or very steady, I looked for the men who had come in the ship, especially for Heilyn and the Gauls, but they were nowhere to be seen. I decided that they had deserted, as Barbarians often do, and mercenaries usually do, before a battle. But, if our army had formed a line, so had the High King's, and what a line. It overlapped ours at both ends, not because there were many more men in it than ours, but because their men were spreading out so as to have room to run away, while ours, having nowhere to run to, were clinging together for warmth. But that was the enemy's first line, and there were three more of the same strength behind that.

Later they made songs about that day which claimed that we were outnumbered by twenty or thirty to one. It always feels like that, even if they're only three to two, because all the spare men go loose and you never know where they're going to come from next. At my best count, they were four to one at most, and fifty chariots to our forty, and we were better off for chariots because we had all the trained horses. Men were running about, pulling off the covers to show the painted sides, and harnessing the horses and fitting the scythe blades to the sides – not to the wheels, of course – which discourage anyone from getting close enough in to hamstring the horses. Of course, someone always tries it and ends up in seventeen pieces.

The few chariots we had ready were already out in front of the foot, and to my surprise they were singing the old song we so often hear at the Circus before a race, when the charioteers are trying to get their spirits up. The words were a reasonable translation of what we are used to:

> Throw an obol on the grass,
> Save a Charioteer's ass:
> Yarahoo-oo …! Yarahoo!!
> Throw an obol on the grass and be saved.

These were nothing like the racing chariots you bet on, though. They had two men, one small and light to drive, and the other big and strong to do the fighting. It was he who needed the big shield, to cover him from shoulder to calf – his shins were behind the low wicker sides. He had a long-edged sword for slashing at anyone who got near enough, though the scythe blades made sure that nobody did, so he had for his main weapon a bundle of javelins. If you have ever tried throwing a spear from a moving chariot, you will realise that the vehicle's main effect is on morale. The charioteers were thinking of their own morale; they sang:

> Riding by the Liffey,
> Hear the warrior wail,
> Save me, Chieftain, save me,
> All Connaught's on my tail.
> Throw an obol to the sky.
> Why should charioteers die?
> Yarahoo …! Yarahoo!!
> Throw an obol in the sky and be saved.

And all our line of foot screamed, 'Yarahoo!!' to keep up their spirits, and they needed it, with the High King's chariots riding out in front of his line, and getting their dressing straight, no fuss, no sweat, very careful, as if they were riding in a triumph, not going into action.

A fine sight it is, a line of chariots, and lucky you are that you will never see it the way I saw it, coming on at you at the trot, very earnest and deadly and full of all the confidence in the world. There I stood on the mound, and I could see the line of them rolling on, the hooves very quiet in the ground soft still after the previous day's rain. They were spreading out on my right and my left and obviously going to lap around me on either side.

The High King's chariots covered the half-mile between the two hosts quite slowly, when you consider they were all eager to fight, but they were saving their horses for that last dash, when you can let them strain as they will against the rope loops about their necks and it does not matter if they half-strangle themselves now. Our little group, twenty ready now against their fifty, came forward in a bunch on our left. They hoped there at least to stop the enemy curling round to come against our foot from the flank. They were very steady, waiting to be loosed at the last moment in a spoiling death ride in the hope of slowing the enemy down before they crashed into our infantry. Some of the latter were already drifting away: the others were none too steady.

Then suddenly, out of the willow scrub on my right, a group of men stood up, shouting and screaming some kind of challenge, mother naked most of them, except for their swords and helmets. Oh, yes, I knew who these were. I did not only recognise Heilyn and Callum, my fellow rowers, and all the other men from the ship: these, I knew, were the Gesatae that Caesar and Tacitus tell us about, warriors vowed to death and so fighting with no protection, to ensure it comes. But an opponent who is not defending himself, but intent on killing you, is very hard to deal with, and if you can kill one of them, then it is clear that you are a hero yourself. So it was no wonder that the chariot line carried out a manoeuvre which does not sound impressive till you try it, remembering now it was being done at the canter, and the whole squadron moving faster and faster, with each warrior wanting to be the first to draw blood and every driver wanting to satisfy him. The whole line of fifty chariots changed front half-left and swept towards the right of the mound, leaving our

477

chariots facing nothing and all our infantry on the right exposed to the full fury of the charge which twenty Gesatae would do nothing to halt, however hard they died.

And then, as the first chariots, because the line was ragged now and had lost its dressing, entered the scrub of dwarf willow, one of them tipped over on a broken wheel, and the horse of another fell, and a third swerved hard left and crashed into a fourth. And into the jumble of smashed chariots the rest hurtled, and in the twinkling of an eye the scrub was full of broken wheels and snapped poles, of kicking horses rolling on their backs tangled in their harnesses, and men trying to get free and throwing down their swords and shields as they dodged the flailing hooves. And the Gesatae were among them at once, and a hundred or more of the foot from our line. In that moment, whatever happened later, the battle was won, and it was Heilyn who had done it, Heilyn and the Gauls from the ship, and Callum the Hairy, the only Irishman among them. They had stretched ropes among the scrub, to trip the horses, and thrown down spikes to hurt their feet, and dug deep holes to break their legs, and scattered big stones to break the chariot wheels. Like all battles, it was won the night before by men who thought: I was not the only sober man that night, nor the only sleepless one.

The few chariots that survived went west like the wind, the drivers urging on the horses in terror. Into the ranks of the High King's army they swept, unstoppable, and before they could be slowed down they had caused as much damage as if they had been enemies, not friends in distress. They punched a wide hole in the line, and now it was the Westerners who were beginning to slip away. The crows cawed impatiently. The Gods Below had begun to taste their feast. They would not rest, now, till they had had their fill of lives. There were few men on that field who saw Beltain again. Few men on either side.

I waited for our own chariots, and now there were thirty of them, to charge in their turn, but they hesitated. Out from the turmoil of the High King's line came a single chariot. I looked at it with the keen sight of the one-eyed man. It was the High King himself, there was no doubt of it. Tall in his chariot, with his long black hair trailing behind him in the wind from beneath his shining helm, Gold

478

gleaming on his neck and wrists, his mail flashing where it caught the sun, his great bronze shield shining red, he came charging alone towards us, and our chariots hung waiting there. Out from our line to meet him rode the Setanta, the Champion of the North.

It was like something out of Homer, and I saw it all from where I stood on the mound. The two chariots rolled on towards each other. The men in the lines were shouting and screaming. I had half a mind to try and get back to start some betting going, but then I reflected, if the North lost who would there be to pay me?

Round and round the mound the chariots raced, in opposite directions, the Setanta with the sun, the High King widdershins. Each driver kept the other on his left as they passed twice on each circuit. Twice on each circuit they passed and each time they passed the warriors threw their spears. Five times the spears were cast, and five times both missed.

Then, on the sixth pass, each man threw his last spear. I was watching the Setanta, and as the horses nearly collided and then swerved violently apart, I saw him stagger as a spear bit deep into his shoulder. I followed him on, but when I looked back to the High King, I saw that his driver was spitted, and he fell forward over the front of the chariot among the horses' feet. The beasts kicked and stumbled, and the chariot overturned, and the High King of all Ireland rolled in the dust.

In the time it takes to tell, the Setanta's chariot was all the way around the mound again, and when he saw the wreck, the Setanta clapped his driver on the back, and the little man pulled up the horses in their own length, and that takes strength. The Setanta leapt down, pulling out the spear and throwing it away, any way; it nearly skewered *me*.

The Setanta was white with passion, and his hair, stiffened and streaked with dye and grease and whitewash, stuck out behind him like a horse's mane. The veins were big on his forehead, his eyes almost started out of his head, his mouth was distorted into that square shape you see on the statues of the Furies, and his limbs were flailing like an octopus's: you'd have sworn there was never a bone in his body. Blood was running down his arm, but if he was in pain, the High King was worse. *He* was half stunned still from his fall, but he groped for his sword

479

and shield on the ground, and then he came to his feet. But as soon as he put his weight on his left ankle, it gave under him, for he must have twisted it hitting the ground all in a bundle as he had. He staggered again, trying to hop on his right leg, and the Setanta was on him at once smashing his shield into the King's face, and hacking and chopping at him as he went down.

The King squirmed on the soft grass, all cut up with hooves and already splashed with the Setanta's blood. The Setanta danced over him, screaming like a wild thing, and hacking and stabbing at him aimlessly, tearing through leather and mail, almost for the mere sake of hurting the man. But this man could not be hurt any more. The body turned into a bloody mess as the Setanta hit it again and again, with edge and with point, in full view of both armies, who all stood still and silent as the grave. Even the crows had ceased to caw.

At last, the Setanta bent down and cut once, carefully. He stood up, holding the High King's head, all gashed and bleeding, and took it to his chariot and tied it by the long black hair to the pole. Why else does a warrior wear his hair so long? While this had been going on, the driver had taken no notice but had calmly changed the horses. The Setanta stepped again into his chariot. And then all his army shouted, and for the first time I heard his name. He was safe now, no witchcraft could hurt him, I could hear it and remember it, as they all bellowed:

'Cuchullain! Hero of the North, Cuchullain!'

The charioteers were now all in line, all forty of them. They began to sing:

> Throw a neckplate or a pin,
> Save a charioteer's skin.
> Yarahoo …! Yarahoo!!
> Throw the Gods Below a pin, and be saved.

The chariot line began to move forward, Cuchullain the Champion of Ulster in the centre, slowly at first. The whole area where they had waited sparkled as if covered with dew. Every man had indeed thrown down some jewel of Gold or silver, a cloak-pin or a kilt-pin, a necklace or an armlet, jewelled and shining, as an earnest for his safe return.

Chapter Four

There wasn't much of a battle, if you are thinking of a civilised battle, where two armies clash in a long line of fighting men, pushing and striking at each other, till one line goes back and back, dwindling and shrinking and the last of them die where they are because they have nowhere that their honour will allow them to go back to any more. In Barbarians' wars, the real business of a battle is over beforehand. By some means or other, a duel between witches or between leaders, one side is convinced by the other that it has lost, before ever a blow is struck by the rank and file. Then the losing side runs away, and very sensibly too. Their enemies run after them and kill all they can catch, and that is not many. Most men who die in battle are struck in the back. Any man who is willing to turn and fight when he has to will be let alone.

Before our chariots were within spear throw of the army of the West, their front line broke and ran, and so did the support lines when they saw there was no protection in front of them. The chariots ran into the shapeless mob and right through them. The scythe blades caught a few men, and the warriors in the chariots stabbed as far as their spears would reach and occasionally threw them at a tempting target if it stood still, but not often because they were afraid of running out of spears. Our foot followed them, almost as much of a mob as the defeated enemy, but going more slowly as soon as they reached where the front line had been, because they kept on bending down to pick up weapons thrown away, and to rob the few bodies. As this undisciplined mass came level with the mound, they drew me with them, waving my axe. Such is the power of a crowd.

I found myself running shoulder to shoulder with Heilyn, who had, sensibly, not stayed naked any longer than it had taken to tempt the chariots against him. I looked at him through the tangle of hair and whiskers and the grease of a winter in the hills. After a few paces, I said to him in Greek:

'Are we running all the way? This mail is heavy.'

'Slow down, then,' replied Aristarchos. We did, and watched both armies disappearing into the distance. We paused to look at the body of the High King. He still had all his jewels: Cuchullain would return to strip him later. His sword lay near him. I looked at that. The weapons we had brought from Britain in the ship had been old-fashioned, native work a century old. This sword was far older in design, whoever had made it, and whenever. It was long and two-edged, pointless or hardly pointed, the sides running parallel almost down to the tip. The hilt was topped by a pommel of Gold, a Golden ball through which the iron tang protruded, to be turned over and hammered down again. The iron, though, was poor, not even as good as Roman, let alone as good as the fine metal the Germans use. Any good iron in the islands, I had been told, was kept for chariot tyres. The High King had fallen at the last on his sword: the blade bent under his weight.

I might have taken a few souvenirs, for Cuchullian owed them to me, but old women were already coming out to crouch around the body, old women in dusty black, their white hair streaming down their blacks, with the lice moving in it like a ceaseless wave. They sang the death song, in a high reedy tune, the tune that the witches had sung to us on the sea shore. I watched them a little: then I thought, 'Even Rhiannon will come to this'. And it was a death song I too had sung all night on the mound. I left the women to the dead I had made.

Other corpses were scattered over the plain. This was no Cannae, but it was enough. All had been struck in the back. Most had been robbed of their weapons already, and some of their heads. Those men of the North who had not been armed out of the ship had gone into battle armed only with their thick cudgels pulled out of the hedge and with their knives. Now everyone had a sword, and there were shields and to spare, and even a few mail shirts cast off by those who felt that the time taken to strip was worth exchanging against the extra speed after it.

The crows were already busy on the dead. These souls of evil men found no famine for their wicked beaks. They could afford now to take the eyes alone, and be filled. The rest would be eaten soon enough. The wolves were slinking out of the woods on the edge of the rout, tearing at the men who lay, living or dead where the armies had passed. When night fell the mangy starving beasts would come further. I looked at my companion. We had both seen battlefields before. We had no need to rob: we had no wish to stay. I asked:

'Which way is Tara?'

'The way nobody is going,' Aristarchos answered, pointing a little north of west. 'I've never captured a city by myself.'

'No more have I,' I agreed. 'Do you think we could sack it? You might even get a mural crown.'

We turned half right and made for the cluster of huts a mile or so away. There was nobody to stop us. I stuck my axe through my belt. Aristarchos sheathed his sword. We slung our shields on our backs. He asked me, casually:

'How was Africanus when last seen?'

'Thriving. The ships should be nearly all ready by now. The Second will embark by the end of June, and the Twentieth will be here in August, weather permitting.'

'Splendid. Now we have scattered the armies of the West and South. By midsummer I shall have the army of the North spread over half the island, with concentration impossible. Before the end of the year, the whole island will be part of the Empire.'

'Yes,' I nodded. 'It will be this year in Tara for the Second, at last.'

We swaggered into Tara. Not alone. A dozen or so of the winded, or windier, footmen had fallen in behind us. Entry into Tara at the head even of this bedraggled little vanguard of a victorious army would have been impressive if only there had been a city for us to enter. When we came close the cluster of huts became a scattering of houses, spread over a mile of country, all mixed up with barrows and mounds and earthworks of doubtful purpose, middens and manure heaps and furnaces, smithies and fields of barley and vegetable plots, and animals grazing, pigs and cows, and dogs and children running everywhere.

There were a lot of people around, men and women too, most of them busy at one thing or another, weaving or beating iron or bronze, or chipping away at wood, and one or two bards, sitting with what looked a little like lyres but weren't, obviously practising their spontaneous improvisations for a feast to come. Our miserable little army killed the first two lads they came to, minding pigs, but all the other people around looked so shocked that they stopped killing at once and clung together in a little group and looked embarrassed.

Aristarchos and I went up to a large and comfortable woman who was boiling soup over an open fire.

'And a fine day it is indeed,' Aristarchos said to her, in a conversational manner.

'It is that: but it was raining it was yesterday, to be sure.' She straightened up and looked at us. 'And who was it that won, then?'

'Us, of course. The North.'

'Indeed. I was thinking, I was, that that was how it would be.' I wondered whether she had had a bet on it, but I remembered that the Irish are very little given to gambling, which was why the King of Leinster's Gesa must weigh so hard on him. She asked:

'And what was it became of the High King?'

'Cuchullain cut his head off.'

'Indeed, and improve him vastly I'm sure it would, for it was a face like a bladder of lard he had on him. And if he lost the battle and lived, then it would be dreadful bad luck for him for the rest of his life, and he might have lived for many years.'

The logic confused me. Still, there seemed method in it. I asked:

'Does this happen often?'

'Constantly. Isn't it the three High Kings we've had in the one year, and never a grain of sense among the three of them? And none of them properly consecrated, although when I think of it although the rite is so well known there is never a king that has followed it so exactly that there is arguing he can ever be that he is High King with no shadow of doubt. And when it does happen, it is a terrible time we have finding the horses, and it is white mares they have to be, pure white, every time.'

484

'You have to find the horses every time?' I didn't find it possible to believe what they told me about the way the High King wedded his kingdom, I still preferred to think of the bridal chase I had seen among the Britons.

'And who else would there to be doing it? Why, do we not live here rent free for that very purpose, to be finding the horses for the High King, and to be making the Feast of Tara for him, and to be forging his sword, and to be making his coffin if indeed there is enough of him left to need a coffin. Mind you, whenever there is a battle, there are usually one or two of us that do get killed, but it is by accident only and not through malice, and it is worth a little risk, you will agree, thinking of all the other advantages of living here.'

'Oh, yes, there must be great advantages in living here,' I agreed. These were quite a familiar people, slaves of the God, living around the Temple, and serving the Priest King, whoever happened to be Priest King for the time being. I asked:

'And where is it that the High King is living?'

'Why, 'tis in his own kingdom that he lives, and it is to Tara that he only comes on the Feast of Tara, and to the Hall of Tara that he and his warriors will go after the battle for the feast. And sure, it is there you will be wanting to go now, is it not?'

'And if it was wanting to go there we were, then which way is it we would be needing to go, now?' The rhythm of their language, even of their way of – no, not thought, a Barbarian cannot think, let us say of their pondering and puzzling – it was infectious. Besides, obviously nothing of any value was to be gained by staying here.

'Why, it is past the mound that the hall is. And if after the feast tonight there is nowhere to sleep that you are finding, then it is in my house that you are welcome to sleep the night.

'Oh, good!' Aristarchos and I both exclaimed together, and then we glared at each other because there is something about the air of the island that is very relaxing to both physique and morals, though it is a fine and keen edge it puts on wit and logic and understanding. But she went on:

'And it is my husband that will be very glad to meet you. That is Cullain over there at the smithy. The one bending horseshoes out of billets of cold iron.'

'It must be very strong teeth he is having,' I was moved to remark.

'Indeed, and it was a strong man he was in his prime,' was her answer. We bade her good day and walked on towards the mound, and round it to the hall. We both spoke together. I said:

'There ought to be some pickings of Gold and silver here, if no one has been here before.'

Simultaneously, Aristarchos remarked:

'I wonder if there will be anything to eat.'

We both laughed. Aristarchos said:

'There is the difference between the soldier and the merchant; you want something to sell, and I want food. But there is nothing to buy, and no one to sell to, and we neither of us had any breakfast.'

We soon caught up with our little band who had gone on in front while we had been talking to the woman. They were straggling forward in an irresolute way, looking about them like worshippers at Delphi, impressed by everything they see, from statues to horse droppings. We two took care only to speak Greek when they could not hear us. We led them round the mound and came to the Hall of Tara.

This hall was the biggest of its kind I had ever seen. It was of the usual British type, round but very big. The roof was held on circles of posts. There were seventeen posts in each circle, and there were nine circles one outside the other. We went in. The hall was empty. No Gold, no silver. Not even good wool cloth hung on the walls. Only the bare oak pillars and the mud-and-wattle walls and the rough thatch. Later we heard talk of pulling it down and rebuilding it in the new Roman style some of the Irish had seen overseas, with straight walls, but there was no thought of making the hall as it stood at all good to look at or comfortable.

Inside, there was a big fire in the centre, venting its smoke through a hole in the ceiling, and bales of hay and baulks of wood strewn around haphazard for people to sit on, around the fire and in the alcoves. Otherwise there was nothing. It was bare as a barn. There is something in the Irish character which forbids them to make their places of worship at all ornate or richly decorated.

486

Outside the hall, though, were big open fires, and men were roasting huge bloody carcases whole on spits. Others were baking bread of a kind, flat barley cakes on flat stones. Aristarchos went over and picked up a loaf and tore it in half. We stood and wolfed it, hot and fresh. Someone handed us a pot of barley beer, and we shared that too, swig and swig about. One of the cooks looked up and asked:

'And is it waiting for the feast you are, then?'

'And for what else would we be waiting?' Aristarchos answered. 'Would you not be wanting to know who it is that won, and who it is that will be feasting here?'

'And why should I worry my head about that? There's little difference to us, one king wins or the other king wins. And indeed, it is always the new king that it is that is winning.'

It was now a little after noon. Aristarchos and I took our bread and bear, and we lay on our backs on the side of the Mound of Tara, a great grave mound of the men of old that is the centre and the heart of Tara. We lay and we looked up into the dark blue clear sky, all flecked with the burning white clouds of May, with never a fleck of grey on them. The air was so clear, with never a trace of mist, it might have been at home.

And so I and Aristarchos were like two small boys again, let out from lessons, and with nothing to do but to lie and watch the clouds. We teased each other as boys do, in our childhood dialects, though we had never known each other as boys; he in clumsy Thracian, I in the purer Greek of the Old City, the best form of the Koine that every civilised man speaks. We pelted each other with the heads of the grasses, and we blew the first seeds of the dandelions in each other's faces, and we played guessing games with the petals of the daisies. And after a while even this intellectual exercise was too exhausting. We lay still and listened to the birds singing, and watched the sparrows come for the crumbs of the barley loaf. I remembered all the birds I had ever seen, and these birds that swarmed about on the Mound of Tara, they were bolder and they were more numerous than any other flock, and they were of all kinds, and it was as if Rhiannon again stood with us. But for no reason, there were two things I was certain of. First, that Rhiannon would not come to

487

me now, however many birds came winging to me from the countries of the dead, each singing, singing, to try to send some message of love and sorrow to those the soul had left behind, and frantic that no man could understand. And yet, a second thing came into my thought, and I was as certain too of this: that it was Rhiannon indeed who had sent these flocks about me in Tara, as a sign that neither in life nor in death would I ever be free of her to whom I was given, of her who was given to me.

And drowsier we grew, and even those thoughts melted in sleep. The afternoon lasted a thousand years, a thousand happy, happy years. This was the high peak of all our lives, for Aristarchos and myself. It was the high peak of all our time in Ireland, and never again would such achievements crown our dreams. This day we had fought a great battle and seen it won. We had taken the enemy's capital. The whole Island of the Blessed was at our feet. Blessed indeed were we in that day.

Chapter Five

Suddenly I was awake. The birds rose in a cloud above us, their singing that had charmed us to sleep, that singing sweeter than the song of women, changed to a frantic scolding of terrified creatures, souls that now remembered that it was true, that all was finished, that never again would they talk as humans, that henceforward they had no words to speak, only the twitter twitter of ghosts. The sun was westering and lower. I nudged Aristarchos awake. He followed me to kneel before the Druid who stood over us on the summit of the mound. He was old, an old, old man. His scanty hair was white and thin on his scalp. His skin was soft with the tenderness of age. The mistletoe on his breast was berryless. I thought back to things Taliesin had said, and I knew from that who it was who wore the leaf without the berry, and I trembled before him. I knew who this must be. I knew the name.

'Cathbad,' I said. 'You must be Cathbad.'

'Mannanan, who are not Mannanan' – the Awen was on him, on the greatest Druid of the Island of the Blessed. I could tell it from the light in his eyes, from the rhythmic chant in which he declaimed, not poetry, but prose—' Son of Lear who are not Son of Lear, Dark Son of the Bright Sun, Bright Star that light the stars below, I know who you have been, I know who you will be, and that you do not. Sorrow and trouble you will bring on the Island of the Blessed, but the whole blame is not at your door.

'Listen to me, then, Mannanan. Stay within the plain of Tara! Do not cross the river in the south, or the river in the north, or the great bog that lies to the west. Here in the plain of Tara I can keep your head for you by day, and by night it is the Gods Below who will see you safe in the dark, because it is the darkness that you serve now, who once served the Sun. But once you leave this

489

place, then neither man nor gods can save you, and your doom, and the blame for it, will lie on your own head.'

The Druid passed on. What he said had meaning and truth enough, but I laughed at his warning as I led Aristarchos into the hall. Once the legions came, how could the gods of the Irish harm me? If in this island I once burned incense before the bust of His Sacred Majesty, what could the spirits of the bogs and the rivers do?

I forgot it all as we entered the Hall of Tara. A horde of men sat about on the bales of straw and the tree trunks. Cuchullain the Setanta sat in the place of honour, looking south across the fire out of the door of the hall. The warriors from the chariots sat on his left hand and on his right in a circle around the fire facing it, and their drivers sat next to the fire, singeing themselves and keeping the heat off their masters. It is a thankless task to drive a chariot, and no work for a gentleman. But there was no place in the circle for Aristarchos or me, or for the hairy Callum or the other men who came ashore from the ship.

The villagers of Tara had stacked piles of wooden platters near the door, and we took one each and squeezed as near to Cuchullain as we could, and that was not very near. We only got into an alcove behind him. Nobody took very much notice of us or of the others of the Fianna, which annoyed me, and I began to think as little of Cuchullain as I had of the Legate of the Second Legion. And then I remembered what had happened to *him*, and I was happier.

The food was, let us say … different. The Britons eat what they grow, mutton almost entirely, with oat bread and beer brewed from wheat. They don't let principle interfere with their appetites except where goose is concerned. But the Irish have a fine idea of what is fitting for a noble to eat. The peasant may eat beef if he likes (while the Briton may drink milk, but when he kills a bull it is for the tallow, not the meat) and he may eat barley bread, and so does the noble most of the time, when he is at home and only being a herder himself with his clansmen. But when he is, so to speak, being an active noble, and going to war, or celebrating it, then he wants to eat in a manner fitting for a gentleman, as he thinks his father ate before they began to be

490

bothered with all this business of the tiresome care of cattle and crops. Then he eats, not what he has killed himself, since this would take up too much energy and time that would otherwise be better expended on eating, but on what he thinks would not be beneath his dignity to chase and kill himself.

The carcases they had been roasting outside on the spits, so big they were that they were not fully cooked yet, were deer. Not red deer, or fallow, but the great elks of the deep forests, almost all gone now in Britain but still roaming in plenty in the dark woods of Ireland, as they do in Germany. This is the beast that the great dogs, which are the only export of Ireland, are trained to bring down. So, at the feast, we ate venison, because tradition said that it was a dish that a noble might eat. Great lumps of the half-raw meat were dumped on our platters, and we sank our teeth into it and stuffed our mouths, and cut it off close to our lips, and chewed for dear life till we could breathe again. We washed it down with beer and all kinds of unnameable native drinks.

Somebody dropped on my platter what looked a bit like a boiled baby. Aristarchos tore off a leg and tried it.

'Badger,' he pronounced. He knew the taste all right, he said; a man who had seen active service like he had knew the taste of many strange dishes. This was the only special treatment I had that day: only I had a boiled badger given me, and Callum, and no one else. I did not know then why.

I stripped the badger carcase; not bad, but not good – two at a meal would be too much, you may like to know, if you are planning a party. And we finished a hare apiece, and I had a hedgehog baked in clay, so that his prickles came off, and a spit of roasted larks, hoping that Rhiannon would not hear about it, down there wherever she was in the South-East. And we had a bowl of stewed mushrooms between us, Aristarchos and I, and he looked a bit doubtful, but, I assured him, I knew my fungi, and besides, how could there be any harm in mushrooms in the Island of the Blessed, where there is neither harmful serpent nor any other dangerous thing, except wolves and bears, and they are so near to man that they do not count. How else do you think that the land got its name?

Then the serious drinking started, after the food was half

gone, and the singing. All the songs were melancholy and sad, enough to make a warrior weep, and that is what they did. Then a Bard called Amairgen stood up and sang an interminable song about all the earlier invasions of the Island of the Blessed, and how our invasion was the most glorious of all, and I was very hurt that he made it sound as if Cuchullain had brought over the sea all the men who fought with him, and he named none but the champion, as one would expect in an epic. But I was even more vexed that nobody asked me to sing. At last, it seemed that even if I were to sing, there was no one sober enough to hear me, and so I pulled Aristarchos to his feet, for he was as drunk as anyone, and I was terrified in case he began to talk in Greek, and back we went to the hut where the smith and his wife were, indeed, waiting for us. But it was not as luxurious as you might think because we had the room left in the hut after the smith and his wife, and their nine children and his five apprentices and seven other warriors, and the pigs had all got in before us. Mind you, next day we sent four of the warriors packing, and we killed one of the little pigs: all black the piglets were too, which some people might not like, but which suited me.

Next day, late next day, when at least some of my companions were in a fit state to talk, I tried to have a word with Cuchullain. There was the question of the Gold to discuss, and that would be a question of the conquest of the South-East, and that was where Rhiannon was. There would be no need to hurry yet; no harm would come to her among the Irish, I knew, not to a princess of an ancient house of Britain, not to the Mother of Those Below. But once the legions landed, there was no knowing what the Irish might not do to keep her out of harm's way – her very presence in the island, they would think, would be a lodestone to draw Roman vengeance on them. They had no real idea what the Empire was about, or what the army was for. They saw it not as a great union of peace and trade, held together by an army of engineers and builders and messengers and administrators: they thought of it as a despotism in other interests than their own, symbolised by the fierce shield wall of the legion. The Irish knew well the rule of their own custom: but the rule of law that we live under in the Empire was beyond their comprehension.

However, there was no talking to Cuchullain, now the battle was over. He was surrounded all the time by his fine friends from the North, who came in to Tara all the day, more and more of them. Clan chiefs and pirates they were who raided the coasts of Britain and Gaul, and each other, but who were too cautious to risk the battle, because that was only for desperate men who had nothing to lose: they were ready enough now to share the pickings and rule all Ireland. The only man of importance who had been in the Fianna was Callum the Hairy, and he was the chief of the poorest and most desperate nation of all the North.

But the chiefs who came down brought their own warbands, and though many of those were only armed with cudgels or with knives tied on to the ends of poles, there were enough swords and spears dug out of hiding, now it was safe, to have filled our ship twice over. And there were slingers too, and if only they had come earlier, we would not have had those moments of terror when the chariots came at us, because I am sure that a squadron of slingers and another of men with long pikes would break up any charge.

But even the Northerners who came with their cudgels tucked under their arms were enough to frighten me away from Cuchullain. And not only me. The two dozen who had hidden out with him in the hills all winter, even Callum, who came at last in the ship and fought well in the battle, won it for him really, they could not get near to speak to him either. And this went on for day after day, and the longer it went on the worse it got, more and more important princes coming down from the North, and Cuchullain always too busy to talk, and we men from the ship now even shut out of the nightly feasts in the hall, where there was no room for any of us, even for Callum, and getting our food where we could, and not many of the smith's little black pigs left. And why wait, I asked, like this, why wait?

'We're waiting to collect the army for one thing,' said Aristarchos, who as Heilyn was getting his orders from someone who got them from someone who got them from some northern prince who occasionally saw Cuchullain. 'He won't sweep into the West with a little band like we beat their king with. Cuchullain wants to raise an army big enough to pour across the plain and crush all three of the other Kingdoms, and any army they can raise now. The Ulstermen want to do to the South what the South did to them. The Queen of Connaught has a new husband already, they say, and she claims that he is the High King now by right of marriage. But Conchobar says that he is High King because he was married to her first, and because they finished half the enthroning ceremony on him before the Westerners came sweeping into Tara to spoil it and Maeve went off with the King of Connaught. So now, the King of Ulster is on his way here to finish his consecration, and when he has done that, when he is married again to Ireland, then he can go back home safe to the North again, while we do the work.'

'We do the work, as usual.'

'We do, that. Have you noticed that they don't use any money here in Ireland?'

'No more they do,' I agreed. 'I suppose they do any trade they can by barter.'

'Oh, no. They have a currency, of sorts. The smaller unit is a cow.'

'And what is the larger? A dead elk?'

'No. Four cows, one slave woman they say. I have a feeling that the Ulstermen intend a certain amount of inflation. And a debasement of the higher unit. By the time they finish, they hope to have a woman for two cows, and a horn of ale for two women.'

There, I thought, you have the whole lack of system in Barbarian life exposed. To a Barbarian, a slave is something to use for pleasure. We in the Empire know that nothing a slave does is equal in quality to what a free man does, whether you are thinking of a mason or a miner or a sailor or a ploughman or a prostitute. Therefore they use slaves in ones or twos, in bed or kitchen. But we use slaves only in large groups, and only in tasks which no free man will do, which no freed man will continue in. And if there were anything better than the fickle, mischievous, unhealthy slave to give us the power we want to break stone or pull ploughs or build, then we would use it. But there is, and can be, nothing else in nature that will ever serve.

It was the end of May when the King of the North arrived.

494

He had taken his time, but now he came galloping into Tara in his chariot as if he were in a dreadful hurry to be enthroned as High King, or to finish his enthronement. And this, the people of Tara said, was wrong. By rights he ought to wait to the Feast of Tara at Samain to be enthroned, and to argue that his enthronement had begun at a Samain and been interrupted was surely better cause for waiting for Samain and starting again rather than finishing it out of season. And sure, had not the last three High Kings who had been enthroned out of season died a violent death? But, I reminded them, had the last forty-three kings not died a violent death, however and whenever enthroned? But, no, the people of Tara said, that was pure coincidence.

And sure, they told me, was it not necessary for the High King to receive the sovereignty at the hands of a woman, and that the right woman, and was not the right woman missing and had she not shown clearly that there was no High Kingship she would be giving to Conchobar now, and was it not only his word alone that we had that she had ever given it to him? So there were some that agreed with the King of Ulster, that it was only necessary for him to carry out those ceremonies that had been omitted, and others said that there was nothing for it but to begin again from the beginning, and with this last party it was said that Cathbad held. As for Cathbad, some said that he thought thus because the Queen of the West had paid him, and others said it was because the part of the ceremony that would be taken as done was the bull sacrifice, and he wanted his fill of the beef, which otherwise he would be unable to taste.

But the King of Ulster had his way, and the day after he arrived he was enthroned under the same blue sky, because there had been no rain since the day that we had marched to the battle across the mud of the horse pastures. I woke early and I climbed up with some other warriors on the top of the great mound, because I realised now that there would be no special treatment for me, whatever I was owed, unless I demanded it in some spectacular way, and I was not doing that while Cuchullain could in any way plead that he was bound by his overlord. The mound was a trifle far off to see everything in detail, but at least I got there. I saw the new High King ride up in his chariot, driving it himself,

495

and showing his skill by passing so close to a standing stone that the felloe of the wheel scraped it and threw out sparks and yet the chariot did not overturn. But he did not do the other feat that was expected, driving his chariot between two other standing stones, because, some said, he had already done it once before, or because others said, he was afraid that the stones would catch him and crush him between them as they were supposed to do if anyone who was not by rights High King rode between them.

The King dismounted then and went to the flat stone on which he was to be enthroned, and they brought the white mare that the smith's wife had spoken of. I will not tell what happened then, because there are things a man may stomach to do in darkness in the rites of a mystery, but to do it in broad day in sight of ten thousand people as the High King must do – I will not speak of it. I will only say that I was sorry for the horse.

After it was over, the King killed the mare with the slash of an iron knife across her throat. Then he went from his stone to the cooking fire outside the Wall of Tara, and from that he went twenty paces to the west. There he piled brushwood for a new fire, and returning to the standing stone he had ridden by he struck fire from it with his sword – and not really his own sword, but the sword with which by proxy he had won the High Kingdom, and with which his champion had cut off the old High King's head – he struck more sparks to kindle timber, and that he carried back to light a new fire.

They put three stones about the new fire, and on this a massive iron cauldron, and by the working of it I could see that this had been made in Britain and brought across the sea, though whether by trade or by theft I do not know: I think by theft. They had this full of boiling water already, or we might have waited all day for the next part of the ceremony. The King began to joint the mare, and of course other men helped after the first cut of the royal knife. They hacked her into gobbets which they dropped into the cauldron, and they boiled the meat for some little time. Then when the King and some of his more favoured warriors and nobles, like Cuchullain, had eaten a little, His Majesty threw the rest into the crowd, lump by lump, and the men fought for them.

496

I did not join in this struggle, but Aristarchos did, and he came to me a little after licking his bloody fingers, because the flesh had not had time to be thoroughly cooked or even more than blanched on the surface. The riot merged with no further ceremonial into the feast in the Hall, to which neither he nor I nor any of the Gauls who came in the ship had been invited, and so we all went back to the smith's house, and there we found a cauldron of our own, and in it we put one of the little pigs and a couple of hares and a calf that we happened to come on by accident when nobody was looking our way because they were so engrossed in a fight between two of the Gauls who made more than enough noise to cover us and get up an appetite of their own. The cauldron we boiled on the smithy fire, and at last had it well cooked. There was not enough to drink, though, till one of the Gauls went off and reconnoitred the kitchen, and came back laden with mead jars, good stuff intended for the High King's own cup.

We sat there outside the smithy, which was only a booth open at two sides, and ate and drank, and talked about the good times one could have in Britain, and about how kings who wanted to keep their thrones paid their debts, and how at least that was a lesson Caesar had learnt, and how profitable it must be to serve in the Praetorian Guard at the death of an Emperor, all that was what we were saying, when the people of the village of Tara began to join us, and we had to talk more carefully, though they all agreed with us. We were all beautifully, ecstatically depressed, a fine contrast to the chieftains in the hall, who were, by the sound of it, in the grip of a different kind of ecstasy. Suddenly there was a movement in the circle, and the songs died. Cathbad the Druid had sat down with us.

I had never seen the Druid in all his splendour sit so near a smithy, or come so near meat cooked in a pot of iron. But this was no ordinary night, and this no ordinary place. He sat there in silence, and we all looked at him and waited to hear what he would say.

We waited for Cathbad to say something, or to recite some poem that would give us, even in a Delphic form, his real thoughts, because there are limits to the things a Priest can say

497

to an all-powerful King. But he just sat and watched us, and listened to the small talk that sprang up again, how this man had killed three great chieftains in the battle, and how that one might have done better if only a cursed useless chariot had not got in his way, and men compared the armlets and collars they had taken from the enemies they had killed, and indeed this was what we had talked about every night for weeks now. Then all of a sudden Cathbad spoke, and spoke to me.

'Mannanan, whether you stay within the plain of Tara and keep your life, or whether you go out of the plain, and risk it, is all one to me. But it will all end in tears, and it is your doing, but there is no blame at your door: it is fated.'

And then, in the way Druids have, he was gone, and we did not see him again, that night or after.

Chapter Six

There was a whole week of feasting, and even on the day after the last feast there was still no one but myself who was both ready and eager to march into the South and West. You can fight a battle with a headache, but you cannot march a mile. But the day after that, the new High King rode north to safety in Ulster, and the Champion of Ulster led the army of Ulster out of Tara, to conquer the island for the High King, and to bring back for him cattle and women without number, and most important of all, among them the Queen of Connaught for his bed and her cattle for his table or for his stud.

Cuchullain, then, led his army down to the river that was the southern boundary of the plain of Tara, and even in that country of no roads there were at least fords here and there, and the army had to come down to one ford and to one ford only. The chariots were at the head of the host, my chariots, all gilded and painted and set with gems, my chariots that I had brought in my ship, that I had bargained for and paid for, that I had broken a legate for, my chariots. And in the first chariot, with the head of the High King that was hanging by its hair from the pole, and other heads with it now, stood Cuchullain.

The Champion did indeed make a fine sight. He wore his particolour hair long down his back, as a challenge to whoever should want to take his head. So, I remembered, did Pryderi wear his. This, I thought, is how Pryderi would like to ride, at the head of an army, sweeping a country bare of women and food and beasts, and it is only for preventing this that he has this hatred for Rome. Oh, yes, war is a fine thing for nobles and leaders, even in defeat; but for the defeated, or the weak on either side, there is little to be said for it, and if you can think what that little is, then tell me, because I cannot think what it is.

499

Cuchullain now spurned the civilised luxury of a shirt. He wore only the long strip of saffron-coloured cloth wound round his body, held together by fine brooches of Gold and silver. This dress set off the muscles of his arm and back, rippling under the armlets and chains that he wore, of precious metals only; nothing so poor as bronze for him. The sword that had killed the High King he had given to Conchobar, and now he wore an old sword, brought down from the North, hidden away from the army of Connaught when it had tried to disarm the North as the Romans had disarmed all Britain. This was the oldest sword I had ever seen, a long chariot sword, double-edged for slashing, but this one pointed too. There was no ball to the pommel. Instead there spread out from the top of the hilt two wide horns of Gold, curling up like a new moon in the sky, and the tips of the horns studded with tiny chips of gems so that they glittered as the light came on them from all directions. And the bottom of the scabbard was likewise ornamented with horns, this time of gilded bronze for the harder wear as the chape bumped on the ground or the sides of the chariot, though it would be seldom that the sword would be worn except in the chariot. It was slung from a sword belt that went over his right shoulder, and was anchored to the garment he wore, but round his waist he wore a noble's belt in the British fashion, a chain of bronze gilt that went round his body four or five times before it was caught by a clasp.

Behind him came his army. You have seen a civilised army on the march, or at least you have seen soldiers, small detachments marching to join their station or stepping out proudly in a review. Are you thinking of those straight lines, dressed from the right, taking their step from the standard-bearer? You will conjure up those scarlet cloaks, all of a length, the line of shields held, however it breaks a man's arm, all level topped. You will imagine the helmets, shining like so many suns, the legionaries' topped with spike or knob according to regiment, the centurions proudly tossing their scarlet plumes of horsehair. The breastplates shine, scoured smooth with brick dust, and the faces are shaved close as if they too were scoured, and every neck cropped, and crown too, so that no hair shows outside the helmet. Those are the two things that you will remember, every man is alike, and every man is clean.

That will not do for your picture of a Barbarian army, Irish or German. Every man is dressed differently, as he pleases, only that a fashion may run for a little through some clan or nation and give them at least a skim of likeness. The helmets they wear are of a hundred different kinds, knobbed or spiked or crested, round or pointed, with cheek-pieces or not, sometimes beaten out of one piece, sometimes built up of plates of metal on a cap of boiled leather, and whether it is of bronze or of iron is a matter of choice. Then some men will wear mail, and some do not, according to whether they have been lucky in war or in inheritance or in theft, and for cloaks they wear what length and colour they can catch. But you must not imagine this equipment as shining, because how can bronze shine when it is green with verdigris, or iron sparkle when it is pitted with rust? The cloaks hide their colours under dirt and grease, and every man wears his beard long for want of will to cut it, and his hair long as a challenge. And this army will not march in ranks, or in any order, but will push along in a great heaving crowd, every man only taking care that he is always near to his lord to recognise him.

So Cuchullain rode at the head of this crowd of warriors, by the way I knew that he would come, and there at the ford I waited for him. And when he stopped there, all his men came up and crowded close to hear what I said, as I knew they would.

Where the track came down to the ford, I had dug a hole. There was no need to seek out a standing stone of a burial mound: here was the boundary between the Plain of Tara and the rest of the Island of the Blessed, and every boundary is a place of mystery. Beside the road to the ford I had dug a hole, dug it with a stick sharpened in the fire. I dug the hole knee-deep before I was satisfied, and I heaped the earth on the south side, the unlucky side. I stood on the west side of the hole, and I barred the way to Cuchullain and his advancing army. He rode up to me in his chariot, and saw me there. The hood of my seal-skin cloak was drawn over my face, but he knew me, and he knew too, and all his soldiers knew, why I held in my left hand a screaming black piglet, the runt of the litter, and in my right a knife roughly chipped of flint. Cuchullain saw the kicking squealing pig, and he stopped.

'How then, Mannanan!' he cried. 'Have you not had enough blood?' He gestured around. This was the way that the army of the West had fled, and the ground was covered with corpses. Some the wolves and the buzzards had torn: most had been stripped. Now the ribs showed through the rotting flesh, three weeks dead. The bellies had burst: there was a stench over everything. There was nobody whose duty it was to bury them. So they were not buried.

'I do not drink blood,' I replied loudly, so that all the host could hear me. 'But I know those who do. Those Below, the thirsty ones, shall they be filled tonight?' and I drew the blunt back of the stone knife across the piglet's throat. Cuchullain looked long at me. He saw my hair plastered down with fat, and it might well have been corpse fat for all he knew, and stuck with the feathers of the black cock. One half of my face was blackened with the ash from the fire, and one painted scarlet with a dye I had with me. From my red cheek glared my one black eye, and from the black cheek shone the red of a ruby. And Cuchullain saw, and all his army saw, that the blood of the black pig would flow into the pit, and I would curse all his army and himself and deliver them to the Gods Below as I had delivered the High King. Cuchullain changed his tune, and asked what I wanted.

'Pay your debts, Setanta, pay your debts!' For he was still arrogant, with his army behind him. Now the battle was won there was no need for him to think that he could escape paying those that had won it for him. 'Before you came here, before I armed you, before I gave you your triumph and your kingdom, you promised me my pay. All the Gold in Ireland, all the Gold of all the mines, you promised me. You promised, Setanta, and you have not paid it yet. What have you promised the men behind you, and will you ever pay it? Pay me my Gold, Setanta, and then pay them!'

He did not dare refuse me, or try to put it off, there in front of all his army who had heard it. There is nothing will make an army melt away as fast as the rumour that the pay chests are empty. If that happened, then indeed he would feast with the Gods Below. Every man watched him and watched me with my hand on my knife. Cuchullain turned to his host and called:

'Who will go with this man into Leinster?'

A big man came forward, and beneath the hair it was possible to recognise Callum that had pulled the skin boat with me. Now his face was painted and his hair stuck with feathers so that he would have drawn attention anywhere in Britain, where he had before been merely an unusually hairy and dirty man. Now, though, he could dress for what he was, the prince of a little kingdom somewhere far away, and with him he brought his own kinsmen, perhaps five hundred of them, and almost every man of them had joined us on that first day. There was little enough attention he had had from the High King, though, for all that, or from the Champion till now.

'Callum the Hairy,' Cuchullain addressed him. 'Ravage Wicklow, and take Mannanan to the Rivers of Gold.'

I stood beside Callum, and we watched the host of Ulster pass, great crowds of ragged hungry men, ill armed and ill tempered, even now, and looking not for excitement or for glory but for loot, only for loot. Only in the middle of them marched a dozen proud and fierce men, well armed, Heilyn and his Gauls. Close behind the leading chariot they strode, ready to keep each others' back, or their leader's back. And as they went, so I saw pass for the last time the Champion of Ulster.

Nor did Conchobar ever see his nephew again.

I trudged south with Callum the Hairy, passing the river last of all, and while the host turned west up river, we turned east towards the sea. There were, as I said, about five hundred of us, and not a man whose name or whose face I knew except Callum. I had my axe in my hand, and my cloak on my back, and a little bag at my waist with my belongings, like a few spare eyes in case we were invited to a feast. I asked Callum where he came from.

'From far up there,' he said, pointing to our left. 'It is on the coasts opposite the Picts that we are living and it is across the sea that it is we would rather be raiding, because it is a fine land that the Picts have, and easy it would be to take it from them, but it is silver in plenty they have that lets them keep men always under arms in case we come, and the bread that those men ought to be growing they can buy for them.'

They were a crafty people, these men of Callum's, part of a

503

nation of the Irish who called themselves Scots. They did not worship any living being, but their sacred thing, they said, was a ship, a stout wooden ship that had once cast itself up on their shores and had given them much silver, and been the foundation of such prosperity as they had. Besides, they said, it was more convenient to worship a ship, since there was no chance of sinning by eating it.

When we crossed the river, we passed into the land where Cathbad could no longer, as he said, protect me, but I remembered how little power he had seemed to have even in the land of Tara, and I laughed at him. There was nothing he could do to protect me that I could not do myself.

We marched on, our men singing the rousing chorus of 'Erch, the Bastard King of Leinster'. When we could smell the sea, we came to a village, a collection of huts by the water. We turned out the whole place in a twinkling, women and pigs and cattle. Beyond the village was a strong place, a rath as they call it, an earthwork around a circular farmyard, and a fence on top of the bank, and a gate in the fence that we easily broke in. The men in the rath we killed very easily, but there was nothing inside worth taking. The prince of the place was already dead across the river, and his women had fled to the west. Some of his own peasants had taken the rest of his belongings, mead mostly, and shut themselves inside the rath to enjoy them. Some of our men were for burning the place down, but Callum would not allow them.

'For indeed,' he told them, 'it is bringing our families down here we will be, and I will be king of this place, and I will reign from this rath myself.'

There we spent the first night, and when we went south we left a band of young men to hold it, and there we sent all the cattle that we stole, and there we agreed to meet if we were scattered. The young men had the women of the place to comfort them, and the pigs to eat. But we turned south into the narrow plain between the mountains and the sea, and all I could think of was Gold. I hardly remembered at all that down there in the South, by the sea, somewhere, was Rhiannon, and that is what Cathbad could not protect me from once I was out of the plain of Tara. For in the Plain, I thought of glory and honour and the rule of law and of love: but once I was across the river, there was nothing I remembered but Gold.

There was no one in that plain that expected our coming. I wondered why. Callum listened to me wondering as one listens to the prattling of a child, and then in pity teaches it to wipe its nose.

'Indeed, it is the country of the Eastern King that we are coming into, the country of Leinster. It was not to the taste of the king of this and to go to fight at Tara, for he has not been in this island for a year or two, but he has been wandering across the seas, and some say inside the Empire. But now he has come back, and he has brought him back a wife too, from among the Iceni, and a hard time of it he must have been having in making his rule felt again. For it is a proud people the Brigantes are, and impatient of any king.'

'But – the Brigantes!' I protested. 'They live in Britain.'

'So do some of them, and some of them live in Gaul, and the finest and oldest branch of the nation live here, although it is arguing and quarrelling they are always over which *is* the oldest and finest branch.'

Now I began to realise why Caw had been so unperturbed when we told him that Rhiannon had been stolen away by the Irish. And now, too, I first began to wonder whether she had, in her own mind, been stolen or rescued. From now on, when I thought of her, as I did infrequently, I only wondered when I should reach her in her palace in the capital of the Brigantes, when we should at last fall, as I thought we would, into each other's arms.

We went south, like a thunderstorm. We slept each night in the villages we sacked, with the widows and daughters of the men we killed, if we could catch any to kill, which was not often, or if not, then with the wives and daughters they kindly left us. And we ate their cows and pigs, but not many of them, because our real interest was in collecting a great herd together on the banks of the river beneath the fence of Callum's new rath. We spread out too, and covered all the country between the mountains and the salt sea, and we were no longer an army of five hundred men, but a scatter of companies of fifty or so, each just

505

enough to settle a village. In these villages there were few men, I noted, however many women we might find. But almost every day, almost every hour, I would ask Callum:

'When do we come to the rivers of Gold?'

And he would answer in that ingratiating way that Barbarians have, when they know that the answer will be unwelcome and they do not want to hurt your feelings by telling you the truth:

'Soon, soon. Tomorrow, the next day, the day after.'

I realised, but slowly, that he had no more idea of where the Gold was than I had. Till at last we forded a little stream running east from the sea, as we did a dozen times a day, and I scraped my toes into the sandy bottom. I stopped dead there, with the mountain water icy cold half way up my calves, and I shouted in joy. Oh, yes, I'd seen sand like that before, the sands of the Maeander are like that, where Midas gathered his Gold, and gathered it all up, so that there is no Gold there any more. But this was Gold sand all right. I stopped where I was, I did that, and I bent down and I plunged my arms to the elbow in the bitter stream and I brought up a fistful of sand. I held it in my cupped hands, and then I swilled it round in my palm, watching for the glint of mica and I saw it, and then I knew that I had come to the Rivers of Gold.

'Callum!' I called to him. 'Callum! Is this the first of the rivers of Gold?'

'Rivers of Gold? Why, all the rivers of the Eastern Kingdom are rivers of Gold, that's what they call them. Why do you think that this is the first?'

'But look at the sand!'

'Sand? Why, it's just sand, like any sand. All sand is the same. What has that got to do with Gold? Come on, we'll hurry on to the next river and you can play in the sand there.'

I had no choice but to follow him. That afternoon we reached the next river, where it ran low among the rocks in the summer, cold from the mountain tops that we could see, and there was a big village. There were a few men there, whom we killed, because they didn't run fast enough, and a lot of women. But while the rest of the party rearranged the politics, not to speak of the morals of the place, I took a flat platter with a high rim out of a

506

house, and I knelt by the river bank, where there was a little backwater with a beach of clean sand. And there I washed for Gold. I knelt there and I put handfuls of sand into the platter and whirled it round till the sand and the water climbed the side and swished over, and I looked in the bottom of the dish for the heavier metal that should be left there. I knelt there in the gravel and I panned and panned, while the sun went behind the hills, and even on a June evening the air grew chilly. And at last, when some of Callum's men came, to call me for supper they said, but they had never done such a thing before, and it was only out of curiosity that they walked so far out of the village, I was able to show them at last a tiny glimmer of Gold, a patch of Gold grains on my palm, enough to gild a third of the nail of my little finger.

It was Gold, real Gold, and all Callum's men, and their leader, crowded to see it, Irish Gold that they had never known, only heard of and not believed in. They made a celebration of it, or tried to, though in reality they did not think as much of the Gold as they did of the cattle they found, since the cattle they were getting for nothing, and the Gold was taking work, that they could see, and the metal I had got in all those hours of kneeling was not enough to buy the hind teat of a barren cow. But because I was jubilant, they rejoiced with me, and we drank late into the night, and looked out over the plain between us and the sea that was dotted with our own fires, and the hills that were bare of the fires of our enemies.

Next morning I went to Callum, because none of our men were in a condition to march, and it was not only the drink that did it, but sheer fatigue, overwork both on the road by day and in bed by night. I said:

'I want some women.'

'And wasn't it enough women we were having last night? There was that fat black-haired bitch with the green eyes—' twas a dreadful game she was having with me, a dreadful game. Oh, Mannanan, it is an awful thing for a man to have to say, but it's too old I think that I am getting for this life. And anyway, what is it you would be doing with a woman in the daytime?'

'No, it's nothing like that, Callum. I want a lot of women, and

I want them to work. You can have them all back for the night. Old ones will do. I'll be staying here for a little, and I want them to work.'

'And it's staying here I think we will all be, for a little while too, the way I'm feeling.' And stay we did, and the men were happy enough, for they had food and drink in plenty and women to wait on them hand and foot. But they let me have about thirty of them, assorted ages, to work during the day.

That first morning of work, I had all the women out by the stream. I made sure that each of them had a trencher or a platter with a rim or a shallow bowl or something like that to work with, not always the best things for panning, but they had to do with what they had, and they soon learned not to bring what would only make hard work. I showed them what to do, whisking the pan around and around. They all looked at me blankly for a bit. Then one of them said, in a bright but witless way:

'Oh, yes, like in the Gold dance.'

'The Gold dance?' I asked. 'What's that?'

'Oh, like this,' they all said together, and straight away they began to dance, and to sing a wailing song. It was a very complex dance, with many figures and a great deal of repetition, and in between each figure, or when they were not dancing principal parts, as some of them did, they were all the time panning, panning with their hands, though none of them picked up the pans they had, or seemed to know that they should. The first few figures I did not see, because I was too busy scattering salt and chewing garlic, and crossing knives and generally making myself secure against any spells they might be weaving. It would, of course, have been foolhardy to have tried to stop the dance in the middle, or all the stored-up power from the first measures would have been split out on me, and there is no knowing what I might not have turned into. But it was tempting, because the dance lasted a full hour of a summer's day.

Some of the figures were quite intelligible. They panned, and they worked bellows, and they poured out of crucibles, and they beat leaf thin with hammers, oh yes, you could have been a goldsmith as good as any in the world to have done all they danced. Then half of the women became traders from over the sea, and

508

brought things to trade for the gold. They had cloth, in long strips, and jars of wine to drink, and cattle to milk, and most welcome, it seemed, of all, they brought the cauldrons, of bronze and of iron, to boil the food in. For you cannot boil a dinner in a cauldron of Gold, any more than in a cup of wood. And all the time, they made this continual panning motion, while they made their sacrifices and poured out their oblations, and charmed the rain down on to the hills to fill their streams.

When they had finished, I said:

'Right, now! You know what to do. Get on with it!'

They all looked at me, blank again.

'What, in the river? Put our feet in cold water?' They were horrified. 'We'd catch our slow deaths if we did, and die coughing and groaning and spitting blood. If cold water touches your skin, then it is death, slow death, and if it is hot water, then it is a quick death.'

Looking at them I could see how firmly they believed this. It was no time to try to convince them by argument. I had borrowed a whip of bull's hide from Callum, and I cracked it in the air above my head.

'I don't care what you think, or how you die. Into the river you go.' What I would have done if they hadn't gone, I don't know, I hadn't the heart to flog them, they were too stupid, but first one and then another waded gingerly into the stream.

'And what is it we are to do now we are here?' one asked. Heaven preserve me from ever again having to make women work.

'You know all about it. Get down there on your knees and wash for Gold.'

'Oh, he's mad,' one woman said, and another, a pert lass and very good in bed, I found, but no use at all in a practical situation, giggled and told me, in a confidential way:

'You don't get Gold out of streams, dear. You get Gold from over the sea. You have to find a city, and then you can dig it up out of the rocks between the houses. And they say the Romans will give Gold for dogs. I wouldn't mind seeing a few Romans around here, I wouldn't, be a change from you Northerners.'

'Oh, no you wouldn't,' another girl corrected her. 'Those

Romans all smell of olive oil, they drink it instead of beer, they do, whatever it is.'

'Then if you can't get Gold out of the river,' I argued and that was a sad mistake, to argue with them, 'where do you think the river got its name? Why do you call it the Gold River?'

'Oh, that's just its name,' they all choroused. 'There's a Red River and a Black River, and so there's a Gold River, or so the Bards tell us. Names don't mean anything.'

'But your dance – why do you call it the Gold dance?'

'Why not? Every dance has to have a name, or you wouldn't know which dance you were doing, would you?'

The more they talked, the more I became convinced that it was true, that they had forgotten what the dance was about. It was all one with the fundamentally irreligious approach they had to dancing. They had really forgotten that the rivers were full of Gold. But they had danced the Gold dance so often, I thought, that it was a miracle that there was any room left for the waters to flow between the mounds of precious metal. They had danced it forty or fifty times a year, every year. The words didn't matter, they told me, they made them up as they went along, about village scandals, and they would soon have some words sufficiently disrespectful to fit my case.

I drove them down into the water, cracking my whip, and I split them up into small groups, choosing the most likely places. I went from group to group all the day, watching to make sure that they were all panning in the right way, and ducking those who weren't. I was sure that they were doing it right. But there was not the glimmer of Gold in the pans, not a sparkle of bright metal, nothing but sand, sand, sand. I couldn't understand it all. It was *just* possible that they had been filching it away and hiding the dust, but it didn't seem possible after I had had the most likely thieves working naked for a few hours, so that they had nowhere to put the stuff. There was no Gold. Thirty women to pan a stream for a whole day and no profit – it was incredible.

We washed that stream for four days, working from the sea back into the hills up to the source. Nothing, not a speck. Mica we found, and plenty of that, but no Gold. The sand was right. The rocks were right. The water was right. Perhaps the earth had stopped breeding it, I thought, but that doesn't happen without the intervention of some God, and there would have been some memory, however garbled in the telling, of that.

There might be Gold in other rivers, I thought, and the women might know of it. They said they didn't. I threatened to have them tied and flogged, but by now our men were so demoralised that all they and the women did at this was roar with laughter. That was one of the troubles in Ireland, nobody took war seriously, and they had even less respect for trade. Irreligious, as I said.

So we moved south, to the other rivers of Gold, and we panned a fresh river every day, with fresh women. Every village had the Gold dance, and we had them dance it till their feet nearly wore off. Perhaps the words of the song, I thought, were more important than the women said they were, but it was past trying now to find out what it was. And they didn't know what the sacrifice was. I tried a number of things, pigs, dog, hen, child, and even once a sickly foal that would have died anyway but even so it was expensive. And yet there was never the smallest little nugget. I didn't try snake, because there are none in Ireland, but if ever you are going that way you might take a snake with you and try. There's not much hope, but at least it would be conclusive.

And then it came to the sixth morning, and we were on the edge of the sixth river, and I had all the women of the village out on the bank, and we had danced the dance, and I was telling them what to do, and here were a couple of cracks of the whip to be going on with – and I was interrupted. Someone was laughing at me. I glared at the crowd, and they all edged away, in the way frightened people have, from the offender. And the worst of it was that they were afraid of her, not of me, that was plain. She was an old woman, very old, with not a tooth in her head, and not much hair on it, shrivelled and bent, and the very look of her frightened me as much as it did the women. For this was someone as old as the women who had cursed us as we landed, and much more evil, and it would not need any queen to bribe her to curse a man – she would do it out of spite and amusement. I snarled at her – my temper was wearing thin now – and I asked:

'And what do you think there is to laugh at? Just you keep quiet, or I'll be storing the Gold dust in skin bags – your skin.'

511

But she kept on cackling and screeching, till at last she had had her laugh out, and then she pointed at me and cried hoarsely:

'The Gold, the Gold, the Gold is gone, there's none for you to find. The Gold, the Gold, the Gold is gone, all washed away to the salt salt sea, swirled away to the cod and the conger, sunk to the weed and shells at the bottom. It's gone, it's gone, it's washed away!'

Up to now, I had refused to believe it. And it was flung in my face, and all at once I knew it was true. Perhaps, men had washed and washed these streams till all the Gold was taken, all smelted down into the collars and bracelets that were now all buried in the graves of the Isle of Britain. It was possible. But no, I could not believe that. I looked at the women, and I knew better. Out of their greed, they had danced the streams dry. In impious laughter they had danced the Gold dance for its own sake, and not for the Gold, and they had, through a myriad repetitions, danced all the Gold out of the hills and down the streams, out into the deep deep sea. In one instant, there alone with all those women on the river bank, I understood all the story of the Gold of Ireland, and in that instant I realised that there was that in Ireland which I would have done better to have prized and sought before all the Gold in Ireland, and she was still here somewhere to the south of me. And I looked across the stream to the land of the Brigantes of Ireland and I prepared to march forward towards Rhiannon and my life, when all at once there was a tumult.

Tumult is a nice and glorified and poetic word for it, and too dignified for that noise. There was the bellowing of a thousand rather anxious cattle, the screaming of five hundred rather frightened women, and the deep panting of as many terrified warriors running north for all they could go. The whole mob came sweeping past us where we stood, a little above the ford where they had to cross, and we watched them come over the river. And bringing up the rear, blowing aside his whiskers to urge his people on, looking like Death, Death received and Death bestowed, was Callum. He gestured to the ridge behind, where the tips of spears caught the sun.

'Run, run!' he cried. 'The Brigantes are on us!'

Chapter Seven

So began that dreadful flight that lasted, as far as I was concerned, for two whole days and two whole nights. For others it lasted longer, for they crossed the river into the Plain of Tara, and for others it ended sooner in a spear thrust or slashing swing of a sword.

At first we formed a great square of movement, men and cattle, pushing north as fast as we could trot. An easy pace, you think? Oh, yes, easy enough for an unarmed man for an hour or so, with nothing at the end of it but a crown of laurel or a horn of ale. But to keep it up for days, with a coat of mail and a helmet, and a sword or an axe or a spear, and with your own life as the prize, why, that's another thing.

Behind us as we went we left our trail, a great belt of land where the grass was eaten and trampled, and the houses burnt, the fences about the paddocks and the folds pushed over, the fruit trees cut down, the wells fouled and the fords muddied. Soon we were leaving other things, bags of food and water bottles, spare shoes and bronze bowls and cloaks, and mine among them. And then, more sinister, mail coats, and helmets, and at last shields and spears and swords thrown down by men who only wanted to run. We left men as well as women gasping by the wayside, with knees or ankles twisted in the mud, or their soles worn into raw blisters, or snorting or spewing blood. I could never understand what came over the women, for they ran as fast as the men even when no one guarded them. They urged the cattle on, they rushed forward to captivity as if it were the goal and object of their lives. Caught up, they were, I suppose, by the general frenzy around them.

I know that I was. I belted along for the first few miles as hard as I could go without falling over the cows in front of me. After a while, though, I remembered Socrates at Delium, and I went faster till I could catch up with Callum.

'We wouldn't have to run so fast,' I shouted to him, 'if we could discourage the Brigantes.'

Callum considered this for a few hundred paces. He was a realist. He didn't slow down till the next ford. Then he stopped at the water's edge and looked at the men who were passing. We were by now well in the front of the retreat, being by nature more determined than our followers. Callum caught one man by the arm, and then another. He was not indiscriminate. He let most of the fugitives go by. He collected about thirty men. None of them were in their first youth, but they were strong men, heavy-handed and savage. Every man of them still had his weapons, and held them as if he knew what these things were for.

We waited in the bushes above the ford, on the south bank of the river, till most of the rout were over and the first pursuers appeared. Young men they were, running lightly and easily, scarcely out of breath, delighted at outrunning their elders, which experience had taught me is never a thing to do in war if you want to live. Their spears were already bloodied and they slung heads at their belts, taken from men too tired and broken to resist. We were different. Youngsters, I said. They had no chance. We charged down on them, and though they tried hard to remember how they had been taught to fight, we killed eleven of them before you could shout a warcry. We only had two wounded. We took the heads, of course, because it was the thing to do, not because we could afford to carry trophies, and indeed we dropped them down the next well we came to. You see, the sight of his friends' bodies, headless laid out in a neat row across his path is enough to make any man wonder whether precedence is so important.

We pushed on. It had begun to rain, breaking the long dry spell that had begun with the Battle before Tara. I could only hope that the rain had the same effect on our pursuers' spirits as it had on ours. I fought seven times in those two days and two nights. Five times we laid ambushes, and twice we were ourselves attacked, for the Leinstermen soon called back all the lads from the forefront of their army, and those who came on after us

were old warriors like ourselves. And what I could not understand was that some of them bore wounds already, sword cuts a
few weeks old, and yet the army of Leinster had not come against
us before Tara, and I wondered what had been happening in the
Eastern Kingdom. I was glad that I had once been taught the
finer points of using an axe by a Lombard, not named Bert, and
I soon had heads enough to hang all round my belt by their long
hair, if I had wanted them.

When we held the field, we took the heads of the enemy and
also we picked up the bodies of our own dead. And their heads
we took too, and carried them with us till we could scrape a little
hole in the earth and bury them out of sight. Because you cannot
leave your comrade's head for his enemies to hack off roughly
and insult, and at the last stick up on a stake for the crows to peck
out the eyes.

But we ran most of the time, and there was nothing that I had
to eat but a piece of dried beef that I picked out of the mud, and
a quarter of a barley loaf and two raw carrots I took from some
women who were fools enough to let me see they had food. We
were no longer now a solid square of movement. The men in
front were hastening to get their beasts out of the Eastern Kingdom and across the plain of Tara and home into the North, and
each made the best speed he could and took the easiest path,
while Callum the Hairy played the prince's part and held back
the pursuit, and gave them time. We were but the wreck of an
army now, and the warbands of Leinster roamed among us at
will and cut off first this herd and then that.

Sometime in the darkness of the second night, I fought for
the eighth time. There were only six left with Callum then.
Some had been killed, and some had fallen with weariness, and
some were just lost in the dark or in the press of cattle. Men
rushed at us out of the darkness, and split us, so that every one of
us was fighting alone, and I the most alone, twisting and turning
always the same way to guard my blind side and striking at
shadows with my two-foot axe. I spun and dodged, and ran to
escape, because there comes a time always when there is no more
to do than run, and you must give up and acknowledge that there
is no more that you can do. I blundered westward, or so I

thought, up hill and over bog and through copses, till at last I tripped over a root and I fell flat on my face into a hollow in the ground, and I lay there winded and sobbing with shame and terror and fatigue, and there at last I slept.

When it was well light I awoke. We had been on the left flank of the retreat. I had wandered far out, into the shoulders of the hills. I got cautiously to my hands and knees and looked down the slope. Far away was the great scar that the herds had cut across the pastures, and the ruin of dead beasts and dying men and wailing women, and the crows and buzzards and the wolves gaining all the profit of the night. But otherwise there was no army to be seen. The pursuit had swept on. There was nobody now to be afraid or to cast cowardice in my teeth. The host of Callum the Hairy had gone and so had the army of the King of Leinster, gone on north towards the river which I could see in the far distance. Across the river lay the Plain of Tara. There I might be safe. Cathbad would protect me there.

Chapter Eight

I began to make my way to the north, moving carefully from one clump of trees to another, trying to keep out of sight. I shivered for want of my cloak as much as from fear, and I turned my head this way and that lest anyone, or anything, should come up on my blind side unseen. I kept moving. I was not only afraid of men. There were wolves around.

But I did not look round enough for all my care. I came at last to a place where I could lie in a hollow and see through the parted grass the mound and the rath which Callum had marked to be his own, above the river. The rath looked empty enough. There was no movement above the fence. There was some smoke, but a fire need not mean living men: I had seen enough burning houses in my time, and families dead around their own dinner a-cooking. The pursuit had turned inland along the banks of the rivers hours ago.

I lay and watched for a time. When I was beginning to think it might be safe enough to go forward and see if there was anything to eat inside the rath, there was a noise behind me, of someone clearing his throat. I whirled round and on to my feet, my axe at the ready, blade vertical before my face, my hacked and battered shield on my arm. A man stood in front of me, ten yards away, his sword at his side, his arms folded. He was not really seven feet high, he only looked it, in his pointed helmet, centuries old, with a bunch of red ribbons threaded through the ring on top. Heilyn Aristarchos had given me warning of his coming lest I killed him. Lest *I* killed *him* – I laughed bitterly at the thought.

'Well?' he asked me in a dull toneless voice. 'Where is all the Gold?'

'There is no Gold,' I replied. 'Have you anything to eat?'

He brought a lump of roast venison, dried and dusty, out of the fold of his cloak. We divided it equally, every scrap. I told him my tale. His was the same. But at least all Callum's men were of one mind, and they tried to drive together one huge herd to drive back to Ulster. But the men who went with Cuchullain into the West did not even do that. As each man found he had enough cows or women to suit him, he would leave the army and go home with them. And as the host went west, so they spread out and the whole army dwindled away, not to nothing, because Cuchullain still kept together his chariots, and the Gauls who had come with Aristarchos held with him, and another band of the Setantii, Irishmen. And these were all that were left to face the wrath of Queen Maeve as she came in a second cloud of chariots against them out of the West. And then Cuchullain had done as Callum did, and fought skirmish after skirmish to hold the Connaught men off the wreck of his army. But as he retreated so his army grew, because like a snowball it swallowed up the stragglers who had no cattle, and soon the skirmishes were more like battles, but the retreat went on for all that.

'Then, two nights ago,' he told me, 'I took a small band off to the right of the road, to try to draw the Queen south after us. We fought with their right flank near dusk, and we were cut to pieces. We scattered in the dark, and here I am at my rendezvous, for it was at this rath that I promised to meet my Gauls. If any are alive: I am almost certain none are.'

'Who were they?' I was bold to ask.

'Oh, Setantii, all right,' he assured me, 'all related to Cuchullain. But how was he to know that every one was a soldier, sworn to Caesar, three of them of the rank of standard-bearer, and every one anxious to hang on his breastplate such Phalerae as would make every legion and every regiment of horse in the Army salute us as we passed. And there is still hope we may have it yet. This rath – where better for the legions to build Praetorium, and govern all Ireland?'

'Soon it will be done,' I assured him. 'Just think, now all the roads of Britain are scarlet with the marching troops, coming down to the boats on the edge of the Irish Sea. All we need do now is to reach the landing beaches before Tara, and wait till the ships appear. When the Liffey itself is full of galleys, then we can come out and collect our praises and our crowns for settling all Ireland in such a turmoil they will never notice what is happening till they are conquered.'

'I hope my Gauls will see it. But they know the ways of this kind of war as well as I do. Make for the rendezvous, and then carry on, and never wait for the men who may never come. But they may be in the rath.'

We trudged down, miserable, through the fine rain that never stopped, and we climbed the path to the gate in the long fence. The gate itself still lay on the ground where it had fallen when Callum himself, under a rain of stones instead of water, had cut through the leather hinges with his sword. The village between the rath and the river had been burnt, but inside the courtyard the houses still stood. There might be food there. We looked at each other. Then Aristarchos nodded.

'There may be food. We'll go in.'

We moved forward, through the open gate into the court. We could see nobody about. And then, there was a shout, and we turned to see a dozen men in the open gate, warriors, splashed with the mud and blood of a three days' pursuit. And in front of them he stood. He was big and grossly fat. His black-and-white-striped shirt was stained with moss. His hair, now grown long down his back, was streaked with whitewash. Picking a chicken carcase he held in both his hands, his royal state made obvious by the massive Gold collar around his neck, stood Gwawl, the Badger King of Leinster.

There he stood, triumphant in the gateway. He spat chicken bones at our feet, and he laughed. He said, in Latin, to taunt me the more:

'Well, Mannanan-Photinus! Who is it now that controls the Gold of Ireland? You have the Monopoly Deed: but I have the monopoly of you. This is my day of victory at last. You cheated me between Bonnonia and Rutupiae. You hid in the mists in the Channel, and my ships missed you. You rolled me like dung in the streets of Londinium. Now it is my turn to do what I like.'

'Do what you will,' I told him. 'Your days are numbered.'

'But at what a number,' he insisted. 'Soon your days will be gone. Do you wonder why I do not kill you now, myself? I promised my cousin, Rhiannon, when I saved her from you, that I would not kill you, nor harm a hair of your head, and no more I will. But I have also promised my other cousin, Maeve, that I will send you to her, bound, and that I will do. And she has her own ideas of sport, and it is not quickly that you will die, nor easily.'

And there was no doubt that he would do it, and there was no knowing how long it would take the legions to bring the Queen to heel. And by then we would be dead. I still held my axe, and Aristarchos his sword, but there were a hundred men in the rath now, with poles and nets, to take us alive like wild beasts. My own skill with axe and shield had brought me alive out of the first stage of the retreat from the rivers of Gold. There was no cheating in Ireland. Now I must bring us both alive out of the Island of the Blessed with my own unaided brain. There was only one thing left now to fight Gwawl with. I called on the man's Gesa. I said:

'Gwawl, or whatever name the Irish call you, I call on you to play against me. Play me three games of Fichel. At each game I wager my head if I lose, but if I win, then you must give me what I ask, or play another game.'

Gwawl looked at me hard, and then he called in a tone of anger to his men:

'Find me a Fichel board.'

And they routed about among the ruins of the strong-hold, and they came to us with a Fichel board, the board of the Fichel of the Nine Men.

Now this Fichel is played on a board that is nine squares to the side, as other Fichel games are played on boards that are of seven or eleven squares each way, or on oblong boards of different sizes. And it is played without dice or the least interposition of chance or of divine favour. In this game, one player has the king, who at the start stands in the middle, and the other has the eight men who stand in the four corners in pairs. And the king must move one square at every turn, and the men one square only at a move. The task of the men is so to hem in the king that he cannot move, but the king, if he can, may kill the men if he catches them alone. Now the object of the game is not the same for the two sides. The men can win only if they kill the king. But if the king is still alive by the end of whatever number of moves the players have agreed, then the king has won.

So it was that I sat at the Fichel board to play against Gwawl. And it was I that took the king for each game, since, I pointed out, I had come alone into the rath as the king into the Fichel board, outnumbered and shut in.

Now, the first game we played was a Fichel of seventeen moves, the Game of the Warrior, and a speedy game was it with a sure end. Because Gwawl was not used to my style, in twelve moves, six to him and six to me, I had killed four of his eight men, and there was no hope that the others could hem me in. Still, he would not surrender, being a king himself, and he played out the last sterile moves while his men watched by the flickering light of the fire, because the dusk had now fallen.

When all the seventeen moves were played, Gwawl glared at me. He asked:

'What then is it that you are wanting of me?'

'That instead of giving me to Queen Maeve, you send me and my man here' – because it was easier to pretend that Aristarchos was someone of no importance – 'back alive to Cuchullain.'

'That I will do,' said Gwawl, because he was bound by his Gesa to respect his wager and to pay it, whatever other promise he must break. But there spoke a voice from the darkness beyond the fire:

'That you cannot do.'

We stood, and we all looked into the shadows, and it was Cathbad the Druid who stood there, and we knew him by the white of his robe and by his voice and not by his face, which was swollen with weeping for all the dead of Ireland that had fallen because I had come to seek Gold. He stood there, and he began to intone a poem, in the terse evocative style that was even now old-fashioned and dying out in favour of the complex rhythmical metres that imitated hexameters:

The rain fell on the pastures at the end of the cattle drive,
The cows lowed, the bulls tore the ground.
All Ulster shouted to urge the beasts over the river –
The Champion's shouts, the heart's sound.

He rode in his Chariot, his eyes started from his head,
The Grey Horse struck who ran.
He thrust with his spear, they fell before him –
Hero of Ulster, the greatest man.

Blood was on Gold and on silver and on enamel,
The mud dried on his face:
Thirsty with death he looked for water and saw
A pool in a reedy place.

The Champion left his chariot and bent to drink:
Beneath his hands, water is red.
The reeds rustled, he threw his spear and saw
The otter shield on the face of the dead.

Three women cooked over a fire by dry thorns.
They told him, 'Take, eat!'
True to his Gesa, he gnawed the bone, and asked:
'Dog,' they said, 'this day is sweet.'

At the ford, the last of the cattle are crossing,
Erc says, 'Give me thy spear.'
True to his Gesa, the Champion hurls it.
When did Erc know fear?

On foot to the standing stone is the road of the Champion.
His own spear pierces his shield.
With a prince's belt he ties himself to the pillar.
Standing he cannot yield.

The hosts of Callum urge the cattle over the river:
Conchobar's chariots mass beyond the ford.
The host of Connaught dare not cross to meet them –
The Champion holds his sword.

Lugaid goes forward, brave, to deal the last stroke.
The Champion's head on the sand.

The sword falls from his shoulder – beneath the pillar
Earth receives Lugaid's hand.

The Hosts of Maeve roll forward into the river,
At her pole, a head.
The Champion's hand they throw in the face of all Ulster –
Emain knows Cuchullain is dead.

There was a long silence. When we looked again, Cathbad
was gone. I pulled myself together. Who was dead, was dead, I
told Gwawl, as harshly as I could:

'If you cannot pay your debts, King, then you must play
again.'

And this time, we sat down to the Fichel of fifty-one moves,
the Game of Champions, the longest that is commonly played.
It must be obvious to you, now, that the more moves the less
chance there is that the king will live. Yet it is possible to play the
game of the fifty-ones moves, if you play well, and not to lose, if
you hold the king, and if you are wise and cautious and at the
same time bold. And play well I did that evening, with the circle
of savage warriors to watch us, breathing over me and watching
my style with interest, because there was not a man of them but
was fair mad on the game.

After twenty-three moves, I killed one of Gwawl's men,
though now he had played me once before it was harder to catch
him. After forty-seven moves, I killed another. And at the fifty-
first move, when he thought he had me, I wafted the king gently
out of his grasp, and that was the end, and all the Leinstermen
who stood behind me saw it.

'Pay your debts, King Gwawl. Let us both, my man and I, go
to Tara, and let us stay there in the Plain and be fed by the people
of the village till there come an Eagle to feed us.'

'Aye, and it is a long time that it is that you will be waiting,'
Gwawl sneered at us, laughed at us. 'What makes you think that
the Eagles will ever come now?'

'Now?' I echoed.

'Aye, now. Do you think that you are the only one to know
that the Eagles follow trade? The nightmare it is that follows all

the Kings of Ireland, and not the High King only, through all their waking watchful nights. That is our terror, the thought of a Roman in every village of Ireland, stealing all our poor pennies to send back to enrich your incense-filled temples in Rome. No that shall never be while there is an Irish King alive.

'It was only by chance that I heard of it. If Cuchullain will go to Eboracum and to Londinium, to learn wisdom, I thought, why should I not go to Rome itself, and see for myself what made the oil-eaters so greedy? And so I did ... And even there I should not have learnt what was going on if my Gesa had not driven me to gamble, and to meet that pretty fool with the Monopoly in his pocket. Ready he was to boast about it. I soon settled him. But you, Photinus, you were more trouble, and yet I would have done for you too, if not for Pryderi ... If you had stayed in Londinium, I would have had you when the nights got dark. But I had no chance out there on the road, and in the Mere, with all *his* friends about you. Pryderi!' Gwawl spat. 'That two-and-a-half-obol king of a half-obol kingdom, and even that in pawn to the Roman, for all he is so proud of his crown and so careful of his people. Just because my young men have been raiding along the coasts of Dyfed, and how else shall they marry without heads to buy their brides with, and because the Romans have not been able to stop us as they promised, he takes it into his head to help any scheme that will bring down all the thrones of Ireland, and have us all in the same state that he is in. There was no hope of defeating him to get at you. But in spite of him, we knew all about you, we learned every detail of your plan and every change in your mind.'

'That cannot be,' I told him, and yet I knew it was true, that he did know everything, and I knew, and I *would* not know, and yet I did know, who it was that had told him, that had sat with Pryderi and me so long and so often by the fireside in the Mere, who knew all that Pryderi knew – and yet there were things she could not know, because I had not even told Pryderi.

'Rhiannon told us,' he shouted at me, in triumph. 'She sent us news of everything you said, by this messenger or that, men or birds or spirits, how should you know or how should you care? And when she knew the time, then she came to me, and I brought

524

her off safely into this land of all her kinsman. And then, there was nothing to do, but to wait till you and Cuchullain came to waste both the armies of the North and of the West. When that was done, I could come out myself and become High King of Ireland, and who better for it than I who had saved the Island of the Blessed?'

'And what good will it do you?' I asked him. There was no harm in talking now, he knew enough. 'It is little comfort being the High King will be to you when the legions come. It happened to Vercingetorix after Alesia fell, and it will happen to you. A short walk in the Triumph, and then – into the Mamertine. Do you know it? A stone box, thirty feet square, with a spring in one corner, that keeps it always damp. But you will not feel rheumatism there, oh no, you won't stay long enough. Four men to hold you and one to twist the rope, slowly … slowly … and your eyes burst out … and the noise in your ears … and then, into the Great Sewer with what is left.'

He still laughed at me, strutting and threatening.

'And what makes *you* think that the legions will ever come? How do you think they will sail now? Aye, we knew that they would come soon, who wouldn't know, with the hammers and the axes going and the ships building in every creek? But the day that Cuchullain held the white mare for Conchobar to mount, that day Rhiannon did our business for us. That day she raised the Brigantes, that day she set all North Britain aflame from sea to sea. How can the Second and the Twentieth sail, if the Sixth is threatened?'

Aristarchos spoke for the first time.

'There are legions and to spare in Gaul and in Germany to hold down the Brigantes and let the others sail.'

Gwawl went on.

'Do you think we Barbarians are as disunited as politicians in Rome? On that same day, there was war from the mouth of the Rhine to the mouth of the Danube. That very day, the Marcomen sacked Vindabonum, and now they are pressing to Aquileia. There are no reinforcements for Britain.'

'Oh, my regiment!' said Aristarchos. 'Oh, my Rangers! To go to war, and I not there to lead you!'

'The regiment you raised among the Brigantes? How else do you think Vindabonum fell but when they deserted? Mutiny against Rome to them was loyalty to Rhiannon. They will pass across the land of the Chatti and through the Friesians across the North Sea, and will fight against the legions before the harvest.'

'I do not believe it,' said Aristarchos. 'It is not true. There is no rebellion. You are lying to make us despair.' He did not say 'Frighten us'; he did not know the word.

Someone stepped forward. I knew him, stout and middle-aged. He had been the other of the two men with the Mouse. Now he had a sword cut on the face, his ear was hanging by a strip of skin, and the unwashed blood was black. He held a bundle on his outstretched forearms, a scarlet Roman cloak folded under and up and over what might have been a great dish. The cloak was a fine one. It was not what the quartermaster issues, but made to measure of close-woven wool, light and warm together, fit for a tribune, or for a very senior centurion.

'This one died well. I killed him myself.'

He turned back the edges of the cloak. It covered a shield, oblong and convex; the leather was hacked and gashed. In the hollow of the shield was a sword, legionary pattern, the edge gapped, the point turned. There was half of a staff of vine wood, snapped off. There was a bundle of Phalerae. I had seen them before. And black and woolly haired, the lips drawn back from the shining teeth in an awful grimace of rage and shame and pain, I saw the head of Caius Julius Africanus.

'It is true. When the Primus Pilus carries a shield and fights in the ranks, the legion is all but lost.' Aristarchos wrapped his cloak about his face, and wept. The middle-aged man went on.

'Now there is no one to stop us in the Island of Britain. We have burnt every ship on the Western Coast. The legions will not come.'

Now I knew why the army of Leinster had not come against us at Tara, why they had not been there to hold back the host of Callum the Hairy, so that their villages would not be burnt and their cattle not stolen. They had been at sea, saving Ireland, whatever the cost to Leinster, as Rhiannon had saved Ireland, whatever the cost to Britain.

526

I had no time to weep, not for the hand of Cuchullain in the dust, not for Africanus, fallen in the front rank. I had no time to weep for the treachery of Rhiannon. It is the surest mark of love, that it betrays, and how could I ever think otherwise? I could only face Gwawl and tell him:

'If you cannot pay your debts, King of Leinster, then you must play again.'

It was well dark when we played our third game of Fichel, the Game of Kings, the game of a hundred and nineteen moves. The Leinstermen stood round with their flaring torches, that brought smoke as well as light to the gaming board, and they counted the moves, shouting the numbers.

'Twenty-one!' and the king moved away in his constant circling.

'Twenty-two!' and one man came to back another that would have been killed otherwise.

The king turned and twisted, the eight men dodged and shuffled like wolves about an elk in winter, but I had too much of the wolf in my blood to die like an elk. Let me tell you this, it is easier to control one man on the board or on the battlefield than eight. It was late. Gwawl was tired from days of pursuit, by land and by sea, from battles and marches, from judgements and decisions. He played most of the time with half his men, he missed his chances.

'Seventy-eight!' and the men stood on three sides of the king.

'Seventy-nine!' and the king moved to threaten two men at once.

'Eighty!' and Gwawl saw the danger, but imperfectly, and moved one man back to where he was safe, when he should have brought a third man to guard them both.

'Eighty-one!' and the king struck, and a man rolled on the ground.

This reminded Gwawl that he had four men he had hardly used at all, and he began to move them to where he thought they might be of help in containing the king, and soon he lost another. But now my eyes were smarting from the smoke of the torches and the fire, and the sweat on my face had little to do with the heat of the logs and turf. My king dodged and feinted and moved spasmodically from edge to centre and back again to edge.

527

'A hundred and nine!' and I erred, and the king was stopped, trapped, if only Gwawl had wit to see it, he was dead next move, and I had lost, lost for myself, what was worse, lost for Aristarchos.

'A hundred and ten!' and he had learned his lesson too well, and he was more eager to guard his own piece than to attack mine.

'A hundred and eleven!' and the king was away, and safe for another move.

But there was still time. The six men pressed and pushed. The king was harried. Three moves left now, to each side, and he was too near the edge of the board for comfort or confidence. Two moves each side, and he was pressed back towards the corner. One move each. Gwawl's last, and had he been more alert he would have seen his chance. But the very man he moved to block the king's way exposed another to vengeance.

'A hundred and nineteen,' cried all the Leinstermen together. The king, in his last move, struck, and struck true.

Gwawl sat rigid, looking at his board. Aristarchos sighed a long sigh. I could not move. We all three slept a little where we sat. I felt as empty as I had on the Night of the Thorn. The Leinstermen stood around us and watched, silent. Africanus stared at us from glazed, unclosing eyes. Suddenly, there was the sound of a cock crowing, the only cock left for miles uneaten, his neck unwrung. We all three blinked our eyes open into the new day. I said to Gwawl:

'Pay your debts, King of Leinster. Give us a boat, sound and dry, and food and drink, that we two may return to whence we came.'

'Go, then, to the Gods Below,' he answered. 'I give you the mercy you showed me at Rutupiae.'

But he was more merciful. They brought us down to the sea-beach where we ate a scanty meal of stale barley bread, and mouldy beef, and water from the river, muddied and fouled by the crossing of great armies high inland. The corpses of men and horses bobbed past us into the salt water. The Leinstermen ate no better than we two did.

They found us a big skin boat, and there was no saying it was not good enough, because it was in boats like this that the army of Leinster had crossed the sea to the Isle of Britain. More bread and meat they put in it, and a big jar of beer they found, the only beer for miles. They left us all we had, our weapons, and my bag with my spare eyes and my dice and other trifles. And then Gwawl came to me with my cloak, my sealskin, and he apologised that it was soiled, because he had had to kill the man who picked it up to get it back for me. And his own cloak, of bearskin from the edge of the Summer Country, he gave to Aristarchos.

Gwawl and his men got into other boats. The middle-aged man took Africanus's white shield, and stood on the beach. The Irishmen paddled out to sea, towing us with them. Far out beyond the ninth wave they took us, till, low as we were in the water, we could no longer see the white shield on the shore. All the boats but one left us. Only Gwawl remained, and he leant over to me. He shouted against the south-west wind: 'One last thing. What was the answer to that riddle?'

'What riddle?'

'The one you asked me on the judgement mound of Arberth? What is both black and white and neither in earth or in sky?'

'Oh, that,' and I laughed, because it was such a little thing to remember through all the months of context and plotting and battle. 'You'll never be a Druid. Why, that was yourself, black hearted, white-clad, standing head in clouds on the mound above the Earth. And another thing, King of Leinster!'

'What?' He was drifting away now, towards the shore.

'Give up gambling – you haven't got the head for it.'

529

Chapter Nine

For seven days and nights we tossed on the seas, between the Island of the Blessed and the Island of the Mighty. At first we tried to head the boat eastward, across the south wind. We paddled silently, our teeth clenched in the bitterness of defeat, saying nothing because neither of us would admit aloud what we both knew, that we could no more paddle that boat to Britain than we could fly.

And that boat *could* have flown. Light as a feather, wicker-framed and leather-covered, it hopped and bobbed across the wave tops in the hard wind. The seas broke beneath us. We could not be swamped, but we were covered in spray. Our clothes dried stiff and white. The barley bread was soaked in salt water, the dried beef was drenched in brine till it would have outlived a mummy. We drank mouthfuls of the beer. It was a diuretic which drained the water from our blood. Both Aristarchos and I had thirsted before. We licked the rain water from the bottom of the boat before the spray splashed in to pollute it. For want of pebbles we sucked spare eyes from my bag – he a ruby, I an amethyst, and that was a strange precaution, for how were we to get drunk?

Only, before we shut our mouths against speech and thirst, Aristarchos said:

'Already they sing their songs about Cuchullain: they will sing none about us.'

'They will sing our deeds and give them to Cuchullain,' I told him. 'Almost every Bard has made his own song, and altered the plain truth of the deeds to fit his own metre. Did you ever see the Setanta able to tell one horse from another? But a hero must have a horse that can be named. And each Bard makes his song fit what his Lord wants to hear, and there will in one generation be a hundred songs of Cuchullain. Yet each Bard will swear that he sings the true and authentic facts of the case, handed down word-perfect from eyewitnesses. At last, someone will write the song down, as Homer did, and write one particular Bard's song among many. And then there will be only one song about Cuchullain, and every other Bard will alter his own song to accord with the true, the written word. All the other tales will soon be forgotten, and we with them.'

'Forgotten and accursed, because defeated.'

'What kind of Briton are you dressed up to be? If you were really a native of the Island of the Mighty, then you would say that defeat is the surest sign of virtue and that failure shows how you enjoy the favour of the Gods. Gwawl has succeeded. He has challenged the might of Rome all across Europe, and he has saved his island, and there is little doubt that he will rule it when Maeve and Conchobar have torn out each others' throats. But no one in Ireland will remember him, and the Britons will know his name only as someone that Pryderi rolled in the mud, and they will invent reasons why that is how the game of the Badger in the Bag was first played. And Pryderi the King will be forgotten, except that as a king he wandered unknown through cities that did not know him, and that with some shadowy companion called Mannanan he cheated shoemakers and shield-makers. And there will be a shadowy memory that Madoc was a sea captain and that Heilyn once sailed in a ship, Caw will only be remembered as the father of his many sons. All will be forgotten, except that dying man bound to the standing stone.'

We spoke no more. By night we lashed ourselves to the single thwart by our belts, and clung on, besides, wakeful, lest we be overturned and drowned in our sleep. By day we took it in turns, one to sleep and one to beat off the birds who would have taken the bread from our mouths if we had had any bread, and the eyes from our heads if they had a chance. It was the salmon mallet we used for this.

We were drifted north by the winds and the tides. We passed close enough to some shore, to the eastward, to see great mountains, miles high. Another time we came near to a rocky coast with seals lying on the beaches, but the tide carried us off, and we watched it dwindle bluer and bluer through the day.

Then, on the eighth day, when we were very weak and not inclined to talk even had our lips been dry enough, I was awake and Aristarchos was asleep, and I realised that we had some peace. The gulls and the gannets had ceased to torment us: they no longer dived at our eyes. Instead, I could see them circling ahead of us, a tower of white feathers above some object moving across the water, as yet invisible from our little boat so close to the surface.

And then, as the seabirds came nearer, I began to see it all, lifting above the close horizon. First the tip of a mast, flying a pennant chequered with yellow and black. Then a great dark lug-sail, the sail of a ship on a broad reach, crossing us from starboard to port, and heading east across the north-west wind.

'A ship!' I shouted to Aristarchos. I shook him awake, I thrust the paddle into his hand. 'A ship! A ship, paddle to it, paddle to the ship!'

And paddle to it we did, and we shouted through our cracked dry throats, and now we could see the gunwales and heads above them, and she lost way and came round towards us into the wind, finer and finer as they made towards us as best they could. And what other ship would we see so far out at sea, and what other ship would we meet at such a time? A ship of the Venetii, a ship built long ago on the coasts of Gaul, a ship that Aristarchos knew as well as I. We shouted, we shouted, and we tried to believe we recognised the voices that shouted back to us.

We came alongside, under her lee, crossing her bow, and someone threw us a rope. I looked up into his face, and it was a face I had not expected to see on the salt water. He no longer squinted, but it was the man I knew, from the inn at Bonnonia, who drew fish and made strange allusions. He helped us aboard, first Aristarchos; and I could hear his cracked cries of surprise and then the gurgling as he drank – he was never very dainty. Then I hauled myself up the side on a rope, and hands clutched me to help me over the bulwarks.

'Come on, boy,' said Madoc. 'Saved us a lot of trouble them birds have. Thought it was I did we'd have to go all down the coast of Ireland to find you.'

'Who shall drink of this water shall thirst again, but he who drinks of the cup of life shall never thirst,' said the man from Bonnonia. That, I thought, was a typical Brit saying, except that to my mild surprise he said it in Greek, a Greek with a Jewish accent, but the dialect of one of the smaller islands, Leros or Patmos or Cos. I snatched at the jug and half drained it before I saw whose hands had offered it.

'Not too greedy, now,' said Pryderi. 'It wouldn't be very dainty if we had you burst over the floor.'

'Not floor, deck,' I corrected him. I wasn't going to have him treat me as if I were a landsman. Now I was in my proper place, as he had been on the road. I looked around that lovely ship, lovely as a woman, I thought, lovely as Rhiannon. Oh, a splendid place to be, on the open sea, clear of all the plots and double dealing of the land. My spirits were rising again, as I drank, and cleaned a chicken leg and tore at a cake of oat bread. Now, I was in a ship, and I was my own master again, and among seamen. The only real landsman I could see was Aristarchos, and it was only for him that Pryderi would have to choose his words. I looked aft. Beside the steersman, in a short white tunic, unspotted, of course, by the marks of toil, stood Taliesin.

'What use is he?' I asked.

'Very useful he do be in recognising the stars,' Madoc assured me, but he went on, 'or at least he will be if ever we get a clear night and any stars to recognise.'

'And how many more have you got like this?' I asked testily. I felt I had a right to know. I had after all, been promised the use of this ship for the summer's trade and I was at least entitled to have it for this return voyage.

'Only four men forward, like this one here,' said Madoc, waving at the man from Bonnonia, and speaking with the familiar tone of someone trying to delay the impact of bad news. 'And aft, there's five of us, and now you.' He hesitated, unsure of how to explain himself, and he was saved the trouble. Out of the cabin under the poop came Cicva.

'Well, at least we'll have some good food in this tub, as far as the cooking goes,' I admitted, grudgingly prepared to forgive the presence of a woman in a ship, seeing it was this sensible and competent queen. But then behind Cicva, yawning and stretching arms as if fresh from sleep, and shocking that was, too, being only a couple of hours before noon, why, who else would it be, with all those ghastly birds around us, but Rhiannon.

'If she's in this flaming ship,' I told them angrily, 'then it's me for the skin boat again. Hoist it out!'

'Shame on you!' scolded Cicva. 'And wasn't it Rhiannon herself who made us come out to sea again after we'd all got safe into the North among the Picts, out of reach of those filthy Romans with all their pillaging and atrocities that they're doing everywhere, delighted they are too that they've got an excuse. We took my little Mannanan up there to be fostered with his Aunty Bithig and home up there with my Grandfather Casnar I would have been pleased enough to stay, but no, out to sea she would go, and it was never letting her go by herself I could be, not with these old goats that call themselves sailors.'

Rhiannon came up to me, all smiling and shining, and looked at me in a proprietorial fashion, as if she had never done me a wrong. I glared at her.

'Why do you look at me like that, Mannanan, when I have saved your life a hundred times?' she asked. 'Did I not send all the birds of the sea to find you, and to hover above you like a tall mast with a fine flag on it, so that we could see you from afar and sail down to pick you out of the water? I belong to you, Mannanan, and after all I have suffered I still return to you when I could so easily be free of you for ever.'

'Traitor,' I told her. I was not angry, this was past the point of anger. 'You have betrayed me to my ruin, and may yet betray me to my death. And you have been the death of good men all up and down the edges of the Empire. What more trouble will you bring on me and on Caesar?'

'I might have been the death of one man at any time,' she answered, 'and saved all other blood. There was never a moment, Mannanan, from the day you saw me first in Londinium to the day you set sail for Ireland, when anything but my word stood between you and swift and silent death. There were men enough ready to kill you, Mannanan, eager to kill you. But I took an oath from Gwawl, and from all the men of the Brigantes, that there should not be a hair of your head touched. How do you think a

534

one-eyed man lives in battle? You were safer facing the host of Gwawl than leading the host of Ulster.'

'And Maeve?'

'A hard woman she is, and cruel, and not one to give up her prey. But I made her swear, at the least, that if she had you in her power, she would keep you alive till I came, and then, we stand together, Mannanan – what can prince or queen or emperor do to harm us?'

I heard her voice and I looked into her eyes. I took her hand and I turned to my friends.

'Whither do we go now?'

'Not back to the Picts,' said Aristarchos. 'They will have my head, and I still have my own uses for it.'

'If we continue south,' Madoc declared, 'we will be on the shores that belong to Callum the Hairy, and it is already one ship of mine that he has trapped and looted, and I do not want to be in a second.'

'If we go south east,' Pryderi told us, 'then it is neither I nor Rhiannon nor Taliesin will live long, nor die slowly, if we meet the legions in the field.'

'And they are looking for me in Britain,' said the man from Bonnonia, to whom this conversation was of interest, 'for blasphemy and treason combined, in that I refused to burn incense before the statue of the Emperor.'

I ignored him. If a man could bring himself to do such a horrid and unprincipled thing as that, then what did he deserve but the punishment decreed by law, whatever that may be. I spoke only to the others.

'I have seen a map, and I have spoken to astronomers who know. Ireland lies half-way between Britain and Spain. Let us then sail west, passing north of Ireland, and in a few days we shall be in the harbour of Gades.'

I took the steering oar from Grathach's hand. They then trimmed the sail. I had the breeze on my right cheek.

'West, then,' I cried. 'West, due west, and home!'

THE END

Places mentioned in the text with their modern names

Bonnonia	Boulogne
Bordigala	Bordeaux
Calleva	Silchester
Corinium	Cirencester
Cunetio	Marlborough
Deva	Chester
Dubris	Dover
Durovernum	Canterbury
Eboracum	York
Glevum	Gloucester
Isca	Caerleon
Lindum	Lincoln
Londinium	London
Lugdunum	Lyons
Lutetia	Paris
Massilia	Marseilles
Noviomagus	Chichester
Pontes	Staines
Rutupiae	Richborough
Sulis	Bath
Venta	Caerwent

MEN WENT
TO CATTRAETH

In Memoriam
Roger Berkshire

Author's Note

This is a work of the imagination, not of history, nor yet a translation. We know nothing about the Battle of Cattraeth, neither when it was fought, nor against whom, nor where, apart from what we read in the surviving ninety-seven elegies which go under Aneirin's name. We do not even know how long after the battle they were written down in their present form. But this is the setting in which the battle must have taken place.

The chapter headings and their translations are taken from the edition of John Williams ab Ithel, published in 1852.

1

Carasswn disgynnu yg Cattraeth gessevin
Gwert med yg kynted a gwirawt win

I could wish to have been the first to shed my blood in Cattraeth
As the price of the mead and the drink of wine in the Hall.

I wish that I had been the first to shed my blood before Cattraeth. But it is now that I pay the price for the wine and mead of
the feasts in Mynydog's Hall. Late, indeed, I came to the feasts.

I came in the afternoon to sight of the Rock of Dumbarton. I
had with me Aidan, son of Cormac King of the Northern Coasts,
whose Judge I had been through the winter. Not a King like you
find in the South. We walked across all his Kingdom to hear his
people's quarrels and judge them and settle the prices in five
days. He had perhaps, in a desperate time, four hundred men
who could bear arms, and those arms would only be their axes,
or scythe-heads tied to long poles. There were only five swords
in the whole Kingdom, and one cape of mail that Cormac wore.
But he was a King, just as Evrog the Wealthy was King in Dumbarton, and Uther in Camelot, Theodoric in Rome and Zeno in
Byzantium and Clovis in Gaul.

I climbed the rock of Dumbarton with Aidan before me and
Morien the charcoal-burner whose father no one knew behind
me. Steep that rock is, and the path is beaten earth, not stone cut
into steps as they say is the path to Camelot. All the harder for
an enemy, Evrog used to say. All the harder for his own men,
labouring up with bags of salt and casks of water, with carcasses
of meat and dried salmon and bales of hay for the horses. All the
harder too for the horses when they were brought down to exercise in the plain. And hard for me.

541

Yet that hard climb up the rock was for me the beginning of my journey to Cattraeth. From this place, Evrog ruled his vast kingdom, Strathclyde and Galloway to the borders of Cumbria. He was hard pressed by the Scots who came flooding in from Ireland, and it was certain that if they did not come to stay this year, then they would some day soon. So had Cormac's father come thirty years ago. In the East, Evrog was always at loggerheads with Mynydog King of Eiddin, although they never came quite to open war: their enmity was more a matter of pinpricks and cattle-raids and hiring poets to sing satires and scurrilous verses against each other. And now, the Savages who had taken the attention of the King of Eiddin for long enough were come far west enough to attack Galloway from the South. This was, I thought a more serious thing than any settlements of the Scots from Ireland, because they were all Christian and worshipped the Virgin: and the people there are the same as we are, only differing in their way of speech, honouring poets and smiths and all makers far above any soldier or King. But the Savages do not live in this Roman way, and there is no understanding them.

Yet Evrog was cheerful enough all the time I knew him, saying that there was no other way for a King to live in such a situation. If once he stopped to shed a tear he would weep for ever.

Evrog's Gatekeeper knew me well. He was Cynon, son to Clydno who was King Mynydog's Judge. Cynon had been to the South beyond the wall, and had learned to read several words of obvious utility like *deus* and *rex* and *poena* and *tributum* from Cattog the Wise in the School of Illtud. He had seen great cities with his own eyes, Chester and Gloucester and Caerleon. But he had not wished to be a Bishop, as he could easily have been, since he had no wish to live walled up and at the beck and call of any little monk who wanted to be ordained, so he came home, and was now Captain of the Household to Evrog. Now, they tell me, Cynon is a great man, and for all that his arm is crooked at the elbow and cannot strike a blow, he stands as Judge at Arthur's throne. Seeing me, as he was coming out of the Hall to blow the horn for the King's dinner, he shouted out the words I did not want to hear, 'Make way for Aneirin! Behold the Chief Bard of the Isle of Britain. Stand aside all, that the greatest Poet of Rome may pass!'

Once I would have thought that my due, less than my due

indeed, and everyone in the Island knew it, and there was no boasting in acknowledging the truth. But now – I was no longer a Bard, though the bitter words were spoken and could not be called back.

I walked through the gate into the Dun of King Evrog, all set around with spiked logs the height of a man, with stables for a hundred horses and three hundred men, safe against the Irish. Evrog's Hall was not of stone as are palaces in the South, with pillars of marble and roofs sheeted with gold and the walls covered with magic pictures. Not even Evrog here in the North could pay for those workmen from far away to bring their magic to his Dun: no man born in the Island has the art now of cutting stone by spells. He had lately new built the Hall in the Roman manner, with straight sides and a rounded end in which he set his High Table. The logs of the walls were thick and the chinks well stuffed with mud and seaweed, and the thatch was of oatstraw, which is better than reeds.

Evrog was wealthy. He showed his wealth, hanging tapestry from the walls and weapons from the pillars. He showed forty swords, and with mail and axes and spears he could send forth a Household, mounted, of a hundred men, and this was, at the time, more than any King had ever done in the Island from the beginning of time. So the whole of this immense Hall, forty or fifty paces long, glittered with iron. It glittered, because beside the fire in the centre Evrog would burn rush lights, dipped in tallow, twenty or thirty at a time, to light the feast. You will understand therefore that a feast in Evrog's Hall was a scene of magnificence such as few even in the South see more than once in a year.

I went in and sat low at the table. All Evrog's great landowners were there, looking at me, and knowing me, and saying nothing, seeing that I was sitting where I wanted to sit. They thought perhaps that I was come to recite a Satire on Evrog paid for by Mynydog, or even by some Irish King, that would do half the business of a war. I have destroyed whole armies in my time with my verses: before I rode to Cattraeth.

Then Cynon, standing now at the High Table, for would you have him sit outside all the time and miss his supper, blew his horn again, and the great ones of Evrog's Court filed in.

Evrog's Judge came first, and then his Butler and his Treasurer, his Steward and his Manciple, his Bailiff and the Master of his Horse, the more important coming later. There was a harper in the Hall, but no Bard, since Evrog's Bard had died the year before, so that Evrog entered, and his Queen with him, and his principal guest last of all.

When the Queen went to pour the first cup for Cynon, and then for her King, as is right, I bowed my head low so that the man who now sat at Evrog's right should not see me. But he did see me, and spoke to the King. Then Cynon, drinking, blew the Horn for the third time, and the King called out. 'The knife is in the meat, and the drink is in the cup. Let no man enter but who is skilled in craftsmanship and preeminent in his art. And if there is any one such in the Hall, let him come and sit at my right hand.'

Now, these are conventional words which every King in all the Empire says when he sits to eat. But this evening, Evrog shouted it out, and Cynon answered loudly, because in those days he had knowledge and no wisdom, like myself, 'Forward Aneirin! Forward the Pre-eminent Chief Poet of the Isle of Britain.'

The men around me seized my elbows and pushed me forward. There was no use my protesting or refusing. They would only have lifted me up and carried me bodily to the High Table. They would have taken my denials only as posings, as if I were any common bard who earned his bread by measure, singing from Hall to Hall and Court to Court. I, Aneirin, never said that I was anything but a great poet: the truth was too clear for anyone to deny. Now I was no longer a poet. But to have explained that to the men around me was too difficult. It was easier to obey than to make a scene.

At the High Table, I sat where they put me, where *he* had first sat, though I had to wait a little while they brought in from the King's sleeping house the Chair he himself had awarded me, the Chair in which no one else was ever allowed to sit. And they made *him* sit on the King's other hand, who ought to have sat in the highest place of honour. For he was Precent.

A strong man was Precent. Not tall, he was a head shorter than I was, but strongly built. Heavy, and strong above all. Some men of that build are only fat, but Precent, why, he could carry off a young ox, and the yoke and chains on it. He used to have sport, seeing how thick a rod of iron he could twist like a rope. The short black hairs bristled on his arms, and his black curls

544

were blacker, sleeked down with goose-grease. His black eyes sparkled in the light of the wax candles they had placed on the table in front of the King, two of them in a precious bronze candlestick. There is no one now who knows where bronze is mined or from what kind of rock it is smelted.

Now the Queen was withdrawn, Peredur served us with mead; young Peredur that is, Evrog's seventh son, who is now such a great man in Arthur's Hall. He was named after his uncle, Peredur Ironarms, Master of Evrog's Horse.

Oh, a strong man was Precent, in all civilised arts. A strong man for breaking a horse, for throwing a steer for gelding. A strong man was he for riding all day with the herd or for running the fells to gather in the sheep. He was a man strong for stalking deer all day in the drizzling rain, or for pitching sheaves into a wagon in the harvest sun. Today he had ridden from Eiddin all the width of Alban, and still there he sat at table, bright as a button. He was young, and so were we all then, young and strong.

Precent talked to Evrog all through the meal, or across us both to the Queen who sat by me. I kept my head down and said nothing. The others did not find this strange, even though they had not seen me all winter. They did not ask me where I had been. Only Precent said to the King, 'Aneirin's got the awen on him tonight. There's a fine poem we'll get from him when he has finished eating.'

But I knew I could never have the awen on me again.

When the meal was finished, Evrog beat on the table. While the mead went round again, and the Queen withdrew, as was the custom in Strathclyde, the King said loud so that all could hear the distinction between conversation overheard and an announcement made. 'Now that the great and principal guest, unexpected though he was, has been fed, tell me, Precent, King of the Picts: why is it you have come tonight into the Kingdom of Strathclyde seeing that for so long you were gatekeeper to my rival Mynydog?'

Precent went red in the face, and cleared his throat loudly, and drowned the frog in mead. He was always longwinded in his speeches, and clumsy in his choice of words, so I hoped that he would offend nobody: and while he talked I would withdraw my mind and think of Bradwen in Eiddin. Precent began well enough.

'A man I am, a man. Gatekeeper to Mynydog I was, and it is

545

some of you I have kept out of his sheepfolds before now, as well you all know. With what little strength I have, I did what I could.'

'Who stole the gadflies off Morddwydtywyllon's cow?' someone shouted. I think it was Peredur Ironarms, because he was always put out to think there could be anybody stronger than he was. It rather put Precent off his speech, and he shouted angrily, losing his composure and thickening his Pictish vowels.

'It is not a matter of cows I am come about, but the matter of the life and death of the Isle of Britain.' His bellow cut through the laughter, and the men below us quietened, sensing in his tone some emotion they had not expected in him.

'It is more than cows you will get if you listen to me. Glory and honour and praise I am come to tell you about, and offer to you all for little effort. Mynydog King of Eiddin is a generous man, though no one calls him "wealthy" to his face, and a proud man too. Those who do him service in one campaign may swagger and be proud all the rest of their lives and tell their children, "I was there". It is men he wants, warriors excelling in weapons, youths exulting in war.'

'Aye, he wants us to steal our own cows for him,' sneered someone from lower down the hall. Precent pretended he didn't hear it, but nevertheless he countered at once.

'In battle against the bloody Loegrians let us loose our blades, not shedding brothers' blood. Savages from over the Ocean, in the salt seas washed, not in sweet baptism bathed, they neither serve the Holy Virgin nor venerate her saints. They persecute her Bishops and betray her priests, thieves of bells are they and burners of thatch. There is nothing that the Holy Virgin desires more than that we should kill them and drive them from this Island.'

A noble of Mynydog's ought to know that, I thought. There was a hermit in the wood behind Mynydog's Hall, and the King had spent good silver to send this man to Iona and have him made a priest, and had bought a book for him to read, so that he could tell Mynydog the days for Easter and Assumption and the other great feasts, and so that he could have his dead prayed for. Not to be outdone, Evrog had sent one of his nephews, Gelorwid, to Iona, but him, for some reason, I could see sitting in the hall that night, not dressed as a hermit. Precent went on.

'I know that now the Savages trouble you little. It is the Scots out of Ireland who, you think, are your only foes. But believe you this. If the Savages from over the sea are not fought and beaten and crushed and driven utterly out of this island, then when the Kings of Ireland come again with their armies, it is the Savages they will fight before this rock, and not Romans. Because we will be dead before our time. And that will not be in ten generations or in two, but it will be the year after next if they wait so long. Carlisle has fallen. Will Dumbarton be the next?

'Strike not at the nearest foe, but at the most dangerous. Mynydog will fight them, whether you wish or not. If there is any man here who thinks himself skilful and strong enough to come and fight the Savages with us, let him stand up and ride out with me, to share in the glory and honour and profit of this war. But do not come if there is any thought in your minds that it will be an easy campaign against a weak foe. Cunning in the field they are, and ruthless in war. How cruel, let Aneirin tell you. Silence for Aneirin, Pre-eminent Chief Bard of the Isle of Britain!'

I did not stand. I looked bleakly at the table before me, seeing the grain of the scrubbed pine. I had known it, I ought not to have come into a King's Hall, or into the company of anyone who knew who I was, till I had come again to Bradwen. I sat and stared at the backs of my hands on the table. At last I said, and they all hushed to listen to me, as if I had been singing for an englyn, or intoning a triad, 'I am not a Bard. I am no longer a poet. I will make no more songs. I have sung for the last time.'

The silence continued, only for the sound of indrawing breath. Evrog asked, 'What do you mean?'

'I mean what I say,' I told him. This was the first time I had told the truth about this in public. It was the first time I had told a King I would make no more poems, no more music to glorify his Kingdom, no more satires against his enemies. I still looked at my hands on the table. I would not look into the faces in front of me. To think that I, Aneirin, who had sung to every King in the North, was abashed in front of this audience.

'You all know the law as well as I do. Naked weapons must not be brought into the presence of a Bard. More. If a sword is drawn before a Bard, and blood is shed in his sight, then he is unclean, and he may not sing again that night. Think, then, what happened to me. More than swords were bared before me. Spears and saxes fought above me. The blood of my friends and my kinsmen flowed over me. The blood of Savages stained me. And that not once but twice. How then can I be a poet again? How can I ever sing again in all my life?'

'Nonsense,' Evrog told me. He could treat it lightly. The generous King had never felt terror, shame, pain like this. 'Nonsense,' he said, 'I'll have my priest up here to cleanse you in the morning. And if he can't do it, we'll take you to the Monastery, where they have a Bishop, and he will be able to do something. You have been baptised, haven't you? If we have to do that all over again, then I'll stand Godfather and the Queen will be your Godmother. Then you can come here and be my Bard – I can't get used to being without one.'

I shook my head. Even if it were possible, was he really thinking that he could get the greatest poet of the Roman world to be his household Bard, to write satires on his enemies and lullabies for his grandchildren in return for bed and board? It was not possible.

'Priests and Poets have nothing to do with each other. The Church hates poetry. Priests are men of writing. Bards sing, they do not write. A Priest would only read something over me out of a book. What good would that do?'

Precent spoke quickly. Trying to cover my embarrassment, unerringly he chose the wrong thing to say.

'Look, all of you! If there is nothing else will make you angry, see what the Savages have done to the greatest Poet of the age. A Poet is the greatest ornament any Kingdom can have, and Aneirin is so great that he belongs not to any one King, but to all the Romans of the Island. Think of all he did in those first few years of his flowering, while still a lad. Who of you has never sung his songs at the reaping, or never recited his verses to the plough team? Who has not walked a dozen miles to hear him sing to the harp or to challenge him to compose on a theme at first hearing? And now, he sits here and says he will not sing again.

'Look at him, Aneirin, Son of Manaw Gododdin, grandson to Cunedda, cousin to Mynydog Gododdin King of Eiddin. The blood of the greatest houses of North Britain, of South Britain within the Wall, of Ireland, flows in his veins. Sent from the South to be fostered he was, as I was from among the Picts in the house of Eudav the Tall, who lived beneath the Wall. Safe we were there, our parents thought, from the Irish, to learn all the arts of civility. We grew up there, he and I and Bradwen the daughter of Eudav.

'Ah, what a youth was Aneirin. Did you know there was one, once, who could outrun Precent? There he sits now as often he sat at the end of the long field, waiting for me to catch up. Did you know there was once one who could outwrestle even Precent? There he hangs down his head, as once he pressed my shoulders to the grass.'

Now, Precent was launched. Three cups of mead, we used to say, and Precent will charm the horns from a stag. Six cups of mead, and Precent will charm the moon from the sky. And not all by boredom, either, though partly – it is not a finished orator you would be calling him.

'All this he set aside to be a bard. These hands you have heard on the harp-strings, how often have they guided the team across the headlands. That voice you have heard sing, it has called the cattle home many a time, or spread the news of cattle-thieves on the moors – aye, and raiders from Strathclyde at that. His first songs I heard when we were still children, when we spent the happy summers in the leafy huts, watching the sheep on the green fells.

'It was to Eudav's house that Aneirin would return, long after he became a man, long after he became welcome in every Hall and every Dun North of the Wall, long after the Kings in the South would have given much to have him live there, in Cardigan or Camelot; long after I had returned to my father's seat among the Picts, long after Bradwen herself had gone to Mynydog's court. And that was when the Savages first came so far North. They came through the Wall. They burnt Eudav's house above Eudav's bloody trunk, and his head they carried away before his cattle. And with the cattle they took away Aneirin, to be their slave and their butt.

'That was a year ago. We heard of it, all of us, all across the Kingdom of Eiddin, across the lands of the Gododdin, into the realm of the Picts. Before the harvest was in the ear, I, Precent, made war. I brought my own men, Romans and Picts together,

and we gathered men in Eiddin. I led the Household of Mynydog the ever-victorious, pre-eminent in war. A hundred men in
mail I led out, an invincible array. Who could stand before us?
Who could resist us? The Savages fled, the Pagans would not
wait for us. We swept across the land of Mordei, and brought the
bones of Eudav for Bradwen to bury in Eiddin. And southwards
from Eudav's Hall, where they thought they were safe, the Savages were clearing the blessed forests to plant their vile wheat.
There we found Aneirin, the greatest poet of the world. In fet-
ters and in misery they kept him in a hole in the ground. We
brought him gently back to Eiddin where we hoped to keep him
and heal him. Before we knew, he had gone from us, into the
North, silent. From then till now we have heard nothing of him.
Now I find him in Strathclyde, and he says that he will not sing
again because of what the Savages did to him. Do you want to
hear him sing again? Then listen to me!

'Mynydog has decided. For once and for all, the menace of
the Savages must be driven from the borders of Eiddin and of
Strathclyde. The House of the Gododdin will do that. The King
of Eiddin has begun to call about him a Household of the young
men of his Kingdom, and not of his Kingdom only. It is a Household such as the world has never seen before. Any young man
from any place may come to join it, if only he is a Roman and
worships the Virgin. If a man is thought fit to join us, then
Mynydog will give him a sword and mail, a helmet, two shirts
and a cloak. And Mynydog will entertain his Household in his
Hall for a year and a day from the time he began to call them
together. And when the time is over, and it will not be so long
now, and not many feasts for you to take part in, then Mynydog's
Household will honour their vow and go down to clear the land
of Mordei from the Savages for ever, and further all across Bernicia to meet the army of Elmet. There is still room at our feasts
for those who are fit to join us. Who will come?'

There was silence, a long silence. Precent would not have made
such an appeal in that Hall, unless he had agreed it before with the
King. Yet there was silence. Even after Evrog said, 'If I were young,
I would go. But now I am too old, and if I must die, then it will be
on the steps of my own Dun,' still there was silence. Precent looked

at me, asking me, silently, to speak. I looked at my hands. Wars had nothing to do with me. I was going to Bradwen in Eiddin, not to war. Someone asked from the bottom of the Hall, 'And have any-body come to join you from other Kingdoms, real like?'

'Oh, come and see them,' Precent invited. 'Men there are from Mona, who speak strange and sibilant, as if they had aden-oids. Syvno has brought them, and you all know of him, whose father was Astrologer to Vortigern the Good. And men from the Mountains that look on Mona, who cannot understand how it rains so little in Eiddin.' This caught at me, these would be my own people. 'And men from Dyfed and Gwent, forest walkers who have stripped every hedge in Eiddin to make their ash bows. Don't like wind, they don't. And men from the Summer Coun-try, where Uther Pendragon rules.'

This last took them all, caused head wagging and whispering.

'More, there are men from over the seas. There are soldiers from Little Britain, in Gaul, who went over with the Legions to conquer Rome, and did it, and never came back till now. Not many of them with us, but some.'

There was more murmuring. But still no one said he would come. Peredur Ironarms put it bluntly, what the hindrance was.

'Do you expect that we will come to ride under you as Cap-tain of Mynydog's Household? How many of my cousins have you not killed, Pict King?'

'I am not the Captain of this Household. I will ride, but I will serve.' There was a sound of astonishment. 'There will be another Captain. His name I will not tell you. If you are too proud to ride except for a name, then it is too proud you are to ride at all.'

And then Evrog spoke again.

'Too old I said I was to go. But if any man of my household wants to go, he may, and he can return to me when the campaign is over, and keep all his booty, and he may boast as he likes of what he did, and no man may contradict him, who did not go with him. And I will send Mynydog thirty suits of mail, and helmets for thirty men, and thirty swords' – and here there was another taking of breath through the Hall, because this was a royal gift again, and would leave half the pillars bare – 'and twenty billets of good iron to beat spearheads out of, and forty horses all broken with their harness and saddles and three sets of shoes apiece. And this so that my Cousin may grant arms to his Household.'

Never had anyone thought that Evrog and Mynydog could be on such terms of friendship. There must be peace for one to send such gifts to the other, at this moment when the Irish raged along the coasts. Cynon stood.

'If Mynydog raises such a Household, what do I do here?'

This, I guessed, had already been arranged. Evrog told him, 'You need not ask arms of Mynydog. I have given you a sword and mail to guard my gate. Take them, and bring them back again to me.'

Peredur Ironarms was on his feet.

'So long as Precent is not leader of the war band,' he said in that lazy insolent way that his nephew, I hear, has after him, 'it will be no objection my friends will be having if I ride alongside this Pict to look after him.'

There was a roar of laughter at this, and Precent went a purple colour, but still he sat chewing the ends of his moustaches and answered mildly.

'We will ride together then, and count the heads of the Savages we drive on to each others' swords.'

Now it was this mildness of Precent's, this willingness to accept provocation, that convinced the men of Strathclyde that there was something special about the expedition. Gelorwid, Evrog's other nephew, stood up, and talked like a hermit preaching a sermon, but that was the fault of the way he had been brought up. 'There is the evil that Morgan preached, that a man can choose his life, and take good or evil as he wishes. But every man does only what God has laid up for him. It may seem to him that he chooses. God in the beginning laid out the world and fixed for every man the way he should go, and how he should die. Maybe, I will be a priest and a hermit after all, maybe not. God has already chosen for me.' His face and his voice brightened. 'I have learnt a few prayers, and I will come and say those to you. Looking at the men who insist on going, I am sure that a little virtue and sound doctrine will be necessary. And I have not forgotten the swordplay I learnt at my father's knee, when I was able to beat Peredur when I liked, and I am sure that I can now—'

With that there was a hubbub, but several of the rougher

grooms bellowed from the back of the Hall, so as to cut down the opposition, 'Quiet all of you, give the lad a chance, let him talk!'

They hoisted Aidan on to the table, and he cried out in his Irish-accented British tongue, his voice not long past breaking, 'I am a King's son, and I deserve a sword and a coat of mail, even if I have three elder brothers who are without arms. I will come with you and fight because I want a sword!'

There was a shout of applause, and now there were a whole crowd of men shouting to be heard. Among them, I could recognise Morien, shouting, 'I shall burn them out, burn them out!'

Then the songs began, and the Harper tried to choose the tunes, but he was shouted down as they sang the old songs, songs of war made long before I ever sang of peace, 'Heads on the Gate', and 'The Toad's Ride', 'The Hunting of the Black Pig', and 'Blood on the Marshes'. Tomorrow would be the preparation, the saddling of the horses and the packing of soft bags, the farewells to mothers and the parting gifts from sweethearts, the choosing of clothes for riding and of clothes for feasting, and the giving away of things one would need after because they would be easy to loot and better for it. But tonight was the time for singing and drinking, and the old songs rolled in the rafters. Under the sound of the music and laughter, Precent and Evrog leant towards me.

'Will you come too?' Precent asked. 'Foster-brother, dearer than a brother, will you ride into Mordei and the land of the Savages? Will you guard my back?'

'In war,' I asked bitterly, 'what would I do? What place has the ox in the stampede?'

'If you are a poet, come and sing for us and make our deeds immortal. If you are not a poet, come and kill Savages.'

'I do not know,' I said. It was true. I could not think what I would do, except that I would not ride to war against the Savages. 'I will come to Eiddin, if I can.'

'I will give you a horse,' offered Evrog. 'You may have it whether you go to war or not, whether you go to Eiddin or not. It is yours for all the pleasure you have given me over the years.'

'Then I will come to Eiddin,' I agreed. I meant that I would ride to Bradwen. I did not know that I was riding to Cattraeth. Gelorwid was right. It was our fate.

2

Gredyf gwr oed gwas
Gwrhyt am dias
Meirch mwth myngvras
A dan vordwyt megyrwas
Ysgwyt ysgauyn lledan
Ar bedrein mein vuan
Kledyuawr glas glan
Ethy eur aphan

He was a man in mind, in years a youth,
And gallant in the din of war:
Fleet, thick-maned chargers
Were ridden by the illustrious hero.
A shield, light and broad,
On the flank of his swift slender steed.
His sword was blue and gleaming,
His spurs were of gold.

It was three days riding from Dumbarton to Eiddin, across the lowlands. It was the first riding I had done for more than a year. I rode the brown gelding that Evrog had given me, a good enough horse, not perhaps the best in his stable, but a steady beast under me as if he had sympathy with me. It did not hurt as much to sit astride him as I feared.

There were nine young men, beside Precent and myself. We did not ride, only, because we led the rest of the forty horses Evrog sent. Three horses to a man is not too great an allowance for a campaign. There would be none to steal from the Savages, because they find it hard enough to manage oxen – even oxen can escape

554

them. Even Arthur could not have defeated them had they been mounted, because they came about him as lice about a hairy dog.

The horses carried the iron rods and bars, ready for the smith to hammer out into spear-points. Axes and swords with their edges sharp to cut a wisp of lamb's wool, they are different. You have to get a real smith to beat out those, who has served his seven years of apprenticeship and has learned to make the edge straight and beat in the charcoal to the spongy iron they bring us from the bogs of Shetland.

Swords are work for craftsmen, as are songs. They are not made by brawn and the hard striking of the great hammer, any more than by a sweet voice or the oft repeating of rhymes. In each the skill is knowing what to say, where to strike. Any man could beat out here the strips of iron that make the rim of a helmet and the arches to frame the hard leather cap. But sending iron for swords would be no use if Mynydog had no swordsmiths, and the likelihood was he had too few workers even to use the iron Evrog had sent him. So swords Evrog sent too, long horsemen's swords of blue smooth iron, to give reach to a man who leans forward to strike at an enemy below.

Lighter than the swords and the iron bars were the shields. A shield-frame is not difficult to make, but it takes time to weave the great oval basket, lightly dished, and time Mynydog did not have. The frames were covered with leather, but unpainted. A man must decide for himself what he wants painted on his shield, and if he can get the iron, whether he wants it rimmed or not; most of us did not want iron on our shields, to tire our arms.

Swords take skill to make, and shields take time. Mail takes both. A mail shirt is not made in a hurry for one campaign. More jeweller's work it is than smith's. You hammer out the iron bars into long wires, a little thicker than oatstraws. Each ring has four more rings linked through it, and each of these into four more. A thousand rings are so linked and you have a little sheet like knitted wool, large enough to shield a man's breast from the flight of an arrow. So weeks and weeks of work will make at last a strip of fabric in iron, and if you fold it you have a sleeve. A shirt has two sleeves, and the body will take as much work as a dozen sleeves. Then after a year, a smith, working small and

555

quiet, ring after monotonous ring, may have enough mail to clothe a man for war. And all that time, the smith must be fed.

A mailed shirt is a precious thing, not easily or cheaply bought, and I did not think that all the Kingdoms of the North could muster five hundred. Yet Evrog had been better than his promise, and had sent forty of them, each worth the purchase of a man's life. I knew, we all knew, how bare he left his own armoury, with the Scots at his gate. These shirts he sent to Mynydog. He did not give them to his own young men. If they were to be Mynydog's men for this campaign, then Mynydog must give them their arms. To Mynydog of Eiddin they went: I went to Bradwen in Eiddin.

We rode under the rock of Eiddin, beneath the steep North Face that rises sheer from the meadows and the marshes, a mile from the Forth. The watchers on the walls of the Dun, at the western end of Eiddin, turned their eyes from the fishing boats to watch us come and try to count us and guess who we were and where we came from. When they recognized the squat figure of Precent, never graceful on a horse, they began to wave and to shout at us, and we waved back.

By the time we had reached the eastern end of Eiddin, and turned south between it and the Giant's Throne, as we called it then, to ride up the long slope to the village beneath the rampart, they were all out, women and children, shouting to Precent, throwing flowers at him, and beneath his horse's hooves. The children fed the tired beast with handfuls of grass, and the smallest ones pulled at his stirrups and at his heels, and called him to look at them; and when he did, they were overcome with shyness and hid their faces or turned away.

They were all glad to see Precent. Nobody looked at the rest of us. It was plain that young men on horses came in every day, always fresh men, every draft like the last. There was no novelty in that, in men they had never seen before. But Precent coming home, Precent himself, oh, that was different, even if he had been gone only a week from Eiddin. Precent coming home, now, that was something to sing about. So they sang, and our young men sang with them. I did not sing. I did nothing. I did not even hide my face. No one looked at me.

We turned in between the two rows of little houses that edge the last mile of the path to the Dun, the King's mile from his Hall to his farm. We heard a horn blow, Gwanar's horn, I knew, who had succeeded Precent at the gate. It was noon, Mynydog would be sitting on his Mound of Judgement, before the gate of the Dun. Now any of his people, any free man of the Isle of Britain, could come to him where he sat with Clydno his Judge by his side to tell him what was true law and what was not. Every day he sat, like every King, to hear complaints of one man against another, or against the King, and do justice, in the Roman manner.

Precent led the file of men and horses up the slope. I dismounted, and let a small boy hold the reins of my brown gelding. This entrance had nothing to do with me. I would not ride up the slope behind Precent. I would not be his gift to Mynydog. I had as much right in Eiddin as any man, as much right as Mynydog himself. I was a freeman of the Isle of Britain, and I would give myself where I wished. I would give myself to Bradwen, and what she told me I would do. I let Precent ride on.

I looked about Eiddin from under my hood. It had altered little in the winter I had been away. But it had altered. The houses were the same. The people were the same, the women as talkative, the children as shrill, the men as silent, as they had been a year ago; only all a year older. A year makes a great difference to a child. You do not recognise a child you knew a year ago, he has changed; and he will not recognise you – he has more important things to fill his mind than the comings of grown-ups. But apart from the people, Eiddin had changed. Every other house was now a smithy, with men beating out spear- and arrowheads, and strips of iron for helmet-brims and shield-rims and for bits and stirrups. You cannot expect a smith who works on his farm and only lights his forge once a week, if that, and then only to straighten a bent ploughshare or edge a wooden spade – you cannot expect him to think of welding mail rings or beating the edge of a sword.

But busy they all were. They were men from the South, from the border of Mordei, from Mordei itself and even from Bernicia. Their own smithies the Savages had burnt, and they had fled north to Eiddin, to the only King who seemed strong and determined enough to promise that one day they would return to the

557

lost lands. These smiths from the South sweated the bitterness of defeat into their weapons: their fires smelt of revenge. I watched their work. I had no feeling whatsoever. It was one thing to think of war by the candle-light of Evrog's Hall. It was different here, in the clear light of day, in a place so well known. It was different here, where Bradwen lived.

At the bottom of the hill was Mynydog's farm. It was a cluster of barns and stables and pigsties, and a fold for the lambing. There was another smithy there, with men who could have made mail, because they were skilful enough, but they had enough work of their own. There was also a wheelwright's shop and a waggoner's yard. All the carts of the Kingdom were made there. Mynydog lived well on his carts. And between the farm and the slopes and steeps of the Giant's Throne and the river, stretched the fields where Mynydog ran his horses as my father did in the pastures of Cae'r Ebolion before Aber-Arth.

Now, though, there were more barns than I could remember, many more, great longhouses. Some of them were well thatched and all the cracks in their walls sealed, and they had stood the winds of winter as I could see from their colour. Others were new, their timbers still showing white from the axe, and their roofs hardly thatched, but covered hurriedly with leafy boughs, not enough to keep out the summer showers, let alone the drenching rains of autumn. These would not last. They were no more substantial than the booths we used to build when we were young, to sleep in through the summer nights when we were herding the sheep out on the high moors.

But they were not shepherds who slept in these huts. With the older barns, there would be room for two hundred, or more. A young man on campaign does not look for comfort in space. The nearer he sleeps to his comrades, the warmer he lies and the safer he feels. And there were more than two hundred. I could see them out on the meadows, forming into three lines, fifty yards apart, in the true Roman way. Far away they were, too far to see any one man clearly, to make out more than that they were horsemen, drilling.

Someone, then, was drilling the King's Household like a regiment of cavalry, real cavalry like they have in the Empire, mail-clad from head to foot, fit to face the Goths. Yes, you could see the sheen of their helmets, and above them a long shimmer of red, a glowing streak across the top of each line.

I had been standing long enough. By now Precent would have spoken to Mynydog. What he said did not matter. Aneirin did not depend on any man's words. Somewhere past the Judgement Mound, Bradwen would be waiting for me. I walked towards her, up the long gentle hill to the gate of the Dun.

Before the gate, long ago, earth was heaped up to form the Mound, and the grass was green on it. Mynydog's throne was set on the mound, so that seated his shoulders were above the heads of standing men. He wore the scarlet robe of state, that his father had received from Vortigern the Good, who was King of all the Romans on the Isle of Britain, before the Savages came and Hengist struck him dead at his own board. Across Mynydog's knees lay unsheathed the sword of the Kings of Eiddin, an old blade, made by magicians, the hilt of bronze stretched out in two wide horns above the pommel.

On his head, Mynydog wore the Crown of the House of Gododdin. Precious beyond belief, it was all of silver, and covered with a film of gold, so that it sparkled to strike awe into all who saw it. There is a cross of gold on the summit, and the rim is set with precious stones of great value, garnets and amethysts and fine crystal won in battle from the Picts and the Irish Scots long before the Wall was made.

There were a great number of people about the King. Beside him stood Clydno the Judge, his ivory staff tipped and bound with silver, his robe bound with ermine like a King's, and his head bare, to show that even a Judge goes in subjection to a King, though the King obeys the law.

Clydno's face was still glowing with the pleasure of seeing his son again after three years. Cynon stood at the foot of the Mound, with Precent. As I went up the hill, and saw the Mound ahead, so Aidan came down, and Morien, Gelorwid and Peredur Ironarms. Mynydog, I saw, had not waited, nor had he been niggardly with Evrog's gift. They came armed in mail, and helm and unpainted shield, and each had a sword. Only a King may grant arms, and only to his own followers. A young man I used to know, called

Gwion Catseyes, led them down to the huts in the King's farm-yard. They did not notice me, or see me, not even Gwion. They were too happy, they were now men, and warriors.

I came nearer to the Judgement Mound. I had to push my way through the crowd. Nobody recognised me. They were not expecting me. Nobody, I thought, would know me unprompted. Nobody will be glad that I have returned, except Bradwen. Bradwen will be glad to see me, however old and weak I have come to look, however long I have been away, whether I make songs or not. Bradwen will know me, she will be glad to see me come home. For Eiddin is my home, now that Eudav's Hall is burnt. I will not ride out, whatever Precent may think I meant at Evrog's table. I said nothing there. I only said that I would return to Eiddin. I meant that I would return to Bradwen. I did not promise to go to Mynydog's war, whoever is the Captain of the Household. I will sit here in Eiddin, and watch the armies ride out, and then I will have some peace, with Bradwen, and perhaps I may even learn to sing again.

I came to the front of the crowd, and all at once there was someone who knew me. Mynydog's little nephew was there, four years old, or perhaps just turned five, I can't remember, son of Mynydog's sister Ygraine, though who his father was, whether her husband Gorlois or someone else, was more than anyone liked to guess at. He had been sent here to be fostered in the North as I had been, and for the same reasons, first that it was safe here, and second that nobody seemed to care what became of him. His half-sister Gwenllian had come with him, fourteen years old when she carried the baby into Eiddin in her arms.

The little boy was Mynydog's only nephew, and the King was very fond of him, as indeed everyone was in Eiddin. You would have expected him to be quite spoiled, but in spite of all the fuss and petting he was still the most loving and patient child you ever heard of. Perhaps it was his sweet and equable temper and his feelings for justice, even at that age. Of course, he had his favourites, and I, once, had been one. He was sitting on his little stool at the foot of the throne, as he had already started to do the year before. He was very good, for only four, an age when it is a penance to sit still for any time at all. But still he sat, his palms on his knees, and listened to every case.

I came forward then, towards the foot of the mound, and I did not know if Cynon had been as free with his tongue as in Dumbarton, or if Precent had listened to what I told him. You could never keep Precent quiet in the old days. I did not know if I were expected or unexpected, a surprise to the King or one awaited and prepared for. I never found that out. As soon as I came to the front of the crowd, it was the little boy who saw me and remembered me. Yes, at four years old, after a whole year, and that is a very long time in a child's life, a quarter of it, he remembered me, and that shows how marvellous he was, even as a child. He stood up and shouted, ''neirin! 'neirin! Look what I got! I got a sword, a real sword. Arthgi made it.'

And it was a real sword, only of wood, of course, just right for his size, and Arthgi had taken some care in the carving and in making the little scabbard of leather that the child was so proud to wear at his belt. He waved it at me, and the whole crowd turned to look at me, the King and all his Officers. I stood there silent, and they too were all silent, and even the little boy stopped shouting, and looked about him guiltily for a moment as if he had done something to be blamed for, although that would have been impossible for him in Eiddin, even when he was little. And still is. But the silence was only for a moment.

Mynydog rose from his throne and came down the Mound of Judgement. I know that you will say that it is not much for a Poet to boast about, that a King embraced him; rather, it is for a King to boast that a Poet allowed his embraces. A King's embrace is not an honour: it is what you expect if you have a mastery of language and can make songs and satires and hymns of praise, and if you can hold in your tongue the fame of every man you meet, and can determine how even the greatest king will be remembered. By the Poets who sat in his Hall is a King's greatness judged. Mynydog was a great King, great as Vortigern the Wise. Even Arthur will depend on the Poets to be remembered.

But for Mynydog to embrace me was different. We embraced, as two men, one old, one young, as two close, too close kinsmen. Whatever had happened, it was meaningless compared to the bonds that held us together, that still drew us together till he died, whenever he died, because I never knew. Or how.

'Welcome again, Bard of the Island of the Mighty,' was what he said. I answered, 'I am no longer a Poet'.

I did not have to talk to him as simply as I did to Evrog, explaining or hiding things that could not easily be explained. Mynydog was wiser than his own Judge and cleverer than his own Fool, and he could foretell the future better than his own Astronomer, and he could do that as well by firelight as by starlight, and as well in daylight as in the dark. He knew what I meant. He did not need to be persuaded. He only repeated, 'Welcome, well come again into Eiddin, Aneirin of the Gododdin.' He looked round at his people. He asked, as always at the end of the hour of Judgement, 'Is there peace?'

We all answered, 'There is peace.'

Mynydog sheathed the sword of the House. Gwanar, as always at Clydno's elbow, his axe in his belt, raised his trumpet and blew the horn for the ending of the court. The people who had come to seek justice or to see justice done to others went back each to his own village in Eiddin or Alban or the edge of Mordei. They would have justice. With Mynydog to proclaim the law, and Clydno to tell it, and Gwanar to execute it, there was always justice in Eiddin. Mynydog with his left hand took my arm, and the little boy, shy now, sensing only that something had happened to mar the happiness of those whose only care for most of his life had been for his happiness from minute to minute, he put his hand into my other hand and pressed himself close to my thigh, rubbing against me as we walked like a cat.

In silence we walked to the gate of the Dun, and nobles of the Court walked behind. Just before the Gate they broke off, and went to their own houses within the Dun or outside it. I thought, soon, in a moment, in the courtyard beyond the gate or in the doorway of the Hall, I will see Bradwen. Then I will be well come indeed. Once I see her, it will all be over and my journey will be at an end. She will heal everything. But I did not know that my journey was already to Cattraeth, and there would be no returning. For the King stopped in the gate and said, 'Let us wait here. Someone is coming up the Hill whom you must meet.'

I looked towards the village. The Horsemen were dismounting in the farmyard and breaking into little knots, unsaddling their horses and rubbing them down with handfuls of grass and throwing blankets over them. That I could guess, even though I could see only a little at that distance. My sight was keener then than it is now. Only one man out of all that host was riding between the houses now. We waited for him.

This then must be the man Mynydog had chosen out of all the men he knew to lead his army into the Mordei, and farther South. Who was it? Who was the man whom Precent had refused to name? Who had been chosen before Precent to be Captain of the Household of Eiddin, whom Precent was willing to follow? No one, I was sure, out of the Kingdom of the Gododdin. But from farther away? Who could have come to Eiddin across the lands and seas that the Savages and the Irish ravaged? Were there heroes from among the South Britons, or from the other Romans of Gaul and Italy, of whom I had not heard? I waited and I watched. Mynydog and I did not speak. We knew each other too well. We stood, and half my mind was on the scene before me, and half was on Bradwen, and surer and surer was I that when I saw her, it would make all well.

The rider came nearer, walking his weary beast up the slope, his greyhounds trotting behind. And then, when he dismounted and let a groom take horse and dogs, I saw the Ravens on his shield and I knew, before Mynydog said, 'Now we see the long awaited meeting, between the two greatest men of all the Isle of Britain, between Aneirin the Pre-eminent Bard, and Owain, son of Mark.'

Yes, this was Owain, King Mark of Cornwall's son, Tristram's brother. There has been trouble there, and it would not have happened had not Owain come to Eiddin, to ride with us all to Cattraeth. But Owain *had* come North, flaunting his Ravens, at Mynydog's call, as if they alone would clear the Savages out of the Eastern coasts, and peck the Loegrians clear out of the Island. (Ravens we said they were. He said no, they were a smaller bird, a chough, that lives in the sea-cliffs of Cornwall, but they looked like Ravens to us, and the Ravens we called them always.)

It was this Raven flag and this Raven shield that men would follow: they had all heard of them. Oh, I thought, this is a shrewd move, to bring in from outside *this* man to lead us, the men of Eiddin, mingled as we were already with men from other kingdoms of the North, and with men dispossessed from lands south of the Wall. There would be no favourites, with this foreigner to lead us, a man of blood as good as any among us, and better. To lead us, I asked myself? No, to lead them. My business was not with Owain, but with Bradwen.

A big man, Owain, seventeen hands high and a half. You will not find his match for strength today among the nobles who follow Arthur. It would have been no trouble for Owain to have killed Bladulf – he could have done it in his sleep. It would have been no trouble for Owain to have killed a thousand Savages, if he had met them in fair fight. They could never have overcome him except by treachery. No, not Owain.

But it was not strength alone that drew us to Owain. Handsome he was, more handsome than any man who has ever lived. I have never seen Arthur in his manhood, but I am sure he is never as handsome as Owain. Corn was the colour of his hair, corn with the touch of gold that gives it life, not the dull yellow tow of the Savages. And his eyes were of that ice-blue, cold and flaming by turns. Only to look into his eyes while he spoke, and it was no trouble to believe what he said, if he told you that black was white, and no danger to obey him though he told you to leap into a blazing fire. And it was that he had us do in the end, and worse: and gladly we did it. It was his beauty that struck me in that moment of meeting, and his strength, as he ran the last furlong of the way to us, uphill, and in his mail faster than many a man can run fresh and unladen on level ground.

He knew of me too. He had heard my verses often, and I had heard his praises sung. He looked me in the eye as he heard my name, and I knew what he thought. He asked himself if I were more than a witless minstrel who can string words together for a bed or a meal, but can no more understand the real meaning of the line he sings or guess what the sounds rouse in his hearers' souls than the smith can swing the sword he forges or feel the terror that comes to the beaten warrior who sees the iron shear down at him for the last time.

'Well?' he asked. He made no ceremony of greeting. Kings in the South are different, I suppose, or at least their sons are. 'Are you come to fight, or are you only going to sing about us who do?'

I refused to be riled, or drawn into a false move.

'I have come here to decide how to spend a spoilt life.'

'There is no better way to forget that than in spoiling other lives,' he told me. It is easy to speak like that if you do not know the meaning of spoiling. In any case, I thought, I will soon see Bradwen. Then there will be no more talk of spoilt lives. Then my life will be complete again. The nearer I came to meeting her, the plainer it was for me to see, that all the strange thoughts I had in those days, of being a Judge in the North the rest of my days, or of going down south to my father's people, or into Ireland to my mother's family or farther still into Little Britain or Gaul, or into Africa, anywhere I was not known, or even, the maddest thought of all, going on this campaign, or any campaign – these were all empty air and froth. Bradwen would take me to her and comfort me, and make me whole again. With Bradwen nothing changed. I was so near her, she so near me, and yet I had for form's sake to stand here and fence in words with this big foreign man.

'There have been lives enough spoilt already,' I said. 'For most of them, there is no asking anybody now to repair the damage. Not all the wars that you can wage in a lifetime will put one head back again on its shoulders once levelled or make one maimed body fruitful. You may lead your army where you will, there will be no end to blood. Why don't you live out your own life in peace on some cliff-top farm and be thankful that you yourself have not suffered.'

'And that from you, Aneirin?' He seemed genuinely surprised. 'You've got more cause for vengeance than any man alive. I offer you the chance to shed blood for blood and chain men who chained you. How delightful it will be when we lead Bladulf through the gates of Eiddin with his hands tied behind his back! When we do that, he will be the last Savage left alive in the Isle of Britain. Then we can put all our strength against the real enemy – the Irish. But what shall we do with Bladulf when we catch him? Shall we blind him and set him to grind oat-flour for the rest of his days to spare women's hands? Shall we set him loose on the sea in a boat to die of thirst? Shall we sink him to his neck in a manure heap to cook to death? You shall choose, Aneirin. It's only fair, you have suffered more from the Savages than any man alive. How they must have rejoiced to have the Pre-eminent Chief Bard of all the Island in their hands—'

'It made no difference,' I corrected him. 'They had no Poets, and certainly would take no notice of them if they had. They aren't like us. For us poetry is the whole reason why men live. Not for them. Besides, they don't know one Briton from another. I was nothing more than another pair of arms and legs that might have their uses on the farm.'

What uses, I did not tell him. It would have been too shameful, there in the open gate. Besides, he knew it without my telling. I could see it in his eyes, so full of pity and of angry pride that such a poet should have lived in our nation.

I did not tell him that they had shackled me to the plough-beam with the ox, and whipped me to break up the stubborn land – our land. With the ox I had pulled the heavy cart of stones picked from the cornfield. With the ox, loaded and goaded, I had walked the weary round to tread the wheat from the ear. And if Precent had not come, then I would have ended up like the old ox, they would have killed me at the end of the summer, and on the night of the Holy Souls they would have fed my worn-out body to the dogs. Was there anyone here who knew the whole truth of it, the truth I would not be even able to tell Bradwen?

There was nobody who could know, and yet, I felt, Owain did know. That was how he led us. He could always make it plain that he knew how you suffered and how you felt, whoever you were, whatever you had been. A man like that you can follow and feel no shame, even if you are as noble as he is, and though you know that you can surpass him in a dozen ways. And there was no way in which any of us could surpass Owain.

'That is all I ask of you,' he answered. 'All I need is another pair of arms and legs to ride with me into the South. Another pair of thighs to grip a horse, and another right arm to cast a spear, and another head to wear a helm. Look, I have had all our helmets set with red feathers, as great generals did in the days of the Legions.'

He was like any soldier, he thought that things of this kind, red feathers and shining helmets were important. And yet, though I knew this was all nonsense, for a moment I wavered, I was on the point of saying yes. I almost answered, 'Yes, I will come with you as a soldier against the Savages, I will add another head of red plumes for the Savages to count. I will do this even though I know that I will be cutting myself off for ever from the company of the Bards of the Island, that by delivering the stroke of Justice I disqualify myself for ever from Judgement.'

I was on the very point of saying all that, and of a sudden I thought of Bradwen, and I knew I could not go. She would never have me go, she would never let me leave her, now I had come back to Eiddin. She would know what to think of all this talk of glory and revenge. Bradwen the Wise Maiden men called her; cool and clear-thinking she was. She would have made a good poet, if it were lawful for a woman to make verses. It is only emotion that stands between a woman and the Muse. Any man who can look at life clear and cold and bleak, as it is, and not be deceived by his own desires and fears, can be a poet. The rest is a mere matter of words and metres: the rest is only a game of sounds. So I replied to Owain instead. 'There are plenty of heads in the lowlands, and in the mountains too, who would be glad to wear your pretty feathers. For every man Precent brought from Dumbarton, he turned back nine, because this one was too old, or this one too young, here a married man and here an only son, and there a man who limped but not enough to stop him doing a hard day's work behind the plough or in a boat. Take them, Owain, hard men used to war, and they will help you more than a hundred poets.'

I expected to hear him tell me they would not do because they were too valuable, but that my useless arm would stop a blow as well as any. In any army, there are only two or three men who kill the enemy, the rest cluster around to shield the champion from the blows of the enemy champions. But what Owain said now was, 'Empty heads, Aneirin, empty heads. In such a campaign, as we go on, there is too much work for me to do myself. In a host like this, I will need a Judge, Aneirin, to tell the law and judge our disputes. You know all the laws of the Island, of every part of the land, and you can help me make this Household of Mynydog's into one army.'

'But Cynon is going with you, and he knows enough law for your purpose. He has learnt it from his father.'

'If that were all the law I needed, I would not worry. I have

Cynrig of Aeron with me, too, but I need more law than he knows.'

This was something to hear. Cynrig was a prince of Aeron, but not heir to the Kingdom, because he was a second son. Now, to be thought superior as a Judge to this Cardi man was something. Owain added, 'But he cannot be my Judge, because when he came, first his elder brother Cynddelig followed, out of jealousy. And then the younger brother came, Cynrain, to keep the peace between them, and they do not thank him for it. And that, Aneirin, is why I need a wiser Judge than Cynon, and one whose reputation is wider.'

That I could understand. But still I told him, 'I do not think myself wise enough yet for that.'

Owain did not try to rebut this argument, or any I ever used. He neither quarrelled with men, nor set up counter-arguments. Instead, he would always find another way to put his case. If only he had acted in war as he did in peace, and shown the same maturity in the face of steel!

'These Savages you have up here in the East, they are a funny people. I've never met them before. I've had enough to do, fighting the Irish.'

This was how he had got his reputation, at war with the Irish who came by sea all along the Western coasts. Down in Demetia, they had even begun to settle and till the soil and build villages, dispossessing the Romans they found living there, as the Savages had done in Bernicia and were trying to do in the debatable land of Mordei. It was the Irish who were the enemy in the land. Now Arthur has utterly destroyed the Savages, he must show his real quality by beating the Irish. If they are not stopped they will first conquer this land, and then cross the seas and bring all the Empire under their rule, as far as Byzantium.

'Yet,' Owain went on, 'the Irish are not so different although they have their own uncouth language. They worship the Virgin, and obey laws like ours, and they know that the true aim of a kingdom is to nurture poets. And there is no shame in marrying them.' He knew, and I knew, that each of us was born of the lawful union of a Royal House of the Roman Island of Britain with a Royal House of the Island of the Blessed. He could not speak scornfully about the Irish for his own sake, let alone for mine.

'But these Savages. They are something quite outside the whole range of humanity. The Church has no doubt that they are not men but devils. It is forbidden to speak of holy things to them, and we all agree that they are no more capable of baptism than my dog. And I have had some very reasonable and cultured dogs in my time.'

He laughed, and I had to laugh with him. That was another thing about Owain, that helped men to obey him, against their inclinations. He could destroy the tension of an embarrassing moment, not to flee the judgement point, you understand, but to step back and approach in another way. Even his laugh was an argument. Nothing was wasted. Once he had taken on himself a task, then everything he did and said was part of that task. He went on, still smiling.

'But these Savages, lack of Baptism is no penance to them. They do not know what God is, and they worship nothing.'

I could not understand how a man could be so wise and yet so ignorant. I corrected him.

'They worship demons. They have a wind demon, called Odin, and they can sail to us only when he favours them. And they have a fire demon called Thor, and it is his magic which gives them those terrible swords which cut through three thicknesses of mail. And another demon called Baldur who makes their wheat grow. All these they worship. They make offerings to them under trees.'

'Do they, indeed. You learned all this when you were a prisoner. All just by watching them?'

'No, they told me about it, boasting of how the demons would overthrow and eat up the Virgin and the Saints.'

'They spoke our language to you, then, did they?'

'Oh, no they cannot speak the tongue of the Angels like us, not Latin, because their tongues are too short.'

'Then how did you learn this?'

'Oh, I had to learn their language, enough at least to speak a little to answer when they taunted me, and to obey the orders they gave me.'

'So you speak their language. And you know their ways.'

I did not see the trap Owain had set, and I boasted, though the Virgin knows that all I said was the truth.

'As well as any man. I know how they dress, and how they make that wheat bread, and how they sit to eat; all this by watching, because they fed me with the dogs.'

Owain sprung his trap. 'Think, Aneirin, how few men there are in all the earth who know the Savages' tongue. Can you name another? Even one other? Think of it, Aneirin. We have come together to fight these people, and we know no more about them than if they lived on the other side of the Ocean. Should we hunt them like deer, lying out on the high moors and crawling on our bellies till we can shoot them with the crossbow? Or ought we to wait till winter and then poke them out of their lairs like bears, with long poles and fire? As long as we don't know anything about them, they'll continue to settle and breed till they outnumber us. I don't want you with us for the sake of your arms, Aneirin, not even for your skill with the crossbow, which we have all heard about. I want you to come because you only can tell us about our enemies and guess what they are going to do.'

I saw what he meant, and what he wanted. For another moment I was on the point of agreeing. Then I thought of Bradwen. I had not seen her yet, though a number of Mynydog's people had come out of the houses in the Dun and stood about at a distance to watch the first meeting of Owain and Aneirin. I had not seen Bradwen among them, I had not even heard her voice. I only half listened to Owain, I had most of my attention on the sounds from the Hall, in the hopes of hearing at last the long-loved tones. I thought of Bradwen and of how she would welcome me, and I answered – and I was quite sincere in this, it was what I felt, it was not a mere excuse:

'I have been a winter as a Judge. Before that I was a Poet. I have had enough of telling other people what they ought to do, and letting them do it by themselves. I have had seven years in which I have taken part in no action. If I were to come with you, I would not come as a mere adviser. I would want a more active part. But there's no need for me to come with you for that. I can tell you all I know before you set out for the campaign, and even teach half your soldiers enough of the Savages' tongue for all your needs. But I will not come. I have had enough of wandering. I will stay here in Eiddin.'

Mynydog the King, who had been standing by all this time, listening and not saying anything, now spoke.

'If it is an active part you want, Aneirin, then I can help you to one. I will give you arms. You can have my own shirt of mail, that I brought back from the South, when I rode in the Household of Vortigern the Handsome. And I have a helmet, too, I picked up after a battle against the Irish – oh, a bloody day that was, for we killed twenty-seven of them and lost seventeen men ourselves. Was ever such carnage seen in the Island? They will keep your head safe, and turn a spear. And a shield-frame and leather I can give you, to paint for yourself.'

I wondered a moment what I should paint on my shield. A wolf? An eagle? But why wonder. I would never paint a shield, nor carry one. I would spend the summer, all the campaigning time, here in Eiddin with Bradwen. She would be glad to have me here, whatever had happened to me, whatever other men did, whatever other men said. This offer of Mynydog's was a trick, to make me feel a coward that I did not go. I told the King, 'I will not take your arms. I have been a Bard too long to think of breaking what I have always preserved. Find some greater hero to wear your arms, King Mynydog.'

'That is a pity,' Owain came in. 'I would have liked you to come with me. I know who I would rather take to war, if I had the choice – a clever man who is not used to fighting or a stupid man who is. I would take the clever man because ...'

His voice went on. I did not listen. I looked beyond him, across the courtyard. Bradwen came from the Hall. She wore a dress of red, the colour she always liked. At the hem her feet twinkled in their shoes of red and yellow, leather of Cordoba, paid for with their weight in silver. She had a chain about her neck, that I had once given her, made of silver with an amethyst hanging from it, and I had had it from a Pictish Lord far in the North, on the shore opposite Orkney, for singing him a satire on the Lord of Orkney who was, let us not say his enemy because there are no enemies among Romans, but, at least let us say, not his best friend. She wore it still.

The bracelets on her wrists Precent had given her, bronze patterned with red enamel and set with garnets and precious red glass. He had taken them from an Irishman who had come East under the Wall to the boundaries of Mynydog's Kingdom. He ought not to have come so far from his ships. Precent had caught him and left few of his men alive. These armlets were the best the Irish had, and they were voted to Precent as the bravest of the Household that Mynydog had sent. He had come straight back to Eudav's Hall and given them to Bradwen. That was what she was to me, even to men brought up with her as brothers.

She came down the steps towards us, her blue eyes shining with love and anticipation, her black curls blowing in the breeze as they always did, for gales haunt the crest of Eiddin. She came to us, stately and dignified, standing as she did only half a head shorter than me, and taller than Precent. Oh, she would have been a Queen in any Kingdom, she would have been the greatest lady in any Court, Caerleon or Camelot or Byzantium itself. This, I thought, is what I have been longing for, all this time in the North by the bitter sea. I had been ashamed to come and face her when they had brought me home from my prison among the Savages. But now, just to see her again was enough to show me that all I dreaded, all that made me afraid to look her in the face, all the pain and grief I suffered was only a construction of my own mind. It was a fiction of the Poet's thoughts, that will seek out the complete and hidden meaning of any action, and find significance where there is none. She will welcome me, I thought, she who has been longing for me to return, thinking of me all through the winter, as she used to do, she said, in the old days when I wandered the length of the Isle of Britain, north of the Wall. Now, I could tell her what she meant to me, of how I too had been thinking of her and longing for my return. And I watched her come to me.

Bradwen did not see me. She reached out and took Owain's arm. With the merest gesture of formal courtesy to the King, she drew away from him the Son of Mark, the Raven Shielded, the Glorious, the Supreme Warrior in his armour, his plumed helm in the crook of his other arm. She led off from us the Victor over the Irish, the Deliverer of the Kingdom of Eiddin. Together they walked away from us.

I said to Mynydog, 'Grant me thy arms, my Uncle and my King.'

Gwyr a aeth gatraeth oed fraeth eu llu
Glasved eu hancwyn a gwenwyn vu

Men went to Cattraeth, talkative was the host,
Blue mead was their liquor, and it proved their poison.

So I came home to Mynydog's Household. Oh, it was a fine life in the King's Hall. As one of the family, I slept in the Hall, where I had always been used to sleep: in a wall bed, on the North side, that they had kept empty all through the winter in case I should come back without warning. The new straw was clean and dry, the old being turned out on to the floor.

I know that a King's Hall in the North is not like one in the South, in the twenty-eight cities of the Island; there were only twenty-six we counted in those days, because the Savages had slighted Carlisle. And they had taken York and burnt it, they had destroyed its Palaces and Churches, and pulled down the walls, and that they were to regret when Uther came against them: but that was later. Down there, in the Halls of common Kings, the roof-columns are of marble, all streaked in bright colours, and in the Hall of the Emperor in Byzantium the pillars are of gold, and in his private rooms they are of precious stones, garnet and diamond, ruby and pearl, sardonyx and opal, as is said in the book of the Blessed John which I have heard read. And the walls are painted with strange scenes, so that a man might think that there were no walls at all, but that he looked straight out into the woods and the pastures.

The pillars of Mynydog's Hall were of pinewood, holding the stout oak roof-tree. The walls were of oak frames and willow withies woven tight, and the chinks well packed with clay. They were hung with red cloth, and every pillar gleamed with mail and blades, helmets and bright-painted shields. Mine among them. Not perhaps that fine mail the Legions wear at Byzantium, fine as knitted wool and so light – in a coat of that mail, a man may run a whole day's journey, and fight at the end of it, and pursue through the next day, and at the end be no more tired than if he wore a linen shirt over his skin. Our mail was heavier: but it served.

The walls of Mynydog's Dun served us, too. They were not like the walls of the cities in the South. Camelot, they say, is a splendid place, and what is Camelot beside Cardigan, or Kenfig? Caerwent, I have heard about. It is only the port of Camelot, and yet there are walls about it seven times the height of a man, and as thick as they are high. The great bastions that look out over the Severn Sea are as high again as the walls. So great is Caerwent that a man may come into it by the North Gate and walk south. For a day he will walk through the entry of the city, and for a day he will cross the centre of the city, and on the evening of the third day, if he walk straight ahead all the time and never turn out of his way, he may reach the South Gate and go down to the water and get into his skin boat and sail away. From the water, he may turn and look back at the city, as we may look back at Eiddin from the Forth. The roofs of the houses are covered with tiles of shining gold, not the oatstraw we grow for thatch, and fixed with nails of silver, not weighted down with stones and ropes.

Eiddin was not a rich town like that, but a little huddle of houses on the hilltop. We heard of the great cities from men who came to us from the South, Cardi men who came with Cynrig, thin slight men with delicatesmall feet, used to treading daintily on the marshy mountain-tops where there is barely a fingernail's depth of the soil on the hard and barren rock. They live nearest to the Irish and suffer from them most. They dare not leave a pin outside their house at night in case some roving sea thief leaps ashore to take it, smelling the slightest booty from the further shore. Saving and careful they have to be, from their poor land and their uncertain tenure, and so they have a reputation for meanness, for demanding full value for anything they give. But they give full value, too, let the dead testify.

The men who had come with Owain from Cornwall were

different again, and you could tell them by seeing them before you heard them talk. They were as fond of cream as the Cardi men of cheese, and they were the ones to ask for lobsters since they had a supernatural skill in catching them, knowing where to put the pots even on this strange shore. To mead they preferred a hard strong cider made from the juicy apples they grow down there in the far South, where, they told us, there is never snow or frost, and the summer days are always sunny and the winter nights are short. They told us true, and so did the men who came from Little Britain.

Most of the Household, for all that, came from Mynydog's own Kingdom. Some were from Eiddin, the centre of the Kingdom, around the rock itself, south of the Forth. Others came from Mordei, the debatable land, that lay south of Eiddin and north of the Wall, north of the Wood of Celidon. Here waves of Savages came and went like the tide, and every sweep, like the tide, they receded a little less, and so they ate the Kingdom away. Men were still willing to talk of fighting for Mordei. None, until Owain, talked of fighting for Bernicia.

There were men in the Household who counted themselves as Bernician by descent. They were not born there, but anywhere in Eiddin, or north of the Forth in Alban to the borders of the Picts. At least they remembered the names of the farms their grandfathers had in Bernicia, or at most where those farms had been. The land was lost. The Savages had settled there, from the Wall as far as the Humber. It was a generation since they had laid waste York. They blocked the road that ran south from Eiddin, through the Wall, past Cattraeth and York, to Lincoln and the Romans of Elmet. And once, they said, it had even been safe for a woman to travel all along that road, with no more than a dozen armed men for an escort. That was the road we now had to open.

We still told of the great feat of Cynon, four years before, when he had returned from the South, all the way by land, bringing Gwenllian out of Uther's Camelot, clutching her half-brother to her, a tiny baby. Now he was the thriving boy we all loved. Then there were still Romans living in Carlisle, but the Savages burnt the place hardly a month after Cynon had passed. Now it was only safe for single men, or parties of not more than two or three, to travel up the west coast in skin boats, looking out for the Savages on land and the Irish by sea, making a detour around the lost shore to come from Mona to Strathclyde. But the Household would now regain Bernicia, and perhaps even Deira too, between us and Elmet. And then the road would run from Eiddin to Camelot itself.

No men came to join the Household from Elmet. Elmet men had enough to do.

Each Squadron had men from all these regions, all mixed together. Never before had any King raised such a Household, bringing in riders from all over the Island, and beyond. The most any King had done before was, perhaps, to have a man from a kingdom near by to be Captain of his Household, as Evrog had kept Cynon. Now we had so many different Kingdoms together, Owain insisted that each Squadron should include men from each region, all mixed up together.

'If a Squadron come all from one place,' he used to say, 'then it will be full of relations. It won't be long before we have Squadrons fighting each other instead of the Savages. We must learn to trust each other in war and peace. Quarrels between kinsmen are the curse of the Roman race and the downfall of the Island.' So he said, glaring at Cynddelig and Cynrig. Owain was Tristram's brother, King Mark's son.

Because of this idea of his, Owain would frequently change us around in the Squadrons, taking whole sections of ten men from one Squadron and putting them into another, even in the middle of the day's exercise.

'In the middle of a battle,' he would say, teaching us quietly and patiently, but never leaving us without the conviction that it was he who understood it all better than we did, 'Squadrons break up, and men rally about whatever centre offers. You must always be able to depend on your neighbour in the line to do the right thing, even if you have never seen him before, and this is quite possible in such a huge army as this. Who ever saw three hundred and fifty men mounted in the field before?'

We always rode in pairs, of course. Usually I had Aidan with me, to keep my back, but Owain often had us change our riding partners.

The most noble of us all had command of the Squadrons. There were more of them than there were Squadrons, and they too took it in turns, by Owain's order, to lead. At the beginning of each day in the field, I, as Judge of the Household, would draw tokens out of a helmet to see who should command that day and who should obey. So, not only did we all get used to the voices of different commanders, but we all of us, however noble became used to obeying. Even Cynddelig, on occasion, served under Cynrig: but it took all Owain's arts to bring that to pass.

Always, Owain led the seven Squadrons together. No one ever took Owain's place. Sometimes Precent or Cynddelig would exercise two or three Squadrons together, but never all seven. It was Owain who was Captain of the Household.

And then, after the heat of the field, after the confusion of the exercise through the morning, after the quiet of the afternoon when we sit and mend out harness or our armour or home our sword-edges, or just sit and watch the birds in the sky, then would come the feast in Mynydog's Hall. That Hall was a vast building, as big, I am sure, as any Arthur has in Camelot. Seventy of us could eat there, sitting at the tables or perched on the beds fixed against the wall. Woe betide any warrior who spilt mead on my pillow. I have satirised men for less.

A whole Squadron, fifty men, would eat in the Hall each night. The other Squadrons would eat in the houses where they slept, or outside on the grass. They had as much meat as they could eat there, served on platters of oatcake, and mead to swim in. They did not cook for themselves, or serve themselves. A crowd of young men like that, all unmarried, to look after themselves when they were just about to go off to the wars? Never! Every girl in the Kingdom came drifting down to the Rock of Eiddin, sooner or later, to hang round the huts trying to get herself a soldier. So, anything one of our lads wanted done, the girls would do for him. They'd mend shirts, sew up leather seams, wash clothes. If you walked down between the huts any summer evening before supper, you fell over men everywhere, lying with their heads in the laps of the girls combing out their long hair for lice.

Then, after supper, the stars would come out in the clear sky, and even in summer the darkness is cool and the dew is wet. The

Household had their long houses to sleep in, that Mynydog had built for them so that they would not catch cold. But as for those poor motherless girls, so far from home, who cared where they slept? Who cared, indeed? Why, the Household cared, they cared all right. Out of charity, they took them in, they sheltered them, they lavished on them all the affection of which, obviously, their mothers had deprived them. If they were not deprived, what were they doing here? Why else would they have come down, relay after relay of them, walking purposefully down from the hills and over the river. And then they would, after three days, or a month, go walking for days home again, back to the farms they came from. There they could boast to the boys who were left of how they had seen the Household of Mynydog, how they had seen for themselves what *men* were like. They might boast to their mothers, or even to their fathers, though this last is doubtful. But as they walked back they would certainly boast to the other girls they passed, latecomers, hurrying down to the rock of Eiddin, all haste and anxiety to reach the huts before the Household rode out against the Savages.

Oh, yes, it was a fine life in King Mynydog's Household, a fine life indeed. Many of the young men had been there since the year previous, coming in for the barley harvest or just after it. Life was a perpetual feast, night after night. They said that the best girls had been the ones who came down in the early days, when the Household was new and small, and there were only a few men to work themselves to death lavishing love and affection on the poor things and run off their feet to do it. Oh, those were the days, Graid and Hoegi told me, cherishing the memory, licking their lips.

And for all this fine living, what in return? Nothing very much, riding on fine horses, hunting in the hills, always hunting. Because at the end of the year, on top of all this good treatment, all these luxuries, they would have the honour and the glory of a battle, and the name of the men who had driven the Savages out of the Island of Britain. Mead, Mynydog gave his Household, and we in our turn would give him our strength and our glory, so that his name would live for ever, and ours with his because we were *his* Household.

So we hunted. We hunted, day after day, because Owain said we should.

'This is how we will fight them,' he told us. 'We will round them up like deer on the high moors and hunt them down, throwing our spears at them. There will be no difficulty.'

'But it won't be like that,' I objected at last. 'They don't live up there on the high moors. They stay close around their farms. If we meet them, they will be in large bodies. They will stand and form a shield-wall.'

'So perhaps they did when you saw them,' Owain corrected me. 'But then they were attacking, banding together to make war on us. We will catch them when they are not ready to fight.'

'But you will need infantry to break these shield-walls,' I persisted.

'We will have infantry for all the good they are,' sneered Owain, and everyone within earshot laughed at men who fought on foot like Savages. 'They will do for mopping up and consolidating afterwards, or for holding the spare horses. You can fight with them if you prefer, Aneirin.'

I held my peace. It was always the same in the Hall, too, where I dined every night, being of the Family, as did those of Royal blood. The other warriors dined each once a week, so that every man could say of his King that he was on dining terms with him. Some, of course, were used to dining in a Royal Hall. Others had won their way into the Household by their own skill and strength, as had Morien the Charcoal-burner, and nobody knew who his father was. And it was a question even as to whether he was more use back in the woods than in the Household. To make a sword from the bars Evrog had sent would take the weight of two sheep in charcoal: and ten times as much to caseharden the bars beforehand, and twenty times as much to smelt the ore before that again. Still, he was admitted of the Household and was honoured by eating with the King and being called by name in the Hall.

Most men would wash and put on their clean shirts for this day in the week, but we who dined in the Hall every night did not take so much trouble. Except Cynrig of Aeron, who was always dainty, cleaning his nails always with his knife before he cut his meat. He washed his arms and feet almost every day, and would often put on a clean shirt for no reason at all but that he had slipped in the mud or put his elbow into a pile of horse-dung. Or if he had tumbled in the marsh and the shirt was wet through and spattered with slime, instead of drying it by the fire and putting it on again like any ordinary man, he would not be satisfied if he could not have a clean shirt to wear and persuade someone else to wash the old one. He was quite shameless about that, and would even, if he could find no one else, try to coax Gwenllian to wash it for him. But she never would. She always washed mine, every week, and said that was enough for her, taken up as she was with looking after her half-brother. But Cynrig had plenty of shirts, being a wealthy prince, and he could afford it.

Oh, they were fine evenings in Mynydog's Hall. Every evening was a Whitsun Day. The King would have them light as many rush dips as did Evrog the Wealthy, and on Sundays or on Ascension Day he would have lit candles of wax and tallow all around, so that the light should be clear and steady. The clear gleam lightened the hangings on the walls, so that they seemed to float above us like clouds, or close us in like shimmering mists; and through the mists the armour glittered like lightning on the mountains. By that light we could eat and drink, and Mynydog could see how each man behaved himself when the mead was set before him, a cup when he sat down, and a cup when the meat was set before us, and a cup when the platters were cleared away and the singing and the story-telling began. For every man, sometime in that year, spoke or sang in the Hall, so that we should each learn all the songs of the Island and understand that all of us who speak the tongue of the Angels are one nation.

Bradwen always sat at Mynydog's table and poured the mead first for the Captain of the Household and then for the King, Mynydog's Queen long being dead. Yet I thought it was Gwenllian's duty by right, since she and not Bradwen was of Royal blood. Perhaps she was ignored because she had come among us from the South as almost a child, and it was as a child that people still treated her, out of habit. Only I, who had been away so long, saw that she was now a woman.

She still behaved, often, like a child, standing back timidly to let an older man go first, not taking her proper precedence like a lady of rank. She was always surprised to see a warrior stand back to let her pass. She was still very shy of strangers, however familiar they showed themselves with the court – or with her. She always came running into the Hall late, from putting her little brother to bed in the house on the north side of the court where they slept. Sometimes, even, the little rascal would not settle but would evade the maidservant who minded him and come creeping himself into the Hall and insinuate himself on to her knee, or even on to mine, because I always sat next to her.

She would sit by me till late. If the little boy had come sliding out to listen to the stories and the songs, she would wait till he fell asleep on her lap or mine, and then slip off with him to his bed and come back to me again. After the third cup had been poured, the Household would drift away from the Hall, each man coming up to bid the King good night and receive from the Royal Hands a jug of the King's own mead, made from the heather honey with a taste of its own. We older men would stay, those sitting lower in the hall moving up to it on the lower side of the high table, opposite the King, so that we formed a ring. Bradwen would stay with us, and talk. And Gwenllian would stay, too, watching Bradwen.

We would all listen to Bradwen. Wise as a man, Bradwen would talk like a man and help us to plan the war, where we who were princes and nobles sat with the King and with Diarmaid, the Irishman, the wild man, who alone was able to pass between the King of Eiddin and the King of Elmet in Lincoln, crossing the Irish Sea twice to avoid the Savages. This man was a close friend of Cynddelig, riding and talking with him a great deal in those days. He knew the King's plans as well as any of us. Mynydog would tell us again and again what he wanted us to do, how we should strike south while the host of Elmet came north.

'We will have them,' he would say, 'like a horseshoe, between hammer and anvil.'

'I have never seen the horseshoe move on the anvil,' I told the King at last one night, when we were all there. 'The Savages will move. They won't stay to be attacked.'

'They won't realise what is happening,' Bradwen told me at once. 'We will be too fast for them. The news will spread only slowly from farm to farm, not as fast as we will move.'

'It's not a matter of news spreading,' I objected. 'They have a King, Bladulf, to call them together.'

'All the better,' said Owain. 'If they were to come together, then the first army to attack will hold them so tight that the later comers, whether they be Elmet or Eiddin, will take them by surprise from behind. Then they will run.'

'They won't run,' I warned him.

'They will. It's only in fables that Savages will stand in line to fight. Who ever heard of it in real life?'

'Who ever heard of a real battle in this Island?' I retorted. 'There have been raids, of the Savages on us or of us on the Savages. But never a full battle with one army drawn up against another in open field. That is what we must – no, not expect, this is not a foreboding I have – what we must bring about, somehow. If we cannot bring their men together in such a battle, then we cannot destroy them.'

'They'll never come together,' Owain insisted.

'They will. I know, I have lived with them.'

'Oh, you have only lived in one place. Perhaps you only met the boastful ones. They won't come together to face us. You'll see. I've had more wars than you have had hot dinners. You come along and see what really happens, and then you can start to sing again, and sing about that. That's your trade.'

He laughed. Bradwen laughed too. Precent grinned. There was laughter everywhere after so much mead. Why did I not argue on, insist, bellow at him, 'But that's why you wanted me to join you, to tell you what they were like, to tell you the difference between these Savages and the Irish you are used to fighting'? Because it was Owain who spoke to me, and there was nothing Owain said that I could not believe, did not believe even against the evidence of my own senses and my memory.

Only Gwenllian did not laugh at me.

4

An gelwir mor a chynnwr ym plymnwyt
Yn tryvrwyt peleidyr peleidyr gogymwyt

We are called! The sea and the borders are in conflict,
Spears are mutually darting, spears equally destructive.

When we were ready, we went on Patrol, Squadron by Squadron, down the coast from Eiddin. I went under Cynon, whether to give Cynon practice in Command or to give us practice in obeying Cynon I was not quite sure. The decision was Owain's. On this ride, Cynrig, like me, obeyed Cynon.

We rode easy, unworried. On this ride we stayed within Mynydog's Kingdom, where no Savages had settled, and where they raided little. It was good practice in itself for the great journey. We rode in the Roman fashion. Owain had drilled us again in riding abreast, in a long line, in walking or trotting or galloping together with no man falling far behind the line or pushing ahead. But on the march we went in Roman fashion, in column, always riding in pairs, to guard each others' backs. Aidan always rode with me on this journey, since he knew me best of all.

We slept each night at farms. Fifty strong, no more, we could always find room to sleep in the stables and the barns. Roofs were not absolutely necessary that summer. It was a long, fine, hot summer, a better summer than any I have seen since. The people were glad to see us. We showed at least that Mynydog was willing to help them guard their fields from the Savages. It was not merely a matter of the King demanding things from them, though he demanded enough, and all Kings did that. He would guard them in return, and there were few Kings to do that.

We did not need to carry food with us. We hunted the high

moorlands inland of the farms, and most days we could count on sighting deer, and then we would ride out in two long wings, one starting the deer into the other, so that we could thin out a few of the bucks. Other times we could loose our greyhounds at hares, or fly our hawks at grouse or duck or a variety of other birds, all good eating. The barley harvest had started, and the people on the farms had no time to hunt, so they were glad to have the fresh meat we brought them. They gave us oat cakes and lettuces, onions and radishes to go with the meat. And they would always be ready to roast us a sheep or three, or bring out the great cauldrons for a mutton stew, to put new life into dead men. You need a hot meal after a day in the saddle, however hot a day it has been already. It is dusty on the road in summer, but when you dismount, and the sun is beginning to go down, you remember now that you have been sweating all day into your flannel shirt, and the cold and the shivers grip you. That's when you need the hot soup and the meat in it, and the fine sharp taste of onions. We would be so eager for it we would hardly strip off our mail: we always rode fully armed, so that our horses, as well as we, could get used to the weight.

What we did not eat hot in the night, we took away with us cold in the morning. In the middle of the day, with four hours riding behind you, and another four hours ahead, there is nothing to keep your heart up like a slab of cold roast mutton, with the crisp white fat in it, firmly breaking between your teeth. They were wonderful days, that summer. We would sit out in the noon sun to eat, the hobbled horses grazing around us. We lay on our backs, and watched the high clouds over us. We played 'She loves me – she loves me not' with the daisy flowers, and blew dandelion fluff into other men's faces, and covered our friends' backs with the bared seedheads of the grass. We would practise the songs we knew, and dance, men with men, the dances of every Kingdom in the Island of Britain. For songs are the same everywhere, since we speak the same language, from Wick to Cornwall, but every Kingdom has its own dances.

They were peaceful days, and we were all friends. I had little work as a judge, because there were no disputes. You may find it difficult, nowadays, hearing of all the quarrels and rivalry of Arthur's Household, to believe that there were no quarrels ever in the Household of Eiddin: but it is true. It is easy enough to keep from quarrelling, when there are enough girls to go round, and meat for everybody, and enough mead but not too much. Sometimes there were arguments about precedence of families or the pride of pedigrees, and it was then that I had to work my memory to bring back the order of the Houses of the Island. But above all, what kept us from quarrelling was the thought, always, that we were the greatest Household that any King had ever raised, and that it was our destiny to ride South and deliver all the Island from the Savages. And if that was our aim, then why should we quarrel over lesser things? We were consecrated, set aside, for this great enterprise and for this holy aim. The Virgin kept us in peace.

What we practised thus in harmony in the day, we sang and danced in earnest at night, in the fenced farmyards with the girls around us to join in, to learn the new choruses we brought them, and to make themselves perfect in the new steps and unfamiliar rhythms of Gwent or Little Britain. Oh, they were merry nights indeed, around the big fires the people lit for us, coming in from three or four miles away, from their own farms to the places where we slept.

Yes, the nights were merry, and the farmers poured out the mead for us, what mead they had left, and they gave it willingly. They had paid, already, that year, a treble tax of mead to Myny-dog, and a treble tax of grain for three years, and of wool the same. This had fed and clothed the whole Household for one year, giving each man his feasts, and his three shirts and his sad-dlecloth and his red cloak. And mutton, too, besides wool: they had sent their sheep in to mix with the game we hunted for our-selves. They had thinned their flocks for the Household, and never grudged it.

Besides the meat and the wool, there was the leather too. The mail of a coat will keep the edge or the point from tearing the skin. It will not stop the force of a blow. A good stroke with an axe, or even with a staff or an iron bar, landing on a body pro-tected only by iron, will break a bone. You see men, too, dying slowly from a ruptured spleen after a blow in the back, or cough-ing up frothy blood with their ribs splintered into their lungs, and dying just the same, and even men with their backbones broken, who live, may live a long time, but cannot move. And sometimes a blow will not itself break the skin, but force the broken ends of the bone out into the air of day.

So when the smiths have made you a mail shirt, you must stitch it to a lining of boiled leather, stiff and unyielding. Always remember to have five or six more layers of boiled oxhide over the shoulders. This will save you from a downward stroke to break the collarbone: also, it stops you raising your arm too high in excitement, and taking a point into the armpit. The farmers all down the coast, now, went without shoes, and they guided their horses with ropes of straw, because for three years they had sent all their ox-hides to Mynydog. All this had stiffened our mail: because of this we could afford, every man of us, to ride in high leather boots, and tuck into them breeches of two thicknesses of leather to keep our shins safe in battle or in the briars.

But you need more padding than that. Stiff leather does little more than muffle the blow and spread it over your whole trunk rather than on a narrow line. Even then, a well-placed stroke might leave you winded, rolling and gasping on the ground, and hoping in your agony that some one of your comrades would come up and stand over you. What we used to do was to wear two sheepskin jerkins under the mail, one with the fleece outside, the other with the fleece next to the body to soak up the sweat. You did sweat under all that, and when your shirt dried at night, you would find it in the morning white and stiff with the salt, to stop a blow on its own. I had to wash my shirt at the end of every week, and that is why Mynydog had given us so many. It was the fashion, too, to wear scarves around the neck, if you could get them, to stop the armour chafing as well as to soak up the sweat, and at the end of the day's ride it was nothing for a man to take his scarf off and wring it out and see a stream of water pour from it to make a puddle at his feet. Men would get their sweethearts to make them scarves in the colours of their families or their kings. So because of the shirts we wore, and the sheepskins we had under the mail, and the saddle-cloths we sat on, and the leather jerkins they made for the infantry, the farmers down the coast and up into the hills had all to make do with their old coats a year longer, through the rain and the snow, or lie a layer colder in their winter beds.

These were the people who had paid for the Household. They had done it all with poor tools, and not enough. A year earlier, even before they had ridden down to rescue me and avenge Eudav, when Mynydog was still only planning this campaign in secret in his own mind, Precent and Gwanar had ridden around every farm in the Kingdom, looking for iron, taking away all the metal the farmers could spare, and some they could not. Precent picked up any old spade, or fork with broken tines: or if there were a farm cart that nobody was actually using at the time, and Gwanar could attract all the attention his way, then Precent would take the iron tyres and the chains and the swingle-rings. A broken ploughshare was a great find, and the nails out of a pair of shoes not too little to take. These farmers had paid, then, in iron as well as in labour. Later in the summer they would be ready, many of them, to pay in time, and in blood, because they were willing to march as infantry with the Household down to the South. They had paid all that the Household had cost, these farmers, and when we came riding by they were pleased to see how all their goods had been spent.

They *were* glad to see us. They had paid, they saw, for an army gathered from all the Kingdoms of Britain, and farther, because we had those men from Little Britain across the sea. They saw our army with their own eyes, riding up and down the coast as far as the edge of Mordei, to press back the Savages, however they came, by land or sea. This was what they wanted. Mynydog had not wasted all the taxes they had sent him, and they were satisfied, and more than satisfied, to see us. We meant to them freedom from fear and anxiety. So nothing was too good for us, who had come to fight for them, nothing too lavish even though they starved themselves. Just to see men who had come such immense distances, from Orkney or from Cornwall even, places they had only heard of from wandering poets like me, come just to defend them, why, it made them sing all night, even sober.

We rode an easy way, east and south, under the blue sky of a hot June, looking out over the blue seas, at a few white clouds, at a little white foam. The wind blew, lightly, from west of south.

When at last we came to the end of our ride, to the border of Mordei, the debatable land, we saw smoke blown out over the sea.

We looked south, across the empty country where no one lived any more. The stone castles that our fathers had built were empty. Those walls can keep out the Savages all right, because they do not know how to attack them, or how to build them, and they are afraid of what they do not understand, instead of wanting to understand it and conquer it like a civilised man: but how can a man live in a castle when he dares not walk as far as his own cabbage-patch, let alone ride his sheep-walks, for fear of being killed without warning by men who sit all the time motionless in the woods, watching him. Nobody lived in Mordei, not our people, not the Savages. But somewhere down there, perhaps as far south as the border between Mordei and Bernicia, there was a fire, so huge a fire that though it was too far to see flames, we could watch the smudge of dirty smoke rising high in the air and drifting out to sea.

'What is it?' Aidan asked. 'Are they burning up all the world?'

'They would if they could,' I answered him. 'They have powerful wizards, who make their strong swords. I have heard it said that there is an Island in the northern seas where their demons have set the mountains on fire.'

'It's evil, whatever it is,' Cynrig agreed. He never liked to talk about magic. Perhaps he was too ashamed of his family who had their own dealings with the Little People who live under the sea near Cardigan. He turned away from us on the hillcrest, and shouted to the rest of the Squadron who had not thought it worth the effort to climb with us, and were grazing their horses in the dead ground behind us.

'Come up here! All of you, come on! Come and see the evil these Savages are bringing on us. They say you can burn the stones in Bernicia, and that is how the legions held the country. I think that this is what the Savages are doing, burning the land itself to spoil it for us.'

The men strolled up the rise to look, chatting as they came and falling silent as they saw the smoke.

'Burn all the Isle of Britain, they will,' breathed Aidan, full of a kind of pride at having been the first to see it. 'Demons they are, indeed. What do they look like? Do they look anything like men?'

'Never seen one, boy?' Cynon smiled at him. 'Like men, they are, only horns they do have, or so they say who never saw any, let alone killed any. And watch out for the females, they're worse. You'll see them, soon enough, horns and all. Come on, then, if you've all had a good look. We don't want to spend too much time watching here for nothing to come. Cynrig, you get them mounted again.'

We straggled down the slope. Morien stayed longest, looking fascinated at the smoke till the last. We laughed at him. He looked seriously at me.

'Burn the whole country,' he breathed. 'Aye, that would be a fine thing to do. Scorch them out of the way, I'd like to do that. And I will, too. You wait.'

We laughed at him the more. I pulled myself up on to my horse, a brown gelding that I had broken myself three years before and Eudav had given me, and Mynydog had kept for me. I walked out to my place, right marker, and waited while the others finished fussing over their harness and got themselves up into their saddles. Then Cynrig bellowed the orders like a true Roman, as Owain had taught him, trying to sound like Owain – we all tried to sound like Owain in those days:

'On your marker, into line … walk! Right … turn! In extended column of pairs … walk! … *March!*'

Going north, for the first hour, I rode as Scout, Aidan as always by me.

'No, never seen any of these Savages, I haven't,' he told me. 'Have they *got* tails, then? Really? Have they really got tails?'

'It all depends. If you are frightened of them, then you'll see tails on them, if they've got them or not.'

'And horns?'

'Oh, yes, horns, of course.' I smiled at him, smiled, not laughed. 'And so have some of us. Why, Aidan, you're a horned man yourself.'

He looked at me suspiciously, puzzled, while we rode a few paces. Then he began to grin.

'Horns? On my helmet, you mean?'

'Yes, on your helmet. And so do they on theirs. But we put whatever we like on our helmets, horns and wings and wheels and moons and stars. They always put horns.'

'But … Aneirin, is it true that they boil living men in their big pots and eat them?'

'Nonsense! Even Savages aren't as bad as that. The Picts used to do that, once upon a time, but you've never seen Precent eat anybody, have you? And, anyway, who ever saw a pot big enough to boil a whole man in. You could never make one, not even out of iron.'

'But they used to have them in Ireland. Everybody knows that. The old Kings used to keep them, and they used to boil their dead soldiers to life again after battles.'

'Tales, Aidan, tales. Men like me make them up.'

'But you haven't been in Ireland, have you, to see? I know people who have been, and they've told me about it. I hope the Savages haven't got one of those Irish cauldrons. Still I hope too I get a chance to see one of those Savages alive before we start killing them. Just to tell about after, like.'

'Little chance of that,' I told him. But even so, he was the first, a few steps later, to see the ship, and the Savages in it. We had come to the head of a steep path winding down the face of the cliff into the bay. It was too steep for a horse, but farther on, between the rocky headland where we stood and the more northern spur of rock, both jutting out into the sea, with the waves breaking at their feet over the cruel stones, sand-dunes ran down to the water's edge. From the cliff, we could look down into the ship, drifting in gently against the light wind, on the last hour of the rising tide, between the horns of the cliff its own dragon head horned.

It was a Savage ship, I could see that. It was bigger than any vessel we Romans build, huge, immense, fifteen or twenty paces long at least. They have wizards to conjure these ships together, making the sides firm with planks of oak because they have not the wisdom to sew leather as civilized people do. They glue the planks together with Roman blood, and sew them with the sinews of Christians.

Aidan, riding ahead, saw it first, and called me to look. He was amazed, saying it was some King's Hall that had fallen into the water. He was more alarmed when he heard it was a ship. I shouted back to Cynrig, but he, leading the main body, was too far back to hear. I told Aidan, 'You ride back and tell Cynon. I'll go on, and find an easy way down there. I think we can ride over the dunes to meet it.'

'Don't go by yourself down there, not by yourself!' Aidan was terrified. 'They'll bewitch you.'

'Better they bewitch one than two,' I laughed at him. 'I'll sing them a satire.' But when he had gone, I remembered that I would sing no more satires. Yet, as I rode down to the beach among the marram and the sea holly, I thought what satire I would have sung, and what the rhyme structure would have been, and what pattern of alliteration would have been most effective in quelling a wizard.

When I had found a smooth way down through the dunes, firm for the horse's feet, the ship had already grounded, some way out, stuck on a sandbank, with the water still all around her. The tide was near its peak, and soon would be hanging, as it does, for an hour. I watched the ship, leaning over on its side, till the leading riders, Aidan leading Cynon and Cynrig and a score of others, came galloping over the sand to me, screaming and shouting as if they were going into battle or driving deer into the nets. I shouted back at them to be quiet, and they settled down, some of them sitting with us and others wandering about up and down the beach on foot. They poked in the seaweed and drift-wood, and filled their helmets with mussels and winkles. Caso spread out his red cloak on the sand and went to sleep in the sun. At least they were quiet, and let us alone to listen for any voices out of the ship.

'*Is* there anyone in it?' Cynon asked, when for a long time we had heard and seen nothing.

'There must be,' I answered. 'I think I saw something from the cliff. Yes, I am sure that I saw people in it.'

'How many were there?'

'I do not know.'

'Think! Were they men or women? Or both? Were they armed? Did you see their weapons shine? Did they move about? Did they look up at you, or wave?'

591

'I do not know. I cannot remember.'

'Did you not try to count them?'

'I never thought.'

'Then what did you think?'

'I remember that. I looked down from the cliff, and I saw the water so blue, against the rocks so grey like shining iron, and spattered with the white foam so clean. And on that pure sea, the ship lay dirty brown, like a ... like a turd, come floating in to foul our pure sand.'

'Oh, a nice poetic thought that was, to be sure. But it's with a soldier's eye you've got to be looking at things now. Fine verse it would make, to be sure, but it don't help the the first boys to go up there, now, do it? How do we know what's waiting for them?'

'All right,' I said shortly. I was nettled by Cynon's sneering, his blunt words. It was more like Precent. It was Owain we tried to be like; but in stress and action, it was Precent we imitated. 'I'm going up first.'

'Oh, no you're not,' Cynrig told me. 'We're not losing our Judge so early. I'm going into it first, I and ... Caso. Caso! *Caso!* Kick him awake, somebody. Come here, boy, and bring your sword. Now, who else would—'

But at that moment the noise started, a blurred indistinct half-moan, half-grumble, from inside the ship. Then a head appeared over the bulwarks, two feet above our faces, and looked down at us. It was a man. At least, it had once been a man and not a woman. He was old, in his forties at least. His hair and his uncut beard were turning from yellow to grey in themselves, but over this they were streaked white with sea salt from the dried foam. The salt was encrusted too on his face, clinging in the layer of grease with which he had tried to protect skin from the drying wind and the sun. He hung there, his face just above the gunwale, and croaked at us, and croaked, and croaked. It was difficult, but at last I could tell Cynon, 'He's asking for water.'

'Oh, it's water he wants, is it? All right, boys, let him have his water.'

Cynrig and Caso rode out into the sea, as far as the ship. Mounted, they could have leant over the bulwarks. They did not go as near as that, only close enough to catch the old man by the

592

arms and drag him over the side, to drop him, face down, into the salt waves. He rolled over, spluttering and retching, trying to hold his head out of the water, which was only ankle deep. Everybody laughed. He got up on to his hands and knees, and crawled a little of the way towards the land. Then he collapsed again. Aidan ran barefooted into the little waves and, catching him by the legs, dragged him backward on to the dry shore. Then Aidan poured some water from his flask into the dry mouth.

'Clean that bottle well after him, lad,' Cynon advised him. Cynrig, dismounting by Aidan, asked me, 'What's he trying to say now?'

Even after drinking, when I was kneeling by him, the old man was difficult to follow. I was able, at last, to say, 'An ox, he seems to be talking about an ox. He wants us to take care of an ox.'

'Got an ox, then, have they?' asked Cynon. 'Have a look, boys!'

There were at least a dozen men now who had ridden or waded out to the ship. At Cynon's word, they gingerly heaved themselves up to look into the ship. Then they began jumping in with shouts of discovery.

They were very gentle with the ox. First of all, Hoegi passed his helmet full of water up into the ship for it. Then they hoisted it out and down into the knee-deep water. It could hardly walk, but they urged it up the sand, to where Morein had lit a fire of brushwood. They brought out, too, three young pigs, and these men had to carry.

'Anything more?' Cynon shouted.

'Lots of iron,' Caso replied. There was, too, a great deal. Six or eight of the curved knives they used for wood-splitting or fighting came first, a little longer than a man's forearm, single-edged and curved. Then there was a hay-fork, two wooden spades edged with iron, three axes, a hammer, two sickles and a scythe. A whetstone Caso thrust through his belt. There was a quern, which they threw into the water. Against it, our men broke a large number of pots and dishes, coarse and clumsy, and bad in colour. Hoegi cut the stays, and then Caso beat the tabernacle to pieces with his axe, so that the mast and yard, with the tatters of sail, fell over the side to be dragged to the shore.

'Any people there?' Cynon asked.

'No, no people at all,' Caso replied. 'Some Savages, though.'

'How many? Dead or alive.'

'Some dead, some alive. Most betwixt and between.'

'But how many?' Cynon asked again.

'How many?' I asked the old man.

'We were thirty,' he answered.

'Fifteen up here,' Caso shouted. But Cynon looked down at the old man and snarled, 'Tell us more!'

'Tell us more!' I repeated in his language. He shut his mouth, firmly, defiantly in a straight line.

'All right, then, hold your tongue if you want to,' Cynon shouted at him, and from the saddle kicked the old man in the back so that he fell forward again on his face in the sand. Meanwhile, men were bringing clothes out of the ship, and bags of household stuffs that they spread out on the beach for us to share out. There were cloaks and shirts, and instead of the togas we wear kilted around our bodies down to our knees the Savages use trousers of cloth to walk about in, as we wear leather breeches to ride. There were some pieces of jewellery in the bags, and I managed to snatch a ring with a stone in it, though what the stone was, and whether it was brass or gold or even bronze the ring was made of, I had not time to see.

Then the soldiers lifted out of the ship, with difficulty, two big leather bags, full to bursting with something that squeezed and shifted. They balanced the sacks on the gunwale, and Caso slashed one of them with his sword, bringing out a handful of grain which he passed over to me.

'Seed corn,' I told him. 'For wheat.'

'Let it grow in the sand!' laughed Cynon. The old man watched as we emptied both sacks into the water. The grain floated, a scum on the surface, spreading out to hide the blue of a wide stretch of the shallow sea, dirtying it, stealing its beauty from us, just like the Savages who brought it.

Last of all, we could see half a dozen of our men heaving and straining till something of great weight fell over the side and splashed into the water. And there it sank into the soft sand, and proved very troublesome to those who tried to bring it out onto the firmer beach. But they did it, and pulled the heavy thing

594

up the beach to the fire. It was a Savage plough, with a beam of oak as thick as a man's body, and a pole of ash: the wheels were iron-tyred, and the share of iron, too, three times the size of a real civilised share. It was built to cut deep furrows in the clay, so that the Savages could plant wheat, that evil plant, which grows in the bad soils where oats run rank and thick. It was too heavy for a horse: it was what the ox was for.

The old man followed us with his eyes as we pulled the plough towards the fire. When he looked up the beach, he gave a wail at what he saw. There they were butchering the ox, and getting the joints ready to roast on a spit that Morien the forest man had made out of the poles of the mast and the yard. Cynon dismounted and shook the old Savage.

'Talk!' he said fiercely. Like so many Eiddin men, he had a few words of the Savages' tongue, not enough to carry on a conversation, but enough to follow, vaguely, what was said in common talk. 'Talk! Where from?'

The old man looked blankly at him. It was wilful insolence, he must have understood Cynon, he had shouted loud enough.

'It's no good,' I told Cynon. 'He *won't* talk, he just won't.'

'Won't he then?' growled Morien. He and Caso grasped the old man under the armpits and dragged him to the fire. Morien took hold of his foot and held it close to the flames, till the filthy cloths in which he wrapped his legs began to char and the leather in his bursting shoes, salt-soaked, curled back and singed and steamed.

'Talk!' ordered Cynon. 'Here, push it right in! Talk! There, that's loosened him. Give him some water, somebody, or Aneirin won't be able to hear him. Now, then, what's he got to say?'

'He says they come from far across the sea, very far,' I explained to my comrades. 'They used to live in a very flat lowland, on the edge of the sea, by marshes and lagoons. He says it is not good land for men to live in. They cannot grow much wheat, and have to kill birds and animals for food. The water is rising. Some of the marshes used to be fields when he was a boy. They can no longer grow enough wheat to live. They cannot go away inland, because they are afraid of the people who live there. So they have set out to sea to find a new land.'

'Then they had better think about another new land,' ruled Cynon. 'They have no place in ours. Let them try Ireland.'

I listened to the rest of the old man's story, putting it as well as I could into the language of the Island of Britain. He said:

'We bought this ship from our chieftain. We gave him all the amber beads we had, and two pieces of gold that my mother's mother had stored away, and three silver buckles and a bronze pot. We were thirty in it, myself and my brother, our sons and their wives, and some children. We had never been on the sea before, any of us, ever, only on little boats in the marsh. We suffered on the first day, and some of us ever after, always being sick, spewing up what we had to eat, burning and blistering in the sun and the wind. We thought that it would be a short voyage, only three weeks, that is what they told us who had been here and come back, only three weeks to Britain with a good east wind. We thought we would have an east wind, because we had sacrificed to the Wind God a sow, and a white horse that we bought with our old ox and two cows. We drove them into the sea, and cut their throats so that the blood drifted out towards the West, and the way the ship would go, and we thought that would bring us an east wind and good luck in all the voyage.

'Then, as soon as the wind began to blow from the East, at the end of the spring, we set out to sea. Oh, we thought it was a great thing, to be out on the sea, just to point the ship before the wind and glide to a new land, with no work, no effort to move us on. At first, it was all a long feast: we ate and drank as much as we liked, even though it all went to waste over the side. But after a week, the wind changed, and began to blow from the West, and the ship went every-which-way whence and whither. Only sometimes at night could we make out the stars, and never in the day did we see the sun through the cloud, the thick cloud that never rained on us, so we never knew, in the end, which way we ought to go.

'And soon, there was no food. And after that, no water. The little water we had, the last of it, we kept for the ox and the pigs. The children died first. Then the old. My brother died the first, and then his wife, and mine. But towards the end, it was the young men and women who began to fall away and dwindle.

I was the only one who had still strength to look over the side when I heard you speak, and knew we were safe.

'Still, in spite of all, we had kept the ox alive. It was all we had to help us break the ground and grow food. We brought all the tools we had, so that we could clear the scrub and plant our wheat. We were not afraid of the hard work in clearing the forests, but at least we knew there would be plenty of empty land we could settle on. Nothing el[[s]]e in this Island, but enough land. It was late in the season, we knew, for setting out, but as long as we had the ox alive, and the seed corn, we would be able to grow enough to keep us through the winter and begin early next spring. That work we were prepared for, and starvation through next winter. But not the thirst on the water: that was too much.'

'How then would you live through the summer, till your harvest was gathered?' I asked him. Oh, but I knew how they would live. We would see them all over the civilised land, little bands of them, sometimes only one or two men, sometimes whole families, in rags, drifting from door to door, begging for old clothes, for food, for drink, for anything. If there were children with them, oh, they were expert at pinching them to make them cry and draw pity from our women.

I had seen Bradwen herself feed them, a hundred times, down in Eudav's Hall, and at the end they had come back and burnt the Hall for her charity. That was what they wanted, to find a woman alone in a house, all the men out in the oat patches or farther out with the sheep. The would sit, all quiet and still, not saying a thing, watching her every move till her nerves began to shred. Then they would start, picking up a few things here and there, always with one eye for the men coming back so that they would have time to run into the woods. And if she protested, they would threaten her, and seize whatever else they could see, and if she did not protest, they would take the same things, but more slowly. And at the end, if nobody came back in time to frighten them away, they would take her as well, raping her on her own hearth, often on her own bed, perhaps four or five of them in turn. Oh, yes, that was how we had seen the Savages live through the summer, before they went home to their own harvest of wheat in August. That was how this man was going to live, dress it up how he might.

'We would live somehow,' the old man told me. 'Somehow. There are some of our own people settled, they told us, almost everywhere along this coast, wherever we came ashore. We would go to the nearest chief, and ask him for protection and food, and promise him support in return – as we promise you our loyalty for the food you will give us. That will ensure us a little wheat, enough to keep us alive through the winter, just alive. But besides, there are the forests. Oh, yes, they are full of food for the taking, everybody knows that. There is fruit there, hanging from every tree, and honey, as much as any family can want. The pigs run where they wish in those woods, and belong to no one, and they will come to be killed when you call. And deer, too, so tame that you can catch them with your hands as you walk in the woods, and they would do, though there is no human being who would eat deer meat for choice. Nobody can starve in this great and empty land. It's fertile, too. It has never been tilled. A man has only to scratch a furrow with his plough, and plant six grains of wheat, and at the summer's end, even if it is a bad summer, he will have six bushels. We have heard all about it from men who have been here, and returned to being over their sweethearts or their children or their parents. And the weather here, we know about that too. It is never bitter cold here, like it is in the homeland, and the snow never lies for weeks together, deep as a man's thigh. And there is never drought, never a lack of rain to swell the crop. Oh, this is a glorious land, a splendid land – and all empty.'

And then he turned angrily, sweeping us, myself, Cynon, Cynrig, Caso, Morien, with a furious look.

'And what have we done to you? What has changed? When first our people came here you welcomed us. Those first comers, you took them in, and fed them, and let them wander far into the country, up to the source of the great river in the South, till they found good clay land to plant their wheat. You were glad enough to have them then, to have more men in your empty Island. And they were no different from us, no better, no worse, three generations ago, I remember, myself, the talk about Hengist, how he sailed, in my grandfather's time. He came, and your Kings welcomed him, too, and made him a King like themselves. The poorest Prince in Jutland, he was, a laughing-stock all over the mainland, and yet you welcomed him and gave him a Kingdom. If you took men in before, why do you not now?'

'There is no room for you,' I told him. 'The land is full. There is no land to spare.'

'But no, but no! This island is empty. We know that. All the world knows it. All the Romans have gone. They went away, by tens of thousands, by tens of tens of thousands, in our grandfathers' time, all of them streaming away across the narrow sea, back into Gaul to quarrel among themselves and fight the Franks and the Goths. They left the Island empty. The Romans pulled down the walls of the cities, and stripped the gold from the roofs and the silver from the gates, and they sailed away with all their wealth. We have not come hoping to find treasure to carry off ourselves; we know it is all gone. But the Romans left the land, they could not carry that off. We need the land to grow our food. Give us the land, so that our children will not starve, like those we left behind in Jutland. Why will you not give us the empty land the Romans left?'

It was Cynon who answered him. I translated as he spoke, even running on ahead, sometimes, because there was only one answer, whoever framed it.

'There is no empty land. The Romans have not left. *We* are Romans.' He stood there, in his red cloak, the red feathers blowing in his helm, proud as Owain. 'The legions, yes, they left, and that was fifty, sixty years ago, to conquer all the world. What does that matter? What does it mean? North or south of the Wall, this Island is Roman. Roman it shall ever be. From Wick to Cornwall we keep the Roman faith, the Roman laws. We live and think as Romans. And this Roman land is not yours to settle in, nor ours to give you. It is a land we must keep for our children, so that they can live as Romans live. If we were not Romans, we would live like wild beasts, in the woods, as you do.'

The old man looked at us. At me, the go-between, still thin and frail after the year I had spent as the Savages' slave. At Cynrig, fastidiously picking the lice out of a Savage shirt, and flicking them into the fire. At Cynon, rock steady, his feet wide apart on the sand, one hand on his sword, the other holding the rib of beef from which he picked the meat with his strong even teeth. At the rest of the Squadron, eating beef around the fire, cooking mussels in a bucket, paddling in the sea, collecting more driftwood, or even just sleeping in the sun. In the heart of the fire, the ploughshare glowed red through and through.

He asked: 'What shall we do now? How shall we live? You have stripped the clothes from our backs. You have broken our plough, and killed the poor ox that was to pull it, that was dearer to us than our children, because we kept it alive though they died. You have scattered our seed corn into the sea, that we thought dearer than our own lives, because we starved rather than eat it. You cannot do all that to us, and not feed us. Let us have water, at least, just a little water – there are some still alive in the ship. Give them water! And then, food! You must give them food, you must let us have food. How else shall we live?'

I gave him Cynon's answer, before Cynon spoke it.

'We do not care how you live, so long as you do not live here.'

At Cynon's sign, Cynrig and Caso took the old man by the arms and dragged him down the beach again to the water. Those of us who were still awake followed, in a jeering, shouting, mocking throng. Some were on foot; others, like myself, rode. By the ship, now almost surrounded by wet sand, because it was a little past the ebb, we stopped. Four men took the old man by the arms and legs, and swung him back and fore, back and fore … and at last, they flung him high into the air. He fell limbs threshing, into the bottom of the ship, landing on the loose planks with a rattle and a crash, screaming in pain and then moaning.

'Push her off, boys!' Cynon shouted. Men crowded to put their shoulders to the sides and slide the vessel down off the sandbank into the water. I looked down from my horse into the ship. There was a huddle of bodies lying in the bottom, half in and half out of the bilge-water showing where our men had torn up the deck-planks in their search for treasure, or iron.

The Savages looked back at me. They did not move, they did not speak, they only looked at me with drying eyes that had little life left in them. One was a man of about my own age, hardly covered by a few rotten rags, his lips puffed and scarred, his body

600

scattered with open sores and running boils. There was a girl of, perhaps, fifteen – it was hard to tell, she was so dried out, but I judged by the budding breasts under the strands of matted yellow hair. There was an old woman, with no teeth left. They were all starving, pot-bellied, their ribs showing, their skin hanging loose on bodies grown too small for it, and dried and shrivelled and peeling. They did not cry for help, or moan in their misery. They did not move even. Only the old man writhed on his broken bones, head lower than his feet. They just looked at me, all of them, with their great empty eyes, blue stones sunk in dark pits. There may have been fifteen: I did not count.

I dropped from my horse into the water. I linked arms with Aidan, and we too put our shoulders against the side of the ship to shove. She was moving already, but even though more and more men came down to help us, she was heavy, sinking into the soft sand. But the half liquid sand soon began to help us much as it hindered, and suddenly she began to feel lighter, to lift as she slid farther and farther off the sand and into the ebbing water that began to snatch her from us. She would drift away from us now, out to sea, out to the narrow gap between the two arms of the cliff which fell grinning into the waves. Pushing, we were up to our waists as we fell into the deeper water, and we laughed and splashed and ducked our friends' heads and played like children.

Then, as the ship began to pull out of our hands, so that not all our weight now could hold her straight, then, with a scream and a shout, Morien came riding down the beach and into the sea. He had rubbed his face with charcoal, so that he looked like a Pict. He flogged his mare into the; when the cold sea touched her belly she whinnied and voided herself. In his left hand, Morien whirled a torch, made of dry wood and wrapped round with some of the old rags out of the ship. He waved it violently to keep the flames alive. He flung it up high into the air, and we watched it circling and falling into the ship as it moved slowly out of our reach.

I stood with Cynon by the fire where the soldiers were now burning the offal and the bones and scraps, raising a stench and a cloud of black smoke. Cynon said, 'There was no need for what

601

Morien did, no need at all.' He had grown up on this coast. 'Watch her go, now.'

We did watch her, as she spun slowly round in the ebb, the smoke rising from her steady and black in the air. There was no sound from her, not that we could hear from that distance, over the laughter of our men dancing on the sands. The ship was moving faster and faster, towards the gap between the cliffs, towards the open sea. Morien and Caso were using the poles that had once been the mast and yard to push the ploughshare out of the fire. The wood had all burnt away from it, leaving only the metal, a huge lump of red-hot iron for which our smiths would be glad. It, with the iron tyres, would make ten or twelve swords, or at least twice as many spearheads. The ploughshare glared its heat into our faces, and the air danced between us and the ship, so that she seemed to shiver already on the calm water. Cynon murmured to me:

'Now, it takes her.'

We watched her, and it did take her. The current took her, and whirled her faster and faster, not out through the gap to the open sea, but towards the rocks, the fire racing down to the waterline with the draught her own motion made. Caso threw a bucket of water over the ploughshare to cool it to carry, spoiling its temper so that it would never now cut into our Roman land. The steam rose in front of us, hissing and whistling like mussels alive, stewing in their own juice in a bucket: for a moment it hid the ship from us completely. When it cleared, she had struck, on a rock still hidden by the tide, twenty paces from the foot of the cliff. She had struck hard, with the fire now down to the rubbing strake, and in an instant she had broken apart, and the fire quenched, and that steam, far from us, rose silent.

That was the end of the Savages, men, women, and, if there were any, children too, though I never heard one of them speak, or even saw them move, except the old man, and he was no loss to us. A meal we got out of it, a snack rather, for the noon halt, for a young ox, half starved, and three little pigs fed no better will hardly give a mouthful between fifty men. And we got out of it some iron, and the hide of the ox would cover a shield for someone, and the pigskin would give a pair of shoes for riding.

And there was enough tallow for a night's candles in Mynydog's Hall, and clothes to give away to the farmers we passed on the way back. And best of all, the Savages were gone with the ebb, drowned, or burnt before, and not to come in again till the next high tide. But by then we would be gone, too, dancing around the fires in a farmyard, and flirting with the girls for whose safety we had gone to war. We at least left the beach clear, the ashes buried, the sand swept over all.

Other patrols found the same, almost every week now in the sailing season. That was the first duty of the Household, to scour the shore for the Savages. Cynddelig's Squadron found a big party of them, who had come ashore the winter before, and built themselves houses close to the sea, and hung on there unnoticed till they had seen their new-sown wheat break the soil. Cynddelig killed them, he and his Squadron, every one. He brought back iron and bronze and silver, clothes and ox-hides, more than we had found. Yet, however we kept the coast, the smoke still rose from Bernicia.

On all that, I might have made a satire, if I had still been a Poet, and this is the satire I would have sung though I could not:

'There is no more to power than wealth.
Wealth does not come to those without power,
Or power fall into the hands of the poor man,
Except he spend effort and blood and shame:
For no new wealth can ever be created
And Power is indivisible and single.
Those who have wealth have more heart to fight to retain it,
Than those who have not to struggle to take it from them.'

This was the satire I could have made. But whether I sang it or not, it was true. It was to keep our own wealth and power that we went to Cattraeth.

603

5

Pan gryssei garadawc y gat
Mal baed coet trychwn trychyat

When Caradoc rushed into battle,
It was like the tearing onset of the woodland boar.

It was not every day we drilled, or rode out to the coast. We did not drill on Sundays, or on Holy Days, or Feasts, or when we had worked very hard the day before. There were many days when the Household did nothing, or when those who felt like it would ride out to hunt, to get some venison to eke out our mutton and salmon.

I remember the last time. I went hunting from Eiddin. I came from the Hall on a fine hot morning, for in that year every day of summer was fine and hot and dry. In the courtyard, Precent was talking sternly to Mynydog's nephew.

'So, as soon as anybody makes you a bow and arrow, *what* is it you said you were going to do?'

'I a hunter, I going to hunt the cat.'

'Oh, no! You mustn't hurt the poor cat, now, must you. What has the poor cat done to you?'

'But I a hunter, I shoot her.'

'Why don't you shoot a dog, instead? There's poor old Perro, here, why don't you shoot him?'

'He's too big. I a hunter, I shoot Pussy.'

'But it's the King's Cat, lad. You know what you'll have to do if you shoot the King's Cat? You have to pile corn over her till she's all covered up. Have you got enough corn to do that?'

'But I want to be a hunter. I want to go hunting. Men go hunting. I'm a man.' Satisfied with the logic of four years old, he turned and saw me. 'Aneirin! Will you take me hunting?'

I couldn't say no to him, not straight out. I couldn't offend him, and no more could Precent. So I answered, 'Go and ask Gwenllian if she'll come, and if she will, then you ask her to take you. But don't tell her I said so.'

Off he went, bubbling with it, and of course he told Gwenllian I said he could come hunting, which he had never been before, and that I said Gwenllian was to bring him. She hunted sometimes, but not as often as Bradwen who hunted almost every day, as skilled as any man at it, and strong enough to stay out with us all day. But deceived by the little boy's joy, Gwenllian did come out, saying, 'Just to please him, let me ride along behind the main party with him on my saddle-bow, so he can see.'

So we were, literally, saddled with him for the day. We rode out a good strong party, led by Bradwen and Owain. Precent did not come, staying behind to drill one half of the Household. Still, there were nearly forty of us, with dogs, and we were ready to take anything we could find for our supper. We cast round to the south of the Giant's Seat, Gwenllian and I riding together at the rear of the party. As we went, I heard her singing to the little boy one hunting song after another, but the one he wanted to hear again and again, as children will, was one I had made for him myself, long ago, and I was surprised first that he, and then that Gwenllian, should remember it.

'What shall Daddy bring you back from the mountain,
What shall he bring you down from the glen?
He'll bring you a salmon, a wild boar, a roebuck,
Speckly eggs from the grey moorhen.

'Daddy will lay his spear on his shoulder,
Daddy will sling his bag on his back:
Through the deep forest and over the mountain,
Daddy will follow the old hunting-track.

'Daddy will take his net and his crossbow,
Dogs Giff and Gaff will run at his side,
He'll go by the Ridgeway and under the waterfall,
The way he once went to bring back his bride.'

It was only doggerel, and I was ashamed of it, ashamed of having sung it first, ashamed that anyone else should remember it. I told Gwenllian so.

'Why, what is the matter with you, Aneirin? It is a very nice little song, and I am grateful to you for making it, because I can rely on it to get him to sleep when nothing else will. And here we are, on a fine July morning, and I still can't get a smile out of you, and I haven't done since you came home in May. What is it, now, what is it?'

I rode still in silence. She waited a little, then again: 'What is the matter, Aneirin? It is plain to me, but it will not be plain to you until you speak about it.'

I looked around in the clear air, down to the level land below us, for we sat our horses on the lower slopes of the hill and watched the rest of the hunt spread out across the plain, colourful and clear and sparkling. I watched Bradwen pass out of sight behind a thicket, and then my eye was dazzled by the stone in Gwenllian's ring, the one out of the Savage ship, that I had given and that I hear she wears still at Arthur's court, an emerald they say it is, set in gold. I said:

> 'My love said farewell to me in May,
> With a greeting she bade me goodbye.
> Now conversation forbids communication,
> Courtesy tempers the violence of feeling,
> The clamour of passion is barred out by custom.
> A wall clear as glass she has built around her,
> And she mewed herself with ravens, not with hawks.
> My love said farewell to me in May.

'And you are no longer a poet?' she asked me. 'Is that why? Is it because of her that you no longer make concise sayings, that you no longer count the syllables and the feet, that you no longer balance opposites, compare white with black, contrast like with like?'

'No, it is—'

'Do not tell me. I know the laws, I know, I know, I know! But the laws never bade a man strain after what no one could reach.

606

Go on, tell me that peace is always beyond a poet's reach. I think I understand it. You cannot sing unless you feel that you are badly treated. And now you have made yourself feel so badly treated that you dare not sing. What a song we shall have out of you in the end!'

'There will be no more poems.'

'And have you not just said me one? You must have been rankling over that one a long time, Aneirin, to have it out so perfect. It has spoiled you, being a poet, Aneirin, and such a great one. You have never known a failure till now. But do you think you are the only one to yearn after Bradwen? Why do you think that Cynon went away, so far away, first into the South, and then, after he brought me back, away again into Strathclyde, but because of her. If you had had to hear his lovesick yearning across the length of Britain as I had to, then you'd know that you weren't the only man who loved Bradwen. And why do you think that Gelorwid wants to be a hermit? He was up here with me last week, trying to choose a spot for his cell. This place was too cold, and that too windy, and another too damp, and another too close to the llan where Mynydog's own hermit lives already: but the main trouble with them all was that he wanted to have the best of both worlds, and to have a cell where he would see Bradwen. And Precent, why does he prefer to stay here and be Mynydog's gatekeeper, when he could rule his own Kingdom among the Picts?'

'But I had thought—'

'That she would have chosen the Pre-eminent Bard of the Island before them? But she did not, Aneirin. She knew you all as brothers, she did not think of you as suitors. But when the pre-eminent soldier of the Island came into the North—'

'Why, yes, then,' I finished for her. 'He did not come for the price, but he took the price eagerly, the price that Mynydog offered him, the price Bradwen was willing to pay, not the wide lands Eudav held by the Wall – what is that to a Prince of Cornwall? No, there was also Bradwen's white body to wallow in, in his bed.'

'And are there no other white bodies, Aneirin? And no other lands, no other homes? Will you waste yourself for ever because Bradwen loves, and not you?'

607

But before I could answer, we heard the horns close to us. The deer, flushed out, came past below. The little boy shouted in excitement, and waved the little spear Arthgi had made for him. Without a word spoken, Gwenllian and I set in our heels, and swept down on a buck on the edge of the herd. I whistled, and old Perro, baying, cast round to the other side of the buck, to head him into us, so that in a few strides we were running parallel with him, a few yards away. I held back till I heard Gwenllian give the word to her half-brother, and saw his toy spear flung – a miss, of course, but still he cast at a deer. I threw my own, straight to the heart – but there, I had had practice. The buck fell, and we pulled up our horses and dismounted.

Gwenllian caught Perro by the collar, and held him back, while I cut the buck's throat. The little boy wandered off a little to pick flowers, not having much taste to see me rip up the stomach to clean the carcase, pushing the steaming tripes away for the dog.

The horses stood still some paces away, as they had been trained. I knelt among the blood and ordure, my arms stained to the elbow. Gwenllian stood over me, and asked again, as if we had not ridden half a mile, and killed, 'And are there no other girls, Aneirin?'

And again, there was interruption. Perro growled, a horn sounded urgently from far away. I looked up. Running towards us flushed by the hunt from his sleep in the wood, was a boar. Head down, slavering, grunting and wheezing horribly, it was a horrid sight. Dangerous always, the more dangerous now not being clouded by pain or unusual anger, it was a threat I had to face.

'The child!' I shouted. He was well away from us. I seized my spear, and ran towards him. I whistled to Perro, and the old dog, well trained, went straight for the boar like a stone rolling down a mountain. I reached the little boy, and snatched him up, struggling because he saw no reason why he should be taken from his contemplation of a grasshopper. Almost as soon as I had him, Gwenllian galloped to me. I passed her brother to her.

'Ride!' I called. She went like the wind. I looked again at the boar. The dog's blood red on his tusks, he was coming at me, roaring. I couched the spear and went down towards him, at the run, because there is no waiting for this beast. I picked my spot – and suddenly, between me and my prey, between the boar and his prey, there came a horse, and Bradwen, splendid in her haste and rage, shouting the hunting cries like trumpets sounding, came charging to save me from no danger, no danger at all. She rode between me and my adversary, and I saw her arm strike, the spear flash down. The boar changed his line, turning away, and, as Bradwen pulled up her horse, I watched it go, fast, the spear trailing from its haunch. That stroke had done little damage, except perhaps to us, because the boar, hunted before, wise to what we could, would, do, was now above all enraged.

'Cut it off! After it! Cut it off!' I shouted to Bradwen, but she hesitated, waited to lean over me and ask, 'Are you hurt at all?'

'No, no. But the boar, after it – do not let it get into the thicket!'

But it was too late, the beast was already out of sight in a clump of thorn-bushes. And then, because things happen as fast in the hunt as they do in battle, and fortunes change as suddenly and as senselessly, there were a host of horsemen around us, Gelorwid and Owain, and Mynydog's Chief Huntsman, Caradog.

'We'll have to go in there on foot,' Caradog warned me.

'I'll go in,' said Owain at once.

'If you wish,' I told him. It was my beast, but it was beyond my pride to say so in front of Bradwen. 'I shall back up.'

'I don't need anyone else,' said Owain. 'I have hunted enough boars in my time, and there is no need for more than one man.'

'Let me come with you,' Bradwen put in. But I was saved argument by Caradog, who only observed, 'Two in, on foot, and the rest mounted around the thicket. That is the rule here. Bradwen, take anything that comes out beyond that withered tree.'

Owain said no more. He went in front of me into the thicket. The thorn-branches tore at our clothes, at our faces. The grass in the spaces between the trees was rank and thick. The trees were in full leaf now in late July. We could see little, we could only listen and smell for him, snuffle like a dog for the scent of pig sweat and ordure. It is better to do this without dogs: they only confuse the hunter, and harm the boar little. With a bear, however, I would take dogs.

We moved silently, Owain well in front, along the path, picking here and there a spot of blood, smears only. This one was not badly hurt, not bleeding badly at all. Dangerous, then.

It was very silent. The thing was somewhere, waiting for us, waiting to charge. Owain was out of my sight around the corner of the path when it happened. I heard it come, a horrible snarling shriek, and the shout from Owain, the trampling of the feet and the breaking of branches. I had the moment of space to lean back into the thorns, out of its track, and as the boar passed me, I leaned over and struck down, into the spine, the way we do here in the North. And it rolled, dead and still, with no further ado. There was no danger, no difficulty, as Owain had said. But Owain? He came down the path, from where the boar had come, still shaken from the wind of the beast as it had charged him, and missed. It was his luck to be taken by surprise, so that he had had no time to strike, and little to dodge: it was my luck that his shout had warned me, given me time to strike.

We carried the boar back to Eiddin, with the deer, for that night's feast. I sat with Gwenllian, and the little boy hid under the table between us and sucked at a marrow bone, with plenty of meat on it, that I slipped down to him. We three ate venison. But in the place of honour, Owain ate the hero's portion, the thigh, of the boar: and shared it with Bradwen.

That was how we rode out to Cattraeth, as to a hunt. We thought the Savage no more dangerous than a boar, and to our leader we gave all the honour and the praise for all that we did.

6

Gwyr a aeth gatraeth yg cat yg gawr
Nerth meirch a gwryrnseirch ac ysgwydawr
Peleidyr ar gychwyn a llym waewawr
A llurugeu claer a chledyuawr

Men went to Cattraeth in marshalled array and with shout oj war,
With powerful steeds and dark brown harness and with shields,
With uplifted javelins and piercing lances,
With glittering mail and swords.

The Household of the Virgin rode out of Eiddin on the Feast of
the Holy Virgin. The oat harvest was gathered, the barley was
in, the sheep-shearing was over. Early in that morning we had
heard the bell from the wood, where Mynydog's hermit offered
his sacrifice.

Before we rode out, Clydno numbered us. We who rode that
day from Eiddin were three hundred men and one. Each of us
rode a horse, and led one, or sometimes two. Each of us was
armed. Never in the whole history of war, never in all the tale of
the Island of Britain, had such wealth been spent to send so great
a host into the field. Not even an army of the wealthy Kings of
Strathclyde had cost so much.

Each of us wore a red cloak. Red is a wide word, a general
colour. Some were red as the russet autumn leaves. Others were
red as the flower of the campion shy against the grass in spring.
Owain's cloak was as red as the holly berry, a crimson we could
see easily in any press of men, and the plume of his helmet was
of the same colour.

My cloak was old and faded by the rain and the wind, till it
looked like a bank of foxgloves, blowing in the hedges of the wet

and clement west from which I had come. This was a cloak the Warden of Carlisle had given me, for singing a marriage song for his daughter, before the Savages had swept into his city, in a great raid, and killed him and his son-in-law, and carried off his daughter into slavery. For years I had kept this cloak in a chest in Mynydog's palace, against my own wedding-day. Now I wore this western colour to ride to war in the East.

We were not the whole army that marched out of the gate of the Dun, that morning, and that had to come in again: by one and one, after we were numbered, so that we could ride out again for the last time. Ten days before, Cynddelig of Cardigan had ridden out with sixty men of the Household, and two thousand peasants on foot. Each of these men carried a long spear and a wooden shield, whether covered with leather or not, and most of them had hand axes or long cook's knives at their belts. They all had coats of boiled leather, enough to stop a thrust, or at least break its force: and the leather cap, rarely reinforced with hoops of metal. None of them could afford a coat of mail, and if they had ever had armour then Mynydog had long taken it away to give to one of his Household. The infantry had gone ahead by the long road along the coast, where the farms were frequent. They went slowly, and would stop only where there was easy water, because they drove in front of them a flock of sheep, for them and us to live on on the road, till we came into Bernicia and could eat what we took from the Savages. Mordei the invaders had ravaged: in Bryneich they had settled. There would be food enough there.

By the borders of the Mordei we were to meet with the foot and with the sheep. We had chosen the place. It would take Cynddelig ten days at least to reach the place on the drovers' road down the coast, where we had caught the Savages on the beach. He would go south beyond that. We of the Household would take only three days to cross the high moorland, too badly watered to risk the herd; we would head always south-east, to reach Eudav's Hall under the Wall. Then we would sweep along the Wall, and north again into the Mordei till we had cleared the way for the infantry and their animals.

The Savages had not yet settled north of the Wall: enough of our men went into the debatable land to tell us that. Only their raiding bands came North, after the wheat harvest, when they felt full of food and beer, and vain enough to think of coming to steal from anyone richer than they were. We were rich enough to stop that when we felt like it, and the time was now. Or they would come in the spring, before the sowing, when they were desperate not only for riches but for very food, and would dare anything to gain even a mouthful of our seed oats or the starved and bony cattle kept alive through the winter. These were the times when, most years, they were most dangerous. Usually they would not raid this time of the year, when the wheat was ripe for the harvest, and every sensible man would be sitting safe at home, sharpening his sickle and mending his barn, treading down the clay on his threshing floor and rehinging his flail. This was the time that Precent had caught them the year before, sweeping down on them from the North without warning, burning the barns over the rats' heads, and finding a hundred other captives besides myself to bring back to the safe and pleasant North.

But just because it was this time the year before that Precent had gone to war it was just possible that they would choose this time to raid north into Mordei to meet us. Therefore we would clear the whole land in front of the infantry.

There had been little ceremony when the infantry marched away, partly because there is not much you can do in dignity when you are driving a thousand sheep, besides oxen and pigs: partly because the infantry, though the most numerous, are the least important part of an army, coming only to support the horsemen of the Household, to consolidate what the cavalry have won. The day that the Household rode out was the real day of the departure of the army.

Rank on rank we rode out past Mynydog on his throne. As we passed him we cried, 'Hail to the King, the Commander!' in the Roman way. Because we *were* a Roman Army, even though we rode through the Wall into the Empire to make war. Many of us, like Cynrig and Owain and myself, had been born in the Empire, wherever we had been fostered after that. Others had been born outside the Empire, and fostered in it, in great cities like Corinium or Kenfig. So we were as Roman an Army as had ever come out of the North.

Because we were Romans, also, we passed before the Llan in the woods where Mynydog's hermit had been told to pray for us, and we showed there that we were Romans, because we served the Roman Gods. As we passed we shouted, 'All hail to the Virgin!' and we waved our helmets crosswise. Many, too, called on the saints they worshipped, on Josephus or Jesus or Albanus or Spiritus. Gelorwid, who was wise in these things, called on a saint called Veron Icon.

Between the gate of Mynydog's Hall, and the Llan, all around the Judgement Mound where the King himself sat, we passed the people of Eiddin. Not everyone in the Kingdom was there, of course, although it seemed like it. Besides those who lived close round the Dun there were people who came in from farms even three days' journey away to see the Household ride out. Oh, yes, that was the day for cheering. A herd of cattle and a flock of sheep and a crowd of farmhands, even with spears in their hands, you could see those any day: but the whole Household, more mounted men than anyone had ever seen, riding out in all their splendour, that was the sight of a lifetime.

Besides, there was none of us but had a father or a mother or a sweetheart somewhere in the crowd. Clydno waved his staff to Cynon, and led the cheering. People cut the boughs of trees, and threw them before our horses' hooves, so that the iron shoes rustled in leaves instead of clattering, and struck no sparks from the granite setts.

My little friend, Mynydog's nephew, was not sitting at his Uncle's feet to see us ride. Before we marched, he had come into the courtyard of the Dun to see us saddling up and mounting, and he had wandered round among us, the only child we would have allowed to do such a thing. He tripped over harness and spilled packed bags, and walked fearless under the very bellies of the great horses, and we all thought it clever of him to do things like that. We all made much of him, of course, picking him up and kissing and tossing him from one to another, squealing with delight. Then Precent challenged him with:

'What are you then? Is it a bear you are?'

614

'Yes, I a bear, I a big brown bear. I eat you!' And he growled in a most bearlike way.

'No, boy,' Precent told him. 'Bears don't eat trees. Bears eat honey, and I'm a tree. You climb up this tree, and see if you can find any honey.'

So the little lad climbed up on to Precent's shoulder, convinced that he was going up by his own efforts, and that Precent had not lifted him at all, and, of course, on the shoulder there was a piece of honeycomb. He ate that. Then he wanted to climb every tree in the wood, and of course on every shoulder he found something good, honeycomb or cheese or dried fruit or meat.

Suddenly, he began to look very thoughtful. I knew the signs, so I picked him up, which was daring in the circumstances, and carried him out of the Dun, and we hid behind Mynydog's throne, unoccupied as yet, while he got rid of what he had eaten. I gave him a long drink, then, from my bottle, which pleased him immensely, because it was a *man's* bottle. It was, I think, the only bottle of water in the whole army, because all the others were weighed down with bottles not of water: the mead they carried had taken all the honey of a kingdom of beehives.

When the little lad had rinsed out his mouth of the nasty taste, and then had a long drink of the cool clear water, he was eager to go back and climb all the trees again. Children are quick to recover, and this one would never own that he was beaten. But while I was trying to persuade him that even a bear can eat too much honeycomb (and loth he was to believe it), and that is how they get caught, then caught my little bear was. Gwenllian came round the mound, having consulted Syvno the astrologer to find us, I am sure, and seized him from me. She scolded us both roundly: me for forcing sweets on the child, him for letting me persuade him to eat it, and nothing was further from what we both had done.

Still, he clung to me, and gave me a long hug and a kiss. I asked him, 'What shall I bring you back from the wars? Shall it be a bracelet or a collar of gold?'

'Bring me a Savage man,' he told me.

'To ride on?' I teased him, 'Or to eat?'

'I bear – I eat him.' And he growled and chuckled by turns,

and then he threw his arms around me and kissed me again. But Gwenllian whisked him away, and carried him back into the Hall, to wash the honey off his face, since he had got it up to the eyebrows, and to put a clean shirt on him, because the one he had, fresh on that morning, was already as filthy as if he had worn it a month and been a scullion in the kitchen all that time.

I went back to finish saddling up and found that Aidan had done it for me. I rode my brown gelding that day, because I knew I could depend on him. My strawberry roan mare I would ride in battle, but on the road I had her as a pack beast, not heavily laden, but carrying what I had, and there was not much of that. I took only the two horses, but there were many who took three, to carry all their jars of mead. Precent, like me, had only his charger to lead, though he would have drunk a river of mead, and not been satisfied.

'If you take too much,' he told me, approvingly, 'it only gets stolen, or left behind in the chase, and that comes to the same thing. If I want a fresh horse, I will get one easily enough after the first skirmish, and the mead on it too.'

Owain did not travel as light. He was a Prince, a Prince of Cornwall, and Precent was only a Lord of the Picts in the North, and I was nothing but a failed bard and an apprentice Judge, whatever my family might be. But Owain was a Prince. He rode on the biggest horse in the Household, a black, thirteen hands high. The son of a King rode behind him and carried his Raven banner. Cynrig is now himself King in Cardigan, and behind the seven walls of Cardigan he rules that city, with all its massive wealth. But when he rode out with the Gododdin, he owned that Owain was supreme, greater in skill and valour and in pride of family. Never has Cynrig the King been more glorious than the day when he reflected the glory of Owain.

Cynrain the brother of Cynrig led Owain's packhorses, six of them, for how could the Commander of a Household hold less state, or travel without his silver cup and his plate, and enough mead to reward his followers for valour? Owain had with him five greyhounds, that ran at his horse's heels, and made wide circles around him, raising every hare for miles, but being well trained they never gave tongue. And at Owain's saddle hung his crossbow, the only bow in the Household, because it was Owain's pleasure to hunt thus, but we would hunt the Savages like deer, with the thrown spear.

A Prince of Cornwall could never wear helm on such a day or in so important a parade. It was necessary that we should all see him to recognise him, and so it was Caso who carried it in front of him. Owain's hair curled red upon his shoulders. Over his mail he wore a shirt of red; on it Bradwen had embroidered the black ravens of Cornwall, with their long curved bills and legs in a different red. And his shield, too, bore the ravens. A King he looked as he led us out, more kingly than any man before or since who has ever commanded an army in the Island of Britain. Not even Arthur in his empery can look more kingly. And Arthur is not a King.

Before Owain led us out, when we were mounting, Gwenllian came back with a nice clean boy in her arms, for him to give me another goodbye hug and kiss. She held him up to me, and he squeezed me tight, but keeping his other arm around Gwenllian as children do he pulled her face close against mine. Kissing him I kissed her, and she kissed me. And weeping as women always weep when men go out to war, she wet my face and shoulders. Into my hands she pushed something warm and soft. Then she hid her eyes behind the little boy, and ran from the yard.

Gwenllian's gift was a scarf, of soft wool, striped green and white, the colours of my house, the younger branch of the Gododdin, the colours that my brother wears who is King in Mona. It could not have been made for any else but me, could not have been worn by anyone else in the Household.

So out of the Dun the Household rode, and saluted King Mynydog on his throne. Rank on rank were we of oval shields, each painted as its owner pleased. Precent carried a wolf's head, and all the little boys and girls who ran alongside us pointed at it and howled horribly, but still they threw flowers at Precent. It was always flowers they threw to him. Other shields were harder to imitate. Horses or crows were not too difficult, but who knows what sounds a dragon makes, or a lion? And there were other beasts shown which are entirely mythical, like the elephant that has two tails and two fundaments, and the tiger striped in yellow and blue. And Morien carried a painted flaming brand, so lifelike that the flames flickered before our eyes and we could almost smell the smoke.

No one, of course, had painted a bear. Even in those days, as now, the Bear was worn by no one but the House of Uther. And then there was no one of that House of an age to ride with us: if there had been, would not Owain have yielded his place to him? But even if there had been, not all that pride of family could have dimmed Owain's glory.

My shield had a ground of white. I had painted it in green, an oxhead. What else for me?

The boys ran alongside us and howled and barked, and at me they mooed, not telling an ox from a cow. The women and the grown girls stood still to watch. Many of them wept, as women often do when a Household goes out to war, whether it be to battle or to a mere patrol along a peaceful border. Others were silent, tense, thin-lipped. But it was the men, the youths grown enough to watch the sheep on the hills, but not yet old enough to ride with us, the men too old to stand the long days in the saddle, with battle at the end, and it is not very old in years you must be to be too worn out for such a campaign, and between them, the young men of our own age who were not chosen to ride, or even march with the infantry, because some must be left to thresh the oats and barley just harvested, and to bale the wool newly sheared, and to net the fish for drying and to tend the oxen, so that the women will not starve through the next winter – the men, it was the men who shouted and cheered as we went by.

This did not trouble the horses. Time and time again we had had all these men out with us, and men from farms farther from Eiddin, to shout and clash metal and run about among us waving flags. Now the horses were used to it. They would stand stock still, or run quiet and steady, in the clamour of battle.

Nor were the horses disturbed at the singing of the Household. First, when we were still close to Eiddin, when the women and children still ran close to us, we sang respectable songs, the songs they expected us to sing. These were marching songs of the days of old, that the armies of the Gododdin had sung when they marched to make war on Rome, and songs too that the

Romans had sung when they marched north of the Wall to fight against Eiddin. And this, too, was proper. We were the newest Army of Rome, marching against an enemy who had never owned the might of Rome, nor served the Roman Virgin.

At last, we left behind even those who were the most loth to lose us to sight. On the flank of the Giant's Seat, where we had hunted, and lain in the sun to dream, Gwenllian sat her horse with the little lad on her saddle-bow to wave goodbye to us at the last. Clydno was there, too. Not Mynydog. He sat his throne till we had all passed, and gone down the hill, and past his farm, and out of his sight, and out of sound, while he strained at the last to hear what could never again be heard in Eiddin, the sound of the Household. Then, I am told, he wrapped his cloak around his face, and wept, and no one dared to speak to him for the rest of the day. But these our other dearest friends sat still, where we could see them when we looked back, for hours, while our column wound up through the woods and out on to the moors.

When we had left them behind, the songs changed. The men sang newer songs, or perhaps they were older songs, bawdier songs and bloodier songs anyway, about the short-comings in bed and battle of Bladulf, and Hengist, and of the Kings of the Irish that had come into the Island before, and that we had fought before, and beaten before. These were songs they sang at the nets, and on the sheep walks. You do not sing on the hunt, only after. I thought that singing at this time was too like singing on the edge of the forest, when you may frighten the deer away. Our prey, now, we did not want to frighten away, but rather to gather together to face us. But who was I to object? I was only the Judge.

At midday, we halted to rest our horses. Now most of us took off our mail shirts and bundled them in our red cloaks to sling across the backs of our spare horses. Mail is too heavy to wear without cause, unless you are fighting or on parade. Our helmets we could sling at our saddles. While our horses cropped the grass, we filled the helms with the ripening whinberries: the blackberries were still red.

When we remounted, one squadron rode still armed, ahead of the rest of the Household, and spread out in a long line of little groups of three or four, a mile from flank to flank. Here, so close to Eiddin, there was no real need for this, but it was good practice. The squadrons took it in turn and turn about, half a day at a time, to ride in the skirmishing line.

Owain with his Standard rode between the Skirmishers and the first concentrated squadron. In case of alarm we could see, from his waving Standard, whether we were to form line to right or to left or equally on either side of our Commander.

Precent always led the Skirmishers. I rode every day with Cynon. His squadron always kept the rear. In an alarm we were not to join the line, but to ride behind it, in the centre, as a reserve. Which is the harder, to lead an army in a massed assault, or to restrain skirmishers and bring them back into the line when they wish to scatter and pursue, or to hold a squadron ready, watching the fight, till the time is ripe to throw them in? I do not know.

This first day, however, we had no thought of battle, nor the next. We rode across the high moorlands and between the groves in the quiet valleys as if we were riding for pleasure, or for hunting. Often men let loose their hawks at grouse, or files or even whole squadrons broke from the line to ride shouting after greyhounds that had started a hare.

Time and again we passed little huts of boughs in the lee of hills or on the edge of little woods, where the youngsters spent the lazy days of summer herding the sheep. The boys we passed out on the hills in groups of two or three. They spurred their rough ponies to ride with us a little, joining in our songs. The girls at the huts looked up from their endless gossiping over the cooking-fires and the spinning-wheels to wave at us, and shout good wishes. One would have thought that huge armies like ours, six whole squadrons, passed every day, we disturbed them so little.

In the evening we came down to a lonely farm, where Precent had already stored up food for us, sides of smoked bacon, cheeses and butter, oatcakes that the people of the place had spent, all that day baking for us. Best, there was mead for all. We slept in the woods above the farm. Some of us built little huts of boughs, as we had done when we were young and kept the sheep in summer. But most of us heaped beds of cut bracken or heather, and rolled ourselves in our scarlet cloaks. In August it was still warm enough for it to be no hardship for us to sleep with no other blanket in the open air. The horses were tethered in long lines, after they had been watered by squadrons in the stream and fed with oats.

Next day, we went on with our summer ride, under the blue sky flecked with hardly a cloud. On that morning we rode careless as before across the southern valley of the Kingdom of Eiddin, and now we climbed the hills that were the border between Eiddin and the debatable land of Mordei. In these hills, we did not see boys, or girls. The shepherds, when we met them, were grown men, well mounted and armed at least as well as the worst armed of the Household. They wore jerkins of stiff boiled leather, and capes of mail. Most carried swords. They looked keenly at us, keenly but with pleasure, because they hoped that our passing would mean that they would be free next year from this boys' work. Under the threat of the Savages, men had to guard the sheep.

That evening, in the hot and yellow August sunset, we came down to another farm. Here again we found food and drink waiting for us and for the horses. Again we lay to sleep by squadrons in the woods, making our beds as we wished. But this was not merely a second night like the first. Tonight, it was not the boys of the farm who watched our horses, and it was not only the wolves we were afraid of. Tonight, Gwion Catseyes and his squadron watched the horses, some sleeping in their mail while others lay awake out on the wide moor, turn and turn about.

We did not light fires that night. The first night, the girls had come out from the farm to flirt with the men watering the horses. Some of them, too, did more than flirt, and slept close to our fires. But tonight we all slept alone, as well as a man may sleep alone in an army of three hundred, camped beneath the stone walls of a tower where no women live. There were worse than wolves to watch for, and these vermin no fires would frighten. The fence round the farm was not a matter of rails and posts, but a rampart of logs, seven feet high, the upper ends sharpened in the fire. This night not even Morien lit a fire, whether to cook food or to sharpen a stake: fires can be seen at night farther than smoke by day.

621

We did not light fires that night. The first night we had been in Eiddin. This night, there was no certainty where we were: this was debatable land.

In the misty dawn we rose to ride again. Now, too, we brought out of the barn what Precent had packed down there, load by load through the summer, to save us the trouble of carrying it ourselves. We packed more than mead now on our spare horses. Each of us had bacon and cheese and oatmeal to feed him for a fortnight. That kind of food is easy to carry: no man of the Household died of hunger.

The heat haze lay before us as we rode south through the empty heather hills. Here there were no more sheep, and no more shepherds. Sometimes hunting parties came as far south as this, but not often, and if they did, they sang about it afterwards as if it were a battle. It was too deep into the debatable land. The deer thrived there.

Still Precent led the skirmish line ahead of us: still Cynon and I led the rearguard. Any man who fell so far behind the main body as to hear *our* voices knew that he was too slow and spurred forward. We rode light enough, all of us, and no horse foundered. Now we were singing the other songs, the songs we knew were of older and bloodier wars, wars before the Romans. 'The Hunting of the Black Pig', we sang, and 'Heads on the Gate', 'The Toad's Ride', and 'Blood in the Marshes'. We were a happy confident Army, the Household of Mynydog King of Eiddin, and we did not care what Savages heard us coming. Besides, we were riding to Cattraeth, though we did not know it.

Ny wnaeth pwyt neuad mor dianaf
Lew mor hael baran llew llwybyr vrwyhaf
A chynon laryvronn adon deccaf

No hall was ever made so faultless,
Nor was there a lion so generous, a majestic lion on the path,
   so kind,
As Cynon of the gentle breast, the most comely lord.

On the last morning of our approach ride, we roused ourselves in the wood on the north side of the; we slept there in the dead ground, while Gwion watched beyond us to the South. We had slept in our mail, let it rust or not. Our horses we had hobbled by our heads, and we fed them on the oats we carried. We poured water from our flasks into our helmets for the beasts to drink. We did not show ourselves outside the wood till it was time.

When we rode out again, it was Cynon's squadron that, for the first time, rode in the skirmish line, and that for the same reason that it had kept the rear the other days, that it had in it the hardest and the toughest men, used to war and fighting and travel. Not all of them were like that. Precent, on the far right of the line, rode with Aidan, to cover him, as due to his Royal blood. I rode with Cynon, and we stayed on the far left, ahead of the others.

We came to the edge of the wood, and looked across the valley to the Wall. It ran before us, miles ahead, a grey line across the green country. Below the wall there was a wood. A strange wood. In August other woods were green. This wood was brown and grey, as if in winter. The woods below us, this side of the stream, were indeed green. Between the edge of the nearer wood and the stream had once been Eudav's Hall, and the paddocks where he ran his horses. Destruction had been complete: I could not be sure where it had been, the house where I grew up.

We walked our horses down the moorland slope, over the grass cropped now by deer, and not by sheep. I rode as one does in the scouting line, on Cynon's left, five horse-lengths behind him. The light changed as we passed beneath the oak trees, dappling patches of shadow with streaks of sun. Hard light, indeed, to see a deer, let alone tell the points: hard light to aim an arrow or a spear. Quiet, too: I have lain, before now, in the wood, and seen five horsemen pass twenty paces from me, and if I had not been turned that way to see them I would never have known it. Therefore our heads were never still as we rode, turning and twisting to see all round us, all the time.

I knew every inch of this forest, in light or dark: I knew all the sounds there ought to be. There was not a hollow where I had not crouched to loose a bolt at deer or hare, or to watch the badgers playing in the full moon. I had ridden here with Bradwen and Precent till I knew every pothole, every soft place where a horse or a man might stumble. I knew, almost, every fallen branch that might crack underfoot, excepting only those of last winter. Our hooves hardly rustled the leaves, or broke the mushrooms, the millers and the redcaps, left to overgrow and turn gross. No civilised man had been here, or they would have been gathered. Cynon, too, had known these woods before, when they were still safe for a little girl to go out with the dawn to come back with a kerchief full of blewits.

It was hard to see deer, here in the August woods. It was hard to see men, too. Sometimes I lost sight of Cynon, or he of me, as we moved or halted by turns, passing or repassing each other.

There was no watching here for deer, or men. The deer had not gone by, we saw no droppings or the birds that would search them for undigested seeds. We would not see the deer here: we sniffed the air for them. Then I smelt it. I raised a hand to Cynon. He rode past me towards the smell of wood-smoke, halting by a hazel-bush, listening for anything that might have alarmed the birds. I came past him, a few yards farther, while he watched me.

I leant down from the saddle to see what they had left. There was a live fire somewhere ahead, but not here: these ashes were

624

too cold to smell of smoke. Last night's? The night before? I rode a little farther, to where they had slept, curled up on heaps of bracken. At least a dozen of them by the space they had flattened. One had left a torn shred of cloth, half a blanket, ragged and dirty, the colour hidden beneath the crusted filth. And there was a scatter of bones too, deer bones, picked clean and polished. These had been hungry men, who had killed by chance at the end of a long and profitless day, and then gorged themselves on the meat, half-cooked, charred at best, and left nothing but the guts that the flies buzzed over. How many men to devour a small deer like that? A dozen? A score?

I moved forward, into the stench. Man droppings, not deer droppings. Fresh. This morning's. Last night's fire, then, lit only to cook on, then prudently dowsed. But another one, somewhere, still burning? I sat still, still as I could, looking round me, listening, sniffing. Were there eyes on my back? Were men watching me from the shadows under the trees, or from the branches over me? And if there were would they stay hidden as long as I could watch? Some men say that you can feel eyes on the back of your neck. Perhaps you can if you are expecting them. I was not positively expecting them: I merely wondered if they were there.

I waved. Cynon came forward, rode past me and halted well ahead. I did not expect eyes. But neither did I expect to find in all Britain a man so poor that he would risk his life for that filthy scrap of blanket. For the sake of that rag, he thought it worth the risk to run across behind me, from cover to cover, picking it up as he went. So fast, he thought he would not be seen. But I heard him come, and I turned to see him pull at the blanket where it had caught on a snag of a fallen branch. It held only for a moment, but it was time enough to end his life. It was an easy throw. The spear took him as he bent, in the back below the short ribs. I saw the point come out below the navel. He rolled on the ground, his knees jerking to his chin, clutching behind him at the shaft, vomiting blood, calling for his mother. There had been no mistake. This was no Briton.

If I had gone back, as I was tempted, I would have been a dead man. If I had dismounted, in mercy to finish him off, in greed to recover my spear, they would have killed me. The screams brought the other Savages out of hiding. There *were* a score of them, nearly, and they rushed at us out of holes in the ground and from behind piles of leaves, from the bushes where they hid as we passed, hoping that we would pass and let them be.

Most of them went at Cynon, sitting his horse still, his head turned away from me, guarding me from that direction from which they did not come. They went at him when I should have guarded him. Before he had a moment to turn, they had his steed by the head and him by the legs, jerking and pulling him from side to side, rocking him out of the saddle. He stabbed at them with his spear, not having time to draw his sword, and they beat at him with what they had, billhooks and axes and cudgels.

I had time to draw my sword before the Savages reached me. I cut down the first who snatched for my bridle, and I spun the roan on her hind legs to scatter the others, giving myself space to ride to Cynon. I shouted a rallying cry:

'I ni, i ni, i ni! Awn, Awn, Awn! dere 'ma!' And from all round, I heard the forest answer

'Awn! 'na ni! Awn! Awn!'

But they were still far away, and now the Savages had Cynon on the ground, cutting and hacking at him while he tried to cover his face with his shield and stabbed up blindly with his spear. But an axe put an end to that as I crashed into them, the mare pushing aside one man with blood streaming from his eyes and another doubled up and clutching his groin.

I cut to this side and that, caracolling my horse around Cynon where he lay bleeding, hoping that my mount would not step on him. I had to be sure that they did not play the same game with me. I found that the enemy were not mailed. My sword cut through shirt and flesh and bone, and I heard them scream. But, screaming, they still held on, beating at me in senseless rage that overcame their fear, and grasping at me from all sides as though nothing but physical contact, the violence of nails and teeth, would satisfy them. Then one of them had his fingers over the edge of my shield, jerking at me, and I nearly went down, but suddenly there were horses all round me, mail shirts and red plumes and words that I could understand. The hands slipped

626

from the rim of the shield, and suddenly there was no fighting, only Morien and a dozen others sitting their horses or sliding down to bend over Cynon.

We dragged the kill over by the heels to lay them in a long line, like hares or fallow deer at the end of the hunt. But this was the beginning of the killing, I knew. Twenty-two altogether, old and young: not a bad day, if only they *had* been deer. They had nothing worth winning – their patched shirts of soft leather, their worn-out blankets rolled and slung on their backs, tied with odds and ends of knotted string, their shoes, those that had them, with the dead toes sticking stiffly out. Only two of them had the long curved knives from which they get their name, the saxes which did Hengist's work for him on the night of the long knives, and brought Vortigern the Great to ruin for a time. Otherwise, they had iron-edged spades, three hedging-hooks and five axes, and with that they had settled Cynon.

We stripped the mail from him, and cut the shirt from the bloody shoulder. He had been struck there either with axe or billhook, between elbow and shoulder, where it is hard to pad the mail without clogging the arm. The flesh was mashed and the bone, at last broken, thrust splintering through the skin. I had never till then seen such a horrible wound. I saw worse later. Cynon, however, drinking mead, was soon able to sit up and speak, gasping, which is better than lying still and groaning.

While a committee of those who claimed to know what to do about wounds debated their incompatible opinions, I cleaned the blood from my sword with the torn blanket that had been the cause of the fight. The first Savage had stopped writhing. I set my foot on his neck to pull out my spear. This was the first man I had looked on that I had killed: now I could never be a poet again, whatever was said. I looked at him. He might have been fifteen, or a little older. The flies were already gathering in his open blue eyes. The yellow hair was blackened with soot of some kind. A man poor enough to want that blanket wore no shoes.

Morien sniffed in the air for something other than blood. He called me:

'Let us see what they were about.'

627

It was not far to a well-remembered clearing. Here were stacks of cut alderwood. The turves were piled ready. We followed our noses. A quarter of a mile farther, in the next clearing, the unwatched kilns smouldered. Charcoal they were making, for the Savage smiths to beat out swords against us. This forest, at least, from now on, we could forbid them.

This was the first skirmish of the campaign. Precent rallied the skirmishers to move on. Now I led the left wing with Morien: others could help Cynon. We found more stacked timber, more kilns, but no more men nor sign of any: it was just the one band that had come into our wood.

We rode down the slope from the edge of the wood to the paddocks above Eudav's Hall. Now the grass in the paddocks grew high and thick because there were no horses to keep it down, or even sheep, only the shy deer and the hare. We stumbled on the dry-stone wall, now hidden under the green, that marked the edge of the inner paddock.

Here the angle of the wall was formed by a huge boulder of granite. It was one of the Dwarves that long ago came down from the North in anger to push aside the wall. But the Magician Vergil, fearing for his handiwork, had stood on his tower and turned them all to stone where they had slept. South and West from the Dwarf Stone we had stacked the thin slabs of slate to make the paddock fence, down to the river side. And standing on the Dwarf Stone, I looked towards the river – yes, there had once been Eudav's Hall.

There was no Hall now. I rode across to it by the little stream. Nothing, now, but a mound of charred thatch and rotten beams, bright green now, the grass growing stronger and rank on it as it does when we have burnt off the heather. Below that rubbish, somewhere, was the hearth where they had cut off Eudav's head, his blood spilling on me as I sang. In one instant the world had spun, from a happy night of song and dance and argument, and mead and mutton. The Savages had burst in, screaming and stabbing about them, stinking of wheat, filthy with grease. Before I could rise, my hands still on the harp, they had struck me down, with a cudgel, as they struck down Cynon.

We brought Cynon down to the edge of the wood above the

paddock, where we built our huts for the night. He was pale and sweating, biting his lips not to scream with the pain. Someone had bound the arm to stop the bleeding, and splinted it to save the smashed bone. To this day, Cynon stands as Judge beside Arthur's chair with one arm stiff and useless. But on that morning he spoke as slowly and clearly and deliberately as he does now when he gives judgement, though his teeth chattered between the words. Owain debated what to do.

'You must go back,' he said. 'Hard though it is. But you can go back in honour because you have killed two of the vermin. Your squadron can ride back with you as a Hero, to give you triumph.'

Cynon, sweating, looked at Owain in surprise.

'Full of men you must be in Cornwall, then, and empty of glory, to talk of honour for killing charcoal-burners, and send fifty men to escort one.'

'It is your due, to ride into Eiddin in triumph, in your shining armour, your shield at your side. And it is not safe to send you across the moors with fewer men than that: you might meet more of these scavengers.'

Cynon spat. 'Shining armour!' he grunted. He called, 'Hoegi!' This was a lad, a poor man from the heather hills, who rode in the rear rank of Cynon's squadron because he had only a cape of mail over his shoulders, and had refused to take a whole shirt from the King if it meant one man less to ride with the Household. All the same, he had killed Irishmen on the coast. 'I shall not wear this shirt again before the spring.' Cynon pushed the bundle of armour at Hoegi. 'My horse will run the faster without it, and it will keep your kidneys warm. I am sorry it has been torn a little: only sew up the leather of the sleeve and it will serve.' Thus Cynon the Courteous.

'I will not wash your blood from it with water,' said Hoegi, knowing that a speech was called for, 'nor yet with the blue mead, but with the blood of savages.'

Courteous as Owain was Cynon, but blunt as Precent he could be.

'Wash it as you like, boy, but do it before it starts to smell, for your comrades' sake. But call Graid, and the two of you ride with me through the wood and see that I do not fall off.'

629

'Ride with him to Eiddin, and see him safe to his father!' Owain ordered. But Cynon over-ruled him.

'Just send me to the crest. Then I can reach a shepherd's booth by night, if I ride this horse hard.' He turned now to Owain. 'I am one man wasted to this army already. We must waste no more.' He stood up, holding to Precent's arm. 'If these boys are going to be back with you before night, then we will have to start now.'

I pressed his hand, and so did all who could get near him, because we all believed that he would die there on the high moors. Hoegi and Graid rode with him through the wood and over the crest on to the high moors, and watched him far across the heather. We all prayed that he would indeed reach a shepherd's hut before he fell from pain and; but we did not think he would. I have not seen him since.

I did not ride with him. I did not even wait to see him go. I rode the other way, south, across the river, with Morien and a strong patrol, to see what was there now. I splashed across the ford, where I had so often lain flat as a child to tickle trout under the flat stones, or netted salmon.

We went across the southern river meadows, that were flooded every winter and so came up fat and green every spring, food for horses though not for sheep. Then we entered the Brown Wood. I called it that to myself since I had first seen it that morning, lying a long greydun shadow below the Wall. When I was young we had called it the Cobnut Wood, because it was that we went there for in the autumn. It was, then, a place to go to hunt squirrels, if you wanted a good cloak of rich red fur for the; and it was good for the pigeons that eat so well in a pie. Then, if you could lie quiet for an hour or so, dead still, you would see them all come. The tree-creeper would spread himself flat against the bark and scuttle up and down, the wood-pecker would nod, nod, nod against the rotten bough. You might even see the mice run. And if there was anywhere to see the Little People, it was in that; though I never did.

That was before the Savages came. Now they had blasted and fouled the forest. It had happened the spring before, when they burnt Eudav's Hall and dragged me off to pull their plough.

They had brought their single-edged knives, two feet long from hilt to tip, not pointed, but heavy, curved, for hedging or reed-cutting. They had cut the saplings and the lighter trees, the cobnuts above all, and stacked them, and burnt them down for charcoal to beat more axes to kill more forests.

They had not the strength to cut down the larger trees. Instead, they had gone from tree to tree, from oak to ash to elm, from each stripping the bark, from as high as they could reach down to the ground, all round the trunk. If you do that in the late spring, after the leaves have sprouted, then through the summer the tree will dry slowly and the leaves will turn brown and fall. Before the autumn, you will look at a winter forest, see-ing the summer sun through bare boughs. The next spring, the leaves will not bud again. The trees will be dead.

This forest, now, in high summer, was a winter forest. So the Savages destroy the very seasons of the year. On some trunks the Dead Men's Ears stood out, in places the rot was speckled and red. But there were neither leaves nor nuts nor acorns. Beneath our feet, indeed, the grass and the brambles grew, and the new shoots of the alder and the hazel were green, but one spring's growth and no more. There might still be sparrows, and, if you waited to see, there were perhaps still mice. But all the life of the high forest was gone. The squirrels no longer quarrelled and shrieked, we could not hear the rattle of the woodpecker that carries so far. No dove called 'Coo-coo-cooroo' for deer. Wild cat and fox cannot live on mice; they too had gone. All this the Savages had done.

Nothing so devastating had happened since the Wall had been built. We came out of the Brown Wood and looked up, ourselves, at the Wall, standing as still and as thunderstruck as had the animals that found it first, the hare and the deer that saw it set across their feeding-grounds, across their ancient trails, the wolf and the bear and the badger seeing that it made safe the beasts that lived to the south. Five times the height of a man it stands, and twice as thick, all made of stones so heavy that a man cannot lift them. It was raised in one night, complete from sea to sea, by the Magician Vergil, at the bidding of King Hadrian. This was one of the works that Hadrian did for the pleasure of his leman Cleopatra.

The Savages, we knew, were afraid of magic, not being safe-guarded by the Virgin: therefore they do not hold the Wall, and neither do they ever walk on it. They would not be watching us. There was, besides, nothing for them to watch except a dying forest. So we could in safety, turn our backs on the Wall, and see the dun swathe of death spread east of us and west, for miles. Beyond the river we could see the Household clearing the pad-dock around Eudav's Hall, and building the huts in which we would sleep for several nights. Axes rang on timber and ham-mers on post and rail, as the horse lines were laid out. The law of Rome had returned to the land below the Wall.

Soon this land would be settled and Roman again. But before that we would ourselves carry the Law of Rome, the eternal Just-ice and the Divine Vengeance, beyond the Wall. Not only the Law of Rome: the Roman pipes sounded to us from the pad-docks, chanters and drones made by skill and art no Savage can comprehend. And more than Roman music we would take: to the sound of the Pipes, Gelorwid sang the Virgin's Hymn.

8

Yr eur a meirch mawr as med medweint
Namen ene delei o vyt hoffeint
Kyndilic aeron wyr enouant

Notwithstanding Gold, and fine steeds, and intoxicating mead,
Only one man of these, who loved the world, returned,
Cynddelig of Aeron, a Novantian hero.

There was no hiding that the might of Rome had ridden again out of the North to Eudav's Hall. Through the three days that followed we raised a new Hall within sight of the old. Stables, cowsheds, houses were built, and for the Hall itself, oak trunks were sunk into the ground for pillars, and stout beams laid across them for roof-trees. At the last we bound reeds for thatch to the rafters. Three hundred men worked in joy to raise a house for Bradwen. For Bradwen and for Owain.

On the fourth day, Owain called us together, the noblest that is, Precent and Cynrig of Aeron and Peredur Ironarms and myself, and young Aidan out of courtesy.

'I know that the Infantry will have reached the heights above the river at the eastward end of the Wall,' he told us. 'Tomorrow we will ride out and down the river to meet them. We will clear the way for Bradwen and then bring her back in triumph to her house.'

There was sense in this. In a day's ride we could sweep the valley from Eudav's Hall to the sea. There were no Savages for a day's ride to the West, our Patrols had been able to tell us that, and they had not come against us from beyond the Wall, as they would surely have done if they had been watching. It would be safe to leave the new Hall unguarded. If the Savages were between us and the sea in force, then we would need the whole House-hold. So we would all ride, to meet Bradwen, who had not seen us ride out because we had already seen her ride out before us, with the Infantry and Gwenabwy the son of Gwen to guard her. When we met the Army, a hundred foot would come with Brad-wen to bring her cattle to the Hall and to stay with her till Owain returned. The rest of the Foot, and the sixty horsemen who were with them, would march south with us of the Household, into Bernicia and even into Deira, and reconquer it, terrible as the wrath of God.

We rode early. We turned east, out of the valley and up on to the high and windy moors. We went parallel to the Wall over the new-blooming heather. After the first hour we crossed the road that the Romans had built to carry up their tribute to the Kings of Caledon. Every year, in those days, the King of the Romans sent the King of Caledon his own weight and the weight of his Queen, and the weight of his Judge and the weight of his Bard, in fine gold. I had seen once a piece of this gold, and it was clear that it had come from the King of Rome, because he had put his own face on it, and letters which were his name. That was for fear that the Caledonians would some day ride out of their wood and come down again into the Empire, as they had done so often before, and burn Rome about the Emperor's head. It was the wood of Caledon that the Savages had now begun to kill.

Through the morning we veered away from the Wall, passing here and there the farms left empty, the houses falling into ruin. We followed the line of a little river that ran east and came down from the moors by a valley so well known to us in stories that it had no name of its own, but was simply referred to as the Dingle. But, name or no name, it was up the Dingle that the army would come to meet us.

Now we looked out from the edge of the high moorlands across the land of Mordei, from where the people had long fled. On either side of the stream we saw again the signs of the Savages. The woods were dead, every tree ringed with the cruel saxes, dead and withered away. The deer had gone out of these woods on to the high moors. The land was dead. The land had been killed.

We sat by the stream in the appointed place, two or three

hours before sunset. I was with the vanguard, and as soon as I had snatched a few mouthfuls of bread and mead and hot bacon I rode forward to take some to Gwion Catseyes, who was our most forward picket. He was sitting on the ground at the edge of the wood, looking across the narrow meadow to the river and across it and another meadow to the woods, the dead woods, beyond that. He was hidden behind a dead alder clump, covered with blackberry thorns. We hobbled our horses and left them a few paces behind us, and we sat and ate and chatted.

Then of a sudden we heard horses. We had never heard of a Savage who rode a horse; nevertheless, we slipped back among the dead trees and mounted again. We peered through the brittle leafless twigs of the alder and poised our spears to throw.

There were two horsemen, riding one behind the other, not quite a spear's cast apart. That we could tell by listening. It was how we had been drilled. Good, I thought, these are the advance scouts of Cynddelig's force. Somewhere behind them there will be the first knot of the horse, spread out well, and then a regiment on foot. After that there will be the sheep to feed us all the way into Bernicia. With them will be the cattle that Bradwen is bringing to stock her new Hall. She has black cows to give milk, so that when we return we will be met with new-made butter, and cheese: and she has a bull to service them. She will have spare horses for her shepherds, and hunting dogs and watch dogs, and pigs to find their own beech mast and acorns in her woods. She'll live well enough through the coming winter, with a hundred men, and more when we come back, to live in the Hall and work for her, and to break new farms all through the debatable land. Next summer, the land will be full of Romans again, men who fled to the kind and wealthy North when the Savages burst in on them in years before. Next spring, their wives will come too: but for the present, Bradwen will be the only woman in Mordei.

The host would be moving, a great horde of men and beasts that would trample the grass and eat it wherever they went, leaving a trail a mile wide. And mingled with it, company by company, the men of Eiddin and the men of Mordei would march, and the last horsemen would ride the flanks or close up the rear. Here we would be ready to meet them. Here we would take the lead, a great army of horse and foot, to regain Bernicia.

Thirty years the Savages had been in Bernicia, living and breeding. Time and again they had swept into Mordei, turning it into a debatable land, but never in such strength as in the spring of last year. Now we could hold Mordei, and sweep into Bernicia, so that at worst this year that would be debatable land. Next year, who knew, we might hunt and fish and shear our sheep as far as York, into Deira itself, as far down as the borders of Elmet, where we could talk with Christian men again.

These, I thought, will be the forward scouts. If the wind had been easterly, I would have been able to hear already the noise of all the host. There would have been the noise of the cattle, and the sheep would have baa'd my eardrums in. I listened as hard as I could, in the silence of that hot summer afternoon, and I could have sworn, from one moment to another, that I could hear them coming.

The leading horseman was almost level with us. His comrade had halted, far back, too far back for what we had been taught. I had mounted, and now I rode out of the woods to him. Gwion remained hidden, his spear couched ready to throw. But there would have been no need for that. I was near enough.

This leading horseman turned to us. For the first time I saw his face, when he lifted his head, and I knew him. Gwenabwy son of Gwen it was, to whom Mynydog had given command of the men who were to stay with Bradwen throughout the winter. He was scarlet cloaked, and his shield was white, with no badge or sign, since he said that a man who had lost his land to the Savages had no right to an identity till he regained it. Gwen's land it was we were on now, between Eudav's and the sea.

He rode wearily, on a tired horse. He looked like a charcoal-burner, like Morien when I first met him, because he was covered, cloak and face, horse and all, in black soot. He barely looked at me as I came down to him, only to see that I wore red and was a friend. He did not even raise his shield from crupper to shoulder, or shift his grip on his spear, or kick his scabbard free to draw his sword.

'Well met, Gwenabwy!' I shouted to him. 'How far behind are the others?'

'In the name of the Virgin, Aneirin,' he answered me, 'have you anything for us to eat?'

I laughed at him.

'Why, Gwenabwy, have you eaten all the sheep? I hope that there are no more of you as hungry as this, because we cannot feed three thousand out of what we are carrying in our saddle-bags, whatever the saints did.'

'I am not jesting, Aneirin. Have you any food? There are no more of us.'

'No more? Why? Have you been defeated? When was the battle?'

'There was no battle.' Gwenabwy waved back to the other rider, still sitting hunched in the saddle by a dead thorn tree. The horse stumbled forward a few steps, the way a steed does when it is dead tired and well blown: then it stopped again.

'Who is it, Gwenabwy? Who is with you?' He did not answer. I put oatcake and cold bacon into his hands, and left him with Gwion. I rode down the meadow along the bank of the little stream. The other horse had made a few more steps, and then stopped; the rider still sat, his head bowed, his body still shrunken into his scarlet cloak. This is the way men sit after they have had three days in the saddle, herding the sheep away from the edge of a racing heather fire. As long as you are riding, you feel nothing, and you always look fresh, however grimed with smoke and dust. But this is the way you slouch down when the sun sets on the last day and the sheep are safe: or burnt.

I went down to this rider, weary long before sunset, on this shaggy horse, its coat caked with the mud of a dozen river crossings, and covered with black ash over that. It stood now on the edge of the stream, too tired even to bend and crop the thick grass under its nose, or even to drink. I rode close to see who this was, mail showing below the red cloak, and an unfamiliar helmet, pointed and hung with purple ribbons, and with a hanging curtain of mail protecting the face at both sides and the neck behind. I could not see the face, because of this mail, till I rode close. Then I saw. It was Bradwen.

637

9

O gyurang gwyth ac asgen
Trenghis ni diengis bratwen

In the engagement of wrath and carnage,
Bradwen perished, she did not escape.

We sat by the fire and passed round the mead jar. In the beginning of dusk, we heard the story. Bradwen told it.

'All went well for the first days. We moved along the coast, a few miles only between each dawn and sunset. Each night we halted by a farm, and the people made us welcome. They always took me in to sleep under a roof. When we passed farms during the day, everyone came out to watch the Army go by. When the horsemen came, they would throw flowers in our path and cheer and sing.

'Three thousand men and a thousand animals do not pass like a cat. We ate the grass from the pastures, and broke the paddock fences. We muddied the farmers' streams, and emptied their wells and left unbearable heaps to windward of their houses. We stole their hens, and enticed their daughters. Their sons came running out to join us. One Army is like another. It could not have been worse for the people south of Eiddin if we had been a horde of Savages. They endured all the unpleasantness of war without the bloodshed. And they had paid for all this. And for nothing.

'Each night, the soldiers sang around the fires they made from broken fences and the planks from barns and the very doors of the houses. The farm people did not miss their doors because they had come out to sing with us. They forgave us the havoc we caused because we were going to the South to fill up the empty land of Mordei. First we would defeat the Savages that threatened them. Then we would live there as a barrier to keep them safe for ever.

'But, at last, we crossed the river. We went out of Eiddin into Mordei. The debatable land was empty. Now we stopped where farms had been. They had been deserted. Not burnt, just left. The doors were closed, the barns cleared, the cattle driven away. They were left by people who had had plenty of warning, and who thought they would soon be back. They were the men who marched with us, the regiments of the Mordei, who had gone to fill empty farms in the North. They had left their houses here in order, the buckets at the wellheads, the pitchforks in the racks by the mangers.

'But in a year, a thatched roof grows weeds, and in two or three winters, unrepaired, the thatch falls in and the rafters rot, and the unprotected walls crumble. The buckets were green with mildew and red with the spotted rot. The tines of the forks had rusted string-thin. Thistles and groundsel, dandelions and couch grass choked the gardens, starving out the lettuce and the carrots, the turnips and the leeks, that, self-grown, might yet have lived a few more years. Yet still, we found apples reddening on the unpruned branches: still, the rowanberries ripened at the forsaken doors.

'A day or two farther south, we came on houses that were left in haste. They had been burnt, and fallen in heaps of rubble. You only knew where they were if someone, riding over a mound by chance, felt the difference in the tread of his mount. The Savages had not only burnt the houses and the barns. They had filled in the wells, too, and they had uprooted the orchards. They had even cut down the friendly rowans before the doors. It was now that the infantry began to turn back.'

'The men of Eiddin cannot be trusted,' said Owain, firmly. He looked around him, then, and hastily qualified, 'The peasants, that is, for the nobles are as warlike and as honourable as any, as they will soon have a chance to show. But these cravens saw what the Savages had done, and it was enough to make them run away, and leave the men of Mordei to win back their own land.'

'No,' said Bradwen, a Mordei woman. 'It was the Mordei men

who returned first. They had lived too long in the clement and peaceful North, where the farms are fertile and the winters mild and the land long clear. There they had pastures for the taking, and space to hunt, and they themselves lived in the houses their fathers had built. Their wives and their children were safe in the North. When they came back into Mordei, they saw what they would have to do if they wished to take their old lands once again. They saw all the work they would have to do, sweating over the sickle and the axe, trenching and clearing, building the paddock walls afresh, and raising new roof-trees. And that work, the work of years, never free from fear. All those years of working armed, their swords always at their sides, the spears hanging in their straps on cart or plough, or leaning against the stable door or in the chimney corner. They would never have a night free from fear, never a night without a watchman waking over them, and themselves never able to sleep for fear the watchman dozed. This was not what they had marched for. They went back. There comes a time, Owain, when lost land is not worth the effort of regaining it, unless it is regained for a certainty. Certainty we could not give them.'

It was half a lifetime ago she said that. Now we have certainty. The Savages are put down all over the land of Britain. Mordei was the last land to be reconquered. Arthur with the Army of the South pinned the hateful ones there between themselves and the Armies of the North, Picts and Strathclyde men, in the wood of Caledon. Now he has resettled all Mordei, and given it to Mordred to rule. There will be peace in Britain for ever.

'They went back,' Bradwen said. She was not bitter, not rancorous, she did not raise her voice or let any emotion cloud it. She did not judge them, she merely said what they had done, and that was judgement enough. 'They did not go back singly. That would have been easier to accept, the flight of single men, frightened, weak, not daring to tell their comrades who will wake with the sun to find the familiar mounds of blankets gone from their sides, slipped away from the dying fire Just before the morning. They look back from the edge of the woods just when the birds begin to sing. They half regret what they have done, and think there is still time to go back, to tell how they were taken short and went into the bushes, or to find some other tale, and they wonder what tale of the many will sound the best. But they never do go back. And they go home alone. A wise Commander does not count his troops at night.

'But this was worse. The sun would rise, and whole companies would go. They would awake, and without a word would form up as if to advance, and, instead, would march the other way, into the North. Other companies, regiments, turned back at the noon halts, or even in the middle of the morning. Always they took the beasts they had driven so far. What they told the farmers they repassed I cannot think. What they told Mynydog I do not care.

'Then we came into the region of the dead forests. Now the men of Eiddin began to turn back. The men of Mordei had come to reconquer Mordei, and when they saw Mordei, and it was not what they remembered, they left reconquest to others. But the men of Eiddin expected to see a conquered land. They did not come to win it back for themselves, and they did not care if anyone lived there or not. They had come to clear the Savages from what should be now dead ground, a belt of space for armour. They had come to fight, and to destroy the Savages before they came further.

'Iron the men of Eiddin were willing to face, and the strength of humans, the shock of shields and the agony of battle, where some are brave and some flee and every man is different, and each man, in the end, fights alone and dies alone. But then they saw the dead forest. All across our front, from the hills to the sea, stretched the line of withered trees. A man may fell an apple-tree in spite, or even, demented by fury, hack at a rowan. It takes more than fury, it takes time and patience to ring a tree, and strip the bark away as high as a man can reach. And this was not one tree, but a thousand thousand trees. It was blind malice that stopped the Mordei men. It was the care and patience of all that witless horde, working for weeks on end, all across Mordei, like the spread of a blight. They had quietly, thoroughly killed the kind forest, that shelters our beasts, that gives us nuts and berries and hides the deer we eat. They killed the trees that should have given us fuel and house timbers for a hundred years. All this they destroyed in malice. And the Eiddin men turned back, all in one night.

'The sight of the wasted farms turned back the men of Mordei. The sight of the dead forest turned back the men of Eiddin. But it was the burnt forest that was the end of Cynddelig and his sixty horsemen. They endured till then.

'After the trees die, and the leaves wither, when the trunks are dried through and through, the Savages set light to the forest. We came out of the dead forest into the burnt land. The charred stumps still stood, sometimes knee high. The ground was covered deep in wood ash. It had been grey after the; now it was blackened with rain. It was too deep, the ash, for even the coarsest grass to sprout. Now the wood is cleared, the Savages will come, next year, to heave out the stumps and plough the ground to plant their filthy wheat.' She looked around her. 'These brambles have not long to live.

'There were no brambles in the burnt forest, no food for man nor horse. Neither grass nor berries nor mushrooms, neither deer nor squirrels. That was why Cynddelig turned back. He said to me, "Mynydog gave me these warriors and all their armour, costly beyond belief. If we go farther and the horses founder, then it will all be lost. I will take the squadron back." Three days ago, he went. We have had little food from then till now.'

'But you did not go back?' My voice showed it was the reason, not the fact, that I questioned.

'I had said that I would meet Owain at this place, and ride with him to my father's Hall, the Hall that was my father's, and is mine, and will be his.'

'And you, Gwenabwy? Why did you not turn back?'

'I don't know, boy. I just came on, like I said I would, to the old Hall.' A heavy slow man, Gwenabwy, not a fast thinker, but one it was always good to have at your back. I turned again to Bradwen.

'Where did you get this mail?'

I ran my hand over the shirt, lying over the log on which we sat. Most men wear mail made of rings that might slip on to a girl's little finger. The mail I wore was counted fine: the rings would have been tight on the fingers of a month-old baby. The rings of Bradwen's mail would have slipped on to the leg of a thrush, and been a snug fit there. Such mail, they say, all the front rank of Arthur's Household wear now, but it was rare in those days. It was foreign work, made by Goths or Persians far in Africa. The leather beneath the mail was boiled hard and ridged and crested like a stickle-back. A point would not pierce the iron: a blow would be broken by the leather.

'This,' she told us, proudly, 'was a shirt that King Majorian of Rome sent as a gift to my father Eudav, one that he stripped from the body of Attil, King of the Scyths, after he killed him with his own hand. Eudav thought it was too new-fashioned for him to wear, and sent it to Mynydog to hang in his Hall as a trophy, till someone worthy of it should come to claim it. But I thought to bring it back so that someone could wear it to defend my Hall.'

Some of the Household made a hut for Bradwen out of dead boughs and withered leaves. We others slept in our cloaks on the bare ground. We took turns about to watch the horses. I drew the turn before dawn. Down on the river meadow, where we had lit our fire, far from the dead trees, I saw Owain still sitting on the log, thinking what next to do.

10

Oed dor diachor diachor din drei
Oed mynut wrth olut ae kyrchei
Oed dinas e vedin ae cretei

The entrance to Din Drei was not guarded,
There was a mountain with riches for those who should approach it,
And there was a city for the army that should venture to enter.

The next day, Owain led us west again, up the valley the way we had come, and then on to the High Moors, towards Eudav's Hall, that I supposed we must now call Bradwen's Hall, or perhaps even Owain's Hall. I rode, for preference, with Precent, in the van.

'Go back, then, we must,' Precent grumbled to me. 'There is no going on this campaign without the foot. Sorry it is I am to be going home without blooding my spear, but there it is. We will have to do it next year. You did well enough, Aneirin, you did more damage to the Savages than all the rest of us put together. Next time, we shall have a champion in you.'

'We shall see,' I told him. We jogged along. We might easily have made Eudav's Hall before the evening, but a little after noon, the flank guard on the right sighted a whole herd of deer, and a squadron went off on to the hunt. They cast round upwind of them, and drove the whole herd down on to our spears. We singled out twenty-six fat bucks, and that was enough for the Household: the rest we let run against next time some Roman felt hungry. It is only a Savage who kills except to eat at once.

This took up time, and by sunset we were nowhere near the Hall. We halted for the night on the old Roman road, looking across to the way through the Wall. We ate well of roasted venison, even though it had not been hung, and there was enough

644

for us all. What with the thrill of the hunt and the smell of the meat cooking, there was a holiday air about the whole Household, more now than ever before. They sat in circles around the fires, and as always, when they were gravy up to the eyebrows, they passed around the mead jars and sang the old songs, one circle singing against another. We the leaders sat around Owain, to hear him, and not, at that, to hear him sing. But he only wanted to hear us. At last Peredur Ironarms asked him, straight out, 'Only one question now, Owain. Do Bradwen stay here on her farm, or do she go back to Eiddin now?'

'I will not go back.' She was firm. We ignored her.

'Someone will have to stay here with her if the men of Mordei do not come. I'll call for volunteers among the squadrons. Hard it will be to find them, I'm sure.' Precent laughed broadly. But Owain said thoughtfully, 'Hard it will be to find men who will give up the glory.'

'What glory is there in riding back tamely to Eiddin with nothing done?' asked Gwion. 'Braver surely it is to stay here on the very edge of the Savages' land, and I am thinking there is not a man who will not stay.'

'Aye,' countered Owain. 'What glory indeed?'

'What will you do, then?' we all asked him together.

'I swore an oath to King Mynydog, that I would go into Bernicia and fight against the Savages. I have not yet entered Bernicia, and I have not fought.'

'But not this year,' insisted Precent. 'Next year, perhaps.'

'Why not this year?'

'There are no infantry. It would be pointless to fight against the Savages with no foot.'

'I have fought the Irish with no foot to back me. And we won.'

'You will not chase these like Irish pirates,' I warned him.

'They will stand to fight, whether we ride or march against them. I have seen them, and I have heard them.'

'Oh, you have only seen a few of them,' Owain pushed me aside. 'Perhaps you heard them, but they were boasting to terrify you. I saw the ones you killed a few days ago, and I saw that there will be no trouble. You settled four yourself, before anyone came to help you.'

'Did I? I only remember twisting and turning where I could and striking out whether I could see anything to hit or not. And in the end, it took a score of us, in armour, to settle a score of them, naked. And Cynon is dead now, most likely.'

'We bought twenty dead, cheap enough, at that price.'

'They were charcoal-burners, not soldiers.'

'All these Savages are warriors, they are brought up to nothing else. Among us, our mothers pray that we will grow up to be poets and the pride of our families and our Kingdoms. Savage mothers only pray their sons will be good fighters. And they live on a handful of wheat a day. So underfed, it is no wonder that though they are all ready to fight, any of us is as good as a dozen of them, and that on foot. Mounted, this Household can destroy any army they can bring.'

'So it is your opinion,' Precent asked him, 'that we ought to go on against the Savages?'

'I have no opinions. I only say what I know.'

'And what do you know?'

'I know that I swore an oath to King Mynydog, that I would go into Bernicia and fight with the Savages.' He did not say 'and you swore too'. He only went on, 'Nothing was said about the infantry. Much was said about the King of Elmet. Shall we leave him to fight alone?'

There was silence for a little while. Then Gwion, from his corner, said, 'So we ride on.'

'Aye,' said Precent. 'So we ride on.'

'So we ride on,' Owain confirmed. 'Tomorrow we will go down the old road through the Wall, and burn their havods on the moors above the valleys. Then we will sweep down into the valleys, and burn their farms before they can call their men together. We shall leave the country a desert and ride through them to Elmet.'

'They do not build havods,' I told them. 'Their young men and women do not go up to the hills in summer to tend the sheep. And they do not live in single farms. They cluster their houses together, and live in crowds of a hundred people and more in one place.' I was unwise enough to add, 'I have seen them.'

'Perhaps they did so live, *where* you saw them,' Owain

answered me, whom he had brought because I had knowledge beyond his own. 'But you were only in one place, in a Dun. No man could bear to live as near as that to his neighbours, except in the Dun of a King who can force them not to quarrel with him. If farms are close together, then their owners are enemies: it is a law of nature, we know it well enough. We will burn their farms in the valleys and be in York before they know we are on them.'

'So we ride on,' said Cynrig.

'I will tell them.' Owain, Bradwen with him, walked across to the nearest fire. We sat silent, listening to the shout from the men there, and the bursts of laughter after it. Owain went on to the next fire.

'And if Owain would not ride on,' I asked those left with me. 'Would any of us go alone?'

'I would go, if I went alone,' said Cynrig. 'Because Cynddelig turned back.'

'I came for a fight,' Peredur Ironarms laughed about it. 'I will go on till I have one, and then I can tell Evrog the Wealthy about it, and keep the arms he gave me.'

'Turn back?' This was Gwenabwy. 'Never thought of it till now, boy.'

I looked at Precent. He answered, 'So we ride on. Now we are all dead men. But it is what we came for.'

'I sang of war enough,' I told them, 'and mourned over my betters who fell. Now I will feel death for myself, and let who will sing my elegy.'

Owain returned. All the fires were blazing up high as the songs and laughter that mocked the summer stars. Syvno looked up, and read the planets for us. Victory he prophesied from them, and booty, and no loss. Owain listened, and then said, 'True it is, good things lie ahead: the best of our lives is to come. And because of that, not all should sing. Some there are that will have to stay behind, to guard Bradwen.'

'Guard me?' she asked.

'We cannot leave you alone on your farm. Either you must go back to Eiddin, or someone must stay with you till we ride back to your own Hall. We will raise such a swarm of wild bees about

647

us that they may try to sting us back over the border. We spent a lot of sweat in building you a new house; if burnt it must be, it would be a pity if you were inside it. Either go back to Eiddin, and that would mean only half a dozen men to ride with you, or stay in your Hall and I will leave you a squadron.'

'If you are going to ride into Bernicia, then you will need every man you can take.'

'Go back to Eiddin, then it will weaken us the less.'

'It is strengthening you need.'

'We cannot wait for strengthening. No more will come.'

'One rider more would be welcome.'

'There are no more riders. We are all the Household that will ride. We have no friends till we reach Elmet.'

'I have my father's helmet and mail. I have a sword, too.'

'A woman cannot fight.' The argument was between Owain and Bradwen, between them alone, but we listened.

'I can ride as well as any man, and as long in the day. Ask Aneirin, or Precent. Riding is the most part of soldiering – I know, I have watched you. And I have killed deer – is it harder to kill a man?'

'A deer cannot hurt you.'

'A wild boar will. I have killed them, too. My father had no son. But I gave him all a son could, in love and loyalty. Now let me give him trophies. Will you deny the right of the heir to avenge the father?'

'Whoever heard before of a woman riding to war?'

'And why else do you think I came? Why else do you imagine I brought this armour, hiding it, and a sword wrapped in my cloak? Think, as I do, of all the women that have died in war. Let me have some satisfaction for all the women the Savages have killed, some recompense for all the ruined farms we passed, a red reward for rowans all cut down.'

'Eudav is dead, now, Bradwen. It is my duty to protect you from folly, even your own.'

'Where better for me to be protected than riding at your side?'

Owain looked at us, sitting around them. We looked back, Cynrig and Precent and I, bleakly. This dispute was not ours.

648

The outcome did not matter. We knew that who came, who rode, would not return, and that was our fate, settled by the Virgin. Only Gwenabwy said, 'It is an omen, better than Syvno's stars. We rode out on the day of the Virgin. Let a virgin ride with us that fight for the Virgin.'

'Ride with us, then,' said Owain at last. 'Carry my banner instead of Cynrig, so that in battle the host will rally round you and keep you safe. Ride with us, Bradwen, the Wise Woman, sign sent from God.'

So it was for pride, and the love of Owain, that we rode at last to Cattraeth.

11

Bu trydar en aerure bu tan
Bu ehut e waewawr bu huan
Bu bwyt brein bu bud e vran

There was a noise in the mount of slaughter, there was fire,
Impetuous were the lances, there was a gleam like the sun,
There was food for the ravens, there the ravens did triumph.

At dawn we rode forward, towards the Wall. Where the road passed through the Wall there had once been a City, a place of great houses and castles and palaces, raised in the twinkling of an eye out of the ground by the Magician Vergil, when the King's Mistress saw here, on the Wall that she had demanded, no place of pleasure for her to spend one night. And she had slept there one night, and one night only, in a city peopled only for that one night: and when she had awakened in the morning, and passed on, all the people that had come to the City rode away likewise. And so the whole place fell into ruin.

What this town had been called by the woman who had asked for it, no one knew. We called it Din Drei. All the gold had been stripped from the roofs, stolen by the soldiers of false King Arcady. Only the walls of the houses were left. The plaster had fallen in heaps, and the grass grew in the earth of the floors. Some say that if you will scrape away the beaten earth of the floors of the Roman houses, you will find there buried beneath them flat pictures of their gods in coloured stone. It is an act of virtue before the Virgin to find them and destroy, but here we had no time. Only we found in many places stone figures of those devils, weather-beaten and green with moss. Where we could without too much trouble, we broke off their hands and their noses, to the glory of the Virgin and her Son and the Dove.

Nothing moved now in Din Drei, Only rats lived there, and foxes, and wild birds. It was twenty years since any civilised men had passed through the Wall here at the Eastern end, though until the Savages burnt Carlisle there had been occasional traffic at the West. We rode through the dead city, the first Roman Army for many years, and out into Bernicia.

I rode with Precent now, always at his stirrup behind the line of scouts, who spread out on either side of the road. So, we agreed, he and I should ride every day, whichever squadron were the skirmishers. Behind us, close in front of the first squadron of the line, Owain would ride. Bradwen was always with him, the raven banner sewn to a light spear, not the stout staff. Behind were the other squadrons, in line ahead, Cynrig now leading Cynon's squadron. Gwion Catseyes always rode behind the last squadron.

Beyond the town, we followed the Roman road at first, though after a day or two we left it and kept across the open moorland. The road was overgrown now with grass, but it still felt and sounded different under the horses' hooves. If you got down here, and scraped with a knife, you would find the big stones of the old road-surface. We left this paved way to head West of South, while it went East of South into the valleys.

The skies were grey and clouded early in the day. By noon, however, when the Wall was far behind, there was only blue above, and the sun in our eyes. We all rode armed, now, of; we were ready to fight. Our flank scouts were half a mile to either side of the road we followed, looking for prey, like the booths of shepherds. As I had told Owain, they did not find any. Savages do not keep many sheep, and only for the wool: instead of lads, they have grown men, who follow the flock on foot and keep them in sight of the farm all day. But what was strange was that we caught none of the usual bands of straggling Savages, bound one way or another across the hills to beg and scavenge on the West coast. At this time of the year, we ought to have caught scores of them going back for the wheat harvest. But there were none, as if, for some reason, they had all rushed home already.

All that first day we rode quietly, not singing, and we found nothing and saw no one. There was not a living soul up there on the high moors to give warning of our coming. North of the Wall, in good sheep country like that, we could have seen the flocks everywhere, and twenty times in a day we would have had the youngsters come out of their booths to welcome us, to talk to us and ask who we were, and who we were related to, and if we had any news of their families. But Savages do not send their children to be fostered by friends and relations far away, as all civilised men do, even Irish, but they allow sons to grow up alongside their fathers, knowing them well, and having no one tied to them by blood and fosterhood in strange places. The Savages do not love the high moors as we do. They leave them desert.

That night we slept in our cloaks on the ground, as we had done since we left Eiddin. But from that night on, we took turns in hanging our cloaks on a frame of spears to make a tent for Bradwen. My cloak was always among them.

There were more days that we rode south. Still the sky was grey at dawn, and cleared later and later every day. The Household could not sing when there was no sun. The emptiness of the moors that should have been full of life weighed on us. Only here and there a rowan showed where once there had been a house.

'Have they fled before us already?' Owain asked. 'How did they know we were coming?'

'This is how they live,' I told him. 'They leave the hills empty, and they farm the valleys.'

'Perhaps they did where you were, because they were hiding in the valleys for fear of us. But people do not live in valleys when they have moorlands to grow their sheep on. There is nothing for sheep to graze in the marshy valleys.'

'These are not people,' I told him. 'These are Savages. You must not expect them to behave in a human manner.'

But Owain did not answer.

Then, an hour before a dusk of an empty day, Precent and I sat our horses with the left flankers in a clump of bushes and looked down at last into a valley. The sun was behind us: nobody could look into it to see us. Precent waved, and Owain cantered over to us to look.

'Look down there,' I said. 'That is how they live. You see? The oblong wooden houses, all in a square, round an open space with a pond in it. Then there are the fields, long and narrow, stretching round the houses. Not all of them are cultivated. I wonder why? That is wheat growing there. It is ripe, and they are harvesting. See where they have cut that field, and stacked the sheaves? They are loading the oxcarts to bring the sheaves back to the threshing-floor. The Savages are going home from the fields now. Can't you smell the cooking-fires? The smoke hangs in a sheet above the yellow roofs—'

'I can see what I can see.' Owain was curt. But Precent marvelled. 'What a way to live, all crushed on top of each other, hugger-mugger. Nothing but noise and people all the time.'

Owain had waved his arm, and the squadrons had spread out on either side of us. Half a dozen men fell back from each to hold the spare horses. Precent gestured the flankers to spread out farther, much farther, to sweep round the village on either side. We still sat, watching the people down there walking home from work, singing, probably, though we could not hear them. It was all very still and peaceful. I thought of Eudav's Hall before the Savages came, and I looked at Bradwen, holding the standard behind Owain, and Gwenabwy of the white shield behind her. No one there had yet seen us, and thought that we could be here. Owain drew his sword.

'For One and the Virgin!' he shouted. 'Free the Isle of Britain!'

Shouting and screaming, the Household charge forward, down the slope that formed the edge of the moor into the valley. We enveloped the village and its people, lapping them in on every side, as they stopped where they were and turned to stare at us a moment, before they realised what it was, and began to run here and there, each away from what he had been facing, like ants, aimlessly. They had never seen anything like this, a Roman Army all cloaked and plumed in red and sweeping against them out of the empty hills. They ran, they all ran, not away from us, or even at us, but just in whatever direction they were facing when they started to run, till some random thing turned them to run another way, because there was no direction from which we were not coming at them, all furious with the vengeance of Rome. As our beaters had herded in the deer a few days before, so our flankers now herded them in for the killing. Among the deer, we had killed only the beasts we needed, and left the rest to breed. Not so here. We cut them down in the killing place.

Sometimes there were men and boys who turned and tried to fight with their sickles and ox-goads. More often they ran, and in either case they died when we came on them. We left them lying, only bending to take back our spears or drag aside bodies which lay where they might frighten the horses. I saw where three or four of them stood on an ox-wagon with axes and hedging-knives, ready to defend themselves and do us what harm they could. I rode at them, finding Aidan with me, and we threw our spears from a distance and saw one fall into his fellows, upsetting them. And, not stopping, we were on them before they could push his body aside, being more concerned with his hurt than with defending themselves, and slashing at them with our long swords, we soon had them tumble into the oxen's heels. We cut through the straps of the harness, and drove the oxen before us, leaving the men writhing on the sheaves till Morien came riding up swinging a flaming torch to set fire to the dried corn.

We herded the oxen into a corner, and killed them, all of them. We brought all the wagons that were not already burning, and the ploughs, and all their weapons and tools into the centre of the village, and we had a good fire to roast our meat. We could find no oat flour, but some of our lads turned out wheat flour and tried to make cakes of that, backing them on the hot plough-shares. Few of us could stomach the stuff. We found jars of the yeast they use to turn the wheat into bread, and we threw that into the fire. We found some mead in the houses, and a great deal of beer, a drink that many of the Household had not seen before, and they were astonished at its strength. All in all, we had the means to celebrate our first victory. We fed our horses on the standing corn.

We had killed all the men we found in the village, and anyone else who seemed too eager to run or fight. The rest of the women we penned in a corner with some hurdles, and let them watch us eat. Tow-haired sluts they were, greasy and ill-dressed, weeping and wailing. But after we had eaten, and drunk all the beer, there were a few of the House-hold who found lust overcame sensibil-

654

ity, and all night long there were screams and laughter to disturb those of us who slept in the biggest house.

This house was divided into two rooms, and we made Bradwen a bed in the inner room, and Gwenabwy slept across the door. We leaders who were too proud to pollute ourselves in the pen sat by the fire, and passed around the mead-jar and planned the next day.

'Let us reach the old road again,' urged Precent. 'Four days riding down there, easy going, and we will reach Elmet, and there we will find whole battalions of foot to support us on the way back. And on the way, one way or the other, we can clear the filth out of York.'

Owain ignored him. Instead he asked us all, 'Do you remember the songs they used to sing of this valley?'

'Gloomy and wet it was in winter, so they say,' answered Cynrig. 'But in summer, pleasant and beautiful to hunt in.'

'Ah, the summer game that was here.' Gwion had heard this. 'Elk lived here, the size of two horses, with horns that would have served as oars for a ten-man boat. Elks like that would feed a whole village. And stags of twenty points. Red deer and roe deer you could find too—'

'And wild boar as well.' That was Gwenabwy. 'The taste of a wild sucking-pig! And where there was all that game, there would be wolf too, and bear, all the fur you could want.'

'Birds of all kinds, too, winter and summer. You would never fly your hawk for nothing, in a place like this. And in the winter, with the streams in a sullen flood, and the whole valley a marsh – pike in the deep pools, roach and gudgeon ....' Even Precent was drawn in, against his will.

'Now, look what they have done to it. It is enough to make a man weep.' Owain could sound as bitter as you liked, when he wanted to, and it was not all pretence. 'All our lovely marshes they have drained away, to leave the ground as dry as the top of a table. And cut down are all our trees, and the groves where we used to wander. And what do they do, when they have killed the trees, and burned them, as we have seen them do this year in Mordei? They pull out the stumps and they plough the ground level, to turn the fruitful forest into barren wheatfields. And that is how they can live, on a handful of wheat a day, a swarm of brown ants, witless, blind, toiling away with no art, no poetry. It is a sin against the Virgin and against God, to multiply cattle, or people, or crops, without heed. For the earth is the Lord's, and he gave it to us to keep, and not to destroy. It is only Christians who protect even the wolf.

'And how else do they live? They do not keep sheep, nor do they spare any space for the gentle cow, that gives milk, and cheese. They only keep as few as they can to raise oxen to drag the plough. And when they have worn out the ox, they kill him for the tallow and the hide only, because they eat no meat, ask Aneirin if it is not true. And that is how they manage to live here, and to grow, so that in two generations they multiply from one boatload to a nation. They will swamp us if we do not stop them. We have to undo all they have done. After that, we must bring the Army of their nation to battle, so that we can destroy them utterly in one place. And, in a few years, we and our sons will hunt in this valley again.'

For four days, then, we raged in the valleys, the one that runs East to the sea, and the one that goes South to York. We treated every village as we treated the first one. When we left that first village, we burnt every house. We had thrown the ploughshares and every weapon and tool that we found into the fire where we cooked our meat, and that not only destroyed the costly work of the wheelwright – ask Mynydog's men how difficult is the wheelwright's task – but it also spoiled the temper of the iron. What metal we could pick out of the ashes, the next morning, we dropped into the well, and threw in as many bodies as we could find, to pollute it. Others we flung into the pond where they watered the cattle. We burnt the corn in the barns, and smashed the querns with hammers – their hammers.

Most of this was Morien's work. After he had set the houses on fire, he made a bundle of clothes he had found in a house, and smeared them in tallow, and tied them behind his horse with a long, long rope. Then we lit the cloths, and he galloped, the flaming torch behind him, through the corn fields, and set the the evil wheat alight where it grew.

We kept the spades that were in the houses, though, and we blocked up all the ditches along the edges of the fields, and broke in all the banks. We made the women work at this before we killed them in case they should breed, and for the sake of all the women the Savages had killed in the Mordei and Bernicia, in our time and in our fathers', and who had had no sons.

When Morien had shown how best to do all this, and he had given lonely thought to this in the woods by his kilns, we spread out by squadrons and did the same all across the land, till I grew tired of the sight of smoke and the taste of half-cooked beef and of wheat cakes, and the sight of the square houses in their long fields. In four days, a hundred villages burnt, and in none of them did we leave more than a few wailing children. The wolf and the bear, the kite and the buzzard came flocking into the houses for easy meat. Why should they not feast, and why should we not feed them? They were *our* wolves, *our* kites.

We left a trail of death and destruction everywhere the Household of Mynydog rode, and there was no one more hard in vengeance, more cruel, more thorough in searching out anything that could be of value to destroy it, than Bradwen. She led us to make a ruin of fruitful fields and happy villages for the sake of the Virgin. In ten years, or five, when the trees and the grass had grown again, and the waters of the winter floods had passed across them, the ugly straight fields would be changed to pleasant marsh, a land that Romans could hunt in and make their home. But first, what we did would be more hideous than anything the wheat-growers had accomplished. Before beauty could return, we had to make devastation.

What people we found we killed, with their livestock, and showed them no mercy. Mostly we found that when they saw the smoke of the next village rise in the still hot air they would flee, hiding in the little woods they had left, seeking refuge in what they had wanted to destroy. They did not resist. There was a thing that puzzled me, though it did not seem of any importance to Owain.

'There are no men,' I told him, 'or very few, and those either very old or very young, like those we left behind when the Army marched out of Eiddin.'

'The men heard us coming and went away without waiting for urging, running faster than the women,' he answered lightly. 'Or else there are few men among the Savages, as we have few whole rams among the flock of sheep, because one male of them can serve a whole flock of females.'

'This not to laugh at,' I insisted. 'No men, and, in the houses I have seen, never a spear, and not one shield or mail coat. And seldom even an axe or a hedging-knife.'

'They are not used to proper arms. They fight naked, like the animals.'

I was stung at last. 'Perhaps that is how the Irish fight, and how you won your famous victories. I tell you, these Savages are as well armed as we are, and fight as well, and that you will find out soon enough. I have been asking the women where the men have gone.'

'You got no answer. These witless brutes have no memory of anything that happened longer ago than yesterday.'

'They said all the men have gone off to a war. Somewhere, Owain, the Savages have gathered a great many. It is true, the women don't know where, North or South, but somewhere there is a horde of Savages on the march. Let us hope that they have gone south against Elmet, because if they have gone into Mordei by the coast road, and missed us, then we will never feast in Eiddin again.'

But Owain only laughed at me, and because he *was* Owain, our leader, I laughed with him, and believed him when he said there was no such army, only a tale the women had made up to hide the cowardice of their men. But they had made up the same tale in every village.

It was the end of the fourth day on which we laid waste the valleys, and we had returned to the place from which we had started. Our squadrons had gone north and east, north to the Border, and east to the sea, almost. Only half a squadron had gone south, probing gently down the road which we would follow, to York and Elmet. The leader of this section was Dyvnwal, whom we called Vrych, the Speckled, because of his freckles, and he had painted his shield white covered with spots of red to match his nickname: and that is all I remember about him, because he was a quiet man. It was on the morning of the fifth day, on which Precent had hoped we would be in Elmet, that we saw this section coming up the Roman Road towards us. Owain rode to meet them, like a King in Venery, with his Judge and his Huntsman and his Standard-bearer, in myself and Precent and Bradwen. When we came near to them, we saw that there were only a dozen red cloaks, instead of forty, and no spare horses, and the chargers they were riding well blown.

They came rushing to us as we rode down to meet them on the empty road, among the empty blackened fields of burnt wheat, all shouting and talking at once.

'A battle,' they shouted. 'We have been in a battle! Against the Savages!'

Owain shouted at them to be quiet. 'Where is Dyvnwal?' he kept on asking. 'Where are the others?'

There was a greater hubbub. Geraint, a man from the South, seemed the most coherent, and I tried to follow his voice against the others.

'We came on a village some time after noon. We rode around it and into it. There was no one there. Not a soul. Not a woman, or a child. Still we did not think it unusual. You never know what customs these Savages have. We dismounted—'

'All of you?' I asked.

'All of us. We went through their houses. They had taken their jewels with them. No silver. We pulled the ploughs together close to the biggest house. We heaped corn on it. And the yeast. We piled the benches over the ploughs. We brought the blankets and clothes out of the houses. We put on the tallow. Then Dyvnwal bent to kindle the fire. There was a shouting in our ears. They were on us.'

'Many of them?'

'They made noise for ten thousand. They were many more than we were. We each had ten to fight. They were in mail. They had those short swords. We had left our shields with our horses. We tried to get back to the horses. We had to cut our way through. I killed two: at least, I struck them and they fell. I think we here are all that reached the horses. If they had stampeded our mounts they would have had us all. We got into line. We charged back into the village. There was nothing we could do for the others. Dead, all of them. A heap of Savages around them. The Savages could not stand up to us mounted. They ran when we returned. We saw that those who had come into the village were the advance guard of an Army. They were in hundreds, thousands. We set the houses alight. We came for you.'

'You returned and left your comrades there?' Owain was sharp, scornful.

'If we had dismounted to recover the bodies, it would have been a glorious deed. Who would have sung us for it? We would have died ourselves. We came back to warn you.'

'I told you the men had gone away to war,' I told Owain. 'It was South they went, and perhaps they have already fought against Elmet. Now they are returning. The road South is blocked. We will not reach Elmet now, or even York.

'The road South may be blocked, but we will still take it.' Owain turned to Precent. 'The squadrons are coming in on us now, as we ordered. Meanwhile, push some scouts down the road for a mile or two.' He ignored Geraint and his; in fact, he never spoke to them again, as if they had shamed themselves, though no one who saw the hacked shields and the gapped blades, and the blood up to their elbows, could doubt that they had fought.

That night, we slept spread across the road in an arc, a mile from horn to horn, with our fires burning and tended by sentries who watched for the Savages. But they did not attack that night. So, in the morning, we rode down the Roman Road in our usual order.

The skirmishers saw the enemy about two hours after dawn. They called back, and Precent and I rode across to where we could see the enemy. They were a little group of men, fifty at most, standing full in the road, waiting. Owain came forward with two squadrons, through the skirmish line, and charged down on them. There was no difficulty there. When the horsemen were within a hundred paces of them, they broke and ran in all directions, and were cut down again as they fled. We reformed, and moved again down the road.

We came on more groups like this. 'Marching north to meet us, all hugger-mugger, every man his own general,' said Owain. I did not think so, but I held my peace. They had more the look of a rearguard, to keep us off the main army while it found somewhere better to fight. But now I knew better than to contradict Owain, because he was our leader, and always right.

Sometimes, they would hear us coming first, and then they would get into some kind of order across the road, and try to hold a line when we rode at them. But we always got round the flanks. If we caught them strung out, they would run before we could get at them, scattering all across the country. As we moved South, they stiffened. They stood longer. Once a group ran, as a body, into a wood. Half a dozen horsemen followed them into the trees. Only two returned. They told of men who leapt out of the undergrowth to hamstring the horses, or dropped from the trees on to the riders. Owain did not order anyone to recover the bodies.

But all this slowed us down. Late in the afternoon, when we had covered barely ten miles, we came in sight of the village where Geraint had fought. Where the road went past the smoking ruins, not through them, there was a stake new set in the ground. On it was the head of Dyvnwal Vrych. It was not freckles now that marked his face but the cuts of knives. His private parts were thrust between his locked teeth. The ravens had already had his eyes.

There we slept that night. We lay in our armour, waiting an attack. Only half of us slept at any time. Those who lay down nestled close to their horses, and not only for; we knew, those who mounted first would live. Before we slept Owain talked to us.

'Now we know the spirit of the Savages,' he told us. 'They will not stand to face us. All we have to do is to show a bold face to them and they will run away. Only remember, do not fight their kind of battle. They want to catch us dismounted in small groups, or lure us into the woods. If you are ready to fight that way, like Savages, then there is no way out, because they are too many for us. We have to use our superior skill and equipment. They cannot ride, and they will not stand up to a man on horseback. Today we have won our first victory. They tried to stop us. They could not. They will never stop us, because we bring civilisation back to the valleys. In two days' time, we will retake York. In four days, we feast in Elmet.'

But Precent spoke to me quietly, in the dark, by the horses.

'A victory is when the whole of an Army runs away, not when even the smallest part of it stands and dies where it fights. We have defeated no one, because they were never afraid of us. Even when they ran, they were only taunting us.' He stood up. 'Hey, Syvno! Have you read the stars tonight? Will there be a battle tomorrow?'

'No, no battle,' Syvno cried back, confidently. 'Tomorrow will be just like today. We will ride through them, and there will be a feast after it, and you and I will toast each other.'

'Then look to all your harness straps,' Precent warned me quietly, lest Syvno hear. 'Telling the stars is as easy as telling the weather.'

12

Peleidyr en eis en dechreu cat
hynt am oleu bu godeu beleidryal

In the first onset his lances penetrate the target,
And a track of light is made by the aim of the darting of his spears.

At dawn, we came down from the fires where we had slept, chewing as we rode on cold bacon and wheat cakes, and drinking from our jars of mead so that we would fight with that last taste of home in our mouths. We crossed the South-flowing river, where the Romans had built a bridge. Now it had fallen, leaving only the columns on the banks, and there were no Magicians in the Island who could raise it again. Behind us, the burning thatch laid low across the land a ceiling of black smoke under a roof of grey cloud. We were not opposed.

We moved up from the river, Precent and I on the road itself, the skirmishers spread out on either side of us. We saw the town before we saw the enemy who lay in front of it. The old town was there, near the bridge. The houses were roofless. The Savages had built their village a half mile away. They never live in the towns, even when they find them empty and waiting. They prefer to stay outside the walls, or if, very bold, they come within the walls, they place their houses in the pleasant gardens where the real people of the place once grew their leeks and radishes. Savages never live in house of stone. They cannot mend the roofs when tiles fall, or hang doors again on metal hinges. Besides, they believe that all the houses are made by Magicians, and that if they come within doors they will fall a prey to the magic. And better it would be if they did.

The town had once been surrounded by a wall. It was ruined

662

now, and often collapsed into a continuous mound, rather than a rampart. There was a gentle slope of rubble in the ditch that went round the walls. The weeds came close to the walls on three sides, not on the one that faced the river.

'Gone,' said Precent, waving towards the town. 'All gone, the people who lived there once. No one even remembers the name of the place.'

'Oh, yes, they do,' I told him. 'The name is clear, where the old road crosses the river. How does it go? I think I remember:

> 'Constantine here held his court.
> Cold the hearth, hosts unkind.
> Women weep for Cattraeth, silenced.'

'Who first sang that? Did you?'

'No, I do not know who was the first. It is an old song. By the language, it is from before the Savages came. Perhaps the town has been desolate before. Why do you ask?'

'Because it is the first verse I have heard you speak for more than a year.'

I did not answer. I felt that I had been unguarded. What had softened me? The heat of the battle yesterday perhaps, the sight of the dead. And which dead had moved me most? Dyvnwal Vrych, eaten by the crows? The corpses, stiff, thrown into the ponds and wells? Or that first boy, barefoot, in Eudav's woods?

But between where we sat and the two places, the town on the one hand and the village on the other, the enemy stood. To our left, the ground sloped down to the river. The pools shining black under the leaden sky, the rushes standing up like clumps of savage spears, showed that this was bogland. It was no ground to ride horses over. To our right, there was another wood, a rare sight in that land, but whether they were afraid again of magic, or whether they left it to feed their swine, or whether perhaps the ground was too poor for wheat, I do not know. At any rate, it was dense wood, with bushes undergrowing the trees. We had had enough of that the day before. Horsemen would not enter that wood. They had taught us that. The space between the wood's edge and the river swamp was five hundred paces, not

663

less, perhaps seven hundred, certainly not as much as a thousand. Through that space led the road. Through that space we had to go. And in that gap stood Bladulf.

Oh, yes, I was sure it was Bladulf, even at that distance. I had seen him the once, and that once was enough. A giant, he was. There are giants among the Savages. We count a man tall at seventeen hands: they mostly top eighteen, and only Owain of all the Household came to that. And Bladulf stood half a head taller than any of his army. His yellow hair hung braided to his waist, not cut like a Christian, and he had wound black rags into the braids so that he could be told from behind. He wore a helmet of bronze, not iron, shining red through the gloom of that day. Over the crest of it ran a high ridge, worked to show a wolf's face above his own. The wolf's paws reached down to cover his nose and to spread out where they might guard his cheeks. This was no Savage work, but stolen somewhere in Gaul. He wore mail to the thigh, and trousers of stiff leather like ours.

'He will not move quickly in those,' I told Precent.

'He does not mean to run,' Precent agreed. 'That one will stand where he stands, whether his men stay with him or not. Watch that sword. He will try to come up at you under your shield. Do not let him attack you on the shield side.'

We could see, even from here, that Bladulf had a real sword, long and double-edged and pointed, such as few of his men carried. This was a sword a man could strike with, putting his weight behind the point to thrust. This was no edge that a village smith could beat out, to spoil by cutting hay or splitting wood or cracking lobster claws. I wondered where he had stolen it. It was no Roman work, too long, too big.

Owain came to us. We three rode forward, close enough to see faces. The Savages did not move, just stood firm. They began to make a noise, beating on their shields, and taking up a rhythmical chanting shout, bellowing in chorus one word again and again, perhaps a hundred times, before they found another word.

'What is the word they cry?' Owain asked.

'*Blood*,' I told him.

'Then the Bloodfield let this place be,' he told me. But it was Cattraeth, all the same.

Cynrig joined us, and Peredur Ironarms.

'Eight to one, would you say, or ten?' asked Precent. He counted nice enough, seeing they were well pressed together all across our front, and three or four lines deep in most places, close on each other's heels. But Owain replied, 'Nearer twenty to one, counting us all together, horse-holders and all. Hear that, Aneirin, hear that, twenty to one, and sing it. Oh there shall be glory for us this day, honour and glory for us all.'

We looked close at the Savages, standing there in line, waiting for us. All giants they were, that is true, all of them far taller than most of us. Many of them in the front rank had a piece or two of mail to hide their shoulders or their breasts. Most of them had the saxes they used on their farms, too long to be called knives, too short for swords, and too useful to be kept only for battle. Besides there was a forest of spears, and axes as well. And every man had a shield, not oval and leather-covered like ours but round and heavy, of limewood planks joined together, with iron-bosses deep and pointed, and iron rims a hand wide. They looked a dirty lot, all dressed in their undyed garments of grey or brown coloured only with grease and dirt, a line of dun ants, frugal as the ants, not knowing what art or poetry or civilisation is, need-ing only each man his handful of wheat to live. Satisfied with that little, too.

Behind Bladulf, a mocking parody of Bradwen, a soot-daubed giant carried his banner. It was black, long and narrow, the edges stiffened with willow-canes, so that it stood out for us to see all the day, and never dropped on the staff. It was embroidered with a dragon, in white. His helmet did not, however, show the drag-on's wings, but the horns they liked to wear. In the rear rank, there were men with neither helmet nor even a cap of wool or leather, and these were Aidan's horned men indeed, because they had twisted their braids in tallow to stand out like stiff horns before their heads. A strange people, among whom a horned man had honour. And we could smell them, too, even at that dis-tance, the strange almost-sweet smell of wheat flour, leavened with yeast.

'How do we take them, Owain?' Cynrig asked. It was some-thing, that we were able to sit there, within a spear's cast of the enemy line, and discuss what we would do, as calmly as if we were in the paddocks under the Giant's Seat.

'As we always planned,' Owain answered. He did not move, though, but sat still a moment, looking at the long dun line of swaying chanting warriors. The rhythm of their voices was a seductive, diverting thing, numbing thought. But under that strange deliberate assault, not on the body but on the senses, Owain still was able to plan, to change his mind.

'No, not as we always planned it. Precent, I want you to command the reserve Squadron.'

'That was not what you promised me.'

'I do not break promises lightly. Twenty to one there may be, but it cannot yet be the whole host of the Savages. It may well be that Bladulf has hidden men in the wood, to try to take us in the rear when we attack. If they do, I want my most experienced commander to be ready for them.'

'I take it Bradwen will ride with us, then?' I asked.

'I cannot ride into battle without my standard. It is my ravens that will drink blood today, and peck out eyes tonight.'

'I will carry your standard,' Cynrig offered.

'Will you dare to try to take it from her?' Owain asked him. 'I have tried to persuade her, but she insists that she will fight. I have told her to ride in the second line, not the first, in case the standard is captured. It is the only argument she will listen to. Gwenabwy and a dozen others will keep close around her. I think she will be safer in the second line than in the reserve, if there should be an attack from the wood. If you want to go and argue yourself, then you can, but I have little hope that you will change her mind.'

There was no more to say. Only Owain asked, 'Their shout has changed. What are they saying now?'

'*Victory*, they are bawling, over and over again, *Victory*.'

'For whom? Go with God, my friends.'

We turned again and joined our squadrons. Precent, Cynrig and I rode together to the reserve line. Between us and the leading squadrons rode; Gwenabwy rode close at her right hand, and Cynrain at her left. As we rode back, though, I heard Precent ask Owain, 'Am I to use my own discretion when to throw in the reserve?'

'No! Charge when you see we have broken through, or when you hear me call to you. Otherwise, sit still!'

Owain rode forward again. We saw him speak to Bradwen before he went to his own place at the centre of the front rank. The chant of the Savages rose louder and louder. From our ranks rose only the voice of Gelorwid, in the words of the Virgin's Hymn. We were ready to put down this proud Bladulf from his throne.

Then we of the reserve stood beside our horses and watched the opening of the battle. The Household spread out in two lines, one behind the other. The Savages suddenly fell silent, keeping their breath for the fight. Owain rode in the centre, in the gap between the two front squadrons. Oh, there is never a sight in all the world like an army of cavalry riding into action, all gleaming in red and shining iron, all the gay shields bobbing and the pennants flying, the plumes tossing as they went forward, silent now as the enemy.

Owain did not ride at the whole of the enemy's line, as he could have done if he had spread out his men as far as they would go. He made his soldiers ride knee to knee, where they could help each other, but not so close that they could not move. They trotted steadily across the empty field, an eye always for bad ground or molehills or traps dug for us by night. And the Savages waited for us, not running forward to meet our people. A spear's throw from the enemy line, the Household halted. The men of the first rank raised their arms, and a shower of spears fell on the enemy. Immediately, the second line rode forward, squeezing through the gaps in the first line, only Owain and Bradwen keeping their places. The men of the second line, now in the front, threw their spears, and then, with swords drawn, rode forward again at the walk, crushing and pressing against the Savage front as if to push it aside by sheer force. But as our men threw their spears, so did the enemy, and sword rang against sword, and long pikes thrust from where swords could not reach. I saw men fall from their saddles, and riderless horses rear in the press and trot back, where they could, saddlecloths blackened with blood or their riders trailing by the feet from the stirrups.

The lines were locked for as long as it took Gelorwid, at my

667

elbow, to repeat twice the Virgin's Prayer that he had learnt from a hermit in the South. But, at length, we heard above the din, above the screech of the Savages, the shouts of the Household, the braying of horns, the screams of men struck down, and the clatter of sword against shield and spear against mail, the voice of Owain, splendid as a trumpet of silver. We saw the second line of horsemen, pressing behind their leaders, slacken, and then the Raven banner came back towards us, and Owain riding behind it, and all the rest of our horsemen following it, in a streaming rout.

Any leader can carry men with him into an attack. Only an Owain can lead them away from the enemy, and then halt them where he pleases. The Raven banner halted where it had stood before, and the squadrons re-formed around it. Again, Owain led them forward, not now at the centre of the enemy's line but at their right flank, our left, where they held their flank against the bog. Now, of course, the ranks were reversed, and it was fresh men who first closed with the line of foot, cutting and slashing at the bearded faces below them, shearing off the tow braids with the tow heads, swords falling in severed hands. Again we would see Owain in the centre of the front line, his plumes tossing, his arms flailing as he dealt out pain and death on either side. Behind him, steady, above his head, the Ravens flew.

Yet, still, the line of foot stood firm, still it neither broke nor bent. Still we could see Bladulf, a head above his men, always meeting the centre of our attack, a demon in flesh. He would not let us pass. Never would Bladulf let us ride through to York, if there were not a man to help him. Oh, it would have been no trouble to Owain to have killed Bladulf: he could have done it in his sleep. There was never a giant that Owain could not have overcome, had he fought against him one to one. But in that press, in the ranks of the wild ones, Owain could not come at him.

At length, again we saw Owain break clear, again we saw the Raven banner retreat. Again we saw our comrades turn their backs on a hail of spears. Again the squadrons reformed. They were fewer now. Bodies lay over all the ground between us and the enemy. The spent horses could not charge again. We stood there, useless and sterile, while the very horseholders of the other squadrons took their places in the line, bringing forward fresh horses for a fresh charge.

Now Owain headed a charge on a narrower front, ten men in line, no more, and twenty deep. Owain rode in the front line. The Ravens flew in the centre of the mass. Now the spears were all thrown. With swords alone the Household rode again for the third charge, and still we of the reserve stood idle, not even mounting because that would have tired our horses. Ever more threatening was the line that stood before us, as dull and lowering as the clouds above us. This battle, I thought, is lost.

The third time, the Household rode up the field, and again Owain led them against the enemy line. At a trot he headed for the centre of the line of shields, and then at the last moment he turned his force half right, to attack the Savages' left flank. At a trot he thrust against the wall of spears, and all the Household with him – except us. The ranks of horse spread out behind their leader, men cutting and hacking overlapped him on either side. The Household was a blunt wedge, pointed at Bladulf, at no one but Bladulf. The Savage line; then, for the first time, it bowed. It bowed, but it did not break. They were pressed back, but their line did not break. There were no gaps. Men thrust in from every side to fill in every vacant place, to pick up every fallen shield.

Now, if a line is stretched, then *somewhere* it must give, somewhere it must thin, somewhere it must weaken.

'Look there!' said Precent. 'See how they strengthen their left flank, not by design, by unthinking necessity. They are thickening at the left. But as each man feels his left flanker shrink away from him, he too edges over, one pace, and then another. At the beginning of the battle, the wall of shields was as strong at either end as in the middle, and four deep. Not a hare could pass. But now on the right they have thinned out to a mere line of sentries.'

'If Owain attacked there,' I replied, ' they would close up again to meet him. And it is what he wants. He has come for glory. The battle to him is more important than the war. If he could send all the Savages back to Jutland with never a blow struck, he would not do it. Oh, a happy man he is today, having his fill of blood, his long count of fallen Savages. And we stand here till he thinks of calling us.'

'If Owain rides to the flank, they will indeed move to meet him. But if he holds them there in strength – have you ever heard of any foot who would stand while cavalry came at them from all sides?'

'Owain said that we were to wait till we heard his voice,' I reminded Precent.

'Indeed, if you will only listen with care you will hear his voice, loud and clear.' Precent laughed from ear to ear, laughed loud enough for Owain to hear there in all the press. 'I am quite sure I can hear him calling me to charge. I can't help it, Aneirin, if you are prematurely deaf. A dreadful affliction that can be, too, for a poet.' He swung into the saddle, and turned to the reserve squadron.

'Into line, now Romans all! One line only, one line. At the canter when we reach them, and no faster. Swords only. Ready now, all of you? Then follow me. Ride, Romans! Ride!'

I rode close to Precent. Aidan was on my left, Cynrig beyond Precent, Gelorwid, Morien, all my friends, rode in line. Behind us, the horseholders, men wearied in the first charge, mounted rested beasts and made a second rank. Geraint led them, still weeping for Dyvnwal Vrych.

War is cruel and a waste, war is vain and useless, war settles nothing, war is a time of misery. So we may all say, on the long march, shut up in a fortress, or in the Hall at the end of a long peace. But in the moment of battle, you do not think of that, true though it may be. There is nothing in your heart but joy, and the happiness of being committed absolutely. And of all ways of fighting, there is nothing like riding in a charge of horse, a line of forty men, knee to knee. Then no man believes in death, no man believes in defeat, no man has any thought for what lies outside the line and beyond the battlefield.

We rode silent. Every head in the enemy line was turned to their left, watching the main action. Our horses' hoofs drummed on the dry ground, threw up the dust of a long drought into our faces. Fifty paces from the Savages, Precent for the first time

670

raised his voice. He gave no words, only a yell of triumph. We shouted with him. We saw the scattered Savages in front of us start, turn to meet us, try to group in threes or fours, and then, seeing how thin they were on the ground, and how little chance they had of stopping us, flee, some into the shelter of their fellows in the centre, and others into the bog, and even into the depths of the river, swimming for the farther bank. And the few that stood to meet us we killed with hardly a break in our stride.

Now the hours that we had drilled below Eiddin were rewarded. Still in line, at the canter, we wheeled, our pivot man halting, our flanker at the gallop. Now the whole of the reserve swept round to come at the backs of the enemy who so bravely faced Owain.

It is true. Did *you* ever hear of infantry who stood while cavalry came at them from all sides? These did not stand. Not even Bladulf stood. He, and the men nearest to him, tried to form a wall, a city as it were, of their shields, and stand as a living fortress. But most of them fled into the wood. Those that stood we ignored. There were enough fleeing for us to cut down from behind. Here and there, two or three of these, overrun, would turn to meet us, striking not at riders but at horses. Now our other Squadrons could break through, where there was no longer a line to meet them, and spread wide over the field. The Bloodfield it was indeed, covered with men, dead or crippled.

Not savages alone. Ahead of us all, alone, near the edge of the wood, I saw a horse fall. A crowd of Savages rallied there to thrust spears into its belly, to swing poleaxes at its fetlocks. The horse came down, screaming, rolling on the rider, and we saw the swords and axes rise and fall in the brief moment before I came up to scatter them. Oh, Gelorwid, Gem of Baptism! You were not born for this. In my grief I cried it aloud. Not for this, your sword-hand cut away, your helmet rolled far, your face beaten in with clubs, your mail shirt wrenched up above your head like the skirt of a raped woman. I had hoped to see you to your marriage bed, not to your grave. You were born for the caresses of a queen, not for the blades of the Savages. I wept for Gelorwid, and sang his elegy, as I struck down those who killed him.

671

Nor was he the only man to fall. Buddvan the son of Bleidd-van, that should have guarded Gelorwid's back, he too lay dead. The white hide of his horse was now as red as his cloak, with his own blood. Blood hid the sheen of his mail. He that once rode through the ranks of the enemy like an eagle through the air, now lay still on the regained earth of Bernicia.

There is no time in battle to weep for those who die. Fight on we must, and show that they have not died in vain, that their death is not empty, that from the arms of the Virgin they need not blame us as sluggards. The Savages fled before us in all directions as we avenged our friends. Only around Bladulf they stood fast, and retreated slowly, step by step, towards the shelter of the wood. Bladulf himself was the rearmost, wielding not a weapon but a flail. With that he swept a space clear behind his men. No horse would be forced into that arc of death, nor would any man walk there.

We left Bladulf and his remnant to hide where they would, and swept forward to take what they had defended. His was the biggest village we had seen. Not the greatest, perhaps, in the number of the houses, but in their size and splendour. The first fugitives had reached it, and now the old men and the women and children were trying to save themselves and their cattle. Neither had they expected defeat. When we burst upon them, they left their animals and tried to save themselves: and could not.

The battle was at an end. Breathless we gathered before Bladulf's Hall. I rode to Owain's side, where he sat, Bradwen still behind him. Precent we had seen among the Savages, leaping and bounding among them like a ball in the game. Now he came to us, panting, wringing the sweat from his scarf. Cynrig, too, joined us, his saddle spattered with blood, but none of his, and Peredur Ironarms, and Aidan, counting the Savages he had killed to make himself a man, and Graid, his arm numbed by Bladulf's flail. And all the others were around us, shouting and cheering and hailing the General whose arm and mind had brought us Victory.

Oh, the sight of Owain on the won field, his face shining as we shouted, 'All Hail to the Commander, the Emperor, the

672

bringer of all luck and fortune!' Only there was no one now to sing praise to the Virgin. Gelorwid was dead.

While some entered the Hall, and the houses around it, and heaped wood and ploughs for a fire, and drove together and slaughtered the animals, others went back to scour the Blood-field. They drove together from here and there a crowd of Savages who were only slightly hurt, or not hurt at all, and who, amazing as it may seem, wished to live even after defeat, and were willing to submit. These they set to dig a grave. With care and tenderness we brought together the bodies of those of the Household who had been killed, and the few who, though unhorsed, still lived. We could not leave anyone for the cruel knives of the Savage women, crawling about the field by night. We buried our dead on the field they had won, and after that we killed the Savages who had dug the grave. We stripped the Savages dead, and brought their armour into the Hall in case anyone thought himself half armed and wanted to take his pick. What was left we would spoil in the fire, with the weapons we found, and then throw into the river, where the Savages might dive for it if they wanted it, and not be sure of finding it. The bodies of the Savage dead we left. This was Bernicia. Were not the wolves here ours to feed?

Victory was almost complete. The road to Elmet was open before us. Only Bladulf was still alive, somewhere in the wood below Cattraeth.

13

Kynt y waet elawr
Nogyt y neithyawr

Thou has gone to a bloody bier,
Sooner than to a nuptial feast.

We feasted our victory in Bladulf's Hall. We did not weep for those who were dead, not for Gelorwid or for Gwion Catseyes, nor yet for Dyvnwal Vrych. There was not room in the Hall to lay their empty places, eighty of them. We drank and ate their share, as they would have wished, and as we wished our comrades to do when we fell. Under the joy of victory and drunkenness of battle, we knew well enough, all of us, that there would be other battles, that Bladulf would return. But not tonight. Tonight he would not come near enough to smell his own pigs roasting.

He was rich, was Bladulf. He would not live on a handful of wheat a day. The couches in his Hall were spread with wool and with furs, soft and warm. We dribbled the dregs of our mead on the couches and wiped the grease from our knives on the sables. They drink out of horns, you know, the Savages, not from cups of pottery or glass, but Bladulf's horns stood in settings of silver.

There was plenty to fill them, too, beer, and mead as well. The bitter beer we washed our hands in, and cleaned the blood from our armour, and groomed our horses and our saddles. Even the horses drank it, but we did not. But the mead, the sweet blue mead, there was enough of that in Bladulf's Hall for us all to drink and be drunk a hundred times over. And we had only one night, or perhaps two, to drink it in, because we soon would move on to Elmet, and leave Bladulf's Hall in a blaze. Tables and blankets would burn, fur and horn would shrivel, painted beams and carved pillars, wool and silver, hemp and flax, all would char away into a waste of nothingness. Why should Bladulf's Hall fare better than Eudav's? But while we had it, we would enjoy it. And we had it.

Only on the top table at the feast we of the Royal families talked of the battle over and the battle to come. Precent and I had ridden over the field after the rout, and we had seen things, noted things, that could not be seen by those who made sure of Bladulf's Hall.

'Where, then, was Elmet?' Precent asked.

'I suppose,' Owain answered between drinking, 'that these are the remnants who came back defeated from Elmet.'

'These men have not fought before this year,' I insisted. 'There were no new wounds, no hacked shields. Dusty they were, and tired, like men who have marched long and fast. But they have not fought.'

'Again, I ask, where was Elmet?' Precent thumped the table in his urgency. 'We have come because Elmet expects us, but where is Elmet?'

'This is the strategy we worked out with Mynydog,' Owain answered easily. 'First we have drawn their army north to meet us, and now they are well engaged with us, the Elmet men will take them in the rear.'

'But why so long?' Precent asked. 'They let us ravage in their valleys for four days. They would not have done so if they had known we were coming. They went south for some reason. They were ready for the Elmet men to come. But they have not fought. Where then are the Elmet men? Did they not come? Or have they made a treaty with the Savages?'

'Or,' put in Peredur, 'have they just melted away and gone home in the night, like the infantry from Eiddin?'

'What does it matter?' shouted Owain, lifting his face from the mead-jar. 'We have beaten the Savages without them. All the better – the more glory for us. We can crow over Elmet for ever now. I wonder how they will have the gall to face us when we ride into Lincoln.'

'We have beaten part of their army,' I warned. 'There are more Savages in Bernicia than the sands of the sea. The men we scattered today could not have half peopled the villages we have burnt already. They were only the fastest, who were the first to come up and face us, in the hope of keeping us out of Bladulf's Hall. There are more coming up, you can be sure. And, worst of all – we did not kill Bladulf. That must be our main concern. When we fight again, we must kill Bladulf: then his army will go home.'

'Let me tell everybody that.' Owain got to his feet, not quite steady, and shouted, 'Listen! Listen to me, all of you!'

Nobody took the slightest notice. Very few even heard him, and they were by now too drunk to take any notice. Owain tried again two or three times, and we beat on the table, but the only effort was that some of the others began to beat their fists on the boards in time with us, and then to sing.

'We'll wait till the morning,' Owain decided at the last. 'When we are ready to move, I'll tell them. I'll give a gold chain to the man who kills Bladulf.'

'You haven't got a gold chain,' Peredur pointed out.

'No, but Mynydog has,' and Owain giggled like a girl, and spilled his drink on to his cloak and tried to brush it off, clumsily.

'Never mind, boy,' Morien shouted. 'Plenty more here.'

He leaned across three or four people to slosh more mead into Owain's cup, and over the table and over everybody and everything in between. And in the state we were all in, we laughed and thought it funny to see the liquor, over the table and over the floor, shining in the light of Bladulf's eandles, forty alight at a time. That night we used the tallow of a hundred oxen.

I saw Bradwen lean over to Owain.

'Now, if you *had* a gold chain, you'd give it to me, wouldn't you?'

'And how do you know I haven't? I was the first in here, wasn't I?'

'No you weren't,' shouted Hoegi from the other end of the table, because Owain, for all his air of telling a secret, leaning over to Bradwen's ear, had forgotten to lower his voice. 'I was the first in here, don't you forget it, and you came next, and ordered me out. Anything you found in here belongs to me.'

Owain and Hoegi shouted at each other from end to end of the table, and Bradwen alternately urged Owain to reply or rolled with helpless laughter at Hoegi's sallies. While this went on, Caradog the Huntsman swept the plates and horns from the table in front of him, and jumping on the board began to dance, keeping time to a wordless song of his own that he sang loud. And nobody took the slightest notice of this, or of the men who had found Savage women somewhere – women will always come where there are soldiers, whoever they are, friend or foe – possessing them wildly on the straw of the Hall floor. And other men slept on the same straw, or bowed across the table, because there is nothing but exhaustion after battle, not only from the heat of moving in armour and the labour of striking and running and riding, but also from the sheer numbness of the cessation of fear. Every man is afraid in battle: but there are few who find that fear strong enough to stop them from fighting.

There were at least three different groups singing in different corners, competing in their various songs to see who could drown the others. In one place, some Mordei men were disputing the possession of a Savage woman, or rather the order of precedence with her, with three lads from Carlisle, and each group were calling their kinsmen to join in, while the woman, unnoticed, crept off, and might have got clear away, but that she stumbled over a man from Aeron, who, too drunk to stand, was still alert enough to pull her down on himself and ravish her there.

I looked round the Hall, and I felt the clear sight of the poet return to me, against all the Law. This, I thought, is where triumph has brought us. This is the prize for victory. There sits Owain in the glory of a battle gained, and barters insults with the bastard of an Irish pirate, to the greater glory of Cornwall, whose King he will be. And Bradwen, the wise Virgin, hangs drunken on his arm, haggling for trinkets, that might have had all the land of Bernicia as well as Mordei to run her horses over, and she with men's blood on her hands. Now, for the first time since I left Eiddin, I heard voices of Romans raised in anger, man against man, regardless of squadron, Mordei men against men from Dyfed, Cardi men against all the North.

Only Precent, I thought, only Precent does not change. He sat opposite me, looking moodily before him. I leaned over to ask him, 'Who is on watch outside? By the noise we are making, every Savage in the island knows what is going on here.'

677

'On watch?' Precent muttered. 'Why, Gwion, he always takes the watch.'

'But Gwion is dead.'

'What's that you say?'

'Dead! Gwion Catseyes is dead. We saw him killed. Don't you remember?'

'Oh, aye, dead then is he? Watch all the better from up there, then, won't he.' And Precent giggled foolishly and suddenly turned aside and spewed up all his supper on the floor, soiling Bradwen's skirts, and she didn't care.

Uyg car yng wirwawr nyn gogyffrawt
O neb o ny bei o gwyn dragon ducawt
Ni didolit yng kynted o ved gwirawt

My friend, in distress we would not have been disturbed,
Had not the white dragon led forth the army,
We should not have been separated in the hall from the
    banquet of mead.

Then I thought, if this is triumph, defeat is better. The fruit of
victory is the death of the soul. Even though now Arthur has
brought the Savages into subjection through all the Island of
Britain, though Mordred rules for him in Bernicia Roman again,
yet after this will come strife and greed and treachery. Because
that is the nature of man.

I got up, holding to the table. I stepped over to the wall, which
was swaying back and fore, and hard to catch at so that I fell
down. I found where I had left my mail, with my sword wrapped
in it, and I put it on. And then I had to take it off and put it on
again, right way round. It was only that night that I noticed what
an ill-made thing it was, because there was an extra lacehole on
one side, and when I laced it up and pulled it tight there was a
fold in the mail which irked my neck. I stuffed Gwenllian's scarf
into the collar to ease it, and then with my helmet in my hand,
still buckling my sword belt, I pushed my way through the
throng of drinking men to the door.

When I got into the cooler night air I felt better. I stood and
thought, and then I looked back into the great Hall, and into the
other houses where our men were sleeping. After a while I decided
that the only man missing was Cynrig. Was Cynrig, then, the only

man to watch over us, and more, over the whole herd of horses in the paddock?

It was true. I found him on the far side of the paddock, moving cautiously from shadow to shadow around the resting herd, as I did myself. I whistled to him, the tune of a harvest song I myself had made. He came and stood beside me in the dark.

'You would guard them better mounted,' I told him.

'There isn't a beast that will carry me now,' he replied. 'We charged and charged again today, and pursued after it. These steeds are all worn out. Not one of them is fit to march tomorrow.'

'We must march. Otherwise, the Savages will catch us here at their mercy.'

'If the horses were fit, what about the men? Will they be able to ride tomorrow, let alone fight? What about yourself? Are you fit to go on?'

'I shall be all right if only I can have some sleep.' It was all I wanted. I was tired, my clothes were still damp with sweat, freezing me as they dried. My head ached, a drilling pain above my left eye. A Savage had stabbed at me with a long spear, to the stomach, and though he had not pierced the mail, yet my midriff was bruised. My thighs and back ached from the hours in the saddle, thrusting and striking. I wanted to sleep. And I was less tired, less badly hurt than many of the men who had ridden in the first assaults. We all wanted sleep.

'If it were not for this banquet,' Cynrig argued, 'we could all sleep.'

'There is always a banquet after a victory. How else would we know that it was a victory?' I pointed out. 'Without the spoils as immediate reward, how would we enjoy war at all?'

'These spoils will spoil us.' Cynrig pointed up to the black sky. 'Pity about these clouds. Syvno would have wanted to forecast another victory for tomorrow. He died well.'

'It is a law of God: men who foretell the fates of others never read their own.'

We stood and watched. Far on the Bloodfield, lights showed, and women wailed seeking their men. Faintly, far away, sometimes horns sounded. Wolf and bear quarreled aloud over the slain. There were more animal noises than one would think. Were some of them not natural? We peered about us.

'Some men,' said Cynrig, 'have slept enough. Cynrain is one. There are others, of my squadron, and of my country. Will you go and fetch them out to watch with me?'

'If I can wake them,' I said, 'I will.'

I slid around the edge of the paddock, as silent as a man in search of badgers in the moonlight. But there was no moonlight, and I feared worse than badgers. Soon I was so near to the Hall that the sound of the feast drowned all the other sounds, rising like a river in spate. As I came between the houses, the doors of the Hall were opened, and half a hundred men poured out, shouting and singing, and seizing me as soon as they saw me.

'A Marriage, a Marriage!' they shouted. 'Come, Aneirin our Judge, and make a Marriage!'

'Put me down!' I told them, because they had lifted me on to their shoulders. 'This is no time for playing. The enemy are around us.'

But they shouted the more. 'A Marriage! A Marriage!' Peredur clutched at my arm as I was carried, and shouted, 'It is true. We are going to have a wedding to crown the day.'

'Owain and Bradwen! Owain and Bradwen!' Others shouted as the crowd bubbled like pot of porridge. Yet there was a little order. One small group of men carried me to the fire of ploughs and wagons, which they revived, and they pulled one cart over and put in it a chair, on which they set me. The rest came out of the Hall, in two streams, and one, carrying Owain, went in one direction, and the other party led by Gwenabwy with Bradwen on his arm went the opposite way. The Roman pipes played, and the marriage songs went up, as the two processions wound round and round the houses, and round and round each other, in and out in the dance we know so well.

'I cannot do this!' I shouted from the eart where I had been lifted. 'I am no priest, I cannot marry!'

'No,' shouted Peredur. 'But you are our Judge. You can marry, there being no priest or hermit.'

This was true. How had this all arisen? Was it a drunken joke, or the outcome of some attempt by Precent or Peredur to change the spirit of the night, to take men's minds off some quarrel? I could not think. I was helpless in the fever that caught us all, all except Cynrig, lonely out there with the horses. There was no sending any of this crowd out to him. They would not hear my voice, or if they did, they would ignore it.

The two processions wound their way around me and about, sunwise and widdershins around the fire, passing away into opposite distances, and then returning to join and approach me, led by Morien carrying a flaming torch. Gwenabwy had Owain on one arm, Bradwen on the other. Adonwy was on the far side of Bradwen, Precent of Owain. They marched, slow and solemn towards me. Was this, then, to be my bitter fate, that I should marry Bradwen, my love, to Owain, her love, my leader? Should mine be the torch to light them to the marriage bed?

What better guests to be at any man's wedding, than the soldiers of Mynydog's Household? In their dusty, bloody mail, their gashed shields, their tattered cloaks of red, they were the finest army that ever was in the Island. These were my friends, my brothers, for whom, with whom, I would fight and die, and yet, they hurt me more than they knew.

But as the procession halted in front of me, seated as a Judge on the cart, the pipes were drowned by the horns. Far we heard Cynrig's voice: 'The horses! The horses!'

The other torches glared on a sudden at the edge of the paddock. The Marriage broke apart before it began. Men ran from the procession towards the lights, towards the horns, to Cynrig fighting in the dark. All that saved us was this, that all the men who had come out in the wedding procession had put on their mail for it. They ran towards Cynrig, ran in one body, and that was their undoing, running into the paddock and across it. For in a moment, the paddock fence that they had put up that evening was broken down in a hundred places, and the whole herd of horses, terrified already by the horns and the shouts, ran away from the soldiers out into the night. At one stroke, we were left without our greatest weapon, our main advantage.

But they found Cynrig, wounded but alive, for he had set his back to a tall tree by the fence where only one man could come at him at one time. And when they found him, when our army

682

was split in two, the Savages attacked again, and came flooding at us into the village.

Before we knew what we were about, they were all among us and around us. It was an attack, then, by an army on two hundred separate men, each one alone. In the first shock, each of us fought alone, trying to hold himself aloof in the strife, trying to take as much and as little as he could of the battle. But soon, the swirling surface of the fight, as I saw it from the cart, began to take some structure, some shape. Men found their riding partners, and set themselves back to back. And then there were groups of four or eight, and then whole sections. At first one section, and then another, set its backs against the cart on which I stood, and the Household began to return from its dissolution, to condense again into an army. This had been the Savages' hope, to take us man by man and kill us each alone. And it was our weeks of drill, under Owain, that saved us from that. It was because we were a Roman army, used to discipline, that we remained an army in that awful night, worse than any dream.

The men who had crossed the paddock formed a squadron around Cynrig, and they charged back as one unit, crashing into the backs of the Savages around the cart. Their effect, in the darkness, was greater than their numbers deserved, and in a short while we were free and clear, the enemy drawing back. We stood on our dead, and on those we had killed, a desperate band in the centre of the village, around the cart, on which now Owain climbed, and we lifted Bradwen up with us. The fire flared higher, and Owain suddenly shouted, 'The houses! Precent, there are men in the houses!'

I jumped down and kept Precent's back, as he gathered two sections. We made a rush at the nearest Savages, and they did not wait for us, but fled out of the village, leaving us a space to enter the great Hall by the main doors. There were men in the houses, men that had been asleep or dead drunk when the attack came, and they were all dead now. Savages were flooding into the Hall through a door in the other end. We tried a charge, and threw them back for long enough to see that there was no one in the place to help. We snatched what fragments of our equipment we could pick up – I took Owain's cross-bow, the only one in the

Household – and then we fell back into the open air, while the Savages came in again to fill the room.

But they gained nothing by it, because when the Hall was full of them, they heard a crackling, and saw that Morien had thrown fire into the thatch, and that while we held one door, Peredur and a dozen men had got round to the other, and though they could not hold it shut completely, they could at least delay the Savages in getting out. The night was cloudy and calm, yet the sparks from the Hall spread every-where, and all the village in a short time was ablaze.

We concentrated again around the cart.

'What now?' Precent shouted to Owain.

'We cannot stay here,' he replied. But what to do he did not say. We none of us knew, but then Cynrig, pushing through to us, said, 'Cattraeth. Let us get to Cattraeth. The Savages cannot fight against walls. If we can get there, we can defy them for a time, and then perhaps we can regain our horses.'

Owain considered for a moment. Then: 'To Cattraeth!' he shouted.

It was not a march I would have liked to undertake in day-light, or mounted, or with a clear head, or fresh. We had none of those advantages. We moved in a curious series of jerks. We would form into a wedge, and rush at the nearest front of the Savages. They would, perhaps, run before us, or, perhaps, they would stand till we pressed them back and broke them. In either case, we then had a little space and time to march in a column perhaps two or three hundred paces in the direction where we hoped Cattraeth lay.

It was a bitter journey. The Savages were all around us. Bigger men than we, they were, and fresher. Their shields were better made for fighting on foot, and many of us threw down our light leather-covered baskets, meant for warding off the thrown spear, and picked up the heavy ironbound planks that stopped a sword thrust or cut with ease. Their swords were shorter than ours, and we could cut at men while out of their reach: their iron was better, though, and few of the saxes would bend as our swords often did. Spears were no great trouble to deal with, because you could get inside the man's thrust and settle him. Few of them were mailed, and there were hardly any helmets. If the Savages had been well armoured, as well as armed, we would not have lived, any of us.

By rush and by stand, we made our way from the blazing houses, where Bladulf's wealth and our own dead together came to ash. Any man who fell, fell. There was no time to help him, and if a man had not good friends, then a slight wound would do for him. It happened at last to me. I was in the front line of an attack, and as we trampled over the bodies of those who had tried to stand in our way, one of them thrust up at me from the ground. His spearpoint went up under my mail, into the muscles of my thigh, and I fell grunting with the pain. Then there were a dozen of them coming at me, and I would have been pegged to death with their spikes if Aidan had not returned to stand over me. Then Precent was with him, and Caradog, and they pulled me to my feet. Precent, the strongest, put my arm around his neck, and aided me to hop back to the main body, where there were helpers in plenty. And lucky it was, that we were then almost in Cattraeth.

15

> Gwr a aeth gatraeth gan wawr
> Wyneb udyn ysgorva ysgwydawr

> Men went to Cattraeth before the dawn,
> But none of them received protection from their shields.

Below the walls of Cattraeth, the Savages had cleared the woods away, and had heaved out the stumps of the trees. They were now busy, day by day, in clearing the scattered stones and bricks from the ground, ready for ploughing, and as we pressed along in the beginning dawn, our ranks were parted, like hairs by a comb, around carts, filled with stones picked up and abandoned where they stood, in mid-work, by men who had run to join a host.

Over the last few hundred paces, the Savages let us alone. We found the gateway in the crumbling walls, and we passed inside, into a city that had been empty for generations. The houses had no roofs, and the grass grew up through the stones of the roads. Men fell down on the hard ground, bleeding, exhausted, sobbing with pain and weariness and disappointment. Owain looked around him in the growing light.

'Courage, my comrades,' he shouted to us. 'Have courage, be cheerful. Our war has just begun. Do not let our hearts go down. The best of our lives is to come.'

We sat up again from where we had thrown ourselves. The sound of his voice was enough to give us hope again, and to persuade us that we could win this war we had come on. Aidan, kneeling by me and binding up the slash in my thigh with my scarf, the only thing I had for him to use, began to smile again. I looked closely at him, and saw the tracks his tears had cut through the dust-caked sweat on his face.

'Now we have an advantage again, greater than we lost with our horses,' Owain continued. 'Savages cannot overcome stone walls. We can hold out here till they grow tired and melt away. Then we can continue our march down to Elmet.'

I believed him, we all believed him. I knew well enough that it was not true. We had not between us food for one square meal all around. We did not know where there was water in Cattraeth. We were no more than a hundred and fifty, half the strength that had marched from Eiddin, half of us wounded, all of us tired, many sleeping still where they had fallen. Now the light was strong enough for us to look through the gate, and see the red cloaks scattered over the field outside. There were one or two heaps that stirred, and yet we were so spent that there was no one willing to go outside and fetch the dying men in. Any man of the Household who could reach Cattraeth on his own, we would be glad to; but we could, would, give them no help. Still, Owain was Owain. What he said was true for us. What he said, we believed, though it was counter to the plain evidence of our senses.

We had silence and a kind of peace for the time between seeing the first rays of the sun on the clouds till the time when it was light enough to tell a red cloak from a green scarf, for the break in the cloud closed in. And then, from far away, we heard them coming. Far away, faintly, the horns blew and the spears beat on the shields, and Savage voices shrieked their strange war cries. Owain stood up, bold, defiant, on the wall to see them come. Precent called men to him, sent them to stand here and there all round the city, to see where the attack came from. But the greater number of us he concentrated by the gateway. Morien and Hoegi took axes and cut down some of the young birches that already stood between the houses, and we pulled them to block the gateway with a breastwork of timber and stones.

The noise of the Savages came closer, resounding through the woods, sounding from all sides, trying to frighten us, to show us that we were surrounded, that they could come at us in overwhelming strength from all sides and bury us in bodies. Yet, we knew that Savages will not rush at walls, cannot scale them and have not the patience to undermine them. If they attacked us at all here, if they did not prefer to sit around and starve us out, they would attack the gate, as they did at York.

And so they did. The noise of the enemy fell silent. For a long period, the field before Cattraeth was so still that the first crows settled on the dead outside the walls. This silence was deliberate. They were testing our nerves, hoping that our hearts would fail with uncertainty. And even in that silence, there were some of us who were so tired, or so calm, that they went to sleep where they waited.

At last there came what we waited for. Out of the woods around us they came, not too many, perhaps a hundred of them. But that hundred was more than enough to threaten us, for all giants they were, the big ones. They pranced on the side of the field, along the hedges, shouting and singing spells and hymns to their demons, winding in and out of each other in long lines, beating their swords on their shields. For besides their shields, these men wore no mail, no helmets, no shirts or breech clouts even. They were stark naked, erect, entranced, rigid as if they were the dead walking. And so they counted themselves. They danced and gyrated senselessly, generating strength and momentum, losing their consciousness, their individuality, their imagination, their fear. These were the poets of war, possessed by the Muse of Hate, composing a satire of destruction, selecting their alliteration of attack, their metre of murder, before they flung themselves, of a sudden, up the slope at us.

These are the most dangerous, men who in their own minds are already dead. A sane man, a whole man – thrust at his eyes and he will sway away his head, cut at his neck and he will guard with his own sword. But men like these naked entranced warriors cannot be deflected, do not waste effort on defending themselves. Their only thought is to kill till they drop, themselves killed. Straight against the gate they came, in a horde, but they did not pass. Some of us sprang on to the breastwork and thrust down at them: others, like myself, stood close to the timbers and pushed them away with spears. Ten men stood higher still, on the walls, while the rest of us passed up to them big stones, torn from the houses and the paved streets, to throw down into the press. The enemy was forced to concentrate all his strength against the gate, where never more than twenty of his men could approach us at one time. There we could hold the Savages, however mad for blood they were. It was a hard fight, a long struggle before the last of the shirtless ones lay dead in the way. They had been able neither to pull down our barrier nor to cross it. But scarcely had the last of them crawled away across the field, than we heard again the rhythmical singing, the tuneless chanting of the Savage army.

They stood in a great horde, as always, on the edge of the woods below us, a long dun line of mindless, faceless blocks, clashing their spears against their shields and thundering out that six-syllable line, whatever it was, again and again. They stamped their feet on the ground till it shook, and the ox-tail tassels that they tie to their spears and on their belts and around their knees waved like marsh reeds in a gale. They shouted, louder, and louder, not moving, as if they wanted to frighten us: to frighten us not enough to run away but enough to draw us out from the shelter of our walls. But we did not move. Owain stood at the centre of the barrier, and the Raven banner still waved over his head. Bradwen still stood firm.

And then, like a ripple of water over the sand, the dun mass began to come nearer to us. Slowly and insignificantly nearer at first, because as fast as they came out of the wood, so others thronged behind them, filling in the space, and soon all the green of the field was turning dun. But they were learning, these Savages. They knew, from that one attempt, that no charge of unsupported men could break into Cattraeth.

Therefore, their wizards came out of the line, and danced against us, trying to harm us with their magic, but they could not, because the Virgin watched over us. But they could bewitch our eyes, and with their posturings and gestures they drew our attention gradually to one end of their line, as Owain had drawn their attention to one end of their line on the Bloodfield. I had climbed, now, up on to the wall, six feet above the ground, and I too watched the dancers, till of a sudden movement the other way caught my eye. I shouted, but by then everybody else had seen it. A crowd of the Savages had taken one of the abandoned carts, full of stones, that lay scattered about the field in front of the gate, the filed they were clearing to plant wheat in. Instead of bringing oxen to pull it, they themselves took it by the pole to push it. More and more of them clustered around it, as we had around the ship, and they rolled it across the ground towards the gate. This was how they had taken York: not able to scale the walls, they had broken in the gate by night, while the garrison slept and thus treacherously murdered them all in their beds. Now they pushed the wagon towards the gate as fast as a man could run, and it was heavy, too, full of stones. We saw at once that if it hit the barricade square on it would scatter the birch-poles and leave a gap for the Savages to rush in by. Clinging to the wall, I lifted stones from the crumbling parapet and threw them at the cart. But Morien had a better device. Who else but he, at this bitter time, would have lit a fire? And it was armed with flame, a flaring torch of his own red cloak, that he leapt on the parapet with me. He waved it round and round his head, till the cart was near enough to throw it. The torch landed on the cart, and flared into the faces of the men on the farther side, run-ning as fast as if they were racing for a pig, and they jerked away, some of them burnt, but most only frightened. And the cart swerved, and turned towards us, losing little speed, and hit the wall below us with a terrible crash.

The ruinous wall crumbled under our feet. I saw it coming, and I jumped away, but my wounded thigh robbed me both of the power to leap and the agility to land. I sprawled on the road of the city beneath the tottering wall. Morien leapt a moment later: but he had already left it too late, and he jumped from a moving surface, so that he covered no distance at all. The stones came down around us, thundering like the tide on a rocky coast in an autumn gale: I felt my ribs crack under the shower, and my knee twisted under me.

And then, following on its thunder, the tide did come in, racing between the horns of the gate as it had between the horns of the cliff, a tide of Savage feet, of Savage voices, of Savage smells, that swept above me as I lay on the ground, as I rolled over and over upon my crushed ribs, the desire to get out of the way, somewhere to safety, overruling the pain. I expected to be stabbed as I lay on the ground, but the men who rushed over me, stepping on my back, were too fixed on a distant prey to bother

690

me. I pulled myself to the wall for a backing, and watched the Savages charge against the line of the Household. Owain held the centre, but, laying about him, as furious as Bladulf with his flail, he was still pressed back. But when I thought he was sure to be overwhelmed, his flanks being eased away from where they depended on the house walls for protection, I heard the cry of the Virgin's name, and Precent charged past me, leading the men from the circuit of the walls. He did not assail directly the backs of the men facing Owain: instead, he flung his force into the gateway, separating the Savages inside the walls from those outside, sending the attackers outside fleeing from the gate by the sheer ferocity of his face and voice. Then, while some hurriedly piled up stones in the gate, others turned on the Savages trapped inside. They killed them all, in time.

Silence came again. It is a vice of the Savages, that, repulsed once, they do not repeat the attack, but withdraw and then come at you again in a different way. Now, there was nothing to remind us that there had been an attack but the piles of dead in the gate, theirs and ours. Aidan came limping to me, and Precent with him, in their own time. It is the first rule of war, to settle with the enemy's wounded before you help your own. I asked them, 'How is Morien?'

Aidan helped me to sit up, and pointed. From under the heap of stones that had been the gatepost of Cattraeth, protruded Morien's feet. No more of him could be seen. I wept. I had brought him to Cattraeth. Morien, who had spread fire upon the enemies of the Romans; now his spark was quenched, the fire of his eyes, that used to dazzle the Savages in battle, was now put out.

It was painful enough to be lifted up to sit. When Aidan put his arm beneath my shoulder and helped me to stand, the pain of my ribs and my leg, when I stood on it, ran through me worse than any sword. I wept aloud, and fainted. I do not know how long I was unconscious, but it was long enough for my comrades to carry me a little way, and take off my mail and bandage me around the body to give some support. They washed my cuts with mead, which was all we had, there only being one well in Cattraeth, and that dry. I looked around me, to see how many of the Household were left here in Cattraeth. I saw only how few we were. Only, Owain still led us, still the Raven banner flew over us. Still Bradwen, unwounded, knelt beside me. Owain came to talk to me.

'There is an end of fighting for you,' he told me. 'There is no weapon you can lift with broken ribs.'

'I can see one weapon I can use,' I replied. I pointed to Owain's crossbow, with a leather bag holding dry strings and twenty quarrels tied to the stock. 'I brought that with me, through the night. At least we have that, whatever else has been lost.'

'Aye, I have lost heavily,' Owain agreed. It is true, I thought, near on two hundred good men have gone, that had mothers and sweethearts to weep for them: all lost, all lost, and the land of Mordei lost with them. But he went on, 'All my baggage, with my two silver cups, and the coronet of a Prince of Cornwall, all lost. And, worst of all, my greyhounds – I have not seen them since the middle of the night march. My poor dogs – I wonder if I will ever see them again.'

That was the measure of Owain, of his humanity, that made us love him – in the wreck of the Household, it was his greyhounds, which he loved, that he wept for. And I? I asked Aidan, 'When you carried me, and I fainted, I did not cry out, did I?'

'Indeed you did, Aneirin,' he answered, 'but any man would have cried in that state.'

'What did I cry?'

'You cried one name.'

'I called for Bradwen?'

'You called for Gwenllian.'

And she, at least, knew nothing of Cattraeth.

16

Disgynnwys en affwys dra phenn
Ny deliit kywyt kywrennin benn
Disgiawr breint vu e lad ar gangen
Kynnedyf y ewein esgynnv ar ystre

He fell headlong down the precipice,
And the bushes supported not his noble head:
It was a breach of privilege to kill him on the breach,
It was a primary law that Owain should ascend up on the course.

The Savages' Herald stood on the green grass before the walls, a scarlet stain on the green. His cloak was red as ours. More scarlet than the poppy was it, more crimson than the brave red blood. Redder it glowed than the flame in a man's thatch, than the sun on a fine morning that tells of evil weather to come. There he stood on the green grass, livid against the green trees. When I closed my eyes to shut him out, I could still see him, a magic green against a curtain of red.

We stood on the wall in the breach where the gate had been, where we had first made a barrier of birch-poles, and which we now had stopped with stones. I sat on a stone, leaning against the parapet, because it hurt me too much to stand.

The Savage came slowly towards us. In his right hand he waved a green branch. His left hand he held empty above his head. Now we could see his clothes beneath the cloak. Once, perhaps, his tunic and trousers had been red also, but now they were patched and darned and scattered with pieces in all colours, yellow and green and blue and brown. Through the unmended rents, and there were many, and few of them new, we could see the flesh. He wore no armour.

No, this was no Judge, no Bard that Bladulf had sent to us as a Herald. The hand that held that green branch had never held an ivory staff, nor played on the man-high harp. On days of audience and at feasts, this man would be close to the throne, without doubt, but he did not sit at the King's side, nor stand behind his throne. Instead, he danced and tumbled before the King. He turned somersaults and walked on his hands. He juggled balls, and balanced sticks on his nose. And when he had finished, he did not even have a seat at table, or a dish and cup to eat and drink from. No, he would sit on his haunches and beg like a dog, and the King would throw him a half-picked bone and a crust of alesoaked bread to gnaw on, if he were pleased. But if the King were not pleased, then the courtiers would know it without telling. They would pelt this man with broken pots and oyster-shells, thrown with malice, to hurt, and laugh to see him leap and dodge and bleed and beg for mercy. This was no Herald who came to talk to us, under the signs of truce, across the field where our dead lay tumbled on the broken stones of the walls of Cattraeth. I told Owain, 'Bladulf has sent us his Jester.'

The envoy came closer, to within shouting distance. He walked daintily, his feet close together. He stopped and called out, '*Frith! Frith!*'

'What is that gibberish?' asked Precent. 'It is like the barking of a dog.'

'He says, "Peace, Peace,"' I told him. 'He wants to parley. Should we let him come any closer? I would not, myself. What will you do, Owain?'

But Precent spoke first, spitting. 'A Jester? I would not soil my tongue. Do not disgrace yourself, my Prince. Let me take a bow and kill him where he stands. It is a weapon I would not use on a man, but on a jester—'

I had a sudden thought. 'No, Precent, if we kill their messenger, will they not then kill one of ours?'

'A messenger to them? A Herald to them?' This was Owain who spoke at last. 'How would we ever wish to send a Herald to those Savages? What would we want to say to them? We have no need to worry about reprisals. All we have to do is to keep ourselves safe here and kill as many as we can, till the Elmet men come up. We can kill this Herald, if we want to, with impunity. But I do not wish to kill him.'

'If we are safe, then we may as well kill him at once,' said Precent. 'It will be one fewer for Elmet to deal with. If we *are* so safe.'

'Safe or not safe, it makes no difference.' Owain was firm of voice. 'There will be no killing of a man who carries a green branch. It is below the honour of a Prince, or at least of a Prince of Cornwall.' He did not say 'whatever the Picts do', but he meant it, and we knew that. 'I will not kill that poor harmless creature.'

'But I am not a Prince of Cornwall, or of anywhere else,' I insisted. 'And this is no poor harmless creature. Look how tall he is. He would not come up to my breast, if I were able to stand. He is a dwarf. And now look again at his face. Do you see it as clear as I do? Hairless and plump it is as a woman's. There was never need for a razor on that face. It is neither man nor woman. It is one of those sexless things that a real man would die rather than touch. Filth is what they are throwing at us. Give me the bow, Precent. You are right. We ought to kill him – it would be an act of virtue before Heaven and the Virgin. A thing like this cannot be a Herald. Let me do it. I am the better shot.'

'Only a harmless, sexless dwarf at best: at worst, a devil,' agreed Precent. 'It would not do the slightest harm to kill him. Owain, let Aneirin kill him if he wants to. Here is the bow. Lay off two fingers for this wind, to the right, and allow for being ten feet above him. Hit him first time, like a deer. If you miss him, he will run and we will have no time for a second shot.'

There was none of all the Savages I wanted more to kill. There was no need to tell Owain how well I knew this one. It would give me a little peace through the long night to come. I cranked back the bow-string, and it hurt me, but the pain of my ribs added strength to my hand. But Owain still held his hand before me so that I could not raise the bow to my shoulder.

'And a Jester,' Precent went on, seeing Owain stand so still. 'Bladulf is doing this as an insult. A Jester? Talk with him, Owain, and all the Kings of Britain will laugh at us. The Household of Mynydog will itself be a jest in every corner of the Empire, a matter for giggling at on feast-days, for mockery in Halls. There is not one of us would ever dare again go into the company of

695

warriors. Jest with him, Owain, and it will be our own honour you will jest away, and our lives too.'

'And what kind of jest would I be if I killed a dwarf?' Owain asked. 'Would *you* want his blood on your hands, Aneirin, grandson of Cunedda? Dwarfish blood, jester blood, will that be a thing to boast about at feasts? Will you take his head to hang on a wall, or his hide to curtain a door? Nobles fight with nobles, I tell you, freemen with freemen. A prince may aim at a King, but there is nobody here so low born or so badly nurtured that he could think of killing a dwarf.'

Owain stood up in the gap in the wall. He waved his arm. The dwarf began to move forward, slowly, cautiously, as if ready at any moment to turn and run. You have seen a bear approach the tethered kid, while you sit in the tree above with your crossbow? So he came towards us. Owain, standing there in full view, took off his helmet. He handed it to Bradwen. She took it. She had said nothing while we argued. Now she spoke, as if she had been saving her words to the end, to when there was nothing left but pleas that Owain might listen to. She said, 'Don't talk with him. There is a treachery in his walk. Look at his gait, soft and wary. A real Herald believes in his green branch: he does not. If he does not trust us, we ought not to trust him. We have seen no enemy so deadly, Owain, since we passed the Wall. Kill him, Owain, or let Aneirin or Precent kill him.' She was almost crying. I had not seen her tears since she was a little girl. 'My love, I want to sit with you again in the Hall of Eiddin. I want to ride with you to Cornwall. Do not risk all that for a whim of your honour. There are few of us here now out of all who started. Anything the Savages do is meant to harm us. Do not talk with him. Let us only wait here till the Elmet men come to us.'

The dwarf had stopped, no more than two lance lengths away. He could tell his danger from the tone of our voices. He was too close, now, to escape if anyone chose to throw a spear at him, or launch a bolt, even if they missed the first time.

Owain looked down at him, proudly, fiercely. Never had I seen him look more kingly. I have never seen any man look more a King. If this is how Kings look in Cornwall, then lucky they are there. I have never seen Gwyddno at his crown-wearing in

Harlech, or Arthur in his Hall at Caerleon in the midst of all the Household of the Kings of Britain, but I swear they can not look half as kingly as Owain did that day. Even now, and there are men who were not born on the day of Cattraeth who have died of old age already, I can shut my eyes, and see him, as he stood in the breach of the walls, looking at all the army of the Savages. His red curls hung down on his shoulders like red snakes, twisting and hissing at the Savages of their own strength. His green eyes showed all the fury of the winter sea, the light sparkled in them like the white foam. From his unlaced mail coat his neck stood out brown and firm, the strong pillar of Britain, to carry that noble head, dear to us as the head of Bendigaid Vran to his followers. So we all looked in love at him, and Bradwen wept, who now knew war, and had seen how many men had died around the Raven banner, that she should come so far unwounded. Owain laughed at the dwarf, who was used to it, surely, and turned his back on him, to say to Bradwen, and to all of us, 'Think who I am, and who is the man you have chosen. Mark's son of Cornwall am I, that shall be King of Cornwall after him. I will lay at your feet, Bradwen, as your dowry, the heads of half a hundred Kings out of Ireland, dead by my sword. And how many heads have I not piled before you in these last days, how much land have I not given back to our own people? I tell you, I am not afraid of any living man—'

'This is not a living *man*,' I had the courage to interrupt him. 'Look at that pale face, the bulging forehead, the chin that curves to nothing under the weak lips, the lank and wispy hair. This is one of the devils out of hell, or a wild beast that Bladulf has tamed to fight for him.'

'If he were a thousand devils, I would not be afraid of him. The Virgin will protect us. Let him come.'

Owain waved at the dwarf. He came forward, still hesitant, dainty on his feet as a faun. Caso and Graid helped me to move along the broken stones so that I might sit beside Owain, my head and shoulders above the parapet. Owain leaned over the broken wall, his elbows on the stone. I was there only to be a mouthpiece, to talk between the two.

The Red Dwarf looked at me, where I could have touched him with my sword-point. He looked close at me, and sneered.

'When we made you dance for us, we did not know that you could sing. We'll have you singing for us soon. The knife it was we took to you the last time. This time it will be the white-hot iron. It sears, the hot iron, it hisses on the skin, and you see the smoke of your own burning and smell yourself roast. Oh, we will hear you sing at the winter feast.'

'Are you trying to frighten me? Think of something else to say, because you are wasting your breath on this.'

'You will be less bold when you hear my message. Ah, you are sweating already from fear, and panting. Too soon my words will come for your comfort.'

I was sweating, it was true, and my face was pale, but it was the pain of my ribs, stabbing at me as I breathed, that made me pant, that caught at my stomach till I wanted to vomit. I turned to Owain.

'He is taunting me. Next, I think he will taunt you, and all of us. We must not show anger, or take offence. He is only a dwarf.' I said this loudly, so that all could hear.

'What does he want?' asked Owain. 'Has he any authority to treat with us, or has he only come to jest?'

'It is a high price he will pay for jesting,' I answered, and my hands beneath the wall trembled on the crossbow. But Precent growled, 'If I were shaped like that, then I would welcome death, and want nothing more than to hurt whole men in dying.'

'Life, Precent, is dear to all,' Bradwen reminded him. Owain bade me, 'Ask him!'

'It may be difficult to find out what he means, rather than what he says.' I turned back to the Dwarf, who had been watching us speak, turning his head from one to another, trying to read our meaning from our eyes, and finding small comfort there. 'What have you come to ask of us? Mind you make your requests politely, now.'

'And mind you tell your master true,' he squealed back at me.

'I serve no master,' I answered him proudly. 'I am a free man and I do what I like.'

'But do you not follow this copper-headed meal-sack?'

'I follow Owain of my own free will. I obey him because I promised to do so – and I did not make that promise to him, or

698

to a King, or to the Virgin. I made it to myself. In obeying Owain, I obey myself. I choose to follow him. After this campaign, I may choose to follow any other chieftain into battle, where ever it takes my fancy, and I will do it so long as it means killing your people.'

'That is the mark of the coward, to pick and choose whom you will follow. The brave man follows the King he is born to serve, and does not ask whether the King be brave or cowardly, wise or foolish. Would you choose to follow a coward? Or a fool?'

'And who are you to talk of courage or of wisdom? Or even of men?'

He bridled, his face paled, he spat venom at me in his words.

'And whose fault is it that I am what I am? Not mine, not any man's. My manhood is this, that by land and sea I follow the King my brother, and my wisdom that by the stars I can tell where we are, and when, and my courage that I stand here alone before you all.'

'Your brother?' and I laughed. This surely, was no more than a figure of speech. All free men are brothers within one nation. And the Savages, all herded together coupling at random at their winter feasts, they could never know who was brother to whom. But yet – the tone of that squeaking voice ... I was Aneirin, the Pre-eminent Bard. I was used, over years, to listening to voices, to judging changes of meaning in the tone. For a winter I had been a Judge in the North. In those months I had heard more truth and more lies than most men in all their lifetime. I asked, not laughing, 'Bladulf is your brother?'

'His was my father, his my mother. So he has sent me, terms you to offer.'

I spoke again to Owain. 'He has authority. This turd is the King's brother. He has terms to offer.'

'No terms,' said Owain shortly. 'This is our land. Tell the Savages to go back where they came from.'

'If they were to try to cross the sea,' objected Precent, 'their numbers would fill it, and more would come walking across on their dead bodies. They breed on their damned wheat like rats in the oat-stack. There is no such simple way out, Owain.' He jerked his head at the Dwarf. 'Ask him his terms.'

Owain did not forbid me again. I asked, trying to frame in the Savages' language the rounded speech I would have made in the tongues of human beings, 'And have you come to offer us a rent of money for your farms, a tale of silver for our ruined pastures, a toll of corn for our lost marshes, and ox-flesh in payment for our lost forests?'

'Better than silver the burden I bear.'

'Gold, then, to bind in our hair and pin in our cloaks?'

'Better than gold to the poor, and sweeter than ale to the thirsty, better than cheers to the minstrel, and fairer than women.'

'What, clown?'

'What, singer? What, what?' He laughed in my face, the wheat-stinking, ale-stinking breath stirred in my hair. 'Life, singer, life is sweeter than all.'

'Offer us what is in your power to give. Here we are and here we stay.'

'Do you still think, then, that others will follow? Do you hope Elmet will come to your rescue? Your King sent a wild man to tell us, that Elmet and Eiddin would march into Deira. First we went south, to the borders of Elmet, wasted a day's march into the country. But the army of Elmet was not in the field, there was no coming against us in battle. That border was safe, we wasted our journey. Then we came North, and settled with you. Do not look for help: there is none coming.'

I looked at him in hate. There was no truth in this. I did not repeat it. I said, 'Our lives are our own. Do you think you can give them to us? And after all this, after so many dead, you expect us to ride away with all undone that we came to do, that we came so far for and have not yet finished?'

'Life, singer, life. Not to ride away. Life only.'

'Life only?' I could not for the moment follow him.

'Life only. There are enough dead men.' We looked at each other closer now. He leaned closer, confidentially, to explain, as if it were some detail in a market, about a horse or a hunting-dog he was selling. 'Men we want to dig out our ditches and clean out our wells, for all are filled in. We want men to reap and to thresh, men to carry and men to pull, men to sweat, to sweat .... You know that, singer, you know that.'

I knew it. He saw my face change.

'Our men are dead, singer, our men are dead. We did not think ever to meet an army like yours. Nothing has satisfied you but blood, nothing but senseless destruction. Too many men are dead, and there is work to do. Axes we have in plenty, trees to cut down. Swords will beat into saxes and sickles, reeds to bundle for thatch. Spearheads will edge spades or spread into pitchforks. Now it is men we lack, fields to clear.'

I turned back to Owain. All the Household were silent to hear. The rain began to fall, began at that moment, light and thin, the rain of summer heat from a grey sky into a steamy day. So silent was the Household that we might have heard the drizzle on the stones.

'No terms,' I said. 'No terms. Slavery only. Nothing else. No terms.'

'Slavery?' Owain looked around him, looked at all the Household, at the men old in wars with the hair worn thin by the helmets, like Precent and Cynrig, at the boys like Aidan and Graid. Last of all he looked, long, at Bradwen. 'Slavery? To these Savages? That is all they offer?'

'You can see why they are so confident and proud,' I reminded him. 'They are all around us, and there are still ten times as many of them as there are of us.'

'Even alive,' he smiled. 'And as many dead, Aneirin. Slavery? To these devils, these demon-worshippers? They have no mercy, no pity. Aneirin, there is more than confidence here, and less. They are anxious to have us disarmed quickly. An army is approaching from Elmet. These monsters do not want to have to fight us on two fronts at once. They want to frighten us into surrender, and into impotence.'

'Slavery, they say, or they will kill us here.'

'Or try to. If they were willing to face the fight, they would attack now, not waste their time offering impossible terms. They say they will kill us? Let them, if they can.'

'What shall I say, then?'

'Let them kill us if they can.' Owain laughed aloud, and so did we all to see him. Oh, there was never a King on his throne had half the majesty of Owain on the walls of Cattraeth, no Queen

701

that ever had half the beauty of Bradwen, dusty and blood-stained, sweating in her mail. 'I will tell him.'

'Don't go too near him.'

'No nearer than I can spit in his face.' Owain leaned over and down past me, down towards the Dwarf.

'Non potest,' he said in Latin, for he spoke that language well as must any ruler of; 'numquam.' And in our own language, the tongue of the Angels, that was spoken in the Garden at the beginning of the World, 'Nage! Dim erioed!' And at last, in the few words I had taught him of the speech of the Savages, 'No, no! Never!'

Have you seen an adder strike? The neck that moves, thrusting forward, the forked tongue stabbing, stinging, pouring venom that will bring low man and horse – so struck the Dwarf. The arm that moved from beneath the cloak, the left hand thrusting forward, the knife not stabbing but cutting, slashing, tearing open the throat – an adder is not so swift, so evil, so silent, so final. A short sax, not two spans long, heavy as an axe, pointless, single-edged, hidden in his ragged sleeve: it did the business.

Thus died Owain, King Mark of Cornwall's son, the hope and strength of all the Isle of Britain. His blood ran down the shining walls of Cattraeth, and stained with new death the dead Roman stones. Mark died with him, and Tristan – Cornwall died. His body fell into the Roman ditch. He never spoke again.

He was a man in years, in mind a youth, and gallant in the din of cruel war. It shall be not my part to tell thy failings, or to reproach thee with our dismal end. Rather shall I make thee live in song, until Rome fades and the world ends. Why did I see thee on thy bloody bier, before I lit thee to thy wedding-couch? My Owain, my beloved friend, my chieftain – at least, thy Ravens will not peck out thy eyes.

Owain's blood poured on my sleeve, and his body tumbled into the ditch. All the Household cried out in sorrow and in horror at the treachery. For a moment, in our bewilderment, all our eyes followed our Leader, our hero, as he died. And no one watched the Dwarf. He ran away down the slope.

After the first cry, there was silence inside the walls of Cat-

702

traeth. Then it was Bradwen who led. She had not cried, she did not weep, for Owain her love that died. Bradwen the Wise, she wasted no time, no effort, on mourning. She needed only the time to set his helmet on her head, the raven plumes gleaming blue-black in the sunless light. Then she leapt over the rubble in the gateway. Gwenabwy followed her, as always.

'Kill the Dwarf!' he shouted. 'Vengeance! Kill the betrayer!'

'No!' answered Precent. 'Stand fast! Stand here within the walls. Do not go outside, where they are waiting for us. That is what they want. Stand fast!'

But there were many men who did not hear him, or, if they did hear him, took no notice. They jumped from the walls or scrambled over the rubble in the gate, sword or axe ready.

'Stop, stop!' Precent shouted. He flung wide his arms in the gate. 'Hold together!'

They took no notice. But I raised the crossbow. I had a heavy quarrel, one fit for bear, with a dropping flight. Aim off, I remembered, two fingers to the right for the wind. The target was plain enough. The Dwarf stood there, stock still, a red shape on the green grass, where he had stopped first. He had no green branch now. He stood, his arms spread wide, an echo of Precent, and waited while Bradwen came down the slope at him, and Gwenabwy, and Geraint, and others, too many others. All were eager to avenge Owain. But that was my task, my duty, my joy.

The Dwarf stood still, and laughed at us, laughed at the death that came at him, helmed and plumed. I found it hard to hold the bow level and steady, my eyes blurred the red shape hard against the green grass, men crossed my sight, red plumes bobbed in the track of my bolt. There was no hurry – he would stand. The only danger now was Bradwen, that she would reach him first. She did not. I slipped the string, the bolt flew. Before the wise woman struck the Dwarf, the iron split his chest, the feathers stood out from the cloak. It was the bolt that killed him, not the blade, though before he touched the ground a dozen swords sank in him.

He died, then. All our hope died with him. With him, and not with Owain. Precent and I looked from the wall, and watched half a hundred of the Household strung out in a long single line across the field. The Red Dwarf did not die in vain, did not stand still in the middle of the field for nothing, that tempted them out of the walls, tempted them out to stand, each man alone, against the horde of Savages that came at them from the woods on every side. Bradwen I saw fall first, a dozen came at her from all sides, and it was Bladulf himself who struck her deathblow, I saw him. Gwenabwy stood above her body, sweeping his sword in wide swathes, as if it were he who held a flail, till he too fell, though when it happened I did not see for the crowd. There was no seeing single men any more in that press. Geraint died then, and Gwydien, and others too many to name. I shot three bolts into the throng, slowly because of my ribs. Before I had hooked the string to my belt for the last bolt, we saw the enemy fall back, at a signal from a horn, to the edge of the wood. Many limped or crawled. More did neither. All the field was covered with dead or dying. Some were ours: most were theirs. The silence came back, the moaning died away.

I looked at Precent. Cynrig came to us.

'How many left?' I asked.

'Not many,' Cynrig told us. 'Not a hundred, now. Most are Picts, or men from the West, or Cardi men who came north with me. The Cornishmen that live, or men of Eiddin, will none of them live long. They are the ones who were too hurt to follow Bradwen. They will follow her soon.'

'How soon?' asked Precent. He looked down the slope. There was no movement now in the wood. 'Will they come at us again now, do you think?'

'No,' Cynrig told him. 'I cannot see them facing us on the walls again. If they thought they could ever take the place that way, they would not have tried treachery. What shall we do now, my Chieftain?'

Cynrig's blood was as good as Precent's, in war he was as experienced. In those words of his, I knew there would be no quarrel. Such disputes about blood and precedence it was that first let the Savages into the Island, and tempted Hengist to enter Britain.

'What shall we do, then?' Cynrig asked again.

'There is no Household that ever kept in the field when the Captain was dead, was there, Aneirin?' Precent asked me. It was true.

704

'Let us go home, then,' said Cynrig. He looked around him at the soldiers who remained, whole and wounded. 'Those who can reach Eiddin, do so. We can do no good here.'

'We must leave here nothing that the Savages can use,' directed Precent. 'But if we are to reach Eiddin before the Savages turn their wrath north against the Dun, we must take nothing that will hinder us on the march.' He turned to me, 'Can you walk, Aneirin?'

I tried to stand. When the weight fell on my ankle, the pain scalded up my leg and into my body, and my ribs seared me like the white hot iron. I was able not to scream as I fell again to the ground. The other men who were wounded looked at me. I called on the Virgin to help me. Then I looked up at Precent, and said loudly, 'I will stay.'

The Picts and Cardi men who could still walk brought together those men who still lived though wounded, and laid them round me, against the walls of a house where I could see through the gateway. No one spoke. We knew, now, all of us, what was to be done. Bitter was defeat that clipped our tongues. We who were to stay stripped off our mail, or others took it from us. Our swords were snapped, the edges of our axes blunted, the points of our spears turned back on the stones of the wall. All these arms were carried to the dry well and thrown down. I still held Owain's crossbow. I had one bolt. I made them leave me that. The rain fell on us: I kept the string dry as well as I could under my cloak.

Four men climbed on to the wall and brought in the body of Owain. The other bodies, it was too dangerous to fetch, that we agreed. Even Bradwen, the glorious Bradwen, we must leave to the wolf and the bear. But not Owain. The three of us wept above his body.

'There was an end to Dyvnwal Vrych,' Cynrig reminded us. 'We saw his head on a pole, because they thought he was a leader. How much more will they dishonour the head of Owain?'

'There is but one thing to do,' Precent agreed, without a discussion, knowing what he was being asked. 'Aneirin has sung us often the song of Bran the Blessed.'

He fetched an axe, whetting it as he came. The men of the

705

Household gathered around us, silent. Only the rasping strokes of the whetstone sounded harsh in our ears. Precent turned on them suddenly, savage, strained to a thread.

'Have you no voices? Will you let the Savages think they have cut all our throats with this one? Sing, all of you, sing! Sing, my children, and let them hear that we are here to fight them still!'

The voices rose in the old songs, the songs of bloody and successful wars. 'The Hunting of the Black Pig' we sang, and 'Heads on the Gate', 'The Toad's Ride' and 'Blood in the Marshes'. A defeated army we were, the remnant of the Household of the King of Eiddin, Mynydog the Magnanimous, and we did not care how many Savages stood to resist our going. Under the music, Precent stood and balanced the axe in his hand. He hesitated.

'I cannot. I loved him too much.'

'Nor I,' said Cynrig. 'Can a King strike a King?'

'I loved him,' I told them. 'He treated me as a man. Not as a Bard, not as a prodigy, not as a marvel of nature, but as a man who loved and hated and felt, as a man who could weep and laugh and kill for himself, and not only in words for others. He loved me as a man who could do things, and in this Household do things no other man could do. For that love, I will not see him dishonoured.'

I took the axe. I could still kneel beside the body. I struck once: with the broad-edged axe, new sharpened, it was enough. The body some of the Picts took and threw down the dry well, with the weapons. Then they heaped stones in the well, jamming great slabs, the work of past ages, the bases of columns, into its mouth, so that it would be beyond the work of a thousand Savages to clear it again. No Savage would dig up his body, or use the iron again.

Cynrig tore the edge of his cloak and washed the head with mead from his flask, cleaning away the blood, closing the eyes. Graid brought a bag of soft leather he had picked up in some village. Cynrig wrapped the head in a cloth, the shirt taken from a dead Cornishman, and slid it into the bag. He drew the string tightly at the mouth and tied it. He offered the bag to Precent.

'No,' Precent told him, 'the honour shall be yours.' I looked at the two faces. Precent had always been a ruddy-faced man,

706

Cynrig sallow and brown. Now both were the same colour, the white that comes from fatigue and desperation. They looked along the line of the men left who could still stand. There was not a man unwounded in the town. Many of them had thrown off their armour, as too heavy, and hidden it. Precent talked to them, to us who would remain, roughly, cheerfully, to hide what we all knew.

'Well, now, who's coming with me, and who's off with the Cardi? He jerked his thumb at Cynrig. 'Most of you will go with him, and go quietly. Cast away north-west there, and make for the river. Then you can get back to Eiddin, in small groups. But I want some of you to come with me the other way, to have a last fling at them. With any luck, we can get down to Elmet in three days. Aidan, will you come and keep my back?'

The boy stepped forward, brave-faced. I was grateful to Precent for that. But I knew that he had been struck in the back with the buttend of a pike in the morning, and although it had then seemed to be no more than a bruise, yet now he was vomiting blood at intervals.

'And Caso?' Precent called.

'Might as well with you as anywhere else,' Caso grunted. How he could stand I could not think. A slash at his waist had near let out his gut: it was only held in by a bandage. So Precent chose twenty men. wounded men, who had not long to live wherever they went. There were sixty others who would go with Cynrig. More than a score of us lay on the ground to watch them make ready. Those who had buried their helmets had kept the plumes to stick in their hair with tallow, so that they would have some Roman thing about them at last. The Picts painted their faces, Precent among them. They separated into little groups of four or five. Men from the squadrons were now mixed up, seeking their own cousins, men from their native Kingdoms. At the last, the great Household of Mynydog, the first Household of all the Isle of Britain, was breaking up.

There was silence again. Nobody had the heart to sing. Only sometimes, from the edge of the wood, came the hoot of the owl or the howl of the wolf. Were they really animals? Or were the Savages signalling to one another? Or were they still there, waiting for us? Or had they all fled, appalled by that last slaughter below the walls? There was no knowing.

'Perhaps,' Precent suggested, 'they are waiting for the dark, to rush us from two sides at once.'

'Then we dodge aside,' said Cynrig, determined that he would be cheerful, 'and let them fight each other.' He pressed my hand. 'The Virgin keep you, Aneirin. One day, come to my Hall in Cardigan, and sing to us of this battle. There will always be a chair for you there, Aneirin, Preeminent Bard of the Island, red-speared battle ravager, war-diademed enemy-subduer.'

I never went there. Men have told me that he still keeps a chair for me, with my name carved on it, in which no other man, no, not even any other bard may sit. But I have never been to Cardigan. I knew then that we would never meet again.

'The Virgin keep your head, Cynrig,' I answered, but he only jested again, 'Which one? I have two to worry about.'

Precent knelt to embrace me.

'Do not weep for Bradwen,' I told him. 'She had her love, and did not live to regret him. Do not weep for me, for my songs live for me. Rather weep for yourself, and for the North, that shall be defeated now we have left it defenceless. Weep for Eiddin, that has spent so much treasure for the sake of the Island, and all for nothing.'

'Not all for nothing.' Precent corrected me. 'What we have done, others will do again, and waste all the North till it is a land fit for hunting again. Every stag that grazes, every moorhen that nests where we have burnt the farms and blocked the ditches is our memorial. It was not in vain. It is not yet over. Cheer up, Aneirin, I brought you out of prison among the Savages once, and I will do it again. We will drink in Eiddin again before the year is out.'

He spoke loud for the other men to hear. But he did weep. I could hardly see him now in the evening light, but I could feel his tears on my face. Or my tears. They were warmer than the rain. The Savages do not weep. They were there somewhere beyond the walls, waiting for us, in the dark. The Household drank the last of their mead. Cynrig put his bottle by my side. I pressed it back into his hand. He would need it more than I. He said nothing more, only went in silence into the dark.

Only when all was silent did I realise that there had been sound. As long as the Household were still in Cattraeth, there was still a rustle of movement. Even men who do not speak and are careful not to make a noise still make a great noise. You notice it only when it stops. We who were left knew when Cattraeth was empty. We lay in soaking rain and listened. For a long time, there was no sound at all, not even the hooting of the owls or the howling of the wolves. Then, all of a sudden, between us and the village, we heard a voice shouting.

'Here am I, Precent, King of the North, Lord of the Picts! Come and face me, if you dare!'

And at once, from that direction, there was the noise of shouting men, and of running, the clatter of armour and the clash of arms, the sogging sound of swords on leather shields. I could hear the noise as men crossed the field before the gate to go towards the village. The noise went on for some time. Then, very suddenly, it died away. There was silence. It was all over, there. There was a long time of quiet. Then far away to the west, the sound of fighting, the blowing of horns and the beating of spears on shields as men tried to call for help. And silence again.

So it went on all night. We lay in silence and listened to fight after fight, some near, some far. None lasted long. How many skirmishes I could not count, nor recognise any voices. Dawn came, a gradual lightening of the cloudy sky over the ceaseless rain. About an hour after dawn, I heard a voice in the woods, screaming.

'Oh, Mam, Mam! Oh, fy Mam i!'

Then it stopped. It was Aidan calling for his mother. He was the last of the Household to fight before Cattraeth.

17

Eurar vur caer krysgrwydyat
Aer cret ty na thaer aer vlodyat
Un ara ae leissyar argatwyt
Adar brwydryat

Carcases of gold mailed warriors lay upon the city walls,
None of the houses nor cities of the Christians any longer
    engaged in;
But one feeble man with his shouts kept aloof
The roving birds.

We lay in Cattraeth in silence through the long day, under the thin
and drenching rain. We waited to die. Death did not come quickly,
or easily. We tore off the bandages from our wounds. My thigh
would not bleed again, though I scratched at the scab with my
nails. The Virgin forbids a man to kill himself: but to seek death is
not the same. Death was near to us all, in any case, as we sweated
in our fevers, and coughed up our lungs out of our chests, but no
one groaned or cried, to give comfort to the Savages who must still
lurk outside. When thirst was too terrible to bear, we sucked the
rain form our clothes. Hunger is easier to withstand: there was no
food left in the town, nothing to eat within our broken walls.

And it was the silence that made me break silence. All these
men who had sung so merrily on the road, or riding into battle,
now lay dead, or awaiting death, in silence. At last I said, bitterly:

'We sang up the road – it was the mead,
That kept our thoughts as slaves.
Shouting over the wheat-eaters we;
Silent, we thirst for our graves.'

710

For a while, no one spoke in answer. Then Gwanar asked, 'Is that all our death song, Aneirin?'

'What other death song do we deserve?' I asked in reply. 'There will be no one to sing it, if there is.'

'A song lives,' groaned Angor, 'even if no one hears it. Sing us our death song, Aneirin. Sing us a lament for us all, for those who have died beyond these walls, and those who are dying here.'

'Sing, Aneirin,' said someone else, in his agony. 'Sing and remind us why we are here, and how we came to our end.'

'How did we come?' I asked. I thought a while, and then:

> 'Exulting, we hurried to this place,
> As if our lives were not short enough:
> To be sold off at a bloody auction,
> And bought for a feast of mead.'

When a man is dying, he is a miser of his words, and careful with his breath. He takes a long time to frame his speeches, and says nothing he does not mean. It was, therefore, a long time before Gwanar said, in reproof, 'It was not all feasting, though glad we were of it.'

'But it is better to remember laughter than sorrow,' I answered him. It took some time to compose, and then I sang:

> 'As we rode to Cattraeth, Gwanar laughed:
> He went to battle jewelled, as for a feast.
> But other laughter died beneath his blade:
> Supporter of the living law – torn by the beast.'

A voice I could scarcely hear above the song of the thrush asked, 'Was it only Gwanar, then, who did well?'

I knew the voice. I had heard it raised in song as he danced on Bladulf's table. Now he lay with both legs broken. No more would I hear his voice in the hunting-field, or in battle. For him, when I could, I sang:

> 'Caradog rushed to battle like a boar;
> Men, witless, fled before his tusks.

Speared, he lies up in a stone thicket:
Brave is the hunter who will follow in.
The questing dogs are silent: for the mead
Of Mynydog's feast has quenched his tongue for ever.'

After a time, he answered, fainter still:
'I shall live though I die. I have a song.'

Sick men think slowly. But soon another voice, close to me, said, 'If Aneirin dies, how shall our songs live?'

And thin and high-pitched as the twittering of the sparrows in the roof I heard them ask all together, cry, plead:

'Live, Aneirin, live and sing our death songs all across the Island. If you live, then we shall live, though we die.'

'I am here with you,' I told them. 'I will live no longer than you do. What good is it to sing?'

But still they whispered in their drying throats:

'Sing us our death songs, Aneirin, sing us to death as our mothers sang us to sleep.' And Gwanar said, and it was the last time he spoke, 'Poetry is the crown of the nation, and the chief product of the Kingdom. If we have died only that a poem is made, then we have died for a better thing than ever we lived for.'

And no one contradicted him, because it was a self-evident truth, as clear to the eye as is the difference between black and white, or the truth that the many is more than the one. This was the truth we proclaimed against all the world, that there is more in life than the mere growing of wheat, and breeding till the whole land is covered by the soles of men's feet, and the blue sky is blackened by the smoke of the smiths' fires, and the song of the little birds is drowned by the harsh voices of men talking in dead-footed prose. Our open, wild land is a poem in itself, even if no man sings in it: and thus we had died to keep it.

The darkness was closing in on us. As night came, then I began the task that has filled all the rest of my life, to sing the death songs of all the Household of the Kingdom of the Gododdin. But that night, I thought only of those who lay around me, and how to give them some happiness, some pride, to take with them when they passed into the hands of the Virgin and all her saints. The nearest man to me rattled in his; as he died he heard:

> 'Those who were merely brave fled before you, Angor:
> Those who were also stubborn you struck down.
> Mailclad they stood in the front line,
> Till you trampled over their bodies.'

And yet, dying, he had the strength to say, 'All is well done. In dying, we have made the Pre-eminent Bard of the Island sing again. Our battle was not lost.'

I sang through the night. As I sang, men answered. At first I wondered that there were so many still alive in the town, so many who called their names and demanded a last song while they still could hear it. But as the Plough revolved above the clouds, the voices were fainter than the owl. Still the rain fell softly on us, chilling to our backbones. And still no Savages came.

With the day, I looked around. The scarlet cloaks did not move, scattered in mounds around me. I lay and shivered, coughing, hot with fever and cold with dying, my bones aching, my breath stabbing me as if it were hot iron in my lungs, my leg numb. I watched the kite and the crow settle on the stones, flutter closer. I did nothing. I needed my little strength for what now I knew only I could do. I could crown and complete all we had done in battle. Suddenly, one arm waved, one weak voice was raised, to drive away the approaching birds. Mirain, with his last strength, guarded us. Now I had time to think of those who had died outside the walls of Cattraeth, who would never hear the death songs.

> 'At our first fight in the valley,
> It was we who set a meal for the birds of prey,
> And satisfied the hunger of the eagles.
> Of all Mynydog's Household who rode out,
> In gold and scarlet mailed form the Dun of Eiddin,
> There was no Roman more renowned than Cynon.'

Because I thought, then, that he had been the first to die.

At last, even Mirain was still. I sang no more. I waited. I could not die yet: the work was not over. And I was rewarded for all my

713

effort, in keeping off death, in refusing to go, at last, to my peace in the Virgin's arms. What had I to do with peace? It was at noon that they came.

I knew they were there, however silent they were, for even after Mirain ceased to wave his arms the birds still kept their distance. And this was an offence to me. These were our kites, our buzzards: why should we not feed them? I too lay as if dead. This was a thicket no hunter entered while the beast lived. There was no matter of courage here, or lack of it: only a common prudence. I knew they would not come too soon. But I knew, too, that they would come, and that only one man could lead them, for shame's sake, if he lived, if Precent had not settled him in the night. And, at last, he came.

I sat upright, propped where Precent had left me, against a pillar, and watched the Savages come to the gap in the wall. Weary men, bloodstained and filthy with two nights and a day of hunting their enemies in the woods and bogs. Huge men, yellow-haired and stinking with sweat and mud, who had fought a long battle, and won it. But they waited at the gap in the wall, till *he* came. Bladulf came, taller than any of them, wearier than any. He stepped, delicately, over Owain's blood in the gap, and stood within Cattraeth, the first of all the Savages to stand there so long and live. He looked about him warily, expecting attack from one side or the other. He muttered charms and spells, and his wizard broke eggs before him, and poured out blood, more blood on that bloody ground, the blood of an ox, to chase away the magic of the Romans. And still I waited, huddled, still as death to the eye, my fingers busy beneath my cloak, my lashes a screen before my sight. I let him come.

He walked forward. His men came behind him. One by one, they turned over the bodies of the Household with the butts of their spears, seeking life and finding none. And at last, he was two spears' length from me. I slipped aside the cloak, and he saw the crossbow, cranked back, the string still taut and dry, my last bolt in the groove, a heavy bolt, fit for bear at this range, or wild boar.

Bladulf did not flinch. He did not move in haste, or cry out. He only said, in a mild surprise, 'There is one still alive.'

'And one to die,' I answered him. And as I jerked my finger to

714

loose the quarrel, someone I could not see, round to my right flank, flung a handful of pebbles in my face, and another on the other side, with a long pole, knocked up the bow.

I sat, in fury and shame, and looked at Bladulf, alive where he, or I, should have been dead. Weaponless, powerless, I had nothing left me but my hate for him. No sword, no long spear, no knife to throw, nothing left to touch him with. He looked at me, and said, 'I know you. You killed my brother.'

The man at his elbow spoke too. He said, 'He killed my brother, too. And my father. And my son.'

'I yield to you, Ingwy,' said Bladulf. 'He is yours. Shall he live or die? And if die, how shall he die?'

Ingwy looked down at me. He was a fat man, streaked with dirt and sweat. He wore a string of amber beads around his neck and copper rings in his ears. He had been weeping, and the tears had made runnels on his face. Black blood was clotted on his arms, and on the naked saxe in his hand. His left ear was cut almost away from his head, and hung by a shred of skin. He hesitated a little. Then:

'What is one more dead among so many? Let him live.'

'I do not want to live,' I replied. 'Let me die.'

'Death is a reward for victory,' said Bladulf. 'Those who are defeated must live, and regret it. Go back and thank your King for me. Where are you hurt?'

I did not answer him. I still do not know whom he counted the victors at Cattraeth. He waved his hand. A number of his men came to me. Ingwy held a horn of beer to my lips, and Bladulf himself offered me a piece of wheat-bread and a piece of cold meat. The wizard knelt down and felt along my leg. He saw first the swollen, misshapen knee. He jabbered like an angry squirrel, and suddenly the men around me held my arms to my sides. I thought that Bladulf had relented, and would give me the death I asked. But the wizard jerked at my leg, and I bit my lips rather than scream at the pain and the sound of grating bone and twisting sinew. But after the sudden pang, the ache was now different in quality, the throb of twisted tissues resting, returning to their proper place, not the strain of muscles under tension, hauled from their proper path by misplaced bones.

Then he looked at the gash in my thigh. He unrolled the bandage, and Gwenllian's scarf fell into the mud, and was disregarded, trodden in. He mumbled his spells, and rubbed the cut with stones and bones and a sword that a man of Bladulf's brought. Then he smeared the wound with grease out of a pot, and wrapped the whole leg in cloth.

Bladulf looked down again at me where I lay and sweated with pain, and he asked me, 'Can you walk?'

I tried to stand. My sides were fire. I could not keep on my feet. Two young men lifted me. They supported me with their arms under my shoulders, pressing on my broken ribs, but I would not cry, even though I wanted to vomit. Slowly they helped me through the gaps in the wall, out on to the green field.

This was a place of blood and death indeed. Here lay the Dwarf, and those who were killed with him: and not only those. From all sides, men were carrying in the dead, Savages and Romans, and laying them in lines, ours near the wall, theirs further away. Other men were working in the wood, cutting down trees. Bladulf asked me, 'How do you burn your dead? What rites do you use?'

'We do not burn. We bury them.'

'Then we will dig for you.'

He called Ingwy and gave him orders. He in turn collected a body of young warriors, and they with axes and spades deepened and widened the ditch beneath the wall, making a long trench. Then, as I watched, they carried into it the bodies of the Household, or those whom they had found. Precent I saw them bring, and Caso, Graid and Aidan, and put them carefully into the earth they had fought for. Bodies they brought from the Bloodfield, three days before, Gelorwid and Gwion. Bodies were carried wrapped in oxhide, that I could not recognise, from fights in earlier days, on the road. Caradog they brought out of Cattraeth, Angor and Geraint and Mirain. Morien they could not bring. Owain they would never find.

There were others, more important, that I could not see. Arthgi was not there, nor Gwyres, or any of the Cardi men who had gone with Cynrig. Perhaps there were twenty men, at most, who had not been killed. No more.

716

As each of the Household was brought to the long grave, the Savages, of course, stripped him of his mail. Why else had they searched for the dead? At least, of this we had often cheated them. Each of us, then, they wrapped in his own red cloak: or, if he had no cloak, then in a cloak of their own, of cloth or fur. Precent they wrapped in a cloak of sable, ermine-edged.

At the last, they took up Bradwen. As a man began to pull the mail shirt from her shoulders, Bladulf shouted, 'Stop! Let her keep it. That at least she has deserved.'

I asked him, 'You knew there was a woman?'

'We expected it. You are ruled by women. We were not surprised that you let a woman taste the luxury of battle. Among us, it has only been allowed, and that seldom, to Goddesses. She was mortal. She did not dishonour you. We will not dishonour her.'

They laid her in the grave, still mailed. All was complete. The rain still fell.

'What sacrifices do you make for the dead?' Bladulf asked me.

'We make no sacrifices. Has there not been sacrifice enough? We commend them to the Virgin, and lament their passing.'

'Then do so!'

I stood a moment, silent. The horde of the Savages gathered round me, looked at me, silent too. I collected myself. I sang:

'In haste from the feasting and the mead we marched to war,
Men used to hardship, spendthrift of our lives.
From Mynydog's Household grief has come to me,
For I have lost my Chieftain and my true friends.
Out of the comfort of a King's Hall we marched,
Where we had horses, and brides, and mead to drink,
Yet only one man turned his back on battle –
Cynddelig of Aeron, shame on him for ever.
I know of no song of battle which records,
So complete a destruction of an Army:
Of the three hundred who rode to Cattraeth,
None will return.
Before we come to earth, we did our duty:
Now may the Blessed Trinity take us home.'

717

I wrapped my cloak around my face. The young men filled in the ditch. I could not weep. Then Bladulf said, 'Turn and see how a warrior ends.'

They had brought their dead together. If we had lost three hundred, as I feared, then they had lost three thousand. I had never seen so many dead men. No battle in this Island, since the beginning of time, had brought so many to a bloody end. They had cut down all the green wood that stood before the walls of Cattraeth. Because the timber was fresh and full of sap, they brought weathered beams and stakes, wagons of dry fir branches and brushwood, barrels of tar from the pine trees, and casks of tallow. They stacked the wood, and laid the bodies on it, layer after layer of timber and dead men. There were as many dead men as living in that place, and there had come, now, crowds of women and children to weep. Besides this, I knew that we had killed almost as many women, and children too young to burn.

When the pyre was complete, there was a noise of trampling. The Savages drove into the place a herd of horses, our horses. They brought only mares, and of these all were either white or near enough to white not be any other colour for certain. And among them, I saw my own strawberry roan. They were of no use to the savages, who cannot ride, and who use ploughs so heavy only an ox can pull them. The wizard, then, cut the throats of all our horses with a spear, and dashed the blood over the dead men. They piled the horses on the wood, and the wizard knocked fire with his spear out of the walls of Cattraeth. And from this he kindled the pyres, the one on which the horses, the ones in which the men lay.

It was now almost night. The roaring flames stood up against the sky, and made all the night light as day. The smell of burning flesh enveloped us. The women wailed and screamed, and cut their faces with knives, and tore their clothes, dancing widdershins around the fire. There were even some who leaped, demented with grief, on to the fire and perished with their men, not quickly or without pain and screaming.

In spite of the rain, the flames roared high into the heavens, so cunningly had the Savages built this pyre, with passages and chimneys to lead the fire from the bottom to the top. The thick smoke blew its stench over all, as black as thunderclouds, a smell of singeing cloth and charring wood, and, above all, of roasting flesh. The wind from the west strengthened, and fanned the heat till ploughshares would have melted in the furnace that was made. The wind, I said, was from the West: the smoke, which in the day a man could have seen from the Wall or from the edge of Mordei, blew east in the darkness, east and out to sea.

And that, I thought, was just. Till the end of the Island, till they rise up on the Day of Judgement, the Household will hold Cattraeth, lying here in the ditch, whence no man will ever move them. They will become one with the Island which is ours, is ours and theirs, by right of birth. Here we are born, and here we die, and here we remain. But the Savages – nothing will be left of them in all the land. After they die, they are blown out over the eastern sea, back to the place from whence they came. The land is ours. They will pass.

I stood there, on the grave of the Household, and watched the end of the Savages who had come to take from us the Isle of the Mighty. The flames flared out into the darkness of the night till it gave way to the greyness of the dawn: and the blackness of the night, displaced, became the blackness of my eyes, and of my soul.

18

Byrr eu hoedyl hir eu hoet ar eu carant
Seith gymeint o loegrwys a ladassant

Short were their lives, long the grief of those who loved them:
Seven times their number of English had they killed.

From the noise of the wedding feast in Bladulf's Hall we awoke
into the dead stillness of Cattraeth. From the noise of the funeral
night before the walls of Cattraeth, I, only I of all the Household, awoke into the noise of Ingwy's Hall. To him, Bladulf had
given me, and to Ingwy, therefore, fell the task of keeping me
alive, as the King had said that I should live. I had rather died,
with the rest of the Household. Or, if I lived, I had rather lived
for ever in Bernicia as a slave, as I had done before, because life
then would not have been long. But Bladulf had said that I must
return to thank my King, and that, therefore, I must do.

I lay for weeks in the noise of Ingwy's Hall. It was Bladulf's
Hall now, too, because we had burnt the King's own village. His
family now had to crowd in and sleep where they could, in the
Hall or in the stables with the oxen, or in the barns on the
unthreshed wheat. There were so many.

Crowds came down, too, from the North. We had killed all
we could find, but there were hundreds, thousands who we had
not found, and they all came down to beg shelter and food for
the winter from their King. We had burnt their houses and stables, and they had nowhere to shelter from the autumn which
had started early with the rain which had fallen on us, dying, in
Cattraeth, and which did not stop. They had nothing to eat. We
had fallen on them at the end of the summer, when they were
living on the very last of the past year's corn. We had spoilt their

harvest for them, burning the reaped grain in their barns, and the ripe wheat in the fields. They came South begging for something to eat. The seed corn was gone, and their fields were flooding as the rain came down, because we had blocked their ditches. They had no tools and no oxen, nothing but their lives, and little use they were to grow wheat with in a hurry.

The nation of Savages, what were left of them, had only the crops of half their land to see them all through the winter. They fed me as they fed themselves. Each of us had a few slices of wheat-bread a day, and the wheat flour itself was bulked out with beechmast and acorns ground with the grain. But they had cut down the wide forests where any man of culture and civility, where any Roman, could find food and clothing for the taking at this time of the year.

These Savages, being tied to one crop, and not knowing how to use the forests of the land, how to hunt deer or how to search for nuts and fruit, faced a whole year on half-rations. A whole year – perhaps longer, if they could not reclaim in that first winter the ruined lands in the North. Famine was near. I have seen famine. I know what it does. I could tell, among the crowds who came to shelter in Ingwy's village, who would die that winter.

All the old people would die: anyone who was over forty would not have the strength for the bitter winter on a crust a day. The young children would die – that is nothing new. In any place, out of three babies born between May and September, only one will see May again. Out of those born between September and May, scarcely one in four will live to the first May. But among these Savages, none of the last year's babies would survive. Their mothers would die, too, starving themselves to save their children, and saving none, nor themselves either. Most of the men wounded in the battle would die. That would have nothing to do with the famine. Their wounds would turn rotten, and stink, and they would grow weaker, and dwindle into death. But until they died, they would have to be fed, uselessly. There would be few Savages' babies the next year: too many fathers had been killed. The raid to Cattraeth had killed far more Savages than had fallen in battle.

Now, as I watched the Savages, I could see what a great victory we few had won, and yet I did not realise it. I realise it now. We had dealt Bladulf and his people such a blow that it would be years, generations perhaps, before they would be strong enough to come again into the debatable land of Mordei. Oh, yes, this defeat of ours had been a victory, a victory such as no King of the Island of Britain had ever won over the Savages. We had our battle: the war was won. I know now that if we had not then so weakened the Savages in Bernicia, then Uther would never have recaptured York as he did a few years after, when Elmet men at last came with him into the; and Arthur would never have reconquered all the Island. The Household died so that all Britain again could be Christian, and so that the blessed language of the Angels could be spoken again from one sea to the other, in Bernicia as in Cornwall, in Kent as in Cardigan. And I saw the victory as I lay in Ingwy's Hall, I saw the seeds of it, if not the details, and blinded by sorrow and shame I did not recognise it. But since then I have recognised it, and by the grace of the Virgin I have seen the seed sprout into a tree.

But in those first days, in Ingwy's Hall, I knew only the bitterness of defeat. I only knew that I lay a prisoner, and that I lived only by the will of my enemies, that I could not decide even my own death. There were Savage girls who looked after me. They turned me in my bed when I was too weak, and they brought me the bread on which we all lived, and they dipped it in the bitter beer when I could not even chew the crust. I was, they told me, days and days too ill to speak intelligibly in any language, days sweating and wasting, and I could remember nothing. The girls gave me brews of herbs the wizard had made to stop the sweating and bring down the fever. And they did all this as carefully and as gently as they looked after their own wounded. And some of us lived, and most of us died. Me, they *made* to live. I knew, if they did not, that this was my punishment, that I although a Bard had taken up arms, and fought and killed.

Bladulf and Ingwy I saw daily, at sunset, when the one tallow dip was lit in the Hall. Then they came in, with all the other men from the fields where it was now too dark for work. Bladulf dressed like the meanest of his subjects, though who was the meanest no one could say, and he worked as they did. He would come in from

722

the dusk, dropping with weariness, his shirt wet with the rain and sweat mingled, his face and hands thick with mud.

When I was able to stand, and walk a few paces, I was allowed – I could easily have been prevented, and was not – to go out of the Hall. Then I found out where it was, because I had been carried there unconscious. It lay north of Cattraeth, being one of the farms we had not had time to burn on the day of the first battle, though we had seen it in the distance. But not a thousand paces away, Morien had fired the corn, and further from it, towards our line of march, we had blocked ditches. The fields were now flooded from the rain, which could not run off. The farms beyond had been burnt.

Here it was that Bladulf worked, as one man among many, taking his part in clearing ditches, in building houses and barns anew, and raising fences. He worked with his hands. I saw him, himself, digging with a spade in a clogged gully, to let the water run down into the river. I saw him again, with axe and nails, setting together the framework for a house, a house for his people, not for himself. Nothing distinguished him from his people who worked around him, but that he did nothing to his own profit.

That is why I would not call Bladulf a King, whatever his birth. It is not the place of a King to work with his hands among his people, or even to tell them what to do from hour to hour. The mark of a King, beyond birth, is wisdom, and after wisdom, wealth. And wisdom cannot be shown in the heat of the day's work, nor wealth gathered there. The place of a King is seated on his Judgement Mound, robed and crowned, listening to his suitors and to his Judge, and, when he has weighed the particular case and the universal law and the precedents, deciding what is now to be done. But the place of a King is to do nothing himself. It is not even the place of a King to ride out to war. That is the task for the Captain of his Household, who may himself be a King some day, although that is irrelevant. If the Captain of the Household of the Kingdom is defeated, then it is no shame to the King, and he can always be replaced. But if the King were to be defeated, then the luck of the Nation is gone, and the Kingdom is at an end. There is no place for a King to die in battle, but on the steps of his own dun, as Evrog Hael did. That is why the

Kings of the Island of Britain did not go out themselves against the Savages, until at last they could send all their Households out to war together, under the one Captain, Arthur.

Bladulf, here, worked as a common man, leading his people and doing himself what he would have every man do. He sent his men miles with the ox-wagons to bring back timber from the hills, because they had long cut down all the trees nearer to where they lived. And he sent the women down into the river-beds to cut reeds for thatch, because we had burnt the straw they would have used. I saw how he made his people work from dawn till the dark came, cheering them on when he needed to, or blustering and threatening them when it was necessary. That showed me how far we had been from victory. Had we killed every man of the Savages but one, and that one Bladulf, then still we would not have had a victory. Had we killed Bladulf, and no other man, then all the Savages would have been scattered and destroyed. Oh, if only Bladulf had stood to meet Owain in the fight. It would have been no trouble for Owain to have killed Bladulf: he could have done it with his little finger. I watched him, and saw that he did not understand the essence and dignity of Kingship. But I saw, too, how he recovered much of what we had destroyed. His life was our defeat.

How many poems have you heard when, after defeat, warriors forgive their foes, fall into sympathy with them, feel more comradeship with them than with those of their own nation who have not ridden to battle? It goes well in a poem. It does not happen in life: it did not happen to me. I watched Bladulf, and I grudged him his life, and I grudged every hour he worked to build his Kingdom new.

Each day, I could walk farther to watch the Savages' Kingdom rise again, stand longer with the Savage girls around me. Slim and delicate, with yellow hair like braided buttercups, their blue eyes mindless, empty, they sported like so many squirrels, so many fauns, and had no more thought for the future. They had nothing to do but attend me. The boys with whom they should have been flirting were dead, or died while we watched them. The corn they should have been grinding was burnt. The querns were silent and the looms were still. War had brought idleness to

724

those who were too young, or too old, or too tender, to strain at raising timbers or digging in mud. These girls, Bladulf's family or Ingwy's, played with me, teasing and flirting, as if I were a toy provided for their; and indeed I might have been that in Bladulf's mind, the only booty saved from the battle.

Theirs was the only gaiety. There were no feasts in that Hall. There was no food or ale to spare, and every man took what he was allowed and tried to find somewhere to sit to eat it, among the great crowd of Savages, men, women and children, who filled the Hall at night. In that continual stench of unwashed wheat-eaters, in the never-ending clamour of shouts and groans, the wailing of children and the quarrels of their parents, I almost lost my reason and my voice. I only kept myself in a whole mind by repeating beneath my breath, the verses I had already made on the men of the Household, and the names of those I would sing if, when I came again to live among men.

There were no feasts. Still, when Bladulf sat to eat, there was a moment of formality, and still, though he worked like all the others, he drank his ale, when there was ale, or his ditchwater when there was none, out of a silver-mounted horn. One night, then, in mid-September, he called me to him when he sat to eat.

'Are you well now? Can you walk?'

'I can walk,' I answered him.

'Then you must go. We can feed you no longer.'

It was true. But it was no thing for a King to say, to a prisoner or to a guest. The excuse was; but the violation of the laws of hospitality was gross. I was, however, in no position to rebuke him. The men in Cattraeth had bidden me live. How else were they to have any memorial?

'I will go, then,' I replied, and stood. It was dark, and far across the river the wolves were howling. Bladulf seized my wrist, and pressed me down again to sit beside him.

'You must go, and take my thanks back to your King.'

'Your thanks?'

'My thanks.'

'For what? Have we then killed the rival who would have supplanted you? Did you send him into the forefront of the battle, as David did among the Romans of old? Or have we thinned out for you a rebellious people who now have no more to do but follow you or die?'

He remained calm, although I taunted him.

'I send you back to thank your King for what he told me.'

This was what I had heard from the Dwarf, but I hardened my face and looked at Bladulf blankly.

'He sent a messenger, a wild man, an Irishman, to tell the men of Elmet to march north against us when you rode south. But that messenger he sent to me also. He told me when you would come. To meet the onslaught of Eiddin and Elmet together we brought down all our people from across the upland moors, and even from Carlisle, that late we won. But we heard that Elmet would come first, and so we marched first against them. When we struck deep into their country, we found that they were not mustered for war. Then, when we were far away, we heard of your raid, and we marched back as fast as we could. We had not thought that so few men could do so much damage. We needed all the men from the uplands to hold you. If we had not marched to Elmet, we would have settled with you sooner: if we had not known you were coming, we could never have gathered, you would have ridden clear to York. For that we thank your King.'

'But it was only treachery that won the day for you,' I reminded him.

'There is no treachery when a man fights for the life of his people, for the future of his Kingdom. Nor was there treachery to which we stooped as low as Mynydog's, who told me that you came, and when. You asked me why I thanked him – ask him why he betrayed you.'

Next day, I set out from Ingwy's village to walk back into the hills. They gave me a spear in case I met wolves, and a knife, and a few loaves of wheat bread. I still had my own cloak. I went west, first, till I could climb up the edge of the high hills. I could look east from the edge of the moorland, into the valleys we had devastated. Where coming south we had seen a hundred pillars of smoke, now there were not ten. The valleys were laid waste. The trees would grow again, the deer and the duck come back, the fields would flood and merge and vanish as if the wheat had never grown. Our sons would hunt again over that land: Mor-

726

dred hunts there now. But at what a price, I thought. I wept for the Household.

I went slowly along the edge of the old road, where I could find it. When I came to a wood, I threw away the wheat-bread they had given me. I would not soil my mouth with it again. The wood-pigeons came to it, and I made a sling out of the edge of my cloak and a small stone. I killed two, and that was enough. I made a fire, and ate again as a free man, a civilised Roman,; I ate fresh meat, game of my own hunting, my own killing, food gained not by sweat and labour of hands but by guile and skill. The fire I lit kept away the bears. It had stopped raining. The corn had rotted in the fields, where there were not enough Savages left alive to cut it and bring it in. Now, too late, the autumn had turned sunny and warm.

A sick man, recovering from a wound, or a wounded man, cannot walk far in one day. What is shelter to the one is shelter to the other. On the third day, I came downwind to a copse, and stalked a deer, inch by inch crawling for an hour till I could cast the spear. Oh, I had meat that night, roasted to eat hot, and to carry away cold. I found a hollow to sleep in, well away from the rest of my kill, and I lit a fire in the dusk to guard me. In the morning I woke shivering, the dew wet on my clothes, and I looked round. On the far side of the hollow where I had not looked in the dusk, I saw a low heap. I went closer. The mail was rusty, the leather green with mildew. Still the bones had not been scattered by the beasts, the rotting flesh still clung to the jaws, the row of even teeth would have told me, even if I had not seen the shield. I wept. Then I sang for him, since there was nothing else I could do:

> 'Tudvlch, driven from his farm – for seven days,
> He slaughtered the Savages.
> His valour should have kept him from harm:
> Now let it keep his memory alive.'

He was the first I found. He was not the last. They were Cardi men, mostly, and a few Picts, who had struggled thus far, either alone or in a band, and had died as they marched. One or two had been buried, and I found the shields set upright to mark the shallow graves. Others had crawled, it seemed, into holes and crannies to die, hiding their pain from their comrades. There were two by the walls of Din Drei, their arms around each other, their swords drawn across their knees. One, by the blue on his face, was a Pict: the other, from the yellow and black of his shield, I knew to be from Menevia, though who I could not tell. Over were the days when I knew every man of the Household by sight, to tell him at a thousand paces. They had died sitting together, men from the opposite ends of the Island, come together to fight against the invader. Now, their backs to the Roman Wall, they still looked to the South, into the lost land of Bernicia. They were the last.

I walked down from the Wall, to the Hall of Eudav the Tall, the Hall of Bradwen, the house where I had grown up, the paddocks where I had learned to ride, the woods where I had first gone to frame in solitude the songs I would sing in Kings' Halls. The old house had burnt. A few weeks ago we had rebuilt it. Now, the work of the Household was undone and all was desolate again. No one lived there. The thatch had kept the house dry, but already the poles of the frame were rotting, since we had never tarred them. We had made it for Bradwen and the men of Mordei, and these last had never come. Would they ever come now? I hoped that they might still come, now that we of the Household had weakened the Savages. But I knew that the hope was in vain. We had not given them that freedom from fear which they had asked. I did not sleep in the Hall. I lay on the ground, under the eye of the stars. My back was to the Dwarf Stone, the friendly Dwarf of our youth, and I faced the dead wood beyond the Wall.

The next day, I climbed the slope beyond, up on to the high ground beyond the woods. A little after noon, I saw before me the white sheep spread from horizon to horizon, a blessed sight, where there are sheep, there are shepherds. Before night I saw smoke, and I came to a hut of boughs. There I slept, as I had so often in my youth, and I had men of my own race, who spoke my own tongue, to look after me. I had returned from Cattraeth.

19

Beird byt barnant wyr o gallon
Diebyrth e gerth e gynghyr

The poets of the world judge those to be men of valour
Whose counsels are not revealed to slaves.

I walked the road between King Mynydog's farm and the gate of
the Dun. The road was silent. The smiths no longer worked at
their anvils, except a man here and there who beat out the iron
tyres for carts and shoes for the horses. The sword-makers were
gone, the sharpeners of iron points, the men who hammered
strips for shield-rims and helmet-brims.

I passed the longhouses where the Household had slept. No
longer were there little groups of men sitting at the doors,
throwing dice or jackstones, playing on the pipes, drinking and
telling stories, boasting of how well they rode, how well they
fought, would fight. The time for boasting had passed. We had
ridden. We had fought. The Household was dead.

I walked between the houses. The children peeped out at me
from the doorways, hiding behind the leather curtains. They
were silent. No one came out to me with flowers to throw before
my feet: Precent would return no more. The parents did not
look at me. They turned their faces aside. Without singing the
women bent at the; silent, the men swung the flails on the
threshing-floor. The Kingdom was in mourning for the Household. I felt a dead man, sitting at his own wake.

King Mynydog sat on his throne, on the Judgement Mound
before the gate of his Dun. No man came now to seek his law.
Clydno stood behind him now, as before. But how should any
decisions be enforced without Gwanar? Mynydog sat alone and

silent, and looked, for ever looked, towards the South, towards the notch below the Giant's Seat where he had seen the House- hold pass away. I stood before him. I leaned on the Savage spear, and I spat upon his feet before anyone who cared to see.

'Is there Peace?' the King asked.

I said nothing. I looked him in the face. I looked down the first. The Mynydog I had known had been a man in his prime. This man was old, his face lined, his hair streaked with grey. Clydno alone answered him, at last:

'There is peace.'

King Mynydog rose from his throne, and came down from his Judgement Mound. He did not offer to embrace me: a rebuff here, in the face of the sun, in the eye of all, would have been too brutal for him to receive, for me to deal. But how otherwise could I have acted? He led me through the gate of the Dun, across the courtyard, into the Hall, in silence.

Dark was Mynydog's Hall. He sat alone at the High Table. Before him burned one tallow dip. The hangings were gone from the walls, to make cloaks for the farm people, to see them through the winter. The arms were gone from the pillars where they had; gone, lost at Cattraeth. There were no weapons in the Kingdom, and few on the Rock of Dumbarton. The Kingdoms were defenceless.

Of the merry crowd who had feasted in the Hall through the summer, only Clydno remained. He sat on the side-table, at Mynydog's right. I sat at the foot of the Hall, far from them. I, only I of all the Household, had returned from Cattraeth, to feast with the King who had sent us.

'The mead is in the cup,' said Clydno, low, his voice weak and broken with long weeping, 'and the knife is in the meat. If there is anyone of pre-eminent skill, or anyone who has a tale of mar- vels to tell, let him speak now.'

I said nothing. Mynydog's cook put food before me, a true Roman meal: a manchet of oatcake, and porridge of oatmeal, salmon dried in the sun and venison roasted on a spit, mutton stewed with onions, blackberries and hazel-nuts and mush- rooms, cheese and butter and heather honey from the mountain hives. I did not touch it, nor the mead in a silver cup. I watched the King eat. And when his third cup was poured, I asked him. 'Why, my Kinsman and my King? Why?'

He did not answer. He only looked at me in wonder, as if he did not know what I was talking about. I spoke again.

'Why, Mynydog, why? There *is* a tale I could tell, of a great Household that was entirely destroyed. It was the Household of all the Kings of Britain, and every Kingdom sent men to serve in it. You spent all the wealth of your Kingdom on it, Mynydog, till there is nothing left, nothing left at all, and there is no more in your house than there is in the house of King Cormac in the empty North. You have ruined your Kingdom, King Mynydog, and all your; and you killed all the men who trusted in you.'

'Cynon returned,' said Clydno. 'Cynrig came back, and two Cardi men and a Pict with him. All were wounded. Three died. Cynrig has gone to the South. Cynon went with him. Three, then, have returned, out of the Household.'

'And Cynddelig?'

'It is said that Cynrig killed him. In Carlisle.'

I asked Mynydog again, 'Why, my King? But why?'

He looked down into his cup. He murmured an epigram I had first sung, years before, when I had made a poem on Vortigern the Great, the Magnificent, the Wise, the Proud, the Unhappy:

> 'Though there be a thousand men in one house,
> Only the King knows in full the cares of war:
> It is the Chief who pays the price for all.'

He looked up at me.

'Do you think there has been one day, one hour, since the Household rode out that I have not looked around the Hall and seen you, every one? I can tell you where every man sits, every man. From the moment you gathered together, I knew the end. There was no end possible for you all but death.'

'And yet you sent us out?'

'I could not let you all go. I told Cynddelig, that if he could find an excuse to turn back with honour then he might save one troop. Even Owain would have saved Cynon's squadron, if

Cynon had been willing. But I knew, whatever I did, all who rode out would die.'

'But, knowing that, you sent us.'

'I sent you.'

'Out to meet the men of Elmet, who did not come.'

'I knew they would not come. They would not follow a Prince of Cornwall. There was always jealousy.'

'And that you knew?'

'I knew.'

'And above that, you betrayed us?'

'I found the means to tell Bladulf that he was threatened from each; and when.'

'And after that, you sent us out. You sent the greatest Army that has ever been gathered here, a Household that any of the Kings of Britain would have been proud of. And you sent us all, deliberately, deceitfully, to a useless death.'

'But it was *my* Household. It was me alone, they came to serve. Even though they followed Owain into battle, it was the Household of Mynydog that rode out. It was not the Household of all the Isle of Britain. Elmet was not there, nor Wight, Ciren or Anderida. Think, Aneirin, what would come if there *were* one Household of all the Island, if all the Kings let their soldiers follow one General, to sweep the Savages back into the sea. But where would there be such a General, to be leader of such a Household?'

'Owain,' I said. 'Owain could have done it. Owain could have led them.'

'Not Owain. Owain was to be King of Cornwall. Would the other Kings have given a mere King such power? The man who will lead the household of the Island must be one with no claim to any throne, but of good blood, nevertheless.

'And all his life, Owain knew he would be a King. That was how he behaved. He knew that you would do whatever he said. And you did, whether what he wanted had any sense in it or not. You followed him, partly, because it never occurred to him that you would do anything else but follow him, and because he had no doubts, you had no doubts. And so you followed him, even though you knew that nothing but death lay ahead. You knew that, did you not? You knew it before you rode out of Eiddin.'

732

'Aye, we knew it.' The Hall of Eiddin was as silent, as dark as the streets of Cattraeth. Men had died; had we been more alive here, in all our feasts?

'Owain was arrogant and proud. The man who will gather together a Household from all the Kings of Britain can have no such spirit. He must be a man who is used to rejection, who will be surprised to find anyone who will follow him, who will never quite expect the love men feel for him. A man who all his life has been pushed, passed from one host to another, always a stranger, never in a land or a Hall of his own, he will be willing to explain humbly, simply, what he wants men to do.'

'There is no such man.' I too looked into my cup as I spoke. My anger now was gone. That *was* how we had followed Owain, blindly, suspending our senses, as we went on a hopeless, useless ride. 'Owain *could* have done it. Any man would have followed Owain, once they had heard him. But for this dream of yours, this desire to prove that Owain's way was wrong, you destroyed him. And you have destroyed your Kingdom. Where now are the arms that should have defended Eiddin? Who now wear those suits of mail? Who now wield the swords your smiths beat out with such patience? Who but the crows benefit from the food your farmers raised and brought in to you? And where now are all those golden warriors, scarlet cloaked, who sat once with me here at table? Where is Precent? Where is Aidan? Where is Cynrain? Where is Bradwen the wisest of all women? And where, above all, is Owain?' I looked around the gloomy Hall. 'Where, now, is Gwenllian? And where, where, is the little boy? Mynydog, where is Arthur?'

'When the Household of Eiddin rode South to fight,' and Mynydog was calm in speech as if he were pronouncing judgement in some case of chance murder between relations or a dispute over land or sheep, 'the host of Bladulf was told. And they were told that the host of Elmet, too, was on the road. They received their challenge, and they came out to meet it. Then, as never before, they faced a threat that might well have driven them into the sea, if Elmet had indeed marched, if all my nation had been faithful, as you were. The Saxons marched, first, to meet Elmet. But when they saw that Elmet was not going to war,

733

they turned to meet you. They expected to fight great battles, and, indeed, even though Elmet did not march, at Cattraeth they fought a greater battle than they would have expected, when only three hundred men faced them. They did not know that our army would be so few. To meet you, they brought back out of the hills their roving bands. There was not a Saxon warrior between the Wall and the Humber who did not face you. All the hill-country, between the Road to the South and the Irish Sea, was empty of them.

'For the first time for four years, a woman and child could travel by land, from Eiddin to Wroxeter, from the House of Mynydog to the House of Uther Pendragon. Gorlois Ygraine's husband is; they are gone who sought the child's life. Now, he can be fostered in his father's country. He will be safer; here, how long can we hold against the Irish who come in from the West and roundabout from the North?'

'For that you spent the Household? To clear the hill-country so that your grandchild could be safer, a little safer, for a few years?'

'For that, Aneirin, for that. This is he, I tell you, who will have the humility to lead the Household of all the Kings of the Island, and the wisdom to know when to fight, and the calmness to command.'

'He alone, of all the Romans in the Island?'

'He alone, to have all that, and be also of blood to attract attention, but yet, by birth, barred from any throne of his own. Syvno saw this, he read it in the stars, Gelorwid knew it, the Virgin told him in his prayers. Even Owain knew it, Owain the Proud, the unteachable, he recognised majesty.'

'And I …?'

'An astronomer may talk of the future, Aneirin, or a Priest, or a soldier. But not a Poet, because a Poet talks only of what is true, what is fact.'

'But am I still a Poet, blood-shedder, steel-bearer?'

'Go out, and ask a holier man than I am.'

Epilogue

Mynydog, then, sacrificed us all, the Household of Eiddin, the three hundred picked warriors of the Isle of Britain, so that, though Eiddin fell, and Dumbarton, yet Britain should live, and Rome live in Britain. I did not believe him then. Since then, I have seen it come true.

My little Arthur rode out as the Captain of a Household of all the Kings of Britain. He led warriors from Cornwall and from Orkney, as Owain did, from Cardigan and from Elmet and from Little Britain beyond the sea. Arthur killed Bladulf beneath the Rock of Eiddin. But no dead Bladulf could bring again to life Mynydog the Merciful, the Wise. Even Bernicia is ours again. Mordred governs it for Arthur and all the kings of Britain. And after Arthur, Mordred will lead the Household.

Still, though, the men of Arthur's Household must ride out in pairs as I did with Cynon. Still they must fight Savage giants in their wheatfields. Still they must find the dragon ships drifting to shore, and destroy them with iron and fire. All we did, they do.

Yet, I have never seen Arthur since, nor Gwenllian. They tell me that she still lives in Arthur's Court, in Camelot, and even Guinevere gives her precedence. Wise she is now as Bradwen ever was, and they say, more beautiful. But she has never married.

I went out that night from the Hall of Mynydog. I walked out across Eiddin and across Strathclyde, and at last I came to the island of the monks. I stood before the Bishop in his cell, silent, and he knew my wish without words and shaved my head in front from ear. I paddled the skin boat across the warlike sea to Dalriada in Ireland, and I walked to the Monastery at Bangor, founded from that older Bangor in my father's kingdom. And for my father's sake the monks took me in. There the monks taught me to read and to write, and there I followed the worship of the Virgin and her son, who likewise went to their Cattraeth.

Seven years after I came to Bangor, the Virgin drove me out again in a dream, to seek a tree which bore three fruits. I wandered till I came to this place, where there was an oak, with acorns on the branches, and a dove's nest in the leaves, and a sow and her litter among the roots. Here I made my llan. I cleared the ground for my garden of beans within the wattle fence. I hung my bell on a branch of the oak tree, and ever since I have remained in my little hut of withies and clay. Here I will stay till I die. And in that time, I have done my penance to the Virgin for my own sins, and for the sins of all who rode with me to Cattraeth.

I am a spoilt warrior, that I returned from a field where my Captain died. Therefore, I cannot work as a man, but only as a hermit. I am a spoilt man, and I cannot be a priest. I am a spoilt poet, who cannot sing, and therefore I must write. That was my penance. I have written down the death songs of all who died at Cattraeth, as I could find vellum. Perhaps they will come at last into the hands of someone who will take them to Arthur, or to Cynrig in Cardigan: perhaps not. Now the three hundred and three songs are ended. I am ready for my own death, so long postponed.

This was the Goddodin, the song of the Household of Eiddin. I, Aneirin, wrote it.

David **John James** (1923–1993)

John James studied philosophy at St David's University College, Lampeter, and also read and completed an MA in psychology at Selwyn College, Cambridge. He became a psychologist for the Ministry of Defence, lecturing on the selection and training of air crews for the RAF at Brampton. In addition to writing he also worked as a teacher and later for the Scientific Civil Service working on aviation problems.

He is known for writing four historical novels set in Roman and early medieval Britain and Europe. He is buried in the graveyard at Strata Florida Abbey in Wales.

A full list of Fantasy Masterworks can be found at
www.gollancz.co.uk